THE TWENTIETH CENTURY

THE VIKING PORTABLE LIBRARY

AMERICAN LITERATURE SURVEY

EDITED BY

Milton R. Stern
The University of Connecticut

AND

Seymour L. Gross
The University of Detroit

COLONIAL AND FEDERAL TO 1800
*General Introduction and Preface by
the Editors*

THE AMERICAN ROMANTICS · 1800–1860
Prefatory Essay by Van Wyck Brooks

NATION AND REGION · 1860–1900
Prefatory Essay by Howard Mumford Jones

THE TWENTIETH CENTURY
Prefatory Essay by Malcolm Cowley

THE
TWENTIETH
CENTURY

REVISED AND EXPANDED

☆
☆　　☆
☆

**WITH A GENERAL INTRODUCTION BY
THE EDITORS AND A PREFATORY ESSAY BY**

Malcolm Cowley

THE VIKING PRESS · NEW YORK

ACKNOWLEDGMENTS

Anderson, Sherwood. *The Triumph of the Egg.* Copr. 1921 by Eleanor Anderson. By permission of Harold Ober Associates, Inc.

Babbitt, Irving. *On Being Creative and Other Essays.* By permission of Houghton Mifflin Company.

Benet, Stephen Vincent. "American Names" from *The Selected Works of Stephen Vincent Benet.* Copr. 1927 by Stephen Vincent Benet, R 1955 by Rosemary Carr Benet. Holt, Rinehart & Winston, Inc. "Invocation" from *John Brown's Body.* Copr. 1927 by Stephen Vincent Benet, R 1955 by Rosemary Carr Benet. Holt, Rinehart & Winston, Inc. By permission of Brandt & Brandt.

Bishop, Elizabeth. "The Man-Moth" from *Poems, North & South* by Elizabeth Bishop. Reprinted by permission of the publisher, Houghton Mifflin Company.

Cather, Willa. *Obscure Destinies.* Copr. 1930, 1932 by Willa Cather. By permission of Alfred A. Knopf, Inc.

Crane, Hart. The Collected Poems of Hart Crane. © R 1961 by Liveright Publishing Corp. and reprinted by their permission.

Cummings, E. E. From *Poems 1923–1954.* Copr. 1923, 1925, 1931, 1940, 1951, 1953, 1954, © 1959 by E. E. Cummings. Copr. 1926 by Horace Liveright, Copr. 1968 by Marion Morehouse Cummings. By permission of Harcourt, Brace & World, Inc.

Dos Passos, John. *USA.* Copr. 1930, 1932, 1933, 1934, 1935, 1936, 1937 by John Dos Passos. Copr. 1946 by John Dos Passos and Houghton Mifflin Company. Copr. © R 1958, 1960 by John Dos Passos.

Dreiser, Theodore. *Free and Other Stories.* Copr. 1918, R 1946 by Mrs. Theodore Dreiser. By permission of G. P. Putnam's Sons.

Eberhart, Richard. *Collected Poems 1930–1960.* © Richard Eberhart 1960. By permission of Oxford University Press, Inc., New York, and Chatto & Windus Ltd., London.

Eliot, T. S. *Collected Poems 1909–1935* by T. S. Eliot. Copr. 1936 by Harcourt, Brace & World, Inc. *Four Quartets.* Copr. 1943 by T. S. Eliot. "Tradition and the Individual Talent" from *Selected Essays: New Edition* by T. S. Eliot. Copr. 1932, 1936, 1950 by Harcourt, Brace & World, Inc. Copr. 1960, 1964 by T. S. Eliot. By permission of Harcourt, Brace & World, Inc., and Faber & Faber, London.

Farrell, James T. *An Omnibus of Short Stories.* Copr. 1942, 1956 by James T. Farrell. By permission of The Vanguard Press.

Fearing, Kenneth. *New and Selected Poems.* Copr. 1956 by Kenneth Fearing. By permission of Indiana University Press.

Fitzgerald, F. Scott. "Winter Dreams" from *All the Sad Young Men.* Copr. 1922, R 1950 by Frances Scott Fitzgerald Lanahan. By permission of Charles Scribner's Sons.

Frost, Robert. From *Complete Poems of Robert Frost.* Copr. 1916, 1923, 1928, 1930, 1934, 1939 by Holt, Rinehart & Winston, Inc. Copr. 1936, 1942, 1944, 1951, © 1956, 1958, 1962 by Robert Frost. Copr. © 1964, 1967 by Lesley Frost Ballantine. Reprinted by permission of Holt, Rinehart & Winston, Inc.

Ginsberg, Allen. "A Supermarket in California," Copr. © 1956, 1959 by Allen Ginsberg. Reprinted by permission of City Lights Books.

Jarrell, Randall. *Little Friend, Little Friend*. Copr. 1945 by Dial Press, Inc. By permission of the author. "Nestus Gurley." Reprinted by permission of Mrs. Randall Jarrell.

Jeffers, Robinson. *Selected Poetry of Robinson Jeffers*. Copr. 1924, 1925, 1928, R 1951, 1953, 1956 by Robinson Jeffers. By permission of Random House, Inc.

Lewis, Sinclair. "The American Fear of Literature," Sinclair Lewis' Nobel Prize Speech, published in 1931 by Harcourt, Brace & World, Inc. By permission of the lawyers for the author's estate, Ernst, Cane, Berner and Gitlin.

Lindsay, Vachel. From *Collected Poems*. Copr. 1913, 1914 by The Macmillan Company, R 1942 by Elizabeth C. Lindsay. By permission of The Macmillan Company.

Lowell, Amy. *Selected Poems*. By permission of Houghton Mifflin Company.

Lowell, Robert. *Lord Weary's Castle*. Copr. 1944, 1946 by Robert Lowell. By permission of Harcourt, Brace & World, Inc. "Skunk Hour." Reprinted with permission of Farrar, Straus & Giroux, Inc. From *Life Studies* by Robert Lowell. Copr. © 1958 by Robert Lowell.

MacLeish, Archibald. "You Andrew Marvell" and "American Letter" from *Poems, 1924–1933*. By permission of Houghton Mifflin Company. "Speech to Those Who Say Comrade" from *Public Speech: Poems*. Copr. 1936, © 1964 by Archibald MacLeish. Reprinted by permission of Holt, Rinehart & Winston, Inc.

Mailer, Norman. "The White Negro, Superficial Reflections on the Hipster." Reprinted by permission of G. P. Putnam's Sons from *Advertisements for Myself* by Norman Mailer. © 1959 by Norman Mailer.

Mencken, H. L. *Prejudices: Third Series*. Copr. 1922 by Alfred A. Knopf, Inc. and reprinted by their permission.

Millay, Edna St. Vincent. *Collected Poems*. Copr. 1923, 1928, 1931, 1951, 1955, 1958 by Edna St. Vincent Millay and Norma Millay Ellis. Harper & Row, Publishers. By permission of Norma Millay Ellis.

Moore, Marianne. *Selected Poems*. Copr. 1935 by Marianne Moore, R 1963 by Marianne Moore and T. S. Eliot. By permission of The Macmillan Company.

O'Neill, Eugene. "The Hairy Ape." Copr. 1922, R 1949 by Eugene O'Neill. Reprinted from *Nine Plays by Eugene O'Neill* by permission of Random House, Inc. Caution: Professionals and amateurs are hereby warned that "The Hairy Ape," being fully protected under the copyright laws of the United States of America, the British Empire, including the Dominion of Canada, and all other countries of the copyright union, is subject to a royalty. All rights, including professional, amateur, motion picture, recitation, public reading, radio broadcasting, and the right of translation into foreign languages are strictly reserved. In its printed form this play is dedicated to the reading public only. All inquiries should be addressed to Richard J. Madden Play Company, 52 Vanderbilt Avenue, New York, N.Y.

Plath, Sylvia. "Daddy" from *Ariel* by Sylvia Plath. Copr. © 1963 by Ted Hughes. Reprinted by permission of Harper & Row, Publishers, and Olwyn Hughes.

Porter, Katherine Anne. *Flowering Judas and Other Stories*. Copr. 1930, 1935, 1958, 1963 by Katherine Anne Porter. By permission of Harcourt, Brace & World, Inc.

Pound, Ezra. *Personae*. Copr. 1926, R by Ezra Pound. By permission of New Directions.

Ransom, John Crowe. From *Selected Poems*. Copr. 1924, 1927, 1945 by Alfred A. Knopf, Inc. and reprinted by their permission.

Robinson, Edwin Arlington. "Miniver Cheevy," "Doctor of Billiards," "For a Dead Lady," and "How Annandale Went Out" from *The Town Down the River*. Copr. 1907, R 1935 by Charles Scribner's Sons and reprinted by their permission. Some other poems from *Collected Poems*.

Copr. 1916, 1920, 1921, 1925 by E. A. Robinson, R 1944, 1948, 1949 by Ruth Nivison, R 1952 by Ruth Nivison and Barbara Holt. By permission of The Macmillan Company.

Roethke, Theodore. "Dolor" from *The Lost Son and Other Poems*. Copr. 1947 by Theodore Roethke. "The Waking" from *The Waking and Other Poems*. Copr. 1953 by Theodore Roethke. By permission of Doubleday & Company, Inc.

Sandburg, Carl. "Grass" from *Cornhuskers*. Copr. 1918 by Holt, Rinehart & Winston, Inc., R 1946 by Carl Sandburg. Some other poems from *Chicago Poems*. Copr. 1916 by Holt, Rinehart & Winston, Inc., R 1944 by Carl Sandburg. By permission of Holt, Rinehart & Winston, Inc. "The People Will Live On" from *The People, Yes*. Copr. 1936 by Harcourt, Brace & World, Inc.; R 1964 by Carl Sandburg. Reprinted by their permission.

Schwartz, Delmore. "Starlight Like Intuition Pierced the Twelve" from *Vaudeville for a Princess*. Copr. 1950 by New Directions and reprinted by their permission. "The True-Blue American" from *Summer Knowledge*. © 1955 by Delmore Schwartz. By permission of Doubleday & Company, Inc.

Scully, James. "Crew Practice." © 1965 The New Yorker Magazine, Inc. Reprinted with their permission.

Shapiro, Karl. *Poems 1940–1953*. Copr. 1943, 1947 by Karl Shapiro. By permission of Random House, Inc.

Southern Agrarians. *I'll Take My Stand* by Twelve Southerners. Copr. 1930 by Harper & Brothers and reprinted by their permission.

Steinbeck, John. *The Long Valley*. Copr. 1938, Copr. © R 1966 by John Steinbeck.

Stevens, Wallace. From *The Collected Poems of Wallace Stevens*. Copr. 1923, 1931, 1935, 1936, 1943, 1951, 1952, 1954 by Wallace Stevens. By permission of Alfred A. Knopf, Inc.

Tate, Allen. From *Poems* (1960). "Ode to the Confederate Dead" and "Death of Little Boys." Copr. 1937 by Charles Scribner's Sons, Copr. © R 1965 by Allen Tate.

Warren, Robert Penn. *Selected Poems 1923–1943*. Copr. 1944 by Robert Penn Warren. By permission of William Morris Agency.

Welty, Eudora. *A Curtain of Green and Other Stories*. Copr. 1941 by Eudora Welty. By permission of Harcourt, Brace & World, Inc.

Wilbur, Richard. *Ceremony and Other Poems*. Copr. 1949 by Richard Wilbur. Originally published in *The New Yorker*. "Advice to a Prophet" from *Advice to a Prophet and Other Poems* by Richard Wilbur. Copr. © 1957 by Richard Wilbur.

Williams, William Carlos. *The Collected Earlier Poems of William Carlos Williams*. Copr. 1938, 1951 by William Carlos Williams. *The Collected Later Poems of William Carlos Williams*. Copr. 1950 by William Carlos Williams. By permission of New Directions Publishing Corporation.

Wilson, Edmund. *The Intent of the Critic*. Copr. 1941 by Princeton University Press and reprinted by their permission.

Wolfe, Thomas. Pp. 155–160 from *Of Time and the River*. Copr. 1935 by Charles Scribner's Sons, Copr. © R 1963 by Paul Gitlin. Reprinted by their permission. *You Can't Go Home Again*. Copr. 1934, 1937, 1938, 1939, 1940 by Maxwell Perkins, as Executor. By permission of Harper & Row, Publishers.

ACKNOWLEDGMENTS

GENERAL
INTRODUCTION

In the spirit of his own time, Emerson insisted that every age must have its original relation to the universe. He reflected an older American belief that no age can hold a mortgage on any future time and that the world is for the living. Our Republic and our national literature share a democratic sense of time in which every age, besides shaping the world that exists, also remakes the past. Given the fact that history is never finally dead, all literary productions of the past can become meaningful in the human mind of the present. What, then, in our living moment, can we see of our identity in the total span of our literature?

One thing stands out clearly: American literature is a rebellious and iconoclastic body of art. The Puritan rebelled against the Anglican, the deist against the Puritan, the romantic against aspects of deism, the naturalist against aspects of romanticism, the symbolist against aspects of naturalism. In each case the rebellion was greeted with cries of outrage and prophecies of doom. It is true that almost any nation's literary history tells the same story: but besides this there is a deeper nay-saying that characterizes American literature and remains constant beneath the shifting faces of rebellion. On the surface it may seem strange that a nation in some ways tending toward a mass identity should produce a literature of which the underlying theme is revolutionary. But when one considers that the artist, with his keener sensibility and articulation, is most aware of tendencies in his society, including those he feels duty-bound to combat, and that the richest heritage of the Republic is its foundation in defense of freedom of the mind, then his rebelliousness becomes natural and inevitable. The American writer's "nay" is but a prelude to his resounding "yea!" uttered in behalf of new experience rather than hoarded conventions.

That constant and subterranean rebellion is a product of many forces which, to this day, make America a puzzle to observers. Our nation was founded in middle-class aspirations that were noble in many ways but still were capable of creating a business culture in which, as Edwin Arlington Robinson has it, "Your Dollar, Dove and Eagle make a Trinity that even you rate higher than you rate yourselves; it pays, it flatters, and it's new." On the other hand, those some aspirations demanded ideologies in which nothing is held to be greater than the integrity and freedom of the individual.

And still more contradictions. An extreme form of individualism, especially to be noted in the late nineteenth century, was a primitive, often savage, social and economic anarchy: each man for himself, but all with a common goal, which was the sack of a continent blessed with incredible resources that beckoned them ever westward. That same predatory impulse, however, was only one sequel to an image of America as the organic Great New West where the ultimate hungers of men's hearts could be satisfied, where the infinitude of human identity could be realized and personality could be fulfilled. Because the Republic faced away from the Old World, it was founded on a faith in experiment, newness, and youth. So founded, it could threaten to create a society in which age is a sin, human value is measured by personal appearance, and the teen-ager becomes the arbiter of popular taste. But this same naïve faith and innocence became something more than a mindless subject for the satire of a Sinclair Lewis: it also suggested an image of the American as a man free from stifling precedent who could break through old barriers in science, belief, and social institutions.

In short, the American writer began to see that there are really two Americas. One is the actual country that shares all the limitations of any human community in the Old World or the New; the other is the ideal America that, as Scott Fitzgerald told us, existed pure only as a wonderful and pathetically adolescent dream. One is a geographic location in the evolution of all human history; the other is a state of being that answers all human hopes. Whenever the ideal was put forward by mistaken patriotism as the real country, American writers protested—sometimes in full and bitter measure, as Mark

Twain, for one, has shown. And whenever the actual America threatened to destroy the ideal, American writers have again protested, with profound, poetic vigor, as Thoreau and Whitman have shown. It is because American culture is precariously and magnificently balanced in a bewildering variety of contradictions that the American writer has remained in a state of protest.

This is not to say that the present editors would return to the critical attitude of the 1930s, which regarded literature as a collection of social documents and interpreted every effort of artistic creation as an economic act. Rather, we think that there is a unifying identity in our cultural and intellectual production that is a deliberate dramatization of our total history. It is from this necessary and sensible orientation, as it seems to us, that we see the iconoclasm of the American writer as a major feature in our literature. What he expresses is a whole-voiced rejection of trammeling orthodoxies, conformities, hypocrisies, and delusions, wherever and whenever they are seen on the national landscape. Keeping that spirit in mind, we offer the following selections from American literature as a record of the continuing exploration that develops into and still speaks to our moment of time.

No student of American literature will feel that he has made a reasonably full perusal of the materials unless he has read complete Hawthorne's *The Scarlet Letter,* Thoreau's *Walden,* Melville's *Moby-Dick,* representative poems from Whitman's *Leaves of Grass,* and a novel or two each of James, Hemingway, and Faulkner. Those authors are most profitably read in full-length works, but before the reading revolution brought about by inexpensive paperback reprints, anthologists were forced to present them in more or less fragmented form. That is no longer necessary. The teacher today can include in his course, in addition to anthologized material, such representative works as those mentioned without feeling that his students are being asked to make an unreasonable expenditure for books.

In view of this change in the practical realities of courses in American literature, we have felt that it was both wise and necessary to omit from our anthology some of the authors who would, in any case, be read under separate cover. By deleting such material, we have been able to provide a wider selection than is usual from other authors, including Edward Taylor, Emily Dickinson, and Stephen Crane, who in many cases would not be read in separate editions. In this revised edition of *American Literature Survey,* we have added some representative works of Melville because it is impossible for students to buy an inexpensive reprint of *Moby-Dick* that also includes some of Melville's shorter fiction. We have added some basic poems by Whitman because in the majority of courses it is not feasible to read the entire *Leaves of Grass* in separate cover. And we have included some work by Henry James for the same reason we included Melville: none of the two or three James novels most commonly assigned is available in a volume that includes his shorter fiction and essays. Given the needs of courses in American literature, we feel that the present volumes maintain a proper balance of materials and meet the widest demands of common practice, flexibility, and usefulness.

As in the first edition of *American Literature Survey,* we have avoided excess editorial apparatus, in the belief that long historical interchapters, copious footnotes, and coercive critical judgments either duplicate or conflict with the teacher's work. The nature of interpretation and emphasis will vary from class to class, from teacher to teacher, and therefore we have been content to provide the student with a basic minimum of biographical, bibliographical, and textual information.

In general the selections are presented chronologically, though not where the logical placement of materials would make strict chronology a meaningless arrangement. In every case we have chosen texts that yield the highest combination of accuracy and readability, a principle which has led us to modernize the spelling and regularize the punctuation of the most reliable texts of some of the early writers. The dates placed after the works indicate publication; a second or third date indicates extensive revisions. In those instances where there has been a significant lapse of time between composition and publication, a "w." stands for date of writing, a "p." for date of publication.

Milton R. Stern
Seymour L. Gross

CONTENTS

PREFACE

By Malcolm Cowley

The new century started badly for American writers. In going over the literary records of the early 1900s, one senses a mood of discouragement that contrasts with the bounce and rebelliousness of the preceding decade. The 1890s had been a time of little magazines and avant-garde publishers, of new critical journals, of the first American little theater, and also of contending literary doctrines. Besides the established realists and local colorists—and besides the best-selling romantic novelists, whom all the younger men despised—there were also naturalists, impressionists, symbolists, decadents, high-minded socialists, Harvard poets (an impressively gifted group), and at least one Veritist, capitalized, in the person of Hamlin Garland, who invented the term. There was talent, there was conviction, there was almost everything, in fact, except a sympathetic audience for outspoken or experimental writing. The lack of an audience proved fatal, and by the end of the decade all this activity had been swept out of sight by what the *Bookman* described, at the time, as a "sudden onrush of ideality and romance which arose like a fresh sweet wind to clear the literary atmosphere. In this resistless new movement toward light and hope and peace," the *Bookman* continued, "those black books were cast aside and forgotten."

It is curious to note how writers can be discouraged by a resistless movement toward light, hope, and ideality. Soon the little magazines vanished with the groups that supported them, and the avant-garde publishers went bankrupt after losing most of their authors. The fact is that many of the rebel authors, and most of their leaders, had died shortly after the turn of the century, stricken in their early prime as if by some contagious blight. Among the careers that suddenly ended were those of Stephen Crane, Frank Norris, Lafcadio Hearn, Trumbull Stickney (the most original of the Harvard poets), James A. Herne (once known as the American Ibsen), and Kate Chopin of New Orleans, who had tried to write an American *Madame Bovary*. There were only a few survivors of this tragic generation. Among them, Theodore Dreiser suffered a prolonged breakdown after *Sister Carrie* was treated by its publisher and its critics as a scandal to be hushed up; he would write no fiction for ten years. Edwin Arlington Robinson was on the edge of succumbing to drink and disheartenment. Hamlin Garland, who also survived, had lost his early convictions; step by by step he was going over to the enemy.

The enemy was of course the Genteel Tradition, which held that no book should be published unless it was a "decent" work that could "safely" be placed on the center table in the parlor and read by proper young girls. "It is the 'young girl' and the family center table," Frank Norris once complained, "that determine the standard of the American short story." He might also have said that they determined the standard of American novels, plays, essays, and poetry. Although his complaint was made in the 1890s, there was no improvement during the early 1900s, when in fact the Genteel Tradition seemed more oppressive than ever. Mark Twain deferred to it, during those years, by reserving most of what he regarded as his serious work for posthumous publication. Edith Wharton was bolder, being encouraged by her wealth and her social position, but she found it more congenial to live in Europe. Although some interesting books were written at home by the muckraking journalists, they were not intended to be permanent. One might say of the decade that almost all the lasting works it produced were either written in Europe (as note Henry James's major novels and the first books of younger writers like Ezra Pound and Gertrude Stein) or else were privately printed, as was *The Education of Henry Adams*.

One might also say that American universities neglected one of their duties during this period—and in fact as late as 1930—by paying almost no attention to American authors, living or dead. They looked fixedly across the

Atlantic. When they offered courses in comparative literature, the comparisons were among the authors of Britain,
France, Germany, Spain, Italy, and sometimes Russia or
Scandinavia. American literature was mentioned, if at all,
as a rather disappointing and altogether colonial branch
of English literature. Undergraduates might easily have
gained the impression that writing was an art that flourished
in Europe and nowhere else. There was indeed a break,
about this time, in the whole tradition of American writing,
and I think the universities helped to produce it by thus
abolishing our literary past.

Writers of the new century would be condemned or
privileged to start over from the beginning, as if nobody
on this continent had ever practiced the art of making
books. As a matter of fact, groups of young writers made
several fresh starts, first in the 1910s, then in the 1920s, and
then again in the 1930s, each time with a different conception of what they should do. I am not proposing to
offer a history of twentieth-century American literature in
capsule form. All I am trying to find is a rough sort of
historical pattern that can be applied to the authors represented or recommended in the present volume, and I might
start by dividing the century into segments of about ten
years each. The division happens to be more than a matter
of convenience. By historical accident almost every decade
of our recent literature seems to possess a mood and
manner of its own, as if writers had been working with
their eyes on the calendar.

Once I thought of comparing the earlier—but not the
later—decades to the early stages of a New England year.
The 1890s, for example, would be a sort of January thaw
in which the sap began to rise before the weather turned
cold again. The ten years after 1900 would be a long
March freeze. But winter doesn't last forever, even in New
Hampshire, and the 1910s would be a sunny week in April,
with flowers bursting forth everywhere under the bare trees.
Some of the flowers had bloomed earlier and had miracu-
lously survived under the snow: I am thinking here of
Dreiser and Robinson, both of whom were rediscovered
at the beginning of the decade. Soon there were younger
rebels to bear them company, and notably there was a
straggling but impressive parade of poets: Frost, Sandburg,
Jeffers, Millay, Lindsay, Masters, Aiken, and Eliot, with

Amy Lowell twirling a cigar like a drum major's baton as she tried to keep them all in step. But there were also new novelists (Cather, Anderson, Lewis), there was at last an admired playwright (Eugene O'Neill), there were brilliant radical journalists (Randolph Bourne, John Reed), and there were critics like Mencken and Van Wyck Brooks, who spoke for the younger men. Brooks in particular played almost the same part in this second renaissance that Emerson had played in the thirties and forties of the preceding century.

In the 1910s there was at last an audience for serious writing, even of a sort not intended for the family center table, and there were also new ways of reaching the audience: new magazines, new publishers, and a profusion of little theaters. It is hard to characterize the extremely varied work of the writers who appeared in the decade. One can say that, with traditions broken, they seemed to owe an extremely small debt to American writers of the preceding century. One can say that they were generally critical in tone—critical, that is, of American life and institutions—but that most of them were moved by an essentially patriotic impulse. They wanted to produce books that would be worthy of this vast and still new country, by virtue of their scope, their newness, and their honesty. Hence, their emphasis was on subject matter, and they paid less than the proper attention to the structure and texture of their writing. There were notable exceptions to this rule—among them Eliot, Frost, and Cather—but in general the writers of the 1910 generation were not models of skilled craftsmanship or of discriminating taste. It was a weakness that would lead to another change in the direction of American letters.

The change became evident in the course of the following decade. There is no good seasonal analogy for the 1920s, but perhaps one could call them a second spring that followed the cold rains of wartime and of the postwar reaction. Once again young writers were starting over from the beginning, with no regard for tradition and without even knowing, in most cases, that such a thing existed in America. They went abroad to write, or many of them did; even those like William Faulkner who stayed at home were deeply affected by European and chiefly French ideals of the literary life. The tradition to which most of their work belongs is ultimately that of Gustave Flaubert, with his belief that writing was more important than living and his addiction to the "quaint mania," as he called it, of wearing himself out in pursuit of the perfect phrase and the unchangeable paragraph. But Proust and Joyce, Pound and Eliot, are writers in the same line, and they all served as models for the work of what became known as the Lost Generation.

Here the most familiar names are those of Faulkner, Hemingway, Fitzgerald, Wolfe, Dos Passos, and Katherine Anne Porter among the novelists, of Cummings, Crane, and Tate among the poets, and of Edmund Wilson among the critics. It is difficult, once again, to characterize the writers of a whole literary period. One might say, however, that their general emphasis was on form rather than subject matter, with the result that they produced better-finished and more complicated works than did most of their immediate predecessors. One might also say that the works—except for those of Dos Passos—are distinguished by intensity and depth rather than by any broad vision of the nation or the world.

Their lack of social vision came to be regarded as an inexcusable weakness and something close to a hanging crime by the young writers who appeared in the early depression years. A new period was beginning, and it is one for which one can find no seasonal comparison. One is tempted to call it a frost in June, when one thinks about the sorrows of the unemployed, but the literary atmosphere of the early years was anything but frosty or discouraged. The young writers of the 1930s were passionately convinced that they could help in their own way to end poverty and change the world. Rejecting all their predecessors except Whitman and Dreiser and John Reed, they started over once again, as the writers of the teens and twenties had done, and they moved in a new direction. At first they called themselves proletarian or revolutionary writers and then, after 1935, social realists. They were primarily concerned neither with form nor, except in appearance, with subject matter. They believed, it is true, that novels and poems should deal with the workers, or proletariat, but their real emphasis was on doctrine. If a book presented the right sort of doctrine—preferably one connected with the inevitable downfall of capitalism, or the triumph of the workers, or the crusade against fascism—they were willing to salute it as a good or sometimes as a great work.

Actually the decade was rich in literary works, but not many of the great or merely good ones were produced by these doctrinal writers. Their poetry was deplorable, and so was most of their prose. The main currents of the time are represented for me by three big novels, all written by somewhat older men. Dos Passos's *U.S.A.* is, among other things, an attack on monopoly capitalism, written around the thesis that human values are destroyed by the inevitable concentration of wealth in a few hands. "Yes, we are two nations," the author says at last, referring to the rich and the poor; and he finds no hope for decent ordinary people, whether they choose to be radical or to be conservative. *The Grapes of Wrath* was almost the last of the proletarian novels, and it is the only one out of hundreds that is read today. Unlike *U.S.A.* it is a hopeful book, expressing the spirit of the decade as a whole; it assumes that the workers will triumph when they learn to unite. *For Whom the Bell Tolls,* published in 1940, is the one masterly American novel that deals with the anti-fascist crusade. Its hero sacrifices himself for a cause and thereby wins a respite from time and mortality; in the seventy hours before death he lives as full a life as he might have lived in seventy years. But the author and his readers know that the cause of the Spanish Republic was a lost one and that the hero's sacrifice was wasted. The decade of hope was ending in despair and disillusionment.

Our simple pattern of changing decades is obscured after 1940. Partly that is because the war was an interregnum in the literary world; young writers were busy in uniform, and everybody was waiting for them to come home and express themselves in completely new books. When the war novels began to appear by scores and then by hundreds, they mostly proved disappointing, at least to those who had been hoping for revelations. Some of them had brute power, of the sort possessed by *The Naked and the Dead* or *From Here to Eternity,* but it did not seem to be under the author's control. Though most of the other war novels were honest and surprisingly craftsmanlike, they added more to our knowledge of how soldiers felt and acted than they did to American literature.

It was not fiction by younger writers that flourished in the postwar years and almost as late as 1960; rather it was criticism that became a field of discovery where new methods were applied and old masterpieces were reinterpreted. The principal labor, however, was one of consolidation. For the first time critics surveyed American writing of the twentieth century in relation to what had gone before. Universities joined in the work—in fact most of the critics were now professors, as were many of the new poets—and it was conducted on a grand scale. What emerged from the survey was a demonstration that American literature was more consistent and more unified than anyone had suspected in the past. Almost every existing current or tendency could be followed back into the nineteenth century, and some, it was shown, had started in colonial days. There was something in common between Hawthorne and Faulkner, for example, as there was between Whitman and Hart Crane; and Hemingway's best work was written in a mid-American prose style that critics traced back through Mark Twain to the old Southwestern humorists. In the same way the social realists of the 1930s had points of resemblance with the muckraking novelists of the early 1900s, and the 1920s repeated the 1890s on a grander scale.

And the 1960s? By the beginning of the decade it was clear that there would be a reaction against the academic tradition in criticism and poetry. Once again young writers were rebelling against their predecessors, and they were speaking of themselves as "alienated" or "disaffiliated," or, for a time, simply as "beat." There was even a growing body of poetry and fiction written from a new point of view. It was the work of writers who had started over from the beginning, but that was what many of their predecessors had done, and it was part of an American pattern too.

THE TWENTIETH CENTURY

THEODORE DREISER

(1871–1945)

As a sign of the changing nature of American letters, Ford Madox Ford considered it most significant that a man named Dreiser could become the dominant writer of his time—a man who was the son of European immigrants, and who came, not from Boston or Cambridge, but from Terre Haute, Indiana.

Dreiser's father was a bitter failure, although an industrious and pious man; his mother was simple and warm-hearted. The family expected that thrift, industry, and sobriety would lead to the attainment of the American dream, and following opportunity and hope, they moved from town to town in Indiana. Young Dreiser's expectations and disappointments pitched up and down with each move, as each new beginning failed to bring the fulfillment of the Horatio Alger promise. With each move a deep sense of life's bitterness, struggle, and mystery grew in his brooding sensibility. His imaginative life developed from an inner merger of natural necessity, disappointment, and American anticipation.

Without finishing high school, he set out for Chicago when he was sixteen. There he held many modest jobs, from dishwashing on up, always contemplating in his slow and sensitive way the meaning of his city experience. That experience combined an excited sense of a new world whose unlimited future was in the making with a recognition of the huge distance between the lip service paid to public morality and the actualities of human drives, motives, and behavior. Chicago gave Dreiser his themes of heredity, social power, and money in all their complex ramifications.

He entered the University of Indiana but left after one year—

the University environment seemed to him too removed from life—and returned to Chicago, where, on the *Daily Globe*, he began his newspaper career in 1892. Later he continued newspaper work in St. Louis, Cleveland, and Pittsburgh.

In 1900 he became involved in the publication difficulties of *Sister Carrie*. At the insistence of Frank Norris, Doubleday, Page & Co. printed an edition, but on second thought decided that public sale was too risky, since Dreiser's naturalistic exposition might incur charges of obscenity against the publisher. Unable to break the contract, Frank Doubleday simply refrained from distributing what he had printed, and Dreiser learned again about the war that social respectability wages against a man's attempt to articulate what he sees to be social truth. The publication of *Sister Carrie* in London in 1901 encouraged another American edition in 1906, but the book did not really enjoy a wide presentation to American readers until its edition of 1912, a year after the appearance of *Jennie Gerhardt*, when Dreiser was suddenly established as a major light in the literary galaxy.

By that time, he had given up newspaper reporting. He became a successful magazine writer in New York, but the *Sister Carrie* affair made him unpopular with editors. He suffered a nervous breakdown, then continued his magazine work; after joining the Butterick publications, he became editor of *The Delineator* in 1907. In 1910 he forsook editorial work in order to devote his undivided time to his novels. *The Financier* appeared in 1912, followed by *The Titan* in 1914 and *The "Genius"* in 1915. These books revealed Dreiser's community with and difference from the naturalism of such a writer as London. Although Dreiser's novels also deal with the sensational superman—either of enormous financial and social power or of high artistic gifts—they indicate that even the hero cannot stand against the superior strength of social groups or the incomprehensible and overwhelming interplay of cosmic forces. Dreiser has often been called America's first naturalist, because he relentlessly and honestly created for his characters natural and recognizable motivations and circumstances rather than an idealized or exceptional world.

His Chicago experiences, together with his readings in Balzac, Spencer, and Huxley, led him to see the universe (one might use the word "God") as a vast impersonal force, a "chemism," working in all forms of life as a grinding and irresistible impulsion toward self-preservation and development. To stop struggling is to die; to act as an Emersonian self-reliant individual, in accordance with the developmental urges within oneself, is to expose oneself to social sanctions. Dreiser saw that the rich and powerful are able to buy what every man needs, but that the poor man often becomes the outcast or the criminal. Yet all men are driven by the same necessities. Love and beauty, the tangible expressions of a living response to the ruthless cosmic will, become commodities subject to wealth, and one's human identity becomes the consequence of power relationships. Given these ideas, Dreiser found enormous discrepancies between American professions of democracy and America's commercial characteristics, between individualism and conformity, between the self and society, between nature and the repressive "decencies" of American civilization. Consequently, Dreiser's particularly American status grows out of his recognition of the difference between the American image and the American actuality. If there is any agreement in the critical consensus about Dreiser, it is that his stubborn, meticulous piling of detail upon detail evokes the density of certain aspects of American experience and gives his fiction an indelible integrity that raises it above the awkwardness of his craftsmanship.

In *An American Tragedy* (1925), Dreiser explored the plight of individuals caught between universal and American forces by creating a character who had neither internal nor external power to satisfy the necessities that drove him. In the consequent soul-hunger, desperation, and eventual destruction of an ordinary person, Dreiser questioned the moral purpose of natural forces as well as those of the Republic. Yet there remains in all of Dreiser's work a queerly Emersonian, almost mystical romanticism, which seems to imply that cosmic will, though blind, dumb, and indifferent, may yet develop man to a point where his body, mind, and heart will be united. At that transcendent moment, man will be able to become truly civilized, and, throwing off the slough of artificial and destructive repressions, will be able to create the truly organic society. Thus, Dreiser's importance lies not only in his documentation but also in his continuing the complex strains of American rebellion extending from the Transcendentalists to the "hip" and the "beat."

Another aspect of Dreiser's modern temper is shown in his social and political books, such as *Dreiser Looks at Russia* (1928) and *Tragic America* (1931). Increasingly, he found in socialism and controlled state planning the possibility of a humanizing of society (however limited) in the face of the impersonal and often antihuman, seemingly chaotic force of creation itself. He was never able to reconcile his mutually exclusive views that man is capable of rational control of society and that both life and man are probably finally irrational.

Among the titles of Dreiser's books, and in addition to those mentioned above, are *A Traveller at Forty* (1913); *Free and Other Stories* (1918); *The Hand of the Potter* (1918); *Hey Rub-a-Dub-Dub* (1920); *A Book about Myself* (1922), reissued as *Newspaper Days; Chains* (1927); *My City* (1929); *Dawn* (1931), about his boyhood; *The Bulwark* (1946); and *The Stoic* (1947).

There is no collected edition of Dreiser's works. Accounts of the man and his writing are to be found in H. L. Mencken, *A Book of Prefaces* (1917); S. P. Sherman, *On Contemporary Literature* (1917); E. Boyd, *Portraits: Real and Imaginary* (1924); P. H. Boynton, *Some Contemporary Americans* (1924); B. Rascoe, *Theodore Dreiser* (1925); S. P. Sherman, *The Main Stream* (1927); D. Karsmer, *Sixteen Authors to One* (1928); E. D. McDonald, *A Bibliography of the Writings of Theodore Dreiser* (1928); R. Michaud, *The American Novel To-day* (1928); G. B. Munson, *Destinations* (1928); J. C. Squire, ed., *Contemporary American Authors* (1928); T. K. Whipple, *Spokesmen* (1928); V. Orton, *Dreiserana: A Book about His Books* (1929); J. B. Cabell, *Some of Us* (1930); N. Foerster, ed., *Humanism in America* (1930); D. Dudley, *Forgotten Frontiers: Dreiser and the Land of the Free* (1932); G. J. Nathan, *The Intimate Notebooks of George Jean Nathan* (1932); B. Rascoe, *Prometheans* (1933); F. M. Ford, *Portraits from Life* (1937); C. Van Doren, *The American Novel* (1940); R. H. Elias, *Theodore Dreiser: Apostle of Nature* (1949); L. Åhnebrink, *The Beginnings of Naturalism in American Fiction* (1950); L. Trilling, *The Liberal Imagination* (1950); F. J. Hoffman, *The Modern Novel in America* (1951); F. O. Matthiessen, *Theodore Dreiser* (1951); M. Geismar, *Rebels and Ancestors* (1953); B. Gelfant, *The American City Novel* (1954); A. Kazin and C. Shapiro, eds., *The Stature of Theodore Dreiser* (1955); K. Lynn, *The Dream of Success* (1955); C. Walcutt, *American Literary Naturalism* (1956); R. H. Elias, ed., *The Letters of Theodore Dreiser*, 3 vols. (1959); L. Campbell, ed., *Letters to Louise: The Letters of Theodore Dreiser to Louise Campbell* (1959); J. T. Farrell, ed., *Theodore Dreiser* (1962); C. Shapiro, *Theodore Dreiser: Our Bitter Patriot* (1962); P. L. Gerber, *Theodore Dreiser* (1964); L. E. Hussman, "The Spiritual Quest of Theodore Dreiser," *Dissertation Abstracts*, XXV (1964); L. F. Schmidtberger, "The Structure of the Novels of Theodore Dreiser," *Dissertation Abstracts*, XXVI (1965); W. A. Swanberg, *Dreiser* (1965); M. Tjader, *Theodore Dreiser, A New Dimension* (1965); and L. Ziff, *The American 1890s* (1966).

The Second Choice

SHIRLEY DEAR:

You don't want the letters. There are only six of them, anyhow, and think, they're all I have of you to cheer me on my travels. What good would they be to you—little bits of notes telling me you're sure to meet me—but me—think of me! If I send them to you, you'll tear them up, whereas if you leave them with me I can dab them with musk and ambergris and keep them in a little silver box, always beside me.

Ah, Shirley dear, you really don't know how sweet I think you are, how dear! There isn't a thing we have ever done together that isn't as clear in my mind as this great big skyscraper over the way here in Pittsburgh, and far more pleasing. In fact, my thoughts of you are the most precious and delicious things I have, Shirley.

But I'm too young to marry now. You know that, Shirley, don't you? I haven't placed myself in any way yet, and I'm so restless that I don't know whether I ever will, really. Only yesterday, old Roxbaum—that's my new employer here—came to me and wanted to know if I would like an assistant overseership on one of his coffee plantations in Java, said there would not be much money in it for a year or two, a bare living, but later there would be more—and I jumped at it. Just the thought of Java and going there did that, although I knew I could make more staying right here. Can't you see how it is with me, Shirl? I'm too restless and too young. I couldn't take care of you right, and you wouldn't like me after a while if I didn't.

But ah, Shirley sweet, I think the dearest things of you! There isn't an hour, it seems, but some little bit of you comes back—a dear, sweet bit—the night we sat on the grass in Tregore Park and counted the stars through the trees; that first evening at Sparrows Point when we missed the last train and had to walk to Langley. Remember the tree-toads, Shirl? And then that warm April Sunday in Atholby woods! Ah, Shirl, you don't want the six notes! Let me keep them. But think of me, will you, sweet, wherever you go and whatever you do? I'll always think of you, and wish that you had met a better, saner man than me, and that I really could have married you and been all you wanted me to be. By-by, sweet. I may start for Java within the month. If so, and you would want them, I'll send you some cards from there—if they have any.

Your worthless
ARTHUR

She sat and turned the letter in her hand, dumb with despair. It was the very last letter she would ever get from him. Of that she was certain. He was gone now, once and for all. She had written him only once, not making an open plea but asking him to return her letters, and then there had come this tender but evasive reply, saying nothing of a possible return but desiring to keep her letters for old times' sake—the happy hours they had spent together.

The happy hours! Oh, yes, yes, yes—the happy hours!

In her memory now, as she sat here in her home after the day's work, meditating on all that had been in the few short months since he had come and gone, was a world of color and light—a color and light so transfiguring as to seem celestial, but now, alas, wholly dissipated. It had contained so much of all she had desired—love, romance, amusement, laughter. He had been so gay and thoughtless, or headstrong, so youthfully romantic, and with such a love of play and change and to be saying and doing anything and everything. Arthur could dance in a gay way, whistle, sing after a fashion, play. He could play cards and do tricks, and he had such a superior air, so genial and brisk, with a kind of innate courtesy in it and yet an intolerance for slowness and stodginess or anything dull or dingy, such as characterized—but here her thoughts fled from him. She refused to think of any one but Arthur.

Sitting in her little bedroom now, off the parlor on the ground floor in her home in Bethune Street, and looking out over the Kessels' yard, and beyond that—there being no fences in Bethune Street—over the "yards" or lawns of the Pollards, Bakers, Cryders, and others, she thought of how dull it must all have seemed to him, with his fine imaginative mind and experiences, his love of change and gaiety, his atmosphere of something better than she had ever known. How little she had been fitted, perhaps, by beauty or temperament to overcome this—the something—dullness in her work or her home, which possibly had driven him away. For, although many had admired her to date, and she was young and pretty in her simple way and constantly receiving suggestions that her beauty was disturbing to some, still, he had not cared for her—he had gone.

And now, as she meditated, it seemed that this scene, and all that it stood for—her parents, her work, her daily shuttling to and fro between the drug company for which she worked and this street and house—was typical of her life and what she was destined to endure always. Some girls were so much more fortunate. They had fine clothes, fine homes, a world of pleasure and opportunity in which to move. They did not have to scrimp and save and work to pay their own way. And yet she had always been compelled to do it, but had never complained until now—or until he came, and after. Bethune Street, with its commonplace front yards and houses nearly all alike, and this house, so like the others, room for room and porch for porch, and her parents, too, really like all the others, had seemed good enough, quite satisfactory, indeed, until then. But now, now!

Here, in their kitchen, was her mother, a thin, pale, but kindly woman, peeling potatoes and washing lettuce, and putting a bit of steak or a chop or a piece of liver in a frying pan day after day, morning and evening, month after month, year after year. And next door was Mrs. Kessel doing the same thing. And next door Mrs. Cryder. And next door Mrs. Pollard. But, until now, she had not thought it so bad. But now—now—oh! And on all the porches or lawns all along this street were the husbands and fathers, mostly middle-aged or old men like her father, reading their papers or cutting the grass before dinner, or smoking and meditating afterward. Her father was out in front now, a stooped, forbearing, meditative soul, who had rarely anything to say—leaving it all to his wife, her mother, but who was fond of her in his dull, quiet way. He was a patternmaker by trade, and had come into possession of this small, ordinary home via years of toil and saving, her mother helping him. They had no particular religion, as he often said, thinking reasonably human conduct a sufficient passport to heaven, but they had gone occasionally to the Methodist Church over in Nicholas Street, and she had once joined it. But of late she had not gone, weaned away by the other commonplace pleasures of her world.

And then in the midst of it, the dull drift of things, as she now saw them to be, he had come—Arthur Bristow—young, energetic, good-looking, ambitious, dreamful, and instanter, and with her never knowing quite how, the whole thing had been changed. He had appeared so swiftly—out of nothing, as it were.

Previous to him had been Barton Williams, stout, phlegmatic, good-natured, well-meaning, who was, or had been before Arthur came, asking her to marry him, and whom she allowed to half assume that she would. She had liked him in a feeble, albeit, as she thought, tender way, thinking him the kind, according to the logic of her neighborhood, who would make her a good husband, and, until Arthur appeared on the scene, had really intended to marry him. It was not really a love-match, as she saw now, but she thought it was, which was much the same thing, perhaps. But, as she now recalled, when Arthur came, how the scales fell from her eyes! In a trice, as it were, nearly, there was a new heaven and a new earth. Arthur had arrived, and with him a sense of something different.

Mabel Gove had asked her to come over to her house in Westleigh, the adjoining suburb, for Thanksgiving eve and day, and without a thought of anything, and because Barton was busy handling a part of the work in the despatcher's office of the Great Eastern and could not see her, she had gone. And then, to her surprise and strange, almost ineffable delight, the moment she had seen him, he was there—Arthur, with his slim, straight figure and dark hair and eyes and clean-cut features, as clean and attractive as those of a coin. And as he had looked at her and smiled and narrated humorous bits of things that had happened to him, something had come over her—a spell—and after dinner they had all gone round to Edith Barringer's to dance, and there as she had danced with him, somehow, without any seeming boldness on his part, he had taken possession of her, as it were, drawn her close, and told her she had beautiful eyes and hair and such a delicately rounded chin, and that he thought she danced gracefully and was sweet. She had nearly fainted with delight.

"Do you like me?" he had asked in one place in the dance, and, in spite of herself, she had looked up into his eyes, and from that moment she was almost mad over him, could think of nothing else but his hair and eyes and his smile and his graceful figure.

Mabel Gove had seen it all, in spite of her determination that no one should, and on their going to bed later, back at Mabel's home, she had whispered:

"Ah, Shirley, I saw. You like Arthur, don't you?"

"I think he's very nice," Shirley recalled replying, for Mabel knew of her affair with Barton and liked him, "but I'm not crazy over him." And for this bit of treason she had sighed in her dreams nearly all night.

And the next day, true to a request and a promise made by him, Arthur had called again at Mabel's to take her and Mabel to a "movie" which was not so far away, and from there they had gone to an ice-cream parlor, and during it all, when Mabel was not looking, he had squeezed her arm and hand and kissed her neck, and she had held her breath, and her heart had seemed to stop.

"And now you're going to let me come out to your place to see you, aren't you?" he had whispered.

And she had replied, "Wednesday evening," and then written the address on a little piece of paper and given it to him.

But now it was all gone, gone!

This house, which now looked so dreary—how romantic it had seemed that first night *he* called—the front room with its commonplace furniture, and later in the spring, the veranda, with its vines just sprouting, and the moon in May. Oh, the moon in May, and June and July, when he was here! How she had lied to Barton to make evenings for Arthur, and occasionally to Arthur to keep him from contact with Barton. She had not even mentioned Barton to Arthur because—because—well, because Arthur was so much better, and somehow (she admitted it to herself now) she had not been sure that Arthur would care for her long, if at all, and then—well, and then, to be quite frank, Barton might be good enough. She did not exactly hate him because she had found Arthur—not at all. She still liked him in a way—he was so kind and faithful, so very dull and straightforward and thoughtful of her, which Arthur was certainly not. Before Arthur had appeared, as she well remembered, Barton had seemed to be plenty good enough—in fact, all that she desired in a pleasant, companionable way, calling for her, taking her places, bringing her flowers and candy, which Arthur rarely did, and for that, if nothing more, she could not help continuing to like him and to feel sorry for him, and, besides, as she had admitted to herself before, if Arthur left her—. . . Weren't his parents better off than hers—and hadn't he a good position for such a man as he—one hundred and fifty dollars a month and the certainty of more later on? A little while before meeting Arthur, she had thought this very good, enough for two to live on at least, and she had thought some of trying it at some time or other—but now —now—

And that first night he had called—how well she remembered it—how it had transfigured the parlor next this in which she was now, filling it with something it had never had before, and the porch outside, too, for that matter, with its gaunt, leafless vine, and this street, too, even— dull, commonplace Bethune Street. There had been a flurry of snow during the afternoon while she was working at the store, and the ground was white with it. All the neighboring homes seemed to look sweeter and happier and more inviting than ever they had as she came past them, with their lights peeping from under curtains and drawn shades. She had hurried into hers and lighted the big red-shaded parlor lamp, her one artistic treasure, as she thought, and put it near the piano, between it and the window, and arranged the chairs, and then bustled to the task of making herself as pleasing as she might. For him she had gotten out her one best filmy house dress and done up her hair in the fashion she thought most becoming—and that he had not seen before—and powdered her cheeks and nose and darkened her eyelashes, as some of the girls at the store did, and put on her new gray satin slippers, and then, being so arrayed, waited nervously, unable to eat anything or to think of anything but him.

And at last, just when she had begun to think he might not be coming, he had appeared with that arch smile and a "Hello! It's here you live, is it? I was wondering. George, but you're twice as sweet as I thought you were, aren't you?" And then, in the little entryway, behind the closed door, he had held her and kissed her on the mouth a dozen times while she pretended to push against his coat and struggle and say that her parents might hear.

And, oh, the room afterward, with him in it in the red glow of the lamp, and with his pale handsome face made handsomer thereby, as she thought! He had made her sit near him and had held her hands and told her about his work and his dreams—all that he expected to do in the future—and then she had found herself wishing intensely to share just such a life—his life—anything that he might wish to do; only, she kept wondering, with a slight pain, whether he would want her to—he was so young, dreamful, ambitious, much younger and more dreamful than herself, although, in reality, he was several years older.

And then followed that glorious period from December to this late September, in which everything which was worth happening in love had happened. Oh, those wondrous days the following spring, when, with the first burst of buds and leaves, he had taken her one Sunday to Atholby, where all the great woods were, and they had hunted spring beauties in the grass, and sat on a slope and looked at the river below and watched some boys fixing up a sailboat and setting forth in it quite as she wished she and Arthur might be doing—going somewhere together—far, far away from all commonplace things and life! And then he had slipped his arm about her and kissed her cheek and neck, and tweaked her ear and smoothed her hair—and oh, there on the grass, with the spring flowers about her and a canopy of small green leaves above, the perfection of love had come—love so wonderful that the mere thought of it made her eyes brim now! And then had been days, Saturday afternoons and Sundays, at Atholby and Sparrows Point, where the great beach was, and in lovely Tregore Park, a mile or two from her home, where they could go of an evening and sit in or near the pavilion and have ice-cream and dance or watch the dancers. Oh, the stars, the winds, the summer breath of those days! Ah, me! Ah, me!

Naturally, her parents had wondered from the first about her and Arthur, and her and Barton, since Barton had already assumed a proprietary interest in her and she had seemed to like him. But then she was an only child and a pet, and used to presuming on that, and they could not think of saying anything to her. After all, she was young and pretty and was entitled to change her mind; only, only —she had had to indulge in a career of lying and subterfuge in connection with Barton, since Arthur was headstrong and wanted every evening that he chose—to call for her at the store and keep her downtown to dinner and a show.

Arthur had never been like Barton, shy, phlegmatic, obedient, waiting long and patiently for each little favor, but, instead, masterful and eager, rifling her of kisses and caresses and every delight of love, and teasing and playing with her as a cat would a mouse. She could never resist him. He demanded of her her time and her affection without let or hindrance. He was not exactly selfish or cruel, as some might have been, but gay and unthinking at times, unconsciously so, and yet loving and tender at others— nearly always so. But always he would talk of things in the future as if they really did not include her—and this troubled her greatly—of places he might go, things he might do, which, somehow, he seemed to think or assume that she could not or would not do with him. He was always going to Australia sometime, he thought, in a business way, or to South Africa, or possibly to India. He never seemed to have any fixed clear future for himself in mind.

A dreadful sense of helplessness and of impending disaster came over her at these times, of being involved in some predicament over which she had no control, and which would lead her on to some sad end. Arthur, although plainly in love, as she thought, and apparently delighted with her, might not always love her. She began, timidly at first (and always, for that matter), to ask him pretty, seeking questions about himself and her, whether their future was certain to be together, whether he really wanted her— loved her—whether he might not want to marry some one else or just her, and whether she wouldn't look nice in a pearl satin wedding-dress with a long creamy veil and satin slippers and a bouquet of bridalwreath. She had been so slowly but surely saving to that end, even before he came, in connection with Barton; only, after *he* came, all thought of the import of it had been transferred to him. But now, also, she was beginning to ask herself sadly, "Would it ever be?" He was so airy, so inconsequential, so ready to say: "Yes, yes," and "Sure, sure! that's right! Yes, indeedy; you bet! Say, kiddie, but you'll look sweet!" but, somehow, it had always seemed as if this whole thing were a glorious interlude and that it could not last. Arthur was too gay and ethereal and too little settled in his own mind. His ideas of travel and living in different cities, finally winding up in New York or San Francisco, but never with her exactly until she asked him, were too ominous, although he always reassured her gaily: "Of course! Of course!" But somehow she could never believe it really, and it made her intensely sad at times, horribly gloomy. So often she wanted to cry, and she could scarcely tell why.

And then, because of her affection for him, she had finally quarreled with Barton, or nearly that, if one could say that one ever really quarreled with him. It had been because of a certain Thursday evening a few weeks before about which she had disappointed him. In a fit of generosity, knowing that Arthur was coming Wednesday, and because Barton had stopped in at the store to see her, she had told him that he might come, having regretted it afterwards, so enamored was she of Arthur. And then when Wednesday came, Arthur had changed his mind, telling her he would come Friday instead, but on Thursday evening he had stopped in at the store and asked her to go to Sparrows Point, with the result that she had no time to notify Barton. He had gone to the house and sat with her parents until ten-thirty, and then, a few days later, although she had written him offering an excuse, had called at the store to complain slightly.

"Do you think you did just right, Shirley? You might have sent word, mightn't you? Who was it—the new fellow you won't tell me about?"

Shirley flared on the instant.

"Supposing it was? What's it to you? I don't belong to you yet, do I? I told you there wasn't any one, and I wish you'd let me alone about that. I couldn't help it last Thursday—that's all—and I don't want you to be fussing with me—that's all. If you don't want to, you needn't come any more, anyhow."

"Don't say that, Shirley," pleaded Barton. "You don't mean that. I won't bother you, though, if you don't want me any more."

And because Shirley sulked, not knowing what else to do, he had gone and she had not seen him since.

And then sometime later when she had thus broken with Barton, avoiding the railway station where he worked, Arthur had failed to come at his appointed time, sending no word until the next day, when a note came to the store saying that he had been out of town for his firm over Sunday and had not been able to notify her, but that he would call Tuesday. It was an awful blow. At the time, Shirley had a vision of what was to follow. It seemed for the moment as if the whole world had suddenly been reduced to ashes, that there was nothing but black charred cinders anywhere—she felt that about all life. Yet it all came to her clearly then that this was but the beginning of just such days and just such excuses, and that soon, soon, he would come no more. He was beginning to be tired of her and soon he would not even make excuses. She felt it, and it froze and terrified her.

And then, soon after, the indifference which she feared did follow—almost created by her own thoughts, as it were. First, it was a meeting he had to attend somewhere one Wednesday night when he was to have come for her. Then he was going out of town again, over Sunday. Then he was going away for a whole week—it was absolutely unavoidable, he said, his commercial duties were increasing—and once he had casually remarked that nothing could stand in the way where she was concerned—never! She did not think of reproaching him with this; she was too proud. If he was going, he must go. She would not be willing to say to herself that she had ever attempted to hold any man. But, just the same, she was agonized by the thought. When he was with her, he seemed tender enough; only, at times, his eyes wandered and he seemed slightly bored. Other girls, particularly pretty ones, seemed to interest him as much as she did.

And the agony of the long days when he did not come any more for a week or two at a time! The waiting, the brooding, the wondering, at the store and here in her home —in the former place making mistakes at times because she could not get her mind off him and being reminded of them, and here at her own home at nights, being so absent-minded that her parents remarked on it. She felt sure that her parents must be noticing that Arthur was not coming any more, or as much as he had—for she pretended to be going out with him, going to Mabel Gove's instead—and that Barton had deserted her too, he having been driven off by her indifference, never to come any more, perhaps, unless she sought him out.

And then it was that the thought of saving her own face

by taking up with Barton once more occurred to her, of using him and his affections and faithfulness and dullness, if you will, to cover up her own dilemma. Only, this ruse was not to be tried until she had written Arthur this one letter—a pretext merely to see if there was a single ray of hope, a letter to be written in a gentle-enough way and ask-for the return of the few notes she had written him. She had not seen him now in nearly a month, and the last time she had, he had said he might soon be compelled to leave her awhile—to go to Pittsburgh to work. And it was his reply to this that she now held in her hand—from Pitts-burgh! It was frightful! The future without him!

But Barton would never know really what had transpired, if she went back to him. In spite of all her delicious hours with Arthur, she could call him back, she felt sure. She had never really entirely dropped him, and he knew it. He had bored her dreadfully on occasion, arriving on off days when Arthur was not about, with flowers or candy, or both, and sitting on the porch steps and talking of the railroad busi-ness and of the whereabouts and doings of some of their old friends. It was shameful, she had thought at times, to see a man so patient, so hopeful, so good-natured as Barton, de-ceived in this way, and by her, who was so miserable over another. Her parents must see and know, she had thought at these times, but still, what else was she to do?

"I'm a bad girl," she kept telling herself. "I'm all wrong. What right have I to offer Barton what is left?" But still, somehow, she realized that Barton, if she chose to favor him, would only be too grateful for even the leavings of others where she was concerned, and that even yet, if she but deigned to crook a finger, she could have him. He was so simple, so good-natured, so stolid and matter of fact, so different to Arthur whom (she could not help smiling at the thought of it) she was loving now about as Barton loved her—slavishly, hopelessly.

And then, as the days passed and Arthur did not write any more—just this one brief note—she at first grieved hor-ribly, and then in a fit of numb despair attempted, bravely enough from one point of view, to adjust herself to the new situation. Why should she despair? Why die of agony where there were plenty who would still sigh for her—Barton among others? She was young, pretty, very—many told her so. She could, if she chose, achieve a vivacity which she did not feel. Why should she brook this unkindness without a thought of retaliation? Why shouldn't she enter upon a gay and heartless career, indulging in a dozen flirtations at once—dancing and killing all thoughts of Arthur in a round of frivolities? There were many who beckoned to her. She stood at her counter in the drug store on many a day and brooded over this, but at the thought of which one to begin with, she faltered. After her late love, all were so tame, for the present anyhow.

And then—and then—always there was Barton, the humble or faithful, to whom she had been so unkind and whom she had used and whom she still really liked. So often self-reproaching thoughts in connection with him crept over her. He must have known, must have seen how badly she was using him all this while, and yet he had not failed to come and come, until she had actually quarreled with him, and any one would have seen that it was literally hopeless. She could not help remembering, especially now in her pain, that he adored her. He was not calling on her now at all—by her indifference she had finally driven him away —but a word, a word—she waited for days, weeks, hoping against hope, and then—

The office of Barton's superior in the Great Eastern terminal had always made him an easy object for her blandishments, coming and going, as she frequently did, via this very station. He was in the office of the assistant train-despatcher on the ground floor, where passing to and from the local, which, at times, was quicker than a street-car, she could easily see him by peering in; only, she had carefully avoided him for nearly a year. If she chose now, and would call for a message blank at the adjacent telegraph-window which was a part of his room, and raised her voice as she often had in the past, he could scarcely fail to hear, if he did not see her. And if he did, he would rise and come over—of that she was sure, for he never could resist her. It had been a wile of hers in the old days to do this or to make her presence felt by idling outside. After a month of brooding, she felt that she must act—her position as a deserted girl was too much. She could not stand it any longer really—the eyes of her mother, for one.

It was six-fifteen one evening when, coming out of the store in which she worked, she turned her step disconsolately homeward. Her heart was heavy, her face rather pale and drawn. She had stopped in the store's retiring-room before coming out to add to her charms as much as possible by a little powder and rouge and to smooth her hair. It would not take much to reallure her former sweet-heart, she felt sure—and yet it might not be so easy after all. Suppose he had found another? But she could not be-lieve that. It had scarcely been long enough since he had last attempted to see her, and he was really so very, very fond of her and so faithful. He was too slow and certain in his choosing—he had been so with her. Still, who knows? With this thought, she went forward in the evening, feeling for the first time the shame and pain that comes of decep-tion, the agony of having to relinquish an ideal and the feeling of despair that comes to those who find themselves in the position of suppliants, stooping to something which in better days and better fortune they would not know. Arthur was the cause of this.

When she reached the station, the crowd that usually filled it at this hour was swarming. There were so many pairs like Arthur and herself laughing and hurrying away or so she felt. First glancing in the small mirror of a weighing scale to see if she were still of her former charm, she stopped thoughtfully at a little flower stand which stood outside, and for a few pennies purchased a tiny bunch of violets. She then went inside and stood near the window, peering first furtively to see if he were present. He was. Bent over his work, a green shade over his eyes, she could see his solid genial figure at a table. Stepping back a mo-ment to ponder, she finally went forward and, in a clear voice asked.

"May I have a blank, please?"

The infatuation of the discarded Barton was such that it brought him instantly to his feet. In his stodgy, stocky way he rose, his eyes glowing with a friendly hope, his mouth wreathed in smiles, and came over. At the sight of her, pale, but pretty—paler and prettier, really, than he had ever seen her—he thrilled dumbly.

"How are you, Shirley?" he asked sweetly, as he drew near, his eyes searching her face hopefully. He had not seen her for so long that he was intensely hungry, and her paler beauty appealed to him more than ever. Why wouldn't she have him? he was asking himself. Why wouldn't his persistent love yet win her? Perhaps it might. "I haven't seen you in a month of Sundays, it seems. How are the folks?"

"They're all right, Bart," she smiled archly, "and so am I. How have you been? It has been a long time since I've seen you. I've been wondering how you were. Have you been all right? I was just going to send a message."

As he had approached, Shirley had pretended at first not to see him, a moment later to affect surprise, although she was really suppressing a heavy sigh. The sight of him, after Arthur, was not reassuring. Could she really interest herself in him any more? Could she?

"Sure, sure," he replied genially; "I'm always all right. You couldn't kill me, you know. Not going away, are you, Shirl?" he queried interestedly.

"No; I'm just telegraphing to Mabel. She promised to meet me to-morrow, and I want to be sure she will."

"You don't come past here as often as you did, Shirley," he complained tenderly. "At least, I don't seem to see you so often," he added with a smile. "It isn't anything I have done, is it?" he queried, and then, when she protested quickly, added: "What's the trouble, Shirl? Haven't been sick, have you?"

She affected all her old gaiety and ease, feeling as though she would like to cry.

"Oh, no," she returned; "I've been all right. I've been going through the other door, I suppose, or coming in and going out on the Langdon Avenue car." (This was true, because she had been wanting to avoid him.) "I've been in such a hurry, most nights, that I haven't had time to stop, Bart. You know how late the store keeps us at times."

He remembered, too, that in the old days she had made time to stop or meet him occasionally.

"Yes, I know," he said tactfully. "But you haven't been to any of our old card-parties either of late, have you? At least, I haven't seen you. I've gone to two or three, thinking you might be there."

That was another thing Arthur had done—broken up her interest in these old store and neighborhood parties and a banjo-and-mandolin club to which she had once belonged. They had all seemed so pleasing and amusing in the old days—but now. . . . In those days Bart had been her usual companion when his work permitted.

"No," she replied evasively, but with a forced air of pleasant remembrance; "I have often thought of how much fun we had at those, though. It was a shame to drop them. You haven't seen Harry Stull or Trina Trask recently, have you?" she inquired, more to be saying something than for any interest she felt.

He shook his head negatively, then added:

"Yes, I did, too; here in the waiting-room a few nights ago. They were coming down-town to a theater, I suppose."

His face fell slightly as he recalled how it had been their custom to do this, and what their one quarrel had been about. Shirley noticed it. She felt the least bit sorry for him, but much more for herself, coming back so disconsolately to all this.

"Well, you're looking as pretty as ever, Shirley," he continued, noting that she had not written the telegram and that there was something wistful in her glance. "Prettier, I think," and she smiled sadly. Every word that she tolerated from him was as so much gold to him, so much of dead ashes to her. "You wouldn't like to come down some evening this week and see 'The Mouse-Trap,' would you? We haven't been to a theater together in I don't know when." His eyes sought hers in a hopeful, doglike way.

So—she could have him again—that was the pity of it! To have what she really did not want, did not care for! At the least nod now he would come, and this very devotion made it all but worthless, and so sad. She ought to marry him now for certain, if she began in this way, and could in a month's time if she chose, but oh, oh—could she? For the moment she decided that she could not, would not. If he had only repulsed her—told her to go—ignored her— but no; it was her fate to be loved by him in this moving, pleading way, and hers not to love him as she wished to love—to be loved. Plainly, he needed some one like her, whereas she, she—She turned a little sick, a sense of the sacrilege of gaiety at this time creeping into her voice, and exclaimed:

"No, no!" Then seeing his face change, a heavy sadness come over it, "Not this week, anyhow, I mean" ("Not so soon," she had almost said). "I have several engagements this week and I'm not feeling well. But"—seeing his face change, and the thought of her own state returning—"you might come out to the house some evening instead, and then we can go some other time."

His face brightened intensely. It was wonderful how he longed to be with her, how the least favor from her comforted and lifted him up. She could see also now, however, how little it meant to her, how little it could ever mean, even if to him it was heaven. The old relationship would have to be resumed in toto, once and for all, but did she want it that way now that she was feeling so miserable about this other affair? As she meditated, these various moods racing to and fro in her mind, Barton seemed to notice, and now it occurred to him that perhaps he had not pursued her enough—was too easily put off. She probably did like him yet. This evening, her present visit, seemed to prove it.

"Sure, sure!" he agreed. "I'd like that. I'll come out Sunday, if you say. We can go any time to the play. I'm sorry, Shirley, if you're not feeling well. I've thought of you a lot these days. I'll come out Wednesday, if you don't mind."

She smiled a wan smile. It was all so much easier than she had expected—her triumph—and so ashenlike in consequence, a flavor of dead-sea fruit and defeat about it all, that it was pathetic. How could she, after Arthur? How could he, really?

"Make it Sunday," she pleaded, naming the farthest day off, and then hurried out.

Her faithful lover gazed after her, while she suffered an intense nausea. To think—to think—it should all be coming to this! She had not used her telegraph-blank, and now had forgotten all about it. It was not the simple trickery that discouraged her, but her own future which could find no better outlet than this, could not rise above it apparently, or that she had no heart to make it rise above it. Why couldn't she interest herself in some one different to Barton? Why did she have to return to him? Why not wait and meet some other—ignore him as before? But no, no; nothing mattered now—no one—it might as well be Barton as any one, and she would at least make him happy and at the same time solve her own problem. She went out into the train-shed and climbed into her train. Slowly, after the usual pushing and jostling of a crowd, it drew out toward Latonia, that suburban region in which her home lay. As she rode, she thought.

"What have I just done? What am I doing?" she kept asking herself as the clacking wheels on the rails fell into a rhythmic dance and the houses of the brown, dry, endless city fled past in a maze. "Severing myself decisively from the past—the happy past—for supposing, once I am married, Arthur should return and want me again—suppose! Suppose!"

Below at one place, under a shed, were some market-gardeners disposing of the last remnants of their day's wares—a sickly, dull life, she thought. Here was Rutgers Avenue, with its line of red street-cars, many wagons and tracks and counterstreams of automobiles—how often had she passed it morning and evening in a shuttle-like way, and how often would, unless she got married! And here, now, was the river flowing smoothly between its banks lined with coal-pockets and wharves—away, away to the huge deep sea which she and Arthur had enjoyed so much. Oh, to be in a small boat and drift out, out into the endless, restless, pathless deep! Somehow the sight of this water, to-night and every night, brought back those evenings in the open with Arthur at Sparrows Point, the long line of dancers in Eckert's Pavilion, the woods at Atholby, the park, with the dancers in the pavilion—she choked back a sob. Once Arthur had come this way with her on just such an evening as this, pressing her hand and saying how wonderful she was. Oh, Arthur! Arthur! And now Barton was to take his old place again—forever, no doubt. She could not trifle with her life longer in this foolish way, or his. What was the use? But think of it!

Yes, it must be—forever now, she told herself. She must marry. Time would be slipping by and she would become too old. It was her only future—marriage. It was the only future she had ever contemplated really, a home, children, the love of some man whom she could love as she loved Arthur. Ah, what a happy home that would have been for her! But now, now—

But there must be no turning back now, either. There was no other way. If Arthur ever came back—but fear not, he wouldn't! She had risked so much and lost—lost him. Her little venture into true love had been such a failure. Before Arthur had come all had been well enough. Barton, stout and simple and frank and direct, had in some way—how, she could scarcely realize now—offered sufficient of a future. But now, now! He had enough money, she knew, to build a cottage for the two of them. He had told her so. He would do his best always to make her happy, she was sure of that. They could live in about the state her parents were living in—or a little better, not much—and would never want. No doubt there would be children, because he craved them—several of them—and that would take up her time, long years of it—the sad, gray years! But then Arthur, whose children she would have thrilled to bear, would be no more, a mere memory—think of that!—and Barton, the dull, the commonplace, would have achieved his finest dream—and why?

Because love was a failure for her—that was why—and in her life there would be no more true love. She would never love any one again as she had Arthur. It could not be, she was sure of it. He was too fascinating, too wonderful. Always, always, wherever she might be, whoever she might marry, he would be coming back, intruding between her and any possible love, receiving any possible kiss. It would be Arthur she would be loving or kissing. She dabbed at her eyes with a tiny handkerchief, turned her face close to the window and stared out, and then as the environs of Latonia came into view, wondered (so deep is romance): What if Arthur should come back at some time—or now! Supposing he should be here at the station now, accidentally or on purpose, to welcome her, to soothe her weary heart. He had met her here before. How she would fly to him, lay her head on his shoulder, forget forever that Barton ever was, that they had ever separated for an hour. Oh, Arthur! Arthur!

But no, no; here was Latonia—here the viaduct over her train, the long business street and the cars marked "Center" and "Langdon Avenue" running back into the great city. A few blocks away in treeshaded Bethune Street, duller and plainer than ever, was her parents' cottage and the routine of that old life which was now, she felt, more fully fastened upon her than ever before—the lawn-mowers, the lawns, the front porches all alike. Now would come the going to and fro of Barton to business as her father and she now went to business, her keeping house, cooking, washing, ironing, sewing for Barton as her mother now did these things for her father and herself. And she would not be in love really, as she wanted to be. Oh, dreadful! She could never escape it really, now that she could endure it less, scarcely for another hour. And yet she must, must, for the sake of—for the sake of—she closed her eyes and dreamed.

She walked up the street under the trees, past the houses and lawns all alike to her own, and found her father on their veranda reading the evening paper. She sighed at the sight.

"Back, daughter?" he called pleasantly.

"Yes."

"Your mother is wondering if you would like steak or liver for dinner. Better tell her."

"Oh, it doesn't matter."

She hurried into her bedroom, threw down her hat and gloves, and herself on the bed to rest silently, and groaned in her soul. To think that it had all come to this!—Never to see him any more!—To see only Barton, and marry him and live in such a street, have four or five children, forget all her youthful companionships—and all to save her face before her parents, and her future. Why must it be? Should it be, really? She choked and stifled. After a little time her mother, hearing her come in, came to the door—thin, practical, affectionate, conventional.

"What's wrong, honey? Aren't you feeling well tonight? Have you a headache? Let me feel."

Her thin cool fingers crept over her temples and hair. She suggested something to eat or a headache powder right away.

"I'm all right, mother. I'm just not feeling well now. Don't bother. I'll get up soon. Please don't."

"Would you rather have liver or steak to-night, dear?"

"Oh, anything—nothing—please don't bother—steak will do—anything"—if only she could get rid of her and be at rest.

Her mother looked at her and shook her head sympathetically, then retreated quietly, saying no more. Lying so, she thought and thought—grinding, destroying thoughts about the beauty of the past, the darkness of the future—until able to endure them no longer she got up and, looking distractedly out of the window into the yard and the house next door, stared at her future fixedly. What should she do? What should she really do? There was Mrs. Kessel in her kitchen getting her dinner as usual, just as her own mother was now, and Mr. Kessel out on the front porch in his shirt-sleeves reading the evening paper. Beyond was Mr. Pollard in his yard, cutting the grass. All along Bethune Street were such houses and such people—simple, commonplace souls all—clerks, managers, fairly successful craftsmen, like her father and Barton, excellent in their way but not like Arthur the beloved, the lost—and here was she, perforce, or by decision of necessity, soon to be one of them, in some such street as this no doubt, forever and—. For the moment it choked and stifled her.

She decided that she would not. No, no, no! There must be some other way—many ways. She did not have to do this unless she really wished to—would not—only—. Then going to the mirror she looked at her face and smoothed her hair.

"But what's the use?" she asked of herself wearily and resignedly after a time. "Why should I cry? Why shouldn't I marry Barton? I don't amount to anything, anyhow. Arthur wouldn't have me. I wanted him, and I am compelled to take some one else—or no one—what difference does it really make who? My dreams are too high, that's all. I wanted Arthur, and he wouldn't have me. I don't want Barton, and he crawls at my feet. I'm a failure, that's what's the matter with me."

And then, turning up her sleeves and removing a fichu which stood out too prominently from her breast, she went into the kitchen and, looking about for an apron, observed:

"Can't I help? Where's the tablecloth?" and finding it among napkins and silverware in a drawer in the adjoining room, proceeded to set the table.

1918

WILLA CATHER
(1873–1947)

Although she was born near Winchester, Virginia, Willa Cather was to become identified through her writing with the Midwest and Southwest, in which her imaginative memory found the American good society. When she was a child of nine, her family moved with her to Red Cloud, Nebraska, where she soon began to show literary promise. Inspired by her luckily exceptional public school teachers, she went on to the University of Nebraska, where she was editor of the student literary magazine; she was graduated in 1895.

Like many other young Americans, she looked at first to the metropolitan East as the enchanted land which would offer an exciting alternative to the cultural and topographical flatness of the heartland. She worked for the Pittsburgh *Daily Leader* from 1896 to 1901, began to publish stories and poems in 1900, and from 1901 to 1906 taught English at Pittsburgh Central High School and at Allegheny High School across the river.

Her first book was *April Twilights*, a collection of verse that appeared in 1903. It was followed two years later by *The Troll Garden*, a book of short stories. Her publishing ventures brought her to *McClure's Magazine*, where she was an editor from 1906 to 1912, when at last she felt able to give all her time to writing novels. The crucial influence on this decision was exerted by Sarah Orne Jewett, who advised her to concentrate on her fiction and on the locales and characters she knew best in the very being of her personal history if she was to write anything lasting. Encouraged, Miss Cather published her first novel, *Alexander's Bridge*, in 1912, and then, heeding Miss Jewett's advice, turned to her own Midwestern semi-frontier milieu.

As she did so, she found herself returning not only in space but in time. In the ordering reconstruction of the writer's mind, her prairie years became a beautiful life in which traditional values were reaffirmed in the face of bitter odds. The fight to remain human and fiercely in love with living despite the antagonism of harsh and laborious necessity gives her characters, her Neighbor Rosicky and the others like him, a glow of purpose and serenity that sharply differentiates them from the driven characters in the naturalistic novels she despised.

Miss Cather, identifying herself as a realistic writer, took issue with the naturalists in two other important areas. First of all, she did not agree with the rebellious social attitudes that permeate most naturalistic fiction; in her flow back into the past, she became conservative to the extent that she championed the constructive and humane aspects of old, established order and values. The accelerated pace of change and transience in contemporary life made her uncomfortable, and she retreated to other places and other times for an alternative to the modern, urban world. Second, she disliked the detail-piling of such naturalists as Dreiser. In *Not Under Forty* (1936), a volume of critical essays and reminiscences, she articulated her idea of "the novel démeublé"—the novel pared free of details, stripped bare and uncluttered, so that the author and reader could concentrate their attention on the nuances of emotional development in the life of the central character.

Shortly after *Alexander's Bridge,* she published *O Pioneers!* (1913), which treated the locale she had known best, as did *The Song of the Lark* (1915) and *My Antonia,* one of her best novels, which appeared in 1918. Two volumes of short stories, *Youth and the Bright Medusa* (1920) and *Obscure Destinies* (1932), bracketed the novels of the twenties: *One of Ours* (1922); *A Lost Lady* (1923), her last Nebraska novel; *The Professor's House* (1925); *My Mortal Enemy* (1926); and *Death Comes for the Archbishop* (1927). In the last of these, with its New Mexico setting, as in *Shadows on the Rock* (1931), laid in seventeenth-century Quebec, Miss Cather dramatized her basic themes and attitudes. The evocation of the past as something alive and viable in the significance of its traditions becomes not only local color in the best sense, but also an exploration of the conditions of human permanence.

In addition to the titles mentioned above, her works include *Lucy Gayheart* (1935); *Sapphira and the Slave Girl* (1940), *The Old Beauty and Others* (1948); and *On Writing* (1949).

Editions and accounts of the woman and her work are to be

found in A. Fields, ed., *The Letters of Sarah Orne Jewett* (1911); T. K. Whipple, *Spokesmen* (1928); R. Rapin, *Willa Cather* (1930); G. Hicks, "The Case against Willa Cather," *English Journal*, XXII (1933); L. Trilling, "Willa Cather," *New Republic*, XC (1937); *The Novels and Stories of Willa Cather*, 13 vols. (1937–1941), Library Edition; E. and L. Bloom, "Willa Cather's Novels of the Frontier: A Study in Thematic Symbolism," *American Literature*, XXI (1949); J. Jessup, *The Faith of Our Feminists* (1950); J. R. Shively, ed., *Writings from Willa Cather's College Years* (1950); M. R. Bennett, *The World of Willa Cather* (1951); D. Daiches, *Willa Cather: A Critical Introduction* (1951); E. K. Brown (completed by L. Edel), *Willa Cather: A Critical Biography* (1953); E. Lewis, *Willa Cather Living* (1953); E. S. Sergeant, *Willa Cather* (1953); F. Hoffman, *The Twenties* (1955); J. H. Randall III, *The Landscape and the Looking Glass* (1960); E. and L. Bloom, *Willa Cather's Gift of Sympathy* (1962); B. Slote, ed., *April Twilights* (1962); A. E. Schmittlein, "Willa Cather's Novels," *Dissertation Abstracts*, XXIV (1963); C. M. Fox, "Revelation of Character in Five Cather Novels," *Dissertation Abstracts*, XXIV (1964); D. Van Ghent, *Willa Cather* (1964); R. Giannone, "Music in Willa Cather's Fiction," *Dissertation Abstracts*, XXV (1964); Sr. P. D. Charles, "Love and Death in the Novels of Willa Cather," *Dissertation Abstracts*, XXVI (1965); Sr. C. Toler, "Man as Creator of Arts and Civilization in the Works of Willa Cather," *Dissertation Abstracts*, XXVI (1965); and M. R. Bennett, ed., *Willa Cather's Collected Short Fiction, 1892–1912* (1965).

Neighbor Rosicky

1

When Doctor Burleigh told neighbour Rosicky he had a bad heart, Rosicky protested.

"So? No, I guess my heart was always pretty good. I got a little asthma, maybe. Just a awful short breath when I was pitchin' hay last summer, dat's all."

"Well now, Rosicky, if you know more about it than I do, what did you come to me for? It's your heart that makes you short of breath, I tell you. You're sixty-five years old, and you've always worked hard, and your heart's tired. You've got to be careful from now on, and you can't do heavy work any more. You've got five boys at home to do it for you."

The old farmer looked up at the Doctor with a gleam of amusement in his queer, triangular-shaped eyes. His eyes were large and lively, but the lids were caught up in the middle in a curious way, so that they formed a triangle. He did not look like a sick man. His brown face was creased but not wrinkled, he had a ruddy color in his smooth-shaven cheeks and in his lips, under his long brown moustache. His hair was thin and ragged around his ears, but very little grey. His forehead, naturally high and crossed by deep parallel lines, now ran all the way up to his pointed crown. Rosicky's face had the habit of looking interested,— suggested a contented disposition and a reflective quality that was gay rather than grave. This gave him a certain detachment, the easy manner of an on-looker and observer.

"Well, I guess you ain't got no pills for a bad heart, Doctor Ed. I guess the only thing is fur me to git me a new one."

Doctor Burleigh swung round in his desk-chair and frowned at the old farmer. "I think if I were you I'd take a little care of the old one, Rosicky."

Rosicky shrugged. "Maybe I don't know how. I expect you mean fur me not to drink my coffee no more."

"I wouldn't, in your place. But you'll do as you choose about that. I've never yet been able to separate a Bohemian from his coffee or his pipe. I've quit trying. But the sure thing is you've got to cut out farm work. You can feed the stock and do chores about the barn, but you can't do anything in the fields that makes you short of breath."

"How about shelling corn?"

"Of course not!"

Rosicky considered with puckered brows.

"I can't make my heart go no longer'n it wants to, can I, Doctor Ed?"

"I think it's good for five or six years yet, maybe more, if you'll take the strain off it. Sit around the house and help Mary. If I had a good wife like yours, I'd want to stay around the house."

His patient chuckled. "It ain't no place fur a man. I don't like no old man hanging round the kitchen too much. An' my wife, she's a awful hard worker her own self."

"That's it; you can help her a little. My Lord, Rosicky, you are one of the few men I know who has a family he can get some comfort out of; happy dispositions, never quarrel among themselves, and they treat you right. I want to see you live a few years and enjoy them."

"Oh, they're good kids, all right," Rosicky assented.

The Doctor wrote him a prescription and asked him how

his oldest son, Rudolph, who had married in the spring, was getting on. Rudolph had struck out for himself, on rented land. "And how's Polly? I was afraid Mary mightn't like an American daughter-in-law, but it seems to be working out all right."

"Yes, she's a fine girl. Dat widder woman bring her daughters up very nice. Polly got lots of spunk, an' she got some style, too. Da's nice, for young folks to have some style." Rosicky inclined his head gallantly. His voice and his twinkly smile were an affectionate compliment to his daughter-in-law.

"It looks like a storm, and you'd better be getting home before it comes. In town in the car?" Doctor Burleigh rose.

"No, I'm in de wagon. When you got five boys, you ain't got much chance to ride round in de Ford. I ain't much for cars, noway."

"Well, it's a good road out to your place; but I don't want you bumping around in a wagon much. And never again on a hay-rake, remember!"

Rosicky placed the Doctor's fee delicately behind the desk-telephone, looking the other way, as if this were an absent-minded gesture. He put on his plush cap and his corduroy jacket with a sheepskin collar, and went out.

The Doctor picked up his stethoscope and frowned at it as if he were seriously annoyed with the instrument. He wished it had been telling tales about some other man's heart, some old man who didn't look the Doctor in the eye so knowingly, or hold out such a warm brown hand when he said good-bye. Doctor Burleigh had been a poor boy in the country before he went away to medical school; he had known Rosicky almost ever since he could remember, and he had a deep affection for Mrs. Rosicky.

Only last winter he had had such a good breakfast at Rosicky's, and that when he needed it. He had been out all night on a long, hard confinement case at Tom Marshall's, —a big rich farm where there was plenty of stock and plenty of feed and a great deal of expensive farm machinery of the newest model, and no comfort whatever. The woman had too many children and too much work, and she was no manager. When the baby was born at last, and handed over to the assisting neighbor woman, and the mother was properly attended to, Burleigh refused any breakfast in that slovenly house, and drove his buggy—

the snow was too deep for a car—eight miles to Anton Rosicky's place. He didn't know another farm-house where a man could get such a warm welcome, and such good strong coffee with rich cream. No wonder the old chap didn't want to give up his coffee!

He had driven in just when the boys had come back from the barn and were washing up for breakfast. The long table, covered with a bright oilcloth, was set out with dishes waiting for them, and the warm kitchen was full of the smell of coffee and hot biscuit and sausage. Five big handsome boys, running from twenty to twelve, all with what Burleigh called natural good manners,—they hadn't a bit of the painful self-consciousness he himself had to struggle with when he was a lad. One ran to put his horse away, another helped him off with his fur coat and hung it up, and Josephine, the youngest child and the only daughter, quickly set another place under her mother's direction.

With Mary, to feed creatures was the natural expression of affection,—her chickens, the calves, her big hungry boys. It was a rare pleasure to feed a young man whom she seldom saw and of whom she was as proud as if he belonged to her. Some country housekeepers would have stopped to spread a white cloth over the oilcloth, to change the thick cups and plates for their best china, and the wooden-handled knives for plated ones. But not Mary.

"You must take us as you find us, Doctor Ed. I'd be glad to put out my good things for you if you was expected, but I'm glad to get you any way at all."

He knew she was glad,—she threw back her head and spoke out as if she were announcing him to the whole prairie. Rosicky hadn't said anything at all; he merely smiled his twinkling smile, put some more coal on the fire, and went into his own room to pour the Doctor a little drink in a medicine glass. When they were all seated, he watched his wife's face from his end of the table and spoke to her in Czech. Then, with the instinct of politeness which seldom failed him, he turned to the Doctor and said slyly, "I was just tellin' her not to ask you no questions about Mrs. Marshall till you eat some breakfast. My wife, she's terrible fur to ask questions."

The boys laughed, and so did Mary. She watched the Doctor devour her biscuit and sausage, too much excited to eat anything herself. She drank her coffee and sat taking in everything about her visitor. She had known him when he was a poor country boy, and was boastfully proud of his success, always saying: "What do people go to Omaha for, to see a doctor, when we got the best one in the State right here?" If Mary liked people at all, she felt physical pleasure in the sight of them, personal exultation in any good fortune that came to them. Burleigh didn't know many women like that, but he knew she was like that.

When his hunger was satisfied, he did, of course, have to tell them about Mrs. Marshall, and he noticed what a friendly interest the boys took in the matter.

Rudolph, the oldest one (he was still living at home then), said: "The last time I was over there, she was lifting them big heavy milk-cans, and I knew she ought not to be doing it."

"Yes, Rudolph told me about that when he come home, and I said it wasn't right," Mary put in warmly. "It was all right for me to do them things up to the last, for I was terrible strong, but that woman's weakly. And do you think she'll be able to nurse it, Ed?" She sometimes forgot to give him the title she was so proud of. "And to think of your being up all night and then not able to get a decent breakfast! I don't know what's the matter with such people."

"Why, mother," said one of the boys, "if Doctor Ed had got breakfast there, we wouldn't have him here. So you ought to be glad."

"He knows I'm glad to have him, John, any time. But I'm sorry for that poor woman, how bad she'll feel the Doctor had to go away in the cold without his breakfast."

"I wish I'd been in practice when these were getting born." The doctor looked down the row of close-clipped heads. "I missed some good breakfasts by not being."

The boys began to laugh at their mother because she flushed so red, but she stood her ground and threw up her head. "I don't care, you wouldn't have got away from this house without breakfast. No doctor ever did. I'd have had something ready fixed that Anton could warm up for you."

The boys laughed harder than ever, and exclaimed at her: "I'll bet you would!" "She would, that!"

"Father, did you get breakfast for the doctor when we were born?"

"Yes, and he used to bring me my breakfast, too, mighty

nice. I was always awful hungry!" Mary admitted with a guilty laugh.

While the boys were getting the Doctor's horse, he went to the window to examine the house plants. "What do you do to your geraniums to keep them blooming all winter, Mary? I never pass this house that from the road I don't see your windows full of flowers."

She snapped off a dark red one, and a ruffled new green leaf, and put them in his buttonhole. "There, that looks better. You look too solemn for a young man, Ed. Why don't you git married? I'm worried about you. Settin' at breakfast, I looked at you real hard, and I seen you've got some grey hairs already."

"Oh, yes! They're coming. Maybe they'd come faster if I married."

"Don't talk so. You'll ruin your health eating at the hotel. I could send your wife a nice loaf of nut bread, if you only had one. I don't like to see a young man getting grey. I'll tell you something, Ed; you make some strong black tea and keep it handy in a bowl, and every morning just brush it into your hair, an' it'll keep the grey from showin' much. That's the way I do!"

Sometimes the Doctor heard the gossipers in the drugstore wondering why Rosicky didn't get on faster. He was industrious, and so were his boys, but they were rather free and easy, weren't pushers, and they didn't always show good judgment. They were comfortable, they were out of debt, but they didn't get much ahead. Maybe, Doctor Burleigh reflected, people as generous and warmhearted and affectionate as the Rosickys never got ahead much; maybe you could not enjoy your life and put it into the bank, too.

II

When Rosicky left Doctor Burleigh's office, he went into the farm-implement store to light his pipe and put on his glasses and read over the list Mary had given him. Then he went into the general merchandise place next door and stood about until the pretty girl with the plucked eyebrows, who always waited on him, was free. Those eyebrows, two thin India-ink strokes, amused him, because he remembered how they used to be. Rosicky always prolonged his shopping by a little joking; the girl knew the old fellow admired her, and she liked to chaff with him.

"Seems to me about every other week you buy ticking, Mr. Rosicky, and always the best quality," she remarked as she measured off the heavy bolt with red stripes.

"You see, my wife is always makin' goose-fedder pillows, an de' thin stuff don't hold in dem little down-fedders."

"You must have lots of pillows at your house."

"Sure. She makes quilts of dem, too. We sleeps easy. Now she's makin' a fedder quilt for my son's wife. You know Polly, that married my Rudolph. How much my bill, Miss Pearl?"

"Eight eighty-five."

"Chust make it nine, and put in some candy fur de women."

"As usual. I never did see a man buy so much candy for his wife. First thing you know, she'll be getting too fat."

"I'd like dat. I ain't much fur all dem slim women like what de style is now."

"That's one for me, I suppose, Mr. Bohunk!" Pearl sniffed and elevated her India-ink strokes.

When Rosicky went out to his wagon, it was beginning to snow,—the first snow of the season, and he was glad to see it. He rattled out of town and along the highway through a wonderfully rich stretch of country, the finest farms in the county. He admired this High Prairie, as it was called, and always liked to drive through it. His own place lay in a rougher territory, where there was some clay in the soil and it was not so productive. When he bought his land, he hadn't the money to buy on High Prairie; so he told his boys, when they grumbled, that if their land hadn't some clay in it, they wouldn't own it at all. All the same, he enjoyed looking at these fine farms, as he enjoyed looking at a prize bull.

After he had gone eight miles, he came to the graveyard, which lay just at the edge of his own hay-land. There he stopped his horses and sat still on his wagon seat, looking about at the snowfall. Over yonder on the hill he could see his own house, crouching low, with the clump of orchard behind and the windmill before, and all down the gentle hill-slope the rows of pale gold cornstalks stood out against the white field. The snow was falling over the cornfield and the pasture and the hay-land, steadily, with very little wind,

—a nice dry snow. The graveyard had only a light wire fence about it and was all overgrown with long red grass. The fine snow, settling into this red grass and upon the few little evergreens and the headstones, looked very pretty.

It was a nice graveyard, Rosicky reflected, sort of snug and homelike, not cramped or mournful,—a big sweep all around it. A man could lie down in the long grass and see the complete arch of the sky over him, hear the wagons go by; in summer the mowing-machine rattled right up to the wire fence. And it was so near home. Over there across the cornstalks his own roof and windmill looked so good to him that he promised himself to mind the Doctor and take care of himself. He was awful fond of his place, he admitted. He wasn't anxious to leave it. And it was a comfort to think that he would never have to go farther than the edge of his own hayfield. The snow, falling over his barnyard and the graveyard, seemed to draw things together like. And they were all old neighbors in the graveyard, most of them friends; there was nothing to feel awkward or embarrassed about. Embarrassment was the most disagreeable feeling Rosicky knew. He didn't often have it,—only with certain people whom he didn't understand at all.

Well, it was a nice snowstorm; a fine sight to see the snow falling so quietly and graciously over so much open country. On his cap and shoulders, on the horses' backs and manes, light, delicate, mysterious it fell; and with it a dry cool fragrance was released into the air. It meant rest for vegetation and men and beasts, for the ground itself; a season of long nights for sleep, leisurely breakfasts, peace by the fire. This and much more went through Rosicky's mind, but he merely told himself that winter was coming, clucked to his horses, and drove on.

When he reached home, John, the youngest boy, ran out to put away his team for him, and he met Mary coming up from the outside cellar with her apron full of carrots. They went into the house together. On the table, covered with oilcloth figured with clusters of blue grapes, a place was set, and he smelled hot coffee-cake of some kind. Anton never lunched in town; he thought that extravagant, and anyhow he didn't like the food. So Mary always had something ready for him when he got home.

After he was settled in his chair, stirring his coffee in a big cup, Mary took out of the oven a pan of *kolache* stuffed with apricots, examined them anxiously to see whether they had got too dry, put them beside his plate, and then sat down opposite him.

Rosicky asked her in Czech if she wasn't going to have any coffee.

She replied in English, as being somehow the right language for transacting business: "Now what did Doctor Ed say, Anton? You tell me just what."

"He said I was to tell you some compliments, but I forgot 'em." Rosicky's eyes twinkled.

"About you, I mean. What did he say about your asthma?"

"He says I ain't got no asthma." Rosicky took one of the little rolls in his broad brown fingers. The thickened nail of his right thumb told the story of his past.

"Well, what is the matter? And don't try to put me off."

"He don't say nothing much, only I'm a little older, and my heart ain't so good like it used to be."

Mary started and brushed her hair back from her temples with both hands as if she were a little out of her mind. From the way she glared, she might have been in a rage with him.

"He says there's something the matter with your heart? Doctor Ed says so?"

"Now don't yell at me like I was a hog in de garden, Mary. You know I always did like to hear a woman talk soft. He didn't say anything de matter wid my heart, only it ain't so young like it used to be, an' he tell me not to pitch hay or run de corn-sheller."

Mary wanted to jump up, but she sat still. She admired the way he never under any circumstances raised his voice or spoke roughly. He was city-bred, and she was country-bred; she often said she wanted her boys to have their papa's nice ways.

"You never have no pain there, do you? It's your breathing and your stomach that's been wrong. I wouldn't believe nobody but Doctor Ed about it. I guess I'll go see him myself. Didn't he give you no advice?"

"Chust to take it easy like, an' stay round de house dis winter. I guess you got some carpenter work for me to do. I kin make some new shelves for you, and I want dis long time to build a closet in de boys' room and make dem two little fellers keep dere clo'es hung up."

Rosicky drank his coffee from time to time, while he considered. His moustache was of the soft long variety and came down over his mouth like the teeth of a buggy-rake over a bundle of hay. Each time he put down his cup, he ran his blue handkerchief over his lips. When he took a drink of water, he managed very neatly with the back of his hand.

Mary sat watching him intently, trying to find any change in his face. It is hard to see anyone who has become like your own body to you. Yes, his hair had got thin, and his high forehead had deep lines running from left to right. But his neck, always clean-shaved except in the busiest seasons, was not loose or baggy. It was burned a dark reddish brown, and there were deep creases in it, but it looked firm and full of blood. His cheeks had a good color. On either side of his mouth there was a half-moon down the length of his cheek, not wrinkles, but two lines that had come there from his habitual expression. He was shorter and broader than when she married him; his back had grown broad and curved, a good deal like the shell of an old turtle, and his arms and legs were short.

He was fifteen years older than Mary, but she had hardly ever thought about it before. He was her man, and the kind of man she liked. She was rough, and he was gentle,—city-bred, as she always said. They had been shipmates on a rough voyage and had stood by each other in trying times. Life had gone well with them because, at bottom, they had the same ideas about life. They agreed, without discussion, as to what was most important and what was secondary. They didn't often exchange opinions, even in Czech,—it was as if they had thought the same thought together. A good deal had to be sacrificed and thrown overboard in a hard life like theirs, and they had never disagreed as to the things that could go. It had been a hard life, and a soft life, too. There wasn't anything brutal in the short, broad-backed man with the three-cornered eyes and the forehead that went on to the top of his skull. He was a city man, a gentle man, and though he had married a rough farm girl, he had never touched her without gentleness.

They had been at one accord not to hurry through life, not to be always skimping and saving. They saw their neighbors buy more land and feed more stock than they did, without discontent. Once when the creamery agent came to the Rosickys to persuade them to sell him their cream, he told them how much money the Fasslers, their nearest neighbors, had made on their cream last year.

"Yes," said Mary, "and look at them Fassler children! Pale, pinched little things, they look like skimmed milk. I had rather put some color into my children's faces than put money into the bank."

The agent shrugged and turned to Anton.

"I guess we'll do like she says," said Rosicky.

III

Mary very soon got into town to see Doctor Ed, and then she had a talk with her boys and set a guard over Rosicky. Even John, the youngst, had his father on his mind. If Rosicky went to throw hay down from the loft, one of the boys ran up the ladder and took the fork from him. He sometimes complained that though he was getting to be an old man, he wasn't an old woman yet.

That winter he stayed in the house in the afternoons and carpentered, or sat in the chair between the window full of plants and the wooden bench where the two pails of drinking-water stood. This spot was called "Father's corner," though it was not a corner at all. He had a shelf there, where he kept his Bohemian papers and his pipes and tobacco, and his shears and needles and thread and tailor's thimble. Having been a tailor in his youth, he couldn't bear to see a woman patching at his clothes, or at the boys'. He liked tailoring, and always patched all the overalls and jackets and work shirts. Occasionally he made over a pair of pants one of the older boys had outgrown, for the little fellow.

While he sewed, he let his mind run back over his life. He had a good deal to remember, really; life in three countries. The only part of his youth he didn't like to remember was the two years he had spent in London, in Cheapside, working for a German tailor who was wretchedly poor. Those days, when he was nearly always hungry, when his clothes were dropping off him for dirt, and the sound of a strange language kept him in continual bewilderment, had left a sore spot in his mind that wouldn't bear touching.

He was twenty when he landed at Castle Garden in New York, and he had a protector who got him work in a tailor shop in Vesey Street, down near the Washington Market. He looked upon that part of his life as very happy. He became a good workman, he was industrious, and his wages were increased from time to time. He minded his own business and envied nobody's good fortune. He went to night school and learned to read English. He often did overtime work and was well paid for it, but somehow he never saved anything. He couldn't refuse a loan to a friend, and he was self-indulgent. He liked a good dinner, and a little went for beer, a little for tobacco; a good deal went to the girls. He often stood through an opera on Saturday nights; he could get standing-room for a dollar. Those were the great days of opera in New York, and it gave a fellow something to think about for the rest of the week. Rosicky had a quick ear, and a childish love of all the stage splendor; the scenery, the costumes, the ballet. He usually went with a chum, and after the performance they had beer and maybe some oysters somewhere. It was a fine life; for the first five years or so it satisfied him completely. He was never hungry or cold or dirty, and everything amused him: a fire, a dog fight, a parade, a storm, a ferry ride. He thought New York the finest, richest, friendliest city in the world.

Moreover, he had what he called a happy home life. Very near the tailor shop was a small furniture-factory, where an old Austrian, Loeffler, employed a few skilled men and made unusual furniture, most of it to order, for the rich German housewives, uptown. The top floor of Loeffler's five-story factory was a loft, where he kept his choice lumber and stored the odd pieces of furniture left on his hands. One of the young workmen he employed was a Czech, and he and Rosicky became fast friends. They persuaded Loeffler to let them have a sleeping-room in one corner of the loft. They bought good beds and bedding and had their pick of the furniture kept up there. The loft was low-pitched, but light and airy, full of windows, and good-smelling by reason of the fine lumber put up there to season. Old Loeffler used to go down to the docks and buy wood from South America and the East from the sea captains. The young men were as foolish about their house as a bridal pair. Zichec, the young cabinet-maker, devised every sort of convenience, and Rosicky kept their clothes in order. At night and on Sundays, when the quiver of machinery underneath was still, it was the quietest place in the world, and on summer nights all the sea winds blew in. Zichec often practiced on his flute in the evening. They were both fond of music and went to the opera together. Rosicky thought he wanted to live like that forever.

But as the years passed, all alike, he began to get a little restless. When spring came round, he would begin to feel fretted, and he got to drinking. He was likely to drink too much of a Saturday night. On Sunday he was languid and heavy, getting over his spree. On Monday he plunged into work again. So he never had time to figure out what ailed him, though he knew something did. When the grass turned green in Park Place, and the lilac hedge at the back of Trinity churchyard put out its blossoms, he was tormented by a longing to run away. That was why he drank too much; to get a temporary illusion of freedom and wide horizons.

Rosicky, the old Rosicky, could remember as if it were yesterday the day when the young Rosicky found out what was the matter with him. It was on a Fourth of July afternoon, and he was sitting in Park Place in the sun. The lower part of New York was empty. Wall Street, Liberty Street, Broadway, all empty. So much stone and asphalt with nothing going on, so many empty windows. The emptiness was intense, like the stillness in a great factory when the machinery stops and the belts and bands cease running. It was too great a change, it took all the strength out of one. Those blank buildings, without the stream of life pouring through them, were like empty jails. It struck young Rosicky that this was the trouble with big cities; they built you in from the earth itself, cemented you away from any contact with the ground. You lived in an unnatural world, like the fish in an aquarium, who were probably much more comfortable than they ever were in the sea.

On that very day he began to think seriously about the articles he had read in the Bohemian papers, describing prosperous Czech farming communities in the West. He believed he would like to go out there as a farmhand; it was hardly possible that he could ever have land of his own. His people had always been workmen; his father and grandfather had worked in shops. His mother's parents had lived in the country, but they rented their farm and had a hard time to get along. Nobody in his family had ever owned any land,—that belonged to a different station of life altogether. Anton's mother died when he was little, and he was sent into the country to her parents. He stayed with them until he was twelve, and formed those ties with the earth and the farm animals and growing things which are never made at all unless they are made early. After his grandfather died, he went back to live with his father and stepmother, but she was very hard on him, and his father helped him to get passage to London.

After that Fourth of July day in Park Place, the desire to return to the country never left him. To work on another man's farm would be all he asked; to see the sun rise and set and to plant things and watch them grow. He was a very simple man. He was like a tree that has not many roots, but one tap-root that goes down deep. He subscribed for a Bohemian paper printed in Chicago, then for one printed in Omaha. His mind got farther and farther west. He began to save a little money to buy his liberty. When he was thirty-five, there was a great meeting in New York of Bohemian athletic societies, and Rosicky left the tailor shop and went home with the Omaha delegates to try his fortune in another part of the world.

IV

Perhaps the fact that his own youth was well over before he began to have a family was one reason why Rosicky was so fond of his boys. He had almost a grandfather's indulgence for them. He had never had to worry about any of them—Except, just now, a little about Rudolph.

On Saturday night the boys always piled into the Ford, took little Josephine, and went to town to the moving-picture show. One Saturday morning they were talking at the breakfast table about starting early that evening, so that they would have an hour or so to see the Christmas things in the stores before the show began. Rosicky looked down the table.

"I hope you boys ain't disappointed, but I want you to let me have de car tonight. Maybe some of you can go in with de neighbors."

Their faces fell. They worked hard all week, and they were still like children. A new jack-knife or a box of candy pleased the older ones as much as the little fellow.

"If you and Mother are going to town," Frank said,

"maybe you could take a couple of us along with you, anyway."

"No, I want to take de car down to Rudolph's, and let him an' Polly go in to de show. She don't git into town enough, an' I'm afraid she's gittin' lonesome, an' he can't afford no car yet."

That settled it. The boys were a good deal dashed. Their father took another piece of apple-cake and went on: "Maybe next Saturday night de two little fellers can go along wid dem."

"Oh, is Rudolph going to have the car every Saturday night?"

Rosicky did not reply at once; then he began to speak seriously: "Listen, boys; Polly ain't lookin' so good. I don't like to see nobody lookin' sad. It comes hard fur a town girl to be a farmer's wife. I don't want no trouble to start in Rudolph's family. When it starts, it ain't so easy to stop. An American girl don't git used to our ways all at once. I like to tell Polly she and Rudolph can have the car every Saturday night till after New Year's, if it's all right with you boys."

"Sure it's all right, Papa," Mary cut in. "And it's good you thought about that. Town girls is used to more than country girls. I lay awake nights, scared she'll make Rudolph discontented with the farm."

The boys put as good a face on it as they could. They surely looked forward to their Saturday nights in town. That evening Rosicky drove the car the half-mile down the road to Rudolph's new, bare little house.

Polly was in a short-sleeved gingham dress, clearing away the supper dishes. She was a trim, slim little thing, with blue eyes and shingled yellow hair, and her eyebrows were reduced to a mere brush-stroke, like Miss Pearl's.

"Good-evening, Mr. Rosicky. Rudolph's at the barn, I guess." She never called him father, or Mary mother. She was sensitive about having married a foreigner. She never in the world would have done it if Rudolph hadn't been such a handsome, persuasive fellow and such a gallant lover. He had graduated in her class in the high school in town, and their friendship began in the ninth grade.

Rosicky went in, though he wasn't exactly asked. "My boys ain't goin' to town to-night, an' I brought de car over fur you two to go in to de picture show."

Polly, carrying dishes to the sink, looked over her shoulder at him. "Thank you. But I'm late with my work tonight, and pretty tired. Maybe Rudolph would like to go in with you."

"Oh, I don't go to de shows! I'm too old-fashioned. You won't feel so tired after you ride in de air a ways. It's a nice clear night, an' it ain't cold. You go an' fix yourself up, Polly, an' I'll wash de dishes an' leave everything nice fur you."

Polly blushed and tossed her bob. "I couldn't let you do that, Mr. Rosicky. I wouldn't think of it."

Rosicky said nothing. He found a bib apron on a nail behind the kitchen door. He slipped it over his head and then took Polly by her two elbows and pushed her gently toward the door of her own room. "I washed up de kitchen many times for my wife, when de babies was sick or somethin'. You go an' make yourself look nice. I like you to look prettier'n any of dem town girls when you go in. De young folks must have some fun, an' I'm goin' to look out fur you, Polly."

That kind, reassuring grip on her elbows, the old man's funny bright eyes, made Polly want to drop her head on his shoulder for a second. She restrained herself, but she lingered in his grasp at the door of her room, murmuring tearfully: "You always lived in the city when you were young, didn't you? Don't you ever get lonesome out here?"

As she turned round to him, her hand fell naturally into his, and he stood holding it and smiling into her face with his peculiar, knowing, indulgent smile without a shadow of reproach in it. "Dem big cities is all right fur de rich, but dey is terrible hard fur de poor."

"I don't know. Sometimes I think I'd like to take a chance. You lived in New York, didn't you?"

"An' London. Da's bigger still. I learned my trade dere. Here's Rudolph comin', you better hurry."

"Will you tell me about London sometime?"

"Maybe. Only I ain't no talker, Polly. Run an' dress yourself up."

The bedroom door closed behind her, and Rudolph came in from the outside, looking anxious. He had seen the car and was sorry any of his family should come just then. Supper hadn't been a very pleasant occasion. Halting in the doorway, he saw his father in a kitchen apron, carrying dishes to the sink. He flushed crimson and something flashed in his eye. Rosicky held up a warning finger.

"I brought de car over fur you an' Polly to go to de picture show, an' I made her let me finish here so you won't be late. You go put on a clean shirt, quick!"

"But don't the boys want the car, father?"

"Not tonight dey don't." Rosicky fumbled under his apron and found his pants pocket. He took out a silver dollar and said in a hurried whisper: "You go an' buy dat girl some ice cream an' candy tonight, like you was courtin'. She's awful good friends wid me."

Rudolph was very short of cash, but he took the money as if it hurt him. There had been a crop failure all over the country. He had more than once been sorry he'd married this year.

In a few minutes the young people came out, looking clean and a little stiff. Rosicky hurried them off, and then he took his own time with the dishes. He scoured the pots and pans and put away the milk and swept the kitchen. He put some coal in the stove and shut off the draughts, so the place would be warm for them when they got home late at night. Then he sat down and had a pipe and listened to the clock tick.

Generally speaking, marrying an American girl was certainly a risk. A Czech should marry a Czech. It was lucky that Polly was the daughter of a poor widow woman; Rudolph was proud, and if she had a prosperous family to throw up at him, they could never make it go. Polly was one of four sisters, and they all worked; one was bookkeeper in the bank, one taught music, and Polly and her younger sister had been clerks, like Miss Pearl. All four of them were musical, had pretty voices, and sang in the Methodist choir, which the eldest sister directed.

Polly missed the sociability of a store position. She missed the choir, and the company of her sisters. She didn't dislike housework, but she disliked so much of it. Rosicky was a little anxious about this pair. He was afraid Polly would grow so discontented that Rudy would quit the farm and take a factory job in Omaha. He had worked for a winter up there, two years ago, to get money to marry on. He had done very well, and they would always take him back at the stockyards. But to Rosicky that meant the end of everything for his son. To be a landless man was to be a wage-earner, a slave, all your life; to have nothing, to be nothing.

Rosicky thought he would come over and do a little carpentering for Polly after the New Year. He guessed she needed jollying. Rudolph was a serious sort of chap, serious in love and serious about his work.

Rosicky shook out his pipe and walked home across the fields. Ahead of him the lamplight shone from his kitchen windows. Suppose he were still in a tailor shop on Vesey Street, with a bunch of pale, narrow-chested sons working on machines, all coming home tired and sullen to eat supper in a kitchen that was a parlor also; with another crowded, angry family quarrelling just across the dumbwaiter shaft, and squeaking pulleys at the windows where dirty washings hung on dirty lines above a court full of old brooms and mops and ash-cans. . . .

He stopped by the windmill to look up at the frosty winter stars and draw a long breath before he went inside. That kitchen with the shining windows was dear to him; but the sleeping fields and bright stars and the noble darkness were dearer still.

V

On the day before Christmas the weather set in very cold; no snow, but a bitter, biting wind that whistled and sang over the flat land and lashed one's face like fine wires. There was baking going on in the Rosicky kitchen all day, and Rosicky sat inside, making over a coat that Albert had outgrown into an overcoat for John. Mary had a big red geranium in bloom for Christmas, and a row of Jerusalem cherry trees, full of berries. It was the first year she had ever grown these; Doctor Ed brought her the seeds from Omaha when he went to some medical convention. They reminded Rosicky of plants he had seen in England; and all afternoon, as he stitched, he sat thinking about those two years in London, which his mind usually shrank from even after all this while.

He was a lad of eighteen when he dropped down into London, with no money and no connections except the address of a cousin who was supposed to be working at a confectioner's. When he went to the pastry shop, however, he found that the cousin had gone to America. Anton tramped the streets for several days, sleeping in doorways and on the

Embankment, until he was in utter despair. He knew no English, and the sound of the strange language all about him confused him. By chance he met a poor German tailor who had learned his trade in Vienna, and could speak a little Czech. This tailor, Lifschnitz, kept a repair shop in a Cheapside basement, underneath a cobbler. He didn't much need an apprentice, but he was sorry for the boy and took him in for no wages but his keep and what he could pick up. The pickings were supposed to be coppers given you when you took work home to a customer. But most of the customers called for their clothes themselves, and the coppers that came Anton's way were very few. He had, however, a place to sleep. The tailor's family lived upstairs in three rooms; a kitchen, a bedroom, where Lifschnitz and his wife and five children slept, and a living-room. Two corners of this living-room were curtained off for lodgers; in one Rosicky slept on an old horsehair sofa, with a feather quilt to wrap himself in. The other corner was rented to a wretched, dirty boy, who was studying the violin. He actually practised there. Rosicky was dirty, too. There was no way to be anything else. Mrs. Lifschnitz got the water she cooked and washed with from a pump in a brick court, four flights down. There were bugs in the place, and multitudes of fleas, though the poor woman did the best she could. Rosicky knew she often went empty to give another potato or a spoonful of dripping to the two hungry, sad-eyed boys who lodged with her. He used to think he would never get out of there, never get a clean shirt to his back again. What would he do, he wondered, when his clothes actually dropped to pieces and the worn cloth wouldn't hold patches any longer?

It was still early when the old farmer put aside his sewing and his recollections. The sky had been a dark grey all day, with not a gleam of sun, and the light failed at four o'clock. He went to shave and change his shirt while the turkey was roasting. Rudolph and Polly were coming over for supper.

After supper they sat round in the kitchen, and the younger boys were saying how sorry they were it hadn't snowed. Everybody was sorry. They wanted a deep snow that would lie long and keep the wheat warm, and leave the ground soaked when it melted.

"Yes, sir!" Rudolph broke out fiercely; "if we have another dry year like last year, there's going to be hard times in this country."

Rosicky filled his pipe. "You boys don't know what hard times is. You don't owe nobody, you got plenty to eat an' keep warm, an' plenty water to keep clean. When you got them, you can't have it very hard."

Rudolph frowned, opened and shut his big right hand, and dropped it clenched upon his knee. "I've got to have a good deal more than that, Father, or I'll quit this farming gamble. I can always make good wages railroading or at the packing house, and be sure of my money."

"Maybe so," his father answered dryly.

Mary, who had just come in from the pantry and was wiping her hands on the roller towel, thought Rudy and his father were getting too serious. She brought her darning-basket and sat down in the middle of the group.

"I ain't much afraid of hard times, Rudy," she said heartily. "We've had a plenty, but we've always come through. Your father wouldn't never take nothing very hard, not even hard times. I got a mind to tell you a story on him. Maybe you boys can't hardly remember the year we had that terrible hot wind, that burned everything up on the Fourth of July? All the corn an' the gardens. An' that was in the days when we didn't have alfalfa yet,—I guess it wasn't invented.

"Well, that very day your father was out cultivatin' corn, and I was here in the kitchen makin' plum preserves. We had bushels of plums that year. I noticed it was terrible hot, but it's always hot in the kitchen when you're preservin', an' I was too busy with my plums to mind. Anton come in from the field about three o'clock, an' I asked him what was the matter.

" 'Nothin',' he says, 'but it's pretty hot, an' I think I won't work no more today.' He stood round for a few minutes, an' then he says: 'Ain't you near through? I want you should git up a nice supper for us tonight. It's Fourth of July."

"I told him to git along, that I was right in the middle of preservin', but the plums would taste good on hot biscuit. 'I'm goin' to have fried chicken, too,' he says, and he went off an' killed a couple. You three oldest boys was little fellers, playin' round outside, real hot an' sweaty, an your father took you to the horse tank down by the windmill an' took off your clothes an' put you in. Them two box-elder trees was little then, but they made shade over the tank. Then he took off all his own clothes, an' got in with you. While he was playin' in the water with you, the Methodist preacher drove into our place to say how all the neighbors was goin' to meet at the schoolhouse that night, to pray for rain. He drove right to the windmill, of course, and there was your father and you three with no clothes on. I was in the kitchen door, an' I had to laugh, for the preacher acted like he ain't never seen a naked man before. He surely was embarrassed, an' your father couldn't git to his clothes; they was all hangin' up on the windmill to let the sweat dry out of 'em. So he laid in the tank where he was, an' put one of you boys on top of him to cover him up a little, an' talked to the preacher.

"When you got through playin' in the water, he put clean clothes on you and a clean shirt on himself, and by that time I'd begun to get supper. He says: 'It's too hot in here to eat comfortable. Let's have a picnic in the orchard. We'll eat our supper behind the mulberry hedge, under them linden trees.'

"So he carried our supper down, an' a bottle of my wild-grape wine, an' everything tasted good, I can tell you. The wind got cooler as the sun was goin' down, and it turned out pleasant, only I noticed how the leaves was curled up on the linden trees. That made me think, an' I asked your father if that hot wind all day hadn't been terrible hard on the gardens an' the corn.

" 'Corn,' he says, 'there ain't no corn.'

" 'What you talkin' about?' I said. 'Ain't we got forty acres?'

" 'We ain't got an ear,' he says, 'nor nobody else ain't got none. All the corn in this country was cooked by three o'clock today, like you'd roasted it in an oven.'

" 'You mean you won't get no crop at all?' I asked him. I couldn't believe it, after he'd worked so hard.

" 'No crop this year,' he says. 'That's why we're havin' a picnic. We might as well enjoy what we got.'

"An' that's how your father behaved, when all the neighbors was so discouraged they couldn't look you in the face. An' we enjoyed ourselves that year, poor as we was, an' our neighbors wasn't a bit better off for bein' miserable. Some of 'em grieved till they got poor digestions and couldn't relish what they did have."

The younger boys said they thought their father had the best of it. But Rudolph was thinking that, all the same, the neighbors had managed to get ahead more, in the fifteen years since that time. There must be something wrong about his father's way of doing things. He wished he knew what was going on in the back of Polly's mind. He knew she liked his father, but he knew, too, that she was afraid of something. When his mother sent over coffee-cake or prune tarts or a loaf of fresh bread, Polly seemed to regard them with a certain suspicion. When she observed to him that his brothers had nice manners, her tone implied that it was remarkable they should have. With his mother she was stiff and on her guard. Mary's hearty frankness and gusts of good humor irritated her. Polly was afraid of being unusual or conspicuous in any way, of being "ordinary," as she said!

When Mary had finished her story, Rosicky laid aside his pipe.

"You boys like me to tell you about some of dem hard times I been through in London?" Warmly encouraged, he sat rubbing his forehead along the deep creases. It was bothersome to tell a long story in English (he nearly always talked to the boys in Czech), but he wanted Polly to hear this one.

"Well, you know about dat tailor shop I worked in in London? I had one Christmas dere I ain't never forgot. Times was awful bad before Christmas; de boss ain't got much work, an' have it awful hard to pay his rent. It ain't so much fun, bein' poor in a big city like London, I'll say! All de windows is full of good t'ings to eat, an' all de push-carts in de streets is full, an' you smell 'em all de time, an' you ain't got no money,—not a damn bit. 1 didn't mind de cold so much, though I didn't have no overcoat, chust a short jacket I'd outgrowed so it wouldn't meet on me, an' my hands was chapped raw. But I always had a good appetite, like you all know, an' de sight of dem pork pies in de windows was awful fur me!

"Day before Christmas was terrible foggy dat year, an' dat fog gits into your bones and makes you all damp like. Mrs. Lifschnitz didn't give us nothin' but a little bread an' drippin' for supper, because she was savin' to try for to give us a good dinner on Christmas Day. After supper de boss say I can go an' enjoy myself, so I went into de streets to listen to de Christmas singers. Dey sing old songs an' make very nice music, an' I run round after dem a good ways, till I got awful hungry. I t'ink maybe if I go home, I can sleep till morning an' forget my belly.

"I went into my corner real quiet, and roll up in my fedder quilt. But I ain't got my head down, till I smell somet'ing good. Seem like it git stronger an' stronger, an' I can't git to sleep noway. I can't understand dat smell. Dere was a gas light in a hall across de court, dat always shine in at my window a little. I got up an' look round. I got a little wooden box in my corner fur a stool, 'cause I ain't got no chair. I picks up dat box, and under it dere is a roast goose on a platter! I can't believe my eyes. I carry it to de window where de light comes in, an' touch it and smell it to find out, an' den I taste it to be sure. I say, I will eat chust one little bite of dat goose, so I can go to sleep, and tomorrow I won't eat none at all. But I tell you, boys, when I stop, one half of dat goose was gone!"

The narrator bowed his head, and the boys shouted. But little Josephine slipped behind his chair and kissed him on the neck beneath his ear.

"Poor little Papa, I don't want him to be hungry!"

"Da's long ago, child. I ain't never been hungry since I had your mudder to cook fur me."

"Go on and tell us the rest, please," said Polly.

"Well, when I come to realize what I done, of course, I felt terrible. I felt better in de stomach, but very bad in de heart. I set on my bed wid dat platter on my knees, an' it all come to me; how hard dat poor woman save to buy dat goose, and how she get some neighbor to cook it dat got more fire, an' how she put it in my corner to keep it away from dem hungry children. Dey was an old carpet hung up to shut my corner off, an' de children wasn't allowed to go in dere. An' I know she put it in my corner because she trust me more'n she did de violin boy. I can't stand it to face her after I spoil de Christmas. So I put on my shoes and go out into de city. I tell myself I better throw myself in de river; but I guess I ain't dat kind of a boy.

"It was after twelve o'clock, an' terrible cold, an' I start out to walk about London all night. I walk along de river

awhile, but dey was lots of drunks all along; men, and
women too. I chust move along to keep away from the
police. I git onto de Strand, an' den over to New Oxford
Street, where dere was a big German restaurant on de
ground floor, wid big windows all fixed up fine, an' I
could see de people havin' parties inside. While I was
lookin' in, two men and two ladies come out, laughin' and
talkin' and feelin' happy about all dey been eatin' an'
drinkin', and dey was speakin' Czech,—not like de Aus-
trians, but like de home folks talk it.

"I guess I went crazy, an' I done what I ain't never done
before nor since. I went right up to dem gay people an'
begun to beg dem: 'Fellow countrymen, for God's sake
give me money enough to buy a goose!'

"Dey laugh, of course, but de ladies speak awful kind to
me, an' dey take me back into de restaurant and give me
hot coffee and cakes, an' make me tell all about how I
happened to come to London, an' what I was doin' dere.
Dey take my name and where I work down on paper, an'
both of dem ladies give me ten shillings.

"De big market at Covent Garden ain't very far away,
an' by dat time it was open. I go dere an' buy a big goose
an' some pork pies, an' potatoes and onions, an' cakes an'
oranges fur de children,—all I could carry! When I git
home, everybody is still asleep. I pile all I bought on de
kitchen table, an' go in an' lay down on my bed, an' I
ain't waken up till I hear dat woman scream when she
come out into her kitchen. My goodness, but she was surprise! She laugh an' cry at de same time, an' hug me and
waken all de children. She ain't stop fur no breakfast; she
git de Christmas dinner ready dat morning, and we all sit
down an' eat all we can hold. I ain't never seen dat violin
boy have all he can hold before.

"Two three days after dat, de two men come to hunt me
up, an' dey ask my boss, and he give me a good report an'
tell dem I was a steady boy all right. One of dem Bohemians was very smart an' run a Bohemian newspaper in
New York, an' de odder was a rich man, in de importing
business, an' dey been travelling togedder. Dey told me how
t'ings was easier in New York, an' offered to pay my passage when dey was goin' home soon on a boat. My boss
say to me: 'You go. You ain't got no chance here, an' I like
to see you git ahead, fur you always been a good boy to

my woman, and fur dat fine Christmas dinner you give us all.' An' da's how I got to New York."

That night when Rudolph and Polly, arm in arm, were running home across the fields with the bitter wind at their backs, his heart leaped for joy when she said she thought they might have his family come over for supper on New Year's Eve. "Let's get up a nice supper, and not let your mother help at all; make her be company for once."

"That would be lovely of you, Polly," he said humbly. He was a very simple, modest boy, and he, too, felt vaguely that Polly and her sisters were more experienced and worldly than his people.

VI

The winter turned out badly for farmers. It was bitterly cold, and after the first light snows before Christmas there was no snow at all,—and no rain. March was as bitter as February. On those days when the wind fairly punished the country, Rosicky sat by his window. In the fall he and the boys had put in a big wheat planting, and now the seed had frozen in the ground. All that land would have to be ploughed up and planted over again, planted in corn. It had happened before, but he was younger than, and he never worried about what had to be. He was sure of himself and of Mary; he knew they could bear what they had to bear, that they would always pull through somehow. But he was not so sure about the young ones, and he felt troubled because Rudolph and Polly were having such a hard start.

Sitting beside his flowering window while the panes rattled and the wind blew in under the door, Rosicky gave himself to reflection as he had not done since those Sundays in the loft of the furniture-factory in New York, long ago. Then he was trying to find what he wanted in life for himself; now he was trying to find what he wanted for his boys, and why it was he so hungered to feel sure they would be here, working this very land, after he was gone.

They would have to work hard on the farm, and probably they would never do much more than make a living. But if he could think of them as staying here on the land, he wouldn't have to fear any great unkindness for them. Hardships, certainly; it was a hardship to have the wheat freeze in the ground when seed was so high; and to have to sell your stock because you had no feed. But there would be other years when everything came along right, and you caught up. And what you had was your own. You didn't have to choose between bosses and strikers, and go wrong either way. You didn't have to do with dishonest and cruel people. They were the only things in his experience he had found terrifying and horrible; the look in the eyes of a dishonest and crafty man, of a scheming and rapacious woman.

In the country, if you had a mean neighbor, you could keep off his land and make him keep off yours. But in the city, all the foulness and misery and brutality of your neighbors was part of your life. The worst things he had come upon in his journey through the world were human, —depraved and poisonous specimens of man. To this day he could recall certain terrible faces in the London streets. There were mean people everywhere, to be sure, even in their own country town here. But they weren't tempered, hardened, sharpened, like the treacherous people in cities who live by grinding or cheating or poisoning their fellow-men. He had helped to bury two of his fellow-workmen in the tailoring trade, and he was distrustful of the organized industries that see one out of the world in big cities. Here, if you were sick, you had Doctor Ed to look after you; and if you died, fat Mr. Haycock, the kindest man in the world, buried you.

It seemed to Rosicky that for good, honest boys like his, the worst they could do on the farm was better than the best they would be likely to do in the city. If he'd had a mean boy, now, one who was crooked and sharp and tried to put anything over on his brothers, then town would be the place for him. But he had no such boy. As for Rudolph, the discontented one, he would give the shirt off his back to anyone who touched his heart. What Rosicky really hoped for his boys was that they could get through the world without ever knowing much about the cruelty of human beings. "Their mother an' me ain't prepared them for that," he sometimes said to himself.

These thoughts brought him back to a grateful consideration of his own case. What an escape he had had, to be sure! He, too, in his time, had had to take money for repair work from the hand of a hungry child who let it go so wistfully; because it was money due his boss. And now, in all these years, he had never had to take a cent from anyone in bitter need,—never had to look at the face of a woman become like a wolf's from struggle and famine. When he thought of these things, Rosicky would put on his cap and jacket and slip down to the barn and give his work-horses a little extra oats, letting them eat it out of his hand in their slobbery fashion. It was his way of expressing what he felt, and made him chuckle with pleasure.

The spring came warm, with blue skies,—but dry, dry as a bone. The boys began ploughing up the wheat-fields to plant them over in corn. Rosicky would stand at the fence corner and watch them, and the earth was so dry it blew up in clouds of brown dust that hid the horses and the sulky plough and the driver. It was a bad outlook.

The big alfalfa-field that lay between the home place and Rudolph's came up green, but Rosicky was worried because during that open windy winter a great many Russian thistle plants had blown in there and lodged. He kept asking the boys to rake them out; he was afraid that their seed would root and "take the alfalfa." Rudolph said that was nonsense. The boys were working so hard planting corn, their father felt he couldn't insist about the thistles, but he set great store by that big alfalfa field. It was a feed you could depend on,—and there was some deeper reason, vague, but strong. The peculiar green of that clover woke early memories in old Rosicky, went back to something in his childhood in the old world. When he was a little boy, he had played in fields of that strong blue-green color.

One morning, when Rudolph had gone to town in the car, leaving a work-team idle in his barn, Rosicky went over to his son's place, put the horses to the buggy rake, and set about quietly raking up those thistles. He behaved with guilty caution, and rather enjoyed stealing a march on Doctor Ed, who was just then taking his first vacation in seven years of practice and was attending a clinic in Chicago. Rosicky got the thistles raked up, but did not stop to burn them. That would take some time, and his breath was pretty short, so he thought he had better get the horses back to the barn.

He got them into the barn and to their stalls, but the pain had come on so sharp in his chest that he didn't try to take the harness off. He started for the house, bending lower with every step. The cramp in his chest was shutting him up like a jack-knife. When he reached the windmill, he swayed and caught at the ladder. He saw Polly coming down the hill, running with the swiftness of a slim greyhound. In a flash she had her shoulder under his armpit.

"Lean on me, Father, hard! Don't be afraid. We can get to the house all right."

Somehow they did, though Rosicky became blind with pain; he could keep on his legs, but he couldn't steer his course. The next thing he was conscious of was lying on Polly's bed, and Polly bending over him wringing out bath towels in hot water and putting them on his chest. She stopped only to throw coal into the stove, and she kept the tea-kettle and the black pot going. She put these hot applications on him for nearly an hour, she told him afterwards, and all that time he was drawn up stiff and blue, with the sweat pouring off him.

As the pain gradually loosed its grip, the stiffness went out of his jaws, the black circles round his eyes disappeared, and a little of his natural color came back. When his daughter-in-law buttoned his shirt over his chest at last, he sighed.

"Da's fine, de way I feel now, Polly. It was a awful bad spell, an' I was so sorry it all come on you like it did."

Polly was flushed and excited. "Is the pain really gone? Can I leave you long enough to telephone over to your place?"

Rosicky's eyelids fluttered. "Don't telephone, Polly. It ain't no use to scare my wife. It's nice and quiet here, an' if I ain't too much trouble to you, just let me lay still till I feel like myself. I ain't got no pain now. It's nice here."

Polly bent over him and wiped the moisture from his face. "Oh, I'm so glad it's over!" she broke out impulsively. "It just broke my heart to see you suffer so, Father."

Rosicky motioned her to sit down on the chair where the tea-kettle had been, and looked up at her with that lively affectionate gleam in his eyes. "You was awful good to me, I won't ever forget dat. I hate it to be sick on you like dis. Down at de barn I say to myself, dat young girl ain't had much experience in sickness, I don't want to scare her, an' maybe she's got a baby comin' or somet'ing."

Polly took his hand. He was looking at her so intently

and affectionately and confidingly; his eyes seemed to caress her face, to regard it with pleasure. She frowned with her funny streaks of eyebrows, and then smiled back at him.

"I guess maybe there is something of that kind going to happen. But I haven't told anyone yet, not my mother or Rudolph. You'll be the first to know."

His hand pressed hers. She noticed that it was warm again. The twinkle in his yellow-brown eyes seemed to come nearer.

"I like mighty well to see dat little child, Polly," was all he said. Then he closed his eyes and lay half-smiling. But Polly sat still, thinking hard. She had a sudden feeling that nobody in the world, not her mother, not Rudolph, or anyone, really loved her as much as old Rosicky did. It perplexed her. She sat frowning and trying to puzzle it out. It was as if Rosicky had a special gift for loving people, something that was like an ear for music or an eye for color. It was quiet, unobtrusive; it was merely there. You saw it in his eyes,—perhaps that was why they were merry. You felt it in his hands, too. After he dropped off to sleep, she sat holding his warm, broad, flexible brown hand. She had never seen another in the least like it. She wondered if it wasn't a kind of gypsy hand, it was so alive and quick and light in its communications,—very strange in a farmer. Nearly all the farmers she knew had huge lumps of fists, like mauls, or they were knotty and bony and uncomfortable-looking, with stiff fingers. But Rosicky's hand was like quicksilver, flexible, muscular, about the color of a pale cigar, with deep, deep creases across the palm. It wasn't nervous, it wasn't a stupid lump; it was a warm brown human hand, with some cleverness in it, a great deal of generosity, and something else which Polly could only call "gypsylike,"—something nimble and lively and sure, in the way that animals are.

Polly remembered that hour long afterward; it had been like an awakening to her. It seemed to her that she had never learned so much about life from anything as from old Rosicky's hand. It brought her to herself; it communicated some direct and untranslatable message.

When she heard Rudolph coming in the car, she ran out to meet him.

"Oh, Rudy, your father's been awful sick! He raked up

those thistles he's been worrying about, and afterwards he could hardly get to the house. He suffered so I was afraid he was going to die."

Rudolph jumped to the ground. "Where is he now?"

"On the bed. He's asleep. I was terribly scared, because, you know, I'm so fond of your father." She slipped her arm through his and they went into the house. That afternoon they took Rosicky home and put him to bed, though he protested that he was quite well again.

The next morning he got up and dressed and sat down to breakfast with his family. He told Mary that his coffee tasted better than usual to him, and he warned the boys not to bear any tales to Doctor Ed when he got home. After breakfast he sat down by his window to do some patching and asked Mary to thread several needles for him before she went to feed her chickens,—her eyes were better than his, and her hands steadier. He lit his pipe and took up John's overalls. Mary had been watching him anxiously all morning, and as she went out of the door with her bucket of scraps, she saw that he was smiling. He was thinking, indeed, about Polly, and how he might never have known what a tender heart she had if he hadn't got sick over there. Girls nowadays didn't wear their heart on their sleeve. But now he knew Polly would make a fine woman after the foolishness wore off. Either a woman had that sweetness at her heart or she hadn't. You couldn't always tell by the look of them; but if they had that, everything came out right in the end.

After he had taken a few stitches, the cramp began in his chest, like yesterday. He put his pipe cautiously down on the window-sill and bent over to ease the pull. No use, —he had better try to get to his bed if he could. He rose and groped his way across the familiar floor, which was rising and falling like the deck of a ship. At the door he fell. When Mary came in, she found him lying there, and the moment she touched him she knew that he was gone.

Doctor Ed was away when Rosicky died, and for the first few weeks after he got home he was hard driven. Every day he said to himself that he must get out to see the family that had lost their father. One soft, warm moonlight night in early summer he started for the farm. His mind was on other things, and not until his road ran by the graveyard did he realize that Rosicky wasn't over there on the hill where the red lamplight shone, but here, in the moonlight. He stopped his car, shut off the engine, and sat there for a while.

A sudden hush had fallen on his soul. Everything here seemed strangely moving and significant, though signifying what, he did not know. Close by the wire fence stood Rosicky's mowing-machine, where one of the boys had been cutting hay that afternoon; his own work-horses had been going up and down there. The new-cut hay perfumed all the night air. The moonlight silvered the long, billowy grass that grew over the graves and hid the fence; the few little evergreens stood out black in it, like shadows in a pool. The sky was very blue and soft, the stars rather faint because the moon was full.

For the first time it struck Doctor Ed that this was really a beautiful graveyard. He thought of city cemeteries; acres of shrubbery and heavy stone, so arranged and lonely and unlike anything in the living world. Cities of the dead, indeed; cities of the forgotten, of the "put away." But this was open and free, this little square of long grass which the wind for ever stirred. Nothing but the sky overhead, and the many-colored fields running on until they met that sky. The horses worked here in summer; the neighbors passed on their way to town; and over yonder, in the corn-field, Rosicky's own cattle would be eating fodder as winter came on. Nothing could be more undeathlike than this place; nothing could be more right for a man who had helped to do the work of great cities and had always longed for the open country and had got to it at last. Rosicky's life seemed to him complete and beautiful.

w. 1928
p. 1930

SHERWOOD ANDERSON

(1876–1941)

One of the seven children of a harness maker, Sherwood Anderson was born in Camden, Ohio. The father, the model of the irresponsible Windy McPherson in Anderson's first novel, soon moved the family to the factory town of Clyde, Ohio, where Anderson had almost all the formal schooling he was to acquire. The emotional, cultural, and aesthetic desolation of his environment furnished Anderson with the materials of his rebellion against the mechanization of human beings in an industrial culture and against the flatness and repressive false respectability of American small towns. The Midwestern settlements that two generations earlier had seemed in the American imagination to be springboards to the great Western Dream became in the national consciousness, through writers like Anderson and Lewis, a slough of joylessness, of spiritual slavery, and of the defeat of human values by commercialism.

Young Anderson worked hard as a factory hand, a painter, and a stableboy. When he was only fourteen, he was thrown entirely upon his own resources by the death of his mother. He drifted from job to job until he joined the army to fight in Cuba during the Spanish-American War. To his own amazement, he returned as a hero, studied for a year at Wittenberg Academy, and then went to Chicago, where he married and became a successful advertising man. From copywriting he went into business for himself, becoming the owner-manager of a paint factory in Elyria, Ohio. The famous legend, as Anderson told it, is that—burning with a sense of misspent energies, lost chances, a larger destiny, and hatred of the businessman's life—one day he suddenly just walked out of the office and abandoned home and job to become a writer in Chicago. Actually, overworked and near nervous collapse, he wandered in a trance to Cleveland, was hospitalized there, and then returned home to conclude his business affairs. Then he took the train to Chicago. There he re-entered the advertising world and soon sent for his family.

While he earned his frustrated living as an advertising copywriter, he was encouraged in his attempts at fiction by members of "the Chicago group"—Carl Sandburg, Edgar Lee Masters, Ben Hecht, and Floyd Dell. His first novel, *Windy McPherson's Son,* was published in 1916. In the next year, in *Marching Men,* he published a proletarian novel which reflected his experience of inequities. He had begun to believe that America was becoming darkly lost in dehumanizing gentility, in conformity, and in superpatriotism. To Anderson, these forces became the enemy that annihilated the possibility of all the ebullient Whitmanesque promise that formed his image of the Republic.

As literary products, however, his novels left much to be desired. Anderson turned to the short story, and with the publication of *Winesburg, Ohio* (1919), he attained a foremost position in contemporary letters. The stories of *Winesburg, Ohio* are perfect examples of Anderson's fiction. The stories abandon traditional ideas of plot and of suspense in favor of the static exposure of character caught in the repressions of the America he knew. Always refracting the careers of his characters through the prism of his own feelings and experiences, Anderson created subjective stories in which inarticulate men and women, craving emotional and spiritual release from the psychic starvation of their public lives, conflict with the containing pressures of social mores. By demanding publicly molded responses instead of basic and honest human expressions, small town life and the machine age emerge as thwarting monsters that cripple people who have sensitivity and feeling. In his stories, Anderson became one of our earliest exponents of Freudian psychology for the explanation of human behavior. He gave first expression to many of our own contemporary themes by substituting for machinery and respectability the therapeutic alternatives of handicraft, nature, and sex. In its insistence that healthy and sane human life is possible only in a natural, organic, and unartificial society, his work indicates the echoing continuation of the concerns voiced by the American Transcendentalists.

In 1920, he moved to New York, where he became a central figure among the *avant-garde* literary and social iconoclasts.

A friend of the novelist, Waldo Frank, H. L. Mencken, and the critic, Paul Rosenfeld, he became conversant with people whose names were associated with such magazines as *Seven Arts*, the *Little Review*, *The Masses* and *The New Republic*. He continued to produce his novels and volumes of short stories—*Poor White* (1920), *Horses and Men* (1923), *The Triumph of the Egg* (1923), and *Dark Laughter* (1925). With the possible exception of *Dark Laughter*, his novels are not artistically equal to his stories. Influenced by Gertrude Stein, whom he met in Paris, he tried to escape traditional literary dialogue as he had escaped traditional plots. He attempted to create natural speech rhythms and colloquial dialects that would subtly indicate, beneath the inarticulateness of the common man, the bursting frenzy for expression and liberation. The evocation of this underlying man was Anderson's chief concern as a writer. In turn an influence upon younger writers—most notably Hemingway and Faulkner—Anderson left his mark upon American letters, not only through that influence but as a pioneer in investigating and dramatizing the effect of national values on little people.

A Story Teller's Story (1924) and *Tar: A Midwest Childhood* (1926) are autobiographical but inaccurate accounts of his experiences. In 1928, returning to small-town life, he became a newspaper publisher in Marion, Virginia, where at one period he was publisher of both the Republican and the Democratic newspapers. On a good-will trip to South America, he died in Panama.

Anderson's works, in addition to those mentioned above, include *Many Marriages* (1923); *Sherwood Anderson's Notebook* (1926); *Hello Towns!* (1929); *Nearer the Grass Roots* (1929); *Perhaps Women* (1931); *Beyond Desire* (1932); *Death in the Woods* (1933); *Puzzled America* (1935); *Plays, Winesburg and Others* (1937); and the posthumous *Sherwood Anderson's Memoirs* (1942).

There is no collected edition of Anderson's works. *The Portable Sherwood Anderson* (1949), edited and with a biographical and critical introduction by Horace Gregory, contains *Poor White* complete, seven stories from *Winesburg, Ohio*, and other stories, reportage, and letters.

Other accounts of the man and his works are to be found in H. Hansen, *Midwest Portraits* (1923); P. Rosenfeld, *Port of New York* (1924); V. F. Calverton, *The Newer Spirit* (1925); C. Van Doren, "Sinclair Lewis and Sherwood Anderson," *Century*, CX (1925); S. P. Sherman, *Critical Woodcuts* (1926); C. B. Chase, *Sherwood Anderson* (1927); N. B. Fagin, *The Phenomenon of Sherwood Anderson* (1927); D. Karsner, *Sixteen Authors to One* (1928); R. West, *The Strange Necessity* (1928); T. K. Whipple, *Spokesmen* (1928); H. Hartwick, *The*

Foreground of American Fiction (1934); M. Cowley, ed., *After the Genteel Tradition* (1937); C. J. McCole, *Lucifer at Large* (1937); P. H. Boynton, *America in Contemporary Fiction* (1940); F. B. Millett, *Contemporary American Authors* (1940); A. Kazin, *On Native Grounds* (1942); F. J. Hoffman, *Freudianism and the Literary Mind* (1945); M. Geismar, *The Last of the Provincials* (1947); P. Rosenfeld, ed., *The Sherwood Anderson Reader* (1947); *The Newberry Library Bulletin* (December, 1948)—an Anderson memorial issue; I. Howe, *Sherwood Anderson* (1951); J. Schevill, *Sherwood Anderson* (1951); C. Walcutt, "Sherwood Anderson: Impressionism and the Buried Life," *Sewanee Review*, LX (1952); H. M. Jones and W. Rideout, eds., *The Letters of Sherwood Anderson* (1953); S. Winther, "The Aura of Loneliness in Sherwood Anderson," *Modern Fiction Studies*, V (1959); M. Geismar, ed., *Sherwood Anderson: Short Stories* (1962); R. Burbank, *Sherwood Anderson* (1964); B. Weber, *Sherwood Anderson* (1964); W. Morris, ed., *Windy McPherson's Son* (1965); G. A. Love, "Sherwood Anderson's American Pastoral," *Dissertation Abstracts*, XXV (1965); and R. L. White, ed., *The Achievement of Sherwood Anderson* (1966).

I Want to Know Why

We got up at four in the morning, that first day in the east. On the evening before we had climbed off a freight train at the edge of town, and with the true instinct of Kentucky boys had found our way across town and to the race track and the stables at once. Then we knew we were all right. Hanley Turner right away found a nigger we knew. It was Bildad Johnson who in the winter works at Ed Becker's livery barn in our home town, Beckersville. Bildad is a good cook as almost all our niggers are and of course he, like everyone in our part of Kentucky who is anyone at all, likes the horses. In the spring Bildad begins to scratch around. A nigger from our country can flatter and wheedle anyone into letting him do most anything he wants. Bildad wheedles the stable men and the trainers from the horse farms in our country around Lexington. The trainers come into town in the evening to stand around and talk and maybe get into a poker game. Bildad gets in with them. He is always doing little favors and telling about things to eat, chicken browned in a pan, and how is the best way to cook sweet potatoes and corn bread. It makes your mouth water to hear him.

When the racing season comes on and the horses go to

the races and there is all the talk on the streets in the evenings about the new colts, and everyone says when they are going over to Lexington or to the spring meeting at Churchill Downs or to Latonia, and the horsemen that have been down to New Orleans or maybe at the winter meeting at Havana in Cuba come home to spend a week before they start out again, at such a time when everything talked about in Beckersville is just horses and nothing else and the outfits start out and horse racing is in every breath of air you breathe, Bildad shows up with a job as cook for some outfit. Often when I think about it, his always going all season to the races and working in the livery barn in the winter where horses are and where men like to come and talk about horses, I wish I was a nigger. It's a foolish thing to say, but that's the way I am about being around horses, just crazy. I can't help it.

Well, I must tell you about what we did and let you in on what I'm talking about. Four of us boys from Beckersville, all whites and sons of men who live in Beckersville regular, made up our minds we were going to the races, not just to Lexington or Louisville, I don't mean, but to the big eastern track we were always hearing our Beckersville men talk about, to Saratoga. We were all pretty young then. I was just turned fifteen and I was the oldest of the four. It was my scheme. I admit that and I talked the others into trying it. There was Hanley Turner and Henry Rieback and Tom Tumberton and myself. I had thirty-seven dollars I had earned during the winter working nights and Saturdays in Enoch Myer's grocery. Henry Rieback had eleven dollars and the others, Hanley and Tom, had only a dollar or two each. We fixed it all up and laid low until the Kentucky spring meetings were over and some of our men, the sportiest ones, the ones we envied the most, had cut out—then we cut out too.

I won't tell you the trouble we had beating our way on freights and all. We went through Cleveland and Buffalo and other cities and saw Niagara Falls. We bought things there, souvenirs and spoons and cards and shells with pictures of the falls on them for our sisters and mothers, but thought we had better not send any of the things home. We didn't want to put the folks on our trail and maybe be nabbed.

We got into Saratoga as I said at night and went to the

track. Bildad fed us up. He showed us a place to sleep in hay over a shed and promised to keep still. Niggers are all right about things like that. They won't squeal on you. Often a white man you might meet, when you had run away from home like that, might appear to be all right and give you a quarter or a half-dollar or something, and then go right and give you away. White men will do that, but not a nigger. You can trust them. They are squarer with kids. I don't know why.

At the Saratoga meeting that year there were a lot of men from home. Dave Williams and Arthur Mulford and Jerry Myers and others. Then there was a lot from Louisville and Lexington Henry Rieback knew but I didn't. They were professional gamblers and Henry Rieback's father is one too. He is what is called a sheet writer and goes away most of the year to tracks. In the winter when he is home in Beckersville he don't stay there much but goes away to cities and deals faro. He is a nice man and generous, is always sending Henry presents, a bicycle and a gold watch and a boy scout suit of clothes and things like that.

My own father is a lawyer. He's all right, but don't make much money and can't buy me things and anyway I'm getting so old now I don't expect it. He never said nothing to me against Henry, but Hanley Turner and Tom Tumberton's fathers did. They said to their boys that money so come by is no good and they didn't want their boys brought up to hear gamblers' talk and be thinking about such things and maybe embrace them.

That's all right and I guess the men know what they are talking about, but I don't see what it's got to do with Henry or with horses either. That's what I'm writing this story about. I'm puzzled. I'm getting to be a man and want to think straight and be O. K., and there's something I saw at the race meeting at the eastern track I can't figure out.

I can't help it, I'm crazy about thoroughbred horses. I've always been that way. When I was ten years old and saw I was growing to be big and couldn't be a rider I was so sorry I nearly died. Harry Hellinfinger in Beckersville, whose father is Postmaster, is grown up and too lazy to work, but likes to stand around in the street and get up jokes on boys like sending them to a hardware store for a gimlet to bore square holes and other jokes like that. He played one on me. He told me that if I would eat a half a cigar I would be stunted and not grow any more and maybe could be a rider. I did it. When father wasn't looking I took a cigar out of his pocket and gagged it down some way. It made me awful sick and the doctor had to be sent for, and then it did no good. I kept right on growing. It was a joke. When I told what I had done and why most fathers would have whipped me but mine didn't.

Well, I didn't get stunted and didn't die. It serves Harry Hellinfinger right. Then I made up my mind I would like to be a stable boy, but had to give that up too. Mostly niggers do that work and I knew father wouldn't let me go into it. No use to ask him.

If you've never been crazy about thoroughbreds it's because you've never been around where they are much and don't know any better. They're beautiful. There isn't anything so lovely and clean and full of spunk and honest and everything as some race horses. On the big horse farms that are all around our town Beckersville there are tracks and the horses run in the early morning. More than a thousand times I've got out of bed before daylight and walked two or three miles to the tracks. Mother wouldn't of let me go but father always says, "Let him alone." So I got some bread out of the bread box and some butter and jam, gobbled it and lit out.

At the tracks you sit on the fence with men, whites and niggers, and they chew tobacco and talk, and then the colts are brought out. It's early and the grass is covered with shiny dew and in another field a man is plowing and they are frying things in a shed where the track niggers sleep, and you know how a nigger can giggle and laugh and say things that make you laugh. A white man can't do it and some niggers can't but a track nigger can every time.

And so the colts are brought out and some are just galloped by stable boys, but almost every morning on a big track owned by a rich man who lives maybe in New York, there are always, nearly every morning, a few colts and some of the old race horses and geldings and mares that are cut loose.

It brings a lump up into my throat when a horse runs. I don't mean all horses but some. I can pick them nearly every time. It's in my blood like in the blood of race track niggers and trainers. Even when they just go slob-jogging

along with a little nigger on their backs I can tell a winner.
If my throat hurts and it's hard for me to swallow, that's
him. He'll run like Sam Hill when you let him out. If he
don't win every time it'll be a wonder and because they've
got him in a pocket behind another or he was pulled or
got off bad at the post or something. If I wanted to be a
gambler like Henry Rieback's father I could get rich. I
know I could and Henry says so, too. All I would have to
do is to wait 'til that hurt comes when I see a horse and
then bet every cent. That's what I would do if I wanted to
be a gambler, but I don't.

When you're at the tracks in the morning—not the race
tracks but the training tracks around Beckersville—you
don't see a horse, the kind I've been talking about, very
often, but it's nice anyway. Any thoroughbred, that is sired
right and out of a good mare and trained by a man that
knows how, can run. If he couldn't what would he be
there for and not pulling a plow?

Well, out of the stables they come and the boys are on
their backs and it's lovely to be there. You hunch down on
top of the fence and itch inside you. Over in the sheds the
niggers giggle and sing. Bacon is being fried and coffee
made. Everything smells lovely. Nothing smells better than
coffee and manure and horses and niggers and bacon frying and pipes being smoked out of doors on a morning like
that. It just gets you, that's what it does.

But about Saratoga. We was there six days and not a soul
from home seen us and everything came off just as we
wanted it to, fine weather and horses and races and all. We
beat our way home and Bildad gave us a basket with fried
chicken and bread and other eatables in, and I had eighteen
dollars when we got back to Beckersville. Mother jawed
and cried but Pop didn't say much. I told everything we
done except one thing. I did and saw that alone. That's
what I'm writing about. It got me upset. I think about it
at night. Here it is.

At Saratoga we laid up nights in the hay in the shed
Bildad had showed us and ate with the niggers early and at
night when the race people had all gone away. The men
from home stayed mostly in the grandstand and betting
field, and didn't come out around the places where the
horses are kept except to the paddocks just before a race
when the horses are saddled. At Saratoga they don't have

paddocks under an open shed as at Lexington and Churchill Downs and other tracks down in our country, but saddle the horses right out in an open place under trees on a
lawn as smooth and nice as Banker Bohon's front yard here
in Beckersville. It's lovely. The horses are sweaty and
nervous and shine and the men come out and smoke cigars
and look at them and the trainers are there and the owners,
and your heart thumps so you can hardly breathe.

Then the bugle blows for post and the boys that ride
come running out with their silk clothes on and you run
to get a place by the fence with the niggers.

I always am wanting to be a trainer or owner, and at
the risk of being seen and caught and sent home I went to
the paddocks before every race. The other boys didn't but
I did.

We got to Saratoga on a Friday and on Wednesday the
next week the big Mullford Handicap was to be run. Middlestride was in it and Sunstreak. The weather was fine and
the track fast. I couldn't sleep the night before.

What had happened was that both these horses are the
kind it makes my throat hurt to see. Middlestride is long
and looks awkward and is a gelding. He belongs to Joe
Thompson, a little owner from home who only has a half-
dozen horses. The Mullford Handicap is for a mile and
Middlestride can't untrack fast. He goes away slow and
is always way back at the half, then he begins to run and
if the race is a mile and a quarter he'll just eat up everything and get there.

Sunstreak is different. He is a stallion and nervous and
belongs on the biggest farm we've got in our country, the
Van Riddle place that belongs to Mr. Van Riddle of New
York. Sunstreak is like a girl you think about sometimes
but never see. He is hard all over and lovely too. When
you look at his head you want to kiss him. He is trained
by Jerry Tillford who knows me and has been good to me
lots of times, lets me walk into a horse's stall to look at him
close and other things. There isn't anything as sweet as that
horse. He stands at the post quiet and not letting on, but
he is just burning up inside. Then when the barrier goes up
he is off like his name, Sunstreak. It makes you ache to see
him. It hurts you. He just lays down and runs like a bird
dog. There can't anything I ever see run like him except
Middlestride when he gets untracked and stretches himself.

Gee! I ached to see that race and those two horses run, ached and dreaded it too. I didn't want to see either of our horses beaten. We had never sent a pair like that to the races before. Old men in Beckersville said so and the niggers said so. It was a fact.

Before the race I went over to the paddocks to see. I looked a last look at Middlestride, who isn't such a much standing in a paddock that way, then I went to see Sunstreak.

It was his day. I knew when I see him. I forgot all about being seen myself and walked right up. All the men from Beckersville were there and no one noticed me except Jerry Tillford. He saw me and something happened. I'll tell you about that.

I was standing looking at that horse and aching. In some way, I can't tell how, I knew just how Sunstreak felt inside. He was quiet and letting the niggers rub his legs and Mr. Van Riddle himself put the saddle on, but he was just a raging torrent inside. He was like the water in the river at Niagara Falls just before it goes plunk down. That horse wasn't thinking about running. He don't have to think about that. He was just thinking about holding himself back 'til the time for the running came. I knew that. I could just in a way see right inside him. He was going to do some awful running and I knew it. He wasn't bragging or letting on much or prancing or making a fuss, but just waiting. I knew it and Jerry Tillford his trainer knew. I looked up and then that man and I looked into each other's eyes. Something happened to me. I guess I loved the man as much as I did the horse because he knew what I knew. Seemed to me there wasn't anything in the world but that man and the horse and me. I cried and Jerry Tillford had a shine in his eyes. Then I came away to the fence to wait for the race. The horse was better than me, more steadier, and now I know better than Jerry. He was the quietest and he had to do the running.

Sunstreak ran first of course and he busted the world's record for a mile. I've seen that if I never see anything more. Everything came out just as I expected. Middlestride got left at the post and was way back and closed up to be second, just as I knew he would. He'll get a world's record too some day. They can't skin the Beckersville country on horses.

I watched the race calm because I knew what would happen. I was sure. Hanley Turner and Henry Rieback and Tom Tumberton were all more excited than me.

A funny thing had happened to me. I was thinking about Jerry Tillford the trainer and how happy he was all through the race. I liked him that afternoon even more than I ever liked my own father. I almost forgot the horses thinking that way about him. It was because of what I had seen in his eyes as he stood in the paddocks beside Sunstreak before the race started. I knew he had been watching and working with Sunstreak since the horse was a baby colt, had taught him to run and be patient and when to let himself out and not to quit, never. I knew that for him it was like a mother seeing her child do something brave or wonderful. It was the first time I ever felt for a man like that.

After the race that night I cut out from Tom and Hanley and Henry. I wanted to be by myself and I wanted to be near Jerry Tillford if I could work it. Here is what happened.

The track in Saratoga is near the edge of town. It is all polished up and trees around, the evergreen kind, and grass and everything painted and nice. If you go past the track you get to a hard road made of asphalt for automobiles, and if you go along this for a few miles there is a road turns off to a little rummy-looking farm house set in a yard.

That night after the race I went along that road because I had seen Jerry and some other men go that way in an automobile. I didn't expect to find them. I walked for a ways and then sat down by a fence to think. It was the direction they went in. I wanted to be as near Jerry as I could. I felt close to him. Pretty soon I went up the side road—I don't know why—and came to the rummy farm house. I was just lonesome to see Jerry, like wanting to see your father at night when you are a young kid. Just then an automobile came along and turned in. Jerry was in it and Henry Rieback's father, and Arthur Bedford from home, and Dave Williams and two other men I didn't know. They got out of the car and went into the house, all but Henry Rieback's father who quarreled with them and said he wouldn't go. It was only about nine o'clock, but they were were all drunk and the rummy-looking farm house was a place for bad women to stay in. That's what it was. I crept up along a fence and looked through a window and saw.

It's what give me the fantods. I can't make it out. The women in the house were all ugly mean-looking women, not nice to look at or be near. They were homely too, except one who was tall and looked a little like the gelding Middlestride, but not clean like him, but with a hard ugly mouth. She had red hair. I saw everything plain. I got up by an old rose bush by an open window and looked. The women had on loose dresses and sat around in chairs. The men came in and some sat on the women's laps. The place smelled rotten and there was rotten talk, the kind a kid hears around a livery stable in a town like Beckersville in the winter but don't ever expect to hear talked when there are women around. It was rotten. A nigger wouldn't go into such a place.

I looked at Jerry Tillford. I've told you how I had been feeling about him on account of his knowing what was going on inside of Sunstreak in the minute before he went to the post for the race in which he made a world's record.

Jerry bragged in that bad woman house as I know Sunstreak wouldn't never have bragged. He said that he made that horse, that it was him that won the race and made the record. He lied and bragged like a fool. I never heard such silly talk.

And then, what do you suppose he did! He looked at the woman in there, the one that was lean and hard-mouthed and looked a little like the gelding Middlestride, but not clean like him, and his eyes began to shine just as they did when he looked at me and at Sunstreak in the paddocks at the track in the afternoon. I stood there by the window— gee!—but I wished I hadn't gone away from the tracks, but had stayed with the boys and the niggers and the horses. The tall rotten-looking woman was between us just as Sunstreak was in the paddocks in the afternoon.

Then, all of a sudden, I began to hate that man. I wanted to scream and rush in the room and kill him. I never had such a feeling before. I was so mad clean through that I cried and my fists were doubled up so my finger nails cut my hands.

And Jerry's eyes kept shining and he waved back and forth, and then he went and kissed that woman and I crept away and went back to the tracks and to bed and didn't sleep hardly any, and then next day I got the other kids to start home with me and never told them anything I seen.

I been thinking about it ever since. I can't make it out. Spring has come again and I'm nearly sixteen and go to the tracks mornings same as always, and I see Sunstreak and Middlestride and a new colt named Strident I'll bet will lay them all out, but no one thinks so but me and two or three niggers.

But things are different. At the tracks the air don't taste as good or smell as good. It's because a man like Jerry Tillford, who knows what he does, could see a horse like Sunstreak run, and kiss a woman like that the same day. I can't make it out. Darn him, what did he want to do like that for? I keep thinking about it and it spoils looking at horses and smelling things and hearing niggers laugh and everything. Sometimes I'm so mad about it I want to fight someone. It gives me the fantods. What did he do it for? I want to know why.

1918

F. SCOTT FITZGERALD

(1896–1940)

Probably more than any other twentieth-century American author, F. Scott Fitzgerald found his materials both in identification with American values of success and in criticism of them. In his life as well as in his vision of America, he was at once the adolescent who wished to clothe himself in all the meretricious appearances of belonging (like Jay Gatsby), the adolescent who believed that the appearances were tickets to the charmed self-fulfillment and total liberation inherent in the American dream (again like Gatsby), and the disenchanted adult who saw that the promissory note of wealth was finally a betrayal of the enlarged humanity which it led the adolescent imagination to expect.

Born in St. Paul, Minnesota, Fitzgerald grew up on the outskirts of the upper-class life that he identified as the target of his endeavors. His education was, significantly, both that of the public school and of the private school. While very young, he was introduced to sophisticated social life, to travel, and the ways of the "very rich," who are "different from you and me." He attended Princeton, where he became a close friend of Edmund Wilson, wrote the libretto of a Triangle Club Show, and contributed to the literary magazine. In 1917 he left college to join the army, and he never completed the work for his degree. Low grades and illness, spoiling his "political" chances at Princeton, contributed to his eagerness to share in the war glamour of the young soldier abroad. But he was never sent overseas. Ever after, he felt that his double failure was a major indication of the extent to which he, as the semi-poor Midwesterner, could never really belong to a dashing, special world for which he so desperately longed but which, paradoxically, he was already beginning to mistrust.

While a young lieutenant stationed in the South, he met Zelda Sayre of Montgomery, Alabama. In Zelda he found the "golden girl" who epitomized for him the romantic and charmed world of his adolescent vision. After separation from the army, Fitzgerald worked as an advertising copywriter in New York, in order to earn the riches that would enable him to marry Zelda and support her in the style which both she and his vision demanded. Then in 1920 his career began: he published *This Side of Paradise*, married Zelda, and was magically tumbled into the center of the Success Circle. In the popular mind and in fact, the Fitzgeralds became the deans and representatives of the jazz age, "the greatest, gaudiest spree in history." As participants, the Fitzgeralds lived extravagantly, sometimes spending more on travel, parties, and liquor than Scott earned —and his earnings were large. His stories, written for the slick magazines—many for the *Saturday Evening Post*— earned as much as $5,000 apiece, and Fitzgerald could be prolific when he wished. In 1920 he collected some of the stories in *Flappers and Philosophers*.

Two years later, he followed the collection with a second novel, *The Beautiful and Damned*, and another collection of stories, *Tales of the Jazz Age*. As readers vicariously identified themselves and the Fitzgeralds with the characters and values of the novels and stories, so the reviewers tended to identify Scott completely with the jazz age. He was thus victimized by his own success. When the spree was over that October, 1929, and the hard, bleak 1930's set in, no one wanted to read about flappers. It was not until the late 1940's that critics began to reappraise Fitzgerald. They discovered that the artistry with which he condemned and pitied his characters—and their values—was at least as significant as his own participation in the age he chronicled, reaching, in its thematic importance, far beyond the limitations of a particular era.

With his impressive income, Scott and Zelda moved to Europe for a few years, and enjoyed frequent trans-Atlantic crossings. In 1925, on the French Riviera that is the setting of *Tender Is the Night*, he wrote *The Great Gatsby*, considered by most critics as his greatest work. But the dissolution of their lives caught up with the Fitzgeralds as the 1930's caught up with America. Zelda became insane (she survived Scott but was burned to death when a wing of the institution she occupied caught fire). Scott's health began to fail, and his literary acceptance diminished. In 1934, with *Tender Is the Night*, he wrote what he thought was his best book; but the critics disagreed. *Taps at Reveille*, another collection of stories, was issued in 1936, but he had to turn to Hollywood for a living. Caught in the very meretriciousnes he had spent his literary life exploring and indicting, he died in 1940, aged forty-four, of a heart attack, leaving unfinished his last novel, *The Last Tycoon*.

In the Fitzgerald revival of the 1940's and 1950's—in which Edmund Wilson (who edited Fitzgerald's own personal testament to destruction, *The Crack-Up*, in 1945), Malcolm Cowley, Budd Schulberg, and Arthur Mizener are the foremost names—Fitzgerald's manuscripts were re-examined. Cowley reorganized *Tender Is the Night* into the final revision that Fitzgerald had been working on when he died, and reissued it in 1951. Perhaps further critical appraisal will decide that *Tender Is the Night* is one of the highest literary productions in the first half of the American twentieth century.

In addition to the works mentioned above, Fitzgerald wrote *The Vegetable: or, From President to Postman* (1923), *All the Sad Young Men* (1926), and *Afternoon of an Author* (1957, A. Mizener, ed.). There is no collected edition of his works.

Accounts of the man and his work are to be found in E. Boyd, *Portraits: Real and Imaginary* (1924); P. Rosenfeld, *Men Seen* (1925); F. B. Millett, *Contemporary American Authors* (1940); "In Memory of Scott Fitzgerald," a symposium, *New Republic*, CIV (1941); D. Parker, ed., with an introduction by John O'Hara, *The Portable F. Scott Fitzgerald* (1945); W. Thorp, ed., *The Lives of Eighteen from Princeton* (1946); M. Cowley, ed., *The Stories of F. Scott Fitzgerald* (1951); A. Kazin, ed., *F. Scott Fitzgerald: The Man and His Work* (1951); A. Mizener, *The Far Side of Paradise* (1951); *Princeton University Library Chronicle*, XII (Summer, 1951)—a Fitzgerald issue; H. Wechsler, *The Theme of Failure in F. Scott Fitzgerald* (1952); M. Cowley, ed., *Three Novels of F. Scott Fitzgerald* (1953); F. J. Hoffman, *The Twenties* (1955); J. Miller, Jr., *The Fictional Technique of Scott Fitzgerald* (1957); A. Mizener, ed., *Afternoon of an Author* (1957); Sheilah Graham, *Beloved Infidel* (1958); M. Bewley, *The Eccentric Design* (1959); A. Gingrich, ed., *The Pat Hobby Stories* (1962); F. J. Hoffman, ed., *The Great Gatsby: A Study* (1962); A. Turnbull, *Scott Fitzgerald* (1962); M. J. Bruccoli, *The Composition of Tender Is the Night* (1963); K. Eble, *F. Scott Fitzgerald* (1963); J. N. Ellis, "The Fragmented Hero in the Novels of F. Scott Fitz-

gerald," *Dissertation Abstracts*, XXIV (1963); W. Goldhurst,
F. Scott Fitzgerald and His Contemporaries (1963); A. Mizener,
ed., *The Fitzgerald Reader* (1963); A. Mizener, ed., *F. Scott
Fitzgerald: A Collection of Critical Essays* (1963); T. F. Staley,
"F. Scott Fitzgerald: A Study of His Development as a Novelist," *Dissertation Abstracts*, XXIII (1963); A. Turnbull, ed.,
The Letters of F. Scott Fitzgerald (1963); K. G. W. Cross,
F. Scott Fitzgerald (1964); K. C. Frederick, "The Short Stories
of F. Scott Fitzgerald," *Dissertation Abstracts*, XXIV (1964);
J. E. Miller, Jr., *F. Scott Fitzgerald, His Art and His Technique*
(1964); M. J. Bruccoli, *F. Scott Fitzgerald Collector's Handlist*
(1965); J. Kuehl, ed., *The Apprentice Fiction of F. Scott Fitz-
gerald* (1965); J. N. Miller, "Romanticism, Irony, and the
Novels of F. Scott Fitzgerald," *Dissertation Abstracts*, XXV
(1965); A. Mizener, *The Far Side of Paradise* (rev. ed., 1965);
S. Perosa, *The Art of F. Scott Fitzgerald* (1965); H. D. Piper,
F. Scott Fitzgerald, A Critical Portrait (1965); A. Turnbull,
ed., *Scott Fitzgerald: Letters to His Daughter* (1965); R. D.
Lehan, *F. Scott Fitzgerald and the Craft of Fiction* (1966);
Sheila Graham, *College of One* (1967); R. Sklar, *F. Scott Fitz-
gerald* (1967); and continuing bibliography in *The Fitzgerald
Newsletter*.

Winter Dreams

Some of the caddies were poor as sin and lived in one-
room houses with a neurasthenic cow in the front yard, but
Dexter Green's father owned the second best grocery-store
in Black Bear—the best one was "The Hub," patronized by
the wealthy people from Sherry Island—and Dexter cad-
died only for pocket-money.

In the fall when the days became crisp and gray, and the
long Minnesota winter shut down like the white lid of a
box, Dexter's skis moved over the snow that hid the fairways of the golf course. At these times the country gave
him a feeding of profound melancholy—it offended him
that the links should lie in enforced fallowness, haunted by
ragged sparrows for the long season. It was dreary, too,
that on tees where the gay colors fluttered in summer there
were now only the desolate sandboxes knee-deep in
crusted ice. When he crossed the hills the wind blew cold as
misery, and if the sun was out he tramped with his eyes
squinted up against the hard dimensionless glare.

In April the winter ceased abruptly. The snow ran down
into Black Bear Lake scarcely tarrying for the early golfers
to brave the season with red and black balls. Without elation, without an interval of moist glory, the cold was gone.

Dexter knew that there was something dismal about this Northern spring, just as he knew there was something gorgeous about the fall. Fall made him clinch his hands and tremble and repeat idiotic sentences to himself, and make brisk abrupt gestures of command to imaginary audiences and armies. October filled him with hope which November raised to a sort of ecstatic triumph, and in this mood the fleeting brilliant impressions of the summer at Sherry Island were ready grist to his mill. He became a golf champion and defeated Mr. T. A. Hedrick in a marvellous match played a hundred times over the fairways of his imagination, a match each detail of which he changed about untiringly—sometimes won with almost laughable ease, sometimes he came up magnificently from behind. Again, stepping from a Pierce-Arrow automobile, like Mr. Mortimer Jones. he strolled frigidly into the lounge of the Sherry Island Golf Club—or perhaps, surrounded by an admiring crowd, he gave an exhibition of fancy diving from the spring-board of the club raft. . . . Among those who watched him in open-mouthed wonder was Mr. Mortimer Jones.

And one day it came to pass that Mr. Jones—himself and not his ghost—came up to Dexter with tears in his eyes and said that Dexter was the ———— best caddy in the club, and wouldn't he decide not to quit if Mr. Jones made it worth his while, because every other ———— caddy in the club lost one ball a hole for him—regularly——

"No, sir," said Dexter decisively, "I don't want to caddy any more." Then, after a pause: "I'm too old."

"You're not more than fourteen. Why the devil did you decide just this morning that you wanted to quit? You promised that next week you'd go over to the state tournament with me."

"I decided I was too old."

Dexter handed in his "A Class" badge, collected what money was due him from the caddy master, and walked home to Black Bear Village.

"The best ———— caddy I ever saw," shouted Mr. Mortimer Jones over a drink that afternoon. "Never lost a ball! Willing! Intelligent! Quiet! Honest! Grateful!"

The little girl who had done this was eleven—beautifully ugly as little girls are apt to be who are destined after a few years to be inexpressibly lovely and bring no end of misery to a great number of men. The spark, however, was perceptible. There was a general ungodliness in the way her lips twisted down at the corners when she smiled, and in the—Heaven help us!—in the almost passionate quality of her eyes. Vitality is born early in such women. It was utterly in evidence now, shining through her thin frame in a sort of glow.

She had come eagerly out on to the course at nine o'clock with a white linen nurse and five small new golf-clubs in a white canvas bag which the nurse was carrying. When Dexter first saw her she was standing by the caddy house, rather ill at ease and trying to conceal the fact by engaging her nurse in an obviously unnatural conversation graced by startling and irrelevant grimaces from herself.

"Well, it's certainly a nice day, Hilda," Dexter heard her say. She drew down the corners of her mouth, smiled, and glanced furtively around, her eyes in transit falling for an instant on Dexter.

Then to the nurse:

"Well, I guess there aren't very many people out here this morning, are there?"

The smile again—radiant, blatantly artificial—convincing.

"I don't know what we're supposed to do now," said the nurse, looking nowhere in particular.

"Oh, that's all right. I'll fix it up."

Dexter stood perfectly still, his mouth slightly ajar. He knew that if he moved forward a step his stare would be in her line of vision—if he moved backward he would lose his full view of her face. For a moment he had not realized how young she was. Now he remembered having seen her several times the year before—in bloomers.

Suddenly, involuntarily, he laughed, a short abrupt laugh—then, startled by himself, he turned and began to walk quickly away.

"Boy!"

Dexter stopped.

"Boy——"

Beyond question he was addressed. Not only that, but he was treated to that absurd smile, that preposterous smile —the memory of which at least a dozen men were to carry into middle age.

"Boy, do you know where the golf teacher is?"

"He's giving a lesson."

"Well, do you know where the caddy-master is?"

"He isn't here yet this morning."

"Oh." For a moment this baffled her. She stood alternately on her right and left foot.

"We'd like to get a caddy," said the nurse. "Mrs. Mortimer Jones sent us out to play golf, and we don't know how without we get a caddy."

Here she was stopped by an ominous glance from Miss Jones, followed immediately by the smile.

"There aren't any caddies here except me," said Dexter to the nurse, "and I got to stay here in charge until the caddy-master gets here."

"Oh."

Miss Jones and her retinue now withdrew, and at a proper distance from Dexter became involved in a heated conversation, which was concluded by Miss Jones taking one of the clubs and hitting it on the ground with violence. For further emphasis she raised it again and was about to bring it down smartly upon the nurse's bosom, when the nurse seized the club and twisted it from her hands.

"You damn little mean old *thing!*" cried Miss Jones wildly.

Another argument ensued. Realizing that the elements of the comedy were implied in the scene, Dexter several times began to laugh, but each time restrained the laugh before it reached audibility. He could not resist the monstrous conviction that the little girl was justified in beating the nurse.

The situation was resolved by the fortuitous appearance of the caddy-master, who was appealed to immediately by the nurse.

"Miss Jones is to have a little caddy, and this one says he can't go."

"Mr. McKenna said I was to wait here till you came," said Dexter quickly.

"Well, he's here now." Miss Jones smiled cheerfully at the caddy-master. Then she dropped her bag and set off at a haughty mince toward the first tee.

"Well?" The caddy-master turned to Dexter. "What you standing there like a dummy for? Go pick up the young lady's clubs."

"I don't think I'll go out to-day," said Dexter.

"You don't——"

"I think I'll quit."

The enormity of his decision frightened him. He was a favorite caddy, and the thirty dollars a month he earned through the summer, were not to be made elsewhere around the lake. But he had received a strong emotional shock, and his perturbation required a violent and immediate outlet.

It is not so simple as that, either. As so frequently would be the case in the future, Dexter was unconsciously dictated to by his winter dreams.

II

Now, of course, the quality and the seasonability of these winter dreams varied, but the stuff of them remained. They persuaded Dexter several years later to pass up a business course at the State university—his father, prospering now, would have paid his way—for the precarious advantage of attending an older and more famous university in the East, where he was bothered by his scanty funds. But do not get the impression, because his winter dreams happened to be concerned at first with musings on the rich, that there was anything merely snobbish in the boy. He wanted not association with glittering things and glittering people—he wanted the glittering things themselves. Often he reached out for the best without knowing why he wanted it—and sometimes he ran up against the mysterious denials and prohibitions in which life indulges. It is with one of those denials and not with his career as a whole that this story deals.

He made money. It was rather amazing. After college he went to the city from which Black Bear Lake draws its wealthy patrons. When he was only twenty-three and had been there not quite two years, there were already people who liked to say: "Now *there's* a boy—." All about him rich men's sons were peddling bonds precariously, or investing patrimonies precariously, or plodding through the two dozen volumes of the "George Washington Commercial Course," but Dexter borrowed a thousand dollars on his college degree and his confident mouth, and bought a partnership in a laundry.

It was a small laundry when he went into it, but Dexter made a specialty of learning how the English washed fine woolen golf-stockings without shrinking them, and within a year he was catering to the trade that wore knicker-bockers. Men were insisting that their Shetland hose and sweaters go to his laundry, just as they had insisted on a caddy who could find golf-balls. A little later he was doing their wives' lingerie as well—and running five branches in different parts of the city. Before he was twenty-seven he owned the largest string of laundries in his section of the country, It was then that he sold out and went to New York. But the part of his story that concerns us goes back to the days when he was making his first big success.

When he was twenty-three Mr. Hart—one of the gray-haired men who like to say "Now there's a boy—" gave him a guest card to the Sherry Island Golf Club for a week-end. So he signed his name one day on the register, and that afternoon played golf in a foursome with Mr. Hart and Mr. Sandwood and Mr. T. A. Hedrick. He did not consider it necessary to remark that he had once carried Mr. Hart's bag over this same links, and that he knew every trap and gully with his eyes shut—but he found himself glancing at the four caddies who trailed them, trying to catch a gleam or gesture that would remind him of him-self, that would lessen the gap which lay between his present and his past.

It was a curious day, slashed abruptly with fleeting, familiar impressions. One minute he had the sense of being a trespasser—in the next he was impressed by the tremendous superiority he felt toward Mr. T. A. Hedrick, who was a bore and not even a good golfer any more.

Then, because of a ball Mr. Hart lost near the fifteenth green, an enormous thing happened. While they were searching the stiff grasses of the rough there was a clear call of "Fore!" from behind a hill in their rear. And as they all turned abruptly from their search a bright new ball sliced abruptly over the hill and caught Mr. T. A. Hedrick in the abdomen.

"By Gad!" cried Mr. T. A. Hedrick, "they ought to put some of these crazy women off the course. It's getting to be outrageous."

A head and a voice came up together over the hill:

"Do you mind if we go through?"

"You hit me in the stomach!" declared Mr. Hedrick wildly.

"Did I?" The girl approached the group of men. "I'm sorry. I yelled 'Fore!' "

Her glance fell casually on each of the men—then scanned the fairway for her ball.

"Did I bounce into the rough?"

It was impossible to determine whether this question was ingenuous or malicious. In a moment, however, she left no doubt, for as her partner came up over the hill she called cheerfully:

"Here I am! I'd have gone on the green except that I hit something."

As she took her stance for a short mashie shot, Dexter looked at her closely. She wore a blue gingham dress, rimmed at throat and shoulders with a white edging that accentuated her tan. The quality of exaggeration, of thinness, which had made her passionate eyes and down-turning mouth absurd at eleven, was gone now. She was arrestingly beautiful. The color in her cheeks was centred like the color in a picture—it was not a "high" color, but a sort of fluctuating and feverish warmth, so shaded that it seemed at any moment it would recede and disappear. This color and the mobility of her mouth gave a continual impression of flux, of intense life, of passionate vitality—balanced only partially by the sad luxury of her eyes.

She swung her mashie impatiently and without interest, pitching the ball into a sand-pit on the other side of the green. With a quick, insincere smile and a careless "Thank you!" she went on after it.

"That Judy Jones!" remarked Mr. Hedrick on the next tee, as they waited—some moments—for her to play on ahead. "All she needs is to be turned up and spanked for six months and then to be married off to an old-fashioned cavalry captain."

"My God, she's good-looking!" said Mr. Sandwood, who was just over thirty.

"Good-looking!" cried Mr. Hedrick contemptuously, "she always looks as if she wanted to be kissed! Turning those big cow-eyes on every calf in town!"

It was doubtful if Mr. Hedrick intended a reference to the maternal instinct.

"She'd play pretty good golf if she'd try," said Mr. Sandwood.

"She has no form," said Mr. Hedrick solemnly.

"She has a nice figure," said Mr. Sandwood.

"Better thank the Lord she doesn't drive a swifter ball," said Mr. Hart, winking at Dexter.

Later in the afternoon the sun went down with a riotous swirl of gold and varying blues and scarlets, and left the dry, rustling night of Western summer. Dexter watched from the veranda of the Golf Club, watched the even overlap of the waters in the little wind, silver molasses under the harvest-moon. Then the moon held a finger to her lips and the lake became a clear pool, pale and quiet. Dexter put on his bathing-suit and swam out to the farthest raft, where he stretched dripping on the wet canvas of the spring-board.

There was a fish jumping and a star shining and the lights around the lake were gleaming. Over on a dark peninsula a piano was playing the songs of last summer and of summers before that—songs from "Chin-Chin" and "The Count of Luxemburg" and "The Chocolate Soldier" —and because the sound of a piano over a stretch of water had always seemed beautiful to Dexter he lay perfectly quiet and listened.

The tune the piano was playing at that moment had been gay and new five years before when Dexter was a sophomore at college. They had played it at a prom once when he could not afford the luxury of proms, and he had stood outside the gymnasium and listened. The sound of the tune precipitated in him a sort of ecstasy and it was with that ecstasy he viewed what happened to him now. It was a mood of intense appreciation, a sense that, for once, he was magnificently attune to life and that everything about him was radiating a brightness and a glamour he might never know again.

A low, pale oblong detached itself suddenly from the darkness of the Island, spitting forth the reverberate sound of a racing motor-boat. Two white streamers of cleft water rolled themselves out behind it and almost immediately the boat was beside him, drowning out the hot tinkle of the piano in the drone of its spray. Dexter raising himself on his arms was aware of a figure standing at the wheel, of two dark eyes regarding him over the lengthening space of water—then the boat had gone by and was sweeping in an immense and purposeless circle of spray round and round in the middle of the lake. With equal eccentricity one of the circles flattened out and headed back toward the raft.

"Who's that?" she called, shutting off her motor. She was so near now that Dexter could see her bathing-suit, which consisted apparently of pink rompers.

The nose of the boat bumped the raft, and as the latter tilted rakishly he was precipitated toward her. With different degrees of interest they recognized each other.

"Aren't you one of those men we played through this afternoon?" she demanded.

He was.

"Well, do you know how to drive a motor-boat? Because if you do I wish you'd drive this one so I can ride on the surf-board behind. My name is Judy Jones"—she favored him with an absurd smirk—rather, what tried to be a smirk, for, twist her mouth as she might, it was not grotesque, it was merely beautiful—"and I live in a house over there on the Island, and in that house there is a man waiting for me. When he drove up at the door I drove out of the dock because he says I'm his ideal."

There was a fish jumping and a star shining and the lights around the lake were gleaming. Dexter sat beside Judy Jones and she explained how her boat was driven. Then she was in the water, swimming to the floating surf-board with a sinuous crawl. Watching her was without effort to the eye, watching a branch waving or a sea-gull flying. Her arms, burned to butternut, moved sinuously among the dull platinum ripples, elbow appearing first, casting the forearm back with a cadence of falling water, then reaching out and down, stabbing a path ahead.

They moved out into the lake; turning, Dexter saw that she was kneeling on the low rear of the now uptilted surf-board.

"Go faster," she called, "fast as it'll go."

Obediently he jammed the lever forward and the white spray mounted at the bow. When he looked around again the girl was standing up on the rushing board, her arms spread wide, her eyes lifted toward the moon.

"It's awful cold," she shouted. "What's your name?"

He told her.

"Well, why don't you come to dinner to-morrow night?"

His heart turned over like the fly-wheel of the boat, and,

for the second time, her casual whim gave a new direction to his life.

III

Next evening while he waited for her to come down-stairs, Dexter peopled the soft deep summer room and the sun-porch that opened from it with the men who had already loved Judy Jones. He knew the sort of men they were —the men who when he first went to college had entered from the great prep schools with graceful clothes and the deep tan of healthy summers. He had seen that, in one sense, he was better than these men. He was newer and stronger. Yet in acknowledging to himself that he wished his children to be like them he was admitting that he was but the rough, strong stuff from which they eternally sprang.

When the time had come for him to wear good clothes, he had known who were the best tailors in America, and the best tailors in America had made him the suit he wore this evening. He had acquired that particular reserve peculiar to his university, that set it off from other universities. He recognized the value to him of such a mannerism and he had adopted it; he knew that to be careless in dress and manner required more confidence than to be careful. But carelessness was for his children. His mother's name had been Krimslich. She was a Bohemian of the peasant class and she had talked broken English to the end of her days. Her son must keep to the set patterns.

At a little after seven Judy Jones came down-stairs. She wore a blue silk afternoon dress, and he was disappointed at first that she had not put on something more elaborate. This feeling was accentuated when, after a brief greeting, she went to the door of a butler's pantry and pushing it open called: "You can serve dinner, Martha." He had rather expected that a butler would announce dinner, that there would be a cocktail. Then he put these thoughts behind him as they sat down side by side on a lounge and looked at each other.

"Father and mother won't be here," she said thoughtfully.

He remembered the last time he had seen her father, and

he was glad the parents were not to be here to-night—they might wonder who he was. He had been born in Keeble, a Minnesota village fifty miles farther north, and he always gave Keeble as his home instead of Black Bear Village. Country towns were well enough to come from if they weren't inconveniently in sight and used as footstools by fashionable lakes.

They talked of his university, which she had visited frequently during the past two years, and of the near-by city which supplied Sherry Island with its patrons, and whither Dexter would return next day to his prospering laundries.

During dinner she slipped into a moody depression which gave Dexter a feeling of uneasiness. Whatever petulance she uttered in her throaty voice worried him. Whatever she smiled at—at him, at a chicken liver, at nothing—it disturbed him that her smile could have no root in mirth, or even in amusement. When the scarlet corners of her lips curved down, it was less a smile than an invitation to a kiss.

Then, after dinner, she led him out on the dark sun-porch and deliberately changed the atmosphere.

"Do you mind if I weep a little?" she said.

"I'm afraid I'm boring you," he responded quickly.

"You're not. I like you. But I've just had a terrible afternoon. There was a man I cared about, and this afternoon he told me out of a clear sky that he was poor as a church-mouse. He'd never even hinted it before. Does this sound horribly mundane?"

"Perhaps he was afraid to tell you."

"Suppose he was," she answered. "He didn't start right. You see, if I'd thought of him as poor—well, I've been mad about loads of poor men, and fully intended to marry them all. But in this case, I hadn't thought of him that way, and my interest in him wasn't strong enough to survive the shock. As if a girl calmly informed her fiancé that she was a widow. He might not object to widows, but——"

"Let's start right," she interrupted herself suddenly. "Who are you, anyhow?"

For a moment Dexter hesitated. Then:

"I'm nobody," he announced. "My career is largely a matter of futures."

"Are you poor?"

"No," he said frankly, "I'm probably making more money than any man my age in the Northwest. I know that's an obnoxious remark, but you advised me to start right."

There was a pause. Then she smiled and the corners of her mouth drooped and an almost imperceptible sway brought her closer to him, looking up into his eyes. A lump rose in Dexter's throat, and he waited breathless for the experiment, facing the unpredictable compound that would form mysteriously from the elements of their lips. Then he saw—she communicated her excitement to him, lavishly, deeply, with kisses that were not a promise but a fulfilment. They aroused in him not hunger demanding renewal but surfeit that would demand more surfeit . . . kisses that were like charity, creating want by holding back nothing at all.

It did not take him many hours to decide that he had wanted Judy Jones ever since he was a proud, desirous little boy.

IV

It began like that—and continued, with varying shades of intensity, on such a note right up to the dénouement. Dexter surrendered a part of himself to the most direct and unprincipled personality with which he had ever come in contact. Whatever Judy wanted, she went after with the full pressure of her charm. There was no divergence of method, no jockeying for position or premeditation of effects—there was a very little mental side to any of her affairs. She simply made men conscious to the highest degree of her physical loveliness. Dexter had no desire to change her. Her deficiencies were knit up with a passionate energy that transcended and justified them.

When, as Judy's head lay against his shoulder that first night, she whispered, "I don't know what's the matter with me. Last night I thought I was in love with a man and to-night I think I'm in love with you——"—it seemed to him a beautiful and romantic thing to say. It was the exquisite excitability that for the moment he controlled and owned. But a week later he was compelled to view this same quality in a different light. She took him in her roadster to a picnic supper, and after supper she disappeared, likewise in her roadster, with another man. Dexter became enormously upset and was scarcely able to be decently civil to the other people present. When she assured him that she had not kissed the other man, he knew she was lying—yet he was glad that she had taken the trouble to lie to him.

He was, as he found before the summer ended, one of a varying dozen who circulated about her. Each of them had at one time been favored above all others—about half of them still basked in the solace of occasional sentimental revivals. Whenever one showed signs of dropping out through long neglect, she granted him a brief honeyed hour, which encouraged him to tag along for a year or so longer. Judy made these forays upon the helpless and defeated without malice, indeed half unconscious that there was anything mischievous in what she did.

When a new man came to town every one dropped out —dates were automatically cancelled.

The helpless part of trying to do anything about it was that she did it all herself. She was not a girl who could be "won" in the kinetic sense—she was proof against cleverness, she was proof against charm; if any of these assailed her too strongly she would immediately resolve the affair to a physical basis, and under the magic of her physical splendor the strong as well as the brilliant played her game and not their own. She was entertained only by the gratification of her desires and by the direct exercise of her own charm. Perhaps from so much youthful love, so many youthful lovers, she had come, in self-defense, to nourish herself wholly from within.

Succeeding Dexter's first exhilaration came restlessness and dissatisfaction. The helpless ecstasy of losing himself in her was opiate rather than tonic. It was fortunate for his work during the winter that those moments of ecstasy came infrequently. Early in their acquaintance it had seemed for a while that there was a deep and spontaneous mutual attraction—that first August, for example—three days of long evenings on her dusky veranda, of strange wan kisses through the late afternoon, in shadowy alcoves or behind the protecting trellises of the garden arbors, of mornings when she was fresh as a dream and almost shy at meeting him in the clarity of the rising day. There was all the ecstasy of an engagement about it, sharpened by his realization that there was no engagement. It was during those three days that, for the first time, he had asked her to marry him. She said "maybe some day," she said "kiss me," she said "I'd like to marry you," she said "I love you"—she said—nothing.

The three days were interrupted by the arrival of a New York man who visited at her house for half September. To Dexter's agony, rumor engaged them. The man was the son of the president of a great trust company. But at the end of a month it was reported that Judy was yawning. At a dance one night she sat all evening in a motor-boat with a local beau, while the New Yorker searched the club for her frantically. She told the local beau that she was bored with her visitor, and two days later he left. She was seen with him at the station, and it was reported that he looked very mournful indeed.

On this note the summer ended. Dexter was twenty-four, and he found himself increasingly in a position to do as he wished. He joined two clubs in the city and lived at one of them. Though he was by no means an integral part of the stag-lines at these clubs, he managed to be on hand at dances where Judy Jones was likely to appear. He could have gone out socially as much as he liked—he was an eligible young man, now, and popular with down-town fathers. His confessed devotion to Judy Jones had rather solidified his position. But he had no social aspirations and rather despised the dancing men who were always on tap for the Thursday or Saturday parties and who filled in at dinners with the younger married set. Already he was playing with the idea of going East to New York. He wanted to take Judy Jones with him. No disillusion as to the world in which she had grown up could cure his illusion as to her desirability.

Remember that—for only in the light of it can what he did for her be understood.

Eighteen months after he first met Judy Jones he became engaged to another girl. Her name was Irene Scheerer, and her father was one of the men who had always believed in Dexter. Irene was light-haired and sweet and honorable, and a little stout, and she had two suitors whom she pleasantly relinquished when Dexter formally asked her to marry him.

Summer, fall, winter, spring, another summer, another fall—so much he had given of his active life to the incorrigible lips of Judy Jones. She had treated him with interest, with encouragement, with malice, with indifference, with contempt. She had inflicted on him the innumerable little slights and indignities possible in such a case—as if in revenge for having ever cared for him at all. She had beckoned him and yawned at him and beckoned him again and he had responded often with bitterness and narrowed eyes. She had brought him ecstatic happiness and intolerable agony of spirit. She had caused him untold inconvenience and not a little trouble. She had insulted him, and she had ridden over him, and she had played his interest in her against his interest in his work—for fun. She had done everything to him except to criticise him—this she had not done—it seemed to him only because it might have sullied the utter indifference she manifested and sincerely felt toward him.

When autumn had come and gone again it occurred to him that he could not have Judy Jones. He had to beat this into his mind but he convinced himself at last. He lay awake at night for a while and argued it over. He told himself the trouble and the pain she had caused him, he enumerated her glaring deficiencies as a wife. Then he said to himself that he loved her, and after a while he fell asleep. For a week, lest he imagined her husky voice over the telephone or her eyes opposite him at lunch, he worked hard and late, and at night he went to his office and plotted out his years.

At the end of a week he went to a dance and cut in on her once. For almost the first time since they had met he did not ask her to sit out with him or tell her that she was lovely. It hurt him that she did not miss these things—that was all. He was not jealous when he saw that there was a new man to-night. He had been hardened against jealousy long before.

He stayed late at the dance. He sat for an hour with Irene Scheerer and talked about books and about music. He knew very little about either. But he was beginning to be master of his own time now, and he had a rather priggish notion that he—the young and already fabulously successful Dexter Green—should know more about such things.

That was in October, when he was twenty-five. In January, Dexter and Irene became engaged. It was to be announced in June, and they were to be married three months later.

The Minnesota winter prolonged itself interminably, and it was almost May when the winds came soft and the snow ran down into Black Bear Lake at last. For the first time in over a year Dexter was enjoying a certain tranquillity of spirit. Judy Jones had been in Florida, and afterward in Hot Springs, and somewhere she had been engaged, and somewhere she had broken it off. At first, when Dexter had definitely given her up, it had made him sad that people still linked them together and asked for news of her, but when he began to be placed at dinner next to Irene Scheerer people didn't ask him about her any more—they told him about her. He ceased to be an authority on her.

May at last. Dexter walked the streets at night when the darkness was damp as rain, wondering that so soon, with so little done, so much of ecstasy had gone from him. May one year back had been marked by July's poignant, unforgivable, yet forgiven turbulence—it had been one of those rare times when he fancied she had grown to care for him. That old penny's worth of happiness he had spent for this bushel of content. He knew that Irene would be no more than a curtain spread behind him, a hand moving among gleaming teacups, a voice calling to children . . . fire and loveliness were gone, the magic of nights and the wonder of the varying hours and seasons . . . slender lips, down-turning, dropping to his lips and bearing him up into a heaven of eyes. . . . The thing was deep in him. He was too strong and alive for it to die lightly.

In the middle of May when the weather balanced for a few days on the thin bridge that led to deep summer he turned in one night at Irene's house. Their engagement was to be announced in a week now—no one would be surprised at it. And to-night they would sit together on the lounge at the University Club and look on for an hour at the dancers. It gave him a sense of solidity to go with her— she was so sturdily popular, so intensely "great."

He mounted the steps of the brownstone house and stepped inside.

"Irene," he called.

Mrs. Scheerer came out of the living-room to meet him.

"Dexter," she said, "Irene's gone up-stairs with a splitting headache. She wanted to go with you but I made her go to bed."

"Nothing serious, I——"

"Oh, no. She's going to play golf with you in the morning. You can spare her for just one night, can't you, Dexter?"

Her smile was kind. She and Dexter liked each other. In the living-room he talked for a moment before he said good-night.

Returning to the University Club, where he had rooms, he stood in the doorway for a moment and watched the dancers. He leaned against the door-post, nodded at a man or two—yawned.

"Hello, darling."

The familiar voice at his elbow startled him. Judy Jones had left a man and crossed the room to him—Judy Jones, a slender enamelled doll in cloth of gold: gold in a band at her head, gold in two slipper points at her dress's hem. The fragile glow of her face seemed to blossom as she smiled at him. A breeze of warmth and light blew through the room. His hands in the pockets of his dinner-jacket tightened spasmodically. He was filled with a sudden excitement.

"When did you get back?" he asked casually.

"Come here and I'll tell you about it."

She turned and he followed her. She had been away—he could have wept at the wonder of her return. She had passed through enchanted streets, doing things that were like provocative music. All mysterious happenings, all fresh and quickening hopes, had gone away with her, come back with her now.

She turned in the doorway.

"Have you a car here? If you haven't, I have."

"I have a coupé."

In then, with a rustle of golden cloth. He slammed the door. Into so many cars she had stepped—like this—like that—her back against the leather, so—her elbow resting on the door—waiting. She would have been soiled long since had there been anything to soil her—except herself—but this was her own self outpouring.

With an effort he forced himself to start the car and back into the street. This was nothing, he must remember.

She had done this before, and he had put her behind him, as he would have crossed a bad account from his books.

He drove slowly down-town and, affecting abstraction, traversed the deserted streets of the business section, peopled here and there where a movie was giving out its crowd or where consumptive or pugilistic youth lounged in front of pool halls. The clink of glasses and the slap of hands on the bars issued from saloons, cloisters of glazed glass and dirty yellow light.

She was watching him closely and the silence was embarrassing, yet in this crisis he could find no casual word with which to profane the hour. At a convenient turning he began to zigzag back toward the University Club.

"Have you missed me?" she asked suddenly.

"Everybody missed you."

He wondered if she knew of Irene Scheerer. She had been back only a day—her absence had been almost contemporaneous with his engagement.

"What a remark!" Judy laughed sadly—without sadness. She looked at him searchingly. He became absorbed in the dashboard.

"You're handsomer than you used to be," she said thoughtfully. "Dexter, you have the most rememberable eyes."

He could have laughed at this, but he did not laugh. It was the sort of thing that was said to sophomores. Yet it stabbed at him.

"I'm awfully tired of everything, darling." She called every one darling, endowing the endearment with careless, individual camaraderie. "I wish you'd marry me."

The directness of this confused him. He should have told her now that he was going to marry another girl, but he could not tell her. He could as easily have sworn that he had never loved her.

"I think we'd get along," she continued, on the same note, "unless probably you've forgotten me and fallen in love with another girl."

Her confidence was obviously enormous. She had said, in effect, that she found such a thing impossible to believe, that if it were true he had merely committed a childish indiscretion—and probably to show off. She would forgive him, because it was not a matter of any moment but rather something to be brushed aside lightly.

"Of course you could never love anybody but me," she continued, "I like the way you love me. Oh, Dexter, have you forgotten last year?"

"No, I haven't forgotten."

"Neither have I!"

Was she sincerely moved—or was she carried along by the wave of her own acting?

"I wish we could be like that again," she said, and he forced himself to answer:

"I don't think we can."

"I suppose not. . . . I hear you're giving Irene Scheerer a violent rush."

There was not the faintest emphasis on the name, yet Dexter was suddenly ashamed.

"Oh, take me home," cried Judy suddenly; "I don't want to go back to that idiotic dance—with those children."

Then, as he turned up the street that led to the residence district, Judy began to cry quietly to herself. He had never seen her cry before.

The dark street lightened, the dwellings of the rich loomed up around them, he stopped his coupé in front of the great white bulk of the Mortimer Joneses' house, somnolent, gorgeous, drenched with the splendor of the damp moonlight. Its solidity startled him. The strong walls, the steel of the girders, the breadth and beam and pomp of it were there only to bring out the contrast with the young beauty beside him. It was sturdy to accentuate her slightness—as if to show what a breeze could be generated by a butterfly's wing.

He sat perfectly quiet, his nerves in wild clamor, afraid that if he moved he would find her irresistibly in his arms. Two tears had rolled down her wet face and trembled on her upper lip.

"I'm more beautiful than anybody else," she said brokenly, "why can't I be happy?" Her moist eyes tore at his stability—her mouth turned slowly downward with an exquisite sadness: "I'd like to marry you if you'll have me, Dexter. I suppose you think I'm not worth having, but I'll be so beautiful for you, Dexter."

A million phrases of anger, pride, passion, hatred, tenderness fought on his lips. Then a perfect wave of emotion washed over him, carrying off with it a sediment of wisdom, of convention, of doubt, of honor. This was his girl who was speaking, his own, his beautiful, his pride.

"Won't you come in?" He heard her draw in her breath sharply.

Waiting.

"All right," his voice was trembling, "I'll come in."

V

It was strange that neither when it was over nor a long time afterward did he regret that night. Looking at it from the perspective of ten years, the fact that Judy's flare for him endured just one month seemed of little importance. Nor did it matter that by his yielding he subjected himself to a deeper agony in the end and gave serious hurt to Irene Scheerer and to Irene's parents, who had befriended him. There was nothing sufficiently pictorial about Irene's grief to stamp itself on his mind.

Dexter was at bottom hard-minded. The attitude of the city on his action was of no importance to him, not because he was going to leave the city, but because any outside attitude on the situation seemed superficial. He was completely indifferent to popular opinion. Nor, when he had seen that it was no use, that he did not possess in himself the power to move fundamentally or to hold Judy Jones, did he bear any malice toward her. He loved her, and he would love her until the day he was too old for loving—but he could not have her. So he tasted the deep pain that is reserved only for the strong, just as he had tasted for a little while the deep happiness.

Even the ultimate falsity of the grounds upon which Judy terminated the enagement that she did not want to "take him away" from Irene—Judy who had wanted nothing else—did not revolt him. He was beyond any revulsion or any amusement.

He went East in February with the intention of selling out his laundries and settling in New York—but the war came to America in March and changed his plans. He returned to the West, handed over the management of the business to his partner, and went into the first officers' training-camp in late April. He was one of those young thousands who greeted the war with a certain amount of relief, welcoming the liberation from webs of tangled emotion.

VI

This story is not his biography, remember, although things creep into it which have nothing to do with those dreams he had when he was young. We are almost done with them and with him now. There is only one more incident to be related here, and it happens seven years farther on.

It took place in New York, where he had done well—so well that there were no barriers too high for him. He was thirty-two years old, and, except for one flying trip immediately after the war, he had not been West in seven years. A man named Devlin from Detroit came into his office to see him in a business way, and then and there this incident occurred, and closed out, so to speak, this particular side of his life.

"So you're from the Middle West," said the man Devlin with careless curiosity. "That's funny—I thought men like you were probably born and raised on Wall Street. You know—wife of one of my best friends in Detroit came from your city. I was an usher at the wedding."

Dexter waited with no apprehension of what was coming.

"Judy Simms," said Devlin with no particular interest; "Judy Jones she was once."

"Yes, I knew her." A dull impatience spread over him. He had heard, of course, that she was married—perhaps deliberately he had heard no more.

"Awfully nice girl," brooded Devlin meaninglessly, "I'm sort of sorry for her."

"Why?" Something in Dexter was alert, receptive, at once.

"Oh, Lud Simms has gone to pieces in a way. I don't mean he ill-uses her, but he drinks and runs around——"

"Doesn't she run around?"

"No. Stays at home with her kids."

"Oh."

"She's a little too old for him," said Devlin.

"Too old!" cried Dexter. "Why, man, she's only twenty-seven."

He was possessed with a wild notion of rushing out into the streets and taking a train to Detroit. He rose to his feet spasmodically.

"I guess you're busy," Devlin apologized quickly. "I didn't realize——"

"No, I'm not busy," said Dexter, steadying his voice. "I'm not busy at all. Not busy at all. Did you say she was —twenty-seven? No, I said she was twenty-seven."

"Yes, you did," agreed Devlin dryly.

"Go on, then. Go on."

"What do you mean?"

"About Judy Jones."

Devlin looked at him helplessly.

"Well, that's—I told you all there is to it. He treats her like the devil. Oh, they're not going to get divorced or anything. When he's particularly outrageous she forgives him. In fact, I'm inclined to think she loves him. She was a pretty girl when she first came to Detroit."

A pretty girl! The phrase struck Dexter as ludicrous.

"Isn't she—a pretty girl, any more?"

"Oh, she's all right."

"Look here," said Dexter, sitting down suddenly. "I don't understand. You say she was a 'pretty girl' and now you say she's 'all right.' I don't understand what you mean —Judy Jones wasn't a pretty girl, at all. She was a great beauty. Why, I knew her, I knew her. She was——"

Devlin laughed pleasantly.

"I'm not trying to start a row," he said. "I think Judy's a nice girl and I like her. I can't understand how a man like Lud Simms could fall madly in love with her, but he did." Then he added: "Most of the women like her."

Dexter looked closely at Devlin, thinking wildly that there must be a reason for this, some insensitivity in the man or some private malice.

"Lots of women fade just like *that*," Devlin snapped his fingers. "You must have seen it happen. Perhaps I've forgotten how pretty she was at her wedding. I've seen her so much since then, you see. She has nice eyes."

A sort of dullness settled down upon Dexter. For the first time in his life he felt like getting very drunk. He knew that he was laughing loudly at something Devlin had said, but he did not know what it was or why it was funny. When, in a few minutes, Devlin went he lay down on his lounge and looked out the window at the New York sky-line into which the sun was sinking in dull lovely shades of pink and gold.

He had thought that having nothing else to lose he was invulnerable at last—but he knew that he had just lost something more, as surely as if he had married Judy Jones and seen her fade away before his eyes.

The dream was gone. Something had been taken from him. In a sort of panic he pushed the palms of his hands into his eyes and tried to bring up a picture of the waters lapping on Sherry Island and the moonlit veranda, and gingham on the golf-links and the dry sun and the gold color of her neck's soft down. And her mouth damp to his kisses and her eyes plaintive with melancholy and her freshness like new fine linen in the morning. Why, these things were no longer in the world! They had existed and they existed no longer.

For the first time in years the tears were streaming down his face. But they were for himself now. He did not care about mouth and eyes and moving hands. He wanted to care, and he could not care. For he had gone away and he could never go back any more. The gates were closed, the sun was gone down, and there was no beauty but the gray beauty of steel that withstands all time. Even the grief he could have borne was left behind in the country of illusion, of youth, of the richness of life, where his winter dreams had flourished.

"Long ago," he said, "long ago, there was something in me, but now that thing is gone. Now that thing is gone, that thing is gone. I cannot cry. I cannot care. That thing will come back no more."

1922

ERNEST HEMINGWAY

(1898–1961)

There is no collected edition of the works of Ernest Hemingway. The stories of *In Our Time, Men Without Women,* and *Winner Take Nothing,* together with some uncollected stories and the play, *The Fifth Column,* were collected in *The Fifth Column and the First Forty-nine Stories.* A uniform edition of the collected works has been under way since 1953. The published works of Hemingway include *Three Stories and Ten Poems* (1923); *In Our Time* (1924, enlarged in 1925); *The Torrents of Spring* (1926); *Today Is Friday* (1926); *The Sun Also Rises* (1926); *Men Without Women* (1927); *A Farewell to Arms* (1929); *Death in the Afternoon* (1932); *God Rest You Merry Gentlemen* (1933); *Winner Take Nothing* (1933); *Green Hills of Africa* (1935); *To Have and Have Not* (1937); *The Spanish Earth* (1938); *The Fifth Column and the First Forty-nine Stories* (1938); *For Whom the Bell Tolls* (1940); *Across the River and into the Trees* (1950); *The Old Man and the Sea* (1953); and *A Moveable Feast* (1964).

Studies of the man and his work are to be found in P. Rosenfeld, *By Way of Art* (1928); L. H. Cohn, *A Bibliography of the Works of Ernest Hemingway* (1931); R. M. Lovett, "Ernest Hemingway," *English Journal,* XXI (1932); L. Kirstein, "The Canon of Death," *Hound and Horn,* VI (1933); G. Stein, *The Autobiography of Alice B. Toklas* (1933); M. Eastman, *Art and the Life of Action* (1934); H. Hartwick, *The Foreground of American Fiction* (1934); W. Lewis, *Men without Art* (1934); J. P. Bishop, "The Missing All," *Virginia Quarterly Review,* XIII (1937); C. J. McCole, *Lucifer at Large* (1937); D. Schwartz, "Ernest Hemingway's Literary Situation," *Southern Review,* III (1938); J. D. Adams, "Ernest Hemingway," *English Journal,* XXVIII (1939); E. Wilson, "Ernest Hemingway: Bourdon Gauge of Morale," *Atlantic Monthly,* CLXIV (1939); E. Johnson, "Farewell the Separate Peace," *Sewanee Review,* XLVIII (1940); C. Van Doren, *The American Novel, 1789–1939* (1940); M. Geismar, "No Man Alone Now," *Virginia Quarterly*

Review, XVII (1941); M. Geismar, *Writers in Crisis* (1942); A. Kazin, *On Native Grounds* (1942); Malcolm Cowley, ed., *The Portable Hemingway* (1944); R. B. West, Jr., "Ernest Hemingway: Death in the Evening," *Antioch Review*, IV (1944); Hemingway Number, *Kenyon Review*, IX (1947); R. Daniel, "Hemingway and His Heroes," *Queens Quarterly*, LIV (1947–1948); G. Snell, *Shapers of American Fiction* (1947); R. P. Warren, "Novelists-Philosophers—X," *Horizon*, XV (1947); D. S. Savage, "Ernest Hemingway," *Hudson Review*, I (1948); W. M. Frohock, *The Novel of Violence in America, 1920–1950* (1950); J. K. M. McCaffery, ed., *Ernest Hemingway: The Man and His Works* (1950); F. J. Hoffman, *The Modern Novel in America, 1900–1950* (1951); H. Levin, "Observations on the Style of Hemingway," *Kenyon Review*, XIII (1951); L. Samuels, *A Hemingway Checklist* (1951); J. A. Atkins, *The Art of Ernest Hemingway* (1952); C. Baker: *Hemingway: The Writer as Artist* (1952, 1956); L. Gurko, "The Achievement of Ernest Hemingway," *College English*, XIII (1952); P. Young, *Ernest Hemingway* (1952); J. McCormick, "Hemingway and History," *Western Review*, XVII (1953); E. Wilson, *The Shores of Light* (1953); F. I. Carpenter, "Hemingway Achieves the Fifth Dimension," *PMLA*, LXIX (1954); E. Fussell, "Hemingway and Mark Twain," *Accent*, XIV (1954); C. A. Fenton, *The Apprenticeship of Ernest Hemingway: The Early Years* (1954); Hemingway Number, *Modern Fiction Studies*, I (August, 1955); C. C. Walcutt, *American Literary Naturalism* (1956); M. D. Zabel, *Craft and Character in Fiction* (1957); J. A. Jones, "Hemingway: The Critics and the Public Legend," *Western Humanities Review*, XIII (1959); D. Sanders, "Ernest Hemingway's Spanish Civil War Experience," *American Quarterly*, XII (1960); J. Brown, *Hemingway* (1961); C. Baker, ed., *Ernest Hemingway: Critiques of Four Major Novels* (1962); C. Clemens, ed., Ernest Hemingway Memorial issue of the *Mark Twain Journal*, XI (1962); L. Hemingway, *My Brother, Ernest Hemingway* (1962); M. Machlin, *The Private Hell of Ernest Hemingway* (1962); R. K. Peterson, "Hemingway: Direct and Oblique," *Dissertation Abstracts*, XXII (1962); M. Hemingway Sanford, *At the Hemingways: A Family Portrait* (1962); K. Singer, *Hemingway, Life and Death of a Giant* (1962); R. P. Weeks, ed., *Hemingway: A Collection of Critical Essays* (1962); J. B. Yokelson, "Symbolism in the Fiction of Ernest Hemingway," *Dissertation Abstracts* XXIII (1962); M. Callaghan, *That Summer in Paris* (1963); J. DeFalco, *The Hero in Hemingway's Short Stories* (1963); G. Z. Hanrahan, *The Wild Years* (1963); Q. Ritzen, *Ernest Hemingway* (1963); E. Rovit, *Ernest Hemingway* (1963); R. H. Sykes, "Ernest Hemingway's Style," *Dissertation Abstracts*, XXIV (1963); C. Baker, *Hemingway: The Writer as Artist* (3rd ed., rev., 1964); R. Escarpit, *Hemingway* (1964); J. Isabelle, *Hemingway's Religious Experience* (1964); N. Algren, *Notes from a Sea Diary: Hemingway All the Way* (1965); R. Asselineau, ed., *The Literary Reputation of Hemingway in Europe* (1965); E. S. Gleaves, "The Spanish Influence on Ernest Hemingway's Concepts . . . ," *Dissertation Abstracts*, XXV (1964); J. F. Kerr, "Hemingway's Use of Physical Setting and Stage Props in His Novels," *Dissertation Abstracts,* XXVI (1965); J. G. Kiley, *Hemingway: An Old Friend Remembers* (1965); R. W. Lewis, *Hemingway on Love* (1965); A. E. Hotchner, *Papa Hemingway* (1966); C. C. Montgomery, *Hemingway in Michigan* (1966); N. A. Scott, Jr., *Ernest Hemingway* (1966); and P. Young, *Ernest Hemingway* (1967).

SINCLAIR LEWIS

(1885–1951)

Lewis was born and raised in Sauk Centre, Minnesota, the town that was to provide his model for the Main Streets full of the Babbitts he satirized. The most influential and famous satirist of his time, he brought to his materials a fine reportorial eye and ear with which to continue the iconoclasm of his generation.

While still a young man, he developed the rebellious attitudes that militated against boosterism, commercialized "idealism," and the subordination of honestly and passionately held values to the advantages of publicity, conformity, and success as defined by the "Rotarian" personality in Lewis's novels. In 1904 he entered Yale, where he was energetic in student literary activities. He interrupted his college career to work his way through the United States, Europe, and Mexico, and also worked for a while as a janitor in Upton Sinclair's experimental colony in socialized living, Helicon Hall. Then he returned to Yale and was graduated in 1908.

After leaving Yale, he was an advertising writer, a publisher's reader, and a contributor to juvenile magazines and the popular slick magazines. With the publication of his first novel, *Our Mr. Wrenn*, in 1914, that checkered literary career was terminated and replaced by free-lancing. The productions of the next five years—*The Trail of the Hawk* (1915), *The Innocents* (1917), *The Job* (1917), and *Free Air* (1919)—were of no special moment, but in 1920 Lewis achieved sudden and total fame with *Main Street*. In this book, the accuracy of his reproduction of American speech, with all its exposures of the speaker, together with the sharp details of the phony and "folksy" culture he evoked, presented a picture too real to be ignored and too satirically compelling not to be hailed with cries of delight and dismay. To some, "Red" Lewis became "red" in every sense; to others, he became the director of a healthily growing American self-consciousness that endowed honest writers with the insight and courage to challenge some of our most cherished institutions: philanthropic organizations, the chamber of commerce, organized religion.

The 1920's saw the publication of his most famous and enduring books: not only *Main Street*, but also *Babbitt* (1922), *Arrowsmith* (1925), *Elmer Gantry* (1927), *The Man Who Knew Coolidge* (1928), and *Dodsworth* (1929). With the possible exception of *It Can't Happen Here* (1935), an examination, later adapted for the stage, of the possible advent of triumphant native fascism, his work of the 1930's and 1940's failed to create the national excitement that had been engendered by his work of the 1920's, the high point of his reputation. In 1926 he refused a Pulitzer Prize, explaining that it was awarded only to "safe" writers in an attempt to sterilize American fiction. In 1930 he became the first American to be awarded the Nobel Prize for literature. Although thereafter his powers and his influence declined, his productivity did not. He continued to write critical novels, such as *Gideon Planish* (1943), a study of fakery in the academic world, and *Kingsblood Royal* (1947), a story of race hatred. These two had a wide sale, but his health, like his reputation, declined, and in 1951, he died in Rome. His ashes were carried back to Sauk Centre.

There is no collected edition of the works of Lewis. In addition to the titles mentioned above, some of his other books are *Mantrap* (1926); *Work of Art* (1934); *Jayhawker: A Play in Three Acts*, written with Lloyd Lewis (1935); *Bethel Merriday* (1940); *Cass Timberlane* (1945); *The God-Seeker* (1946); and *World So Wide* (1951).

Accounts of the man and his work are to be found in S. P. Sherman, *The Significance of Sinclair Lewis* (1922); E. Boyd, *Portraits: Real and Imaginary* (1924); O. Harrison (H. Smith), *Sinclair Lewis* (1925); S. Anderson, *Sherwood Anderson's Notebook* (1926); P. H. Boynton, *More Contemporary Americans* (1927); W. Lippmann, *Men of Destiny* (1927); V. L. Parrington, *Sinclair Lewis: Our Own Diogenes* (1927); R. Michaud, *The American Novel To-day* (1928); J. C. Squire, et al., eds., *Contemporary American Authors* (1928); T. K. Whipple, *Spokesmen* (1928); J. B. Cabell, *Some of Us* (1930); V. L. Parrington, *Main Currents in American Thought*, III (1930); E. M. Forster, *Sinclair Lewis Interprets America* (1932); G. J. Nathan,

The Intimate Notebooks of George Jean Nathan (1932); C. Van Doren, Sinclair Lewis (1933); H. Hartwick, The Foreground of American Fiction (1934); P. H. Boynton, America in Contemporary Fiction (1940); C. Van Doren, The American Novel: 1789–1939 (1940); A. Kazin, On Native Grounds (1942); M. Geismar, The Last of the Provincials (1947); H. Smith, ed., From Main Street to Stockholm (1952); H. Maule and M. Cane, eds., The Man from Main Street: Selected Essays and Other Writings, 1904–1950 (1953); G. Lewis, With Love from Gracie: Sinclair Lewis: 1912–1925 (1955); G. Moore, The Young Rebel in American Literature (1959); M. Schorer, Sinclair Lewis: An American Life (1961); N. Grebstein, Sinclair Lewis (1962); M. Schorer, ed., Sinclair Lewis: A Collection of Critical Essays (1962); M. Schorer, Sinclair Lewis (1963); V. Sheean, Dorothy and Red (1963); M. Bucco, "The Serialized Novels of Sinclair Lewis," Dissertation Abstracts, XXIV (1964); and S. S. Conroy, "The American Culture and the Individual in the Novels of Sinclair Lewis," Dissertation Abstracts, XXVII (1966).

[The American Fear of Literature]

(NOBEL PRIZE ADDRESS)

MEMBERS OF THE SWEDISH ACADEMY,
LADIES AND GENTLEMEN:

Were I to express my feeling of honor and pleasure in having been awarded the Nobel Prize in Literature, I should be fulsome and perhaps tedious, and I present my gratitude with a plain "Thank you."

I wish, in this address, to consider certain trends, certain dangers, and certain high and exciting promises in present-day American literature. To discuss this with complete and unguarded frankness—and I should not insult you by being otherwise than completely honest, however indiscreet—it will be necessary for me to be a little impolite regarding certain institutions and persons of my own greatly beloved land.

But I beg of you to believe that I am in no case gratifying a grudge. Fortune has dealt with me rather too well. I have known little struggle, not much poverty, many generosities. Now and then I have, for my books or myself, been somewhat warmly denounced—there was one good pastor in California who upon reading my "Elmer Gantry" desired to lead a mob and lynch me, while another holy man in the State of Maine wondered if there was no respectable and righteous way of putting me in jail. And, much harder to endure than any raging condemnation, a certain number of old acquaintances among journalists, what in the galloping American slang we call the "I Knew Him When Club," have scribbled that since they know me personally, therefore I must be a rather low sort of fellow and certainly no writer. But if I have now and then received such cheering brickbats, still I, who have heaved a good many bricks myself, would be fatuous not to expect a fair number in return.

No, I have for myself no conceivable complaint to make, and yet for American literature in general, and its standing in a country where industrialism and finance and science flourish and the only arts that are vital and respected are architecture and the film, I have a considerable complaint.

I can illustrate by an incident which chances to concern the Swedish Academy and myself and which happened a few days ago, just before I took ship at New York for Sweden. There is in America a learned and most amiable old gentleman who has been a pastor, a university professor, and a diplomat. He is a member of the American Academy of Arts and Letters and no few universities have honored him with degrees. As a writer he is chiefly known for his pleasant little essays on the joy of fishing. I do not suppose that professional fishermen, whose lives depend on the run of cod or herring, find it altogether an amusing occupation, but from these essays I learned, as a boy, that there is something very important and spiritual about catching fish, if you have no need of doing so.

This scholar stated, and publicly, that in awarding the Nobel Prize to a person who has scoffed at American institutions as much as I have, the Nobel Committee and the Swedish Academy had insulted America. I don't know whether, as an ex-diplomat, he intends to have an international incident made of it, and perhaps demand of the American Government that they land Marines in Stockholm to protect American literary rights, but I hope not.

I should have supposed that to a man so learned as to have been made a Doctor of Divinity, a Doctor of Letters, and I do not know how many other imposing magnificences, the matter would have seemed different; I should have supposed that he would have reasoned, "Although personally I dislike this man's books, nevertheless the Swedish

Academy has in choosing him honored America by assuming that the Americans are no longer a puerile backwoods clan, so inferior that they are afraid of criticism, but instead a nation come of age and able to consider calmly and maturely any dissection of their land, however scoffing."

I should even have supposed that so international a scholar would have believed that Scandinavia, accustomed to the works of Strindberg, Ibsen, and Pontoppidan, would not have been peculiarly shocked by a writer whose most anarchistic assertion has been that America, with all her wealth and power, has not yet produced a civilization good enough to satisfy the deepest wants of human creatures.

I believe that Strindberg rarely sang the "Star-Spangled Banner" or addressed Rotary Clubs, yet Sweden seems to have survived him.

I have at such length discussed this criticism of the learned fisherman not because it has any conceivable importance in itself, but because it does illustrate the fact that in America most of us—not readers alone but even writers—are still afraid of any literature which is not a glorification of everything American, a glorification of our faults as well as our virtues. To be not only a best-seller in America but to be really beloved, a novelist must assert that all American men are tall, handsome, rich, honest, and powerful at golf; that all country towns are filled with neighbors who do nothing from day to day save go about being kind to one another; that although American girls may be wild, they change always into perfect wives and mothers; and that, geographically, America is composed solely of New York, which is inhabited entirely by millionaires; of the West, which keeps unchanged all the boisterous heroism of 1870; and of the South, where every one lives on a plantation perpetually glossy with moonlight and scented with magnolias.

It is not today vastly more true than it was twenty years ago that such novelists of ours as you have read in Sweden, novelists like Dreiser and Willa Cather, are authentically popular and influential in America. As it was revealed by the venerable fishing Academician whom I have quoted, we still most revere the writers for the popular magazines who in a hearty and edifying chorus chant that the America of a hundred and twenty million population is still as simple, as pastoral, as it was when it had but forty million; that in

an industrial plant with ten thousand employees, the relationship between the worker and the manager is still as
neighborly and uncomplex as in a factory of 1840, with
five employees; that the relationships between father and
son, between husband and wife, are precisely the same in
an apartment in a thirty-story palace today, with three
motor cars awaiting the family below and five books on the
library shelves and a divorce imminent in the family next
week, as were those relationships in a rose-veiled five-
room cottage in 1880; that, in fine, America has gone
through the revolutionary change from rustic colony to
world-empire without having in the least altered the
bucolic and Puritanic simplicity of Uncle Sam.

I am, actually, extremely grateful to the fishing Academician for having somewhat condemned me. For since he is
a leading member of the American Academy of Arts and
Letters, he has released me, has given me the right to speak
as frankly of that Academy as he has spoken of me. And in
any honest study of American intellectualism today, that
curious institution must be considered.

Before I consider the Academy, however, let me sketch
a fantasy which has pleased me the last few days in the
unavoidable idleness of a rough trip on the Atlantic. I am
sure that you know, by now, that the award to me of the
Nobel Prize has by no means been altogether popular in
America. Doubtless the experience is not new to you. I
fancy that when you gave the award even to Thomas
Mann, whose "Zauberberg" seems to me to contain the
whole of intellectual Europe, even when you gave it to
Kipling, whose social significance is so profound that it
has been rather authoritatively said that he created the
British Empire, even when you gave it to Bernard Shaw,
there were countrymen of those authors who complained
because you did not choose another.

And I imagined what would have been said had you
chosen some American other than myself. Suppose you had
taken Theodore Dreiser.

Now to me, as to many other American writers, Dreiser
more than any other man, marching alone, usually unap-
preciated, often hated, has cleared the trail from Victorian
and Howellsian timidity and gentility in American fiction
to honesty and boldness and passion of life. Without his
pioneering, I doubt if any of us could, unless we liked to

be sent to jail, seek to express life and beauty and terror.

My great colleague Sherwood Anderson has proclaimed this leadership of Dreiser. I am delighted to join him. Dreiser's great first novel, "Sister Carrie," which he dared to publish thirty long years ago and which I read twenty-five years ago, came to housebound and airless America like a great free Western wind, and to our stuffy domesticity gave us the first fresh air since Mark Twain and Whitman.

Yet had you given the Prize to Mr. Dreiser, you would have heard groans from America; you would have heard that his style—I am not exactly sure what this mystic quality "style" may be, but I find the word so often in the writings of minor critics that I suppose it must exist—you would have heard that his style is cumbersome, that his choice of words is insensitive, that his books are interminable. And certainly respectable scholars would complain that in Mr. Dreiser's world, men and women are often sinful and tragic and despairing, instead of being forever sunny and full of song and virtue, as befits authentic Americans.

And had you chosen Mr. Eugene O'Neill, who has done nothing much in American drama save to transform it utterly, in ten or twelve years, from a false world of neat and competent trickery to a world of splendor and fear and greatness, you would have been reminded that he has done something far wose than scoffing—he has seen life as not to be neatly arranged in the study of a scholar but as a terrifying, magnificent and often quite horrible thing akin to the tornado, the earthquake, the devastating fire.

And had you given Mr. James Branch Cabell the Prize, you would have been told that he is too fantastically malicious. So would you have been told that Miss Willa Cather, for all the homely virtue of her novels concerning the peasants of Nebraska, has in her novel, "The Lost Lady," been so untrue to America's patent and perpetual and possibly tedious virtuousness as to picture an abandoned woman who remains, nevertheless, uncannily charming even to the virtuous, in a story without any moral; that Mr. Henry Mencken is the worst of all scoffers; that Mr. Sherwood Anderson viciously errs in considering sex as important a force in life as fishing; that Mr. Upton Sinclair, being a Socialist, sins against the perfectness of

American capitalistic mass-production; that Mr. Joseph Hergesheimer is un-American in regarding graciousness of manner and beauty of surface as of some importance in the endurance of daily life; and that Mr. Ernest Hemingway is not only too young but, far worse, uses language which should be unknown to gentlemen; that he acknowledges drunkenness as one of men's eternal ways to happiness, and asserts that a soldier may find love more significant than the hearty slaughter of men in battle.

Yes, they are wicked, these colleagues of mine; you would have done almost as evilly to have chosen them as to have chosen me; and as a Chauvinistic American—only, mind you, as an American of 1930 and not of 1880—I rejoice that they are my countrymen and countrywomen, and that I may speak of them with pride even in the Europe of Thomas Mann, H. G. Wells, Galsworthy, Knut Hamsun, Arnold Bennett, Feuchtwanger, Selma Lagerlöf, Sigrid Undset, Verner von Heidenstam, D'Annunzio, Romain Rolland.

It is my fate in this paper to swing constantly from optimism to pessimism and back, but so is it the fate of any one who writes or speaks of anything in America—the most contradictory, the most depressing, the most stirring, of any land in the world today.

Thus, having with no muted pride called the roll of what seem to me to be great men and women in American literary life today, and having indeed omitted a dozen other names of which I should like to boast were there time, I must turn again and assert that in our contemporary American literature, indeed in all American arts save architecture and the film, we—yes, we who have such pregnant and vigorous standards in commerce and science—have no standards, no healing communication, no heroes to be followed nor villains to be condemned, no certain ways to be pursued and no dangerous paths to be avoided.

The American novelist or poet or dramatist or sculptor or painter must work alone, in confusion, unassisted save by his own integrity.

That, of course, has always been the lot of the artist. The vagabond and criminal François Villon had certainly no smug and comfortable refuge in which elegant ladies would hold his hand and comfort his starveling soul and more starved body. He, veritably a great man, destined to outlive in history all the dukes and puissant cardinals whose robes he was esteemed unworthy to touch, had for his lot the gutter and the hardened crust.

Such poverty is not for the artist in America. They pay us, indeed, only too well; that writer is a failure who cannot have his butler and motor and his villa at Palm Beach, where he is permitted to mingle almost in equality with the barons of banking. But he is oppressed ever by something worse than poverty—by the feeling that what he creates does not matter, that he is expected by his readers to be only a decorator or a clown, or that he is good-naturedly accepted as a scoffer whose bark probably is worse than his bite and who probably is a good fellow at heart, who in any case certainly does not count in a land that produces eighty-story buildings, motors by the million, and wheat by the billions of bushels. And he has no institution, no group, to which he can turn for inspiration, whose criticism he can accept and whose praise will be precious to him.

What institutions have we?

The American Academy of Arts and Letters does contain, along with several excellent painters and architects and statesmen, such a really distinguished university-president as Nicholas Murray Butler, so admirable and courageous a scholar as Wilbur Cross, and several first-rate writers: the poets Edwin Arlington Robinson and Robert Frost, the free-minded publicist James Truslow Adams, and the novelists Edith Wharton, Hamlin Garland, Owen Wister, Brand Whitlock and Booth Tarkington.

But it does not include Theodore Dreiser, Henry Mencken, our most vivid critic, George Jean Nathan who, though still young, is certainly the dean of our dramatic critics, Eugene O'Neill, incomparably our best dramatist, the really original and vital poets, Edna St. Vincent Millay and Carl Sandburg, Robinson Jeffers and Vachel Lindsay and Edgar Lee Masters, whose "Spoon River Anthology" was so utterly different from any other poetry ever published, so fresh, so authoritative, so free from any gropings and timidities that it came like a revelation, and created a new school of native American poetry. It does not include the novelists and short-story writers, Willa Cather, Joseph Hergesheimer, Sherwood Anderson, Ring Lardner, Ernest Hemingway, Louis Bromfield, Wilbur Daniel Steele,

Fannie Hurst, Mary Austin, James Branch Cabell, Edna Ferber, nor Upton Sinclair, of whom you must say, whether you admire or detest his aggressive socialism, that he is internationally better known than any other American artist whosoever, be he novelist, poet, painter, sculptor, musician, architect.

I should not expect any Academy to be so fortunate as to contain all these writers, but one which fails to contain any of them, which thus cuts itself off from so much of what is living and vigorous and original in American letters, can have no relationship whatever to our life and aspirations. It does not represent literary America of today—it represents only Henry Wadsworth Longfellow.

It might be answered that, after all, the Academy is limited to fifty members; that, naturally, it cannot include every one of merit. But the fact is that while most of our few giants are excluded, the Academy does have room to include three extraordinarily bad poets, two very melodramatic and insignificant playwrights, two gentlemen who are known only because they are university presidents, a man who was thirty years ago known as a rather clever humorous draughtsman, and several gentlemen of whom—I sadly confess my ignorance—I have never heard.

Let me again emphasize the fact—for it is a fact—that I am not attacking the American Academy. It is a hospitable and generous and decidedly dignified institution. And it is not altogether the Academy's fault that it does not contain many of the men who have significance in our letters. Sometimes it is the fault of those writers themselves. I cannot imagine that grizzly-bear Theodore Dreiser being comfortable at the serenely Athenian dinners of the Academy, and were they to invite Mencken, he would infuriate them with his boisterous jeering. No, I am not attacking—I am reluctantly considering the Academy because it is so perfect an example of the divorce in America of intellectual life from all authentic standards of importance and reality.

Our universities and colleges, or gymnasia, most of them, exhibit the same unfortunate divorce. I can think of four of them, Rollins College in Florida, Middlebury College in Vermont, the University of Michigan, and the University of Chicago—which has had on its roll so excellent a novelist as Robert Herrick, so courageous a critic as Robert Morss Lovett—which have shown an authentic interest in contemporary creative literature. Four of them. But universities and colleges and musical emporiums and schools for the teaching of theology and plumbing and sign-painting are as thick in America as the motor traffic. Whenever you see a public building with Gothic fenestration on a sturdy backing of Indiana concrete, you may be certain that it is another university, with anywhere from two hundred to twenty thousand students equally ardent about avoiding the disadvantage of becoming learned and about gaining the social prestige contained in the possession of a B.A. degree.

Oh, socially our universities are close to the mass of our citizens, and so are they in the matter of athletics. A great college football game is passionately witnessed by eighty thousand people, who have paid five dollars apiece and motored anywhere from ten to a thousand miles for the ecstasy of watching twenty-two men chase one another up and down a curiously marked field. During the football season, a capable player ranks very nearly with our greatest and most admired heroes—even with Henry Ford, President Hoover, and Colonel Lindbergh.

And in one branch of learning, the sciences, the lords of business who rule us are willing to do homage to the devotees of learning. However bleakly one of our trader aristocrats may frown upon poetry or the visions of a painter, he is graciously pleased to endure a Millikan, a Michelson, a Banting, a Theobald Smith.

But the paradox is that in the arts our universities are as cloistered, as far from reality and living creation, as socially and athletically and scientifically they are close to us. To a true-blue professor of literature in an American university, literature is not something that a plain human being, living today, painfully sits down to produce. No; it is something dead; it is something magically produced by superhuman beings who must, if they are to be regarded as artists at all, have died at least one hundred years before the diabolical invention of the typewriter. To any authentic don, there is something slightly repulsive in the thought that literature could be created by any ordinary human being, still to be seen walking the streets, wearing quite commonplace trousers and coat and looking not so unlike a chauffeur or a farmer. Our American professors like their literature clear and cold and pure and very dead.

I do not suppose that American universities are alone in this. I am aware that to the dons of Oxford and Cambridge, it would seem rather indecent to suggest that Wells and Bennett and Galsworthy and George Moore may, while they commit the impropriety of continuing to live, be compared to any one so beautifully and safely dead as Samuel Johnson. I suppose that in the Universities of Sweden and France and Germany there exist plenty of professors who prefer dissection to understanding. But in the new and vital and experimental land of America, one would expect the teachers of literature to be less monastic, more human, than in the traditional shadows of old Europe.

They are not.

There has recently appeared in America, out of the universities, an astonishing circus called "the New Humanism." Now of course "humanism" means so many things that it means nothing. It may infer anything from a belief that Greek and Latin are more inspiring than the dialect of contemporary peasants to a belief that any living peasant is more interesting than a dead Greek. But it is a delicate bit of justice that this nebulous word should have been chosen to label this nebulous cult.

Insofar as I have been able to comprehend them—for naturally in a world so exciting and promising as this today, a life brilliant with Zeppelins and Chinese revolutions and the Bolshevik industrialization of farming and ships and the Grand Canyon and young children and terrifying hunger and the lonely quest of scientists after God, no creative writer would have the time to follow all the chilly enthusiasms of the New Humanists—this newest of sects reasserts the dualism of man's nature. It would confine literature to the fight between man's soul and God, or man's soul and evil.

But, curiously, neither God nor the devil may wear modern dress, but must retain Grecian vestments. Oedipus is a tragic figure for the New Humanists; man, trying to maintain himself as the image of God under the menace of dynamos, in a world of high-pressure salesmanship, is not. And the poor comfort which they offer is that the object of life is to develop self-discipline—whether or not one

112 · SINCLAIR LEWIS

ever accomplishes anything with this self-discipline. So this the whole movement results in the not particularly novel doctrine that both art and life must be resigned and negative. It is a doctrine of the blackest reaction introduced into a stirringly revolutionary world.

Strangely enough, this doctrine of death, this escape from the complexities and danger of living into the secure blankness of the monastery, has become widely popular among professors in a land where one would have expected only boldness and intellectual adventure, and it has more than ever shut creative writers off from any benign influence which might conceivably have come from the universities.

But it has always been so. America has never had a Brandes, a Taine, a Goethe, a Croce.

With a wealth of creative talent in America, our criticism has most of it been a chill and insignificant activity pursued by jealous spinsters, ex-baseball-reporters, and acid professors. Our Erasmuses have been village schoolmistresses. How should there be any standards when there has been no one capable of setting them up?

The great Cambridge-Concord circle of the middle of the Nineteenth Century—Emerson, Longfellow, Lowell, Holmes, the Alcotts—were sentimental reflections of Europe, and they left no school, no influence. Whitman and Thoreau and Poe and, in some degree, Hawthorne, were outcasts, men alone and despised, berated by the New Humanists of their generation. It was with the emergence of William Dean Howells that we first began to have something like a standard, and a very bad standard it was.

Mr. Howells was one of the gentlest, sweetest, and most honest of men, but he had the code of a pious old maid whose greatest delight was to have tea at the vicarage. He abhorred not only profanity and obscenity but all of what H. G. Wells has called "the jolly coarsenesses of life." In his fantastic vision of life, which he innocently conceived to be realistic, farmers and seamen and factory-hands might exist, but the farmer must never be covered with muck, the seaman must never roll out bawdy chanteys, the factory-hand must be thankful to his good kind employer, and all of them must long for the opportunity to visit Florence and smile gently at the quaintness of the beggars.

So strongly did Howells feel this genteel, this New

Humanistic philosophy that he was able vastly to influence his contemporaries, down even to 1914 and the turmoil of the Great War.

He was actually able to tame Mark Twain, perhaps the greatest of our writers, and to put that fiery old savage into an intellectual frock coat and top hat. His influence is not altogether gone today. He is still worshipped by Hamlin Garland, an author who should in every way have been greater than Howells but who under Howells' influence was changed from a harsh and magnificent realist into a genial and insignificant lecturer. Mr. Garland is, so far as we have one, the dean of American letters today, and as our dean, he is alarmed by all of the younger writers who are so lacking in taste as to suggest that men and women do not always love in accordance with the prayer-book, and that common people sometimes use language which would be inappropriate at a women's literary club on Main Street. Yet this same Hamlin Garland, as a young man, before he had gone to Boston and become cultured and Howellsised, wrote two most valiant and revelatory works of realism, "Main-Travelled Roads" and "Rose of Dutcher's Coolly."

I read them as a boy in a prairie village in Minnesota—just such an environment as was described in Mr. Garland's tales. They were vastly exciting to me. I had realized in reading Balzac and Dickens that it was possible to describe French and English common people as one actually saw them. But it had never occurred to me that one might without indecency write of the people of Sauk Centre, Minnesota, as one felt about them. Our fictional tradition, you see, was that all of us in Midwestern villages were altogether noble and happy; that not one of us would exchange the neighborly bliss of living on Main Street for the heathen gaudiness of New York or Paris or Stockholm. But in Mr. Garland's "Main-Travelled Roads" I discovered that there was one man who believed that Midwestern peasants were sometimes bewildered and hungry and vile—and heroic. And, given this vision, I was released; I could write of life as living life.

I am afraid that Mr. Garland would be not pleased but acutely annoyed to know that he made it possible for me to write of America as I see it, and not as Mr. William

Dean Howells so sunnily saw it. And it is his tragedy, it is a completely revelatory American tragedy, that in our land of freedom, men like Garland, who first blast the roads to freedom, become themselves the most bound.

But, all this time, while men like Howells were so effusively seeking to guide America into becoming a pale edition of an English cathedral town, there were surly and authentic fellows—Whitman and Melville, then Dreiser and James Huneker and Mencken—who insisted that our land had something more than tea-table gentility.

And so, without standards, we have survived. And for the strong young men, it has perhaps been well that we should have no standards. For, after seeming to be pessimistic about my own and much beloved land, I want to close this dirge with a very lively sound of optimism.

I have, for the future of American literature, every hope and every eager belief. We are coming out, I believe, of the stuffiness of safe, sane, and incredibly dull provincialism. There are young Americans today who are doing such passionate and authentic work that it makes me sick to see that I am a little too old to be one of them.

There is Ernest Hemingway, a bitter youth, educated by the most intense experience, disciplined by his own high standards, an authentic artist whose home is in the whole of life; there is Thomas Wolfe, a child of, I believe, thirty or younger, whose one and only novel, "Look Homeward, Angel," is worthy to be compared with the best in our literary production, a Gargantuan creature with great gusto of life; there is Thornton Wilder, who in an age of realism dreams the old and lovely dreams of the eternal romantics; there is John Dos Passos, with his hatred of the safe and sane standards of Babbitt and his splendor of revolution; there is Stephen Benét who, to American drabness, has restored the epic poem with his glorious memory of old John Brown; there are Michael Gold, who reveals the new frontier of the Jewish East Side, and William Faulkner, who has freed the South from hoop-skirts; and there are a dozen other young poets and fictioneers, most of them living now in Paris, most of them a little insane in the tradition of James Joyce, who, however insane they may be, have refused to be genteel and traditional and dull.

I salute them, with a joy in being not yet too far removed from their determination to give to the America that has mountains and endless prairies, enormous cities and lost far cabins, billions of money and tons of faith, to an America that is, as strange as Russia and as complex as China, a literature worthy of her vastness.

1930

JOHN DOS PASSOS
(1896–   )

Dos Passos comes from a background almost as varied as the wide panorama offered in his greatest novel. His grandfather was a Portuguese immigrant, yet he himself attended the Choate school in Connecticut; his mother came from a southern family in tidewater Virginia and his father was a New York lawyer; he was born in Chicago, but he spent his childhood shuttling between New York, Mexico, Europe, and Virginia. When he attended Harvard, he adopted the romantic rebelliousness of the young aesthete swooning before the hard, inhuman surface of industrialized society. When he emerged from World War I, he was on his way to becoming a Marxist of militant left-wing tendencies.

Graduated from Harvard in 1916, he prepared for the study of architecture in Spain, but that career was cut short by service in a French ambulance unit, the Italian Red Cross, and the American Medical Corps. The bitter disillusionment occasioned by the war showed up in his fiction (as it did in the writing of all the young authors of his generation and experiences) in *One Man's Initiation* (1920), his first novel, and in *Three Soldiers* (1921). These novels, like *Streets of the Night* (1923), were concerned with the responses of a sensitive young man faced with isolating and potentially dehumanizing experience, be it war, loneliness, or a hypocritical society whose beliefs had been all but commercialized away. *Three Soldiers*, easily the best of the early books, attracted critical attention and was followed by a book of essays, *Rosinante to the Road Again*, and a book of verse, *A Pushcart at the Curb*, both in

1922. Three years later, Dos Passos achieved fame and reputation with *Manhattan Transfer*.

This novel, experimental in technique and purpose, abandoned conventional forms and chronological development in favor of a series of shifting, juxtaposed scenes, which were more concerned with the relations and milieu of the characters than with the traditional problems of characterization as such. In its flash backs and fadeouts, the novel prefigured the technique of his masterwork, *USA* (1937), and in its method, that of the movies, it suggested the influence of industrial technology upon the literary artist. Further, *Manhattan Transfer* indicated Dos Passos' growing concern with social patterns as the central "character" of a novel, rather than with any defined or developing individual personality. In this respect, the novel is a consequence both of Dos Passos' political philosophy at the time and of the conditions of modern civilization out of which that philosophy grew.

USA, the culminating product of the directions of Dos Passos' development, is a trilogy made up of *The 42nd Parallel* (1930), *1919* (1932), and *The Big Money* (1936). Its tremendous breadth of social scene in its chronicling of the first three decades of American twentieth-century life, as well as its tightly controlled experimental form, perhaps make it the greatest "social novel" yet written in the land of its title. Dos Passos innovated unreservedly. The "Newsreel" sections present a run-together of topical headlines suggestive not of distinctly individual news but of a melange of merged historical forces, thus providing a hint of the vast political, economic, and social movements that dimly interrelate the destinies of the book's people. The "Camera Eye" provides a stylistically "Faulknerian" statement of the narrator's roving perception, a subjective over-all reading of the events of the times. The profiles of figures famous in those events provide both a personalization of the contemporary history and a debunking of its slickly popularized appearances.

With *The Adventures of a Young Man* (1939), however, Dos Passos' ideas began to change. In this account of failure to find a lasting set of humane social values in diverse leftist groups, he began to shift from radicalism to liberalism (some critics, with an eye to his treatment of the New Deal, *The Grand Design*, published in 1948, have called it not liberalism but conservatism). In *The Ground We Stand On* (1941) he tried to enunciate his changed ideas by means of a reassessment of American history. With *The Head and Heart of Thomas Jefferson* (1953), it became clear that Dos Passos had abandoned the idea of salvation through social "forces" in favor of the historical kinds of individualism sanctioned by such figures as Roger Williams, Benjamin Franklin, and, pre-eminently, Thomas Jefferson. In what is probably the best of his later books, *Midcentury* (1961), Dos Passos used that individualism to align himself more explicitly with conservative ideologies.

In the 1940's Dos Passos wrote *State of the Nation* (1944) and *Tour of Duty* (1946), reports and sketches of America engaged in World War II, during which he was a foreign correspondent. In 1953 he published another trilogy, *District of Columbia*, including *Adventures of a Young Man*, *Number One*, and *The Grand Design*. In his disenchantment with collectivist ideology and his consequent loss of earlier relatively programatic radicalism, Dos Passos unfortunately seems to have lost some of his creative energy. *District of Columbia* is noticeably inferior to *USA*.

In addition to the titles mentioned above, Dos Passos' works include *The Garbage Man* (1926); *Orient Express* (1927); *In All Countries* (1934); *Three Plays* (1934); *The Prospect before Us* (1950); *Chosen Country* (1951); *Most Likely to Succeed* (1954); *The Men Who Made the Nation* (1957); *The Great Days* (1958); and *World in a Glass* (1966).

There is no collected edition of the works of Dos Passos. Accounts of the man and his work are to be found in G. Hicks, "John Dos Passos," *Bookman*, LXXV (1932); M. Cowley, *After the Genteel Tradition* (1937); C. J. McCole, *Lucifer at Large* (1937); J. Chamberlain, *John Dos Passos: A Biographical and Critical Essay* (1939); P. H. Boynton, *America in Contemporary Fiction* (1940); C. Van Doren, *The American Novel* (1940); J. W. Beach, *American Fiction, 1920–1940* (1941); A. Kazin, *On Native Grounds* (1942); T. K. Whipple, *Study Out the Land* (1943); G. Hicks, "Dos Passos and His Critics," *American Mercury*, LXVIII (1949); J. Potter, *A Bibliography of John Dos Passos* (1950); H. McLuhan, "John Dos Passos: Technique vs. Sensibility," *Fifty Years of the American Novel*, ed. H. C. Gardiner (1951); B. Gelfant, *The American City Novel* (1954); G. Astre, *Thèmes et structures dans l'oeuvre de John Dos Passos* (1956); C. Walcutt, *American Literary Naturalism: A Divided Stream* (1956); R. G. Davis, *John Dos Passos* (1962); W. K. Holditch, "Literary Technique in the Novels of John Dos Passos," *Dissertation Abstracts*, XXII (1962); J. W. Canario, "A Study of the Artistic Development of John Dos Passos . . . ," *Dissertation Abstracts*, XXIV (1964); and D. Fitelson, "The Art of John Dos Passos," *Dissertation Abstracts*, XXV (1964).

FROM

U.S.A.

FROM THE 42nd PARALLEL

Lover of Mankind

Debs was a railroad man, born in a weatherboarded shack at Terre Haute.

He was one of ten children.

His father had come to America in a sailingship in '49,
an Alsatian from Colmar; not much of a money-maker, fond of music and reading,

he gave his children a chance to finish public school and that was about all he could do.

At fifteen Gene Debs was already working as a machinist on the Indianapolis and Terre Haute Railway.

He worked as locomotive fireman,

clerked in a store

joined the local of the Brotherhood of Locomotive Firemen, was elected secretary, traveled all over the country as organizer.

He was a tall shamblefooted man, had a sort of gusty rhetoric that set on fire the railroad workers in their pineboarded halls

made them want the world he wanted,

a world brothers might own

where everybody would split even:

I am not a labor leader. I don't want you to follow me or anyone else. If you are looking for a Moses to lead you out of the capitalist wilderness you will stay right where you are. I would not lead you into this promised land if I could, because if I could lead you in, someone else would lead you out.

That was how he talked to freighthandlers and gandywalkers, to firemen and switchmen and engineers, telling them it wasn't enough to organize the railroadmen, that all workers must be organized, that all workers must be organized in the workers' cooperative commonwealth.

Locomotive fireman on many a long night's run,

under the smoke a fire burned him up, burned in gusty

words that beat in pineboarded halls; he wanted his brothers to be free men.

That was what he saw in the crowd that met him at the Old Wells Street Depot when he came out of jail after the Pullman strike,

those were the men that chalked up nine hundred thousand votes for him in nineteen twelve and scared the frockcoats and the tophats and diamonded hostesses at Saratoga Springs, Bar Harbor, Lake Geneva with the bogy of a socialist president.

But where were Gene Debs' brothers in nineteen eighteen when Woodrow Wilson had him locked up in Atlanta for speaking against war,

where were the big men fond of whisky and fond of each other, gentle rambling tellers of stories over bars in small towns in the Middle West,

quiet men who wanted a house with a porch to putter around and a fat wife to cook for them, a few drinks and cigars, a garden to dig in, cronies to chew the rag with

and wanted to work for it

and others to work for it;

where were the locomotive firemen and engineers when they hustled him off to Atlanta Penitentiary?

And they brought him back to die in Terre Haute

to sit on his porch in a rocker with a cigar in his mouth,

beside him American Beauty roses his wife fixed in a bowl;

and the people of Terre Haute and the people in Indiana and the people of the Middle West were fond of him and afraid of him and thought of him as an old kindly uncle who loved them, and wanted to be with him and to have him give them candy,

but they were afraid of him as if he had contracted a social disease, syphilis or leprosy, and thought it was too bad,

but on account of the flag

and prosperity

and making the world safe for democracy,

they were afraid to be with him,

or to think much about him for fear they might believe him;

for he said:

*While there is a lower class I am of it, while there is
a criminal class I am of it, while there is a soul in prison
I am not free.*

1930

FROM 1919

The Body of an American

Whereasthe Congressoftheunitedstates byaconcurrentresolutionadoptedon the4thdayofmarch lastauthorizedthe Secretaryofwar to cause to be brought to theunitedstatesthe body of an Americanwhowasamemberoftheamericanexpeditionaryforcesineurope wholosthislifeduringtheworldwarandwhoseidentityhasnotbeenestablished for burial inthememorialamphitheatreofthe nationalcemeteryatarlingtonvirginia

In the tarpaper morgue at Chalons-sur-Marne in the reek of chloride of lime and the dead, they picked out the pine box that held all that was left of

enie menie minie moe plenty other pine boxes stacked up there containing what they'd scraped up of Richard Roe

and other person or persons unknown. Only one can go. How did they pick John Doe?

Make sure he aint a dinge, boys,

make sure he aint a guinea or a kike,

how can you tell a guy's a hunredpercent when all you've got's a gunnysack full of bones, bronze buttons stamped with the screaming eagle and a pair of roll puttees?

. . . and the gagging chloride and the puky dirt-stench of the yearold dead . . .

The day withal was too meaningful and tragic for applause. Silence, tears, songs and prayer, muffled drums and soft music were the instrumentalities today of national approbation.

John Doe was born (thudding din of blood in love into the shuddering soar of a man and a woman alone indeed together lurching into

andninemonths sick drowse waking into scared agony and the pain and blood and mess of birth). John Doe was born and raised in Brooklyn, in Memphis, near the lakefront in Cleveland, Ohio, in the stench of the stockyards in Chi, on Beacon Hill, in an old brick house in Alexandria Virginia, on Telegraph Hill, in a halftimbered Tudor cottage in Portland the city of roses,

in the Lying-In Hospital old Morgan endowed on Stuyvesant Square.

across the railroad tracks, out near the country club, in a shack cabin tenement apartmenthouse exclusive residential suburb;

scion of one of the best families in the social register, won first prize in the baby parade at Coronado Beach, was marbles champion of the Little Rock grammarschools, crack basketballplayer at the Booneville High, quarterback at the State Reformatory, having saved the sheriff's kid from drowning in the Little Missouri River was invited to Washington to be photographed shaking hands with the President on the White House steps;—

though this was a time of mourning, such an assemblage necessarily has about it a touch of color. In the boxes are seen the court uniforms of foreign diplomats, the gold braid of our own and foreign fleets and armies, the black of the conventional morning dress of American statesmen, the varicolored furs and outdoor wrapping garments of mothers and sisters come to mourn, the drab and blue of soldiers and sailors, the glitter of musical instruments and the white and black of a vested choir

—busboy harveststiff hogcaller boyscout champeen cornshucker of Western Kansas bellhop at the United States Hotel at Saratoga Springs office boy callboy fruiter telephone lineman longshoreman lumberjack plumber's helper,

worked for an exterminating company in Union City, filled pipes in an opium joint in Trenton, N.J.

Y.M.C.A. secretary, express agent, truckdriver, fordmechanic, sold books in Denver Colorado: Madam would you be willing to help a young man work his way through college?

President Harding, with a reverence seemingly more significant because of his high temporal station, concluded his speech:

We are met today to pay the impersonal tribute;
the name of him whose body lies before us took flight with his imperishable soul . . .

as a typical soldier of this representative democracy he fought and died believing in the indisputable justice of his country's cause . . .

by raising his right hand and asking the thousands within the sound of his voice to join in the prayer:

Our Father which art in heaven hallowed be thy name . . .

Naked he went into the army;

they weighed you, measured you, looked for flat feet, squeezed your penis to see if you had clap, looked up your anus to see if you had piles, counted your teeth, made you cough, listened to your heart and lungs, made you read the letters on the card, charted your urine and your intelligence,

gave you a service record for a future (imperishable soul)

and an identification tag stamped with your serial number to hang around your neck, issued OD regulation equipment, a condiment can and a copy of the articles of war.

Atten'SHUN suck in your gut you c———r wipe that smile off your face eyes right wattja tink dis is a choirch-social? For-war-D'ARCH.

John Doe

and Richard Roe and other person or persons unknown drilled hiked, manual of arms, ate slum, learned to salute, to soldier, to loaf in the latrines, forbidden to smoke on deck, overseas guard duty, forty men and eight horses, shortarm inspection and the ping of shrapnel and the shrill bullets combing the air and the sorehead woodpeckers the machineguns mud cooties gas-masks and the itch.

Say feller tell me how I can get back to my outfit.

John Doe had a head

for twentyodd years intensely the nerves of the eyes the ears the palate the tongue the fingers the toes the armpits, the nerves warm-feeling under the skin charged the coiled brain with hurt sweet warm cold mine must dont sayings print headlines:

Thou shalt not the multiplication table long division, Now is the time for all good men knocks but once at a young man's door, It's a great life if Ish gebibbel, The first five years'll be the Safety First, Suppose a hun tried to rape your my country right or wrong, Catch 'em young, What he dont know wont treat 'em rough, Tell 'em nothin, He got what was coming to him he got his, This is a white man's country, Kick the bucket, Gone west, If you dont like it you can croaked him

Say buddy cant you tell me how I can get back to my outfit?

Cant help jumpin when them things go off, give me the trots them things do. I lost my identification tag swimming in the Marne, roughhousin with a guy while he was waitin to be deloused, in bed with a girl named Jeanne (Love moving picture wet French postcard dream began with saltpeter in the coffee and ended at the propho station);—

Say soldier for chrissake cant you tell me how I can get back to my outfit?

John Doe's
heart pumped blood:
alive thudding silence of blood in your ears
down in the clearing in the Oregon forest where the punkins were punkincolor pouring into the blood through the eyes and the fallcolored trees and the bronze hoopers were hopping through the dry grass, where tiny striped snails hung on the underside of the blades and the flies hummed, wasps droned, bumblebees buzzed, and the woods smelt of wine and mushrooms and apples, homey smell of fall pouring into the blood,

and I dropped the tin hat and the sweaty pack and lay flat with the dogday sun licking my throat and adams-apple and the tight skin over the breastbone.

The shell had his number on it.

The blood ran into the ground.

The service record dropped out of the filing cabinet when the quartermaster sergeant got blotto that time they had to pack up and leave the billets in a hurry.

The identification tag was in the bottom of the Marne.

The blood ran into the ground, the brains oozed out of the cracked skull and were licked up by the trenchrats, the belly swelled and raised a generation of bluebottle flies,

and the incorruptible skeleton,

and the scraps of dried viscera and skin bundled in khaki

they took to Chalons-sur-Marne
and laid it out neat in a pine coffin
and took it home to God's Country on a battleship
and buried it in a sarcophagus in the Memorial Amphitheatre in the Arlington National Cemetery
and draped the Old Glory over it
and the bugler played taps
and Mr. Harding prayed to God and the diplomats and the generals and the admirals and the brasshats and the politicians and the handsomely dressed ladies out of the society column of the *Washington Post* stood up solemn
and thought how beautiful sad Old Glory God's Country it was to have the bugler play taps and the three volleys made their ears ring.

Where his chest ought to have been they pinned
the Congressional Medal, the D.S.C., the Medaille Militaire, the Belgian Croix de Guerre, the Italian gold medal, the Vitutea Militara sent by Queen Marie of Rumania, the Czechoslovak war cross, the Virtuti Militari of the Poles, a wreath sent by Hamilton Fish, Jr., of New York, and a little wampum presented by a deputation of Arizona redskins in warpaint and feathers. All the Washingtonians brought flowers.

Woodrow Wilson brought a bouquet of poppies.

1932

FROM THE BIG MONEY

Tin Lizzie

"Mr. Ford the automobileer," the feature-writer wrote in 1900,

"Mr. Ford the automobileer began by giving his steed three or four sharp jerks with the lever at the righthand side of the seat; that is, he pulled the lever up and down sharply in order, as he said, to mix air with gasoline and

*drive the charge into the exploding cylinder. . . . Mr.
Ford slipped a small electric switch handle and there followed a puff, puff, puff. . . . The puffing of the machine
assumed a higher key. She was flying along about eight
miles an hour. The ruts in the road were deep, but the
machine certainly went with a dreamlike smoothness. There
was none of the bumping common even to a streetcar.
. . . By this time the boulevard had been reached, and
the automobileer, letting a lever fall a little, let her out.
Whiz! She picked up speed with infinite rapidity. As she
ran on there was a clattering behind, the new noise of the
automobile.*

For twenty years or more,

ever since he'd left his father's farm when he was sixteen to get a job in a Detriot machineshop, Henry Ford
had been nuts about machinery. First it was watches, then
he designed a steamtractor, then he built a horseless carriage with an engine adapted from the Otto gasengine
he'd read about in *The World of Science,* then a mechanical buggy with a onecylinder fourcycle motor, that would
run forward but not back;

at last, in ninetyeight, he felt he was far enough along
to risk throwing up his job with the Detroit Edison Company, where he'd worked his way up from night fireman
to chief engineer, to put all his time into working on a
new gasoline engine,

(in the late eighties he'd met Edison at a meeting of
electriclight employees in Atlantic City. He'd gone up to
Edison after Edison had delivered an address and asked
him if he thought gasoline was practical as a motor fuel.
Edison had said yes. If Edison said it, it was true. Edison
was the great admiration of Henry Ford's life);

and in driving his mechanical buggy, sitting there at the
lever jauntily dressed in a tightbuttoned jacket and a high
collar and a derby hat, back and forth over the level ill-
paved streets of Detroit,

scaring the big brewery horses and the skinny trotting
horses and the sleekrumped pacers with the motor's loud
explosions,

looking for men scatterbrained enough to invest money
in a factory for building automobiles.

He was the eldest son of an Irish immigrant who during
the Civil War had married the daughter of a prosperous

Pennsylvania Dutch farmer and settled down to farming
near Dearborn in Wayne County, Michigan;

like plenty of other Americans, young Henry grew up
hating the endless sogging through the mud about the
chores, the hauling and pitching manure, the kerosene
lamps to clean, the irk and sweat and solitude of the
farm.

He was a slender, active youngster, a good skater,
clever with his hands; what he liked was to tend the machinery and let the others do the heavy work. His mother
had told him not to drink, smoke, gamble or go into debt,
and he never did.

When he was in his early twenties his father tried to
get him back from Detroit, where he was working as
mechanic and repairman for the Drydock Engine Company that built engines for steamboats, by giving him forty
acres of land.

Young Henry built himself an uptodate square white
dwellinghouse with a false mansard roof and married and
settled down on the farm,

but he let the hired men do the farming;

he bought himself a buzzsaw and rented a stationary
engine and cut the timber off the woodlots.

He was a thrifty young man who never drank or smoked
or gambled or coveted his neighbor's wife, but he couldn't
stand living on the farm.

He moved to Detroit, and in the brick barn behind his
house tinkered for years in his spare time with a mechanical buggy that would be light enough to run over the
clayey wagonroads of Wayne County, Michigan.

By 1900 he had a practicable car to promote.

He was forty years old before the Ford Motor Company
was started and production began to move.

Speed was the first thing the early automobile manufacturers went after. Races advertised the makes of cars.

Henry Ford himself hung up several records at the
track at Grosse Pointe and on the ice on Lake St. Clair.
In his 999 he did the mile in thirtynine and fourfifths
seconds.

But it had always been his custom to hire others to do
the heavy work. The speed he was busy with was speed

in production, the records records in efficient output. He hired Barney Oldfield, a stunt bicyclerider from Salt Lake City, to do the racing for him.

Henry Ford had ideas about other things than the designing of motors, carburetors, magnetos, jigs and fixtures, punches and dies; he had ideas about sales,

that the big money was in economical quantity production, quick turnover, cheap interchangeable easilyreplaced standardized parts;

it wasn't until 1909, after years of arguing with his partners, that Ford put out the first Model T.

Henry Ford was right.

That season he sold more than ten thousand tin lizzies, ten years later he was selling almost a million a year.

In these years the Taylor Plan was stirring up plantmanagers and manufacturers all over the country. Efficiency was the word. The same ingenuity that went into improving the performance of a machine could go into improving the performance of the workmen producing the machine.

In 1913 they established the assemblyline at Ford's. That season the profits were something like twenty-five million dollars, but they had trouble in keeping the men on the job, machinists didn't seem to like it at Ford's.

Henry Ford had ideas about other things than production.

He was the largest automobile manufacturer in the world; he paid high wages; maybe if the steady workers thought they were getting a cut (a very small cut) in the profits, it would give trained men an inducement to stick to their jobs,

wellpaid workers might save enough money to buy a tin lizzie; the first day Ford's announced that cleancut properlymarried American workers who wanted jobs had a chance to make five bucks a day (of course it turned out that there were strings to it; always there were strings to it)

such an enormous crowd waited outside the Highland Park plant

all through the zero January night

that there was a riot when the gates were opened; cops

broke heads, jobhunters threw bricks; property, Henry Ford's own property, was destroyed. The company dicks had to turn on the firehose to beat back the crowd.

The American Plan; automotive prosperity seeping down from above; it turned out there were strings to it.

But that five dollars a day

paid to good, clean American workmen

who didn't drink or smoke cigarettes or read or think, and who didn't commit adultery

and whose wives didn't take in boarders,

made America once more the Yukon of the sweated workers of the world;

made all the tin lizzies and the automotive age, and incidentally,

made Henry Ford the automobileer, the admirer of Edison, the birdlover,

the great American of his time.

But Henry Ford had ideas about other things besides assemblylines and the livinghabits of his employees. He was full of ideas. Instead of going to the city to make his fortune, here was a country boy who'd made his fortune by bringing the city out to the farm. The precepts he'd learned out of McGuffey's Reader, his mother's prejudices and preconceptions, he had preserved clean and unworn as freshprinted bills in the safe in a bank.

He wanted people to know about his ideas, so he bought the *Dearborn Independent* and started a campaign against cigarettesmoking.

When war broke out in Europe, he had ideas about that too. (Suspicion of armymen and soldiering were part of the midwest farm tradition, like thrift, stickativeness, temperance and sharp practice in money matters.) Any intelligent American mechanic could see that if the Europeans hadn't been a lot of ignorant underpaid foreigners who drank, smoked, were loose about women and wasteful in their methods of production, the war could never have happened.

When Rosika Schwimmer broke through the stockade of secretaries and servicemen who surrounded Henry Ford and suggested to him that he could stop the war,

he said sure they'd hire a ship and go over and get the boys out of the trenches by Christmas.

He hired a steamboat, the *Oscar II,* and filled it up with pacifists and socialworkers,

to go over to explain to the princelings of Europe that what they were doing was vicious and silly. It wasn't his fault that Poor Richard's commonsense no longer rules the world and that most of the pacifists were nuts, goofy with headlines.

When William Jennings Bryan went over to Hoboken to see him off, somebody handed William Jennings Bryan a squirrel in a cage; William Jennings Bryan made a speech with the squirrel under his arm. Henry Ford threw American Beauty roses to the crowd. The band played *I Didn't Raise My Boy to Be a Soldier.* Practical jokers let loose more squirrels. An eloping couple was married by a platoon of ministers in the saloon, and Mr. Zero, the flophouse humanitarian, who reached the rock too late to sail,

dove into the North River and swam after the boat.

The *Oscar II* was described as a floating Chautauqua; Henry Ford said it felt like a middlewestern village, but by the time they reached Christiansand in Norway, the supporters had kidded him so that he had gotten cold feet and gone to bed. The world was too crazy outside of Wayne County, Michigan. Mrs. Ford and the management sent an Episcopal dean after him who brought him home under wraps,

and the pacifists had to speechify without him.

Two years later Ford's was manufacturing munitions, Eagle boats; Henry Ford was planning oneman tanks, and oneman submarines like the one tried out in the Revolutionary War. He announced to the press that he'd turn over his war profits to the government,

but there's no record that he ever did.

One thing he brought back from his trip was the Protocols of the Elders of Zion.

He started a campaign to enlighten the world in the *Dearborn Independent;* the Jews were why the world wasn't like Wayne County, Michigan, in the old horse and buggy days;

the Jews had started the war, Bolshevism, Darwinism, Marxism, Nietzsche, short skirts and lipstick. They were behind Wall Street and the international bankers, and the whiteslave traffic and the movies and the Supreme Court and the ragtime and the illegal liquor business.

Henry Ford denounced the Jews and ran for senator and sued the *Chicago Tribune* for libel,

and was the laughing stock of the kept metropolitan press;

but when the metropolitan bankers tried to horn in on his business

he thoroughly outsmarted them.

In 1918 he had borrowed on notes to buy out his minority stockholders for the picayune sum of seventy-five million dollars.

In February, 1920, he needed cash to pay off some of these notes that were coming due. A banker is supposed to have called on him and offered him every facility if the bankers' representative could be made a member of the board of directors. Henry Ford handed the banker his hat,

and went about raising the money in his own way:

he shipped every car and part he had in his plant to his dealers and demanded immediate cash payment. Let the other fellow do the borrowing had always been a cardinal principle. He shut down production and cancelled all orders from the supplyfirms. Many dealers were ruined many supplyfirms failed, but when he reopened his plant,

he owned it absolutely,

the way a man owns an unmortgaged farm with the taxes paid up.

In 1922 there started the Ford boom for President (high wages, waterpower, industry scattered to the small towns) that was skillfully pricked behind the scenes

by another crackerbarrel philosopher,

Calvin Coolidge;

but in 1922 Henry Ford sold one million three hundred and thirtytwo thousand two hundred and nine tin lizzies; he was the richest man in the world.

Good roads had followed the narrow ruts made in the mud by the Model T. The great automotive boom was on. At Ford's production was improving all the time; less waste, more spotters, strawbosses, stoolpigeons (fifteen minutes for lunch, three minutes to go to the toilet, the Tay-

lorized speedup everywhere, reach under, adjust washer,
screw down bolt, shove in cotterpin, reachunder adjust-
washer screwdownbolt, reachunderadjustscrewdownreach-
underadjust until every ounce of life was sucked off into
production and at night the workmen went home grey shaking husks)

Ford owned every detail of the process from the ore
in the hills until the car rolled off the end of the assemblyline under its own power, the plants were rationalized
to the last tenth-thousandth of an inch as measured by the
Johansen scale;

in 1926 the production cycle was reduced to eightyone
hours from the ore in the mine to the finished salable car
proceeding under its own power,

but the Model T was obsolete.

New Era prosperity and the American Plan
(there were strings to it, always there were strings to it)
had killed Tin Lizzie.
Ford's was just one of many automobile plants.
When the stockmarket bubble burst,
Mr. Ford the crackerbarrel philosopher said jubilantly,
"I told you so.
Serves you right for gambling and getting in debt.
The country is sound."
But when the country on cracked shoes, in frayed
trousers, belt tightened over hollow bellies,
idle hands cracked and chapped with the cold of that
coldest March day of 1932,
started marching from Detroit to Dearborn, asking for
work and the American Plan, all they could think of at
Ford's was machineguns.
The country was sound, but they mowed the marchers
down.
They shot four of them dead.

Henry Ford as an old man
is a passionate antiquarian,
(lives besieged on his father's farm embedded in an
estate of thousands of millionaire acres, protected by an
army of servicemen, secretaries, secret agents, dicks under
orders of an English exprizefighter,

always afraid of the feet in broken shoes on the roads,
afraid the gangs will kidnap his grandchildren,
   that a crank will shoot him,
   that Change and the idle hands out of work will break
through the gates and the high fences;
   protected by a private army against
   the new America of starved children and hollow bellies
and cracked shoes stamping on souplines,
   that has swallowed up the old thrifty farmlands
   of Wayne County, Michigan,
   as if they had never been).

Henry Ford as an old man
is a passionate antiquarian.
   He rebuilt his father's farmhouse and put it back exactly
in the state he remembered it in as a boy. He built a village of museums for buggies, sleighs, coaches, old plows,
waterwheels, obsolete models of motorcars. He scoured
the country for fiddlers to play old-fashioned square-
dances.
   Even old taverns he bought and put back into their
original shape, as well as Thomas Edison's early laboratories.
   When he bought the Wayside Inn near Sudbury, Massachusetts, he had the new highway where the newmodel
cars roared and slithered and hissed oilily past (*the new
noise of the automobile*),
   moved away from the door,
   put back the old bad road,
   so that evening might be
   the way it used to be,
   in the days of horses and buggies.

1936

THOMAS WOLFE

(1900–1938)

The "Altamont" of Wolfe's novels was Asheville, North Carolina, where he was born. His father, a stonecutter fond of poetry and the rhetorical flourish, and his mother, a boardinghouse keeper (Asheville is a resort city in the great Smokies), were the prototypes of Oliver and Eliza Gant. Indeed, all four of Wolfe's novels are autobiographical in that they are intense, romantic records of the people, places, sensations, and experiences that fed Wolfe's enormous sense of expectation, his hunger for fulfillment, and the excitement of his lusty love affair with living. The largeness of Wolfe's sense of possible identity was given an emblem in the gigantic stature of his body. His burning desire for greatness, which he fostered through the intake of experience and the outlet of verbal, dramatic expression, led him into the theater at an early age. When sixteen, he enrolled at the University of North Carolina, became editor of the literary magazine in his senior year, and worked for the Carolina Playmakers, under the gifted direction of Professor Frederick Koch.

The Return of Buck Gavin, written for the Playmakers, became Wolfe's first published work when Koch edited a collection of student plays (*Carolina Folk Plays: Second Series*, 1924). Bent upon the theater, upon graduation in 1920 Wolfe went to Harvard, where, during his work for his M. A., he enrolled in Professor Baker's famous "47 Workshop." Completing his degree in 1922, he traveled in England, France, and the United States. Unsuccessful in his attempts to interest Broadway producers in his plays, he compromised by accepting an instructorship in English composition (the source of some apocryphal and wonderful Wolfeiana) at the Washington Square College of New York University in 1924, a post he held intermittently until 1930. While at N.Y.U., he "completed" a 350,000 word novel that publishers were afraid to accept. Then it was read by Scribner's famous editor, Maxwell Perkins. In an age of hard-boiled realism, this manuscript was a lyrical, uncontrolled, Whitmanesque cry of gusto and yearning that Perkins felt would become, with pruning, one of the most important statements of the American sense of hope, alienation, memory, and voracious-ness for new experience. Working with the author, Perkins helped to put the manuscript into a form that was published in 1929 as Wolfe's first novel, *Look Homeward, Angel.* The response was adulatory. So Wolfe quit N.Y.U., took a Guggenheim fellowship to Europe—his passport to the exits from academe—and wrote furiously. Two years after his return from Europe, Perkins helped him, over a two-year period, to organize the vast bundles of manuscript into another novel centered around the character of Eugene Gant, *Of Time and the River.* In 1935, when *Of Time and the River* finally appeared, Wolfe assem-bled a collection of short pieces in *From Death to Morning,* followed in the next year by *The Story of a Novel,* an account of his life as a man and a writer during the preparation and publication of *Of Time and the River.*

Wolfe then changed publishing houses and heroes, and Eugene Gant became George Webber in *The Web and the Rock,* which appeared one year after Wolfe's death. Edward C. As-well, his new editor, took the rough outline and the unfinished manuscript of a fourth novel, put the manuscript into shape according to the outline, and published it in 1940 as *You Can't Go Home Again.* Further fragments were collected by Aswell the next year in *The Hills Beyond.*

Whatever the critical estimate of Wolfe (since his famous literary argument with F. Scott Fitzgerald about "putting in" and "leaving out," he has been called everything from Amer-ica's greatest lyrical genius to an adolescent and bombastic blowhard), there is no question that his prose is evocative, both in nostalgia and anticipation, of the youthful possibilities of American experience. It is not insignificant that the young al-ways seem to be those who delight the most in Wolfe's prose. All the yearning hunger, the appetite of the emotions and the body, drive his Eugene Gant-George Webber-Thomas Wolfe-American Young Man to a search for self by way of a search for America. The sheer bigness of his hero's capacity—for food, for sex, for brawl, for color, for sensation and for more, more, and more—epitomizes the bigness and mysteriousness of the American land and the American experience, which broods always in the story as a promissory symbol of human amplitude and potential, as well as of alienation in time and place.

Suffering from the complications of pneumonia, Wolfe contracted a brain disease and died when he was only thirty-eight.

Some of his other works are *A Note on Experts* (1939); *Gentlemen of the Press: A Play* (1942); *Mannerhouse* (1948); and *A Western Journal* (1951). There is no collected edition of Wolfe's works.

Accounts of the man and his work are to be found in G. R. Preston, Jr., *Thomas Wolfe: A Bibliography* (1943); J. S. Terry, ed., *Thomas Wolfe's Letters to His Mother* (1943); H. J. Muller, *Thomas Wolfe* (1947); H. Norwood, *The Marble Man's Wife* (1947); P. Johnson, *Hungry Gulliver* (1948); M. Geismar, ed., *The Portable Thomas Wolfe* (1950); R. Walser, ed., *The Enigma of Thomas Wolfe* (1953); T. C. Pollock and O. Cargill, eds., *The Correspondence of Thomas Wolfe and Homer Andrew Watt* (1954); T. C. Pollock and O. Cargill, eds., *Thomas Wolfe at Washington Square* (1954); L. D. Rubin, *Thomas Wolfe, the Weather of His Youth* (1955); E. Nowell, ed., *The Letters of Thomas Wolfe* (1956); F. Watkins, *Thomas Wolfe's Characters* (1957); E. Nowell, *Thomas Wolfe* (1959); M. Wheaton and L. Blythe, *Thomas Wolfe and His Family* (1960); F. F. Finney, Jr., "A Critical Examination of . . . the Fiction of Thomas Wolfe," *Dissertation Abstracts*, XXII (1961); J. C. Gatlin, Jr., "The Development of Thomas Wolfe as a Literary Artist," *Dissertation Abstracts*, XXII (1961); O. C. Lawrence, "Thomas Wolfe: From Individual to Man-Swarm," *Dissertation Abstracts*, XXII (1961); C. H. Holman, ed., *The Thomas Wolfe Reader* (1962); C. H. Holman, ed., *The World of Thomas Wolfe* (1962); R. S. Kennedy, *The Window of Memory: The Literary Career of Thomas Wolfe* (1962); F. E. Skipp, "Thomas Wolfe and His Scribner's Editors," *Dissertation Abstracts*, XXIII (1963); V. Fisher, *Thomas Wolfe as I Knew Him* (1963); T. E. Boyle, "Thomas Wolfe's Myth of America," *Dissertation Abstracts*, XXV (1964); B. R. McElderry, Jr., *Thomas Wolfe* (1964); W. P. Reeves, Jr., "Race and Nationality in the Works of Thomas Wolfe," *Dissertation Abstracts*, XXIV (1964); J. L. Idol, Jr., "Thomas Wolfe's Satire," *Dissertation Abstracts*, XXVI (1965); C. W. LaSalle, "Thomas Wolfe," *Dissertation Abstracts*, XXVI (1965); Thomas Wolfe issue, *Modern Fiction Studies*, XI (1965); and R. Raynolds, *Thomas Wolfe* (1965).

FROM

Of Time and the River

[America]

But this was the reason why . . . [our memories] could never be forgotten—because we are so lost, so naked and so lonely in America. Immense and cruel skies bend over us, and all of us are driven on forever and we have no home. Therefore, it is not the slow, the punctual sanded drip of the unnumbered days that we remember best, the ash of time; nor is it the huge monotone of the lost years, the unswerving schedules of the lost life and the well-known faces, that we remember best. It is a face seen once and lost forever in a crowd, an eye that looked, a face that smiled and vanished on a passing train, it is a prescience of snow upon a certain night, the laughter of a woman in a summer street long years ago, it is the memory of a single moon seen at the pine's dark edge in old October—and all of our lives is written in the twisting of a leaf upon a bough, a door that opened, and a stone.

For America has a thousand lights and weathers and we walk the streets, we walk the streets forever, we walk the streets of life alone.

It is the place of the howling winds, the hurrying of the leaves in old October, the hard clean falling to the earth of acorns. The place of the storm-tossed moaning of the wintry mountainside, where the young men cry out in their throats and feel the savage vigor, the rude strong energies; the place also where the trains cross rivers.

It is a fabulous country, the only fabulous country; it is the one place where miracles not only happen, but where they happen all the time.

It is the place of exultancy and strong joy, the place of the darkened brooding air, the smell of snow; it is the place of all the fierce, the bitten colors in October, when all of the wild, sweet woods flame up; it is also the place of the cider press and the last brown oozings of the York Imperials. It is the place of the lovely girls with good jobs and the husky voices, who will buy a round of drinks; it is the place where the women with fine legs and silken underwear lie in the pullman berth below you, it is the place of the dark-green snore of the pullman cars, and the voices in the night-time in Virginia.

It is the place where great boats are baying at the harbor's mouth, where great ships are putting out to sea; it is the place where great boats are blowing in the gulf of night, and where the river, the dark and secret river, full of strange time, is forever flowing by us to the sea.

The tugs keep baying in the river; at twelve o'clock the Berengaria *moans, her lights slide gently past the piers beyond Eleventh Street; and in the night a tall tree falls in Old Catawba, there in the hills of home.*

It is the place of autumnal moons hung low and orange at the frosty edges of the pines; it is the place of frost and silence; of the clean dry shocks and the opulence of enormous pumpkins that yellow on hard clotted earth; it is the place of the stir and feathery stumble of the hens upon their roost, the frosty, broken barking of the dogs, the great barn-shapes and solid shadows in the running sweep of the moon-whited countryside, the wailing whistle of the fast express. It is the place of flares and steamings on the tracks, and the swing and bob and tottering dance of lanterns in the yards; it is the place of dings and knellings and the sudden glare of mighty engines over sleeping faces in the night; it is the place of the terrific web and spread and smouldering, the distant glare of Philadelphia and the solid rumble of the sleepers; it is also the place where the Transcontinental Limited is stroking eighty miles an hour across the continent and the small dark towns whip by like bullets, and there is only the fanlike stroke of the secret, immense and lonely earth again.

I have foreseen this picture many times: I will buy passage on the Fast Express.

It is the place of the wild and exultant winter's morning and the wind, with the powdery snow, that has been howling all night long; it is the place of solitude and the branches of the spruce and hemlock piled with snow; it is the place where the Fall River boats are tethered to the wharf, and the wild gray snow of furious, secret, and storm-whited morning whips across them. It is the place of the lodge by the frozen lake and the sweet breath and amorous flesh of sinful woman; it is the place of the tragic and lonely beauty of New England; it is the place of the red barn and the sound of the stabled hooves and of bright tatters of old circus posters; it is the place of the immense and pungent smell of breakfast, the country sausages and the ham and eggs, the smoking wheat cakes and the fragrant coffee, and of lone hunters in the frosty thickets who whistle to their lop-eared hounds.

Where is old Doctor Ballard now with all his dogs? He held that they were sacred, that the souls of all the dear lost dead went into them. His youngest sister's soul sat on the seat beside him; she had long ears and her eyes were sad. Two dozen of his other cherished dead trotted around the buggy as he went up the hill past home. And that was eleven years ago, and I was nine years old; and I stared gravely out the window of my father's house at old Doctor Ballard.

It is the place of the straight stare, the cold white bellies and the buried lust of the lovely Boston girls; it is the place of ripe brainless blondes with tender lips and a flowery smell, and of the girls with shapely arms who stand on ladders picking oranges; it is also the place where large slow-bodied girls from Kansas City, with big legs and milky flesh, are sent East to school by their rich fathers, and there are also immense and lovely girls, with the grip of a passionate bear, who have such names as Neilson, Lundquist, Jorgenson, and Brandt.

I will go up and down the country, and back and forth across the country on the great trains that thunder over America. I will go out West where States are square; Oh, I will go to Boise, and Helena and Albuquerque. I will go to Montana and the two Dakotas and the unknown places.

It is the place of violence and sudden death; of the fast shots in the night, the club of the Irish cop, and the smell of brains and blood upon the pavement; it is the place of the small-town killings, and the men who shoot the lovers of their wives; it is the place where the negroes slash with razors and the hillmen kill in the mountain meadows; it is the place of the ugly drunks and the snarling voices and of foul-mouthed men who want to fight; it is the place of the loud word and the foolish boast and the violent threat; it is also the place of the deadly little men with white faces and the eyes of reptiles, who kill quickly and casually in the dark; it is the lawless land that feeds on murder.

"Did you know the two Lipe girls?" he asked. "Yes," I said. "They lived in Biltburn by the river, and one of them was drowned in the flood. She was a cripple, and she wheeled herself along in a chair. She was strong as a bull." "That's the girl," he said.

It is the place of the crack athletes and of the runners who limber up in March; it is the place of the ten-second men and the great jumpers and vaulters; it is the place where Spring comes, and the young birch trees have white and tender barks, of the thaw of the earth, and the feathery smoke of the trees; it is the place of the burst of grass and bud, the wild and sudden tenderness of the wilderness, and of the crews out on the river and the coaches coming down behind them in the motorboats, the surges rolling out behind when they are gone with heavy sudden wash. It is the place of the baseball players, and the easy lob, the soft spring smackings of the glove and mit, the crack of the bat; it is the place of the great batters, fielders, and pitchers, of the nigger boys and the white, drawling, shirt-sleeved men, the bleachers and the resinous smell of old worn wood; it is the place of Rube Waddell, the mighty untamed and ill-fated pitcher when his left arm is swinging like a lash. It is the place of the fighters, the crafty Jewish lightweights and the mauling Italians, Leonard, Tendler, Rocky Kansas, and Dundee; it is the place where the champion looks over his rival's shoulder with a bored expression.

I shall wake at morning in a foreign land thinking I heard a horse in one of the streets of home.

It is the place where they like to win always, and boast about their victories; it is the place of quick money and sudden loss; it is the place of the mile-long freights with their strong, solid, clanking, heavy loneliness at night, and of the silent freight of cars that curve away among raw piney desolations with their promise of new lands and unknown distances—the huge attentive gape of emptiness. It is the place where the bums come singly from the woods at sunset, the huge stillness of the water tower, the fading light, the rails, secret and alive, and trembling with the oncoming train; it is the place of the great tramps, Oklahoma Red, Fargo Pete, and the Jersey Dutchman, who grab fast rattlers for the Western shore; it is the place of old blown bums who come up in October skirls of dust and wind and crumpled newspapers and beg, with canned heat on their breaths: "Help Old McGuire: McGuire's a good guy, kid. You're not so tough, kid: McGuire's your pal, kid: How about McGuire, McGuire—?"

It is the place of the poolroom players and the drug-store boys; of the town whore and her paramour, the tough town driver; it is the place where they go to the woods on Sunday and get up among the laurel and dogwood bushes and the rhododendron blossoms; it is the place of the cheap hotels and the kids who wait with chattering lips while the nigger goes to get them their first woman; it is the place of the drunken college boys who spend the old man's money and wear fur coats to the football games; it is the place of the lovely girls up North who have rich fathers, of the beautiful wives of business men.

The train broke down somewhere beyond Manassas, and I went forward along the tracks with all the other passengers. "What's the matter?" I said to the engineer. "The eccentric strap is broken, son," he said. It was a very cold day, windy and full of sparkling sun. This was the farthest north I'd ever been, and I was twelve years old and on my way to Washington to see Woodrow Wilson inaugurated. Later I could not forget the face of the engineer and the words "eccentric strap."

It is the place of the immense and lonely earth, the place of fat ears and abundance where they grow cotton, corn, and wheat, the wine-red apples of October, and the good tobacco.

It is the place that is savage and cruel, but it is also the innocent place; it is the wild lawless place, the vital earth that is soaked with the blood of the murdered men, with the blood of the countless murdered men, with the blood of the unavenged and unremembered murdered men; but it is also the place of the child and laughter, where the young men are torn apart with ecstasy, and cry out in their throats with joy, where they hear the howl of the wind and the rain and smell the thunder and the soft numb spitting of the snow, where they are drunk with the bite and sparkle of the air and mad with the solar energy, where they believe in love and victory and think that they can never die.

It is the place where you come up through Virginia on the great trains in the night-time, and rumble slowly across the wide Potomac and see the morning sunlight on the nation's dome at Washington, and where the fat man shaving in the pullman washroom grunts, "What's this? What's this we're coming to—Washington?"—And the thin man glancing out the window says, "Yep, this is Washington. That's what it is, all right. You gettin' off here?"— And where the fat man grunts, "Who—me? Naw—I'm goin' on to Baltimore." It is the place where you get off at Baltimore and find your brother waiting.

Where is my father sleeping on the land? Buried? Dead these seven years? Forgotten, rotten in the ground? Held by his own great stone? No, no! Will I say, "Father" when I come to him? And will he call me, "Son"? Oh, no, he'll never see my face: we'll never speak except to say—

It is the place of the fast approach, the hot blind smoky passage, the tragic lonely beauty of New England, and the web of Boston; the place of the mighty station there, and engines passive as great cats, the straight dense plumes of engine smoke, the acrid and exciting smell of trains and stations, and of the man-swarm passing ever in its million-footed weft, the smell of the sea in harbors and the thought of voyages—and the place of the goat cry, the strong joy of our youth, the magic city, when we knew the most fortunate life on earth would certainly be ours, that we were twenty and could never die.

And always America is the place of the deathless and enraptured moments, the eye that looked, the mouth that smiled and vanished, and the word; the stone, the leaf, the door we never found and never have forgotten. And these are the things that we remember of America, for we have known all her thousand lights and weathers, and we walk the streets, we walk the streets forever, we walk the streets of life alone.

1935

FROM

You Can't Go Home Again

[America]

The lives of men who have to live in our great cities are often tragically lonely. In many more ways than one, these dwellers in the hive are modern counterparts of Tantalus. They are starving to death in the midst of abundance. The crystal stream flows near their lips but always falls away when they try to drink of it. The vine, rich-weighted with its golden fruit, bends down, comes near, but springs back when they reach to touch it.

Melville, at the beginning of his great fable, *Moby Dick,* tells how the city people of his time would, on every occasion that was afforded them, go down to the dock, to the very edges of the wharf, and stand there looking out to sea. In the great city of today, however, there is no sea to look out to, or, if there is, it is so far away, so inaccessible, walled in behind such infinite ramifications of stone and steel, that the effort to get to it is disheartening. So now, when the city man looks out, he looks out on nothing but crowded vacancy.

Does this explain, perhaps, the desolate emptiness of city youth—those straggling bands of boys of sixteen or eighteen that one can always see at night or on a holiday, going along a street, filling the air with raucous jargon and senseless cries, each trying to outdo the others with joyless cat-calls and mirthless quips and jokes which are so feeble, so stupidly inane, that one hears them with strong mixed feelings of pity and of shame? Where here, among these lads, is all the merriment, high spirits, and spontaneous gayety of youth? These creatures, millions of them, seem to have been born but half made up, without innocence, born old and stale and dull and empty.

Who can wonder at it? For what a world it is that most of them were born into! They were suckled on darkness, and weaned on violence and noise. They had to try to draw out moisture from the cobblestones, their true parent was a city street, and in that barren universe no urgent sails swelled out and leaned against the wind, they rarely knew the feel of earth beneath their feet and no birds sang, their youthful eyes grew hard, unseeing, from being stopped forever by a wall of masonry.

In other times, when painters tried to paint a scene of awful desolation, they chose the desert or a heath of barren rocks, and there would try to picture man in his great loneliness—the prophet in the desert, Elijah being fed by ravens on the rocks. But for a modern painter, the most desolate scene would be a street in almost any one of our great cities on a Sunday afternoon.

Suppose a rather drab and shabby street in Brooklyn, not quite tenement perhaps, and lacking therefore even the gaunt savagery of poverty, but a street of cheap brick buildings, warehouses, and garages, with a cigar store or a fruit stand or a barber shop on the corner. Suppose a Sunday afternoon in March—bleak, empty, slaty grey. And suppose a group of men, Americans of the working class, dressed in their "good" Sunday clothes—the cheap machinemade suits, the new cheap shoes, the cheap felt hats stamped out of universal grey. Just suppose this, and nothing more. The men hang around the corner before the cigar store or the closed barber shop, and now and then, through the bleak and empty street, a motor car goes flashing past, and in the distance they hear the cold rumble of an elevated train. For hours they hang around the corner, waiting—waiting—waiting——

For what?

Nothing. Nothing at all. And that is what gives the scene its special quality of tragic loneliness, awful emptiness, and utter desolation. Every modern city man is familiar with it.

And yet—and yet——

It is also true—and this is a curious paradox about America—that these same men who stand upon the corner and wait around on Sunday afternoons for nothing are filled at the same time with an almost quenchless hope, an almost boundless optimism, an almost indestructible belief that something is bound to turn up, something is sure to happen. This is a peculiar quality of the American soul, and it contributes largely to the strange enigma of our life, which is so incredibly mixed of harshness and of tenderness, of innocence and of crime, of loneliness and of good fellowship, of desolation and of exultant hope, of terror and of courage, of nameless fear and of soaring conviction, of brutal, empty, naked, bleak, corrosive ugliness, and of beauty so lovely and so overwhelming that the tongue is stopped by it, and the language for it has not yet been uttered.

How explain this nameless hope that seems to lack all reasonable foundation? I cannot. But if you were to go up to this fairly intelligent-looking truck driver who stands and waits there with his crowd, and if you put to him your question, and if he understood what you were talking about (he wouldn't), and if he were articulate enough to frame in words the feelings that are in him (he isn't)—he might answer you with something such as this:

"Now is duh mont' of March, duh mont' of March— now it is Sunday afternoon in Brooklyn in duh mont' of March, an' we stand upon cold corners of duh day. It's funny dat dere are so many corners in duh mont' of March, here in Brooklyn where no corners are. Jesus! On Sunday in duh mont' of March we sleep late in duh mornin', den we get up an' read duh papers—duh funnies an' duh sportin' news. We eat some chow. An' den we dress up in duh afternoon, we leave our wives, we leave duh funnies littered on duh floor, an' go outside in Brooklyn in duh mont' of March an' stand around upon ten t'ousand corners of duh day. We need a corner in duh mont' of March, a wall to stand to, a shelter an' a door. Dere must be *some* place inside in duh mont' of March, but we never found it. So we stand around on corners where duh sky is cold an' ragged still wit' winter, in our good clothes we stand around wit' a lot of udder guys we know, before duh barber shop, just lookin' for a door."

Ah, yes, for in summer:

It is so cool and sweet tonight, a million feet are walking here across the jungle web of Brooklyn in the dark, and it's so hard now to remember that it ever was the month of March in Brooklyn and that we couldn't find a door. There are so many million doors tonight. There's a door for everyone tonight, all's open to the air, all's interfused tonight: remote the thunder of the elevated trains on Fulton Street, the rattling of the cars along Atlantic Avenue, the glare of Coney Island seven miles away, the mob, the racket, and the barkers shouting, the cars swift-shuttling through the quiet streets, the people swarming in the web, lit here and there with livid blurs of light, the voices of the neighbors leaning at their windows, harsh, soft, all interfused. All's illusive in the liquid air tonight, all mixed in with the radios that blare from open windows. And there is something over all tonight, something fused, remote, and trembling, made of all of this, and yet not of it, upon the huge and weaving ocean of the night in Brooklyn—something that we had almost quite forgotten in the month of March. What's this?—a sash raised gently?—a window?—a near voice on the air?—something swift and passing, almost captured, there below?—there in the gulf of night the mournful and yet thrilling voices of the tugs?—the liner's blare? Here—there—some otherwhere—was it a whisper?—a woman's call?—a sound of people talking behind the screens and doors in Flatbush? It trembles in the air throughout the giant web tonight, as fleeting as a step—near—as soft and sudden as a woman's laugh. The liquid air is living with the very whisper of the thing that we are looking for tonight throughout America—the very thing that seemed so bleak, so vast, so cold, so hopeless, and so lost as we waited in our good clothes on ten thousand corners of the day in Brooklyn in the month of March.

. . .

And we? Made of our father's earth, blood of his blood, bone of his bone, flesh of his flesh—born like our father here to live and strive, here to win through or be defeated—here, like all the other men who went before us, not too nice or dainty for the uses of this earth—here to live, to suffer, and to die—O brothers, like our fathers in their time, we are burning, burning, burning in the night.

Go, seeker, if you will, throughout the land and you will find us burning in the night.

There where the hackles of the Rocky Mountains blaze in the blank and naked radiance of the moon, go make your resting stool upon the highest peak. Can you not see us now? The continental wall just sheer and flat, its huge black shadow on the plain, and the plain sweeps out against the East, two thousand miles away. The great snake that you see there is the Mississippi River.

Behold the gem-strung towns and cities of the good, green East, flung like star-dust through the field of night. That spreading constellation to the north is called Chicago, and that giant wink that blazes in the moon is the pendant lake that it is built upon. Beyond, close-set and dense as a clenched fist, are all the jeweled cities of the eastern seaboard. There's Boston, ringed with the bracelet of its shining little towns, and all the lights that sparkle on the rocky indentations of New England. Here, southward and a little to the west, and yet still coasted to the sea, is our intensest ray, the splintered firmament of the towered island of Manhattan. Round about her, sown thick as grain, is the glitter of a hundred towns and cities. The long chain of lights there is the necklace of Long Island and the Jersey shore. Southward and inland, by a foot or two, behold the duller glare of Philadelphia. Southward further still, the twin constellations—Baltimore and Washington. Westward, but still within the borders of the good, green East, that nighttime glow and smolder of hell-fire is Pittsburgh. Here, St. Louis, hot and humid in the cornfield belly of the land, and bedded on the mid-length coil and fringes of the snake. There at the snake's mouth, southward six hundred miles or so, you see the jeweled crescent of old New Orleans. Here, west and south again, you see the gemmy glitter of the cities on the Texas border.

Turn now, seeker, on your resting stool atop the Rocky Mountains, and look another thousand miles or so across moon-blazing fiend-worlds of the Painted Desert and beyond Sierras' ridge. That magic congeries of lights there to the west, ringed like a studded belt around the magic setting of its lovely harbor, is the fabled town of San Francisco. Below it, Los Angeles and all the cities of the California shore. A thousand miles to north and west, the sparkling towns of Oregon and Washington.

Observe the whole of it, survey it as you might survey a field. Make it your garden, seeker, or your backyard patch. Be at ease in it. It's your oyster—yours to open if you will. Don't be frightened, it's not so big now, when your footstool is the Rocky Mountains. Reach out and dip a hatful of cold water from Lake Michigan. Drink it—we've tried it—you'll not find it bad. Take your shoes off and work your toes down in the river oozes of the Mississippi bottom—it's very refreshing on a hot night in the summertime. Help yourself to a bunch of Concord grapes up there in northern New York State—they're getting good now. Or raid that watermelon patch down there in Georgia. Or, if you like, you can try the Rockyfords here at your elbow, in Colorado. Just make yourself at home, refresh yourself, get the feel of things, adjust your sights, and get the scale. It's your pasture now, and it's not so big—only three thousand miles from east to west, only two thousand miles from north to south—but all between, where ten thousand points of light prick out the cities, towns, and villages, there, seeker, you will find us burning in the night.

Here, as you pass through the brutal sprawl, the twenty miles of rails and rickets, of the South Chicago slums— here, in an unpainted shack, is a Negro boy, and, seeker, he is burning in the night. Behind him is a memory of the cotton fields, the flat and mournful pineland barrens of the lost and buried South, and at the fringes of the pine another nigger shack, with mammy and eleven little niggers. Farther still behind, the slave-driver's whip, the slave ship, and, far off, the jungle dirge of Africa. And before him, what? A roped-in ring, a blaze of lights, across from him a white champion; the bell, the opening, and all around the vast sea-roaring of the crowd. Then the lightning feint and stroke, the black panther's paw—the hot, rotating presses, and the rivers of sheeted print! O seeker, where is the slave ship now?

Or there, in the clay-baked piedmont of the South, that lean and tan-faced boy who sprawls there in the creaking chair among admiring cronies before the open doorways of the fire department, and tells them how he pitched the team to shut-out victory today. What visions burn, what dreams possess him, seeker of the night? The packed stands of the stadium, the bleachers sweltering with their unshaded hordes, the faultless velvet of the diamond, unlike the clay-baked outfields down in Georgia. The mounting roar of eighty thousand voices and Gehrig coming up to bat, the boy himself upon the pitching mound, the lean face steady as a hound's; then the nod, the signal, and the wind-up, the rawhide arm that snaps and crackles like a whip, the small white bullet of the blazing ball, its loud report in the oiled pocket of the catcher's mitt, the umpire's thumb jerked upward, the clean strike.

Or there again, in the East-Side Ghetto of Manhattan,

two blocks away from the East River, a block away from the gas-house district and its thuggery, there in the swarming tenement, shut in his sweltering cell, breathing the sun-baked air through opened window at the fire escape, celled there away into a little semblance of privacy and solitude from all the brawling and vociferous life and argument of his family and the seething hive around him, the Jew boy sits and pores upon his book. In shirt-sleeves, bent above his table to meet the hard glare of a naked bulb, he sits with gaunt, starved face converging to his huge beaked nose, the weak eyes squinting painfully through his thick-lens glasses, his greasy hair roached back in oily scrolls above the slanting cage of his painful and constricted brow. And for what? For what this agony of concentration? For what this hell of effort? For what this intense withdrawal from the poverty and squalor of dirty brick and rusty fire-escapes, from the raucous cries and violence and never ending noise? For what? Because, brother, he is burning in the night. He sees the class, the lecture room, the shining apparatus of gigantic laboratories, the open field of scholarship and pure research, certain knowledge, and the world distinction of an Einstein name.

So, then, to every man his chance—to every man, regardless of his birth, his shining, golden opportunity—to every man the right to live, to work, to be himself, and to become whatever thing his manhood and his vision can combine to make him—this, seeker, is the promise of America.

1940

JOHN STEINBECK

(1902–   )

John Steinbeck's experience is an integral part of the materials of his fiction. He was born in Salinas, California, the locale
of much of his writing. His mother was a schoolteacher, his
father the county treasurer. When Steinbeck was graduated
from high school, where he held various jobs during his schooling, he attended Stanford University for four years. His college
years were in many ways enviable. Because he had to finance
himself, he enrolled as a special student, interrupting his
formal education frequently in order to hold diverse jobs, and
he did not work for a degree. The flexibility of his program
allowed him to take only those courses he liked: he specialized
in marine biology.

After his four years at Stanford, he worked his way to New
York on a cattleboat. Failing to find success as a novelist or a
newspaperman, he worked as a bricklayer and returned to
California, where he worked as, among other things, caretaker,
chemist's assistant, and migratory fruitpicker. For a while he
lived in his own boat and caught his own food off Monterey.
It was in many ways a hard life, but free, exciting and not
unpleasant.

His first novel, *Cup of Gold* (1929), was a romantic historical novel of adventure. Like his next two books—*The Pastures
of Heaven*, connected short stories (1932) and *To a God Unknown*, a novel (1933)—*Cup of Gold* brought Steinbeck neither
fame nor fortune. However, in *The Pastures of Heaven*, he first
introduced the regional folk material of his California wander-
ings, and when he used this again in *Tortilla Flat* (1935), he
achieved a sudden fame that was to grow throughout the rest
of the decade. As a writer whose work matured during the de-

pression years, Steinbeck created fiction that tenderly, sometimes sentimentally, announced the indestructibility of the common and laboring folk. For Steinbeck, they became a human symbol of natural process viewed from philosophical perspectives that would be recognizable to the Transcendentalists of the romantic era. Whether he writes about the *paisanos* of Monterey or the rural people of the Salinas Valley or Oklahoma, he combines warm humor and regionalism and violence with a realistic technique that produces his own special blend of social protest and mysticism.

Following *Tortilla Flat* were four years of growing popular success for Steinbeck. *In Dubious Battle* appeared in 1936, *Of Mice and Men* and *The Red Pony* in 1937, *The Long Valley* in 1938, and his masterwork, *The Grapes of Wrath*, in 1939. With this output, Steinbeck became the foremost new novelist in American fiction during the 1930's. He has since written a number of works of large variety (one of the fullest statements of his beliefs is *Sea of Cortez* 1941), in some cases—such as *Cannery Row* (1945) and *Sweet Thursday* (1954)—returning to his California "lovable bums." But he has not yet again reached the heights he scaled in *The Grapes of Wrath*, although some feel that he came close to it in *The Winter of Our Discontent* (1961), a mordant criticism of declining American values, disguised in comedy.

In addition to the titles mentioned above, Steinbeck's books include *Saint Katy the Virgin* (1936); *Their Blood Is Strong* (1938); *The Forgotten Village* (1941); *The Moon Is Down* (1942); *Bombs Away* (1942); *The Wayward Bus* (1947); *The Pearl* (1947); *A Russian Journal* (1948); *Burning Bright* (1950); *East of Eden* (1952); *The Short Reign of Pippin IV* (1957); *Once There Was a War* (1958); *Travels with Charley in Search of America* (1962); and *America and Americans* (1966).

The Portable Steinbeck (1943; revised edition 1946), edited by Pascal Covici, with an introduction by Lewis Gannett, contains biographical notes, *Of Mice and Men* and *The Red Pony* complete, eight short stories, selections from six other books, and letters.

Other studies of the man and his work are to be found in H. T. Moore, *The Novels of John Steinbeck* (1939); P. H. Boynton, *America in Contemporary Fiction* (1940); C. E. Jones, "Proletarian Writing and John Steinbeck," *Sewanee Review,* XLVIII (October, 1940); F. B. Millett, *Contemporary American Authors* (1940); J. W. Beach, *American Fiction, 1920–1940* (1941); F. I. Carpenter, "The Philosophical Joads," *College English,* II (January, 1941); E. Wilson, *The Boys in the Back Room* (1941); B. Fairley, "John Steinbeck and the Coming Literature," *Sewanee Review,* L (1942); E. Tedlock, Jr., and C. Wicker, eds., *Steinbeck and His Critics* (1957); P. Lisca, *The Wide World of John Steinbeck* (1958); H. S. Levant, "A Critical Study of the Longer Fiction of John Steinbeck," *Dissertation Abstracts,* XXIII (1962); L. J. Marks, "A Study of Thematic Continuity in the Novels of John Steinbeck," *Dissertation Abstracts,* XXII (1962); H. P. Taylor, Jr., "The Biological Naturalism of John Steinbeck," *Dissertation Abstracts,* XXII (1962); F. W. Watt, *John Steinbeck* (1962); J. Fontenrose, *John Steinbeck* (1963); W. French, ed., *A Companion to* The Grapes of Wrath (1963); J. H. Jackson, ed., *The Short Novels of John Steinbeck* (1963); S. G. Alexander, "Primitivism and Pastoral Form in John Steinbeck's Early Fiction;" *Dissertation Abstracts,* XXVI (1965); John Steinbeck issue, *Modern Fiction Studies,* XI (1965); and W. French, *The Social Novel at the End of an Era* (1966).

The Leader of the People

On Saturday afternoon Billy Buck, the ranch-hand, raked together the last of the old year's haystack and pitched small forkfuls over the wire fence to a few mildly interested cattle. High in the air small clouds like puffs of cannon smoke were driven eastward by the March wind. The wind could be heard whishing in the brush on the ridge crests, but no breath of it penetrated down into the ranch-cup.

The little boy, Jody, emerged from the house eating a thick piece of buttered bread. He saw Billy working on the last of the haystack. Jody tramped down scuffing his shoes in a way he had been told was destructive to good shoe-leather. A flock of white pigeons flew out of the black cypress tree as Jody passed, and circled the tree and landed again. A half-grown tortoise-shell cat leaped from the bunkhouse porch, galloped on stiff legs across the road, whirled and galloped back again. Jody picked up a stone to help the game along, but he was too late, for the cat was under the porch before the stone could be discharged. He threw the stone into the cypress tree and started the white pigeons on another whirling flight.

Arriving at the used-up haystack, the boy leaned against the barbed wire fence. "Will that be all of it, do you think?" he asked.

The middle-aged ranch-hand stopped his careful raking and stuck his fork into the ground. He took off his black hat and smoothed down his hair. "Nothing left of it that isn't soggy from ground moisture," he said. He replaced his hat and rubbed his dry leathery hands together.

"Ought to be plenty mice," Jody suggested.

"Lousy with them," said Billy. "Just crawling with mice."

"Well, maybe, when you get all through, I could call the dogs and hunt the mice."

"Sure, I guess you could," said Billy Buck. He lifted a forkful of the damp ground-hay and threw it into the air. Instantly three mice leaped out and burrowed frantically under the hay again.

Jody sighed with satisfaction. Those plump, sleek, arrogant mice were doomed. For eight months they had lived and multiplied in the haystack. They had been immune from cats, from traps, from poison and from Jody. They had grown smug in their security, overbearing and fat. Now the time of disaster had come; they would not survive another day.

Billy looked up at the top of the hills that surrounded the ranch. "Maybe you better ask your father before you do it," he suggested.

"Well, where is he? I'll ask him now."

"He rode up to the ridge ranch after dinner. He'll be back pretty soon."

Jody slumped against the fence post. "I don't think he'd care."

As Billy went back to his work he said ominously, "You'd better ask him anyway. You know how he is."

Jody did know. His father, Carl Tiflin, insisted upon giving permission for anything that was done on the ranch, whether it was important or not. Jody sagged farther against the post until he was sitting on the ground. He looked up at the little puffs of wind-driven cloud. "Is it like to rain, Billy?"

"It might. The wind's good for it, but not strong enough."

"Well, I hope it don't rain until after I kill those damn mice." He looked over his shoulder to see whether Billy had noticed the mature profanity. Billy worked on without comment.

Jody turned back and looked at the side-hill where the road from the outside world came down. The hill was washed with lean March sunshine. Silver thistles, blue lupins and a few poppies bloomed among the sage bushes. Halfway up the hill Jody could see Doubletree Mutt, the black dog, digging in a squirrel hole. He paddled for a while and then paused to kick bursts of dirt out between his hind legs, and then he dug with an earnestness which belied the knowledge he must have had that no dog had ever caught a squirrel by digging in a hole.

Suddenly, while Jody watched, the black dog stiffened, and backed out of the hole and looked up the hill toward the cleft in the ridge where the road came through. Jody looked up too. For a moment Carl Tiflin on horseback stood out against the pale sky and then he moved down the road toward the house. He carried something white in his hand.

The boy started to his feet. "He's got a letter," Jody cried. He trotted away toward the ranch house, for the letter would probably be read aloud and he wanted to be there. He reached the house before his father did, and ran in. He heard Carl dismount from his creaking saddle and slap the horse on the side to send it to the barn where Billy would unsaddle it and turn it out.

Jody ran into the kitchen. "We got a letter!" he cried.

His mother looked up from a pan of beans. "Who has?"

"Father has. I saw it in his hand."

Carl strode into the kitchen then, and Jody's mother asked, "Who's the letter from, Carl?"

He frowned quickly. "How did you know there was a letter?"

She nodded her head in the boy's direction. "Big-Britches Jody told me."

Jody was embarrassed.

His father looked down at him contemptuously. "He is getting to be a Big-Britches," Carl said. "He's minding everybody's business but his own. Got his big nose into everything."

Mrs. Tiflin relented a little. "Well, he hasn't enough to keep him busy. Who's the letter from?"

Carl still frowned on Jody. "I'll keep him busy if he isn't careful." He held out a sealed letter. "I guess it's from your father."

Mrs. Tiflin took a hairpin from her head and slit open the flap. Her lips pursed judiciously. Jody saw her eyes snap back and forth over the lines. "He says," she translated, "he says he's going to drive out Saturday to stay for a little while. Why, this is Saturday. The letter must have been delayed." She looked at the postmark. "This was mailed day before yesterday. It should have been here yesterday." She looked up questioningly at her husband, and then her face darkened angrily. "Now what have you got that look on you for? He doesn't come often."

Carl turned his eyes away from her anger. He could be stern with her most of the time, but when occasionally her temper arose, he could not combat it.

"What's the matter with you?" she demanded again.

In his explanation there was a tone of apology Jody himself might have used. "It's just that he talks," Carl said lamely. "Just talks."

"Well, what of it? You talk yourself."

"Sure I do. But your father only talks about one thing."

"Indians!" Jody broke in excitedly. "Indians and crossing the plains!"

Carl turned fiercely on him. "You get out, Mr. Big-Britches! Go on, now! Get out!"

Jody went miserably out the back door and closed the screen with elaborate quietness. Under the kitchen window his shamed, downcast eyes fell upon a curiously shaped stone, a stone of such fascination that he squatted down and picked it up and turned it over in his hands.

The voices came clearly to him through the open kitchen window. "Jody's damn well right," he heard his father say. "Just Indians and crossing the plains. I've heard that story about how the horses got driven off about a thousand times. He just goes on and on, and he never changes a word in the things he tells."

When Mrs. Tiflin answered her tone was so changed that Jody, outside the window, looked up from his study of the stone. Her voice had become soft and explanatory. Jody knew how her face would have changed to match the tone. She said quietly, "Look at it this way, Carl. That was the big thing in my father's life. He led a wagon train clear across the plains to the coast, and when it was finished, his life was done. It was a big thing to do, but it didn't last long enough. Look!" she continued, "it's as though he was born to do that, and after he finished it, there wasn't anything more for him to do but think about it and talk about it. If there'd been any farther west to go, he'd have gone.

He's told me so himself. But at last there was the ocean. He lives right by the ocean where he had to stop."

She had caught Carl, caught him and entangled him in her soft tone.

"I've seen him," he agreed quietly. "He goes down and stares off west over the ocean." His voice sharpened a little. "And then he goes up to the Horseshoe Club in Pacific Grove, and he tells people how the Indians drove off the horses."

She tried to catch him again. "Well, it's everything to him. You might be patient with him and pretend to listen."

Carl turned impatiently away. "Well, if it gets too bad, I can always go down to the bunkhouse and sit with Billy," he said irritably. He walked through the house and slammed the front door after him.

Jody ran to his chores. He dumped the grain to the chickens without chasing any of them. He gathered the eggs from the nests. He trotted into the house with the wood and interlaced it so carefully in the woodbox that two armloads seemed to fill it to overflowing.

His mother had finished the beans by now. She stirred up the fire and brushed off the stove-top with a turkey wing. Jody peered cautiously at her to see whether any rancor toward him remained. "Is he coming today?" Jody asked.

"That's what his letter said."

"Maybe I better walk up the road to meet him."

Mrs. Tiflin clanged the stove-lid shut. "That would be nice," she said. "He'd probably like to be met."

"I guess I'll just do it then."

Outside, Jody whistled shrilly to the dogs. "Come on up the hill," he commanded. The two dogs waved their tails and ran ahead. Along the roadside the sage had tender new tips. Jody tore off some pieces and rubbed them on his hands until the air was filled with the sharp wild smell. With a rush the dogs leaped from the road and yapped into the brush after a rabbit. That was the last Jody saw of them, for when they failed to catch the rabbit, they went back home.

Jody plodded on up the hill toward the ridge top. When he reached the little cleft where the road came through, the afternoon wind struck him and blew up his hair and ruffled his shirt. He looked down on the little hills and ridges below and then out at the huge green Salinas Valley. He could see the white town of Salinas far out in the flat and the flash of its windows under the waning sun. Directly below him, in an oak tree, a crow congress had convened. The tree was black with crows all cawing at once.

Then Jody's eyes followed the wagon road down from the ridge where he stood, and lost it behind a hill, and picked it up again on the other side. On that distant stretch he saw a cart slowly pulled by a bay horse. It disappeared behind the hill. Jody sat down on the ground and watched the place where the cart would reappear again. The wind sang on the hilltops and the puff-ball clouds hurried eastward.

Then the cart came into sight and stopped. A man dressed in black dismounted from the seat and walked to the horse's head. Although it was so far away, Jody knew he had unhooked the check-rein, for the horse's head dropped forward. The horse moved on, and the man walked slowly up the hill beside it. Jody gave a glad cry and ran down the road toward them. The squirrels bumped along off the road, and a road-runner flirted its tail and raced over the edge of the hill and sailed out like a glider.

Jody tried to leap into the middle of his shadow at every step. A stone rolled under his foot and he went down. Around a little bend he raced, and there, a short distance ahead, were his grandfather and the cart. The boy dropped from his unseemly running and approached at a dignified walk.

The horse plodded stumble-footedly up the hill and the old man walked beside it. In the lowering sun their giant shadows flickered darkly behind them. The grandfather was dressed in a black broadcloth suit and he wore kid congress gaiters and a black tie on a short, hard collar. He carried his black slouch hat in his hand. His white beard was cropped close and his white eyebrows overhung his eyes like mustaches. The blue eyes were sternly merry. About the whole face and figure there was a granite dignity, so that every motion seemed an impossible thing. Once at rest, it seemed the old man would be stone, would never move again. His steps were slow and certain. Once made, no step could ever be retraced; once headed in a direction, the path would never bend nor the pace increase nor slow.

When Jody appeared around the bend, Grandfather waved his hat slowly in welcome, and he called, "Why, Jody! Come down to meet me, have you?"

Jody sidled near and turned and matched his step to the old man's step and stiffened his body and dragged his heels a little. "Yes, sir," he said. "We got your letter only today."

"Should have been here yesterday," said Grandfather. "It certainly should. How are all the folks?"

"They're fine, sir." He hesitated and then suggested shyly, "Would you like to come on a mouse hunt tomorrow, sir?"

"Mouse hunt, Jody?" Grandfather chuckled. "Have the people of this generation come down to hunting mice? They aren't very strong, the new people, but I hardly thought mice would be game for them."

"No, sir. It's just play. The haystack's gone. I'm going to drive out the mice to the dogs. And you can watch, or even beat the hay a little."

The stern, merry eyes turned down on him. "I see. You don't eat them, then. You haven't come to that yet."

Jody explained, "The dogs eat them, sir. It wouldn't be much like hunting Indians, I guess."

"No, not much—but then later, when the troops were hunting Indians and shooting children and burning teepees, it wasn't much different from your mouse hunt."

They topped the rise and started down into the ranch-cup, and they lost the sun from their shoulders. "You've grown," Grandfather said. "Nearly an inch, I should say."

"More," Jody boasted. "Where they mark me on the door, I'm up more than an inch since Thanksgiving even."

Grandfather's rich throaty voice said, "Maybe you're getting too much water and turning to pith and stalk. Wait until you head out, and then we'll see."

Jody looked quickly into the old man's face to see whether his feelings should be hurt, but there was no will to injure, no punishing nor putting-in-your-place light in the keen blue eyes. "We might kill a pig," Jody suggested.

"Oh, no! I couldn't let you do that. You're just humoring me. It isn't the time and you know it."

"You know Riley, the big boar, sir?"

"Yes. I remember Riley well."

"Well, Riley ate a hole into that same haystack, and it fell down on him and smothered him."

"Pigs do that when they can," said Grandfather.

"Riley was a nice pig, for a boar, sir. I rode him sometimes, and he didn't mind."

A door slammed at the house below them, and they saw Jody's mother standing on the porch waving her apron in welcome. And they saw Carl Tiflin walking up from the barn to be at the house for the arrival.

The sun had disappeared from the hills by now. The blue smoke from the house chimney hung in flat layers in the purpling ranch-cup. The puff-ball clouds, dropped by the falling wind, hung listlessly in the sky.

Billy Buck came out of the bunkhouse and flung a wash basin of soapy water on the ground. He had been shaving in mid-week, for Billy held Grandfather in reverence, and Grandfather said that Billy was one of the few men of the new generation who had not gone soft. Although Billy was in middle age, Grandfather considered him a boy. Now Billy was hurrying toward the house too.

When Jody and Grandfather arrived, the three were waiting for them in front of the yard gate.

Carl said, "Hello, sir. We've been looking for you."

Mrs. Tiflin kissed Grandfather on the side of his beard, and stood still while his big hand patted her shoulder. Billy shook hands solemnly, grinning under his straw mustache. "I'll put up your horse," said Billy, and he led the rig away.

Grandfather watched him go, and then, turning back to the group, he said as he had said a hundred times before, "There's a good boy. I knew his father, old Mule-tail Buck. I never knew why they called him Mule-tail except he packed mules."

Mrs. Tiflin turned and led the way into the house. "How long are you going to stay, Father? Your letter didn't say."

"Well, I don't know. I thought I'd stay about two weeks. But I never stay as long as I think I'm going to."

In a short while they were sitting at the white oilcloth table eating their supper. The lamp with the tin reflector hung over the table. Outside the dining-room windows the big moths battered softly against the glass.

Grandfather cut his steak into tiny pieces and chewed

slowly. "I'm hungry," he said. "Driving out here got my appetite up. It's like when we were crossing. We all got so hungry every night we could hardly wait to let the meat get done. I could eat about five pounds of buffalo meat every night."

"It's moving around does it," said Billy. "My father was a government packer. I helped him when I was a kid. Just the two of us could about clean up a deer's ham."

"I knew your father, Billy," said Grandfather. "A fine man he was. They called him Mule-tail Buck. I don't know why except he packed mules."

"That was it," Billy agreed. "He packed mules."

Grandfather put down his knife and fork and looked around the table. "I remember one time we ran out of meat—" His voice dropped to a curious low sing-song, dropped into a tonal groove the story had worn for itself. "There was no buffalo, no antelope, not even rabbits. The hunters couldn't even shoot a coyote. That was the time for the leader to be on the watch. I was the leader, and I kept my eyes open. Know why? Well, just the minute the people began to get hungry they'd start slaughtering the team oxen. Do you believe that? I've heard of parties that just ate up their draft cattle. Started from the middle and worked toward the ends. Finally they'd eat the lead pair, and then the wheelers. The leader of a party had to keep them from doing that."

In some manner a big moth got into the room and circled the hanging kerosene lamp. Billy got up and tried to clap it between his hands. Carl struck with a cupped palm and caught the moth and broke it. He walked to the window and dropped it out.

"As I was saying," Grandfather began again, but Carl interrupted him. "You better eat some more meat. All the rest of us are ready for our pudding."

Jody saw a flash of anger in his mother's eyes. Grandfather picked up his knife and fork. "I'm pretty hungry, all right," he said. "I'll tell you about that later."

When supper was over, when the family and Billy Buck sat in front of the fireplace in the other room, Jody anxiously watched Grandfather. He saw the signs he knew. The bearded head leaned forward; the eyes lost their sternness and looked wonderingly into the fire; the big lean fingers laced themselves on the black knees. "I wonder," he began, "I just wonder whether I ever told you how those thieving Piutes drove off thirty-five of our horses."

"I think you did," Carl interrupted. "Wasn't it just before you went up into the Tahoe country?"

Grandfather turned quickly toward his son-in-law. "That's right. I guess I must have told you that story."

"Lots of times," Carl said cruelly, and he avoided his wife's eyes. But he felt the angry eyes on him, and he said, " 'Course I'd like to hear it again."

Grandfather looked back at the fire. His fingers unlaced and laced again. Jody knew how he felt, how his insides were collapsed and empty. Hadn't Jody been called a Big-Britches that very afternoon? He arose to heroism and opened himself to the term Big-Britches again. "Tell about Indians," he said softly.

Grandfather's eyes grew stern again. "Boys always want to hear about Indians. It was a job for men, but boys want to hear about it. Well, let's see. Did I ever tell you how I wanted each wagon to carry a long iron plate?"

Everyone but Jody remained silent. Jody said, "No. You didn't."

"Well, when the Indians attacked, we always put the wagons in a circle and fought from between the wheels. I thought that if every wagon carried a long plate with rifle holes, the men could stand the plates on the outside of the wheels when the wagons were in the circle and they would be protected. It would save lives and that would make up for the extra weight of the iron. But of course the party wouldn't do it. No party had done it before and they couldn't see why they should go to the expense. They lived to regret it, too."

Jody looked at his mother, and knew from her expression that she was not listening at all. Carl picked at a callus on his thumb and Billy Buck watched a spider crawling up the wall.

Grandfather's tone dropped into its narrative groove again. Jody knew in advance exactly what words would fall. The story droned on, speeded up for the attack, grew sad over the wounds, struck a dirge at the burials on the great plains. Jody sat quietly watching Grandfather. The stern blue eyes were detached. He looked as though he were not very interested in the story himself.

When it was finished, when the pause had been politely

respected as the frontier of the story, Billy Buck stood up and stretched and hitched his trousers. "I guess I'll turn in," he said. Then he faced Grandfather. "I've got an old powder horn and a cap and ball pistol down to the bunkhouse. Did I ever show them to you?"

Grandfather nodded slowly. "Yes, I think you did, Billy. Reminds me of a pistol I had when I was leading the people across." Billy stood politely until the little story was done, and then he said, "Good night," and went out of the house.

Carl Tiflin tried to turn the conversation then. "How's the country between here and Monterey? I've heard it's pretty dry."

"It is dry," said Grandfather. "There's not a drop of water in the Laguna Seca. But it's a long pull from '87. The whole country was powder then, and in '61 I believe all the coyotes starved to death. We had fifteen inches of rain this year."

"Yes, but it all came too early. We could do with some now." Carl's eye fell on Jody. "Hadn't you better be getting to bed?"

Jody stood up obediently. "Can I kill the mice in the old haystack, sir?"

"Mice? Oh! Sure, kill them all off. Billy said there isn't any good hay left."

Jody exchanged a secret and satisfying look with Grandfather. "I'll kill every one tomorrow," he promised.

Jody lay in his bed and thought of the impossible world of Indians and buffaloes, a world that had ceased to be forever. He wished he could have been living in the heroic time, but he knew he was not of heroic timber. No one living now, save possibly Billy Buck, was worthy to do the things that had been done. A race of giants had lived then, fearless men, men of a staunchness unknown in this day. Jody thought of the wide plains and of the wagons moving across like centipedes. He thought of Grandfather on a huge white horse, marshaling the people. Across his mind marched the great phantoms, and they marched off the earth and they were gone.

He came back to the ranch for a moment, then. He heard the dull rushing sound that space and silence make. He heard one of the dogs, out in the doghouse, scratching a flea and bumping his elbow against the floor with every stroke. Then the wind arose again and the black cypress groaned and Jody went to sleep.

He was up half an hour before the triangle sounded for breakfast. His mother was rattling the stove to make the flames roar when Jody went through the kitchen. "You're up early," she said. "Where are you going?"

"Out to get a good stick. We're going to kill the mice today."

"Who is 'we'?"

"Why, Grandfather and I."

"So you've got him in it. You always like to have someone in with you in case there's blame to share."

"I'll be right back," said Jody. "I just want to have a good stick ready for after breakfast."

He closed the screen door after him and went out into the cool blue morning. The birds were noisy in the dawn and the ranch cats came down from the hill like blunt snakes. They had been hunting gophers in the dark, and although the four cats were full of gopher meat, they sat in a semi-circle at the back door and mewed piteously for milk. Doubletree Mutt and Smasher moved sniffing along the edge of the brush, performing the duty with rigid ceremony, but when Jody whistled, their heads jerked up and their tails waved. They plunged down to him, wriggling their skins and yawning. Jody patted their heads seriously, and moved on to the weathered scrap pile. He selected an old broom handle and a short piece of inch-square scrap wood. From his pocket he took a shoelace and tied the ends of the sticks loosely together to make a flail. He whistled his new weapon through the air and struck the ground experimentally, while the dogs leaped aside and whined with apprehension.

Jody turned and started down past the house toward the old haystack ground to look over the field of slaughter, but Billy Buck, sitting patiently on the back steps, called to him, "You better come back. It's only a couple of minutes till breakfast."

Jody changed his course and moved toward the house. He leaned his flail against the steps. "That's to drive the mice out," he said. "I'll bet they're fat. I'll bet they don't know what's going to happen to them today."

"No, nor you either," Billy remarked philosophically, "nor me, nor anyone."

Jody was staggered by this thought. He knew it was true. His imagination twitched away from the mouse hunt. Then his mother came out on the back porch and struck the triangle, and all thoughts fell in a heap.

Grandfather hadn't appeared at the table when they sat down. Billy nodded at his empty chair. "He's all right? He isn't sick?"

"He takes a long time to dress," said Mrs. Tiflin. "He combs his whiskers and rubs up his shoes and brushes his clothes."

Carl scattered sugar on his mush. "A man that's led a wagon train across the plains has got to be pretty careful how he dresses."

Mrs. Tiflin turned on him. "Don't do that, Carl! Please don't!" There was more of threat than of request in her tone. And the threat irritated Carl.

"Well, how many times do I have to listen to the story of the iron plates, and the thirty-five horses? That time's done. Why can't he forget it, now it's done?" He grew angrier while he talked, and his voice rose. "Why does he have to tell them over and over? He came across the plains. All right! Now it's finished. Nobody wants to hear about it over and over."

The door into the kitchen closed softly. The four at the table sat frozen. Carl laid his mush spoon on the table and touched his chin with his fingers.

Then the kitchen door opened and Grandfather walked in. His mouth smiled tightly and his eyes were squinted. "Good morning," he said, and he sat down and looked at his mush dish.

Carl could not leave it there. "Did—did you hear what I said?"

Grandfather jerked a little nod.

"I don't know what got into me, sir. I didn't mean it. I was just being funny."

Jody glanced in shame at his mother, and he saw that she was looking at Carl, and that she wasn't breathing. It was an awful thing that he was doing. He was tearing himself to pieces to talk like that. It was a terrible thing to him to retract a word, but to retract it in shame was infinitely worse.

Grandfather looked sidewise. "I'm trying to get right side up," he said gently. "I'm not being mad. I don't mind what you said, but it might be true, and I would mind that."

"It isn't true," said Carl. "I'm not feeling well this morning. I'm sorry I said it."

"Don't be sorry, Carl. An old man doesn't see things sometimes. Maybe you're right. The crossing is finished. Maybe it should be forgotten, now it's done."

Carl got up from the table. "I've had enough to eat. I'm going to work. Take your time, Billy!" He walked quickly out of the dining-room. Billy gulped the rest of his food and followed soon after. But Jody could not leave his chair.

"Won't you tell any more stories?" Jody asked.

"Why, sure I'll tell them, but only when—I'm sure people want to hear them."

"I like to hear them, sir."

"Oh! Of course you do, but you're a little boy. It was a job for men, but only little boys like to hear about it."

Jody got up from his place. "I'll wait outside for you, sir. I've got a good stick for those mice."

He waited by the gate until the old man came out on the porch. "Let's go down and kill the mice now," Jody called.

"I think I'll just sit in the sun, Jody. You go kill the mice."

"You can use my stick if you like."

"No, I'll just sit here a while."

Jody turned disconsolately away, and walked down toward the old haystack. He tried to whip up his enthusiasm with thoughts of the fat juicy mice. He beat the ground with his flail. The dogs coaxed and whined about him, but he could not go. Back at the house he could see Grandfather sitting on the porch, looking small and thin and black.

Jody gave up and went to sit on the steps at the old man's feet.

"Back already? Did you kill the mice?"

"No, sir. I'll kill them some other day."

The morning flies buzzed close to the ground and the ants dashed about in front of the steps. The heavy smell of sage slipped down the hill. The porch boards grew warm in the sunshine.

Jody hardly knew when Grandfather started to talk. "I

shouldn't stay here, feeling the way I do." He examined his strong old hands. "I feel as though the crossing wasn't worth doing." His eyes moved up the side-hill and stopped on a motionless hawk perched on a dead limb. "I tell those old stories, but they're not what I want to tell. I only know how I want people to feel when I tell them.

"It wasn't Indians that were important, nor adventures, nor even getting out here. It was a whole bunch of people made into one big crawling beast. And I was the head. It was westering and westering. Every man wanted something for himself, but the big beast that was all of them wanted only westering. I was the leader, but if I hadn't been there, someone else would have been the head. The thing had to have a head.

"Under the little bushes the shadows were black at white noonday. When we saw the mountains at last, we cried—all of us. But it wasn't getting here that mattered, it was movement and westering.

"We carried life out here and set it down the way those ants carry eggs. And I was the leader. The westering was as big as God, and the slow steps that made the movement piled up and piled up until the continent was crossed.

"Then we came down to the sea, and it was done." He stopped and wiped his eyes until the rims were red. "That's what I should be telling instead of stories."

When Jody spoke, Grandfather started and looked down at him. "Maybe I could lead the people some day," Jody said.

The old man smiled. "There's no place to go. There's the ocean to stop you. There's a line of old men along the shore hating the ocean because it stopped them."

"In boats I might, sir."

"No place to go, Jody. Every place is taken. But that's not the worst—no, not the worst. Westering has died out of the people. Westering isn't a hunger any more. It's all done. Your father is right. It is finished." He laced his fingers on his knee and looked at them.

Jody felt very sad. "If you'd like a glass of lemonade I could make it for you."

Grandfather was about to refuse, and then he saw Jody's face. "That would be nice," he said. "Yes, it would be nice to drink a lemonade."

Jody ran into the kitchen where his mother was wiping

the last of the breakfast dishes. "Can I have a lemon to make a lemonade for Grandfather?"

His mother mimicked—"And another lemon to make a lemonade for you."

"No, ma'am. I don't want one."

"Jody! You're sick!" Then she stopped suddenly. "Take a lemon out of the cooler," she said softly. "Here, I'll reach the squeezer down to you."

1938

JAMES T. FARRELL

(1904–   )

James T. Farrell came out of the Chicago South Side environment that is the moral, social, economic, and physical landscape of his fiction. For whatever incomprehensible reasons make a man special, Farrell did not succumb to his world, like Studs Lonigan, but, like Danny O'Neill, tried to get it into a perspective that afforded him a wider freedom than that world tended to allow. His parochial-school education was followed by study at the University of Chicago, where he supported himself with a wide variety of odd jobs.

In 1932 he published his first novel, *Young Lonigan*, which, together with *The Young Manhood of Studs Lonigan* (1934) and *Judgment Day* (1935), became the famous Studs Lonigan trilogy (1935).

The world of Studs Lonigan is a world of the lower (mostly Irish) middle class, whose income might be one step above the true slumdweller's, but whose tensions, frustrations, prejudices, narrowness, conformity, shabby respectability, ill-concealed violence, and shallow values create a moral slum. Like many of his characters, Farrell was conditioned by the depression of the 1930's—though he had formed many of his political and social ideas as early as the 1920's—and the purposes lent him by the depression are clear in his writing. Farrell is more explicit and honest about his purposes than many writers care, or dare, to be. Although as a writer he insists upon the difference between sociology and literary art, as a social thinker he also insists that literature is a social function. This is not to say that for Farrell literature is only a programatic preface to social change, but rather that once literature ceases to be a mirror which images society and also discloses its meanings, it loses a major source of its life.

The facet of American society that Farrell best understands is, of course, his own experience of it. Consequently his fiction is a comment upon incipient fascism in American lower middle-class life (*Tommy Gallagher's Crusade*, 1939), upon the possibilities of promise beyond that life (the Danny O'Neill and the Bernard Clare books), and the censorship of hope in that life (the Studs Lonigan books). In his literary criticism—*A Note on Literary Criticism* (1937), *The League of Frightened Philistines* (1945), *Literature and Morality* (1947)—Farrell constantly defends the function of literature as an exploration of human behavior in terms of the natural and environmental circumstances that condition human choice.

In 1936, Farrell followed the Lonigan trilogy with *A World I Never Made*, beginning the Danny O'Neill story, which continued through *No Star Is Lost* (1939), *Father and Son* (1940), *My Days of Anger* (1943), and *The Face of Time* (1953). The Bernard Clare novels, centering on the life of a young writer in New York City, begin with *Bernard Clare* (1946) and continue through *The Road Between* (1949) and *Yet Other Waters* (1952).

In addition to the titles mentioned above, Farrell's works also include *Gas-House McGinty* (1933); *Calico Shoes and Other Stories* (1934); *Guillotine Party and Other Stories* (1935); *Can All This Grandeur Perish?* (1937); *Ellen Rogers* (1941); *$1,000 a Week and Other Stories* (1942); *To Whom It May Concern* (1944); *When Boyhood Dreams Come True* (1946); *The Life Adventurous* (1947); *An American Dream Girl* (1950); *This Man and This Woman* (1951); *Reflections at Fifty, and Other Essays* (1954); *French Girls Are Vicious* (1955); *My Baseball Diary* (1957); *A Dangerous Woman* (1957); and *It Has Come to Pass* (1958).

Accounts of the man and his work are to be found in R. M. Lovett, "James T. Farrell," *English Journal*, XXVI (1937); J. W. Beach, *American Fiction, 1920–1940* (1941); R. Hatfield, "The Intellectual Honesty of James T. Farrell," *College English*, III (1942); I. Howe, "James T. Farrell: The Critic Calcified," *Partisan Review*, XIV (1947); W. M. Frohock, "James Farrell: The Precise Content," *Southwest Review*, XXXV (1950); I. Stock, "Farrell and His Critics," *Arizona Quarterly*, VI (1950); H. C. Gardiner, S.J., ed., *Fifty Years of the American Novel* (1951); C. C. Walcutt, "James T. Farrell and the Reversible Topcoat," *Arizona Quarterly*, VII (1951);

The Coming of Age of A Great Book, collected essays on Studs
Lonigan (1953); B. Gelfant, The American City Novel (1954);
E. Branch, A Bibliography of James T. Farrell's Writings,
1921–1957 (1959); E. M. Branch, James T. Farrell (1963);
R. Mitchell, "James T. Farrell's Scientific Novel," Dissertation
Abstracts, XXIV (1964); L. Wolf, ed., Selected Essays (1964);
I. M. Reiter, "A Study of James T. Farrell's Short Stories and
Their Relation to His Longer Fiction," Dissertation Abstracts,
XXV (1965); and H. H. Dyer, "James T. Farrell's Studs
Lonigan and Danny O'Neill Novels," Dissertation Abstracts,
XXVI (1965).

A Jazz-Age Clerk

I

Jack Stratton worked from ten to eight answering telephone calls in the Wagon Department of the Continental
Express Company. What he liked best about his job was
his lunch hour from one to two. Ordinarily, clerks went
to lunch at twelve o'clock, and he believed that people seeing him on the streets between one and two might figure
that he was a lad with a pretty good job, because one
o'clock was the time when many businessmen took their
lunch in order to avoid the noonday jams in the Loop.

One sunny day in early spring Jack went out to lunch.
He felt good. He would have felt even better if only his
faded powder-blue suit were not so old, and if only it were
already the next pay day, because then he hoped to be able
to make a down payment and get a new suit on the install-
ment plan. When he had got this powder-blue suit, he'd
thought that it was the real thing. All the cake-eaters were
wearing them. But it was a cheap suit that had faded
quickly. And his brown hat, fixed square-shaped the way
the cakes were wearing them, was old and greasy from the
stacomb that he smeared on his hair every day. Yes, he
would have been feeling much better if he were dogged
out in a new outfit. Well, he would some day, he decided.
He walked toward Van Buren Street.

It was a narrow, dusty street, with garages, a continental
filling station and terminal, and the rear ends of old office
buildings and restaurants. On the other side he spotted
a girl, and told himself that she was so hot she could start

a new Chicago fire all by herself. He snapped his fingers and watched her pass. Daddy! He burst into song:

Teasing eyes, teasing eyes,
You're the little girl that sets my heart afire . . .

Teasing! He expressed his feelings with a low whistle. He guessed that working in the Loop had its advantages. At least there were plenty of shebas to look at. He shifted his gait into a hopping two-step. Self-conscious, he checked himself. People might laugh at him in the street, just as Gas-House McGinty, Heinie Mueller, and some of the others in the office laughed at him. Some day he would like to show them, clean up on a few of the wise-aleck clerks. And he would, too! They were dumb, that was all, and they didn't know what was the real thing in the world today. They didn't have enough sense to be cake-eaters. And nick-naming him Jenny, like they had. Some day he would Jenny them! He began walking in a kind of waltzing dance step, his body quivering as he moved. Another song burst into his thoughts, Tiger Rose.

Sadness and self-pity drove the half-sung chorus out of his mind. He wanted girls, a girl, and he wanted money to spend on clothes so that he could impress the broads, and to spend on dances, dates, going places. But he was only making eighty-five dollars a month. That was more than he had expected when he started looking for a job, and he couldn't kick. He knew fellows who only made their fifteen a week. But his pay wasn't any too much. And since his old man was out of work, most of his jack had to go to his mother toward keeping up the home. Gee, he wished that the old man would find another job, and then he could have a little more to spend.

He saw an athletically built blonde, who was just bow-wows, the kind to look at and weep. He jerked his shoulders in rhythm and sang:

I'm runnin' wild, I'm runnin' wild,
I lost control . . .

Now, if there would only be some mama like that in the restaurant, and if he could only get next to her.

The restaurant where he usually ate was owned by a Greek, and was a small establishment with a tile floor and an imitation marble counter. He took a counter seat in the front, several stools removed from the nearest customer. Kitty, the slatternly peroxide-blonde waitress, greeted him with a yellow-toothed yawn, and at the same time she rubbed a fat hand over her low forehead. He looked up at her face; it was crusted with powder.

"Hello," he said.

A customer got up and went to the glass case to pay his check. Kitty left Jack, collected, rang the cash register, deposited the silver in the drawer, and returned. The expression on her face was stupid, bored. Jack snapped his fingers, rolled his eyes, and sang a jazz song.

"What yuh want today, Dapper Dan?" she asked.

"Ham and coffee."

Swinging her head sidewise, she shouted the sandwich order to the chef. Other customers left and she collected. He was the only one remaining in the restaurant. Suddenly he was conscious of his shabbiness. He reached down to touch the raggedy cuffs of his bell-bottom trousers. He felt the thinness at the right elbow of his coat. Kitty slid a ham sandwich at him, and then she slopped a cup of coffee across the counter.

"Big times tonight!" he said while applying mustard to his sandwich.

"Huh?" she mumbled lifelessly.

"Dance at the South Hall out in Englewood where I live," he said, biting into his sandwich.

"Takin' yours along?" she asked lackadaisically.

"I told her to keep the home fires burning tonight. I like a little variety and change, sister."

His shoulders swung to the singing of a few lines from The Darktown Strutters' Ball.

"Cancha sing something that's new," Kitty said petulantly.

"I just learned this one this week at the Song Shop on Quincy Street. Listen!"

> No, no, Nora, nobody but you, dear,
> You know, Nora, yours truly is true, dear . . .

"Aha!" he interrupted with a leer.

> And when you accuse me of flirting

"Like that?" he interpolated with a lascivious wink.

> I wouldn't, I couldn't, I love you so,
> I've had chances, too many to mention . . .

"Always get chances," he interposed.

Never give them a bit of attention.
No, no, Nora. No? No?

"Nice tune," Kitty said dopily as Jack bent down to drink coffee.

"Fast! And tonight I'm grabbing myself a keen number and stepping myself right up over those blue clouds into heaven."

"You're conceited."

He finished his sandwich. His coffee cup was half full. He looked at the cuts of pie in the dessert case before him. He dug his hand into his right trouser pocket. He swallowed his coffee in one gulp and slid off the stool. He paid Kitty fifteen cents, which she rang up.

"Toodle-oo!"

" 'Bye, sheik," she said patronizingly.

II

Overhead, the elevated trains thundered, drowning out the racket of street traffic. He stood on the sidewalk, hands in pockets, hat tilted, watching the crowd. He decided that today he'd sit in the lobby of a good hotel instead of going to the Song Shop and listening to the new tunes being sung. It would be restful.

If he only had on decent clothes, he could sit in a lobby and seem like a young fellow, maybe, with a rich old man or a good job that paid a big salary. A man in a hurry bumped into him and, hastening on, snottily suggested that he quit taking up the whole sidewalk. Jack looked after him, shrugged his shoulders, laughed. He bent his eyes on the moving legs of a girl ahead of him. He realized that if he got his shoes shined, he would improve his appearance. He hated to spend the dime, though, because when he got home tonight he could shine his own shoes. But his appearance would be improved, and he wouldn't look quite so poor. It was all in accordance with the principles of clever dressing. Always have on something new, outstanding or shiny, a loud tie, a clean shirt, a new hat, shined shoes, and then something else you were wearing that was shabby wouldn't be so noticed. He applied his principle by dropping into a shoe-shine parlor.

A young Negro energetically shined his shoes, and Jack day-dreamed about how he would stroll nonchalantly into the lobby of the Potter Hotel and find himself a chair that he could slump into, just so natural. He could spread his legs out so that the first thing anyone noticed about him would be his shined shoes. His thoughts leaped. Wouldn't it be luck if ᵣ ne ritzy queen fell for him! It would just be . . . delicious. Daddy! His mood lifted.

Adventure-bound, hopeful and gay, he hustled toward the new Potter Hotel. His courage deserted him as he passed the uniformed doorman who stood with a set and frowning face, seeming to tell Jack that he wasn't wanted. He paused at the entrance to the enormous lobby, with its gold decorations, its hanging diamond-like chandeliers, its lavish display of comfortable furniture. He told himself in awe that it was like a palace. He noticed men and women, sitting, standing, moving around, talking, reading newspapers, and for a moment he felt as if he were in a moving picture world, the hero in a picture walking into this hotel lobby like a palace fit for the richest of kings or businessmen. He skirted several bellboys and found a chair in a corner, but it was not obscure, because there was a passageway all round the lobby and many people would pass him while he sat. A feeling of awe, as if he were in a church where talking was not permitted, filled his consciousness. He wished that he hadn't come here where he didn't belong, and at the same time he was glad that he'd come.

Several yards away from him he noticed a gray-haired man in a gray suit, whose pleasingly wrinkled face seemed calm, contented, mellowed. He tried to make himself seem as calm and as it ease as this man. For want of something to do, he ran the palm of his hand through his greasy hair; it was meticulously parted in the center. He sedulously drew out his dirty handkerchief to wipe the grease off his hand. To his right, he heard a well-dressed fellow discussing the stock market with a friend. A bellboy wended in and out, intoning:

"Call for Mr. Wagner . . . Call for Mr. Wagner . . . Call for Mr. Wagner . . . Call for Mr. Wagner . . . Mr. Wagner please . . ."

He was unable to chase out his confusion of feelings in this alien atmosphere of the well-dressed, the well-fed, the prosperous. He wished he could live a life that had as much glitter as there must be in the lives of these people. He thought how some day he wanted to be able to sit in a swanky hotel lobby like this one, well-dressed, and have a bell hop pass along calling out his name. He tried to visualize himself, a little older, a successful rich business- man in the lobby with the bellboy droning for him.

"Call for Mr. Stratton . . . Call for Mr. John Stratton . . . Call for Mr. John Stratton . . . Mr. John Strat- ton . . ."

And it would be some millionaire on the wire waiting to close an important deal that would net him a hand- some piece of change. He'd close the deal and come back to wait for a mama. Maybe she'd be some hot movie ac- tress like Gloria Swanson who would be like the sweet- heart of the world in her pictures. And he would be wait- ing for this movie actress more beautiful than even Gloria Swanson, thinking how when he had been nothing but a punk clerk at the express company he'd come to sit in the same lobby, wearing shabby clothes, dreaming of the day when things would happen to him.

He watched a tall and handsome young fellow stroll by. Must be collegiate! Must have had his gray suit made to order and have paid fifty, seventy-five bucks for it, maybe even more. The threads of his daydream suddenly snapped. All the confidence went out of him, so that he felt shaky, trembly. He wished again that he hadn't come here. He felt as if everyone in the lobby were looking at him, knowing he didn't belong and wanting to see him tossed out on his can. He looked unobtrusively at two snappily dressed young fellows on his left. They were out of earshot, but he wondered what they were saying. They probably had everything they wanted and did anything they cared to do, had automobiles, money on which to date up queens . . . everything. The one wearing a Scotch tweed suit drew out a fat cigar, removed the band, smelled the cigar, bit off the end, lit it like a businessman in a movie. If only his life were that of a hero in the movies! Ah! That was class, the way that fellow in the tweeds had pulled out his cigar and lit it. Yes, when his own dream ship came in and he could afford to smoke four-bit cigars, he would have to remember to light them the way that fellow did.

"Call for Mr. O'Flaherty . . . Call for Mr. Al O'-
Flaherty . . . Call for Mr. Al O'Flaherty . . . Call for
Mr. Al O'Flaherty . . ."

Wouldn't it be the dogs to be paged like that on important business calls! But he had no right even to think
of such things. It wouldn't ever be for him. His lot in life
deepened his wretchedness. He hadn't had anything to
start on. Father and mother with no dough. One year
in high school, and that without clothes, no athletic
ability, no money, nothing that could get him into frater-
nities and make the girls go for him. But, gee, in high
school there'd been all kinds of hot and classy girls! Only
why should they have looked at an unimportant fresh-
man like himself? And anyway, that was all over. Now
he was working at a job with no future. Maybe he ought
to be glad for what he had, but, gee, he couldn't help feeling that some guys got all the breaks, while he got almost
none. All these people, they belonged to a world he would
never enter.

A bellboy coming toward him. Gee! He sat stricken in
a paralyzing fright. He pushed back the dirty cuffs of
his shirt so that they were invisible. He tried to think up
a reason he could give for being in the lobby when the
bell hop came and questioned him. He'd say he was
waiting for somebody who was staying at the hotel. But
they could check up on the name. He'd say he was waiting for a friend coming in from New York who was going to stay here. The bellboy coming! He wanted to get
up and leave. He had no will. He was so afraid that he
began to sweat under the armpits, and his forehead per-
spired. Coming!

The bellboy passed by his chair as if no one were sitting
in it, and bent down to speak with the calm-faced man.
The man rose and followed the bellboy across the lobby.
Jack again pulled out his soiled handkerchief, crushed it
into a ball so that it couldn't be noticed, and wiped his
forehead.

He watched a slim, voluptuous blonde woman cross the
lobby. She was the dogs, the snake's hips, and the stars
all rolled into something in a black dress. Those lips of
hers. She had lip-appeal, sister, lip-appeal, sex-appeal, and
she had it, and she was like a shower of stars. Looked
like a woman some rich bird had put in the velvet. He

followed her tantalizing, sensuous movements with thirsting eyes. She was a trifle taller than he, he guessed . . . but . . . hot . . . She sat down beside a middleaged man in a conservative blue suit, crossed her legs. . . . Legs! Wouldn't he like to have the bucks to buy the most expensive stockings money could buy for those legs! She lit a cigarette and he bet himself that it was an expensive Turkish cigarette. Oh, sister!

Tantalizing, he told himself, not removing his eyes from her legs.

Yes, all he wanted was the money to have a mama like that. There wasn't a movie queen in Hollywood that had a nickel on that one. He imagined that she was his woman, seated beside him, talking to him, saying that she would rather have lunch at the Fraternity Row today. She was saying she was crazy, just crazy, about him and didn't care two cents for anyone else in the world. She was wild for him. . . .

"Call for Mr. Jones . . . Mr. Jones please! . . . Mr. Jones!"

The voice of the bellboy was like a jolt, awakening him. He looked at his Ingersoll watch. Two minutes to two. He'd be late, and Collins, his boss, might bawl the hell out of him, and then all the fellows in the office would razz him, call him Jenny, the drugstore cowboy. He placed his hat on carefully and moved swiftly out of the lobby. Hurrying along the street, he fell into a dance step. Then he ran until he pulled up, winded. Four minutes after two. What excuse could he give Collins? He paused to look at a girl in pink. Nice! He unwittingly broke into song.

I'm Al-a-ba-ma bound . . .

He again worried about himself, thought of the things he wanted and couldn't have. He started running, hoping that Collins wouldn't bawl him out. Two seven!

1932

KATHERINE ANNE PORTER

(1890–   )

Being a descendant of the Daniel Boone family and being the admired center of a literary coterie offer two very different sets of associations. Katherine Anne Porter is the one by the accident of birth; she is the other by virtue of hard work and a magnificently controlled style which has won for her, despite a small output, the respect of scholars and writers. In all, besides some volumes of essays and translations, her high reputation is based upon only five novelettes, three volumes of short stories, and a novel, *Ship of Fools*, upon which Miss Porter worked for many years, and which was greeted with delight by the reviewers when it appeared in 1962.

Katherine Anne Porter was born in Indian Creek, Texas, and was educated in small convent schools in the South, where much of her life has been spent. She read widely and voraciously in her youth and began to write, as she says, "at about three years"; yet she did not attempt to publish anything until she was thirty, when her stories began to appear in both established and experimental literary magazines. She has done newspaper and editorial work in Dallas, Denver, and New York.

Her reputation really began in 1930, when she published *Flowering Judas*, a volume of six stories which was expanded by four more stories in 1935 under the title of *Flowering Judas and Other Stories*. Her fiction reflects her life in the South, in Mexico, California, France, and New York; her opportunities to write and travel were enlarged by a Guggenheim fellowship in 1931 and again in 1938. *Hacienda*, her first novelette, appeared in 1934 and was followed by a second, *Noon Wine*, in 1937. *Noon Wine* was later included with *Old Mortality* and the title piece in *Pale Horse, Pale Rider* (1939); *No Safe Harbor* (1941) completed the list of novelettes. In 1944 Miss Porter issued another collection of short fiction, *The Leaning Tower and Other Stories.*

Through two marriages and many honors Miss Porter has continued to write with complete dedication and absorption. She herself has said that writing is the central meaning and pattern in her life and that almost everything else pales to insignificance beside her art. She has held residenceships and lectureships at several universities, and in 1959 she became the first Glasgow Professor at Washington and Lee.

Her volumes of essays and translations are *Outline of Mexican Popular Arts and Crafts* (1922), *The French Song Book* (1933), *The Itching Parrot* (1942), *The Days Before* (1952), and *A Defense of Circe* (1954).

Studies of Miss Porter's work are to be found in R. P. Warren, "Katherine Anne Porter (Irony with a Center)," *Kenyon Review,* IV (1942); R. B. West, Jr., "Katherine Anne Porter: Symbol and Theme in 'Flowering Judas,' " *Accent,* VII (1947); E. Schwartz, *Katherine Anne Porter: A Critical Bibliography* (1953); H. J. Mooney, Jr., *The Fiction and Criticism of Katherine Anne Porter* (1957); C. Kaplan, "True Witness: Katherine Anne Porter," *Colorado Quarterly,* VII (1959); H. J. Mooney, Jr., *The Fiction and Criticism of Katherine Anne Porter* (rev. ed., 1962); R. B. West, Jr., *Katherine Anne Porter* (1963); R. N. Hertz, "Rising Waters: A Study of Katherine Anne Porter," *Dissertation Abstracts,* XXV (1964); W. L. Nance, *Katherine Anne Porter and the Art of Rejection* (1964); and G. Hendrick, *Katherine Anne Porter* (1965).

Flowering Judas

Braggioni sits heaped upon the edge of a straight-backed chair much too small for him, and sings to Laura in a furry, mournful voice. Laura has begun to find reasons for avoiding her own house until the latest possible moment, for Braggioni is there almost every night. No matter how late she is, he will be sitting there with a surly, waiting expression, pulling at his kinky yellow hair, thumbing the strings of his guitar, snarling a tune under his breath. Lupe the Indian maid meets Laura at the door, and says with a flicker of a glance towards the upper room, "He waits."

Laura wishes to lie down, she is tired of her hairpins and the feel of her long tight sleeves, but she says to him, "Have you a new song for me this evening?" If he says yes, she asks him to sing it. If he says no, she remembers his favorite one, and asks him to sing it again. Lupe brings her a cup of chocolate and a plate of rice, and Laura eats at the small table under the lamp, first inviting Braggioni, whose answer is always the same: "I have eaten, and besides, chocolate thickens the voice."

Laura says, "Sing, then," and Braggioni heaves himself into song. He scratches the guitar familiarly as though it were a pet animal, and sings passionately off key, taking the high notes in a prolonged painful squeal. Laura, who haunts the markets listening to the ballad singers, and stops every day to hear the blind boy playing his reedflute in Sixteenth of September Street, listens to Braggioni with pitiless courtesy, because she dares not smile at his miserable performance. Nobody dares to smile at him. Braggioni is cruel to everyone, with a kind of specialized insolence, but he is so vain of his talents, and so sensitive to slight, it would require a cruelty and vanity greater than his own to lay a finger on the vast cureless wound of his self-esteem. It would require courage, too, for it is dangerous to offend him, and nobody has this courage.

Braggioni loves himself with such tenderness and amplitude and eternal charity that his followers—for he is a leader of men, a skilled revolutionist, and his skin has been punctured in honorable warfare—warm themselves in the reflected glow, and say to each other: "He has a real nobility, a love of humanity raised above mere personal affections." The excess of this self-love has flowed out, inconveniently for her, over Laura, who, with so many others, owes her comfortable situation and her salary to him. When he is in a very good humor, he tells her, "I am tempted to forgive you for being a *gringa. Gringita!*" and Laura, burning, imagines herself leaning forward suddenly, and with a sound back-handed slap wiping the suety smile from his face. If he notices her eyes at these moments he gives no sign.

She knows what Braggioni would offer her, and she must resist tenaciously without appearing to resist, and if she could avoid it she would not admit even to herself the slow drift of his intention. During these long evenings which have spoiled a long month for her, she sits in her deep chair with an open book on her knees, resting her eyes on the consoling rigidity of the printed page when the sight and sound of Braggioni singing threaten to identify themselves with all her remembered afflictions and to add their weight to her uneasy premonitions of the future. The gluttonous bulk of Braggioni has become a symbol of her many disillusions, for a revolutionist should be lean, animated by heroic faith, a vessel of abstract virtues. This is nonsense, she knows it now and is ashamed of it. Revolution must have leaders, and leadership is a career for energetic men. She is, her comrades tell her, full of romantic error, for what she defines as cynicism in them is merely "a developed sense of reality." She is almost too willing to say, "I am wrong, I suppose I don't really understand the principles," and afterward she makes a secret truce with herself, determined not to surrender her will to such expedient logic. But she cannot help feeling that she has been betrayed irreparably by the disunion between her way of living and her feeling of what life should be, and at times she is almost contented to rest in this sense of grievance as a private store of consolation. Sometimes she wishes to run away, but she stays. Now she longs to fly out of this room, down the narrow stairs, and into the street where the houses lean together like conspirators under a single mottled lamp, and leave Braggioni singing to himself.

Instead she looks at Braggioni, frankly and clearly, like a good child who understands the rules of behavior. Her knees cling together under sound blue serge, and her round white collar is not purposely nun-like. She wears the uniform of an idea, and has renounced vanities. She was born Roman Catholic, and in spite of her fear of being seen by someone who might make a scandal of it, she slips now and again into some crumbling little church, kneels on the chilly stone, and says a Hail Mary on the gold rosary she bought in Tehuantepec. It is no good and she ends by examining the altar with its tinsel flowers and ragged brocades, and feels tender about the battered doll-shape of some male saint whose white, lace-trimmed drawers hang limply around his ankles below the hieratic dignity of his velvet robe. She has encased herself in a set of principles derived from her early training, leaving no detail of gesture or of personal taste untouched, and for this reason she will not wear lace made on machines. This is her private heresy, for in her special group the machine is sacred, and will be the salvation of the workers. She loves fine lace, and there is a tiny edge of fluted cobweb on this collar, which is one of twenty precisely alike, folded in blue tissue paper in the upper drawer of her clothes chest.

Braggioni catches her glance solidly as if he had been waiting for it, leans forward, balancing his paunch between his spread knees, and sings with tremendous emphasis, weighing his words. He has, the song relates, no father and no mother, nor even a friend to console him; lonely as a wave of the sea he comes and goes, lonely as a wave. His mouth opens round and yearns sideways, his balloon cheeks grow oily with the labor of song. He bulges marvelously in his expensive garments. Over his lavender collar, crushed upon a purple necktie, held by a diamond hoop: over his ammunition belt of tooled leather worked in silver, buckled cruelly around his gasping middle: over the tops of his glossy yellow shoes Braggioni swells with ominous ripeness, his mauve silk hose stretched taut, his ankles bound with the stout leather thongs of his shoes.

When he stretches his eyelids at Laura she notes again that his eyes are the true tawny yellow cat's eyes. He is rich, not in money, he tells her, but in power, and this power brings with it the blameless ownership of things, and the right to indulge his love of small luxuries. "I have a taste for the elegant refinements," he said once, flourishing a yellow silk handkerchief before her nose. "Smell that? It is Jockey Club, imported from New York." Nonetheless he is wounded by life. He will say so presently. "It is true everything turns to dust in the hand, to gall on the tongue." He sighs and his leather belt creaks like a saddle girth. "I am disappointed in everything as it comes. Everything." He shakes his head. "You, poor thing, you will be disappointed too. You are born for it. We are more alike than you realize in some things. Wait and see. Some day you will remember what I have told you, you will know that Braggioni was your friend."

Laura feels a slow chill, a purely physical sense of danger, a warning in her blood that violence, mutilation, a shocking death, wait for her with lessening patience. She has translated this fear into something homely, immediate, and sometimes hesitates before crossing the street. "My personal fate is nothing, except as the testimony of a mental attitude," she reminds herself, quoting from some forgotten philosophic primer, and is sensible enough to add, "Anyhow, I shall not be killed by an automobile if I can help it."

"It may be true I am as corrupt, in another way, as Braggioni," she thinks in spite of herself, "as callous, as incomplete," and if this is so, any kind of death seems preferable. Still she sits quietly, she does not run. Where could she go? Uninvited she has promised herself to this place; she can no longer imagine herself as living in another country, and there is no pleasure in remembering her life before she came here.

Precisely what is the nature of this devotion, its true motives, and what are its obligations? Laura cannot say. She spends part of her days in Xochimilco, near by, teaching the Indian children to say in English, "The cat is on the mat." When she appears in the classroom they crowd about her with smiles on their wise, innocent, clay-colored faces, crying, "Good morning, my titcher!" in immaculate voices, and they make of her desk a fresh garden of flowers every day.

During her leisure she goes to union meetings and listens to busy important voices quarreling over tactics, methods, internal politics. She visits the prisoners of her own political faith in their cells, where they entertain themselves with counting cockroaches, repenting of their indiscretions, composing their memoirs, writing out manifestoes and plans for their comrades who are still walking about free, hands in pockets, sniffing fresh air. Laura brings them food and cigarettes and a litte money, and she brings messages disguised in equivocal phrases from the men outside who dare not set foot in the prison for fear of disappearing into the cells kept empty for them. If the prisoners confuse night and day, and complain, "Dear little Laura, time doesn't pass in this infernal hole, and I won't know when it is time to sleep unless I have a reminder," she brings them their favorite narcotics, and says in a tone that does not wound them with pity, "Tonight will really be night for you," and though her

Spanish amuses them, they find her comforting, useful. If they lose patience and all faith, and curse the slowness of their friends in coming to their rescue with money and influence, they trust her not to repeat everything, and if she inquires, "Where do you think we can find money, or influence?" they are certain to answer, "Well, there is Braggioni, why doesn't he do something?"

She smuggles letters from headquarters to men hiding from firing squads in back streets in mildewed houses, where they sit in tumbled beds and talk bitterly as if all Mexico were at their heels, when Laura knows positively they might appear at the band concert in the Alameda on Sunday morning, and no one would notice them. But Braggioni says, "Let them sweat a little. The next time they may be careful. It is very restful to have them out of the way for a while." She is not afraid to knock on any door in any street after midnight, and enter in the darkness, and say to one of these men who is really in danger: "They will be looking for you—seriously—to-morrow morning after six. Here is some money from Vicente. Go to Vera Cruz and wait."

She borrows money from the Roumanian agitator to give to his bitter enemy the Polish agitator. The favor of Braggioni is their disputed territory, and Braggioni holds the balance nicely, for he can use them both. The Polish agitator talks love to her over café tables, hoping to exploit what he believes is her secret sentimental preference for him, and he gives her misinformation which he begs her to repeat as the solemn truth to certain persons. The Roumanian is more adroit. He is generous with his money in all good causes, and lies to her with an air of ingenuous candor, as if he were her good friend and confidant. She never repeats anything they may say. Braggioni never asks questions. He has other ways to discover all that he wishes to know about them.

Nobody touches her, but all praise her gray eyes, and the soft, round under lip which promises gayety, yet is always grave, nearly always firmly closed: and they cannot understand why she is in Mexico. She walks back and forth on her errands, with puzzled eyebrows, carrying her little folder of drawings and music and school papers. No dancer dances more beautifully than Laura walks, and she inspires some amusing, unexpected ardors, which cause little gossip, because nothing comes of them. A young captain who had been a soldier in Zapata's army attempted, during a horseback ride near Cuernavaca, to express his desire for her with the noble simplicity befitting a rude folk-hero: but gently, because he was gentle. This gentleness was his defeat, for when he alighted, and removed her foot from the stirrup, and essayed to draw her down into his arms, her horse, ordinarily a tame one, shied fiercely, reared and plunged away. The young hero's horse careered blindly after his stable-mate, and the hero did not return to the hotel until rather late that evening. At breakfast he came to her table in full charro dress, gray buckskin jacket and trousers with strings of silver buttons down the leg, and he was in a humorous, careless mood. "May I sit with you?" and "You are a wonderful rider. I was terrified that you might be thrown and dragged. I should never have forgiven myself. But I cannot admire you enough for your riding!"

"I learned to ride in Arizona," said Laura.

"If you ride with me again this morning, I promise you a horse that will not shy with you," he said. But Laura remembered that she must return to Mexico City at noon.

Next morning the children made a celebration and spent their playtime writing on the blackboard, "We lov ar ticher," and with tinted chalks they drew wreaths of flowers around the words. The young hero wrote her a letter: "I am a very foolish, wasteful, impulsive man. I should have first said I love you, and then you would not have run away. But you shall see me again." Laura thought, "I must send him a box of colored crayons," but she was trying to forgive herself for having spurred her horse at the wrong moment.

A brown, shock-haired youth came and stood in her patio one night and sang like a lost soul for two hours, but Laura could think of nothing to do about it. The moonlight spread a wash of gauzy silver over the clear spaces of the garden, and the shadows were cobalt blue. The scarlet blossoms of the Judas tree were dull purple, and the names of the colors repeated themselves automatically in her mind, while she watched not the boy, but his shadow, fallen like a dark garment across the fountain rim, trailing in the water. Lupe came silently and whispered expert counsel in her ear: "If you will throw him one little flower, he will sing another song or two and go away." Laura threw the flower, and he sang a last song and went away with the flower tucked in the band of his hat. Lupe said, "He is one of the organizers of the Typographers Union, and before that he sold corridos in the Merced market, and before that, he came from Guanajuato, where I was born. I would not trust any man, but I trust least those from Guanajuato."

She did not tell Laura that he would be back again the next night, and the next, nor that he would follow her at a certain fixed distance around the Merced market, through the Zócolo, up Francisco I. Madero Avenue, and so along the Paseo de la Reforma to Chapultepec Park, and into the Philosopher's Footpath, still with that flower withering in his hat, and an indivisible attention in his eyes.

Now Laura is accustomed to him, it means nothing except that he is nineteen years old and is observing a convention with all propriety, as though it were founded on a law of nature, which in the end it might well prove to be. He is beginning to write poems which he prints on a wooden press, and he leaves them stuck like handbills in her door. She is pleasantly disturbed by the abstract, unhurried watchfulness of his black eyes which will in time turn easily towards another object. She tells herself that throwing the flower was a mistake, for she is twenty-two years old and knows better; but she refuses to regret it, and persuades herself that her negation of all external events as they occur is a sign that she is gradually perfecting herself in the stoicism she strives to cultivate against that disaster she fears, though she cannot name it.

She is not at home in the world. Every day she teaches children who remain strangers to her, though she loves their tender round hands and their charming opportunist savagery. She knocks at unfamiliar doors not knowing whether a friend or a stranger shall answer, and even if a known face emerges from the sour gloom of that unknown interior, still it is the face of a stranger. No matter what this stranger says to her, nor what her message to him, the very cells of her flesh reject knowledge and kinship in one monotonous word. No. No. No. She draws

her strength from this one holy talismanic word which
does not suffer her to be led into evil. Denying everything, she may walk anywhere in safety, she looks at
everything without amazement.

No, repeats this firm unchanging voice of her blood;
and she looks at Braggioni without amazement. He is a
great man, he wishes to impress this simple girl who
covers her great round breasts with thick dark cloth, and
who hides long, invaluably beautiful legs under a heavy
skirt. She is almost thin except for the incomprehensible
fullness of her breasts, like a nursing mother's, and Braggioni, who considers himself a judge of women, specu-
lates again on the puzzle of her notorious virginity, and
takes the liberty of speech which she permits without
a sign of modesty, indeed, without any sort of sign, which
is disconcerting.

"You think you are so cold, *gringita!* Wait and see.
You will surprise yourself some day! May I be there to
advise you!" He stretches his eyelids at her, and his ill-
humored cat's eyes waver in a separate glance for the two
points of light marking the opposite ends of a smoothly
drawn path between the swollen curve of her breasts. He
is not put off by that blue serge, nor by her resolutely
fixed gaze. There is all the time in the world. His cheeks
are bellying with the wind of song. "O girl with the dark
eyes," he sings, and reconsiders. "But yours are not dark.
I can change all that. O girl with the green eyes, you
have stolen my heart away!" then his mind wanders to
the song, and Laura feels the weight of his attention being shifted elsewhere. Singing thus, he seems harmless,
he is quite harmless, there is nothing to do but sit patiently and say "No," when the moment comes. She draws
a full breath, and her mind wanders also, but not far.
She dares not wander too far.

Not for nothing has Braggioni taken pains to be a
good revolutionist and a professional lover of humanity.
He will never die of it. He has the malice, the cleverness,
the wickedness, the sharpness of wit, the hardness of
heart, stipulated for loving the world profitably. *He will
never die of it.* He will live to see himself kicked out
from his feeding trough by other hungry world-saviors.
Traditionally he must sing in spite of his life which drives
him to bloodshed, he tells Laura, for his father was a

Tuscany peasant who drifted to Yucatan and married a Maya woman: a woman of race, an aristocrat. They gave him the love and knowledge of music, thus: and under the rip of this thumbnail, the strings of the instrument complain like exposed nerves.

Once he was called Delgadito by all the girls and married women who ran after him; he was so scrawny all his bones showed under his thin cotton clothing, and he could squeeze his emptiness to the very backbone with his two hands. He was a poet and the revolution was only a dream then; too many women loved him and sapped away his youth, and he could never find enough to eat anywhere, anywhere! Now he is a leader of men, crafty men who whisper in his ear, hungry men who wait for hours outside his office for a word with him, emaciated men with wild faces who waylay him at the street gate with a timid, "Comrade, let me tell you . . ." and they blow the foul breath from their empty stomachs in his face.

He is always sympathetic. He gives them handfuls of small coins from his own pocket, he promises them work, there will be demonstrations, they must join the unions and attend the meetings, above all they must be on the watch for spies. They are closer to him than his own brothers, without them he can do nothing—until tomorrow, comrade!

Until tomorrow. "They are stupid, they are lazy, they are treacherous, they would cut my throat for nothing," he says to Laura. He has good food and abundant drink, he hires an automobile and drives in the Paseo on Sunday morning, and enjoys plenty of sleep in a soft bed beside a wife who dares not disturb him; and he sits pampering his bones in easy billows of fat, singing to Laura, who knows and thinks these things about him. When he was fifteen, he tried to drown himself because he loved a girl, his first love, and she laughed at him. "A thousand women have paid for that," and his tight little mouth turns down at the corners. Now he perfumes his hair with Jockey Club, and confides to Laura: "One woman is really as good as another for me, in the dark. I prefer them all."

His wife organizes unions among the girls in the cigarette factories, and walks in picket lines, and even

speaks at meetings in the evening. But she cannot be
brought to acknowledge the benefits of true liberty. "I
tell her I must have my freedom, net. She does not understand my point of view." Laura has heard this many times.
Braggioni scratches the guitar and meditates. "She is an
instinctively virtuous woman, pure gold, no doubt of that.
If she were not, I should lock her up, and she knows it."

His wife, who works so hard for the good of the factory girls, employs part of her leisure lying on the floor
weeping because there are so many women in the world,
and only one husband for her, and she never knows where
nor when to look for him. He told her: "Unless you can
learn to cry when I am not here, I must go away for
good." That day he went away and took a room at the
Hotel Madrid.

It is this month of separation for the sake of higher
principles that has been spoiled not only for Mrs. Braggioni, whose sense of reality is beyond criticism, but for
Laura, who feels herself bogged in a nightmare. Tonight
Laura envies Mrs. Braggioni, who is alone, and free to
weep as much as she pleases about a concrete wrong.
Laura has just come from a visit to the prison, and she
is waiting for tomorrow with a bitter anxiety as if tomorrow may not come, but time may be caught immovably
in this hour, with herself transfixed, Braggioni singing on
forever, and Eugenio's body not yet discovered by the
guard.

Braggioni says: "Are you going to sleep?" Almost before she can shake her head, he begins telling her about
the May-day disturbances coming on in Morelia, for the
Catholics hold a festival in honor of the Blessed Virgin,
and the Socialists celebrate their martyrs on that day.
"There will be two independent processions, starting from
either end of town, and they will march until they meet,
and the rest depends . . ." He asks her to oil and load
his pistols. Standing up, he unbuckles his ammunition belt,
and spreads it laden across her knees. Laura sits with
the shells slipping through the cleaning cloth dipped in
oil, and he says again he cannot understand why she
works so hard for the revolutionary idea unless she loves
some man who is in it. "Are you not in love with someone?" "No," says Laura. "And no one is in love with
you?" "No." "Then it is your own fault. No woman

need go begging. Why, what is the matter with you? The legless beggar woman in the Alameda has a perfectly faithful lover. Did you know that?"

Laura peers down the pistol barrel and says nothing, but a long, slow faintness rises and subsides in her; Braggioni curves his swollen fingers around the throat of the guitar and softly smothers the music out of it, and when she hears him again he seems to have forgotten her, and is speaking in the hypnotic voice he uses when talking in small rooms to a listening, close-gathered crowd. Some day this world, now seemingly so composed and eternal, to the edges of every sea shall be merely a tangle of gaping trenches, of crashing walls and broken bodies. Everything must be torn from its accustomed place where it has rotted for centuries, hurled skyward and distributed, cast down again clean as rain, without separate identity. Nothing shall survive that the stiffened hands of poverty have created for the rich and no one shall be left alive except the elect spirits destined to procreate a new world cleansed of cruelty and injustice, ruled by benevolent anarchy: "Pistols are good, I love them, cannons are even better, but in the end I pin my faith to good dynamite," he concludes, and strokes the pistol lying in her hands. "Once I dreamed of destroying the city, in case it offered resistance to General Ortíz, but it fell into his hands like an overripe pear."

He is made restless by his own words, rises and stands waiting. Laura holds up the belt to him: "Put that on, and go kill somebody in Morelia, and you will be happier," she says softly. The presence of death in the room makes her bold. "Today, I found Eugenio going into a stupor. He refused to allow me to call the prison doctor. He had taken all the tablets I brought him yesterday. He said he took them because he was bored."

"He is a fool, and his death is his own business," says Braggioni, fastening his belt carefully.

"I told him if he had waited only a little while longer, you would have got him set free," says Laura. "He said he did not want to wait."

"He is a fool and we are well rid of him," says Braggioni, reaching for his hat.

He goes away. Laura knows his mood has changed, she will not see him any more for a while. He will send word when he needs her to go on errands into strange streets, to speak to the strange faces that will appear, like clay masks with the power of human speech, to mutter their thanks to Braggioni for his help. Now she is free, and she thinks, I must run while there is time. But she does not go.

Braggioni enters his own house where for a month his wife has spent many hours every night weeping and tangling her hair upon her pillow. She is weeping now, and she weeps more at the sight of him, the cause of all her sorrows. He looks about the room. Nothing is changed, the smells are good and familiar, he is well acquainted with the woman who comes toward him with no reproach except grief on her face. He says to her tenderly: "You are so good, please don't cry any more, you dear good creature." She says, "Are you tired, my angel? Sit here and I will wash your feet." She brings a bowl of water, and kneeling, unlaces his shoes, and when from her knees she raises her sad eyes under her blackened lids, he is sorry for everything, and bursts into tears. "Ah, yes, I am hungry, I am tired, let us eat something together," he says, between sobs. His wife leans her head on his arm and says, "Forgive me!" and this time he is refreshed by the solemn, endless rain of her tears.

Laura takes off her serge dress and puts on a white linen nightgown and goes to bed. She turns her head a little to one side, and lying still, reminds herself that it is time to sleep. Numbers tick in her brain like little clocks, soundless doors close of themselves around her. If you would sleep, you must not remember anything, the children will say tomorrow, good morning, my teacher, the poor prisoners who come every day bringing flowers to their jailor. 1-2-3-4-5—it is monstrous to confuse love with revolution, night with day, life with death—ah, Eugenio!

The tolling of the midnight bell is a signal, but what does it mean? Get up, Laura, and follow me: come out of your sleep, out of your bed, out of this strange house. What are you doing in this house? Without a word, without fear she rose and reached for Eugenio's hand, but he eluded her with a sharp, sly smile and drifted away. This is not all, you shall see—Murderer, he said, follow me, I will show you a new country, but it is far away and we must hurry. No, said Laura, not unless you take my hand, no; and she clung first to the stair rail, and then to the topmost branch of the Judas tree that bent down slowly and set her upon the earth, and then to the rocky ledge of a cliff, then to the jagged wave of a sea that was not water but a desert of crumbling stone. Where are you taking me, she asked in wonder but without fear. To death, and it is a long way off, and we must hurry, said Eugenio. No, said Laura, not unless you take my hand. Then eat these flowers, poor prisoner, said Eugenio in a voice of pity, take and eat: and from the Judas tree he stripped the warm bleeding flowers, and held them to her lips. She saw that his hand was fleshless, a cluster of small white petrified branches, and his eye sockets were without light, but she ate the flowers greedily for they satisfied both hunger and thirst. Murderer! said Eugenio, and Cannibal! This is my body and my blood. Laura cried No! and at the sound of her own voice, she awoke trembling, and was afraid to sleep again.

1930

EUDORA WELTY

(1909–   )

Like her friend and admirer Katherine Anne Porter, Eudora Welty has achieved a large literary reputation despite a relatively small output. Since she published her first story in 1936, Miss Welty has written a novelette (*The Robber Bridegroom*, 1942), two novels (*Delta Wedding*, 1946; *The Ponder Heart*, 1954), and four collections of short stories. But what she has produced has been of an astonishingly consistent and high order of merit, attested to by many awards and fellowships, including a gold medal for fiction from the American Academy of Arts and Letters "in recognition of her skill in the short story and her artistry in the subtle portrayal of character."

Miss Welty has lived most of her life in the place where she was born, Jackson, Mississippi, the locale which has provided her with much of the materials of her best fiction. Like her fellow Mississippian, William Faulkner, Miss Welty has never been a part of any literary coterie, but has gone her own way in the quiet conviction that it is not programs or rules but the private "imagination . . . that calls forth and communicates." Inevitably, after the Mississippi State College for Women, the University of Wisconsin (B.A., 1929), the Columbia University School of Advertising, and a brief stint in the world of advertising and publicity, Miss Welty settled down in her home town to devote herself to the life of a literary artist. Since 1958 she has been an Honorary Consultant in American Letters to the Library of Congress.

As is the case with much present-day Southern writing, Miss Welty's world is peopled by characters so extreme in their plights or beings that their fictional stances tend to strike us as grotesque. But unlike much "Southern Gothic" writing, there is often in Miss Welty's fiction (as there is in "Keela, the Outcast Indian Maiden"), a tenderness without softness for the isolated and bewildered that humanizes her figures without denying the conditions which they symbolize. Whereas popular Southern fiction of the last century sentimentalized its horrors, Miss Welty's sensitivity transforms her nightmares into stories "of beauty and passion and truth."

Miss Welty's four volumes of short stories are: *A Curtain of Green and Other Stories* (1941); *The Wide Net and Other Stories* (1943); *The Golden Apples* (1949); and *The Bride of the Innisfallen and Other Stories* (1955).

Studies of Miss Welty's work are to be found in K. A. Porter's introduction to *A Curtain of Green* (1941); R. P. Warren, "The Love and Separateness of Eudora Welty," *Kenyon Review*, VI (1944); E. Glenn, "Fantasy in the Fiction of Eudora Welty," in Allen Tate, ed., *A Southern Vanguard* (1947); R. Daniel, "The World of Eudora Welty," *Hopkins Review*, VI (1953); H. Morris, "Eudora Welty's Use of Mythology," *Shenandoah*, VI (1955); K. Smythe, "Eudora Welty: A Checklist," *Bulletin of Bibliography*, XXI (1956); S. Gross, "Eudora Welty: A Bibliography of Criticism and Comment," *News Sheets, Bibliographical Society of the University of Virginia* (1960); R. M. Van de Kieft, *Eudora Welty* (1962); S. A. Rouse, "Place and People in Eudora Welty's Fiction," *Dissertation Abstracts*, XXIII (1963); W. U. McDonald, "Welty's 'Keela': Irony, Ambiguity, and the Ancient Mariner," *Studies in Short Fiction*, I (1964); and A. Appel, Jr., *A Season of Dreams: The Fiction of Eudora Welty* (1965).

Keela, the Outcast Indian Maiden

One morning in summertime, when all his sons and daughters were off picking plums and Little Lee Roy was all alone, sitting on the porch and only listening to the screech owls away down in the woods, he had a surprise.

First he heard white men talking. He heard two white men coming up the path from the highway. Little Lee Roy ducked his head and held his breath; then he patted all around back of him for his crutches. The chickens all came out from under the house and waited attentively on the steps.

The men came closer. It was the young man who was doing all the talking. But when they got through the fence, Max, the older man, interrupted him. He tapped

him on the arm and pointed his thumb toward Little
Lee Roy.

He said, "Bud? Yonder he is."

But the younger man kept straight on talking, in an
explanatory voice.

"Bud?" said Max again. "Look, Bud, yonder's the only
little clubfooted nigger man was ever around Cane Springs.
Is he the party?"

They came nearer and nearer to Little Lee Roy and
then stopped and stood there in the middle of the yard.
But the young man was so excited he did not seem to
realize that they had arrived anywhere. He was only
about twenty years old, very sunburned. He talked constantly, making only one gesture—raising his hand stiffly
and then moving it a little to one side.

"They dressed it in a red dress, and it ate chickens
alive," he said. "I sold tickets and I thought it was worth
a dime, honest. They gimme a piece of paper with the
thing wrote off I had to say. That was easy, 'Keela, the
Outcast Indian Maiden!' I call it out through a pasteboard
megaphone. Then ever' time it was fixin' to eat a live
chicken, I blowed the sireen out front."

"Just tell me, Bud," said Max, resting back on the
heels of his perforated tan-and-white sport shoes, "Is this
nigger the one? Is that him sittin' there?"

Little Lee Roy sat huddled and blinking, a smile on
his face. . . . But the young man did not look his way.

"Just took the job that time. I didn't mean to—I mean,
I meant to go to Port Arthur because my brother was
on a boat," he said. "My name is Steve, mister. But I
worked with this show selling tickets for three months,
and I never would have knowed it was like that if it hadn't
been for that man." He arrested his gesture.

"Yeah, what man?" said Max in a hopeless voice.

Little Lee Roy was looking from one white man to
the other, excited almost beyond respectful silence. He
trembled all over and a look of amazement and sudden
life came into his eyes.

"Two years ago," Steve was saying impatiently. "And
he was travelin' through Texas in those ole trucks.—See,
the reason nobody ever come clost to it before was they
give it a iron bar this long. And tole it if anybody come
near, to shake the bar good at 'em, like this. But it couldn't

say nothin'. Turned out they'd tole it it couldn't say nothin' to anybody ever, so it just kind of mumbled and growled, like a animal."

"Hee! hee!" This from Little Lee Roy, softly.

"Tell me again," said Max, and just from his look you could tell that everybody knew old Max. "Somehow I can't get it straight in my mind. Is this the boy? Is this little nigger boy the same as this Keela, the Outcast Indian Maiden?"

Up on the porch, above them, Little Lee Roy gave Max a glance full of hilarity, and then bent the other way to catch Steve's next words.

"Why, if anybody was to even come near it or even bresh their shoulder against the rope it'd growl and take on and shake its iron rod. When it would eat the live chickens it'd growl somethin' awful—you ought to heard it."

"Hee! hee!" It was a soft, almost incredulous laugh that began to escape from Little Lee Roy's tight lips, a little mew of delight.

"They'd throw it this chicken, and it would reach out an' grab it. Would sort of rub over the chicken's neck with its thumb an' press on it good, an' then it would bite its head off."

"O.K.," said Max.

"It skint back the feathers and stuff from the neck and sucked the blood. But ever'body said it was still alive." Steve drew closer to Max and fastened his light-colored troubled eyes on his face.

"O.K."

"Then it would pull the feathers out easy and neat-like, awful fast, an' growl the whole time, kind of moan, an' then it would commence to eat all the white meat. I'd go in an' look at it. I reckon I seen it a thousand times."

"That was you, boy?" Max demanded of Little Lee Roy unexpectedly.

But Little Lee Roy could only say, "Hee! hee!" The little man at the head of the steps where the chickens sat, one on each step, and the two men facing each other below made a pyramid.

Steve stuck his hand out for silence. "They said—I mean, I said it, out front through the megaphone, I said it myself, that it wouldn't eat nothin' but only live meat.

It was supposed to be a Indian woman, see, in this red dress an' stockin's. It didn't have on no shoes, so when it drug its foot ever'body could see. . . . When it come to the chicken's heart, it would eat that too, real fast, and the heart would still be jumpin'."

"Wait a second, Bud," said Max briefly. "Say, boy, is this white man here crazy?"

Little Lee Roy burst into hysterical, deprecatory giggles. He said, "Naw suh, don't think so." He tried to catch Steve's eye, seeking appreciation, crying, "Naw suh, don't think he crazy, mista."

Steve gripped Max's arm. "Wait! Wait!" he cried anxiously. "You ain't listenin'. I want to tell you about it. You didn't catch my name—Steve. You never did hear about that little nigger—all that happened to him? Lived in Cane Springs, Miss'ippi?"

"Bud," said Max, disengaging himself, "I don't hear anything. I got a juke box, see, so I don't have to listen."

"Look—I was really the one," said Steve more patiently, but nervously, as if he had been slowly breaking bad news. He walked up and down the bare-swept ground in front of Little Lee Roy's porch, along the row of princess feathers and snow-on-the-mountain. Little Lee Roy's turning head followed him. "I was the one—that's what I'm tellin' you."

"Suppose I was to listen to what every dope comes in Max's Place got to say, I'd be nuts," said Max.

"It's all me, see," said Steve. "I know that. I was the one was the cause for it goin' on an' on an' not bein' found out—such an awful thing. It was me, what I said out front through the megaphone."

He stopped still and stared at Max in despair.

"Look," said Max. He sat on the steps, and the chickens hopped off. "I know I ain't nobody but Max. I got Max's Place. I only run a place, understand, fifty yards down the highway. Liquor buried twenty feet from the premises, and no trouble yet. I ain't ever been up here before. I don't claim to been anywhere. People come to my place. Now. You're the hitchhiker. You're tellin' me, see. You claim a lot of information. If I don't get it I don't get it and I ain't complainin' about it, see. But I think you're nuts, and did from the first. I only come up here with you because I figured you's crazy."

"Maybe you don't believe I remember every word of it even now," Steve was saying gently. "I think about it at night—that an' drums on the midway. You ever hear drums on the midway?" He paused and stared politely at Max and Little Lee Roy.

"Yeh," said Max.

"Don't it make you feel sad? I remember how the drums was goin' and I was yellin', 'Ladies and gents! Do not try to touch Keela, the Outcast Indian Maiden—she will only beat your brains out with her iron rod, and eat them alive!' " Steven waved his arm gently in the air, and Little Lee Roy drew back and squealed. " 'Do not go near her, ladies and gents! I'm warnin' you!' So nobody ever did. Nobody ever come near her. Until that man."

"Sure," said Max. "That fella." He shut his eyes.

"Afterwards when he come up so bold, I remembered seein' him walk up an' buy the ticket an' go in the tent. I'll never forget that man as long as I live. To me he's a sort of—well— —"

"Hero," said Max.

"I wish I could remember what he looked like. Seem like he was a tallish man with a sort of white face. Seem like he had bad teeth, but I may be wrong. I remember he frowned a lot. Kept frownin'. Whenever he's buy a ticket, why, he'd frown."

"Ever seen him since?" asked Max cautiously, still with his eyes closed. "Ever hunt him up?"

"No, never did," said Steve. Then he went on. "He'd frown an' buy a ticket ever' day we was in these two little smelly towns in Texas, sometimes three-four times a day, whether it was fixin' to eat a chicken or not."

"O.K., so he gets in the tent," said Max.

"Well, what the man finally done was, he walked right up to the little stand where it was tied up and laid his hand out open there and said, 'Come here,' real low and quick, that-a-way."

Steve laid his open hand on Little Lee Roy's porch and held it there, frowning in concentration.

"I get it," said Max. "He'd caught on it was a fake."

Steve straightened up. "So ever'body yelled to git away, git away," he continued, his voice rising, "because it was growlin' an' carryin' on an' shakin' its iron bar like they tole it. When I heard all that commotion—boy! I was scared."

"You didn't know it was a fake."

Steve was silent for a moment, and Little Lee Roy held his breath, for fear everything was all over.

"Look," said Steve finally, his voice trembling. "I guess I was supposed to feel bad like this, and you wasn't. I wasn't supposed to ship out on that boat from Port Arthur and all like that. This other had to happen to me—not you all. Feelin' responsible. You'll be O.K., mister, but I won't. I feel awful about it. That poor little old thing."

"Look, you got him right here," said Max quickly. "See him? Use your eyes. He's O.K., ain't he? Looks O.K. to me. It's just you. You're nuts, is all."

"You know—when that man laid out his open hand on the boards, why, it just let go the iron bar," continued Steve, "let it fall down like that—bang—and act like it didn't know what to do. Then it drug itself over to where the fella was standin' an' leaned down an' grabbed holt onto that white man's hand as tight as it could an' cried like a baby. It didn't want to hit him!"

"Hee! hee! hee!"

"No sir, it didn't want to hit him. You know what it wanted?"

Max shook his head.

"It wanted him to help it. So the man said, 'Do you wanta get out of this place, whoever you are?' An' it never answered—none of us knowed it could talk—but it just wouldn't let that man's hand a-loose. It hung on, cryin' like a baby. So the man says, 'Well, wait here till I come back.' "

"Uh-huh?" said Max.

"Went off an' come back with the sheriff. Took us all to jail. But just the man owned the show and his son got took to the pen. They said I could go free. I kep' tellin' 'em I didn't know it wouldn't hit me with the iron bar an' kep' tellin' 'em I didn't know it could tell what you was sayin' to it."

"Yeh, guess you told 'em," said Max.

"By that time I felt bad. Been feelin' bad ever since. Can't hold onto a job or stay in one place for nothin' in the world. They made it stay in jail to see if it could talk or not, and the first night it wouldn't say nothin'. Some time it cried. And they undressed it an' found out it wasn't no outcast Indian woman a-tall. It was a little club-footed nigger man."

"Hee! hee!"

"You mean it was this boy here—yeh. It was him."

"Washed its face, and it was paint all over it made it look red. It all come off. And it could talk—as good as me or you. But they'd tole it not to, so it never did. They'd tole it if anybody was to come near it they was comin' to git it —and for it to hit 'em quick with that iron bar an' growl. So nobody ever came near it—until that man. I was yellin' outside, tellin' 'em to keep away, keep away. You could see where they'd whup it. They had to whip it some to make it eat all the chickens. It was awful dirty. They let it go back home free, to where they got it in the first place. They made them pay its ticket from Little Oil, Texas, to Cane Springs, Miss'ippi."

"You got a good memory," said Max.

"The way it started was," said Steve, in a wondering voice, "the show was just travelin' along in ole trucks through the country, and just seen this little deformed nigger man, sittin' on a fence, and just took it. It couldn't help it."

Little Lee Roy tossed his head back in a frenzy of amusement.

"I found it all out later. I was up on the Ferris wheel with one of the boys—got to talkin' up yonder in the peace an' quiet—an' said they just kind of happened up on it. Like a cyclone happens: it wasn't nothin' it could do. It was just took up." Steve suddenly paled through his sunburn. "An' they found out that back in Miss'ippi it had it a little bitty pair of crutches an' could just go runnin' on 'em!"

"And there they are," said Max.

Little Lee Roy held up a crutch and turned it about, and then snatched it back like a monkey.

"But if it hadn't been for that man, I wouldn't of knowed it till yet. If it wasn't for him bein' so bold. If he hadn't knowed what he was doin'."

"You remember that man this fella's talkin' about, boy?" asked Max, eying Little Lee Roy.

"Naw suh, I cain't say as I remembas that ve'y man, suh," he said softly, looking down where just then a sparrow alighted on his child's shoe. He added happily, as if on inspiration, "Now I remembas this man."

Steve did not look up, but when Max shook with silent laughter, alarm seemed to seize him like a spasm in his side. He walked painfully over and stood in the shade for a few minutes, leaning his head on a sycamore tree.

"Seemed like that man just studied it out an' knowed it was somethin' wrong," he said presently, his voice coming more remotely than ever. "But I didn't know. I can't look at nothin' an' be sure what it is. Then afterwards I know. Then I see how it was."

"Yeh, but you're nuts," said Max affably.

"You wouldn't of knowed it either!" cried Steve in sudden boyish, defensive anger. Then he came out from under the tree and stood again almost pleadingly in the sun, facing Max where he was sitting below Little Lee Roy on the steps. "You'd of let it go on an' on when they made it do those things—just like I did."

"Bet I could tell a man from a woman and an Indian from a nigger though," said Max.

Steve scuffed the dust into little puffs with his worn shoe. The chickens scattered, alarmed at last.

Little Lee Roy looked from one man to the other radiantly, his hands pressed over his grinning gums.

Then Steve sighed, and as if he did not know what else he could do, he reached out and without any warning hit Max in the jaw with his fist. Max fell off the steps.

Little Lee Roy suddenly sat as still and dark as a statue, looking on.

"Say! Say!" cried Steve. He pulled shyly at Max where he lay on the ground, with his lips pursed up like a whistler, and then stepped back. He looked horrified. "How you feel?"

"Lousy," said Max thoughtfully. "Let me alone." He raised up on one elbow and lay there looking all around, at the cabin, at Little Lee Roy sitting cross-legged on the porch, and at Steve with his hand out. Finally he got up.

"I can't figure out how I could of ever knocked down an athaletic guy like you. I had to do it," said Steve. "But I guess you don't understand. I had to hit you. First you didn't believe me, and then it didn't bother you."

"That's all O.K., only hush," said Max, and added, "Some dope is always giving me the lowdown on something, but this is the first time one of 'em ever got away with a thing like this. I got to watch out."

"I hope it don't stay black long," said Steve.

"I got to be going," said Max. But he waited. "What you want to transact with Keela? You come a long way to see him." He stared at Steve with his eyes wide open now, and interested.

"Well, I was goin' to give him some money or somethin', I guess, if I ever found him, only now I ain't got any," said Steve defiantly.

"O.K.," said Max. "Here's some change for you, boy. Just take it. Go on back in the house. Go on."

Little Lee Roy took the money speechlessly, and then fell upon his yellow crutches and hopped with miraculous rapidity away through the door. Max stared after him for a moment.

"As for you"—he brushed himself off, turned to Steve and then said, "When did you eat last?"

"Well, I'll tell you," said Steve.

"Not here," said Max. "I didn't go to ask you a question. Just follow me. We serve eats at Max's Place, and I want to play the juke box. You eat, and I'll listen to the juke box."

"Well . . ." said Steve. "But when it cools off I got to catch a ride some place."

"Today, while all you all was gone, and not a soul in de house," said Little Lee Roy at the supper table that night, "two white mens come heah to de house. Wouldn't come in. But talks to me about de ole times when I use to be wid de circus—"

"Hush up, Pappy," said the children.

1940

WILLIAM FAULKNER

(1897–1962)

There is no collected edition of the works of William Faulkner. The published works include *The Marble Faun* (1924); *Soldier's Pay* (1926); *Mosquitoes* (1927); *The Sound and the Fury* (1929); *Sartoris* (1929); *As I Lay Dying* (1930); *Sanctuary* (1931); *These 13* (1931); *Idyll in the Desert* (1931); *Salmagundi* (1932); *This Earth* (1932); *Miss Zilphia Gant* (1932); *Light in August* (1932); *A Green Bough* (1933); *Doctor Martino and Other Stories* (1934); *Pylon* (1935); *Absalom, Absalom!* (1936); *The Unvanquished* (1938); *The Wild Palms* (1939); *The Hamlet* (1940); *Go Down, Moses, and Other Stories* (1942); *Intruder in the Dust* (1948); *Knight's Gambit* (1949); *Collected Stories of William Faulkner* (1950); *Notes on a Horse Thief* (1950); *Requiem for a Nun* (1951); *A Fable* (1954); *Big Woods* (1955); R. A. Jelliffe, ed., *Faulkner at Nagano* (1956); *The Town* (1957); C. Collins, ed., *William Faulkner: New Orleans Sketches* (1958); *The Mansion* (1959); and *The Reivers* (1962).

The Viking Portable Faulkner, edited by Malcolm Cowley (1946) is a chronological picture of Yoknapatawpha County and its inhabitants. It contains *Old Man* (from *The Wild Palms*), *Spotted Horses* (from *The Hamlet*), and *The Bear* complete, with selections from *Absalom, Absalom!*, *The Unvanquished*, *The Sound and the Fury*, *Sanctuary*, and *Light in August*, and nine short stories: "A Justice," "Red Leaves," "Was," "Wash," "That Evening Sun," "Ad Astra," "A Rose for Emily," "Death Drag," and "Delta Autumn."

Studies of the man and his work are to be found in G. Hicks, "The Past and the Future of William Faulkner," *Bookman*, LXXIV (1931); A. W. Green, "William Faulkner at Home," *Sewanee Review*, XL (1932); D. Schwartz, "The Fiction of William Faulkner," *Southern Review*, VII (1941); Faulkner Number, *Perspective*, II (Summer, 1949) and III (Autumn, 1950); W. M. Frohock, *The Novel of Violence in America, 1920–1950* (1950); H. M. Campbell and R. E. Foster, *William Faulkner: A Critical Appraisal* (1951); Faulkner Number, *Har-*

vard *Advocate*, CXXXV (November, 1951); W. L. Miner, *The World of William Faulkner* (1952); A. Downer, ed., *English Institute Essays: 1952* (1954); W. Van O'Connor, *The Tangled Fire of William Faulkner* (1954); Faulkner Number, *Modern Fiction Studies*, II (Autumn, 1956); J. B. Meriwether, *William Faulkner: A Checklist* (1957); Faulkner Number, *Princeton University Library Chronicle*, XVIII (Spring, 1957); O. W. Vickery, *The Novels of William Faulkner* (1959); H. H. Waggoner, *William Faulkner: From Jefferson to the World* (1959); F. J. Hoffman and O. W. Vickery, eds., *William Faulkner: Three Decades of Criticism* (1960); W. J. Slatoff, *Quest for Failure: A Study of William Faulkner* (1960); C. Collins, ed., *William Faulkner: Early Prose and Poetry* (1962); S. L. Elkin, "Religious Themes and Symbolism in the Work of William Faulkner," *Dissertation Abstracts*, XXII (1962); O. B. Emerson, "William Faulkner's Literary Reputation in America," *Dissertation Abstracts*, XXIII (1962); I. Howe, *William Faulkner: A Critical Study* (1962); W. P. Sullivan, "William Faulkner and the Community," *Dissertation Abstracts*, XXII (1962); P. Swiggart, *The Art of Faulkner's Novels* (1962); E. K. Brady, "The Literary Faulkner," *Dissertation Abstracts*, XXIII (1962); H. A. Simpson, "The Short Stories of William Faulkner," *Dissertation Abstracts*, XXIII (1962); C. Brooks, *William Faulkner* (1963); B. R. Dowell, "Faulkner's Comic Spirit," *Dissertation Abstracts*, XXIII (1963); J. Faulkner, *My Brother Bill: An Affectionate Reminiscence* (1963); R. W. Kirk and M. Klotz, *Faulkner's People: A Complete Guide and Index to Characters in the Fiction of William Faulkner* (1963); J. L. Longley, Jr., *The Tragic Mask: A Study of Faulkner's Heroes* (1963); T. F. Loughrey, "Values and Love in the Fiction of William Faulkner," *Dissertation Abstracts*, XXIII (1963); C. D. McLaughlin, "Religion in Yoknapatawpha County," *Dissertation Abstracts*, XXIII (1963); K. E. Richardson, "Quest for Faith: A Study of Destructive and Creative Force in the Novels of William Faulkner," *Dissertation Abstracts*, XXIII (1963); I. L. Sleeth, *William Faulkner: A Bibliography of Criticism* (1963); L. Thompson, *William Faulkner* (1963); G. O. Carey, "William Faulkner: Critic of Society," *Dissertation Abstracts*, XXIII (1963); E. M. Holmes, "Faulkner's Twice-Told Tales," *Dissertation Abstracts*, XXIII (1963); M. J. Dain, *Faulkner's County* (1964); R. R. Fazio, "The Fury and the Design," *Dissertation Abstracts*, XXV (1964); V. T. Hornback, Jr., "William Faulkner and the Terror of History," *Dissertation Abstracts*, XXV (1964); J. M. Mellard, "Humor in Faulkner's Novels," *Dissertation Abstracts*, XXV (1964); H. E. Richardson, "William Faulkner: From Past to Self-Discovery," *Dissertation Abstracts*, XXIV (1964); H. Runyan, *A Faulkner Glossary* (1964); J. K. Simon, "The Glance of the Idiot," *Dissertation Abstracts*, XXV (1964); D. Tuck, *Crowell's Handbook of Faulkner* (1964); E. L. Volpe, *A Reader's Guide to William Faulkner* (1964); J. Blotner, comp., *William Faulkner's Library—A Catalogue* (1965); W. M. Brylowski, "Man's Enduring Chronicle: A Study of Myth in the Novels of William Faulkner," *Dissertation Ab-*

stracts, XXV (1965); R. D. Harwick, "Humor in the Novels of William Faulkner," *Dissertation Abstracts*, XXVI (1964); J. W. Hunt, *William Faulkner: Art in Theological Tension* (1965); D. M. Kartiganer, "The Individual and the Community: Values in the Novels of William Faulkner," *Dissertation Abstracts*, XXV (1965); J. B. Meriwether, ed., *Essays, Speeches, and Public Letters of William Faulkner* (1965); A. S. Pollock, "The Current of Time in the Novels of William Faulkner," *Dissertation Abstracts*, XXV (1965); G. K. Smart, *Religious Elements in Faulkner's Early Novels* (1965); W. F. Taylor, Jr., "The Roles of the Negro in William Faulkner's Fiction," *Dissertation Abstracts*, XXV (1964); O. W. Vickery, *The Novels of William Faulkner* (rev. ed., 1965); J. W. Webb and A. W. Green, *William Faulkner of Oxford* (1965); M. Backman, *Faulkner, The Major Years* (1966); M. Cowley, *The Faulkner-Cowley File* (1966); J. Gold, *William Faulkner* (1966); F. Hoffman, *William Faulkner* (1966); M. Millgate, *The Achievement of William Faulkner* (1966); H. Runyan, *A Faulkner Glossary* (1966); R. P. Warren, ed., *Faulkner* (1966); and W. M. Brylowski, *William Faulkner* (1968).

EUGENE O'NEILL

(1885–1953)

If any man was born into the probability of a career in drama, it was Eugene O'Neill. He was born in a New York theater-district hotel, the son of James O'Neill, a celebrated romantic actor whose role in *The Count of Monte Cristo* had brought him national fame. As a lad, Eugene accompanied his father on tour, was educated in various Catholic schools and at the Betts Academy in Stamford, Connecticut, and entered Princeton in 1906. In 1907 he was expelled.

Although he worked occasionally with his father's company, his most dramatic experience came from his wandering through an amazing variety of jobs that took him over the world. He tried everything from gold prospecting to reporting, but primarily he was a seaman who frequented various waterfront dives, brooding, observing, and learning the various ironies that fate played in the seamy lives of his companions. In the winter of 1912–1913 he was hosptalized for tuberculosis, and he spent his time in a Connecticut sanitarium reading a wide sweep of dramatic literature, particularly Ibsen and Strindberg. His illness made him reflect upon his purposes and goals, and when he emerged from this decisive moment of his life, he was a playwright.

In 1914 he enrolled in Professor Baker's famous "47 Workshop" at Harvard, but he soon left. By 1916 he was associated with the Provincetown Players, who produced his one-acters in the Wharf Theater and later in their radical theater in Macdougal Street, Greenwich Village. By 1917–1918 he had begun to attract national recognition when some of his one-act plays were published by Mencken and Nathan in *The Smart Set*, but it was the year 1920 that established O'Neill—his first full-length play, *Beyond the Horizon*, was produced in New York. The enormous advances that the American theater had begun to make in the first two decades of the twentieth century were epitomized in the work of O'Neill. With *Beyond the Horizon*, a powerful, serious, and original literature finally arrived on the American stage.

O'Neill's genius not only brought symbolism, experimental naturalism, and expressionism to the American stage, but it brought the American stage itself into world prominence, allowing our native drama to take its place alongside the productions of the great modern Europeans. As some of his best works began to appear, the 1920's recognized O'Neill to be the chief American playwright. He wrote almost twenty plays in that decade, including *The Emperor Jones* (1921), *The Hairy Ape* (1922), *Anna Christie* (1922), *All God's Chillun Got Wings* (1924), *Desire Under the Elms* (1924), *The Great God Brown* (1926), *Marco Millions* (1927), *Lazarus Laughed* (1927), and *Strange Interlude* (1928). In the 1930's he produced, among other plays, *Mourning Becomes Electra* (1931), *Days without End* (1933), and *Ah, Wilderness* (1933). Then his energies flagged. In 1936 he received the Nobel Prize; the award, however, did not stimulate him to break a silence that lasted until *The Iceman Cometh*, in 1946.

O'Neill had been counted on as a playwright of the highest order for so long that his audiences were disappointed with *The Iceman Cometh* and the works that followed it. Indeed, many feel that O'Neill's promise was never really fulfilled and that the American playwright who will stand with the immortals of drama is yet to be born. Nevertheless, O'Neill comes as close as any. His plays of man caught in a Freudian trap, of man seen through the exposing and experimental eye of the disillusionment that followed World War I, brought American drama a stature it had never before enjoyed.

Undoubtedly O'Neill will be remembered as a playwright of the 1920's and early 1930's. *A Moon for the Misbegotten* was produced in 1952, and the play about the O'Neill family, *Long Day's Journey into Night*, which many critics consider his best play and which he had left to be produced posthumously, was presented in 1956. *A Touch of the Poet* (1957), *Hughie* (1959), and *More Stately Mansions* (1967) complete, so far, the list of posthumous productions.

Some other O'Neill plays are *Thirst and Other One Act Plays* (1914); *Bound East for Cardiff* (1916); *The Moon of*

the Caribbees, and Six Other Plays of the Sea (1919); *Gold*
(1920); *Diff'rent* (1921); *The Straw* (1921); *Welded* (1924);
The Fountain (1926); and *Dynamo* (1929).

Editions and accounts of the man and his work are to be
found in A. Woolcott, *Shouts and Murmurs* (1922); *Complete
Works of Eugene O'Neill*, 4 vols. (1925); R. Sanborn and B. H.
Clark, *A Bibliography of the Works of Eugene O'Neill* (1931);
S. K. Winther, *Eugene O'Neill* (1934); *The Plays of Eugene
O'Neill*, 12 vols. (1934–1935); R. D. Skinner, *Eugene O'Neill*
(1935); B. H. Clark, *Eugene O'Neill* (1947); E. A. Engel, *The
Haunted Heroes of Eugene O'Neill* (1953); A. Boulton, *Part of
a Long Story* (1958); D. V. Falk, *Eugene O'Neill and the Tragic
Tension* (1958); L. Gellert, ed., *The Lost Plays of Eugene
O'Neill* (1958); C. Bowen and S. O'Neill, *Curse of the Misbe-
gotten* (1959); A. and B. Gelb, *O'Neill* (1962); D. Alexander,
The Tempering of Eugene O'Neill (1962); O. Cargill, N. B.
Fagin and W. J. Fisher, eds., *O'Neill and His Plays* (1962);
J. Y. Miller, *Eugene O'Neill and the American Critic* (1962);
C. Leech, *Eugene O'Neill* (1963); J. Gassner, ed., *O'Neill*
(1964); F. Carpenter, *Eugene O'Neill* (1964); J. Gassner,
Eugene O'Neill (1965); J. Y. Miller, *Playwright's Progress*
(1965); and J. H. Raleigh, *The Plays of Eugene O'Neill* (1965).

The Hairy Ape

A Comedy of Ancient and Modern Life
in Eight Scenes

Characters

ROBERT SMITH, "YANK"	A GUARD
PADDY	A SECRETARY OF AN ORGAN-
LONG	IZATION
MILDRED DOUGLAS	STOKERS, LADIES, GENTLE-
HER AUNT	MEN, ETC.
SECOND ENGINEER	

Scenes

SCENE I: The firemen's forecastle of an ocean liner—an
hour after sailing from New York.

SCENE II: Section of promenade deck, two days out—
morning.

SCENE III: The stokehole. A few minutes later.

SCENE IV: Same as Scene I. Half an hour later.

SCENE V: Fifth Avenue, New York. Three weeks later.

SCENE VI: An island near the city. The next night.

SCENE VII: In the city. About a month later.
SCENE VIII: In the city. Twilight of the next day.

SCENE I

SCENE. The firemen's forecastle of a transatlantic liner an hour after sailing from New York for the voyage across. Tiers of narrow, steel bunks, three deep, on all sides. An entrance in rear. Benches on the floor before the bunks. The room is crowded with men, shouting, cursing, laughing, singing—a confused, inchoate uproar swelling into a sort of unity, a meaning—the bewildered, furious, baffled defiance of a beast in a cage. Nearly all the men are drunk. Many bottles are passed from hand to hand. All are dressed in dungaree pants, heavy ugly shoes. Some wear singlets, but the majority are stripped to the waist.

The treatment of this scene, or of any other scene in the play, should by no means be naturalistic. The effect sought after is a cramped space in the bowels of a ship, imprisoned by white steel. The lines of bunks, the uprights supporting them, cross each other like the steel framework of a cage. The ceiling crushes down upon the men's heads. They cannot stand upright. This accentuates the natural stooping posture which shoveling coal and the resultant overdevelopment of back and shoulder muscles have given them. The men themselves should resemble those pictures in which the appearance of Neanderthal Man is guessed at. All are hairy-chested, with long arms of tremendous power, and low, receding brows above their small, fierce, resentful eyes. All the civilized white races are represented, but except for the slight differentiation in color of hair, skin, eyes, all these men are alike.

The curtain rises on a tumult of sound. YANK is seated in the foreground. He seems broader, fiercer, more truculent, more powerful, more sure of himself than the rest. They respect his superior strength—the grudging respect of fear. Then, too, he represents to them a self-expression, the very last word in what they are, their most highly developed individual.

VOICES. Gif me trink dere, you!
'Ave a wet!
Salute!
Gesundheit!
Skoal!
Drunk as a lord, God stiffen you!
Here's how!
Luck!
Pass back that bottle, damn you!

Pourin' it down his neck!

Ho, Froggy! Where the devil have you been?

La Touraine.

I hit him smash in yaw, py Gott!

Jenkins—the First—he's a rotten swine——

And the coppers nabbed him—and I run——

I like peer better. It don't pig head gif you.

A slut, I'm sayin'! She robbed me aslape——

To hell with 'em all!

You're a bloody liar!

Say dot again!

(*Commotion. Two men about to fight are pulled apart.*)

No scrappin' now!

To-night——

See who's the best man!

Bloody Dutchman!

To-night on the fo'ard square.

I'll bet on Dutchy.

He packa da wallop, I tella you!

Shut up, Wop!

No fightin', maties. We're all chums, ain't we?

(*A voice starts bawling a song.*)

> "Beer, beer, glorious beer!
> Fill yourselves right up to here."

YANK. (*For the first time seeming to take notice of the uproar about him, turns around threateningly—in a tone of contemptuous authority.*) Choke off dat noise! Where d'you get dat beer stuff? Beer, hell! Beer's for goils—and Dutchmen. Me for somep'n wit a kick to it! Gimme a drink, one of youse guys. (*Several bottles are eagerly offered. He takes a tremendous gulp at one of them; then, keeping the bottle in his hand, glares belligerently at the owner, who hastens to acquiesce in this robbery by saying.*) All righto, Yank. Keep it and have another. (YANK *contemptuously turns his back on the crowd again. For a second there is an embarrassed silence. Then——*)

VOICES. We must be passing the Hook.

She's beginning to roll to it.

Six days in hell—and then Southampton.

Py Yesus, I vish somepody take my first vatch for me!

Gittin' seasick, Square-head?

Drink up and forget it!

What's in your bottle?
Gin.
Dot's nigger trink.
Absinthe? It's doped. You'll go off your chump, Froggy!
Cochon!
Whisky, that's the ticket!
Where's Paddy?
Going asleep.
Sing us that whisky song, Paddy.
(*They all turn to an old, wizened Irishman who is doz-ing, very drunk, on the benches forward. His face is ex-tremely monkey-like with all the sad, patient pathos of that animal in his small eyes.*)
Singa da song, Caruso Pat!
He's gettin' old. The drink is too much for him.
He's too drunk.
PADDY. (*Blinking about him, starts to his feet resentfully, swaying, holding onto the edge of a bunk.*) I'm never too drunk to sing. 'Tis only when I'm dead to the world I'd be wishful to sing at all. (*With a sort of sad contempt.*) "Whisky Johnny," ye want? A chanty, ye want? Now that's a queer wish from the ugly like of you, God help you. But no matther. (*He starts to sing in a thin, nasal, doleful tone.*)

Oh, whisky is the life of man!
  Whisky! O Johnny! (*They all join in on this.*)
Oh, whisky is the life of man!
  Whisky for my Johnny! (*Again chorus.*)
Oh, whisky drove my old man mad!
  Whisky! O Johnny!
Oh, whisky drove my old man mad!
  Whisky for my Johnny!

YANK. (*Again turning around scornfully.*) Aw hell! Nix on dat old sailing ship stuff! All dat bull's dead, see? And you're dead, too, yuh damned old Harp, on'y yuh don't know it. Take it easy, see. Give us a rest. Nix on de loud noise. (*With a cynical grin.*) Can't youse see I'm tryin' to t'ink?
ALL. (*Repeating the word after him as one with the same cynical amused mockery.*) Think! (*The chorused word has a brazen metallic quality as if their throats were pho-*

nograph horns. It is followed by a general uproar of hard, barking laughter.)

VOICES. Don't be cracking your head wit ut, Yank.

You gat headache, py yingo!

One thing about it—it rhymes with drink!

Ha, ha, ha!

Drink, don't think!

Drink, don't think!

Drink, don't think!

(*A whole chorus of voices has taken up this refrain, stamping on the floor, pounding on the benches with fists.*)

YANK. (*Taking a gulp from his bottle—goodnaturedly.*) Aw right. Can de noise. I got yuh de foist time.

(*The uproar subsides. A very drunken sentimental tenor begins to sing.*)

> "Far away in Canada,
>   Far across the sea,
>   There's a lass who fondly waits
>   Making a home for me——"

YANK (*Fiercely contemptuous.*) Shut up, yuh lousy boob! Where d'yuh get dat tripe? Home? Home, hell! I'll make a home for yuh! I'll knock yuh dead. Home! T'hell wit home! Where d'yuh get dat tripe? Dis is home, see? What d'yuh want wit home? (*Proudly.*) I runned away from mine when I was a kid. On'y too glad to beat it, dat was me. Home was lickings for me, dat's all. But yuh can bet your shoit no one ain't never licked me since! Wanter try it, any of youse? Huh! I guess not. (*In a more placated but still contemptuous tone.*) Goils waitin' for yuh, huh? Aw, hell! Dat's all tripe. Dey don't wait for no one. Dey'd double-cross yuh for a nickel. Dey're all tarts, get me? Treat 'em rough, dat's me. To hell wit 'em. Tarts, dat's what, de whole bunch of 'em.

LONG. (*Very drunk, jumps on a bench excitedly, gesticulating with a bottle in his hand.*) Listen 'ere, Comrades! Yank 'ere is right. 'E says this 'ere stinkin' ship is our 'ome. And 'e says as 'ome is 'ell. And 'e's right! This is 'ell. We lives in 'ell, Comrades—and right enough we'll die in it. (*Raging.*) And who's ter blame, I arsks yer? We ain't. We wasn't born this rotten way. All men is born free and ekal. That's in the bleedin' Bible, maties. But what d'they care for the Bible—them lazy, bloated swine what travels first cabin? Them's the ones. They dragged us down 'til we're on'y wage slaves in the bowels of a bloody ship, sweatin', burnin' up, eatin' coal dust! Hit's them's ter blame—the damned Capitalist clarss!

(*There had been a gradual murmur of contemptuous resentment rising among the men until now he is interrupted by a storm of catcalls, hisses, boos, hard laughter.*)

VOICES. Turn it off!

Shut up!

Sit down!

Closa da face!

Tamn fool! (*Etc.*)

YANK. (*Standing up and glaring at* LONG.) Sit down before I knock yuh down! (LONG *makes haste to efface himself.* YANK *goes on contemptuously.*) De Bible, huh? De Cap'tlist class, huh? Aw nix on dat Salvation Army-Socialist bull. Git a soapbox! Hire a hall! Come and be saved, huh? Jerk us to Jesus, huh? Aw g'wan! I've listened to lots of guys like you, see. Yuh're all wrong. Wanter know what I t'ink? Yuh ain't no good for no one. Yuh're de bunk. Yuh ain't got no noive, get me? Yuh're yellow, dat's what. Yellow, dat's you. Say! What's dem slobs in de foist cabin got to do wit us? We're better men dan dey are, ain't we? Sure! One of us guys could clean up de whole mob wit one mit. Put one of 'em down here for one watch in de stokehole, what'd happen? Dey'd carry him off on a stretcher. Dem boids don't amount to nothin'. Dey're just baggage. Who makes dis old tub run? Ain't it us guys? Well den, we belong, don't we? We belong and dey don't. Dat's all (*A loud chorus of approval.* YANK *goes on.*) As for dis bein' hell—aw, nuts! Yuh lost your noive, dat's what. Dis is a man's job, get me? It belongs. It runs dis tub. No stiffs need apply. But yuh're a stiff, see? Yuh're yellow, dat's you.

VOICES. (*With a great hard pride in them.*)

Righto!

A man's job!

Talk is cheap, Long.

He never could hold up his end.

Divil take him!

Yank's right. We make it go.

Py Gott, Yank say right ting!

We don't need no one cryin' over us.
Makin' speeches.
Throw him out!
Yellow!
Chuck him overboard!
I'll break his jaw for him!

(*They crowd around* LONG *threateningly.*)

YANK. (*Half good-natured again—contemptuously.*) Aw, take it easy. Leave him alone. He ain't woith a punch. Drink up. Here's how, whoever owns dis. (*He takes a long swallow from his bottle. All drink with him. In a flash all is hilarious amiability again, back-slapping, loud talk, etc.*)

PADDY. (*Who has been sitting in a blinking, melancholy daze—suddenly cries out in a voice full of old sorrow.*) We belong to this, you're saying? We make the ship to go, you're saying? Yerra then, that Almighty God have pity on us! (*His voice runs into the wail of a keen, he rocks back and forth on his bench. The men stare at him, startled and impressed in spite of themselves.*) Oh, to be back in the fine days of my youth, ochone! Oh, there was fine beautiful ships them days—clippers wid tall masts touching the sky—fine strong men in them—men that was sons of the sea as if 'twas the mother that bore them. Oh, the clean skins of them, and the clear eyes, the straight backs and full chests of them! Brave men they was, and bold men surely! We'd be sailing out, bound down round the Horn maybe. We'd be making sail in the dawn, with a fair breeze, singing a chanty song wid no care to it. And astern the land would be sinking low and dying out, but we'd give it no heed but a laugh, and never a look behind. For the day that was, was enough, for we was free men—and I'm thinking 'tis only slaves do be giving heed to the day that's gone or the day to come—until they're old like me. (*With a sort of religious exaltation.*) Oh, to be scudding south again wid the power of the Trade Wind driving her on steady through the nights and the days! Full sail on her! Nights and days! Nights when the foam of the wake would be flaming wid fire, when the sky'd be blazing and winking wid stars. Or the full of the moon maybe. Then you'd see her driving through the gray night, her sails stretching aloft all silver and white, not a sound on the deck, the lot of us dreaming dreams, till you'd believe 'twas no real ship at all you was on but a ghost ship like the *Flying Dutchman* they

say does be roaming the seas forevermore without touching
a port. And there was the days, too. A warm sun on the
clean decks. Sun warming the blood of you, and wind over
the miles of shiny green ocean like strong drink to your
lungs. Work—aye, hard work—but who'd mind that at all?
Sure, you worked under the sky and 'twas work wid skill
and daring to it. And wid the day done, in the dog watch,
smoking me pipe at ease, the lookout would be raising land
maybe, and we'd see the mountains of South Americy wid
the red fire of the setting sun painting their white tops and
the clouds floating by them! (*His tone of exaltation ceases.
He goes on mournfully.*) Yerra, what's the use of talking?
'Tis a dead man's whisper. (*To* YANK *resentfully.*) 'Twas
them days men belonged to ships, not now. 'Twas them
days a ship was part of the sea, and a man was part of a
ship, and the sea joined all together and made it one.
(*Scornfully.*) Is it one wid this you'd be, Yank—black
smoke from the funnels smudging the sea, smudging the
decks—the bloody engines pounding and throbbing and
shaking—wid divil a sight of sun or a breath of clean air
—choking our lungs wid coal dust—breaking our backs
and hearts in the hell of the stokehole—feeding the bloody
furnace—feeding our lives along wid the coal, I'm thinking
—caged in by steel from a sight of the sky like bloody apes
in the Zoo! (*With a harsh laugh.*) Ho-ho, divil mend you!
Is it to belong to that you're wishing? Is it a flesh and blood
wheel of the engines you'd be?

YANK. (*Who has been listening with a contemptuous
sneer, barks out the answer.*) Sure ting! Dat's me. What
about it?

PADDY. (*As if to himself—with great sorrow.*) Me time
is past due. That a great wave wid sun in the heart of it
may sweep me over the side sometime I'd be dreaming of
the days that's gone!

YANK. Aw, yuh crazy Mick! (*He springs to his feet and
advances on* PADDY *threateningly—then stops, fighting
some queer struggle within himself—lets his hands fall to
his sides—contemptuously.*) Aw, take it easy. Yuh're aw
right at dat. Yuh're bugs, dat's all—nutty as a cuckoo. All
dat tripe yuh been pullin'——Aw, dat's all right. On'y it's
dead, get me? Yuh don't belong no more, see. Yuh don't
get de stuff. Yuh're too old. (*Disgustedly.*) But aw say,
come up for air onct in a while, can't yuh? See what's hap-

pened since yuh croaked. (*He suddenly bursts forth vehe-mently, growing more and more excited.*) Say! Sure! Sure I meant it! What de hell—— Say, lemme talk! Hey! Hey, you old Harp! Hey, youse guys! Say, listen to me—wait a moment—I gotter talk, see. I belong and he don't. He's dead but I'm livin'. Listen to me! Sure, I'm part of de engines! Why de hell not! Dey move, don't dey? Dey're speed, ain't déy! Dey smash trou, don't dey? Twenty-five knots a hour! Dat's goin' some! Dat's new stuff! Dat be-longs! But him, he's too old. He gets dizzy. Say, listen. All dat crazy tripe about nights and days; all dat crazy tripe about stars and moons; all dat crazy tripe about suns and winds, fresh air and de rest of it—— Aw hell, dat's all a dope dream! Hittin' de pipe of de past, dat's what he's doin'. He's old and don't belong no more. But me, I'm young! I'm in de pink! I move wit it! It, get me! I mean de ting dat's de guts of all dis. It ploughs trou all de tripe he's been sayin'. It blows dat up! It knocks dat dead! It slams dat offen de face of de oith! It, get me! De engines and de coal and de smoke and all de rest of it! He can't breathe and swallow coal dust, but I kin, see? Dat's fresh air for me! Dat's food for me! I'm new, get me? Hell in de stokehole? Sure! It takes a man to work in hell. Hell, sure, dat's my fav'rite climate. I eat it up! I git fat on it! It's me makes it hot! It's me makes it roar! It's me makes it move! Sure, on'y for me everyting stops. It all goes dead, get me? De noise and smoke and all de engines movin' de woild, dey stop. Dere ain't nothin' no more! Dat's what I'm sayin'. Everyting else dat makes de woild move, somep'n makes it move. It can't move witout somep'n else, see? Den yuh get down to me. I'm at de bottom, get me! Dere ain't nothin' foither. I'm de end! I'm de start! I start somep'n and de woild moves! It—dat's me!—de new dat's moiderin' de old! I'm de ting in coal dat makes it boin; I'm steam and oil for de engines; I'm de ting in noise dat makes yuh hear it; I'm smoke and express trains and steamers and factory whistles; I'm de ting in gold dat makes it money! And I'm what makes iron into steel! Steel, dat stands for de whole ting! And I'm steel—steel—steel! I'm de muscles in steel, de punch behind it! (*As he says this he pounds with his fist against the steel bunks. All the men, roused to a pitch of frenzied self-glorification by his speech, do likewise. There is a deafening metallic roar,*

through which YANK's *voice can be heard bellowing.*)
Slaves, hell! We run de whole woiks. All de rich guys dat
tink dey're somep'n, dey ain't nothin'! Dey don't belong.
But us guys, we're in de move, we're at de bottom, de
whole ting is us! (PADDY *from the start of* YANK's *speech
has been taking one gulp after another from his bottle, at
first frightenedly, as if he were afraid to listen, then desperately, as if to drown his senses, but finally has achieved
complete indifferent, even amused, drunkenness.* YANK *sees
his lips moving. He quells the uproar with a shout.*) Hey,
youse guys, take it easy! Wait a moment! De nutty Harp is
sayin' somep'n.

PADDY. (*Is heard now—throws his head back with a
mocking burst of laughter.*) Ho-ho-ho-ho-ho——

YANK. (*Drawing back his fist, with a snarl.*) Aw! Look
out who yuh're givin' the bark!

PADDY. (*Begins to sing the "Miller of Dee" with enormous good nature.*)

"I care for nobody, no, not I,
And nobody cares for me."

YANK. (*Good-natured himself in a flash, interrupts* PADDY
with a slap on the bare back like a report.) Dat's de stuff!
Now yuh're gettin' wise to somep'n. Care for nobody, dat's
de dope! To hell wit 'em all! And nix on nobody else
carin'. I kin care for myself, get me! (*Eight bells sound,
muffled, vibrating through the steel walls as if some enormous brazen gong were imbedded in the heart of the
ship. All the men jump up mechanically, file through the
door silently close upon each other's heels in what is
very like a prisoners' lockstep.* YANK *slaps* PADDY *on the
back.*) Our watch, yuh old Harp! (*Mockingly.*) Come on
down in hell. Eat up de coal dust. Drink in de heat. It's
it, see! Act like yuh liked it, yuh better—or croak yuhself.

PADDY. (*With jovial defiance.*) To the divil wid it! I'll
not report this watch. Let thim log me and be damned.
I'm no slave the like of you. I'll be sittin' here at me ease,
and drinking, and thinking, and dreaming dreams.

YANK. (*Contemptuously.*) Tinkin' and dreamin', what'll
that get yuh? What's tinkin' got to do wit it? We move,
don't we? Speed, ain't it? Fog, dat's all you stand for. But
we drive trou dat, don't we? We split dat up and smash
trou—twenty-five knots a hour! (*Turns his back on* PADDY

scornfully.) Aw, yuh make me sick! Yuh don't belong!
(*He strides out the door in rear.* PADDY *hums to himself,
blinking drowsily.*)
(*Curtain.*)

SCENE II

SCENE. Two days out. A section of the promenade deck.
MILDRED DOUGLAS and her AUNT are discovered reclining in deck
chairs. The former is a girl of twenty, slender, delicate, with a
pale, pretty face marred by a self-conscious expression of dis-
dainful superiority. She looks fretful, nervous, and discontented,
bored by her own anemia. Her aunt is a pompous and proud—
and fat—old lady. She is a type even to the point of a double
chin and lorgnette. She is dressed pretentiously, as if afraid
her face alone would never indicate her position in life. MIL-
DRED is dressed all in white.
The impression to be conveyed by this scene is one of the
beautiful, vivid life of the sea all about—sunshine on the deck
in a great flood, the fresh sea wind blowing across it. In the
midst of this, these two incongruous, artificial figures, inert and
disharmonious, the elder like a gray lump of dough touched up
with rouge, the younger looking as if the vitality of her stock
had been sapped before she was conceived, so that she is the
expression not of its life energy but merely of the artificialities
that energy had won for itself in the spending.

MILDRED. (*Looking up with affected dreaminess.*) How
the black smoke swirls back against the sky! Is it not
beautiful?
AUNT. (*Without looking up.*) I dislike smoke of any
kind.
MILDRED. My great-grandmother smoked a pipe—a clay
pipe.
AUNT. (*Ruffling.*) Vulgar.
MILDRED. She was too distant a relative to be vulgar.
Time mellows pipes.
AUNT. (*Pretending boredom but irritated.*) Did the soci-
ology you took up at college teach you that—to play the
ghoul on every possible occasion, excavating old bones?
Why not let your great-grandmother rest in her grave?
MILDRED. (*Dreamily.*) With her pipe beside her—puff-
ing in Paradise.
AUNT. (*With spite.*) Yes, you are a natural born ghoul.
You are even getting to look like one, my dear.
MILDRED. (*In a passionless tone.*) I detest you, Aunt.

(*Looking at her critically.*) Do you know what you remind me of? Of a cold pork pudding against a background of linoleum tablecloth in the kitchen of a—but the possibilities are wearisome. (*She closes her eyes.*)

AUNT. (*With a bitter laugh.*) Merci for your candor. But since I am and must be your chaperon—in appearance, at least—let us patch up some sort of armed truce. For my part you are quite free to indulge any pose of eccentricity that beguiles you—as long as you observe the amenities——

MILDRED. (*Drawling.*) The inanities?

AUNT. (*Going on as if she hadn't heard.*) After exhausting the morbid thrills of social service work on New York's East Side—how they must have hated you, by the way, the poor that you made so much poorer in their own eyes!—you are now bent on making your slumming international. Well, I hope Whitechapel will provide the needed nerve tonic. Do not ask me to chaperon you there, however. I told your father I would not. I loathe deformity. We will hire an army of detectives and you may investigate everything—they allow you to see.

MILDRED. (*Protesting with a trace of genuine earnestness.*) Please do not mock at my attempts to discover how the other half lives. Give me some sort of groping sincerity in that at least. I would like to help them. I would like to be some use in the world. Is it my fault I don't know how? I would like to be sincere, to touch life somewhere. (*With weary bitterness.*) But I'm afraid I have neither the vitality nor integrity. All that was burnt out in our stock before I was born. Grandfather's blast furnaces, flaming to the sky, melting steel, making millions—then father keeping those home fires burning, making more millions—and little me at the tail-end of it all. I'm a waste product in the Bessemer process—like the millions. Or rather, I inherit the acquired trait of the by-product, wealth, but none of the energy, none of the strength of the steel that made it. I am sired by gold and damned by it, as they say at the race track—damned in more ways than one. (*She laughs mirthlessly.*)

AUNT. (*Unimpressed—superciliously.*) You seem to be going in for sincerity to-day. It isn't becoming to you, really—except as an obvious pose. Be as artificial as you are, I advise. There's a sort of sincerity in that, you know. And, after all, you must confess you like that better.

MILDRED. (*Again affected and bored.*) Yes, I suppose I do. Pardon me for my outburst. When a leopard complains of its spots, it must sound rather grotesque. (*In a mocking tone.*) Purr, little leopard. Purr, scratch, tear, kill, gorge yourself and be happy—only stay in the jungle where your spots are camouflage. In a cage they make you conspicuous.

AUNT. I don't know what you are talking about.

MILDRED. It would be rude to talk about anything to you. Let's just talk. (*She looks at her wrist watch.*) Well, thank goodness, it's about time for them to come for me. That ought to give me a new thrill, Aunt.

AUNT. (*Affectedly troubled.*) You don't mean to say you're really going? The dirt—the heat must be frightful——

MILDRED. Grandfather started as a puddler. I should have inherited an immunity to heat that would make a salamander shiver. It will be fun to put it to the test.

AUNT. But don't you have to have the captain's—or someone's—permission to visit the stokehole?

MILDRED. (*With a triumphant smile.*) I have it—both his and the chief engineer's. Oh, they didn't want to at first, in spite of my social service credentials. They didn't seem a bit anxious that I should investigate how the other half lives and works on a ship. So I had to tell them that my father, the president of Nazareth Steel, chairman of the board of directors of this line, had told me it would be all right.

AUNT. He didn't.

MILDRED. How naïve age makes one! But I said he did, Aunt. I even said he had given me a letter to them—which I had lost. And they were afraid to take the chance that I might be lying. (*Excitedly.*) So it's ho! for the stokehole. The second engineer is to escort me. (*Looking at her watch again.*) It's time. And here he comes, I think.

(*The* SECOND ENGINEER *enters. He is a husky, fine-looking man of thirty-five or so. He stops before the two and tips his cap, visibly embarrassed and ill-at-ease.*)

SECOND ENGINEER. Miss Douglas?

MILDRED. Yes. (*Throwing off her rugs and getting to her feet.*) Are we all ready to start?

SECOND ENGINEER. In just a second, ma'am. I'm waiting for the Fourth. He's coming along.

MILDRED. (*With a scornful smile.*) You don't care to shoulder this responsibility alone, is that it?

SECOND ENGINEER. (*Forcing a smile.*) Two are better than one. (*Disturbed by her eyes, glances out to sea—blurts out.*) A fine day we're having.

MILDRED. Is it?

SECOND ENGINEER. A nice warm breeze——

MILDRED. It feels cold to me.

SECOND ENGINEER. But it's hot enough in the sun——

MILDRED. Not hot enough for me. I don't like Nature. I was never athletic.

SECOND ENGINEER. (*Forcing a smile.*) Well, you'll find it hot enough where you're going.

MILDRED. Do you mean hell?

SECOND ENGINEER. (*Flabbergasted, decides to laugh.*) Ho-ho! No, I mean the stokehole.

MILDRED. My grandfather was a puddler. He played with boiling steel.

SECOND ENGINEER. (*All at sea—uneasily.*) It that so? Hum, you'll excuse me, ma'am, but are you intending to wear that dress?

MILDRED. Why not?

SECOND ENGINEER. You'll likely rub against oil and dirt. It can't be helped.

MILDRED. It doesn't matter. I have lots of white dresses.

SECOND ENGINEER. I have an old coat you might throw over——

MILDRED. I have fifty dresses like this. I will throw this one into the sea when I come back. That ought to wash it clean, don't you think?

SECOND ENGINEER. (*Doggedly.*) There's ladders to climb down that are none too clean—and dark alleyways——

MILDRED. I will wear this very dress and none other.

SECOND ENGINEER. No offense meant. It's none of my business. I was only warning you——

MILDRED. Warning? That sounds thrilling.

SECOND ENGINEER. (*Looking down the deck—with a sigh of relief.*) There's the Fourth now. He's waiting for us. If you'll come——

MILDRED. Go on. I'll follow you. (*He goes.* MILDRED *turns a mocking smile on her aunt.*) An oaf—but a handsome, virile oaf.

AUNT. (*Scornfully.*) Poser!

MILDRED. Take care. He said there were dark alley-ways——

AUNT. (*In the same tone.*) Poser!

MILDRED. (*Biting her lips angrily.*) You are right. But would that my millions were not so anemically chaste!

AUNT. Yes, for a fresh pose I have no doubt you would drag the name of Douglas in the gutter!

MILDRED. From which it sprang. Goodby, Aunt. Don't pray too hard that I may fall into the fiery furnace.

AUNT. Poser!

MILDRED. (*Viciously.*) Old hag! (*She slaps her aunt insultingly across the face and walks off, laughing gayly.*)

AUNT. (*Screams after her.*) I said poser!

(*Curtain.*)

Scene III

SCENE. The stokehole. In the rear, the dimly-outlined bulks of the furnaces and boilers. High overhead one hanging electric bulb sheds just enough light through the murky air laden with coal dust to pile up masses of shadows everywhere. A line of men, stripped to the waist, is before the furnace doors. They bend over, looking neither to right nor left, handling their shovels as if they were part of their bodies, with a strange, awkward, swinging rhythm. They use the shovels to throw open the furnace doors. Then from these fiery round holes in the black a flood of terrific light and heat pours full upon the men who are outlined in silhouette in the crouching, inhuman attitudes of chained gorillas. The men shovel with a rhythmic motion, swinging as on a pivot from the coal which lies in heaps on the floor behind to hurl it into the flaming mouths before them. There is a tumult of noise—the brazen clang of the furnace doors as they are flung open or slammed shut, the grating, teeth-gritting grind of steel against steel, of crunching coal. This clash of sounds stuns one's ears with its rending dissonance. But there is order in it, rhythm, a mechanical regulated recurrence, a tempo. And rising above all, making the air hum with the quiver of liberated energy, the roar of leaping flames in the furnaces, the monotonous throbbing beat of the engines.

As the curtain rises, the furnace doors are shut. The men are taking a breathing spell. One or two are arranging the coal behind them, pulling it into more accessible heaps. The others can be dimly made out leaning on their shovels in relaxed attitudes of exhaustion.

PADDY. (*From somewhere in the line—plaintively.*) Yerra, will this divil's own watch nivir end? Me back is broke. I'm destroyed entirely.

YANK. (*From the center of the line—with exuberant scorn.*) Aw, yuh make me sick! Lie down and croak, why don't yuh? Always beefin', dat's you! Say dis is a cinch! Dis was made for me! It's my meat, get me! (*A whistle is blown—a thin, shrill note from somewhere overhead in the darkness.* YANK *curses without resentment.*) Dere's de damn engineer crackin' de whip. He tinks we're loafin'.

PADDY. (*Vindictively.*) God stiffen him!

YANK. (*In an exultant tone of command.*) Come on, youse guys! Git into de game! She's gittin hungry! Pile some grub in her. Trow it into her belly! Come on now, all of youse! Open her up!

(*At this last all the men, who have followed his movements of getting into position, throw open their furnace doors with a deafening clang. The fiery light floods over their shoulders as they bend round for the coal. Rivulets of sooty sweat have traced maps on their backs. The enlarged muscles form bunches of high light and shadow.*)

YANK. (*Chanting a count as he shovels without seeming effort.*) One—two—tree—— (*His voice rising exultantly in the joy of battle.*) Dat's de stuff! Let her have it! All togedder now! Sling it into her! Let her ride! Shoot de piece now! Call de toin on her! Drive her into it! Feel her move! Watch her smoke! Speed, dat's her middle name! Give her coal, youse guys! Coal, dat's her booze! Drink it up, baby! Let's see yuh sprint! Dig in and gain a lap! Dere she go-o-es. (*This last in the chanting formula of the gallery gods at the six-day bike race. He slams his furnace door shut. The others do likewise with as much unison as their wearied bodies will permit. The effect is of one fiery eye after another being blotted out with a series of accompanying bangs.*)

PADDY. (*Groaning.*) Me back is broke. I'm bate out— bate——

(*There is a pause. Then the inexorable whistle sounds again from the dim regions above the electric light. There is a growl of cursing rage from all sides.*)

YANK. (*Shaking his fist upward—contemptuously.*) Take it easy dere, you! Who d'yuh tinks runnin' dis game, me or you? When I git ready, we move. Not before! When I git ready, get me!

VOICES. (*Approvingly.*) That's the stuff!

Yank tal him, py golly!

Yank ain't afeerd.

Goot poy, Yank!

Give him hell!

Tell 'im 'e's a bloody swine!

Bloody slave-driver!

YANK. (*Contemptuously.*) He ain't got no noive. He's yellow, get me? All de engineers is yellow. Dey got streaks a mile wide. Aw, to hell wit him! Let's move, youse guys. We had a rest. Come on, she needs it! Give her pep! It ain't for him. Him and his whistle, dey don't belong. But we belong, see! We gotter feed de baby! Come on! (*He turns and flings his furnace door open. They all follow his lead. At this instant the SECOND and FOURTH ENGINEERS enter from the darkness on the left with MILDRED between them. She starts, turns paler, her pose is crumbling, she shivers with fright in spite of the blazing heat, but forces herself to leave the ENGINEERS and take a few steps nearer the men. She is right behind YANK. All this happens quickly while the men have their backs turned.*)

YANK. Come on, youse guys! (*He is turning to get coal when the whistle sounds again in a peremptory, irritating note. This drives YANK into a sudden fury. While the other men have turned full around and stopped dumfounded by the spectacle of MILDRED standing there in her white dress, YANK does not turn far enough to see her. Besides, his head is thrown back, he blinks upward through the murk trying to find the owner of the whistle, he brandishes his shovel murderously over his head in one hand, pounding on his chest, gorilla-like, with the other, shouting.*) Toin off dat whistle! Come down outa dere, yuh yellow, brass-buttoned, Belfast bum, yuh! Come down and I'll knock yer brains out! Yuh lousy, stinkin', yellow mut of a Catholic-moiderin' bastard! Come down and I'll moider yuh! Pullin' dat whistle on me, huh? I'll show yuh! I'll crash yer skull in! I'll drive yer teet' down yer troat! I'll slam yer nose trou de back of yer head! I'll cut yer guts out for a nickel, yuh lousy boob, yuh dirty, crummy, muck-eatin' son of a

——(*Suddenly he becomes conscious of all the other men staring at something directly behind his back. He whirls defensively with a snarling, murderous growl, crouching to spring, his lips drawn back over his teeth, his small eyes gleaming ferociously. He sees* MILDRED, *like a white apparition in the full light from the open furnace doors. He glares into her eyes, turned to stone. As for her, during his speech she has listened, paralyzed with horror, terror, her whole personality crushed, beaten in, collapsed, by the terrific impact of this unknown, abysmal brutality, naked and shameless. As she looks at his gorilla face, as his eyes bore into hers, she utters a low, choking cry and shrinks away from him, putting both hands up before her eyes to shut out the sight of his face, to protect her own. This startles* YANK *to a reaction. His mouth falls open, his eyes grow bewildered.*)

MILDRED. (*About to faint—to the* ENGINEERS, *who now have her one by each arm—whimperingly.*) Take me away! Oh, the filthy beast! (*She faints. They carry her quickly back, disappearing in the darkness at the left, rear. An iron door clangs shut. Rage and bewildered fury rush back on* YANK. *He feels himself insulted in some unknown fashion in the very heart of his pride. He roars.*) God damn yuh! (*And hurls his shovel after them at the door which has just closed. It hits the steel bulkhead with a clang and falls clattering on the steel floor. From overhead the whistle sounds again in a long, angry, insistent command.*)

(*Curtain.*)

SCENE IV

SCENE. The firemen's forecastle. YANK'S watch has just come off duty and had dinner. Their faces and bodies shine from a soap and water scrubbing but around their eyes, where a hasty dousing does not touch, the coal dust sticks like black make-up, giving them a queer, sinister expression. YANK has not washed either face or body. He stands out in contrast to them, a blackened, brooding figure. He is seated forward on a bench in the exact attitude of Rodin's "The Thinker." The others, most of them smoking pipes, are staring at YANK half-apprehensively, as if fearing an outburst; half-amusedly, as if they saw a joke somewhere that tickled them.

VOICES. He ain't ate nothin'.
Py golly, a fallar gat to gat grub in him.

Divil a lie.

Yank feeda da fire, no feeda da face.

Ha-ha.

He ain't even washed hisself.

He's forgot.

Hey, Yank, you forgot to wash.

YANK. (*Sullenly.*) Forgot nothin'! To hell wit washin'.

VOICES. It'll stick to you.

It'll get under your skin.

Give yer the bleedin' itch, that's wot.

It makes spots on you—like a leopard.

Like a piebald nigger, you mean.

Better wash up, Yank.

You sleep better.

Wash up, Yank.

Wash up! Wash up!

YANK. (*Resentfully.*) Aw say, youse guys. Lemme alone. Can't youse see I'm tryin' to tink?

ALL. (*Repeating the word after him as one with cynical mockery.*) Think! (*The word has a brazen, metallic quality as if their throats were phonograph horns. It is followed by a chorus of hard, barking laughter.*)

YANK. (*Springing to his feet and glaring at them belligerently.*) Yes, tink! Tink, dat's what I said. What about it? (*They are silent, puzzled by his sudden resentment at what used to be one of his jokes.* YANK *sits down again in the same attitude of "The Thinker."*)

VOICES. Leave him alone.

He's got a grouch on.

Why wouldn't he?

PADDY. (*With a wink at the others.*) Sure I know what's the matther. 'Tis aisy to see. He's fallen in love, I'm telling you.

ALL. (*Repeating the word after him as one with cynical mockery.*) Love! (*The word has a brazen, metallic quality as if their throats were phonograph horns. It is followed by a chorus of hard, barking laughter.*)

YANK. (*With a contemptuous snort.*) Love, hell! Hate, dat's what. I've fallen in hate, get me?

PADDY. (*Philosophically.*) 'Twould take a wise man to tell one from the other. (*With a bitter, ironical scorn, increasing as he goes on.*) But I'm telling you it's love that's in it. Sure what else but love for us poor bastes in the stokehole would be bringing a fine lady, dressed like a white quane, down a mile of ladders and steps to be havin' a look at us?

(*A growl of anger goes up from all sides.*)

LONG. (*Jumping on a bench—hectically.*) Hinsultin' us! Hinsultin' us, the bloody cow! And them bloody engineers! What right 'as they got to be exhibitin' us 's if we was bleedin' monkeys in a menagerie? Did we sign for hinsults to our dignity as 'onest workers? Is that in the ship's articles? You kin bloody well bet it ain't! But I knows why they done it. I arsked a deck steward 'o she was and 'e told me. 'Er old man's a bleedin' millionaire, a bloody Capitalist! 'E's got enuf bloody gold to sink this bleedin' ship! 'E makes arf the bloody steel in the world! 'E owns this bloody boat! And you and me, Comrades, we're 'is slaves! And the skipper and mates and engineers, they're 'is slaves! And she's 'is bloody daughter and we're all 'er slaves, too! And she gives 'er orders as 'ow she wants to see the bloody animals below decks and down they takes 'er!

(*There is a roar of rage from all sides.*)

YANK. (*Blinking at him bewilderedly.*) Say! Wait a moment! Is all dat straight goods?

LONG. Straight as string! The bleedin' steward as waits on 'em, 'e told me about 'er. And what're we goin' ter do, I arsks yer? 'Ave we got ter swaller 'er hinsults like dogs? It ain't in the ship's articles. I tell yer we got a case. We kin go to law——

YANK. (*With abysmal contempt.*) Hell! Law!

ALL. (*Repeating the word after him as one with cynical mockery.*) Law! (*The word has a brazen metallic quality as if their throats were phonograph horns. It is followed by a chorus of hard, barking laughter.*)

LONG. (*Feeling the ground slipping from under his feet —desperately.*) As voters and citizens we kin force the bloody governments——

YANK. (*With abysmal contempt.*) Hell! Governments!

ALL. (*Repeating the word after him as one with cynical mockery.*) Governments! (*The word has a brazen metallic quality as if their throats were phonograph horns. It is followed by a chorus of hard, barking laughter.*)

LONG. (*Hysterically.*) We're free and equal in the sight of God——

YANK. (*With abysmal contempt.*) Hell! God!

ALL. (*Repeating the word after him as one with cynical mockery.*) God! (*The word has a brazen metallic quality as if their throats were phonograph horns. It is followed by a chorus of hard, barking laughter.*)

YANK. (*Witheringly.*) Aw, join de Salvation Army!

ALL. Sit down! Shut up! Damn fool! Sea-lawyer!

(LONG *slinks back out of sight.*)

PADDY. (*Continuing the trend of his thoughts as if he had never been interrupted—bitterly.*) And there she was standing behind us, and the Second pointing at us like a man you'd hear in a circus would be saying: In this cage is a queerer kind of baboon than ever you'd find in darkest Africy. We roast them in their own sweat—and be damned if you won't hear some of thim saying they like it! (*He glances scornfully at* YANK.)

YANK. (*With a bewildered uncertain growl.*) Aw!

PADDY. And there was Yank roarin' curses and turning round wid his shovel to brain her—and she looked at him, and him at her——

YANK. (*Slowly.*) She was all white. I thought she was a ghost. Sure.

PADDY. (*With heavy, biting sarcasm.*) 'Twas love at first sight, divil a doubt of it! If you'd seen the endearin' look on her pale mug when she shriveled away with her hands over her eyes to shut out the sight of him! Sure, 'twas as if she'd seen a great hairy ape escaped from the Zoo!

YANK. (*Stung—with a growl of rage.*) Aw!

PADDY. And the loving way Yank heaved his shovel at the skull of her, only she was out the door! (*A grin breaking over his face.*) 'Twas touching, I'm telling you! It put the touch of home, swate home in the stokehole.

(*There is a roar of laughter from all.*)

YANK. (*Glaring at* PADDY *menacingly.*) Aw, choke dat off, see!

PADDY. (*Not heeding him—to the others.*) And her grabbin' at the Second's arm for protection. (*With a grotesque imitation of a woman's voice.*) Kiss me, Engineer dear, for it's dark down here and me old man's in Wall Street making money! Hug me tight, darlin', for I'm afeerd in the dark and me mother's on deck makin' eyes at the skipper!

(*Another roar of laughter.*)

YANK. (*Threateningly.*) Say! What yuh tryin' to do, kid me, yuh old Harp?

PADDY. Divil a bit! Ain't I wishin' myself you'd brained her?

YANK. (*Fiercely.*) I'll brain her! I'll brain her yet, wait 'n' see! (*Coming over to* PADDY—*slowly.*) Say, is dat what she called me—a hairy ape?

PADDY. She looked it at you if she didn't say the word itself.

YANK. (*Grinning horribly.*) Hairy ape, huh? Sure! Dat's de way she looked at me, aw right. Hairy ape! So dat's me, huh? (*Bursting into rage—as if she were still in front of him.*) Yuh skinny tart! Yuh whitefaced bum, yuh! I'll show yuh who's a ape! (*Turning to the others, bewilderment seizing him again.*) Say, youse guys. I was bawlin' him out for pullin' de whistle on us. You heard me. And den I seen youse lookin' at somep'n and I thought he'd sneaked down to come up in back of me, and I hopped around to knock him dead wit de shovel. And dere she was wit de light on her! Christ, yuh coulda pushed me over with a finger! I was scared, get me? Sure! I tought she was a ghost, see? She was all in white like dey wrap around stiffs. You seen her. Kin yuh blame me? She didn't belong, dat's what. And den when I come to and seen it was a real skoit and seen de way she was lookin' at me— like Paddy said—Christ, I was sore, get me? I don't stand for dat stuff from nobody. And I flung de shovel—on'y she'd beat it. (*Furiously.*) I wished it'd banged her! I wished it'd knocked her block off!

LONG. And be 'anged for murder or 'lectrocuted? She ain't bleedin' well worth it.

YANK. I don't give a damn what! I'd be square wit her, wouldn't I? Tink I wanter let her put somep'n over on me? Tink I'm goin' to let her git away wit dat stuff? Yuh don't know me! No one ain't never put nothin' over on me and got away wit it, see!—not dat kind of stuff—no guy and no skoit neither! I'll fix her! Maybe she'll come down again——

VOICE. No chance, Yank. You scared her out of a year's growth.

YANK. I scared her? Why de hell should I scare her? Who de hell is she? Ain't she de same as me? Hairy ape, huh? (*With his old confident bravado.*) I'll show her I'm better'n her, if she on'y knew it. I belong and she don't, see! I move and she's dead! Twenty-five knots a hour, dat's me! Dat carries her but I make dat. She's on'y baggage. Sure! (*Again bewilderedly.*) But, Christ, she was funny lookin'! Did yuh pipe her hands? White and skinny. Yuh could see de bones trough 'em. And her mush, dat was dead white, too. And her eyes, dey was like dey'd seen a ghost. Me, dat was! Sure! Hairy ape! Ghost, huh? Look at dat arm! (*He extends his right arm, swelling out the great muscles.*) I coulda took her wit dat, wit just my little finger even, and broke her in two. (*Again bewilderedly.*) Say, who is dat skoit, huh? What is she? What's she come from? Who made her? Who give her de noive to look at me like dat? Dis ting's got my goat right. I don't get her. She's new to me. What does a skoit like her mean, huh? She don't belong, get me! I can't see her. (*With growing anger.*) But one ting I'm wise to, aw right, aw right! Youse all kin bet your shoits I'll get even wit her. I'll show her if she tinks she—— She grinds de organ and I'm on de string, huh? I'll fix her! Let her come down again and I'll fling her in de furnace! She'll move den! She won't shiver at nothin', den! Speed, dat'll be her! She'll belong den! (*He grins horribly.*)

PADDY. She'll never come. She's had her belly-full, I'm telling you. She'll be in bed now, I'm thinking, wid ten doctors and nurses feedin' her salts to clean the fear out of her.

YANK. (*Enraged.*) Yuh tink I made her sick, too, do yuh? Just lookin' at me, huh? Hairy ape, huh? (*In a frenzy of rage.*) I'll fix her! I'll tell her where to git off! She'll git down on her knees and take it back or I'll burst de face offen her! (*Shaking one fist upward and beating on his chest with the other.*) I'll find yuh! I'm comin', d'yuh hear? I'll fix yuh, God damn yuh! (*He makes a rush for the door.*)

VOICES. Stop him!
He'll get shot!
He'll murder her!
Trip him up!
Hold him!
He's gone crazy!
Gott, he's strong!

Hold him down!
Look out for a kick!
Pin his arms!

(*They have all piled on him and, after a fierce struggle, by sheer weight of numbers have borne him to the floor just inside the door.*)

PADDY. (*Who has remained detached.*) Kape him down till he's cooled off. (*Scornfully.*) Yerra, Yank, you're a great fool. Is it payin' attention at all you are to the like of that skinny sow widout one drop of rale blood in her?

YANK. (*Frenziedly, from the bottom of the heap.*) She done me doit! She done me doit, didn't she? I'll git square wit her! I'll git her some way! Git offen me, youse guys! Lemme up! I'll show her who's a ape!

(*Curtain.*)

Scene V

SCENE. Three weeks later. A corner of Fifth Avenue in the Fifties on a fine Sunday morning. A general atmosphere of clean, well-tidied, wide street; a flood of mellow, tempered sunshine; gentle, genteel breezes. In the rear, the show windows of two shops, a jewelry establishment on the corner, a furrier's next to it. Here the adornments of extreme wealth are tantalizingly displayed. The jeweler's window is gaudy with glittering diamonds, emeralds, rubies, pearls, etc., fashioned in ornate tiaras, crowns, necklaces, collars, etc. From each piece hangs an enormous tag from which a dollar sign and numerals in intermittent electric lights wink out the incredible prices. The same in the furrier's. Rich furs of all varieties hang there bathed in a downpour of artificial light. The general effect is of a background of magnificence cheapened and made grotesque by commercialism, a background in tawdry disharmony with the clear light and sunshine on the street itself.

Up the side street YANK and LONG come swaggering. LONG is dressed in shore clothes, wears a black Windsor tie, cloth cap. YANK is in his dirty dungarees. A fireman's cap with black peak is cocked defiantly on the side of his head. He has not shaved for days and around his fierce, resentful eyes—as around those of LONG to a lesser degree—the black smudge of coal dust still sticks like make-up. They hesitate and stand together at the corner, swaggering, looking about them with a forced, defiant contempt.

LONG. (*Indicating it all with an oratorical gesture.*) Well, 'ere we are. Fif' Avenoo. This 'ere's their bleedin' private lane, as yer might say. (*Bitterly.*) We're trespassers 'ere. Proletarians keep orf the grass!

YANK. (*Dully.*) I don't see no grass, yuh boob. (*Staring at the sidewalk.*) Clean, ain't it? Yuh could eat a fried egg offen it. The white wings got some job sweepin' dis up. (*Looking up and down the avenue—surlily.*) Where's all de white-collar stiffs yuh said was here—and de skoits —*her* kind?

LONG. In church, blarst 'em! Arskin' Jesus to give 'em more money.

YANK. Choich, huh? I useter go to choich onct—sure— when I was a kid. Me old man and woman, dey made me. Dey never went demselves, dough. Always got too big a head on Sunday mornin', dat was dem. (*With a grin.*) Dey was scrappers for fair, bot' of dem. On Satiday nights when dey bot' got a skinful dey could put up a bout oughter been staged at de Garden. When dey got trough dere wasn't a chair or table wit a leg under it. Or else dey bot' jumped on me for somep'n. Dat was where I loined to take punishment. (*With a grin and a swagger.*) I'm a chip offen de old block, get me?

LONG. Did yer old man follow the sea?

YANK. Naw. Worked along shore. I runned away when me old lady croaked wit de tremens. I helped at truckin' and in de market. Den I shipped in de stokehole. Sure. Dat belongs. De rest was nothin'. (*Looking around him.*) I ain't never seen dis before. De Brooklyn waterfront, dat was where I was dragged up. (*Taking a deep breath.*) Dis ain't so bad at dat, huh?

LONG. Not bad? Well, we pays for it wiv our bloody sweat, if yer wants to know!

YANK. (*With sudden angry disgust.*) Aw, hell! I don't see no one, see—like her. All dis gives me a pain. It don't belong. Say, ain't dere a back room around dis dump? Let's go shoot a ball. All dis is too clean and quiet and dolled-up, get me! It gives me a pain.

LONG. Wait and yer'll bloody well see——

YANK. I don't wait for no one. I keep on de move. Say, what yuh drag me up here for, anyway? Tryin' to kid me, yuh simp, yuh?

LONG. Yer wants to get back at 'er, don't yer? That's

what yer been sayin' every bloomin' hour since she hin-sulted yer.

YANK. (*Vehemently.*) Sure ting I do! Didn't I try to get even with her in Southampton? Didn't I sneak on de dock and wait for her by de gangplank? I was goin' to spit in her pale mug, see! Sure, right in her pop-eyes! Dat woulda made me even, see? But no chanct. Dere was a whole army of plain-clothes bulls around. Dey spotted me and gimme de bum's rush. I never seen her. But I'll git square wit her yet, you watch! (*Furiously.*) De lousy tart! She tinks she kin get away wit moider—but not wit me! I'll fix her! I'll tink of a way!

LONG. (*As disgusted as he dares to be.*) Ain't that why I brought yer up 'ere—to show yer? Yer been lookin' at this 'ere 'ole affair wrong. Yer been actin' an' talkin' 's if it was all a bleedin' personal matter between yer and that bloody cow. I wants to convince yer she was on'y a repre-sentative of 'er clarss. I wants to awaken yer bloody clarss consciousness. Then yer'll see it's 'er clarss yer've got to fight, not 'er alone. There's a 'ole mob of 'em like 'er, Gawd blind 'em!

YANK. (*Spitting on his hands—belligerently.*) De more de merrier when I gits started. Bring on de gang!

LONG. Yer'll see 'em in arf a mo', when that church lets out. (*He turns and sees the window display in the two stores for the first time.*) Blimey! Look at that, will yer? (*They both walk back and stand looking in the jeweler's. LONG flies into a fury.*) Just look at this 'ere bloomin' mess! Just look at it! Look at the bleedin' prices on 'em—more'n our 'ole bloody stokehole makes in ten voyages sweatin' in 'ell! And they—'er and 'er bloody clarss—buys 'em for toys to dangle on 'em! One of these 'ere would buy scoff for a starvin' family for a year!

YANK. Aw, cut de sob stuff! T' hell wit de starvin' family! Yuh'll be passin' de hat to me next. (*With naïve admira-tion.*) Say, dem tings is pretty, huh? Bet yuh dey'd hock for a piece of change aw right. (*Then turning away, bored.*) But, aw hell, what good are dey? Let her have 'em. Dey don't belong no more'n she does. (*With a gesture of sweeping the jewelers into oblivion.*) All dat don't count, get me?

LONG. (*Who has moved to the furrier's—indignantly.*) And I s'pose this 'ere don't count neither—skins of poor,

'armless animals slaughtered so as 'er and 'ers can keep
their bleedin' noses warm!

YANK. (*Who has been staring at something inside—with
queer excitement.*) Take a slant at dat! Give it de once-
over! Monkey fur—two t'ousand bucks! (*Bewilderedly.*)
Is dat straight goods—monkey fur? What de hell——?

LONG. (*Bitterly.*) It's straight enuf. (*With grim humor.*)
They wouldn't bloody well pay that for a 'airy ape's skin—
no, nor for the 'ole livin' ape with all 'is 'ead, and body,
and soul thrown in!

YANK. (*Clenching his fists, his face growing pale with
rage as if the skin in the window were a personal insult.*)
Trowin' it up in my face! Christ! I'll fix her!

LONG. (*Excitedly.*) Church is out. 'Ere they come, the
bleedin' swine. (*After a glance at* YANK'S *lowering face—
uneasily.*) Easy goes, Comrade. Keep yer bloomin' temper.
Remember force defeats itself. It ain't our weapon. We
must impress our demands through peaceful means—the
votes of the on-marching proletarians of the bloody world!

YANK. (*With abysmal contempt.*) Votes, hell! Votes is a
joke, see. Votes for women! Let dem do it!

LONG. (*Still more uneasily.*) Calm, now. Treat 'em wiv
the proper contempt. Observe the bleedin' parasites but 'old
yer 'orses.

YANK. (*Angrily.*) Git away from me! Yuh're yellow,
dat's what. Force, dat's me! De punch, dat's me every
time, see!

(*The crowd from church enter from the right, sauntering
slowly and affectedly, their heads held stiffly up, looking
neither to right nor left, talking in toneless, simpering
voices. The women are rouged, calcimined, dyed, over-
dressed to the nth degree. The men are in Prince Alberts,
high hats, spats, canes, etc. A procession of gaudy ma-
rionettes, yet with something of the relentless horror of
Frankensteins in their detached, mechanical unawareness.*)

VOICES. Dear Doctor Caiaphas! He is so sincere!

What was the sermon? I dozed off.

About the radicals, my dear—and the false doctrines that
are being preached.

We must organize a hundred per cent American bazaar.

And let everyone contribute one one-hundredth per cent of
their income tax.

What an original idea!

We can devote the proceeds to rehabilitating the veil of the temple.
But that has been done so many times.

YANK. (*Glaring from one to the other of them—with an insulting snort of scorn.*) Huh! Huh!

(*Without seeming to see him, they make wide detours to avoid the spot where he stands in the middle of the side-walk.*)

LONG. (*Frightenedly.*) Keep yer bloomin' mouth shut, I tells yer.

YANK. (*Viciously.*) G'wan! Tell it to Sweeney! (*He swaggers away and deliberately lurches into a top-hatted gentleman, then glares at him pugnaciously.*) Say, who d'yuh tink yuh're bumpin'? Tink yuh own de oith?

GENTLEMAN. (*Coldly and affectedly.*) I beg your pardon. (*He has not looked at* YANK *and passes on without a glance, leaving him bewildered.*)

LONG. (*Rushing up and grabbing* YANK'S *arm.*) 'Ere! Come away! This wasn't what I meant. Yer'll 'ave the bloody coppers down on us.

YANK. (*Savagely—giving him a push that sends him sprawling.*) G'wan!

LONG. (*Picks himself up—hysterically.*) I'll pop orf then. This ain't what I meant. And whatever 'appens, yer can't blame me. (*He slinks off left.*)

YANK. T' hell wit youse! (*He approaches a lady—with a vicious grin and a smirking wink.*) Hello, Kiddo. How's every little ting? Got anyting on for to-night? I know an old boiler down to de docks we kin crawl into. (*The lady stalks by without a look, without a change of pace.* YANK *turns to others—insultingly.*) Holy smokes, what a mug! Go hide yuhself before de horses shy at yuh. Gee, pipe de heine on dat one! Say, youse, yuh look like de stoin of a ferryboat. Paint and powder! All dolled up to kill! Yuh look like stiffs laid out for de boneyard! Aw, g'wan, de lot of youse! Yuh give me de eye-ache. Yuh don't belong, get me! Look at me, why don't youse dare? I belong, dat's me! (*Pointing to a skyscraper across the street which is in process of construction—with bravado.*) See dat building goin' up dere? See de steel work? Steel, dat's me! Youse guys live on it and tink yuh're somep'n. But I'm *in* it, see! I'm de hoistin' engine dat makes it go up! I'm it—de inside and bottom of it! Sure! I'm steel and steam and smoke and de rest of it! It moves—speed—twenty-five stories up —and me at de top and bottom—movin'! Youse simps don't move. Yuh're on'y dolls I winds up to see 'm spin. Yuh're de garbage, get me—de leavins—de ashes we dump over de side! Now, what 'a' yuh gotta say? (*But as they seem neither to see nor hear him, he flies into a fury.*) Bums! Pigs! Tarts! Bitches! (*He turns in a rage on the men, bumping viciously into them but not jarring them the least bit. Rather it is he who recoils after each collision. He keeps growling.*) Git off de oith! G'wan, yuh bum! Look where yuh're goin', can't yuh? Git outa here! Fight, why don't yuh? Put up yer mits! Don't be a dog! Fight or I'll knock yuh dead! (*But, without seeming to see him, they all answer with mechanical affected politeness.*) I beg your pardon. (*Then at a cry from one of the women, they all scurry to the furrier's window.*)

THE WOMAN. (*Ecstatically, with a gasp of delight.*) Monkey fur! (*The whole crowd of men and women chorus after her in the same tone of affected delight.*) Monkey fur!

YANK. (*With a jerk of his head back on his sholders, as if he had received a punch full in the face—raging.*) I see yuh, all in white! I see yuh, yuh white-faced tart, yuh! Hairy ape, huh? I'll hairy ape yuh! (*He bends down and grips at the street curbing as if to pluck it out and hurl it. Foiled in this, snarling with passion, he leaps to the lamp-post on the corner and tries to pull it up for a club. Just at that moment a bus is heard rumbling up. A fat, high-hatted, spatted gentleman runs out from the side street. He calls out plaintively.*) Bus! Bus! Stop there! (*And runs full tilt into the bending, straining* YANK, *who is bowled off his balance.*)

YANK. (*Seeing a fight—with the roar of joy as he springs to his feet.*) At last! Bus, huh? I'll bust yuh! (*He lets drive a terrific swing, his fist landing full on the fat gentleman's face. But the gentleman stands unmoved as if nothing had happened.*)

GENTLEMAN. I beg your pardon. (*Then irritably.*) You have made me lose my bus. (*He claps his hands and begins to scream:*) Officer! Officer!

(*Many police whistles shrill out on the instant and a whole platoon of policemen rush in on* YANK *from all sides. He tries to fight but is clubbed to the pavement and fallen*

upon. *The crowd at the window have not moved or noticed this disturbance. The clanging gong of the patrol wagon approaches with a clamoring din.*)
    (*Curtain.*)

SCENE VI

SCENE. Night of the following day. A row of cells in the prison on Blackwell's Island. The cells extend back diagonally from right front to left rear. They do not stop, but disappear in the dark background as if they ran on, numberless, into infinity. One electric bulb from the low ceiling of the narrow corridor sheds its light through the heavy steel bars of the cell at the extreme front and reveals part of the interior. YANK can be seen within, crouched on the edge of his cot in the attitude of Rodin's "The Thinker." His face is spotted with black and blue bruises. A blood-stained bandage is wrapped around his head.

YANK. (*Suddenly starting as if awakening from a dream, reaches out and shakes the bars—aloud to himself, wonderingly.*) Steel. Dis is the Zoo, huh? (*A burst of hard, barking laughter comes from the unseen occupants of the cells, runs back down the tier, and abruptly ceases.*)
    VOICES. (*Mockingly.*) The Zoo. That's a new name for this coop—a damn good name!
Steel, eh? You said a mouthful. This is the old iron house.
Who is that boob talkin'?
He's the bloke they brung in out of his head. The bulls had beat him up fierce.
    YANK (*Dully.*) I musta been dreamin'. I tought I was in a cage at de Zoo—but de apes don't talk, do dey?
    VOICES. (*With mocking laughter.*) You're in a cage aw right.
A coop!
A pen!
A sty!
A kennel! (*Hard laughter—a pause.*)
Say, guy! Who are you? No, never mind lying. What are you?
Yes, tell us your sad story. What's your game?
What did they jug yuh for?
    YANK. (*Dully.*) I was a fireman—stokin' on de liners. (*Then with sudden rage, rattling his cell bars.*) I'm a hairy

ape, get me? And I'll bust youse all in de jaw if yuh don't lay off kiddin' me.

VOICES. Huh! You're a hard boiled duck, ain't you! When you spit, it bounces! (*Laughter.*)

Aw, can it. He's a regular guy. Ain't you?

What did he say he was—a ape?

YANK. (*Defiantly.*) Sure ting! Ain't dat what youse all are—apes? (*A silence. Then a furious rattling of bars from down the corridor.*)

A VOICE. (*Thick with rage.*) I'll show yuh who's a ape, yuh bum!

VOICES. Ssshh! Nix!

Can de noise!

Piano!

You'll have the guard down on us!

YANK. (*Scornfully.*) De guard? Yuh mean de keeper, don't yuh? (*Angry exclamations from all the cells.*)

VOICE. (*Placatingly.*) Aw, don't pay no attention to him. He's off his nut from the beatin'-up he got. Say, you guy! We're waitin' to hear what they landed you for—or ain't yuh tellin'?

YANK. Sure, I'll tell youse. Sure! Why de hell not? On'y —youse won't get me. Nobody gets me but me, see? I started to tell de Judge and all he says was: "Toity days to tink it over." Tink it over! Christ, dat's all I been doin' for weeks! (*After a pause.*) I was tryin' to git even wit someone, see?—someone dat done me doit.

VOICES. (*Cynically.*) De old stuff, I bet. Your goil, huh?

Give yuh the double-cross, huh?

That's them every time!

Did yuh beat up de odder guy?

YANK. (*Disgustedly.*) Aw, yuh're all wrong! Sure dere was a skoit in it—but not what youse mean, not dat old tripe. Dis was a new kind of skoit. She was dolled up all in white—in de stokehole. I tought she was a ghost. Sure. (*A pause.*)

VOICES. (*Whispering.*) Gee, he's still nutty.

Let him rave. It's fun listenin'.

YANK. (*Unheeding—groping in his thoughts.*) Her hands —dey was skinny and white like dey wasn't real but painted on somep'n. Dere was a million miles from me to her—twenty-five knots a hour. She was like some dead

ting de cat brung in. Sure, dat's what. She didn't belong.
She belonged in de window of a toy store, or on de top of
a garbage can, see! Sure! (*He breaks out angrily.*) But
would yuh believe it, she had de noive to do me doit. She
lamped me like she was seein' somep'n broke loose from de
menagerie. Christ, yuh'd oughter seen her eyes! (*He rattles
the bars of his cell furiously.*) But I'll get back at her yet,
you watch! And if I can't find her I'll take it out on de
gang she runs wit. I'm wise to where dey hangs out now.
I'll show her who belongs! I'll show her who's in de move
and who ain't. You watch my smoke!

VOICES. (*Serious and joking.*) Dat's de talkin'!
Take her for all she's got!
What was this dame, anyway? Who was she, eh?

YANK. I dunno. First cabin stiff. Her old man's a millionaire, dey says—name of Douglas.

VOICES. Douglas? That's the president of the Steel Trust,
I bet.
Sure. I seen his mug in de papers.
He's filthy with dough.

VOICE. Hey, feller, take a tip from me. If you want to
get back at that dame, you better join the Wobblies. You'll
get some action then.

YANK. Wobblies? What de hell's dat?

VOICE. Ain't you ever heard of the I. W. W.?

YANK. Naw. What is it?

VOICE. A gang of blokes—a tough gang. I been readin'
about 'em to-day in the paper. The guard give me the
Sunday Times. There's a long spiel about 'em. It's from a
speech made in the Senate by a guy named Senator Queen.
(*He is in the cell next to* YANK's. *There is a rustling of
paper.*) Wait'll I see if I got light enough and I'll read you.
Listen. (*He reads:*) "There is a menace existing in this
country to-day which threatens the vitals of our fair Republic—as foul a menace against the very life-blood of the
American Eagle as was the foul conspiracy of Catiline
against the eagles of ancient Rome!"

VOICE. (*Disgustedly.*) Aw, hell! Tell him to salt de tail
of dat eagle!

VOICE. (*Reading:*) "I refer to that devil's brew of rascals,
jailbirds, murderers and cut-throats who libel all honest
workingmen by calling themselves the Industrial Workers

of the World; but in the light of their nefarious plots, I call them the Industrious *Wreckers* of the World!"

YANK. (*With vengeful satisfaction.*) Wreckers, dat's de right dope! Dat belongs! Me for dem!

VOICE. Ssshh! (*Reading:*) "This fiendish organization is a foul ulcer on the fair body of our Democracy——"

VOICE. Democracy, hell! Give him the boid, fellers—the raspberry! (*They do.*)

VOICE. Ssshh! (*Reading:*) "Like Cato I say to this Senate, the I. W. W. must be destroyed! For they represent an ever-present dagger pointed at the heart of the greatest nation the world has even known, where all men are born free and equal, with equal opportunities to all, where the Founding Fathers have guaranteed to each one happiness, where Truth, Honor, Liberty, Justice, and the Brotherhood of Man are a religion absorbed with one's mother's milk, taught at our father's knee, sealed, signed, and stamped upon in the glorious Constitution of these United States!" (*A perfect storm of hisses, catcalls, boos, and hard laughter.*)

VOICES. (*Scornfully.*) Hurrah for de Fort' of July!
Pass de hat!
Liberty!
Justice!
Honor!
Opportunity!
Brotherhood!

ALL. (*With abysmal scorn.*) Aw, hell!

VOICE. Give that Queen Senator guy the bark! All toged-der now—one—two—tree—— (*A terrific chorus of barking and yapping.*)

GUARD. (*From a distance.*) Quiet there, youse—or I'll git the hose. (*The noise subsides.*)

YANK. (*With growling rage.*) I'd like to catch that Senatoi guy alone for a second. I'd loin him some trute!

VOICE. Ssshh! Here's where he gits down to cases on the Wobblies. (*Reads:*) "They plot with fire in one hand and dynamite in the other. They stop not before murder to gain their ends, nor at the outraging of defenseless woman-hood. They would tear down society, put the lowest scum in the seats of the mighty, turn Almighty God's revealed plan for the world topsy-turvy, and make of our sweet and lovely civilization a shambles, a desolation where man,

God's masterpiece, would soon degenerate back to the ape!"

VOICE. (*To* YANK.) Hey, you guy. There's your ape stuff again.

YANK. (*With a growl of fury.*) I got him. So dey blow up tings, do dey? Dey turn tings round, do dey? Hey, lend me dat paper, will yuh?

VOICE. Sure. Give it to him. On'y keep it to yourself, see. We don't wanter listen to no more of that slop.

VOICE. Here you are. Hide it under your mattress.

YANK. (*Reaching out.*) Tanks. I can't read much but I kin manage. (*He sits, the paper in the hand at his side, in the attitude of Rodin's "The Thinker." A pause. Several snores from down the corridor. Suddenly* YANK *jumps to his feet with a furious groan as if some appalling thought had crashed on him—bewilderedly.*) Sure—her old man—president of de Steel Trust—makes half de steel in de world—steel—where I tought I belonged—drivin' trou—movin'—in dat—to make *her*—and cage me in for her to spit on! Christ! (*He shakes the bars of his cell door till the whole tier trembles. Irritated, protesting exclamations from those awakened or trying to get to sleep.*) He made dis—dis cage! Steel! *It* don't belong, dat's what! Cages, cells, locks, bolts, bars—dat's what it means!—holdin' me down wit him at de top! But I'll drive trou! Fire, dat melts it! I'll be fire—under de heap—fire dat never goes out—hot as hell—breakin' out in de night—— (*While he has been saying this last he has shaken his cell door to a clanging accompaniment. As he comes to the "breakin' out" he seizes one bar with both hands and, putting his two feet up against the others so that his position is parallel to the floor like a monkey's, he gives a great wrench backwards. The bar bends like a licorice stick under his tremendous strength. Just at this moment the* PRISON GUARD *rushes in, dragging a hose behind him.*)

GUARD. (*Angrily.*) I'll loin youse bums to wake me up! (*Sees* YANK.) Hello, it's you, huh? Got the D. Ts., hey? Well, I'll cure 'em. I'll drown your snakes for yuh! (*Noticing the bar.*) Hell, look at dat bar bended! On'y a bug is strong enough for dat!

YANK. (*Glaring at him.*) Or a hairy ape, yuh big yellow bum! Look out! Here I come! (*He grabs another bar.*)

GUARD. (*Scared now—yelling off left.*) Toin de hose on,

Ben!—full pressure! And call de others—and a straitjacket! (*The curtain is falling. As it hides* YANK *from view, there is a splattering smash as the stream of water hits the steel of* YANK'S *cell.*)

(*Curtain.*)

SCENE VII

SCENE. Nearly a month later. An I. W. W. local near the waterfront, showing the interior of a front room on the ground floor, and the street outside. Moonlight on the narrow street, buildings massed in black shadow. The interior of the room, which is general assembly room, office, and reading-room, resembles some dingy settlement boys' club. A desk and high stool are in one corner. A table with papers, stacks of pamphlets, chairs about it, is at center. The whole is decidedly cheap, banal, commonplace, and unmysterious as a room could well be. The secretary is perched on the stool making entries in a large ledger. An eye shade casts his face into shadows. Eight or ten men, longshoremen, iron workers, and the like, are grouped about the table. Two are playing checkers. One is writing a letter. Most of them are smoking pipes. A big signboard is on the wall at the rear, "Industrial Workers of the World— Local No. 57."

(YANK *comes down the street outside. He is dressed as in Scene Five. He moves cautiously, mysteriously. He comes to a point opposite the door; tiptoes softly up to it, listens, is impressed by the silence within, knocks carefully, as if he were guessing at the password to some secret rite. Listens. No answer. Knocks again a bit louder. No answer. Knocks impatiently, much louder.*)

SECRETARY. (*Turning around on his stool.*) What the hell is that—someone knocking? (*Shouts.*) Come in, why don't you? (*All the men in the room look up.* YANK *opens the door slowly, gingerly, as if afraid of an ambush. He looks around for secret doors, mystery, is taken aback by the commonplaceness of the room and the men in it, thinks he may have gotten in the wrong place, then sees the signboard on the wall and is reassured.*)

YANK. (*Blurts out.*) Hello.

MEN. (*Reservedly.*) Hello.

YANK. (*More easily.*) I tought I'd bumped into de wrong dump.

SECRETARY. (*Scrutinizing him carefully.*) Maybe you have. Are you a member?

YANK. Naw, not yet. Dat's what I come for—to join.

SECRETARY. That's easy. What's your job—longshore?

YANK. Naw. Fireman—stoker on de liners.

SECRETARY. (*With satisfaction.*) Welcome to our city. Glad to know you people are waking up at last. We haven't got many members in your line.

YANK. Naw. De're all dead to de woild.

SECRETARY. Well, you can help to wake 'em. What's your name? I'll make out your card.

YANK. (*Confused.*) Name? Lemme tink.

SECRETARY. (*Sharply.*) Don't you know your own name?

YANK. Sure; but I been just Yank for so long—Bob, dat's it—Bob Smith.

SECRETARY. (*Writing.*) Robert Smith. (*Fills out the rest of card.*) Here you are. Cost you half a dollar.

YANK. Is dat all—four bits? Dat's easy. (*Gives the Secretary the money.*)

SECRETARY. (*Throwing it in drawer.*) Thanks. Well, make yourself at home. No introductions needed. There's literature on the table. Take some of those pamphlets with you to distribute aboard ship. They may bring results. Sow the seed, only go about it right. Don't get caught and fired. We got plenty out of work. What we need is men who can hold their jobs—and work for us at the same time.

YANK. Sure. (*But he still stands, embarrassed and uneasy.*)

SECRETARY. (*Looking at him—curiously.*) What did you knock for? Think we had a coon in uniform to open doors?

YANK. Naw. I tought it was locked—and dat yuh'd wanter give me the once-over trou a peep-hole or somep'n to see if I was right.

SECRETARY. (*Alert and suspicious but with an easy laugh.*) Think we were running a crap game? That door is never locked. What put that in your nut?

YANK. (*With a knowing grin, convinced that this is all camouflage, a part of the secrecy.*) Dis burg is full of bulls, ain't it?

SECRETARY. (*Sharply.*) What have the cops to do with us? We're breaking no laws.

YANK. (*With a knowing wink.*) Sure. Youse wouldn't for woilds. Sure. I'm wise to dat.

SECRETARY. You seem to be wise to a lot of stuff none of us knows about.

YANK. (*With another wink.*) Aw, dat's aw right, see. (*Then made a bit resentful by the suspicious glances from all sides.*) Aw, can it! Youse needn't put me trou de toid degree. Can't youse see I belong? Sure! I'm reg'lar. I'll stick, get me? I'll shoot de woiks for youse. Dat's why I wanted to join in.

SECRETARY. (*Breezily, feeling him out.*) That's the right spirit. Only are you sure you understand what you've joined? It's all plain and above board; still, some guys get ʻ wrong slant on us. (*Sharply.*) What's your notion of the purpose of the I. W. W.?

YANK. Aw, I know all about it.

SECRETARY. (*Sarcastically.*) Well, give us some of your valuable information.

YANK. (*Cunningly.*) I know enough not to speak outa my toin. (*Then, resentfully again.*) Aw, say! I'm reg'lar. I'm wise to de game. I know yuh got to watch your step wit a stranger. For all youse know, I might be a plain-clothes dick, or somep'n, dat's what yuh're tinkin', huh? Aw, forget it! I belong, see? Ask any guy down to de docks if I don't.

SECRETARY. Who said you didn't?

YANK. After I'm 'nitiated, I'll show yuh.

SECRETARY. (*Astounded.*) Initiated? There's no initiation.

YANK. (*Disappointed.*) Ain't there no password—no grip nor nothin'?

SECRETARY. What'd you think this is—the Elks—or the Black Hand?

YANK. De Elks, hell! De Black Hand, dey're a lot of yellow backstickin' Ginees. Naw. Dis is a man's gang, ain't it?

SECRETARY. You said it! That's why we stand on our two feet in the open. We got no secrets.

YANK. (*Surprised but admiringly.*) Yuh mean to say yuh always run wide open—like dis?

SECRETARY. Exactly.

YANK. Den yuh sure got your noive wit youse!

SECRETARY. (*Sharply.*) Just what was it made you want to join us? Come out with that straight.

YANK. Yuh call me? Well, I got noive, too! Here's my

hand. Yuh wanter blow tings up, don't yuh? Well, dat's me! I belong!

SECRETARY. (*With pretended carelessness.*) You mean change the unequal conditions of society by legitimate direct action—or with dynamite?

YANK. Dynamite! Blow it offen de oith—steel—all de cages—all de factories, steamers, buildings, jails—de Steel Trust and all dat makes it go.

SECRETARY. So—that's your idea, eh? And did you have any special job in that line you wanted to propose to us? (*He makes a sign to the men, who get up cautiously one by one and group behind* YANK.)

YANK. (*Boldly.*) Sure, I'll come out wit it. I'll show youse I'm one of de gang. Dere's dat millionaire guy, Doug-las——

SECRETARY. President of the Steel Trust, you mean? Do you want to assassinate him?

YANK. Naw, dat don't get you nothin'. I mean blow up de factory, de woiks, where he makes de steel. Dat's what I'm after—to blow up de steel, knock all de steel in de woild up to de moon. Dat'll fix tings! (*Eagerly, with a touch of bravado.*) I'll do it by me lonesome! I'll show yuh! Tell me where his woiks is, how to git there, all de dope. Gimme de stuff, de old butter—and watch me do de rest! Watch de smoke and see it move! I don't give a damn if dey nab me—as long as it's done! I'll soive life for it— and give 'em de laugh! (*Half to himself.*) And I'll write her a letter and tell her de hairy ape done it. Dat'll square tings.

SECRETARY. (*Stepping away from* YANK.) Very inter-esting. (*He gives a signal. The men, huskies all, throw themselves on* YANK *and before he knows it they have his legs and arms pinioned. But he is too flabbergasted to make a struggle, anyway. They feel him over for weapons.*)

MAN. No gat, no knife. Shall we give him what's what and put the boots to him?

SECRETARY. No. He isn't worth the trouble we'd get into. He's too stupid. (*He comes closer and laughs mock-ingly in* YANK'S *face.*) Ho-ho! By God, this is the biggest joke they've put up on us yet. Hey, you Joke! Who sent you—Burns or Pinkerton? No, by God, you're such a bonehead I'll bet you're in the Secret Service! Well, you dirty spy, you rotten agent provocator, you can go back and tell whatever skunk is paying you blood-money for betraying your brothers that he's wasting his coin. You couldn't catch a cold. And tell him that all he'll ever get on us, or ever has got, is just his own sneaking plots that he's framed up to put us in jail. We are what our manifesto says we are, neither more nor less—and we'll give him a copy of that any time he calls. And as for you—— (*He glares scornfully at* YANK, *who is sunk in an oblivious stupor.*) Oh hell, what's the use of talking? You're a brainless ape.

YANK. (*Aroused by the word to fierce but futile struggles.*) What's dat, yuh Sheeny bum, yuh!

SECRETARY. Throw him out, boys. (*In spite of his struggles, this is done with gusto and éclat. Propelled by several parting kicks,* YANK *lands sprawling in the middle of the narrow cobbled street. With a growl he starts to get up and storm the closed door, but stops bewildered by the confusion in his brain, pathetically impotent. He sits there, brooding, in as near to the attitude of Rodin's "Thinker" as he can get in his position.*)

YANK. (*Bitterly.*) So dem boids don't tink I belong, neider. Aw, to hell wit 'em! Dey're in de wrong pew—de same old bull—soapboxes and Salvation Army—no guts! Cut out an hour offen de job a day and make me happy! Gimme a dollar more a day and make me happy! Tree square a day, and cauliflowers in de front yard—ekal rights—a woman and kids—a lousy vote—and I'm all fixed for Jesus, huh? Aw, hell! What does dat get yuh? Dis ting's in your inside, but it ain't your belly. Feedin' your face—sinkers and coffee—dat don't touch it. It's way down—at de bottom. Yuh can't grab it, and yuh can't stop it. It moves, and everything moves. It stops and de whole woild stops. Dat's me now—I don't tick, see?—I'm a busted Ingersoll, dat's what. Steel was me, and I owned de woild. Now I ain't steel, and de woild owns me. Aw, hell! I can't see—it's all dark, get me? It's all wrong! (*He turns a bitter mocking face up like an ape gibbering at the moon.*) Say, youse up dere, Man in de Moon, yuh look so wise, gimme de answer, huh? Slip me de inside dope, de information right from de stable—where do I get off at, huh?

A POLICEMAN. (*Who has come up the street in time to hear this last—with grim humor.*) You'll get off at the station, you boob, if you don't get up out of that and keep movin'.

YANK. (*Looking up at him—with a hard, bitter laugh.*) Sure! Lock me up! Put me in a cage! Dat's de on'y answer yuh know. G'wan, lock me up!

POLICEMAN. What you been doin'?

YANK. Enuf to gimme life for! I was born, see? Sure, dat's de charge. Write it in de blotter. I was born, get me!

POLICEMAN. (*Jocosely.*) God pity your old woman! (*Then matter-of-fact.*) But I've no time for kidding. You're soused. I'd run you in but it's too long a walk to the station. Come on now, get up, or I'll fan your ears with this club. Beat it now! (*He hauls* YANK *to his feet.*)

YANK. (*In a vague mocking tone.*) Say, where do I go from here?

POLICEMAN. (*Giving him a push—with a grin, indifferently.*) Go to hell.

(*Curtain.*)

SCENE VIII

SCENE. Twilight of the next day. The monkey house at the Zoo. One spot of clear gray light falls on the front of one cage so that the interior can be seen. The other cages are vague, shrouded in shadow from which chatterings pitched in a conversational tone can be heard. On the one cage a sign from which the word "Gorilla" stands out. The gigantic animal himself is seen squatting on his haunches on a bench in much the same attitude as Rodin's "Thinker." Yank enters from the left. Immediately a chorus of angry chattering and screeching breaks out. The gorilla turns his eyes but makes no sound or move.

YANK. (*With a hard, bitter laugh.*) Welcome to your city, huh? Hail, hail, de gang's all here! (*At the sound of his voice the chattering dies away into an attentive silence.* YANK *walks up to the gorilla's cage and, leaning over the railing, stares in at its occupant, who stares back at him, silent and motionless. There is a pause of dead stillness. Then* YANK *begins to talk in a friendly confidential tone, half-mockingly, but with a deep undercurrent of sympathy.*) Say, yuh're some hard-lookin' guy, ain't yuh? I seen lots of tough nuts dat de gang called gorillas, but yuh're de foist real one I ever seen. Some chest yuh got, and shoulders, and dem arms and mits! I bet yuh got a punch in eider fist dat'd knock 'em all silly! (*This with genuine admiration. The gorilla, as if he understood, stands upright, swelling out his chest and pounding on it with his fist.* YANK *grins sympathetically.*) Sure, I get yuh. Yuh challenge de whole woild, huh? Yuh got what I was sayin' even if yuh muffed de woids. (*Then bitterness creeping in.*) And why wouldn't yuh get me? Ain't we both members of de same club—de Hairy Apes? (*They stare at each other —a pause—then* YANK *goes on slowly and bitterly.*) So yuh're what she seen when she looked at me, de white-faced tart! I was you to her, get me? On'y outa de cage— broke out—free to moider her, see? Sure! Dat's what she tought. She wasn't wise dat I was in a cage, too—worser'n yours—sure—a damn sight—'cause you got some chanct to bust loose—but me—— (*He grows confused.*) Aw, hell! It's all wrong, ain't it? (*A pause.*) I s'pose yuh wanter know what I'm doin' here, huh? I been warmin' a bench down to de Battery—ever since last night. Sure. I seen de sun come up. Dat was pretty, too—all red and pink and green. I was lookin' at de skyscrapers—steel—and all de ships comin' in, sailin' out, all over de oith—and dey was steel, too. De sun was warm, dey wasn't no clouds, and dere was breeze blowin'. Sure, it was great stuff. I got it aw right— what Paddy said about dat bein' de right dope—on'y I couldn't get *in* it, see? I couldn't belong in dat. It was over my head. And I kept tinkin'—and den I beat it up here to see what youse was like. And I waited till dey was all gone to git yuh alone. Say, how d'yuh feel sittin' in dat pen all de time, havin' to stand for 'em comin' and starin' at yuh —de white-faced, skinny tarts and de boobs what marry 'em—makin' fun of yuh, laughin' at yuh, gittin' scared of yuh—damn 'em! (*He pounds on the rail with his fist. The gorilla rattles the bars of his cage and snarls. All the other monkeys set up an angry chattering in the darkness.* YANK *goes on excitedly.*) Sure! Dat's de way it hits me, too. On'y yuh're lucky, see? Yuh don't belong wit 'em and yuh know it. But me, I belong wit 'em—but I don't, see? Dey don't belong wit me, dat's what. Get me? Tinkin' is hard— (*He passes one hand across his forehead with a painful gesture. The gorilla growls impatiently.* YANK *goes on gropingly.*) It's dis way, what I'm drivin' at. Youse can sit and dope dream in de past, green woods, de jungle and de rest of it. Den yuh belong and dey don't. Den yuh kin

laugh at 'em, see? Yuh're de champ of de woild. But me
—I ain't got no past to tink in, nor nothin' dat's comin',
on'y what's now—and dat don't belong. Sure, you're de
best off! Yuh can't tink, can yuh? Yuh can't talk neider.
But I kin make a bluff at talkin' and tinkin'—a'most git
away wit it—a'most!—and dat's where de joker comes in.
(*He laughs.*) I ain't on oith and I ain't in heaven, get me?
I'm in de middle tryin' to separate 'em, takin' all de woist
punches from bot' of 'em. Maybe dat's what dey call hell,
huh? But you, yuh're at de bottom. You belong! Sure!
Yuh're de on'y one in de woild dat does, yuh lucky stiff!
(*The gorilla growls proudly.*) And dat's why dey gotter put
yuh in a cage, see? (*The gorilla roars angrily.*) Sure! Yuh
get me. It beats it when you try to tink it or talk it—it's
way down—deep—behind—you 'n' me we feel it. Sure!
Bot's members of dis club! (*He laughs—then in a savage
tone.*) What de hell! T' hell wit it! A little action, dat's our
meat! Dat belongs! Knock 'em down and keep bustin' 'em
till dey croaks yuh wit a gat—wit steel! Sure! Are yuh
game? Dey've looked at youse, ain't dey—in a cage?
Wanter git even? Wanter wind up like a sport 'stead of
croakin' slow in dere? (*The gorilla roars an emphatic affirmative,* YANK *goes on with a sort of furious exaltation.*)
Sure! Yuh're reg'lar! Yuh'll stick to de finish! Me 'n' you,
huh?—bot' members of this club! We'll put up one last
star bout dat'll knock 'em offen deir seats! Dey'll have to
make de cages stronger after we're trou! (*The gorilla is
straining at his bars, growling, hopping from one foot to
the other.* YANK *takes a jimmy from under his coat and
forces the lock on the cage door. He throws this open.*)
Pardon from de governor! Step out and shake hands. I'll
take yuh for a walk down Fif' Avenoo. We'll knock 'em
offen de oith and croak wit de band playin'. Come on,
Brother. (*The gorilla scrambles gingerly out of his cage.
Goes to* YANK *and stands looking at him.* YANK *keeps his
mocking tone—holds out his hand.*) Shake—de secret grip
of our order. (*Something, the tone of mockery, perhaps,
suddenly enrages the animal. With a spring he wraps his
huge arms around* YANK *in a murderous hug. There is a
crackling snap of crushed ribs—a gasping cry, still mocking, from* YANK.) Hey, I didn't say kiss me! (*The gorilla
lets the crushed body slip to the floor; stands over it uncer-
tainly, considering; then picks it up, throws it in the cage,*

*shuts the door and shuffles off menacingly into the dark-
ness at left. A great uproar of frightened chattering and
whimpering comes from the other cages. Then* YANK *moves,
groaning, opening his eyes, and there is silence. He mutters
painfully.*) Say—dey oughter match him—wit Zybszko. He
got me, aw right. I'm trou. Even him didn't tink I belonged. (*Then, with sudden passionate despair.*) Christ,
where do I get off at? Where do I fit in? (*Checking himself
as suddenly.*) Aw, what de hell! No squawkin', see! No
quittin', get me! Croak wit your boots on! (*He grabs hold
of the bars of the cage and hauls himself painfully to his
feet—looks around him bewilderedly—forces a mocking
laugh.*) In de cage, huh? (*In the strident tones of a circus
barker.*) Ladies and gents, step forward and take a slant
at de one and only—(*His voice weakening.*)—one and
original—Hairy Ape from de wilds of—— (*He slips in a
heap on the floor and dies. The monkeys set up a chattering, whimpering wail. And, perhaps, the Hairy Ape at last
belongs.*)

(*Curtain.*)

1922

CRITICAL VOICES

Critical voices after World War I all acknowledge the death of an era. Mostly, the tone was experimental. The cynicism was cheap, but the disillusionment was something else again. As Victorian attitudes, proprieties, and gods died under the shells of the German seventy-sevens, the disgust with all the shams of the world that supposedly was going out led to excitement about the possibilities of the world that supposedly was coming in. The excitement, like the cynicism, often was cheap, but the voices of Hemingway, Faulkner, Eliot, Fitzgerald, and the working expatriates sounded new notes whose genuineness transcended the melodramatic or silly or "interested" noises made by the attitudinizing Americans who swarmed aboard the transatlantic steamers to "do" the left bank of the Seine.

In every form and genre the arts burgeoned in fantastic and fascinating experiment, much of it falling into the trashcan reserved for the brummagem of man's creative instincts. What was good transformed Western culture. Yet not all voices were those of experiment, of naturalism, of symbolism, of expressionism, dadaism, surrealism, mysticism, verticalism. The "New Humanists," for example, expressing the reaction, demanded a return to classical clarity and decorum. Their temperamental heirs, the "New Critics," warring (under the early leadership of T. E. Hulme) with the romanticism that was the central impulse of the "experimental sensibility," took exception to the more lenient accommodation of various kinds of literature afforded by critical eclectics.

Simply, the postwar era concentrated into one creative burst the various and differing American critical attitudes which had existed before and which still exist today. Not all the samples included here are confined to that era.

One good example of the postwar defiant excitement and experimentalism was provided by Eugene Jolas's little magazine, *transition* (1927–1938). Eugene Jolas (1894–1952) was more a European than an American: his parents were immigrants from Lorraine and returned there with him when he was two years old. He remained in Europe until he was sixteen, when he returned to America for ten years; from 1921 on he spent his time alternately on the two continents. Given such a background, Jolas was at home in the culture of various Western nations, and with his friend, the American novelist Elliot Paul, he founded *transition* in Paris in an attempt to bring together the writings of international postwar experimentalism. He is included here not because he is a well-known figure, but because his "Manifesto: The Revolution of the Word" is an excellent brief example of the rebellious literary attitudes of the time. Moreover, the dicta of the "Manifesto" lie behind much of modern literature. Appearing in *transition*, number 16–17, it was signed by Kay Boyle, Whit Burnett, Hart Crane, Caresse Crosby, Harry Crosby, Martha Foley, Stuart Gilbert, A. L. Gillespie, Leigh Hoffman, Eugene Jolas, Elliot Paul, Douglas Rigby, Theo Rutra, Robert Sage, Harold J. Salemson, and Laurence Vail.

During the 1920's, the reaction to both a naturalism that saw man trapped in various determinisms and to a romanticism that insisted upon free vent for the passions was led by Irving Babbitt (1865–1933), the acknowledged chief and most formidable of the "New Humanists." Babbitt took his ideas from his great love and knowledge of classical language and literature. Born in Dayton, Ohio, he moved around the country with his family, attended Harvard for his B. A. and M. A. degrees, and studied at the Sorbonne, specializing in Classics and Oriental studies. After teaching in Montana and at Williams College, he became a professor of French and comparative literature at Harvard, where he attracted serious young men who were fascinated by his courses in critical theory and intellectual history.

Babbitt felt that man, through decorum, restraint, discipline, and moderation, could will a control over the romantic, passional impulses, as well as over the seemingly determining circumstances of existence. The laws for man, through will, could have a spiritual fullness that made them different from the laws for things. The modern world, in losing decorum and spirituality, was becoming debased; its literature was becoming unprofound and coarse, emphasizing man's lower nature; its criticism was becoming impressionistic and vague, losing its evaluative usefulness. Supported by such men as Norman Foerster, Paul Elmer More, Harry Haydn Clark, and Stuart Pratt Sherman—most of whom were professors of literature—Babbitt became the center of a raging controversy. Many of the new voices in the arts saw the New Humanism as a recrudescence of a Victorian gentility that was dead but yet to be buried, and the claims of Babbitt had a corpse-stench of reaction in their nostrils. Sinclair Lewis, for instance, complained that American professors liked "their literature clear and cold and pure and very dead." While the controversy often created more heat than light—each "side" often not understanding the other— Babbitt, with his great learning and pedagogic effectiveness, exerted a wide and subtle influence through students as different as Van Wyck Brooks and T. S. Eliot.

His books include *Literature and the American College* (1908), *The New Laokoön* (1910), *The Masters of Modern French Criticism* (1912), *Rousseau and Romanticism* (1919), *Democracy and Leadership* (1924), *On Being Creative* (1932), and *Spanish Character* (1940). Studies of the man and his work are to be found in T. S. Eliot, "The Humanism of Irving Babbitt, *Forum*, LXXX (1928); E. Wilson, "Notes on Babbitt and More," *New Republic*, LXII (1930); E. Wilson, "Sophocles, Babbitt, and Freud," *New Republic*, LXV (1930); F. E. McMahon, *The Humanism of Irving Babbitt* (1931); J. L. Adams, "Humanism and Creation," *Hound and Horn*, VI (1932); P. E. More, "Irving Babbitt," *American Review*, III (1934); G. R. Elliott, "T. S. Eliot and Irving Babbitt," *American Review*, VII (1936); F. Leander, *Humanism and Naturalism* (1937); R. P. Blackmur, "Humanism and Symbolic Imagination," *Southern Review*, VII (1941); F. Manchester and O. Shepard, *Irving Babbitt: Man and Teacher* (1941); R. Kirk, "The Conservative Humanism of Irving Babbitt," *Prairie Schooner*, XXVI (1952); L. Mercier "Was Irving Babbitt a Naturalist?" *New Scholasticism*, XXVII (1953); F. Leander, "Irving Babbitt and the Aestheticians," *Modern Age*, IV (1960); R. Wellek, "Irving Babbitt, Paul More, and Transcendentalism," in M. Simon and T. Parsons, eds., *Transcendentalism and Its Legacy* (1966).

As Babbitt was the leader of the humanists, Henry Louis Mencken (1880–1956) was the most boisterous figure of the gleeful and gusty irreverence that the humanists attacked. Born in Baltimore, he was graduated in 1896 from the Baltimore Polytechnic Institute and went unenthusiastically to work in his father's tobacco business. After three years of this, he began the long newspaper career that was to last for almost 40 years, beginning with the Baltimore *Herald*. From 1914 to 1923, Mencken, together with George Jean Nathan, co-edited the *Smart Set*, to which he had begun contributing as early as 1908. Then in 1923, Mencken and Nathan began the *American Mercury*.

As newspaperman and editor—especially of the *Mercury*—Mencken became the idol of the Jazz Age's "flaming youth," and all the sad young men of the intelligentsia awaited each issue of the *Mercury* to find out what they were attacking and what their views were. A vituperative cynic and a clever debunker of American values, Mencken created a magazine to which a subscription became the sure sign of sophistication and rebellious liberation from the gentility and smugness of what he called the "booboisie." He was the self-appointed dean of the attackers of parochialism, provincialism, patriotism, puritanism, philistinism, and prohibition. His sights were leveled at government by the masses, Congress, censorship, orthodoxy, small towns, clergymen, chambers of commerce, respectability and college professors. He championed, and in various ways influenced and helped "discover," such diverse writers as Theodore Dreiser, Edgar Lee Masters, Carl Sandburg, Eugene O'Neill, Willa Cather, and Sinclair Lewis.

His social and political criticism was basically an exposition of conservatism rather than of the radicalism with which he was identified by his numerous enemies. In his literary criticism, he furnished the humanist critics with an example of the impressionism to which they so bitterly objected. But in all areas of criticism, his influence began to fade in the depression 1930's, which had little time for many of Mencken's attitudes. After his retirement from the editorship of the *American Mercury* in 1933, he became a living memory rather than an active force. He remains a significant figure in American letters primarily for two reasons. One is his effect on the tone of the literature and the times during the 1920's. The second is his *The American Language* (1919), which was given a final revision in 1936 and to which he added two supplements; the first in 1945, the second in 1948. Engaging in the solid scholarship of the professors he delighted in attacking, he produced a reliable and highly enjoyable linguistic study of our native American English, a pioneering work that has proved to be a beginning point for subsequent scholarship.

Mencken's early books included *George Bernard Shaw* (1905) and *The Philosophy of Friedrich Nietzsche* (1908). The more important of his critiques of America and things in general include *A Book of Burlesques* (1916), *A Book of Prefaces* (1917), *Damn! A Book of Calumny* (1918), *In Defense of Women* (1918), the six series of *Prejudices* (1919, 1920, 1922, 1924, 1926, and 1927), *The American Credo* (with George Jean Nathan, 1920), *Notes on Democracy* (1926), *Treatise on the Gods* (1930), and *Treatise on Right and Wrong* (1934). Mencken's autobiographical work includes *Happy Days, 1880–1892* (1940), *Newspaper Days, 1899–1906* (1941), and *Heathen Days, 1890–1936* (1943). General selections of his work include *A Mencken Chrestomathy* (1949); Malcolm Moos, ed., *A Carnival of Buncombe* (1956); *Minority Report: H. L. Mencken's Notebooks* (1956); and R. McHugh, ed., *The Bathtub Hoax and Other Blasts and Bravos from the Chicago Tribune* (1958).

Accounts of the man and his work are to be found in B. Rascoe, et al., *H. L. Mencken* (1920); S. P. Sherman, *Americans* (1922); F. Harris, *Contemporary Portraits* (1923); C. Van Doren, *Many Minds* (1924); V. F. Calverton, *The Newer Spirit* (1925); I. Goldberg, *The Man Mencken* (1925); J. W. Beach, *The Outlook for American Prose* (1926); W. Lippmann, *H. L. Mencken* (1926); E. A. Boyd, *H. L. Mencken* (1927); E. S. Sergeant, *Fire Under the Andes* (1927); B. De Casseres, *Mencken and Shaw* (1930); M. Cowley, ed., *After the Genteel Tradition* (1937); M. Geismar, *The Last of the Provincials* (1947); E. Kemler, *The Irreverent Mr. Mencken* (1950); W. Manchester, *Disturber of the Peace* (1951); C. Angoff, *H. L. Mencken* (1956); *Menckeniana* (1965); W. Nolte, *H. L. Mencken* (1966); and P. Wagner, *H. L. Mencken* (1966).

Related to the humanism of Babbitt and opposed to the impressionism of Mencken stand the beginnings of the "New Criticism." Yet, once the New Critics are introduced, the complexity of developments makes it impossible to talk about "sides," except in the artificially isolated cases of the particular thoughts that particular critics have had at particular times about particular issues. For one thing, in many areas of thought, including literary criticism itself, it is not as though all New Critics agree about all principles; nor is it possible to tell just who the New Critics are any longer, with or without a score card. (The term itself was derived from John Crowe Ransom's *The New Criticism*, 1941). Furthermore, in political and economic thought, "enemies" such as Mencken were in many ways allies at the beginning, particularly as the movement manifested itself in the social ideas borrowed through T. E. Hulme, Ezra Pound, and T. S. Eliot from the thought of the

Comte de Maistre, Charles Maurras, Remy de Gourmont, and the French symbolists, particularly Baudelaire.

In the 1930's, the "Fugitives," writers and thinkers associated with Vanderbilt University in Nashville, Tennessee, began to issue manifestoes that reflected a reaction against industrialism, commercialism, scientism, and mass culture, all of which were associated in their minds with the American democracy of the northern United States. They championed order, hierarchy, and agrarianism, which, for them, was associated with the ante-bellum South. Discounting transatlantic influences for the moment, if the immediate temperamental American parent (not to go back to James Russell Lowell, for instance) of the Southern Agrarians was the New Humanism, Southern Agrarianism, through the fugitives, was the parent of the New Criticism. Yet, since the 1930's, the Southern Agrarians have diverged so on questions of "reaction" and "liberalism," "agrarianism" and "industrialism," "elitism" and "modernism," that one quickly discovers that one is talking about men rather than a movement. Perhaps it is not an evasion to say that the classical temperament which led to the political thought of Southern Agrarianism also led naturally to the formalistic criticism of the New Critics. It might be significant that some of the leading New Critics began their intellectual careers as academic specialists in the neo-classicism of the eighteenth century.

In any event, *I'll Take My Stand,* the manifesto of the Southern Agrarians, is an excellent concentration of the early attitudes of the leading New Critics. Illumination of the movement is to be found in the writings of the most famous signatories of *I'll Take My Stand*: John Crowe Ransom, the group's mentor and most influential figure; Donald Davidson; John Gould Fletcher; Allen Tate; Robert Penn Warren, the most widely known of the group; and Stark Young. The criticism of Cleanth Brooks also is important; he was a member of the "Fugitive" group at Vanderbilt, but did not contribute to *I'll Take My Stand.*

Important works on the "Fugitives" are J. Bradbury, *The Fugitives: A Critical Account* (1958); L. Cowan, *The Fugitive Group: A Literary History* (1959); and R. R. Purdy, ed., *Fugitive's Reunion* (1959). A brief but controversial (and famous) account of the relationship between the "New Criticism" and the Southern Agrarians is to be found in Robert Gorham Davis, "The New Criticism and the Democratic Tradition," *American Scholar,* XVIV (1949—1950).

The historical interpretation of literature is opposed to the New Critical doctrine (now modified or abandoned by many New Critics) that a piece of literature is to be judged as an independent art work regardless of its time or place. Edmund Wilson (1895—   ), developing his methods under the influence of Taine and of his own immediate teacher, Christian Gauss of Princeton, has become a leading exponent of the thought which sees literary criticism, in Wilson's words, as "a history of man's ideas and imaginings in the setting of the conditions which have shaped them."

Combining Freudianism and Marxism in his early work, Wilson has tried to forge a new synthesis of modern methodologies and ideologies for the purposes of history and literary criticism. Because he is a highly evaluative critic, he would not be an "impressionist" in Babbitt's sense. Yet because he is willing to rest aesthetic judgments upon the taste of the highly informed and educated critic, he is considered an impressionist by those "New Critics" whose decalogues demand a demonstrated explication and analysis of the formal relationship of all parts of a literary work.

A native of New Jersey, Edmund Wilson attended Princeton, where he became the friend of F. Scott Fitzgerald, whose *The Crack-up* (1945) he edited. He has been associated with *Vanity Fair* and the *New Masses* as well as *The New Republic* and *The New Yorker*, for the last of which he continues to write.

His books include *Axel's Castle* (1931), an epoch-making study of the symbolist movement; *The American Jitters* (1932); *Travels in Two Democracies* (1936); *The Triple Thinkers* (1938); *To the Finland Station* (1940); *The Wound and the Bow* (1941); *Classics and Commercials* (1950); *The Shores of Light* (1952); and *The American Earthquake* (1958).

In addition to the works mentioned above, accounts of movements in modern American literary criticism are to be found in D. A. Stauffer, ed., *The Intent of the Critic* (1941); S. E. Hyman, *The Armed Vision* (1948); C. Glicksberg, *American Literary Criticism, 1900–1950* (1951); M. D. Zabel, ed., *Literary Opinion in America* (revised edition, 1951); W. V. O'Connor, *An Age of Criticism, 1900–1950* (1952); F. Stovall, ed., *The Development of American Literary Criticism* (1955); J. P. Pritchard, *Criticism in America* (1956); W. Wimsatt, Jr., and C. Brooks, *Literary Criticism: A Short History* (1957); and S. Paul, *Edmund Wilson* (1967).

The nature of experimentalism and criticism following World War II was slow to define itself. The novels that came out of the war, like *The Gallery,* by John Horne Burns, and *The Naked and the Dead,* by Norman Mailer, foreshadowed things to come, but not so much in form as in theme and attitude. Although some war books, like Irwin Shaw's *The Young Lions,* tended to see the aftermath of the war as a process of education into human brotherhood and inter-responsibility—the actualization of a dream of political and social liberalism—writers like Burns and Mailer were educated differently by the war. In varying responses, from nihilism to guarded hopefulness, most of the serious young writers who came out of the war saw the military experience as a metaphor for modern life. They responded in some respects similarly to Hemingway's World War I generation: if they had been conditioned to open-ended expectation, fluidity, and independence in American life, they were shocked and depressed, cynical or annoyed, depending on their vision and temperament. If they had been conditioned to dissent and disenchantment, they found their suspicions intensified: American life was not different in measurable human terms from the qualities of modern life generally.

In the nineteen-fifties, McCarthyism and the Korean War further widened the growing rift between a social and national definition of human personality on the one hand, and on the other the American transcendental radicalism that had always tended to alienate the Emersons and Thoreaus from their social institutions. What happened in the forties and fifties was nothing new: historically American literature has provided the voice for a millenial view of America as a metaphor for ultimate and absolute and experimental liberty.

Consistently, when the American literary imagination repudiates the historical facts of America as a betrayal of the metaphor, the literary hero becomes the Outsider, the Avenger, the Stranger. He becomes the Divine Outlaw, not as the representative American standing against the corrupt Old World, but as the dissenting American standing against his own society. In the 1950's, our literary heroes went "outside" and "underground" with increasing vehemence and frequency. The marginal man as hero, living dangerously on the outskirts of our society—the "hipster"—became part of an international community of dissent which recoiled from the established state as a monolithic power structure steering straight toward dehumanization and nuclear annihilation.

The social personifications of the dissenting hero moved

from the "beatnik" (the late 1940's and early 1950's) to the "hipster" (the mid and late 1950's), to the "hippie" (the early and mid 1960's). Although different emphases give a minimal validity to the labels, there are so many submovements within each group, so many contradictory definitions, and so many unifying cross-currents among them that the labels, finally, offer little help. If any distinction can be made at all, it is the "hipster" who stands out as the dangerous figure— it is he who haunts newspaper cartoons that call for law and order, peace and quiet. It is he who, whether in the civil rights movement or ban-the-bomb activities, is most likely to respond to violence with violence rather than with the withdrawal and intellectualism of the beatnik or with the "love" and gentle anti-intellectualism of the hippie.

This figure, one avatar in a long development of the Stranger in American literature, is described by Norman Mailer, who himself represents the surge of that development in the 1950's and 1960's. Mailer (1923–   ) grew up in Brooklyn, attended Harvard, worked at various odd jobs, and went into the army as a rifleman, serving in the Pacific theater. He took his war experiences, combined them with a hint from *Moby-Dick* (the conquest of Anopopei and its mountain peak was based on the idea of the hunt for the white whale) and with the title of a play he had written about an insane asylum, and in 1948 published *The Naked and the Dead*. The novel brought him immediate fame and popularity. His second novel, smaller but in some ways more ambitious than *The Naked and the Dead,* did not receive as wide or as friendly a reception. Called *Barbary Shore* (1951), the book attempted to examine the personal and political identities of Americans and the general identity of America through a rediscovery of the meanings of history in the revolutionary movements of the twentieth century.

Mailer's third novel, *The Deer Park* (1955), became the controversial center of raging critical claims that it was either unspeakable filth or a heroic breakthrough. With the Korean War, Hollywood, and loyalty investigations as its background, the book attempts to create an existential metaphysic for psychic release of human power, especially through sex. Mailer rewrote the novel as a play, and it was produced in New York in 1967. His other volumes include a book of poems, *Deaths for the Ladies* (1962), three books of essays and short stories, *Advertisements for Myself* (1959), *The Presidential*

Papers (1963), and *Cannibals and Christians* (1966), and two other novels, *An American Dream* (1965) and *Why Are We in Vietnam?* (1967).

Some studies of the man and his work are F. J. Hoffman, "Norman Mailer and the Revolt of the Ego," *Wisconsin Studies in Contemporary Literature,* I (1960); G. A. Schrader, "Norman Mailer and the Despair of Defiance," *Yale Review,* LII (1962); D. Trilling, "Norman Mailer," *Encounter,* XIX (1962); N. Mailer, "Norman Mailer Versus Nine Writers," *Esquire,* LX (1963); H. Dienstfrey, "The Fiction of Norman Mailer," *On Contemporary Literature* (R. Kostelanetz, ed., 1965); and M. Richler, "Norman Mailer," *Encounter,* XXV (1965).

EUGENE JOLAS

Manifesto: The Revolution of the Word

TIRED OF THE SPECTACLE OF SHORT STORIES, NOVELS, POEMS AND PLAYS STILL UNDER THE HEGEMONY OF THE BANAL WORD, MONOTONOUS SYNTAX, STATIC PSYCHOLOGY, DESCRIPTIVE NATURALISM, AND DESIROUS OF CRYSTALLIZING A VIEWPOINT . . .

WE HEREBY DECLARE THAT:

1. THE REVOLUTION IN THE ENGLISH LANGUAGE IS AN ACCOMPLISHED FACT.

2. THE IMAGINATION IN SEARCH OF A FABULOUS WORLD IS AUTONOMOUS AND UNCONFINED.
   (*Prudence is a rich, ugly old maid courted by Incapacity* . . . Blake)

3. PURE POETRY IS A LYRICAL ABSOLUTE THAT SEEKS AN A PRIORI REALITY WITHIN OURSELVES ALONE.
   (*Bring out number, weight and measure in a year of dearth* . . . Blake)

4. NARRATIVE IS NOT MERE ANECDOTE, BUT THE PROJECTION OF A METAMORPHOSIS OF REALITY.
   (*Enough! Or Too Much!* . . . Blake)

5. THE EXPRESSION OF THESE CONCEPTS CAN BE ACHIEVED ONLY THROUGH THE RHYTHMIC "HALLUCINATION OF THE WORD." (Rimbaud)

6. THE LITERARY CREATOR HAS THE RIGHT TO DISINTEGRATE THE PRIMAL MATTER OF WORDS IMPOSED ON HIM BY TEXTBOOKS AND DICTIONARIES.
   (*The road of excess leads to the palace of Wisdom* . . . Blake)

7. HE HAS THE RIGHT TO USE WORDS OF HIS OWN FASHIONING AND TO DISREGARD EXISTING GRAMMATICAL AND SYNTACTICAL LAWS.
   (*The tigers of wrath are wiser than the horses of instruction* . . . Blake)

8. THE "LITANY OF WORDS" IS ADMITTED AS AN INDE-
PENDENT UNIT.

9. WE ARE NOT CONCERNED WITH THE PROPAGATION OF
SOCIOLOGICAL IDEAS, EXCEPT TO EMANCIPATE THE
CREATIVE ELEMENTS FROM THE PRESENT IDEOLOGY

10. TIME IS A TYRANNY TO BE ABOLISHED.

11. THE WRITER EXPRESSES. HE DOES NOT COMMUNICATE.

12. THE PLAIN READER BE DAMNED.
    (*Damn braces! Bless relaxes!* . . . Blake)

IRVING BABBITT

The Critic and American Life

A frequent remark of the French about Americans is:
"They're children"; which, interpreted, means that from
the French point of view Americans are childishly un-
critical. The remark is relevant only in so far as it refers
to general critical intelligence. In dealing with the special problems of a commercial and industrial society
Americans have shown that they can be abundantly critical. Certain Americans, for example, have developed a
critical keenness in estimating the value of stocks and
bonds that is nothing short of uncanny. The very persons, however, who are thus keen in some particular field
are when confronted with questions that call for general
critical intelligence, often puerile. Yet in an age like
the present, which is being subjected to a constant stream
of propaganda in everything from the choice of its religion to its cigarettes, general critical intelligence would
seem desirable.

As a matter of fact, most persons nowadays aspire to
be not critical but creative. We have not merely creative
poets and novelists, but creative readers and listeners and
dancers. Lately a form of creativeness has appeared that
may in time swallow up all the others—creative salesmanship. The critic himself has caught the contagion
and also aspires to be creative. He is supposed to become
so when he receives from the creation of another, con-

ceived as pure temperamental overflow, so vivid an impression that, when passed through his temperament, it issues forth as a fresh creation. What is eliminated in both critic and creator is any standard that is set above temperament and that therefore might interfere with their eagerness to get themselves expressed.

The notion of criticism as self-expression is important for our present subject, for it has been adopted by the writer who is, according to the last edition of the *Encyclopaedia Britannica,* "the greatest critical force in America"—Mr. H. L. Mencken. "The critic is first and last," says Mr. Mencken, "simply trying to express himself; he is trying to achieve thereby for his own inner ego the grateful feeling of a function performed, a tension relieved, a katharsis attained which Wagner achieved when he wrote *Die Walküre,* and a hen achieves every time she lays an egg." This creative self-expression, as practiced by himself and others, has, according to Mr. Mencken, led to a salutary stirring up of the stagnant pool of American letters: "To-day for the first time in years there is strife in American criticism. . . . Heretics lay on boldly and the professors are forced to make some defence. Often going further they attempt counter-attacks. Ears are bitten off, noses are bloodied. There are wallops both above and below the belt."

But it may be that criticism is something more than Mr. Mencken would have us believe, more in short than a squabble between Bohemians, each eager to capture the attention of the public for his brand of self-expression. To reduce criticism indeed to the satisfaction of a temperamental urge, to the uttering of one's gustos and disgustos (in Mr. Mencken's case chiefly the latter) is to run counter to the very etymology of the word which implies discrimination and judgment. The best one would anticipate from a writer like Mr. Mencken, possessing an unusual verbal virtuosity and at the same time temperamentally irresponsible, is superior intellectual vaudeville. One must grant him, however, certain genuine critical virtues—for example, a power of shrewd observation within rather narrow limits. Yet the total effect of his writing is nearer to intellectual vaudeville than to serious criticism.

The serious critic is more concerned with achieving a

correct scale of values and so seeing things proportionately than with self-expression. His essential virtue is poise. The specific benefit he confers is to act as a moderating influence on the opposite insanities between which mankind in the lump is constantly tending to oscillate—oscillations that Luther compares to the reelings of a drunken peasant on horseback. The critic's survey of any particular situation may very well seem satirical. The complaint that Mr. Mencken is too uniformly disgruntled in his survey of the American situation rather misses the point. Behind the pleas for more constructiveness it is usually easy to detect the voice of the booster. A critic who did not get beyond a correct diagnosis of existing evils might be very helpful. If Mr. Mencken has fallen short of being such a diagnostician, the failure is due not to his excess of severity but to his lack of discrimination.

The standards with reference to which men have discriminated in the past have been largely traditional. The outstanding fact of the present period, on the other hand, has been the weakening of traditional standards. An emergency has arisen not unlike that with which Socrates sought to cope in ancient Athens. Anyone who is untraditional and seeks at the same time to be discriminating must almost necessarily own Socrates as his master. As is well known, Socrates sought above all to be discriminating in his use of general terms. The importance of the art of inductive defining that he devised may perhaps best be made clear by bringing together two sayings, one of Napoleon—"Imagination governs mankind"—and one of John Selden—"Syllables govern mankind." Before allowing one's imagination and finally one's conduct to be controlled by a general term, it would seem wise to submit it to a Socratic scrutiny.

It is, therefore, unfortunate that at a time like the present, which plainly calls for a Socrates, we should instead have got a Mencken. One may take as an example of Mr. Mencken's failure to discriminate adequately, his attitude toward the term that for several generations past has been governing the imagination of multitudes—democracy. His view of democracy is simply that of Rousseau turned upside down, and nothing, as has been remarked, resembles a hollow so much as a swelling. A distinction of which he has failed to recognize the importance is that between a direct or unlimited and a constitutional democracy. In the latter we probably have the best thing in the world. The former, on the other hand, as all thinkers of any penetration from Plato and Aristotle down have perceived, leads to the loss of liberty and finally to the rise of some form of despotism. The two conceptions of democracy involve not merely incompatible views of government but ultimately of human nature. The desire of the constitutional democrat for institutions that act as checks on the immediate will of the people implies a similar dualism in the individual—a higher self that acts restrictively on his ordinary and impulsive self. The partisan of unlimited democracy on the other hand is an idealist in the sense of that the term assumed in connection with the so-called romantic movement. His faith in the people is closely related to the doctrine of natural goodness proclaimed by the sentimentalists of the eighteenth century and itself marking an extreme recoil from the dogma of total depravity. The doctrine of natural goodness favors the free temperamental expansion that I have already noticed in speaking of the creative critic.

It is of the utmost importance, however, if one is to understand Mr. Mencken, to discriminate between two types of temperamentalist—the soft and sentimental type, who cherishes various "ideals," and the hard, or Nietzschean type, who piques himself on being realistic. As a matter of fact, if one sees in the escape from traditional controls merely an opportunity to live temperamentally, it would seem advantageous to pass promptly from the idealistic to the Nietzschean phase, sparing oneself as many as possible of the intermediary disillusions. It is at all events undeniable that the rise of Menckenism has been marked by a certain collapse of romantic idealism in the political field and elsewhere. The numerous disillusions that have supervened upon the War have provided a favoring atmosphere.

The symptoms of Menckenism are familiar: a certain hardness and smartness and disposition to rail at everything that, rightly or wrongly, is established and respected; a tendency to identify the real with what Mr. Mencken terms "the cold and clammy facts" and to assume that the only alternative to facing these facts is to fade away into sheer romantic unreality. These and similar traits are becoming so widely diffused that, whatever one's opinion of Mr. Mencken as a writer and thinker, one must grant him representativeness. He is a chief prophet at present of those who deem themselves emancipated but who are, according to Mr. Brownell, merely unbuttoned.

The crucial point in any case is one's attitude toward the principle of control. Those who stand for this principle in any form or degree are dismissed by the emancipated as reactionaries or, still graver reproach, as Puritans. Mr. Mencken would have us believe that the historical Puritan was not even sincere in his moral rigorism, but was given to "lamentable transactions with loose women and fiery jugs." This may serve as a sample of the assertions, picturesquely indiscriminate, by which a writer wins immediate notoriety at the expense of his permanent reputation. The facts about the Puritan happen to be complex and need to be dealt with very Socratically. It has been affirmed that the point of view of the Puritan was Stoical rather than truly Christian, and the affirmation is not wholly false. The present discussion of the relationship between Puritanism and the rise of capitalism with its glorification of the acquisitive life also has its justification. It is likewise a fact that the Puritan was from the outset unduly concerned with reforming others as well as himself, and this trait relates him to the humanitarian meddler or "wowser" of the present day, who is Mr. Mencken's pet aversion.

Yet it remains true that awe and reverence and humility are Christian virtues and that there was some survival of these virtues in the Puritan. For a representative Puritan like Jonathan Edwards they were inseparable from the illumination of grace, from what he terms "a divine and supernatural light." In the passage from the love and fear of God of an Edwards to the love and service of man professed by the humanitarian, something has plainly dropped out, something that is very near the center. What has tended to disappear is the inner life with the special type of control it imposes. With the decline of this inner control there has been an increasing resort to outer control. Instead of the genuine Puritan we then have the humanitarian legalist who passes innumerable laws for the control of people who refuse to control themselves. The activity of our uplifters is scarcely suggestive of any "divine and supernatural light." Here is a discrimination of the first importance that has been obscured by the muddy thinking of our half-baked intelligentsia. One is thus kept from perceiving the real problem, which is to retain the inner life, even though one refuse to accept the theological nightmare with which the Puritan associated it. More is involved in the failure to solve this problem than the Puritan tradition. It is the failure of our contemporary life in general. Yet, unless some solution is reached by a full and free exercise of the critical spirit, one remains a mere modernist and not a thoroughgoing and complete modern; for the modern spirit and the critical spirit are in their essence one.

What happens, when one sets out to deal with questions of this order without sufficient depth of reflection and critical maturity, may be seen in Mr. Sinclair Lewis's last novel [*Elmer Gantry*]. He has been lured from art into the writing of a wild diatribe which, considered even as such, is largely beside the mark. If the Protestant Church is at present threatened with bankruptcy, it is not because it has produced an occasional Elmer Gantry. The true reproach it has incurred is that, in its drift toward modernism, it has lost its grip not merely on certain dogmas but, simultaneously, on the facts of human nature. It has failed above all to carry over in some modern and critical form the truth of a dogma that unfortunately receives much support from these facts—the dogma of original sin. At first sight Mr. Mencken would appear to have a conviction of evil—when, for example, he reduces democracy in its essential aspect to a "combat between jackals and jackasses"—that establishes at least one bond between him and the austere Christian.

The appearance, however, is deceptive. The Christian is conscious above all of the "old Adam" in himself: hence his humility. The effect of Mr. Mencken's writing, on the other hand, is to produce pride rather than humility, a pride ultimately based on flattery. The reader, especially the young and callow reader, identifies himself imaginatively with Mr. Mencken and conceives of himself as a sort of morose and sardonic divinity surveying from some superior altitude an immeasurable expanse of "boobs." This attitude will not seem especially novel to anyone who has traced the modern movement. One is reminded in particular of Flaubert, who showed a diligence in collecting bourgeois imbecilities comparable to that displayed by Mr. Mencken in his *Americana*. Flaubert's discovery that one does not add to one's happiness in this way would no doubt be dismissed by Mr. Mencken as irrelevant, for he has told us that he does not believe in happiness. Another discovery of Flaubert's may seem to him more worthy of consideration. "By dint of railing at idiots," Flaubert reports, "one runs the risk of becoming idiotic oneself."

It may be that the only way to escape from the unduly complacent cynicism of Mr. Mencken and his school is to reaffirm once more the truths of the inner life. In that case it would seem desirable to disengage, so far as possible, the principle of control on which the inner life finally depends from mere creeds and traditions and assert it as a psychological fact; a fact, moreover, that is neither "cold" nor "clammy." The coldness and clamminess of much so called realism arises from its failure to give this fact due recognition. A chief task, indeed, of the Socratic critic would be to rescue the noble term "realist" from its present degradation. A view of reality that overlooks the element in man that moves in an opposite direction from mere temperament, the specifically human factor in short, may prove to be singularly one-sided. Is the Puritan, John Milton, when he declares that "he who reigns within himself and rules passions, desires, and fears is more than a king," less real than Mr. Theodore Dreiser when he discourses in his peculiar dialect of "those rearranging chemisms upon which all the morality or immorality of the world is based?"

As a matter of fact, according to the degree and nature of the exercise of the principle of control, one may distinguish two main types of realism which may be denominated respectively religious and humanistic: as the principle of control falls into abeyance, a third type tends to emerge, which may be termed naturalistic realism. That the decline of the traditional controls has been followed by a lapse to the naturalistic level is indubitable. The characteristic evils of the present age arise from unrestraint and violation of the law of measure and not, as our modernists would have us believe, from the tyranny of taboos and traditional inhibitions. The facts cry to heaven. The delicate adjustment that is required between the craving for emancipation and the need of control has been pointed out once for all by Goethe, speaking not as Puritan but as a clear-eyed man of the world. Everything, he says, that liberates the spirit without a corresponding growth in self-mastery is pernicious. This one sentence would seem to cover the case of our "flaming youth" rather completely.

The movement in the midst of which we are still living was from its inception unsound in its dealing with the principle of control. It is vain to expect from the dregs of this movement what its "first sprightly running failed to give." Mr. Carl Sandburg speaks of the "marvelous rebellion of man at all signs reading 'Keep off.'" An objection to this purely insurrectional attitude is that, as a result of its endless iteration during the past century and more, it has come to savor too strongly of what has been called "the humdrum of revolt." A more serious objection to the attitude is that it encourages an unrestricted and merely temperamental liberty which, paradoxically enough at first sight, affords the modern man no avenue of escape from the web that is being woven about him by the scientific determinist.

Realists of the current type are in point of fact intimately allied with the psychologists,—glandular, behavioristic, and psychoanalytical,—who, whatever their divergences among themselves, unite in their deterministic trend and therefore clash fundamentally with both religious and humanistic realists. The proper method of procedure in defending the freedom of the will would seem to be to insist upon it as a fact of experience, a fact so primary that the position of the determinist involves an evasion of one of the immediate data of consciousness in favor of a metaphysical dream. What is genuinely experimental in naturalistic psychology should of course be received with respect; but the facts of which it takes account in its experiments are unimportant compared with the facts it either neglects or denies. Practically it is running into grotesque extremes of pseudo-science that make of it a shining mark for the Socratic critic.

Here at all events is the issue on which all other issues finally hinge; for until the question of moral freedom— the question whether man is a responsible agent or only the plaything of his impulses and impressions—is decided, nothing is decided; and to decide the question under existing circumstances calls for the keenest critical discrimination. Creation that is not sufficiently supported by such discrimination is likely to prove premature.

One may illustrate from Mr. Dreiser's *American Tragedy*, hailed in certain quarters as the "Mt. Everest" of recent fiction. He has succeeded in producing in this work something genuinely harrowing; but one is harrowed to no purpose. One has in more than full measure the tragic qualm but without the final relief and enlargement of spirit that true tragedy succeeds somehow in giving, and that without resort to explicit moralizing. It is hardly worth while to struggle through eight hundred and more very pedestrian pages to be left at the end with a feeling of sheer oppression. The explanation of this oppression is that Mr. Dreiser does not rise sufficiently above the level of "rearranging chemisms," in other words, of animal behavior. Tragedy may admit fate—Greek tragedy admits it—but not of the naturalistic variety. Confusion on this point may compromise in the long run the reputation of writers more eminent than Mr. Dreiser—for example, of Thomas Hardy. Fatalism of the naturalistic type is responsible in large measure for the atmosphere of futility and frustration that hangs heavily over so much contemporary writing. One finally comes to feel with a recent poet that "dust" is the common source from which

stream
The cricket's cry and Dante's dream.

Anyone who admits reality only in what derives from the dust, whether in a cricket or a Dante, must, from the point of view of the religious or the humanistic realists, be prepared to make substantial sacrifices. In the first place, he must sacrifice the depth and subtlety that arise from the recognition in some form of the duality of man's nature. For the interest that may arise from the portrayal of the conflict between a law of the spirit and a law of the members, the inordinate interest in sex for its own sake promoted by most of the so-called realists is a rather shabby substitute. A merely naturalistic realism also involves the sacrifice of beauty in almost any sense of that elusive term. Closely related to this sacrifice is the sacrifice of delicacy, elevation, and distinction. The very word realism has come to connote the opposite of these qualities. When we learn, for example, that someone has written a realistic study of a great man, we are sure in advance that he has devoted his main effort to proving that "Plutarch lied." The more the great man is reduced to the level of commonplace or worse, the more we feel he has been "humanized."

Mr. Sherwood Anderson has argued ingeniously that, in as much as we ourselves are crude, our literature, if it is not to be unreal and factitious, should be crude likewise. But the writer who hopes to achieve work of importance cannot afford to be too deeply immersed in the atmosphere of the special place and passing moment. Still less can he afford to make us feel, as writers like Mr. Anderson and Mr. Dreiser and Mr. Sinclair Lewis do, that, if there were any lack of vulgarity in what they are depicting they would be capable of supplying the defect from their own abundance. More is involved here than mere loss of distinction. We have come, indeed, to the supreme sacrifice that every writer must make who does not transcend a naturalistic realism. He must forego the hope of the enduring appeal—the hope that every writer worthy of his salt cherishes in some degree. In the absence of humanistic or religious standards, he is prone to confound the real with the welter of the actual, and so to miss what Dr. Johnson terms the "grandeur of generality."

Certain books in the current mode are so taken up with the evanescent surfaces of life that they will survive, if at all, not as literature but as sociological documents. The very language in which they are written will, in a generation or two, require a glossary. So far from imposing an orderly pattern on the raw material of experience, they rather emphasize the lack of pattern. The resulting effect, to borrow a phrase from the late Stephen Crane, who has had a marked influence on the recent movement, is that of a "cluttered incoherency." As an extreme example of the tendency one may cite *Manhattan Transfer* by John Dos Passos. In the name of reality, Mr. Dos Passos has perpetrated a literary nightmare. Such a work would seem to have slight value even

as a sociological document; unless, indeed, one is prepared to admit that contemporary Manhattan is inhabited
chiefly by epileptic Bohemians.

"It is as much a trade," says La Bruyère, "to make
a book as it is to make a clock"; in short, literature is
largely a matter of technique. The technique of *Manhattan Transfer* is as dubious as its underlying philosophy.
Neither can be justified save on the assumption that the
aim of art is to exaggerate the clutter and incoherency
of the mundane spectacle instead of eliciting its deeper
meaning. Technique counts for even more in poetry
than in prose. It would be possible to base on technical
grounds alone a valid protest against the present preposterous overestimate of Walt Whitman. Fundamental questions need, in these very untraditional days, to be critically
elucidated with a view to right definition if the poet is
not to lack technique or still worse, if he is not, like
certain recent practitioners of free verse, to be hagrid-
den by a false technique. It evidently concerns both the
form and substance of poetry, whether one define it with
Aristotle as the portrayal of representative human action,
or whether one define it with Mr. Carl Sandburg as a
"mystic, sensuous mathematics of fire, smokestacks, waf-
fles, pansies, people, and purple sunsets."

There is no doubt much in the America of to-day that
suggests a jazzy impressionism. Still our naturalistic deli-
quescence has probably not gone so far as one might
infer from poetry like that of Mr. Sandburg or fiction like
that of Mr. Dos Passos. The public response to some of
the realistic novels has been considerable: allowance must
be made however for the *succès de scandale,* also for
the skill attained by the modern publisher in the art of
merchandising. The reputation of certain books one might
mention may be regarded as a triumph of "creative" advertising. What has been created is a mirage of masterpieces where no masterpieces are. It is well also to remember in regard to some of the works that have been
most discussed that, so far from being an authentic reflection of the American scene, they are rather a belated
echo of certain European movements. For it is as certain
that in our literary and artistic modes we follow Europe—
usually at an interval of from five to forty years—as it
is that we lead Europe in our bathtubs and sanitary plumbing. Anyone who resided in Paris in the nineties and later

in America, will, as I can testify from personal experience, have the sense of having lived through the same literary fads twice. Mr. Dreiser reminds one of Zola and his school. The technique of Mr. Dos Passos recalls that of the Goncourts. Our experimenters in free verse have followed in the wake not merely of Walt Whitman but of the French symbolists, and so on.

We shall presently begin to hear of certain new developments in French literature and critical thought that point, though indecisively as yet, to a radical departure from what has been the main current since the eighteenth century and in some respects since the Renaissance. It is well that we should become familiar with the writers who reveal in different ways this latest trend—notably with Maritain, Maurras, Lasserre, Seillière, and Benda; for they give evidence of a quality of cerebration that is rare in our own literati. At the same time we should not adopt with our usual docility the total outlook of any of these writers: for no one of them has worked out a point of view exactly adapted to our requirements. In general, it is not fitting that a great nation at the very height of its power should go on indefinitely trailing after Europe. It is time for us to initiate something of our own. This does not mean that we should proceed forthwith to inbreed our own "originality." It means almost the exact opposite. The most original thing one could do nowadays would be to question the whole theory of originality as mere temperamental overflow and self-expression that has prevailed from the "geniuses" of the eighteenth century down to one of our youthful and very minor bards who aspires to "spill his bright illimitable soul."

A genuinely critical survey would make manifest that the unsatisfactoriness of our creative effort is due to a lack of the standards that culture alone can supply. Our cultural crudity and insignificance can be traced in turn to the inadequacy of our education, especially our higher education. Mr. Mencken's attack on the "professors" is therefore largely justified; for if the professors were performing their function properly Mr. Mencken himself would not be possible. One must add in common justice that the professors themselves, or at least some of them, are becoming aware that all is not well with existing conditions. One could not ask anything more perspicacious than the following paragraph from a recent report of Committee G to the American Association of University Professors:

American education has suffered from the domination, conscious or unconscious, direct or indirect, of political and sentimental, as well as educational, theories that are demonstrably false. If the views of some men are to prevail the intellectual life of the country is doomed; everybody except the sheer idiot is to go to college and pursue chiefly sociology, nature study, child study, and community service—and we shall have a society unique only in its mediocrity, ignorance and vulgarity. It will not do to dismiss lightly even so extreme a view as this; it is too indicative. Such influences are very strong, their pressure is constant; and if education has largely failed in America it has been due primarily to them.

In short, as a result of the encroachments of an equalitarian democracy, the standards of our higher education have suffered in two distinct particulars: first, as regards the quality of students; second, as regards the quality of the studies these students pursue. The first of these evils is generally recognized. There is even some prospect of remedial measures. Certain institutions, Harvard, for example, without being as yet severely selective, are becoming more critical of the incompetent student. On the other hand, there seems to be less hope than ever of any righting of the second and more serious evil—the failure to distinguish qualitatively between studies. The main drift is still toward what one may term the blanket degree. (Dartmouth, for example, has just merged its bachelor of arts and bachelor of science.) Yet rather than blur certain distinctions it would have been better, one might suppose, to use up all the letters of the alphabet devising new degrees to meet the real or supposed educational needs of the modern man. To bestow the A.B. degree indiscriminately on a student for whom education has meant primarily a specialization in chemistry and on one for whom it has meant primarily an assimilation of the masterpieces of Greek literature is to empty it of any effective meaning. At the present rate, indeed, the time may come when the A.B. will not throw much more light on the cultural quality of its recipient than it would, if, as has been suggested, it were bestowed on every American child at birth.

It goes without saying that those who have been lower-

ing and confusing educational standards have been pro-
fuse in their professions of "service." A critical examination, not merely of American education but of American
life at the present time will almost necessarily hinge on
this term. The attitude of the Socratic critic toward it is
not to be confounded with that of Mr. Mencken and the
"hard-boiled" contingent. "When a gang of real estate
agents," says Mr. Mencken, "bond salesmen, and automobile dealers gets together to sob for Service, it takes no
Freudian to surmise that someone is about to be swin-
dled." But if one entertain doubts about this current
American gospel, why waste one's ammunition on any
such small fry? Other and more exalted personages than
the members of the Rotary Club at Zenith have, in Mr.
Sinclair Lewis's elegant phrase, been "yipping for Service." If one is to deal with this idea of service Socratically, one needs to consider it in its relation to the two
figures who have rightly been taken to be the most representative in our cultural background—Benjamin Franklin and Jonathan Edwards. Franklin's idea of service is
already humanitarian. Edwards' idea is still traditionally
Christian service not of man but of God. What Franklin
stood for is flourishing prodigiously at the present moment, so much so that he may perhaps be defined in his
chief line of influence as the great superrotarian. What
Edwards stood for is, on the other hand, largely obsolete
or survives only in the form of habits, which, lacking
doctrinal support, are steadily declining along with the
whole Puritan culture.

Intermediary types are possible. One may in one's
character reflect the Puritan background and at the same
time in one's idea of service derive rather from Franklin.
Precisely that combination is found in the most influential of our recent educational leaders—the late President Eliot. A legitimate admiration for his personal qualities should not interfere with the keenest critical scrutiny
of his views about education, for the two things stand
in no necessary connection. Practically this means to
scrutinize the humanitarian idealism that he probably did
more than any other man of his generation to promote.
In this respect most of the heads of our institutions of
learning have been and still are understudies of President
Eliot.

In an address on the occasion of his ninetieth birthday President Eliot warned his hearers against introspection, lest it divert them from a whole-hearted devotion to service. Between this attitude and a religious or humanistic attitude there is a clash of first principles. Both humanism and religion require introspection as a prerequisite of the inner life and its appropriate activity. With the disappearance of this activity what is left is the outer activity of the utilitarian, and this leads straight to the one-sided cult of material efficiency and finally to the standardization that is, according to nearly all foreign critics and many of our own, a chief American danger. We cannot return to the introspection of the Puritan. We shudder at the theology an Edwards would impose as the condition of his "divine and supernatural light." Yet it does not follow, as I have already suggested, that we should reject the inner life itself along with this theology. One may recognize innumerable incidental advantages in the gospel of service and yet harbor an uneasy suspicion withal that in the passage from the older religion to the modern humanitarian dispensation something vital has disappeared, something of which neither the outer working of the utilitarian nor again the expansive sympathy of the sentimentalist can offer an equivalent.

The problem of the inner life is very much bound up with two other problems that are now pressing for solution in our higher education and have as yet found none: the problem of the specialist and the problem of leisure. The man of leisure is engaged in an inner and specifically human form of activity, a form that is, according to Aristotle, needful if he is to compass the end of ends— his own happiness. The question is whether one should consent like the specialist to forego this activity and to live partially and as a mere instrument for the attainment of some outer end—even though this end be the progress of humanity. We are beginning to hear a great deal nowadays about the "menace" of leisure. It has been estimated that with the perfecting of mechanical devices the man of the future will be able to satisfy his material wants by working not more than four hours a day. It is vain to anticipate that the rank and file will use this release from outer activity intelligently unless the leaders, notably those in high academic station, show the way. The notion of true leisure is the ultimate source of the standards of any education that deserves to be called liberal. When even a few of our college and university presidents show that they are thinking to some purpose on the nature of leisure it will be time enough to talk of "America's coming of age."

As it is, our institutions of learning seem to be becoming more and more hotbeds of "idealism." Their failure, on the whole, to achieve standards as something quite distinct from ideals on the one hand, and standardization on the other, may prove a fact of sinister import for the future of American civilization. The warfare that is being waged at the present time by Mr. Sinclair Lewis and others against a standardized Philistinism continues in the main the protest that has been made for several generations past by the temperamentalists, hard or soft, against the mechanizing of life by the utilitarian. This protest has been, and is likely to continue to be, ineffectual. The fruitful opposite of the standardized Philistine is not the Bohemian, nor again the hard temperamentalist or superman, as Mr. Mencken conceives him, but the man of leisure. Leisure involves an inner effort with reference to standards that is opposed to the sheer expansion of temperament, as it is to every other form of sheer expansion.

Perhaps a reason why the standards of the humanist are less popular in this country than the ideals of the humanitarian is that these standards set bounds to the acquisitive life; whereas it seems possible to combine a perfect idealism with an orgy of unrestricted commercialism. It is well for us to try to realize how we appear to others in this matter. Our growing unpopularity abroad is due no doubt in part to envy of our material success, but it also arises from the proneness of the rest of the world to judge us, not by the way we feel about ourselves, but by our actual performance. If we are in our own eyes a nation of idealists, we are, according to our most recent French critic, M. André Siegfried, a "nation of Pharisees." The European, M. Siegfried would have us believe, still has a concern for the higher values of civilization, whereas the American is prepared to sacrifice these values ruthlessly to mass production and material efficiency.

It is easy to detect under this assumption the latest form of a "certain condescension in foreigners." The breakdown of cultural standards is European as well as American. It is not clear that M. Siegfried himself has an adequate notion of the form of effort that can alone serve as a counterpoise to the one-sided activity of the utilitarian. His assertion that Europe, appalled at the American excess of standardization, is inclined to turn from Henry Ford to Gandhi is more picturesque than convincing. At the same time his anatomy of our favorite ideal of service is not without interest. This ideal opposes no effective barrier to our expansiveness. An unchecked expansiveness on the national scale is always imperialistic. Among the ingredients of a possible American imperialism M. Siegfried enumerates the American's "great self-satisfaction, his rather brutal sense of his own interest, and *the consciousness, still more dangerous, of his 'duties' towards humanity."* M. Siegfried admits however that our imperialism is likely to be of a new and subtle essence, not concerned primarily with territorial aggrandizement.

A proper discussion of Mr. Siegfried's position as well as of other issues I have been raising would transcend the limits of an article. My end has been accomplished if I have justified in some measure the statement with which I started as to the importance of cultivating a general critical intelligence. James Russell Lowell's dictum that before having an American literature we must have an American criticism was never truer than it is to-day. The obvious reply to those who call for more creation and less criticism is that one needs to be critical above all in examining what now passes for creation. A scrutiny of this kind would, I have tried to show, extend beyond the bounds of literature to various aspects of our national life and would converge finally on our higher education.

We cannot afford to accept as a substitute for this true criticism the self-expression of Mr. Mencken and his school, unless indeed we are to merit the comment that is, I am told, made on us by South Americans: "They are not a very serious people." To be sure, the reader may reflect that I am myself a critic, or would-be critic. I can only express the hope that, in my magnifying of the critical function, I do not offer too close a parallel to the dancing-master in Molière who averred, it will be remembered, that "all the mistakes of men, the fatal reverses that fill the world's annals, the shortcomings of statesmen, and the blunders of great captains arise from not knowing how to dance."

1928

H. L. MENCKEN

FROM

Prejudices: Third Series

From On Being an American

I

Apparently there are those who begin to find it disagreeable—nay, impossible. Their anguish fills the Liberal weeklies, and every ship that puts out from New York carries a groaning cargo of them, bound for Paris, London, Munich, Rome and way points—anywhere to escape the great curses and atrocities that make life intolerable for them at home. Let me say at once that I find little to cavil at in their basic complaints. In more than one direction, indeed, I probably go a great deal further than even the Young Intellectuals. It is, for example, one of my firmest and most sacred beliefs, reached after an inquiry extending over a score of years and supported by incessant prayer and meditation, that the government of the United States, in both its legislative arm and its executive arm, is ignorant, incompetent, corrupt, and disgusting—and from this judgment I except no more than twenty living lawmakers and no more than twenty executioners of their laws. It is a belief no less piously cherished that the administration of justice in the Republic is stupid, dishonest, and against all reason and equity—and from this judgment I except no more than thirty judges, including two upon the bench of the Supreme Court of the United States. It is another that the foreign policy of the United States—its habitual manner of dealing with other nations, whether friend or foe—is hypocritical, disingenuous, knavish, and dishonorable—and from this judgment I consent to no exceptions whatever, either recent or long past. And it is my fourth (and, to avoid too depressing a bill, final) conviction that the American people taking one with another, constitute the most timorous, sniveling, poltroonish, ignominious mob of serfs and goose-steppers ever gathered under one flag in Christendom since the end of the Middle Ages, and that they grow more timorous, more sniveling, more poltroonish, more ignominious every day.

So far I go with the fugitive Young Intellectuals—and into the Bad Lands beyond. Such, in brief, are the cardinal articles of my political faith, held passionately since my admission to citizenship and now growing stronger and stronger as I gradually disintegrate into my component carbon, oxygen, hydrogen, phosphorus, calcium, sodium, nitrogen and iron. This is what I believe and preach, *in nomine Domini,* Amen. Yet I remain on the dock, wrapped in the flag, when the Young Intellectuals set sail. Yet here I stand, unshaken and undespairing, a loyal and devoted Americano, even a chauvinist, paying taxes without complaint, obeying all laws that are physiologically obeyable, accepting all the searching duties and responsibilities of citizenship unprotestingly, investing the sparse usufructs of my miserable toil in the obligations of the nation, avoiding all commerce with men sworn to overthrow the government, contributing my mite toward the glory of the national arts and sciences, enriching and embellishing the native language, spurning all lures (and even all invitations) to get out and stay out—here am I, a bachelor of easy means, forty-two years old, unhampered by debts or issue, able to go wherever I please and to stay as long as I please—here am I, contentedly and even smugly basking beneath the Stars and Stripes, a better citizen, I daresay, and certainly a less murmurous and exigent one, than thousands who put the Hon. Warren Gamaliel Harding beside Friedrich Barbarossa and Charlemagne, and hold the Supreme Court to be directly inspired by the Holy Spirit, and belong ardently to every Rotary Club, Ku Klux Klan, and Anti-Saloon League, and choke with emotion when the band plays "The Star-Spangled Banner," and believe with the faith of little children that one of Our Boys, taken at random, could dispose in a fair fight of ten Englishmen, twenty Germans, thirty Frogs, forty Wops, fifty Japs, or a hundred Bolsheviki.

Well, then, why am I still here? Why am I so complacent (perhaps even to the point of offensiveness), so free from bile, so little fretting and indignant, so curiously happy? Why did I answer only with a few academic "Hear, Hears" when Henry James, Ezra Pound, Harold Stearns and the *emigrés* of Greenwich Village issued their successive calls to the corn-fed *intelligentsia* to flee the shambles, escape to fairer lands, throw off the curse forever? The answer, of course, is to be sought in the nature of happiness, which tempts to metaphysics. But let me keep upon the ground. To me, at least (and I can only follow my own nose), happiness presents itself in an aspect that is tripartite. To be happy (reducing the thing to its elementals) I must be:

a. Well-fed, unhounded by sordid cares, at ease in Zion.
b. Full of a comfortable feeling of superiority to the masses of my fellow-men.
c. Delicately and unceasingly amused according to my taste.

It is my contention that, if this definition be accepted, there is no country on the face of the earth wherein a man roughly constituted as I am—a man of my general weaknesses, vanities, appetites, prejudices, and aversions—can be so happy, or even one-half so happy, as he can be in these free and independent states. Going further, I lay down the proposition that it is a sheer physical impossibility for such a man to live in These States and *not* be happy—that it is as impossible to him as it would be to a schoolboy to weep over the burning down of his school-house. If he says that he isn't happy here, then he either lies or is insane. Here the business of getting a living, particularly since the war brought the loot of all Europe to the national strong-box, is enormously easier than it is in any other Christian land—so easy, in fact, that an educated and forehanded man who fails at it must actually make deliberate efforts to that end. Here the general average of intelligence, of knowledge, of competence, of integrity, of self-respect, of honor is so low that any man who knows his trade, does not fear ghosts, has read fifty good books, and practices the common decencies stands out as brilliantly as a wart on a bald head, and is thrown willy-nilly into a meager and exclusive aristocracy. And here, more than anywhere else that I know of or have heard of, the daily panorama of human existence, of private and communal folly—the unending procession of governmental extortions and chicaneries, of commercial brigandages and throat-slittings, of theological buffooneries, of aesthetic ribaldries, of legal swindles and harlotries, of miscellaneous rogueries, villainies, imbecilities, grotesqueries, and extravagances—is so inordinately gross and preposterous, so perfectly brought up to the highest conceivable amperage, so steadily enriched with an almost fabulous daring and originality, that only the man who was born with a petrified diaphragm can fail to laugh himself to sleep every night, and to awake every morning with all the eager, unflagging expectation of a Sunday-school superintendent touring the Paris peep-shows.

A certain sough of rhetoric may be here. Perhaps I yield to words as a chautauqua lecturer yields to them, belaboring and fermenting the hinds with his Message from the New Jerusalem. But fundamentally I am quite as sincere as he is. For example, in the matter of attaining to ease in Zion, of getting a fair share of the national swag, now piled so mountainously high. It seems to me, sunk in my Egyptian night, that the man who fails to do this in the United States to-day is a man who is somehow stupid— maybe not on the surface, but certainly deep down. Either he is one who cripples himself unduly, say by setting up a family before he can care for it, or by making a bad bargain for the sale of his wares, or by concerning himself too much about the affairs of other men; or he is one who endeavors fatuously to sell something that no normal American wants. Whenever I hear a professor of philosophy complain that his wife has eloped with some moving-picture actor or bootlegger who can at least feed and clothe her, my natural sympathy for the man is greatly corrupted by contempt for his lack of sense. Would it be regarded as sane and laudable for a man to travel the Soudan trying to sell fountain-pens, or Greenland offering to teach double-entry bookkeeping or counterpoint? Coming closer, would the judicious pity or laugh at a man who opened a shop for the sale of incunabula in Little Rock, Ark., or who demanded a living in McKeesport, Pa., on the ground that he could read Sumerian? In precisely the same way it seems to me to be nonsensical for a man to offer generally some commodity that only a few rare and dubious Americans want, and then weep and beat his breast because he is not patronized. One seeking to make a living in a country must pay due regard to the needs and tastes of that country. Here in the United States we have no jobs for grand dukes, and none for *Wirkliche Geheimräte* [actual privy councilors], and none for palace eunuchs, and none for masters of the buckhounds, and none (any more) for brewery *Todsaufer* [one who tastes for poison] —and very few for oboe-players, metaphysicians, astrophysicists, assyriologists, water-colorists, stylites and epic poets. There was a time when the *Todsaufer* served a public need and got an adequate reward, but it is no more. There may come a time when the composer of string quartettes is paid as much as a railway conductor, but it is not yet. Then why practice such trades—that is, as trades? The man of independent means may venture into them prudently; when he does so, he is seldom molested; it may even be argued that he performs a public service by adopting them. But the man who has a living to make is simply silly if he goes into them; he is like a soldier going over the top with a coffin strapped to his back. Let him abandon such puerile vanities, and take to the uplift instead, as, indeed, thousands of other victims of the industrial system have already done. Let him bear in mind that, whatever its neglect of the humanities and their monks, the Republic has never got half enough bond salesmen, quack doctors, ward leaders, phrenologists, Methodist evangelists, circus clowns, magicians, soldiers, farmers, popular song writers, moonshine distillers, forgers of gin labels, mine guards, detectives, spies, snoopers, and *agents provocateurs*. The rules are set by Omnipotence; the discreet man observes them. Observing them, he is safe beneath the starry bed-tick, in fair weather or foul. The *boobus Americanus* is a bird that knows no closed season—and if he won't come down to Texas oil stock, or one-night cancer cures, or building lots in Swampshurst, he will always come down to Inspiration and Optimism, whether political, theological, pedagogical, literary, or economic.

The doctrine that it is *infra dignitatem* [undignified] for an educated man to take a hand in the snaring of this goose is one in which I see nothing convincing. It is a

doctrine chiefly voiced, I believe, by those who have tried
the business and failed. They take refuge behind the childish notion that there is something honorable about poverty
per se—the Greenwich Village complex. This is nonsense.
Poverty may be an unescapable misfortune, but that no
more makes it honorable than a cocked eye is made honorable by the same cause. Do I advocate, then, the ceaseless,
senseless hogging of money? I do not. All I advocate—
and praise as virtuous—is the hogging of enough to provide
security and ease. Despite all the romantic superstitutions to
the contrary, the artist cannot do his best work when he
is oppressed by unsatisfied wants. Nor can the philosopher.
Nor can the man of science. The best and clearest thinking
of the world is done and the finest art is produced, not by
men who are hungry, ragged and harassed, by by men who
are well-fed, warm and easy in mind. It is the artist's first
duty to his art to achieve that tranquility for himself.
Shakespeare tried to achieve it; so did Beethoven, Wagner,
Brahms, Ibsen and Balzac. Goethe, Schopenhauer, Schu-
mann and Mendelssohn were born to it. Joseph Conrad,
Richard Strauss and Anatole France have got it for themselves in our own day. In the older countries, where competence is far more general and competition is thus more
sharp, the thing is often cruelly difficult, and sometimes almost impossible. But in the United States it is absurdly
easy, given ordinary luck. Any man with a superior air,
the intelligence of a stockbroker, and the resolution of a
hat-check girl—in brief, any man who believes in himself
enough, and with sufficient cause, to be called a journey-
man—can cadge enough money, in this glorious commonwealth of morons, to make life soft for him.

And if a lining for the purse is thus facilely obtainable,
given a reasonable prudence and resourcefulness, then balm
for the ego is just as unlaboriously got, given ordinary
dignity and decency. Simply to exist, indeed, on the plane
of a civilized man is to attain, in the Republic, to a distinction that should be enough for all save the most vain;
it is even likely to be too much, as the frequent challenges
of the Ku Klux Klan, the American Legion, the Anti-
Saloon League, and other such vigilance committees of the
majority testify. Here is a country in which all political
thought and activity are concentrated upon the scramble
for jobs—in which the normal politician, whether he be a

President or a village road supervisor, is willing to renounce any principle, however precious to him, and to adopt any lunacy, however offensive to him, in order to keep his place at the trough. Go into politics, then, without seeking or wanting office, and at once you are as conspicuous as a red-haired blackamoor—in fact, a great deal more conspicuous, for red-haired blackamoors have been seen, but who has ever seen or heard of an American politician, Democrat or Republican, Socialist or Liberal, Whig or Tory, who did not itch for a job? Again, here is a country in which it is an axiom that a business man shall be a member of a Chamber of Commerce, an admirer of Charles M. Schwab, a reader of the *Saturday Evening Post,* a golfer —in brief, a vegetable. Spend your hours of escape from *Geschäft* [business] reading Remy de Gourmont or practicing the violincello, and the local Sunday newspaper will infallibly find you out and hymn the marvel—nay, your banker will summon you to discuss your notes, and your rivals will spread the report (probably truthful) that you were pro-German during the war. Yet again, here is a land in which women rule and men are slaves. Train your women to get your slippers for you, and your ill fame will match Galileo's or Darwin's. Once more, here is the Paradise of backslappers, of democrats, of mixers, of gogetters. Maintain ordinary reserve, and you will arrest instant attention—and have your hand kissed by multitudes who, despite democracy, have all the inferior man's unquenchable desire to grovel and admire.

Nowhere else in the world is superiority more easily attained or more eagerly admitted. The chief business of the nation, as a nation, is the setting up of heroes, mainly bogus. It admired the literary style of the late Woodrow; it respects the theological passion of Bryan; it venerates J. Pierpont Morgan; it takes Congress seriously; it would be unutterably shocked by the proposition (with proof) that a majority of its judges are ignoramuses, and that a respectable minority of them are scoundrels. The manufacture of artificial *Durchlauchten, k. k. Hoheiten* [royal imperial Highnesses] and even gods goes on feverishly and incessantly; the will to worship never flags. Ten iron-molders meet in the backroom of a near-beer saloon, organize a lodge of the Noble and Mystic Order of American Rosicrucians, and elect a wheelwright Supreme Worthy

Whimwham; a month later they send a notice to the local
newspaper that they have been greatly honored by an official visit from that Whimwham, and that they plan to give
him a jeweled fob for his watch-chain. The chief national
heroes—Lincoln, Lee, and so on—cannot remain mere
men. The mysticism of the mediaeval peasantry gets into
the communal view of them, and they begin to sprout
haloes and wings. As I say, no intrinsic merit—at least,
none commensurate with the mob estimate—is needed to
come to such august dignities. Everything American is a
bit amateurish and childish, even the national gods. The
most conspicuous and respected American in nearly every
field of endeavor, saving only the purely commercial (I
exclude even the financial) is a man who would attract
little attention in any other country. The leading American
critic of literature, after twenty years of diligent exposition
of his ideas, has yet to make it clear what he is in favor of,
and why. The queen of the *haut monde* [fashionable world]
in almost every American city, is a woman who regards
Lord Reading as an aristocrat and her superior, and whose
grandfather slept in his underclothes. The leading American musical director, if he went to Leipzig, would be put
to polishing trombones and copying drum parts. The chief
living American military-man—the national heir to Frederick, Marlborough, Wellington, Washington and Prince
Eugene—is a member of the Elks, and proud of it. The
leading American philosopher (now dead, with no suc-
cessor known to the average pedagogue) spent a lifetime
erecting an epistemological defense for the national aesthetic maxim: "I don't know nothing about music, but I
know what I like." The most eminent statesman the
United States has produced since Lincoln was fooled by
Arthur James Balfour, and miscalculated his public support by more than 5,000,000 votes. And the current Chief
Magistrate of the nation—its defiant substitute for czar
and kaiser—is a small-town printer who, when he wishes
to enjoy himself in the Executive Mansion, invites in a
homeopathic doctor, a Seventh Day Adventist evangelist,
and a couple of moving-picture actresses.

IV

All the while I have been forgetting the third of my reasons for remaining so faithful a citizen of the Federation,

despite all the lascivious inducements from expatriates to follow them beyond the seas, and all the surly suggestions from patriots that I succumb. It is the reason which grows out of my mediaeval but unashamed taste for the bizarre and indelicate, my congenital weakness for comedy of the grosser varieties. The United States, to my eye, is incomparably the greatest show on earth. It is a show which avoids diligently all the kinds of clowning which tire me most quickly—for example, royal ceremonials, the tedious hocus-pocus of *haut politique* [political ceremony], the taking of politics seriously—and lays chief stress upon the kinds which delight me unceasingly—for example, the ribald combats of demagogues, the exquisitely ingenious operations of master rogues, the pursuit of witches and heretics, the desperate struggles of inferior men to claw their way into Heaven. We have clowns in constant practice among us who are as far above the clowns of any other great state as a Jack Dempsey is above a paralytic—and not a few dozen or score of them, but whole droves and herds. Human enterprises which, in all other Christian countries, are resigned despairingly to an incurable dullness—things that seem devoid of exhilarating amusement by their very nature—are here lifted to such vast heights of buffoonery that contemplating them strains the midriff almost to breaking. I cite an example: the worship of God. Everywhere else on earth it is carried on in a solemn and dispiriting manner; in England, of course, the bishops are obscene, but the average man seldom gets a fair chance to laugh at them and enjoy them. Now come home. Here we not only have bishops who are enormously more obscene than even the most gifted of the English bishops; we have also a huge force of lesser specialists in ecclesiastical mountebankery—tin-horn Loyolas, Savonarolas and Xaviers of a hundred fantastic rites, each performing untiringly and each full of a grotesque and illimitable whimsicality. Every American town, however small, has one of its own: a holy clerk with so fine a talent for introducing the arts of jazz into the salvation of the damned that his performance takes on all the gaudiness of a four-ring circus, and the bald announcement that he will raid Hell on such and such a night is enough to empty all the town blind-pigs and bordellos and pack his sanctuary to the doors. And to aid him and inspire him there are traveling experts to

whom he stands in the relation of a wart to the Matterhorn
—stupendous masters of theological imbecility, contrivers
of doctrines utterly preposterous, heirs to the Joseph Smith,
Mother Eddy and John Alexander Dowie tradition—
Bryan, Sunday, and their like. These are the eminences of
the American Sacred College. I delight in them. Their
proceedings make me a happier American.

Turn, now, to politics. Consider, for example, a campaign for the Presidency. Would it be possible to imagine
anything more uproariously idiotic—a deafening, nerve-
wracking battle to the death between Tweedledum and
Tweedledee, Harlequin and Sganarelle, Gobbo and Dr.
Cook—the unspeakable, with fearful snorts, gradually
swallowing the inconceivable? I defy any one to match it
elsewhere on this earth. In other lands, at worst, there are
at least intelligible issues, coherent ideas, salient personalities. Somebody says something, and somebody replies.
But what did Harding say in 1920, and what did Cox
reply? Who was Harding, anyhow, and who was Cox?
Here, having perfected democracy, we lift the whole combat to symbolism, to transcendentalism, to metaphysics.
Here we load a pair of palpably tin cannon with blank
cartridges charged with talcum powder, and so let fly. Here
one may howl over the show without any uneasy reminder
that it is serious, and that some one may be hurt. I hold that
this elevation of politics to the plane of undiluted comedy
is peculiarly American, that nowhere else on this disreputa-
ble ball has the art of the shambattle been developed to
such fineness. Two experiences are in point. During the
Harding-Cox combat of bladders an article of mine, dealing with some of its more melodramatic phases, was translated into German and reprinted by a Berlin paper. At the
head of it the editor was careful to insert a preface explaining to his readers, but recently delivered to democracy,
that such contests were not taken seriously by intelligent
Americans, and warning them solemnly against getting into
sweats over politics. At about the same time I had dinner
with an Englishman. From cocktails to bromo seltzer he
bewailed the political lassitude of the English populace—
its growing indifference to the whole partisan harlequinade.
Here were two typical foreign attitudes: the Germans were
in danger of making politics too harsh and implacable, and
the English were in danger of forgetting politics altogether.

Both attitudes, it must be plain, make for bad shows. Observing a German campaign, one is uncomfortably harassed and stirred up; observing an English campaign (at least in times of peace), one falls asleep. In the United States the thing is done better. Here politics is purged of all menace, all sinister quality, all genuine significance, and stuffed with such gorgeous humors, such inordinate farce that one comes to the end of a campaign with one's ribs loose, and ready for "King Lear," or a hanging, or a course of medical journals.

But feeling better for the laugh. *Ridi si sapis,* said Martial. Mirth is necessary to wisdom, to comfort, above all, to happiness. Well, here is the land of mirth, as Germany is the land of metaphysics and France is the land of fornication. Here the buffoonery never stops. What could be more delightful than the endless struggle of the Puritan to make the joy of the minority unlawful and impossible? The effort is itself a greater joy to one standing on the side-lines than any or all of the carnal joys that it combats. Always, when I contemplate an uplifter at his hopeless business, I recall a scene in an old-time burlesque show, witnessed for hire in my days as a dramatic critic. A chorus girl executed a fall upon the stage, and Rudolph Krausemeyer, the Swiss comedian, rushed to her aid. As he stooped painfully to succor her, Irving Rabinovitz, the Zionist comedian, fetched him a fearful clout across the cofferdam with a slap-stick. So the uplifter, the soul-saver, the Americanizer, striving to make the Republic fit for Y.M.C.A. secretaries. He is the eternal American, ever moved by the best intentions, ever running *à la* Krausemeyer to the rescue of virtue, and ever getting his pantaloons fanned by the Devil. I am naturally sinful, and such spectacles caress me. If the slap-stick were a sash-weight the show would be cruel, and I'd probably complain to the *Polizei.* As it is, I know that the uplifter is not really hurt, but simply shocked. The blow, in fact, does him good, for it helps to get him into Heaven, as exegetes prove from Matthew V, ii: *Heureux serez-vous, lorsqu'on vous outragera, qu'on vous persécutera* ["Blessed are ye, when men shall revile you, and persecute you"], and so on. As for me, it makes me a more contented man, and hence a better citizen. One man prefers the Republic because it pays better wages than Bulgaria. Another because it has laws to keep him sober and his daughter chaste. Another because the Woolworth Building is higher than the cathedral at Chartres. Another because, living here, he can read the New York *Evening Journal*. Another because there is a warrant out for him somewhere else. Me, I like it because it amuses me to my taste. I never get tired of the show. It is worth every cent it costs.

That cost, it seems to me, is very moderate. Taxes in the United States are not actually high. I figure, for example, that my private share of the expense of maintaining the Hon. Mr. Harding in the White House this year will work out to less than 80 cents. Try to think of better sport for the money: in New York it has been estimated that it costs $8 to get comfortably tight, and $17.50, on an average, to pinch a girl's arm. The United States Senate will cost me perhaps $11 for the year, but against that expense set the subscription price of the *Congressional Record*, about $15, which as a journalist, I receive for nothing. For $4 less than nothing I am thus entertained as Solomon never was by his hooch dancers. Col. George Brinton McClellan Harvey costs me but 25 cents a year; I get Nicholas Murray Butler free. Finally, there is young Teddy Roosevelt, the naval expert. Teddy costs me, as I work it out, about 11 cents a year, or less than a cent a month. More, he entertains me doubly for the money, first as a naval expert, and secondly as a walking *attentat* [outrage] upon democracy, a devastating proof that there is nothing, after all, in that superstition. We Americans subscribe to the doctrine of human equality—and the Rooseveltii reduce it to an absurdity as brilliantly as the sons of Veit Bach. Where is your equal opportunity now? Here in this Eden of clowns, with the highest rewards of clowning theoretically open to every poor boy—here in the very citadel of democracy we found and cherish a clown *dynasty!*

1922

SOUTHERN AGRARIANS

Donald Davidson, John Gould Fletcher, Henry Blue Kline,
Lyle H. Lanier, Andrew Nelson Lytle, Clarence Nixon,
Frank Lawrence Owsley, John Crowe Ransom,
Allen Tate, John Donald Wade, Robert Penn
Warren, and Stark Young

FROM

I'll Take My Stand

Introduction—A Statement of Principles

The authors contributing to this book are Southerners, well acquainted with one another and of similar tastes, though not necessarily living in the same physical community, and perhaps only at this moment aware of themselves as a single group of men. By conversation and exchange of letters over a number of years it had developed that they entertained many convictions in common, and it was decided to make a volume in which each one should furnish his views upon a chosen topic. This was the general background. But background and consultation as to the various topics were enough; there was to be no further collaboration. And so no single author is responsible for any view outside his own article. It was through the good fortune of some deeper agreement that the book was expected to achieve its unity. All the articles bear in the same sense upon the book's title-subject: all tend to support a Southern way of life against what may be called the American or prevailing way; and all as much as agree that the best terms in which to represent the distinction are contained in the phrase, Agrarian *versus* Industrial. . . .

Nobody now proposes for the South, or for any other community in this country, an independent political destiny. That idea is thought to have been finished in 1865. But how far shall the South surrender its moral, social, and economic autonomy to the victorious principle of Union? That question remains open. The South is a minority section that has hitherto been jealous of its minority right to live its own kind of life. The South scarcely hopes to determine the other sections, but it does propose to determine itself, within the utmost limits of legal action. Of late, however, there is the melancholy fact that the South itself has wavered a little and shown signs of wanting to join up behind the common or American industrial ideal. It is against that tendency that this book is written. The younger Southerners, who are being converted frequently to the industrial gospel, must come back to the support of the Southern tradition. They must be persuaded to look very critically at the advantages of becoming a "new South" which will be only an undistinguished replica of the usual industrial community. . . .

But there are many other minority communities opposed to industrialism, and wanting a much simpler economy to live by. The communities and private persons sharing the agrarian tastes are to be found widely within the Union. Proper living is a matter of the intelligence and the will, does not depend on the local climate or geography, and is capable of a definition which is general and not Southern at all. Southerners have a filial duty to discharge to their own section. But their cause is precarious and they must seek alliances with sympathetic communities everywhere. The members of the present group would be happy to be counted as members of a national agrarian movement. . . .

Industrialism is the economic organization of the collective American society. It means the decision of society to invest its economic resources in the applied sciences. But the word science has acquired a certain sanctitude. It is out of order to quarrel with science in the abstract, or even with the applied sciences when their applications are made subject to criticism and intelligence. The capitalization of the applied sciences has now become extravagant and un-critical; it has enslaved our human energies to a degree now clearly felt to be burdensome. The apologists of in-dustrialism do not like to meet this charge directly; so they often take refuge in saying that they are devoted sim-ply to science! They are really devoted to the applied sci-ences and to practical production. Therefore it is necessary to employ a certain skepticism even at the expense of the Cult of Science, and to say, It is an Americanism, which looks innocent and disinterested, but really is not either.

. . .

The contribution that science can make to a labor is to render it easier by the help of a tool or a process, and to assure the laborer of his perfect economic security while he is engaged upon it. Then it can be performed with leisure and enjoyment. But the modern laborer has not exactly received this benefit under the industrial regime. His labor is hard, its tempo is fierce, and his employment is insecure. The first principle of a good labor is that it must be effective, but the second principle is that it must be enjoyed. Labor is one of the largest items in the human career; it is a modest demand to ask that it may partake of happiness.

. . .

The regular act of applied science is to introduce into labor a labor-saving device or a machine. Whether this is a benefit depends on how far it is advisable to save the labor. The philosophy of applied science is generally quite sure that the saving of labor is a pure gain, and that the more of it the better. This is to assume that labor is an evil, that only the end of labor or the material product is good. On this assumption labor becomes mercenary and servile, and it is no wonder if many forms of modern labor are accepted without resentment though they are evidently brutalizing. The act of labor as one of the happy functions of human life has been in effect abandoned, and is practiced solely for its rewards.

. . .

Even the apologists of industrialism have been obliged to admit that some economic evils follow in the wake of the machines. These are such as overproduction, unemployment, and a growing inequality in the distribution of wealth. But the remedies proposed by the apologists are always homeopathic. They expect the evils to disappear when we have bigger and better machines, and more of them. Their remedial programs, therefore, look forward to more industrialism. Sometimes they see the system righting itself spontaneously and without direction: they are Optimists. Sometimes they rely on the benevolence of capital, or the militancy of labor, to bring about a fairer division of the spoils: they are Cooperationists or Socialists. And sometimes they expect to find super-engineers, in the shape of Boards of Control, who will adapt production to consumption and regulate prices and guarantee business against fluctuations: they are Sovietists. With respect to these last it must be insisted that the true Sovietists or Communists—if the term may be used here in the European sense—are the Industrialists themselves. They would have the government set up an economic super-organization, which in turn would become the government. We therefore look upon the Communist menace as a menace indeed, but not as the Red one; because it is simply according to the blind drift of our industrial development to expect in America at last much the same economic system as that imposed by violence upon Russia in 1917.

. . .

Turning to consumption, as the grand end which justifies the evil of modern labor, we find that we have been deceived. We have more time in which to consume, and many more products to be consumed. But the tempo of our labors communicates itself to our satisfactions, and these also become brutal and hurried. The constitution of the natural man probably does not permit him to shorten his labor-time and enlarge his consuming-time indefinitely. He has to pay the penalty in satiety and aimlessness. The modern man has lost his sense of vocation.

. . .

Religion can hardly expect to flourish in an industrial society. Religion is our submission to the general intention of a nature that is fairly inscrutable; it is the sense of our role as creatures within it. But nature industrialized, transformed into cities and artificial habitations, manufactured into commodities, is no longer nature but a highly simplified picture of nature. We receive the illusion of having power over nature, and lose the sense of nature as something mysterious and contingent. The God of nature under the conditions is merely an amiable expression, a superfluity, and the philosophical understanding ordinarily carried in the religious experience is not there for us to have.

. . .

Nor do the arts have a proper life under industrialism, with the general decay of sensibility which attends it. Art

depends, in general, like religion, on a right attitude to
nature; and in particular on a free and disinterested observation of nature that occurs only in leisure. Neither the
creation nor the understanding of works of art is possible
in an industrial age except by some local and unlikely suspension of the industrial drive.

· · ·

The amenities of life also suffer under the curse of a
strictly-business or industrial civilization. They consist in
such practices as manners, conversation, hospitality, sympathy, family life, romantic love—in the social exchanges
which reveal and develop sensibility in human affairs. If
religion and the arts are founded on right relations of man-
to-nature, these are founded on right relations of man-to-
man.

· · ·

Apologists of industrialism are even inclined to admit
that its actual processes may have upon its victims the
spiritual effects just described. But they think that all can
be made right by extraordinary educational efforts, by all
sorts of cultural institutions and endowments. They would
cure the poverty of the contemporary spirit by hiring experts to instruct it in spite of itself in the historic culture.
But salvation is hardly to be encountered on that road.
The trouble with the life-pattern is to be located at its
economic base, and we cannot rebuild it by pouring in
soft materials from the top. The young men and women
in colleges, for example, if they are already placed in a
false way of life, cannot make more than an inconsequential acquaintance with the arts and humanities transmitted
to them. Or else the understanding of these arts and humanities will but make them the more wretched in their
own destitution.

· · ·

The "Humanists" are too abstract. Humanism, properly
speaking, is not an abstract system, but a culture, the whole
way in which we live, act, think, and feel. It is a kind of
imaginatively balanced life lived out in a definite social
tradition. And, in the concrete, we believe that this, the
genuine humanism, was rooted in the agrarian life of the

older South and of other parts of the country that shared in such a tradition. It was not an abstract moral "check" derived from the classics—it was not soft material poured in from the top. It was deeply founded in the way of life itself—in its tables, chairs, portraits, festivals, laws, marriage customs. We cannot recover our native humanism by adopting some standard of taste that is critical enough to question the contemporary arts but not critical enough to question the social and economic life which is their ground.

· · ·

The tempo of the industrial life is fast, but that is not the worst of it; it is accelerating. The ideal is not merely some set form of industrialism, with so many stable industries, but industrial progress, or an incessant extension of industrialization. It never proposes a specific goal; it initiates the infinite series. We have not merely capitalized certain industries; we have capitalized the laboratories and inventors, and undertaken to employ all the labor-saving devices that come out of them. But a fresh labor-saving device introduced into an industry does not emancipate the laborers in that industry so much as it evicts them. Applied at the expense of agriculture, for example, the new processes have reduced the part of the population supporting itself upon the soil to a smaller and smaller fraction. Of course no single labor-saving process is fatal; it brings on a period of unemployed labor and unemployed capital, but soon a new industry is devised which will put them both to work again, and a new commodity is thrown upon the market. The laborers were sufficiently embarrassed in the meantime, but, according to the theory, they will eventually be taken care of. It is now the public which is embarrassed; it feels obligated to purchase a commodity for which it had expressed no desire, but it is invited to make its budget equal to the strain. All might yet be well, and stability and comfort might again obtain, but for this: partly because of industrial ambitions and partly because the repressed creative impulse must break out somewhere, there will be a stream of further labor-saving devices in all industries, and the cycle will have to be repeated over and over. The result is an increasing disadjustment and instability.

. . .

It is an inevitable consequence of industrial progress that production greatly outruns the rate of natural consumption. To overcome the disparity, the producers, disguised as the pure idealists of progress, must coerce and wheedle the public into being loyal and steady consumers, in order to keep the machines running. So the rise of modern advertising—along with its twin, personal salesmanship—is the most significant development of our industrialism. Advertising means to persuade the consumers to want exactly what the applied sciences are able to furnish them. It consults the happiness of the consumer no more than it consulted the happiness of the laborer. It is the great effort of a false economy of life to approve itself.

. . .

It is strange, of course, that a majority of men anywhere could ever as with one mind become enamored of industrialism: a system that has so little regard for individual wants. There is evidently a kind of thinking that rejoices in setting up a social objective which has no relation to the individual. Men are prepared to sacrifice their private dignity and happiness to an abstract social ideal, and without asking whether the social ideal produces the welfare of any individual man whatsoever. But this is absurd. The responsibility of men is for their own welfare and that of their neighbors; not for the hypothetical welfare of some fabulous creature called society.

. . .

Opposed to the industrial society is the agrarian, which does not stand in particular need of definition. An agrarian society is hardly one that has no use at all for industries, for professional vocations, for scholars and artists, and for the life of cities. Technically, perhaps, an agrarian society is one in which agriculture is the leading vocation, whether for wealth, for pleasure, or for prestige—a form of labor that is pursued with intelligence and leisure, and that becomes the model to which the other forms approach as well as they may. But an agrarian regime will be secured readily enough where the superfluous industries are not allowed to rise against it. The theory of agrarianism is that the culture of the soil is the best and most sensitive of vocations, and that therefore it should have the economic preference and enlist the maximum number of workers.

. . .

These principles do not intend to be very specific in proposing any practical measures. How may the little agrarian community resist the Chamber of Commerce of its county seat, which is always trying to import some foreign industry that cannot be assimilated to the life-pattern of the community? Just what must the Southern leaders do to defend the traditional Southern life? How may the Southern and the Western agrarians unite for effective action? Should the agrarian forces try to capture the Democratic party, which historically is so closely affiliated with the defense of individualism, the small community, the state, the South? Or must the agrarians—even the Southern ones—abandon the Democratic party to its fate and try a new one? What legislation could most profitably be championed by the powerful agrarians in the Senate of the United States? What anti-industrial measures might promise to stop the advances of industrialism, or even undo some of them, with the least harm to those concerned? What policy should be pursued by the educators who have a tradition at heart? These and many other questions are of the greatest importance, but they cannot be answered here.

. . .

. . . in conclusion, this much is clear: If a community, or a section, or a race, or an age, is groaning under industrialism, and well aware that it is an evil dispensation, it must find the way to throw it off. To think that this cannot be done is pusillanimous. And if the whole community, section, race, or age thinks it cannot be done, then it has simply lost its political genius and doomed itself to impotence.

1930

EDMUND WILSON

The Historical Interpretation of Literature

I want to talk about the historical interpretation of literature—that is, about the interpretation of literature in its social, economic and political aspects.

To begin with, it will be worth while to say something about the kind of criticism which seems to be furthest removed from this. There is a kind of comparative criticism which tends to be non-historical. The essays of T. S. Eliot, which have had such an immense influence in our time, are, for example, fundamentally non-historical. Eliot sees, or tries to see, the whole of literature, so far as he is acquainted with it, spread out before him under the aspect of eternity. He then compares the work of different periods and countries, and tries to draw from it general conclusions about what literature ought to be. He understands, of course, that our point of view in connection with literature changes, and he has what seems to me a very sound conception of the whole body of writing of the past as something to which new works are continually being added, and which is not merely increased in bulk thereby but modified as a whole—so that Sophocles is no longer precisely what he was for Aristotle, or Shakespeare what he was for Ben Jonson or for Dryden or for Dr. Johnson, on account of all the later literature that has intervened between them and us. Yet at every point of this continual accretion, the whole field may be surveyed, as it were, spread out before the critic. The critic tries to see it as God might: he calls the books to a Day of Judgment. And looking at things in this way, he may arrive at interesting and valuable conclusions which could hardly be reached by approaching them in any other way. Eliot was able to see, for example—what I believe had never been noticed before —that the French symbolist poetry of the nineteenth century had certain fundamental resemblances to the English poetry of the age of Donne. Another kind of critic would draw certain historical conclusions from these purely

esthetic findings, as the Russian D. S. Mirsky did; but Eliot does not draw them.

Another example of this kind of non-historical criticism, in a somewhat different way and on a somewhat different plane, is the work of the late George Saintsbury. Saintsbury was a connoisseur of wines, he wrote an entertaining book on the subject. And his attitude toward literature, too, was that of the connoisseur. He tastes the authors, and tells you about the vintages; he distinguishes the qualities of the various wines. His palate was as fine as could be, and he possessed the great qualification that he knew how to take books on their own terms and was thus able to appreciate a very large variety of different kinds of writing. He was a man of strong social prejudices and peculiarly intransigent political views, but, so far as it is humanly possible, he kept them out of his literary criticism. The result is one of the most agreeable commentaries on literature that have ever been written. Most scholars who have read as much as Saintsbury don't have Saintsbury's discriminating taste. Saintsbury has been over the whole ground like any academic historian, but his account of it is not merely a chronology: it is a record of fastidious enjoyment. Since enjoyment is the only thing he is looking for, he does not need to know the causes of things, and the historical background of literature does not interest him very much.

There is, however, another tradition of criticism that dates from the beginning of the eighteenth century. In 1725, the Neapolitan philosopher Vico published *La Scienza Nuova,* a revolutionary work on the philosophy of history, in which he asserted for the first time that *the social world* was *certainly the work of man,* and attempted what is, so far as I know, the first social interpretation of a work of literature. This is what Vico says about Homer: "Homer composed the *Iliad in his youth*—that is, in the youth of Greece. Greece was then all aflame with sublime passions, with pride, anger and vengeance. These sentiments are incompatible with dissimulation and do not exclude generosity; Greece admired Achilles, *the hero of force.* Homer composed the *Odyssey* when he was *old,* when the passions of the Greeks were beginning to be cooled by reflection, the mother of prudence. In the time of Homer's youth, the pride of Agamemnon, the insolence and barbarity of Achilles, were what was pleasing to the peoples of Greece. In the time of its old age, they already liked the luxury of Alcinoüs, the delights of Calypso, the sensuous pleasures of Circe, the songs of the sirens, and the pastimes of the lovers of Penelope. How could one possibly assign to the same age manners so competely dissimilar? Plato is so much impressed by this difficulty that, not knowing how to resolve it, he pretends that in his divine transports of poetic enthusiasm, Homer was able to foresee the effeminate and dissolute life of the future. But isn't this to attribute the height of imprudence to him whom he presents as the founder of Greek civilization? To publish an account of such manners before they existed, even though one condemned them at the same time, wouldn't this be to teach people to imitate them? Let us agree rather that the author of the *Iliad* must have long preceded the author of the *Odyssey*—that the former, who came from the northeastern part of Greece, sang of the Trojan War, which had taken place in his part of the country; whereas the latter, who had been born in the southeastern part, celebrated Ulysses, who reigned in that part of the world."

You see that Vico has here explained Homer in terms both of historical period and of geographical origin. The idea that human arts and institutions were to be studied and elucidated as the products of the geographical and climatic conditions in which the people who created them lived and of the phase of their social development through which they were passing at the moment, made great progress during the eighteenth century. There are traces of it even in Dr. Johnson, that most orthodox and classical of critics—as, for example, when he accounts for certain characteristics of Shakespeare by the relative barbarity of the age in which he lived, pointing out just as Vico had done that "nations, like individuals, have their infancy." And by the eighties of the eighteenth century Herder, in his *Ideas on the Philosophy of History,* was writing of poetry that it was a kind of "Proteus among the people, which is always changing its form in response to the languages, manners and habits, to the temperaments and climates, nay, even to the accents of different nations." He said—what could still seem startling even so late as that—

that "language was not a divine communication, but something men had produced themselves." In the lectures on the philosophy of history that Hegel delivered in Berlin in 1822–1823, he discussed the national literatures as expressions of the societies which had produced them—societies which he conceived as great organisms continually transforming themselves under the propulsion of a succession of dominant ideas.

In the field of literary criticism, this historical point of view came to its first complete flower in the work of the French critic Taine, in the middle of the nineteenth century. The whole school of historian-critics to which he belonged—Michelet, Renan, Sainte-Beuve—had been occupied in interpreting books in terms of their historical origins. But Taine was the first to try to apply these principles systematically and on a large scale to a work devoted exclusively to literature. In the Introduction to his *History of English Literature,* published in 1863, he made his famous pronouncement that works of literature were to be understood as the upshot of three interfusing factors: *the moment, the race, and the milieu.* Taine thought he was a scientist and a mechanist who was examining works of literature from the same point of view as the chemist in experimenting with chemical compounds. But the difference between the critic and the chemist is that the critic cannot first combine his elements and then watch to see what they will do: he can only examine phenomena which have already taken place. What Taine actually does is pretend to set the stage for the experiment by describing the moment, the race and the milieu; and then say, "Such a situation demands such a kind of writer." He now goes on to describe the kind of writer that the situation demands, and at the end of the description we discover that we are confronted with Shakespeare or Milton or Byron, or whoever the great figure is—who turns out to prove the accuracy of Taine's prognosis by precisely fitting the description.

There is thus an element of imposture in Taine; but it is a lucky thing that there is. If he had really been the mechanist that he thought he was, his work on literature would have had little value. The truth was that Taine loved literature for its own sake—he was at his best an excellent artist himself—and that he had very strong moral convictions which give his writing emotional power. His mind, to be sure, was an analytic one, and his analysis, though terribly oversimplified, does have an explanatory value. Yet his work was what we call creative. Whatever he may say about chemical experiments, it is evident when he writes of a great writer that the moment, the race and the milieu have combined, like the three sounds of the chord in Browning's poem about Abt Vogler, to produce not a fourth sound but a star.

To Taine's set of elements was added, dating from the middle of the century, a new element, the economic, which was introduced into the discussion of historical phenomena mainly by Marx and Engels. The non-Marxist critics themselves were at the time already taking into account the influence of the social classes. In his chapters on the Norman conquest of England, Taine shows that the difference between the literatures produced respectively by the Normans and the Saxons was partly the difference between a ruling class, on the one hand, and a vanquished and oppressed class, on the other. And Michelet in his volume on the Regency, which was finished the same year that the *History of English Literature* appeared, studies *Manon Lescaut* as a document representing the point of view of the small gentry before the French Revolution. But Marx and Engels derived the social classes from the ways that people made or got their livings—from what they called the *methods of production;* and they tended to regard these economic processes as fundamental to civilization.

The Dialectical Materialism of Marx and Engels was not really so materialistic as it sounds. There was in it a large element of the Hegelian idealism that Marx and Engels thought they had gotten rid of. At no time did they take so mechanistic a view of things as Taine began by professing; and their theory of the relation of works of literature to what they called the *economic base* was a good deal less simple than Taine's theory of the moment, the race and the milieu. They thought that art, politics, religion, philosophy and literature belonged to what they called the *superstructure* of human activity; but they saw that the practitioners of these various departments tended also to constitute social groups, and that they were always pulling away from the kind of solidarity based on economic classes in order to establish a professional solidarity of their own. Furthermore, the activities of the superstructure could influence one another, and they could influence the economic base. It may be said of Marx and Engels in general that, contrary to the popular impression, they were modest, confused and groping, where a materialist like Taine was cocksure. Marx once made an attempt to explain why the poems of Homer were so good when the society that produced them was from his point of view—that is, from the industrial point of view—so primitive; and this gave him a good deal of trouble. If we compare his discussion of this problem with Vico's discussion of Homer, we see that the explanation of literature in terms of a philosophy of social history is becoming, instead of simpler and easier, more difficult and complex.

Marx and Engels were deeply imbued, moreover, with the German admiration for literature which they had learned from the age of Goethe. It would never have occurred to either of them that *der Dichter* [the poet] was not one of the noblest and most beneficent of humankind. When Engels writes about Goethe, he presents him as a man equipped for "practical life," whose career was frustrated by the "misery" of the historical situation in Germany in his time, and reproaches him for allowing himself to lapse into the "cautious, smug and narrow" philistinism of the class from which he came; but Engels regrets this because it interfered with the development of the "mocking, defiant, world-despising genius," *"der geniale Dichter," "der gewaltige Poet"* [the ingenious poet, the powerful poet], of whom Engels would not even, he says, have asked that he should have been a political liberal if he had not sacrificed to his bourgeois shrinkings his truer esthetic sense. And the great critics who were trained on Marx—Franz Mehring and Bernard Shaw—had all this reverence for the priesthood of literature. Shaw deplores the lack of political philosophy and what he regards as the middle-class snobbery in Shakespeare; but he celebrates Shakespeare's poetry and his dramatic imagination almost as enthusiastically as Swinburne did, describing even those pot-boiling comedies —*Twelfth Night* and *As You Like It*—the themes of which seem to him most contemptible, as "the Crown Jewels of English dramatic poetry." Such a critic may do more for a writer by showing him a real man in a real world at a definite moment of time than the impressionist critic of Swinburne's type who flourished in the same period of the late nineteenth century. The purely impressionist critic approaches the whole of literature as an exhibit of bellettristic jewels, and he can only write a rhapsodic catalogue. But when Shaw turned his spotlight on Shakespeare as a figure in the Shavian drama of history, he invested him with a new interest as perhaps no other English critic had done.

The insistence that the man of letters should play a political rôle, the disparagement of works of art in comparison with political action, were thus originally no part of Marxism. They only became associated with it later. This happened by way of Russia, and it was due to special tendencies in that country that date from long before the Revolution or the promulgation of Marxism itself. In Russia there have been very good reasons why the political implications of literature should particularly occupy the critics. The art of Pushkin itself, with its marvellous power of implication, had certainly been partly created by the censorship of Nicholas I, and Pushkin set the tradition for most of the great Russian writers that followed him. Every play, every poem, every story, must be a parable of which the moral is implied. If it were stated, the censor would suppress the book, as he tried to do with *The Bronze Horseman* of Pushkin, where it was merely a question of the packed implications protruding a little too plainly. Right down through the writings of Chekhov and up almost to the Revolution, the imaginative literature of Russia presents the peculiar paradox of an art which is technically objective and yet charged with dynamic social messages. In Russia under the Tsar, all social criticism was necessarily political because the most urgent need from the point of view of the intelligentsia was to get rid of the Tsarist régime. Even the neo-Christian moralist Tolstoy, who pretends to be non-political, is as political in his implications as any because his preaching will inevitably embroil him with the Church, and the Church is an integral part of the tsardom. His pamphlet called *What Is Art?*, in which he throws overboard Shakespeare and a large part of modern literature, including his own novels, in the interests of his intransigent morality, is the example which is most familiar to us of the moralizing Russian criticism; but it was only the most sensational expression of a kind of approach which had been prevalent since Belinsky and

Chernyshevsky in the early part of the century. The critics, who were usually journalists writing in exile or in a contraband press, were always tending to demand of the imaginative writers that they should illustrate bolder morals.

After the Revolution occurred, this situation did not change. The old habits of censorship persisted in the new socialist society of the Soviets, which was necessarily made up of people who had been stamped by the die of the old despotism. We find the peculiar phenomenon of a series of literary groups attempting one after another to obtain official recognition or to make themselves sufficiently powerful so that they could establish themselves as arbiters of literature. Lenin and Trotsky and Lunacharsky had the sense to oppose these attempts: the comrade-dictators of Proletcult or Lev or Rapp would certainly have been just as bad as the Count Benckendorf who made Pushkin miserable, and when the Stalin bureaucracy, after the death of Gorky, got control of this department as of everything else, they instituted a system of repression that made Benckendorf and Nicholas I look like Lorenzo de' Medici. In the meantime, Trotsky, himself a great political writer who had always had an interest in belles-lettres, attempted in 1924, apropos of one of these movements, to clarify the situation. He wrote a brilliant and important book called *Literature and Revolution,* in which he explained the aims of the government, analysed the work of the Russian writers, and praised or rebuked the latter as they seemed to him in harmony or in conflict with the former. Trotsky is intelligent, sympathetic; it is evident that he is really fond of literature and that he knows that a work of art does not fulfil its function in terms of the formulas of party propaganda. But Mayakovsky, the Soviet poet, whom Trotsky had praised with reservations, expressed himself in a famous joke when he was asked what he thought about Trotsky's book—a pun which implied that a Commissar turned critic was unmistakably a Commissar still; and what a foreigner cannot accept in Trotsky is his assumption that it is the duty of the government to take a hand in the direction of literature.

This point of view, indigenous to Russia, has been imported to other countries through the permeation of Communist influence. The Communist press and its literary followers have reflected the control of the Kremlin in all the phases through which it has passed, down to the wholesale imprisonment of Soviet writers which has been taking place since 1935. But it has never been a part of the American system that our Republican or Democratic administration should lay down a political line for the guidance of the national literature. A gesture in this direction lately on the part of Archibald MacLeish, who seems a little carried away by the eminence of his position as Librarian of Congress, was anything but cordially received by serious American writers. And so long as the United States happily remains a nontotalitarian country, we can very well do without this aspect of the historical criticism of literature.

Another element of a different order has, however, since Marx's time been added to the historical study of the origins of works of literature. I mean the psychoanalysis of Freud. This appears as an extension of something which had already got well started before, which had figured even in Johnson's *Lives of the Poets,* and of which the great exponent had been Sainte-Beuve: the interpretation of works of literature in the light of the personalities behind them. But the Freudians made this interpretation more exact and more systematic. The great example of the psychoanalysis of an artist is Freud's own essay on Leonardo da Vinci; but this is pretty much an attempt to reconstruct a straight case history. The best example I know of the application of Freudian analysis to literature is in Van Wyck Brook's book, *The Ordeal of Mark Twain,* in which Brooks uses an incident of Mark Twain's boyhood as a key to his whole career. He has been loudly attacked for this by Bernard de Voto, and he has himself since repudiated the general method on the ground that nobody but an analyst can ever know enough about a writer to make a valid psychoanalytic diagnosis. This is true, of course, and the method has led to bad results where the critic has built a Freudian mechanism out of very slender evidence, and then given us merely a romance based on the supposed working of this mechanism instead of a genuine study of the writer's life and work. But I believe that Brooks had hold of something when he fixed upon that incident of which Mark Twain gave so vivid an account to his biographer—that scene at the deathbed of his father when his mother made him promise that he would not break her heart. If it was not one of those crucial happenings which are supposed to determine the complexes of Freud, it has certainly a typical significance in relation to Mark Twain's whole psychology. The stories that people tell about their childhood are likely to be profoundly symbolic even when they have been partly or wholly made up in the light of later experience. And the attitudes, the compulsions, the emotional "patterns" that recur in the work of a writer are of great interest to the historical critic.

These attitudes and patterns are embedded in the community and the historical moment, and they may indicate its ideals and its diseases as the cell shows the condition of the tissue. The recent scientific experimentation in the combining of Freudian with Marxist method, and of psychoanalysis with anthropology, has had its parallel development in criticism. And there is thus another element added to our equipment for analysing literary works, and the problem grows still more complex.

The analyst, however, is of course not concerned with the comparative values of his patients any more than the surgeon is. He cannot tell you why the neurotic Dostoevsky produces work of immense value to his fellows, while another man with the same neurotic pattern would become a public menace. Freud himself emphatically states in his study of Leonardo that his method does not make any attempt to account for Leonardo's genius. The problems of comparative value remain after we have investigated the Freudian psychological factor just as they do after we have given due attention to the Marxist economic factor and the racial and geographical factors. No matter how thorough and complete our explanations of works of literature may be from the historical and biographical points of view, we must be ready to try to estimate the relative degrees of success attained by the products of the various periods and the various personalities in some such way as Eliot and Saintsbury do. We must be able to tell good from bad, the first-rate from the second-rate. We shall not otherwise write literary criticism at all, but merely social or political history as reflected in literary texts, or psychological case histories from past eras, or, to take the historical point of view in its simplest and most academic form, merely chronologies of books that have been published.

And now how, in these matters of literary art, do we tell the good art from the bad? Norman Kemp Smith, the Kantian philosopher, whose courses I was fortunate enough to take at Princeton twenty-five years ago, used to tell us that this recognition was based primarily on an emotional reaction. For purposes of practical criticism this is a safe assumption to go on. It is possible to discriminate in a variety of ways the elements that in any given department go to make a successful work of literature. Different schools have at different times demanded different things of literature: *unity, symmetry, universality, originality, vision, inspiration, strangeness, suggestiveness, improving morality, socialist realism,* etc. But you could have any set of these qualities that any school of writing demanded and still not have a good play, a good novel, a good poem, a good history. If you identify the essence of good literature with any one of these elements or with any combination of them, you simply shift the emotional reaction to the recognition of the elements. Or if you add to your other demands the demand that the writer must have *talent,* you simply shift this recognition to the talent. Once people find some grounds of agreement in the coincidence of their emotional reactions to books, they may be able to discuss these elements profitably; but if they do not have this basic agreement, the discussion will make no sense.

How, you may ask, are we to distinguish this élite who know what they are talking about? They are self-appointed and self-perpetuating, and they will compel you to accept their authority. Impostors may try to put themselves over, but these impostors will not last. The position of the people who understand writing (as is also the case in every other art) is simply that they know what they know, and that they are determined to impose their opinions by main force of eloquence or assertion on the people who do not know.

But what is the *cause* of this emotional reaction which is the critic's divining-rod? This question has long been an object of study by the branch of philosophy called esthetics, and it has recently been made a subject of scientific experimentation. Both these kinds of investigation of literature are likely to be prejudiced in the eyes of the critic by the fact that they are often carried on by persons who are themselves obviously deficient in literary taste. Yet one should not deny the possible value of explorations in this domain by men of acute minds who take as their given data the esthetic emotions of other men.

Almost everybody interested in literature has tried to explain these emotions to himself; and I of course have my own explanation.

In my view, all our intellectual activity, in whatever field it takes place, is an attempt to give a meaning to our experience—that is, to make life more practicable; for by understanding things we make it easier to survive and get around among them. Euclid, working in a convention of abstractions, shows us relations between the distances of our unwieldy and cluttered-up environment upon which we are able to count. A drama of Sophocles also indicates relations between the various human impulses, which appear so confused and dangerous, and brings out a certain justice of Fate—that is to say, of the way in which the interaction of these impulses is seen in the long run to work out—upon which we can also depend. The kinship from this point of view of the purposes of science and art appears particularly clearly with the Greeks, because not only do both Euclid and Sophocles satisfy us by making patterns, but they make very much the same kind of patterns. Euclid's *Elements* takes simple theorems and by a series of logical operations builds them up to a climax in the square on the hypotenuse. A typical drama of Sophocles makes much the same kind of pattern.

Some writers (as well as some scientists) have a more specific message: not content with such an effort as that of Sophocles to make life appear more sensible, and hence to make it more bearable, they try, like Plato, to explain the conditions for making it something different and better. Other kinds of literature, such as Sappho's lyrics, have less philosophical content than Sophocles. A lyric gives us nothing but a pattern imposed on the expression of a feeling; but this pattern of metrical qualities and of balancing consonants and vowels has the effect of reducing the feeling, however unruly or painful it may seem when we experience it in the course of our lives, to something orderly, symmetrical and pleasing. It also relates it to the more comprehensive scheme, works it into the larger texture, of the body of poetic art. The discord has been resolved, the anomaly subjected to discipline. And this control of his emotion by the poet has the effect at second-hand of making it easier for the reader to manage his own emotions. (Why certain sounds and rhythms gratify us more than others and how they are related to the ideas which they are selected as appropriate for conveying, are questions that may be passed on to the scientist.)

And this brings us back to the historical point of view. The experience of mankind is always changing; and the writer who is to be anything more than an echo of his predecessors must always find expression for something which has not yet been expressed, must master new phenomena which have never yet been mastered. With each such victory of the human intellect, whether in the language of philosophy or the language of poetry, we experience a deep satisfaction: we have been cured of some ache of disorder, relieved of some oppressive burden of uncomprehended events.

This relief that brings the sense of power, and with the sense of power, joy, is the emotion which tells us when we are in the presence of a first-rate piece of literature. But, you may at this point object, are not people often solaced and rejoiced by literature of the trashiest kind? They are: crude and limited people do certainly feel such emotions in connection with work that is limited and crude. The man who is more highly organized and has a wider intellectual range will feel it in connection with work that is finer and more complex. The difference between the emotion of the more highly organized man and the emotion of the less highly organized one is merely a matter of gradation. You sometimes encounter books that seem to mark precisely the borderline between work that is definitely superior and work that is definitely bad—the novels of John Steinbeck, for example. When I was speaking a little while back of the experts who establish the standards of taste, I meant the people who can distinguish Grade A and who prefer it to the other grades.

1941

NORMAN MAILER

The White Negro

Superficial Reflections on the Hipster

Our search for the rebels of the generation led us to the hipster. The hipster is an enfant terrible *turned inside out. In character with his time, he is trying to get back at the conformists by lying low. . . . You can't interview a hipster because his main goal is to keep out of a society which, he thinks, is trying to make everyone over in its own image. He takes marijuana because it supplies him with experiences that can't be shared with "squares." He may affect a broad-brimmed hat or a zoot suit, but usually he prefers to skulk unmarked. The hipster may be a jazz musician; he is rarely an artist, almost never a writer. He may earn his living as a petty criminal, a hobo, a carnival roustabout or a free-lance moving man in Greenwich Village, but some hipsters have found a safe refuge in the upper income brackets as television comics or movie actors. (The late James Dean, for one, was a hipster hero.) . . . It is tempting to describe the hipster in psychiatric terms as infantile, but the style of his infantilism is a sign of the times. He does not try to enforce his will on others, Napoleon-fashion, but contents himself with a magical omnipotence never disproved because never tested. . . . As the only extreme nonconformist of his generation, he exercises a powerful if underground appeal for conformists, through newspaper accounts of his delinquencies, his structureless jazz, and his emotive grunt words.*
—*"Born 1930: The Unlost Generation"*
by Caroline Bird
Harper's Bazaar, February 1957

1

Probably, we will never be able to determine the psychic havoc of the concentration camps and the atom bomb upon the unconscious mind of almost everyone alive in these years. For the first time in civilized history, perhaps for the first time in all of history, we have been forced to live with the suppressed knowledge that the smallest facets of our personality or the most minor projection of our ideas, or indeed the absence of ideas and the absence of personality, could mean equally well that we might still be doomed to die as a cipher in some vast statistical operation in which our teeth would be counted, and our hair would be saved, but our death itself would be unknown, unhonored, and·unremarked, a death which could not follow with dignity as a possible consequence to serious actions we had chosen, but rather a death by *deus ex machina* in a gas chamber or a radioactive city; and so if in the midst of civilization—that civilization founded upon the Faustian urge to dominate nature by mastering time, mastering the links of social cause and effect—in the middle of an economic civilization founded upon the confidence that time could indeed be subjected to our will, our psyche was subjected itself to the intolerable anxiety that death being causeless, life was causeless as well, and time deprived of cause and effect had come to a stop.

The Second World War presented a mirror to the human condition which blinded anyone who looked into it. For if tens of millions were killed in concentration camps out of the inexorable agonies and contractions of superstates founded upon the always insoluble contradictions of injustice, one was then obliged also to see that no matter how crippled and perverted an image of man was the society he had created, it was nonetheless his creation, his collective creation (at least his collective creation from the past) and if society was so murderous, then who could ignore the most hideous of questions about his own nature?

Worse. One could hardly maintain the courage to be individual, to speak with one's own voice, for the years in which one could complacently accept oneself as part of an elite by being a radical were forever gone. A man knew that when he dissented, he gave a note upon his life which could be called in any year of overt crisis. No wonder then that these have been the years of conformity and depression. A stench of fear has come out of every pore of American life, and we suffer from a collective failure of nerve. The only courage, with rare exceptions, that we have been witness to, has been the isolated courage of isolated people.

2

It is on this bleak scene that a phenomenon has appeared: the American existentialist—the hipster, the man who knows that if our collective condition is to live with instant death by atomic war, relatively quick death by the State as *l'univers concentrationnaire*, or with a slow death by conformity with every creative and rebellious instinct stifled (at what damage to the mind and the heart and the liver and the nerves no research foundation for cancer will discover in a hurry), if the fate of twentieth-century man is to live with death from adolescence to premature senescence, why then the only life-giving answer is to accept the terms of death, to live with death as immediate danger, to divorce oneself from society, to exist without roots, to set out on that uncharted journey into the rebellious imperatives of the self. In short, whether the life is criminal or not, the decision is to encourage the psychopath in oneself, to explore that domain of experience where security is boredom and therefore sickness, and one exists in the present, in that enormous present which is without past or future, memory or planned intention, the life where a man must go until he is beat, where he must gamble with his energies through all those small or large crises of courage and unforeseen situations which beset his day, where he must be with it or doomed not to swing. The unstated essence of Hip, its psychopathic brilliance, quivers with the knowledge that new kinds of victories increase one's power for new kinds of perception; and defeats, the wrong kind of defeats, attack the body and imprison one's energy until one is jailed in the prison air of other people's habits, other people's defeats, boredom, quiet desperation, and muted icy self-destroying rage. One is Hip or one is Square (the alternative which each new generation coming into American life is beginning to feel), one is a rebel or one conforms, one is a frontiersman in the Wild West of American night life, or else a Square cell, trapped in the totalitarian tissues of American society, doomed willy-nilly to conform if one is to succeed.

A totalitarian society makes enormous demands on the courage of men, and a partially totalitarian society makes even greater demands, for the general anxiety is greater. Indeed if one is to be a man, almost any kind of unconventional action often takes disproportionate courage. So it is no accident that the source of Hip is the Negro for he has been living on the margin between totalitarianism and democracy for two centuries. But the presence of Hip as a working philosophy in the sub-worlds of American life is probably due to jazz, and its knifelike entrance into culture, its subtle but so penetrating influence on an avant-garde generation—that postwar generation of adventurers who (some consciously, some by osmosis) had absorbed the lessons of disillusionment and disgust of the twenties, the depression, and the war. Sharing a collective disbelief in the words of men who had too much money and controlled too many things, they knew almost as powerful a disbelief in the socially monolithic ideas of the single mate, the solid family, and the respectable love life. If the intellectual antecedents of this generation can be traced to such separate influences as D. H. Lawrence, Henry Miller, and Wilhelm Reich, the viable philosophy of Hemingway fit most of their facts: in a bad world, as he was to say over and over again (while taking time out from his parvenu snobbery and dedicated gourmandize), in a bad world there is no love nor mercy nor charity nor justice unless a man can keep his courage, and this indeed fitted some of the facts. What fitted the need of the adventurer even more precisely was Hemingway's categorical imperative that what made him feel good became therefore The Good.

So no wonder that in certain cities of America, in New York of course, and New Orleans, in Chicago and San Francisco and Los Angeles, in such American cities as Paris and Mexico, D.F., this particular part of a generation was attracted to what the Negro had to offer. In such places as Greenwich Village, a ménage-à-trois was completed—the bohemian and the juvenile delinquent came face-to-face with the Negro, and the hipster was a fact in American life. If marijuana was the wedding ring, the child was the language of Hip for its argot gave expression to abstract states of feeling which all could share, at least all who were Hip. And in this wedding of the white and the black it was the Negro who brought the cultural dowry. Any Negro who wishes to live must live with danger from his first day, and no experience can ever be casual to him, no Negro can saunter down a street with any real certainty that violence will not visit him on his walk. The cameos of security for the average white: mother and the home, job and the family, are not even a mockery to millions of Negroes; they are impossible. The Negro has the simplest of alternatives: live a life of constant humility or ever-threatening danger. In such a pass where paranoia is as vital to survival as blood, the Negro had stayed alive and begun to grow by following the need of his body where he could. Knowing in the cells of his existence that life was war, nothing but war, the Negro (all exceptions admitted) could rarely afford the sophisticated inhibitions of civilization, and so he kept for his survival the art of the primitive, he lived in the enormous present, he subsisted for his Saturday night kicks, relinquishing the pleasures of the mind for the more obligatory pleasures of the body, and in his music he gave voice to the character and quality of his existence, to his rage and the infinite variations of joy, lust, languor, growl, cramp, pinch, scream, and despair of his orgasm. For jazz is orgasm, it is the music of orgasm, good orgasm and bad, and so it spoke across a nation, it had the communication of art even where it was watered, perverted, corrupted, and almost killed, it spoke in no matter what laundered popular way of instantaneous existential states to which some whites could respond, it was indeed a communication by art because it said, "I feel this, and now you do too."

So there was a new breed of adventurers, urban adventurers who drifted out at night looking for action with a black man's code to fit their facts. The hipster had absorbed the existentialist synapses of the Negro, and for practical purposes could be considered a white Negro.

To be an existentialist, one must be able to feel one-self—one must know one's desires, one's rages, one's anguish; one must be aware of the character of one's frustration and know what would satisfy it. The overcivilized man can be an existentialist only if it is chic, and deserts it quickly for the next chic. To be a real existentialist (Sartre admittedly to the contrary) one must be religious,

one must have one's sense of the "purpose"—whatever
the purpose may be—but a life which is directed by one's
faith in the necessity of action is a life committed to the
notion that the substratum of existence is the search, the
end meaningful but mysterious; it is impossible to live
such a life unless one's emotions provide their profound
conviction. Only the French, alienated beyond alienation
from their unconscious, could welcome an existential philosophy without ever feeling it at all; indeed only a French-
man by declaring that the unconscious did not exist could
then proceed to explore the delicate involutions of consciousness, the microscopically sensuous and all but ineffable *frissons* of mental becoming, in order finally to
create the theology of atheism and so submit that in a
world of absurdities the existential absurdity is most coherent.

In the dialogue between the atheist and the mystic, the
atheist is on the side of life, rational life, undialectical
life—since he conceives of death as emptiness, he can, no
matter how weary or despairing, wish for nothing but
more life; his pride is that he does not transpose his weakness and spiritual fatigue into a romantic longing for
death, for such appreciation of death is then all too capable of being elaborated by his imagination into a universe
of meaningful structure and moral orchestration.

Yet this masculine argument can mean very little for
the mystic. The mystic can accept the atheist's description
of his weakness, he can agree that his mysticism was a
response to despair. And yet . . . and yet his argument
is that he, the mystic, is the one finally who has chosen to
live with death, and so death is his experience and not the
atheist's, and the atheist by eschewing the limitless dimensions of profound despair has rendered himself incapable to judge the experience. The real argument which
the mystic must always advance is the very intensity of
his private vision—his argument depends from the vision
precisely because what was felt in the vision is so extraordinary that no rational argument, no hypotheses of
"oceanic feelings," and certainly no skeptical reductions
can explain away what has become for him the reality
more real than the reality of closely reasoned logic. His
inner experience of the possibilities within death is his

logic. So, too, for the existentialist. And the psychopath. And the saint and the bullfighter and the lover. The common denominator for all of them is their burning consciousness of the present, exactly that incandescent consciousness which the possibilities within death has opened for them. There is a depth of desperation to the condition which enables one to remain in life only by engaging death, but the reward is their knowledge that what is happening at each instant of the electric present is good or bad for them, good or bad for their cause, their love, their action, their need.

It is this knowledge which provides the curious community of feeling in the world of the hipster, a muted cool religious revival to be sure, but the element which is exciting, disturbing, nightmarish perhaps, is that incompatibles have come to bed, the inner life and the violent life, the orgy and the dream of love, the desire to murder and the desire to create, a dialectical conception of existence with a lust for power, a dark, romantic, and yet undeniably dynamic view of existence for it sees every man and woman as moving individually through each moment of life forward into growth or backward into death.

3

It may be fruitful to consider the hipster a philosophical psychopath, a man interested not only in the dangerous imperatives of his psychopathy but in codifying, at least for himself, the suppositions on which his inner universe is constructed. By this premise the hipster is a psychopath, and yet not a psychopath but the negation of the psychopath, for he possesses the narcissistic detachment of the philosopher, that absorption in the recessive nuances of one's own motive which is so alien to the unreasoning drive of the psychopath. In this country where new millions of psychopaths are developed each year, stamped with the mint of our contradictory popular culture (where sex is sin and yet sex is paradise), it is as if there has been room already for the development of the antithetical psychopath who extrapolates from his own condition, from the inner certainty that his rebellion is just, a radical vision of the universe which thus separates him from the general ignorance, reactionary prejudice, and self-doubt of the more conventional psychopath. Having converted his unconscious experience into much conscious knowledge, the hipster has shifted the focus of his desire from immediate gratification toward that wider passion for future power which is the mark of civilized man. Yet with an irreducible difference. For Hip is the sophistication of the wise primitive in a giant jungle, and so its appeal is still beyond the civilized man. If there are ten million Americans who are more or less psychopathic (and the figure is most modest), there are probably not more than one hundred thousand men and women who consciously see themselves as hipsters, but their importance is that they are an elite with the potential ruthlessness of an elite, and a language most adolescents can understand instinctively, for the hipster's intense view of existence matches their experience and their desire to rebel.

Before one can say more about the hipster, there is obviously much to be said about the psychic state of the psychopath—or, clinically, the psychopathic personality. Now, for reasons which may be more curious than the similarity of the words, even many people with a psycho-analytical orientation often confuse the psychopath with the psychotic. Yet the terms are polar. The psychotic is legally insane, the psychopath is not; the psychotic is almost always incapable of discharging in physical acts the rage of his frustration, while the psychopath at his extreme is virtually as incapable of restraining his violence. The psychotic lives in so misty a world that what is happening at each moment of his life is not very real to him whereas the psychopath seldom knows any reality greater than the face, the voice, the being of the particular people among whom he may find himself at any moment. Sheldon and Eleanor Glueck describe him as follows:

The psychopath . . . can be distinguished from the person sliding into or clambering out of a "true psychotic" state by the long tough persistence of his anti-social attitude and behaviour and the absence of hallucinations, delusions, manic flight of ideas, confusion, disorientation, and other dramatic signs of psychosis.

The late Robert Lindner, one of the few experts on the subject, in his book *Rebel Without a Cause—The Hypno-*

analysis of a Criminal Psychopath presented part of his definition in this way:

> . . . the psychopath is a rebel without a ˙cause, an agitator without a slogan, a revolutionary without a program: in other words, his rebelliousness is aimed to achieve goals satisfactory to himself alone; he is incapable of exertions for the sake of others. All his efforts, hidden under no matter what disguise, represent investments designed to satisfy his immediate wishes and desires. . . . The psychopath, like the child, cannot delay the pleasures of gratification; and this trait is one of his underlying, universal characteristics. He cannot wait upon erotic gratification which convention demands should be preceded by the chase before the kill: he must rape. He cannot wait upon the development of prestige in society: his egoistic ambitions lead him to leap into headlines by daring performances. Like a red thread the predominance of this mechanism for immediate satisfaction runs through the history of every psychopath. It explains not only his behaviour but also the violent nature of his acts.

Yet even Lindner who was the most imaginative and most sympathetic of the psychoanalysts who have studied the psychopathic personality was not ready to project himself into the essential sympathy—which is that the psychopath may indeed be the perverted and dangerous front-runner of a new kind of personality which could become the central expression of human nature before the twentieth century is over. For the psychopath is better adapted to dominate those mutually contradictory inhibitions upon violence and love which civilization has exacted of us, and if it be remembered that not every psychopath is an extreme case, and that the condition of psychopathy is present in a host of people including many politicians, professional soldiers, newspaper columnists, entertainers, artists, jazz musicians, call-girls, promiscuous homosexuals, and half the executives of Hollywood, television, and advertising, it can be seen that there are aspects of psychopathy which already exert considerable cultural influence.

What characterizes almost every psychopath and part-psychopath is that they are trying to create a new nervous system for themselves. Generally we are obliged to act with a nervous system which has been formed from infancy, and which carries in the style of its circuits the very contradictions of our parents and our early milieu. Therefore, we are obliged, most of us, to meet the tempo of the present and the future with reflexes and rhythms which come from the past. It is not only the "dead weight of the institutions of the past" but indeed the inefficient and often antiquated nervous circuits of the past which strangle our potentiality for responding to new possibilities which might be exciting for our individual growth.

Through most of modern history, "sublimation" was possible: at the expense of expressing only a small portion of oneself, that small portion could be expressed intensely. But sublimation depends on a reasonable tempo to history. If the collective life of a generation has moved too quickly, the "past" by which particular men and women of that generation may function is not, let us say, thirty years old, but relatively a hundred or two hundred years old. And so the nervous system is overstressed beyond the possibility of such compromises as sublimation, especially since the stable middle-class values so prerequisite to sublimation have been virtually destroyed in our time, at least as nourishing values free of confusion or doubt. In such a crisis of accelerated historical tempo and deteriorated values, neurosis tends to be replaced by pyschopathy, and the success of psychoanalysis (which even ten years ago gave promise of becoming a direct major force) diminishes because of its inbuilt and characteristic incapacity to handle patients more complex, more experienced, or more adventurous than the analyst himself. In practice, psychoanalysis has by now become all too often no more than a psychic blood-letting. The patient is not so much changed as aged, and the infantile fantasies which he is encouraged to express are condemned to exhaust themselves against the analyst's nonresponsive reactions. The result for all too many patients is a diminution, a "tranquilizing" of their most interesting qualities and vices. The patient is indeed not so much altered as worn out—less bad, less good, less bright, less willful, less destructive, less creative. He is thus able to conform to that contradictory and unbearable society which first created his neurosis. He can conform to what he loathes because he no longer has the passion to feel loathing so intensely.

The psychopath is notoriously difficult to analyze because the fundamental decision of his nature is to try to live the infantile fantasy, and in this decision (given the dreary alternative of psychoanalysis) there may be a certain instinctive wisdom. For there is a dialectic to changing one's nature, the dialectic which underlies all psycho-analytic method: it is the knowledge that if one is to change one's habits, one must go back to the source of their creation, and so the psychopath exploring backward along the road of the homosexual, the orgiast, the drug-addict, the rapist, the robber, and the murderer seeks to find those violent parallels to the violent and often hope-less contradictions he knew as an infant and as a child. For if he has the courage to meet the parallel situation at the moment when he is ready, then he has a chance to act as he has never acted before, and in satisfying the frustra-tion—if he can succeed—he may then pass by symbolic substitute through the locks of incest. In thus giving ex-pression to the buried infant in himself, he can lessen the tension of those infantile desires and so free himself to remake a bit of his nervous sytem. Like the neurotic he is looking for the opportunity to grow up a second time, but the psychopath knows instinctively that to express a for-bidden impulse actively is far more beneficial to him than merely to confess the desire in the safety of a doctor's room. The psychopath is inordinately ambitious, too am-bitious ever to trade his warped brilliant conception of his possible victories in life for the grim if peaceful attrition of the analyst's couch. So his associational journey into the past is lived out in the theater of the present, and he exists for those charged situations where his senses are so alive that he can be aware actively (as the analysand is aware passively) of what his habits are, and how he can change them. The strength of the psychopath is that he knows (where most of us can only guess) what is good for him and what is bad for him at exactly those instants when an old crippling habit has become so attacked by experience that the potentiality exists to change it, to re-place a negative and empty fear with an outward action, even if—and here I obey the logic of the extreme psycho-path—even if the fear is of himself, and the action is to murder. The psychopath murders—if he has the courage —out of the necessity to purge his violence, for if he cannot empty his hatred then he cannot love, his being is frozen with implacable self-hatred for his cowardice. (It can of course be suggested that it takes little courage for two strong eighteen-year-old hoodlums, let us say, to beat

in the brains of a candy-store keeper, and indeed the act—
even by the logic of the psychopath—is not likely to prove
very therapeutic, for the victim is not an immediate equal.
Still, courage of a sort is necessary, for one murders not
only a weak fifty-year-old man but an institution as well,
one violates private property, one enters into a new relation
with the police and introduces a dangerous element into
one's life. The hoodlum is therefore daring the unknown,
and so no matter how brutal the act, it is not altogether
cowardly.)

At bottom, the drama of the psychopath is that he seeks
love. Not love as the search for a mate, but love as the
search for an orgasm more apocalyptic than the one which
preceded it. Orgasm is his therapy—he knows at the seed
of his being that good orgasm opens his possibilities and
bad orgasm imprisons him. But in this search, the psychopath becomes an embodiment of the extreme contradictions of the society which formed his character, and the
apocalyptic orgasm often remains as remote as the Holy
Grail, for there are clusters and nests and ambushes of violence in his own necessities and in the imperatives and
retaliations of the men and women among whom he lives
his life, so that even as he drains his hatred in one act or
another, so the conditions of his life create it anew in him
until the drama of his movements bears a sardonic resemblance to the frog who climbed a few feet in the well only
to drop back again.

Yet there is this to be said for the search after the good
orgasm: when one lives in a civilized world and still can
enjoy none of the cultural nectar of such a world because
the paradoxes on which civilization is built demand that
there remain a cultureless and alienated bottom of ex-
ploitable human material, then the logic of becoming a
sexual outlaw (if one's psychological roots are bedded in
the bottom) is that one has at least a running competitive
chance to be physically healthy so long as one stays alive.
It is therefore no accident that psychopathy is most prevalent with the Negro. Hated from outside and therefore
hating himself, the Negro was forced into the position of
exploring all those moral wildernesses of civilized life which
the Square automatically condemns as delinquent or evil
or immature or morbid or self-destructive or corrupt.
(Actually the terms have equal weight. Depending on the

telescope of the cultural clique from which the Square
surveys the universe, "evil" or "immature" are equally
strong terms of condemnation.) But the Negro, not being
privileged to gratify his self-esteem with the heady satisfactions of categorical condemnation, chose to move instead in that other direction where all situations are equally
valid, and in the worst of perversion, promiscuity, pimpery,
drug addiction, rape, razor-slash, bottle-break, what-have-
you, the Negro discovered and elaborated a morality of
the bottom, an ethical differentiation between the good and
the bad in every human activity from the go-getter pimp
(as opposed to the lazy one) to the relatively dependable
pusher or prostitute. Add to this, the cunning of their
language, the abstract ambiguous alternatives in which
from the danger of their oppression they learned to speak
("Well, now, man, like I'm looking for a cat to turn me
on . . ."), add even more the profound sensitivity of the
Negro jazzman who was the cultural mentor of a people,
and it is not too difficult to believe that the language of
Hip which evolved was an artful language, tested and
shaped by an intense experience and therefore different
in kind from white slang, as different as the special obscenity of the soldier which, in its emphasis upon "ass"
as the soul and "shit" as circumstance, was able to express
the existential states of the enlisted man. What makes Hip
a special language is that it cannot really be taught—if
one shares none of the experiences of elation and exhaustion which it is equipped to describe, then it seems merely
arch or vulgar or irritating. It is a pictorial language, but
pictorial like non-objective art, imbued with the dialectic
of small but intense change, a language for the microcosm,
in this case, man, for it takes the immediate experiences of
any passing man and magnifies the dynamic of his movements, not specifically but abstractly so that he is seen
more as a vector in a network of forces than as a static
character in a crystallized field. (Which latter is the practical view of the snob.) For example, there is real difficulty
in trying to find a Hip substitute for "stubborn." The best
possibility I can come up with is: "That cat will never
come off his groove, dad." But groove implies movement,
narrow movement but motion nonetheless. There is really
no way to describe someone who does not move at all.
Even a creep does move—if at a pace exasperatingly more
slow than the pace of the cool cats.

4

Like children, hipsters are fighting for the sweet, and their language is a set of subtle indications of their success or failure in the competition for pleasure. Unstated but obvious is the social sense that there is not nearly enough sweet for everyone. And so the sweet goes only to the victor, the best, the most, the man who knows the most about how to find his energy and how not to lose it. The emphasis is on energy because the psychopath and the hipster are nothing without it since they do not have the protection of a position or a class to rely on when they have overextended themselves. So the language of Hip is a language of energy, how it is found, how it is lost.

But let us see. I have jotted down perhaps a dozen words, the Hip perhaps most in use and most likely to last with the minimum of variation. The words are man, go, put down, make, beat, cool, swing, with it, crazy, dig, flip, creep, hip, square. They serve a variety of purposes, and the nuance of the voice uses the nuance of the situation to convey the subtle contextual difference. If the hipster moves through his life on a constant search with glimpses of Mecca in many a turn of his experience (Mecca being the apocalyptic orgasm) and if everyone in the civilized world is at least in some small degree a sexual cripple, the hipster lives with the knowledge of how he is sexually crippled and where he is sexually alive, and the faces of experience which life presents to him each day are engaged, dismissed, or avoided as his need directs and his lifemanship makes possible. For life is a contest between people in which the victor generally recuperates quickly and the loser takes long to mend, a perpetual competition of colliding explorers in which one must grow or else pay more for remaining the same (pay in sickness, or depression, or anguish for the lost opportunity), but pay or grow.

Therefore one finds words like go, and make it, and with it, and swing: "Go" with its sense that after hours or days or months or years of monotony, boredom, and depression one has finally had one's chance, one has amassed enough energy to meet an exciting opportunity with all one's present talents for the flip (up or down) and so one is ready to go, ready to gamble. Movement is always to be preferred to inaction. In motion a man has a chance, his body is warm, his instincts are quick, and when the crisis comes, whether of love or violence, he can make it, he can win, he can release a little more energy for himself since he hates himself a little less, he can make a little better nervous system, make it a little more possible to go again, to go faster next time and so make more and thus find more people with whom he can swing. For to swing is to communicate, is to convey the rhythms of one's own being to a lover, a friend, or an audience, and—equally necessary—be able to feel the rhythms of their response. To swing with the rhythms of another is to enrich oneself—the conception of the learning process as dug by Hip is that one cannot really learn until one contains within oneself the implicit rhythm of the subject or the person. As an example, I remember once hearing a Negro friend have an intellectual discussion at a party for half an hour with a white girl who was a few years out of college. The Negro literally could not read or write, but he had an extraordinary ear and a fine sense of mimicry. So as the girl spoke, he would detect the particular formal uncertainties in her argument, and in a pleasant (if slightly Southern) English accent, he would respond to one or another facet of her doubts. When she would finish what she felt was a particularly well-articulated idea, he would smile privately and say, "Other-direction . . . do you really believe in that?"

"Well . . . No," the girl would stammer, "now that you get down to it, there is something disgusting about it to me," and she would be off again for five more minutes.

Of course the Negro was not learning anything about the merits and demerits of the argument, but he was learning a great deal about a type of girl he had never met before, and that was what he wanted. Being unable to read or write, he could hardly be interested in ideas nearly as much as in lifemanship, and so he eschewed any attempt to obey the precision or lack of precision in the girl's language, and instead sensed her character (and the values of her social type) by swinging with the nuances of her voice.

So to swing is to be able to learn, and by learning take a step toward making it, toward creating. What is to be created is not nearly so important as the hipster's belief that when he really makes it, he will be able to turn his hand to anything, even to self-discipline. What he must do before that is find his courage at the moment of violence, or equally make it in the act of love, find a little more between his woman and himself, or indeed between his mate and himself (since many hipsters are bisexual), but paramount, imperative, is the necessity to make it because in making it, one is making the new habit, unearthing the new talent which the old frustration denied.

Whereas if you goof (the ugliest word in Hip), if you lapse back into being a frightened stupid child, or if you flip, if you lose your control, reveal the buried weaker more feminine part of your nature, then it is more difficult to swing the next time; your ear is less alive, your bad and energy-wasting habits are further confirmed, you are farther away from being with it. But to be with it is to have grace, is to be closer to the secrets of that inner unconscious life which will nourish you if you can hear it, for you are then nearer to that God which every hipster believes is located in the senses of his body, that trapped, mutilated, and nonetheless megalomaniacal God who is It, who is energy, life, sex, force, the Yoga's *prana,* the Reichian's orgone, Lawrence's "blood," Hemingway's "good," the Shavian life-force; "It"; God; not the God of the churches but the unachievable whisper of mystery within the sex, the paradise of limitless energy and perception just beyond the next wave of the next orgasm.

To which a cool cat might reply, "Crazy, man!"

Because, after all, what I have offered above is an hypothesis, no more, and there is not the hipster alive who is not absorbed in his own tumultuous hypotheses. Mine is interesting, mine is way out (on the avenue of the mystery along the road to "It"), but still I am just one cat in a world of cool cats, and everything interesting is crazy, or at least so the Squares who do not know how to swing would say.

(And yet crazy is also the self-protective irony of the hipster. Living with questions and not with anwers, he is so different in his isolation and in the far reach of his imagination from almost everyone with whom he deals in the outer world of the Square, and meets generally so much enmity, competition, and hatred in the world of Hip, that his isolation is always in danger of turning upon itself, and leaving him indeed just that, crazy.)

If, however, you agree with my hypothesis, if you as a cat are way out too, and we are in the same groove (the universe now being glimpsed as a series of ever-extending radii from the center), why then you say simply, ·"I dig," because neither knowledge nor imagination comes easily, it is buried in the pain of one's forgótten experience, and so one must work to find it, one must occasionally exhaust oneself by digging into the self in order to perceive the outside. And indeed it is essential to dig the most, for if you do not dig you lose your superiority over the Square, and so you are less likely to be cool (to be in control of a situation because you have swung where the Square has not, or because you have allowed to come to consciousness a pain, a guilt, a shame or a desire which the other has not had the courage to face). To be cool is to be equipped, and if you are equipped it is more difficult for the next cat who comes along to put you down. And of course one can hardly afford to be put down too often, or one is beat, one has lost one's confidence, one has lost one's will, one is impotent in the world of action and so closer to the demeaning flip of becoming a queer, or indeed closer to dying, and therefore it is even more difficult to recover enough energy to try to make it again, because once a cat is beat he has nothing to give, and no one is interested any longer in making it with him. This is the terror of the hipster—to be beat— because once the sweet of sex has deserted him, he still cannot give up the search. It is not granted to the hipster to grow old gracefully—he has been captured too early by the oldest dream of power, the gold fountain of Ponce de León, the fountain of youth where the gold is in the orgasm.

To be beat is therefore a flip, it is a situation beyond one's experience, impossible to anticipate—which indeed in the circular vocabulary of Hip is still another meaning for flip, but then I have given just a few of the connotations of these words. Like most primitive vocabularies each word is a prime symbol and serves a dozen or a hundred functions of communication in the instinctive dialectic through which the hipster perceives his experience, that dialectic of the instantaneous differentials of existence in which one is forever moving forward into more or retreating into less.

5

It is impossible to conceive a new philosophy until one creates a new language, but a new popular language (while it must implicitly contain a new philosophy) does not necessarily present its philosophy overtly. It can be asked then what really is unique in the life-view of Hip which raises its argot above the passing verbal whimsies of the bohemian or the lumpenproletariat.

The answer would be in the psychopathic element of Hip which has almost no interest in viewing human nature, or better, in judging human nature, from a set of standards conceived a priori to the experience, standards inherited from the past. Since Hip sees every answer as posing immediately a new alternative, a new question, its emphasis is on complexity rather than simplicity (such complexity that its language without the illumination of the voice and the articulation of the face and body remains hopelessly incommunicative). Given its emphasis on complexity, Hip abdicates from any conventional moral responsibility because it would argue that the results of our actions are unforeseeable, and so we cannot know if we do good or bad, we cannot even know (in the Joycean sense of the good and the bad) whether we have given energy to another, and indeed if we could, there would still be no idea of what ultimately the other would do with it.

Therefore, men are not seen as good or bad (that they are good-and-bad is taken for granted) but rather each man is glimpsed as a collection of possibilities, some more possible than others (the view of character implicit in Hip) and some humans are considered more capable than others of reaching more possibilities within themselves in less time, provided, and this is the dynamic, provided the particular character can swing at the right time. And here arises the sense of context which differentiates Hip from a Square view of character. Hip sees the context as generally dominating the man, dominating him because his character is less significant than the context in which he must function. Since it is arbitrarily five times more demanding of one's energy to accomplish even an inconsequential action in an unfavorable context than a favorable one, man is then not only his character but his context, since the success or failure of an action in a given context reacts upon the character and therefore affects what the character will be in the next context. What dominates both character and context is the energy available at the moment of intense context.

Character being thus seen as perpetually ambivalent and dynamic enters then into an absolute relativity where there are no truths other than the isolated truths of what each observer feels at each instant of his existence. To take a perhaps unjustified metaphysical extrapolation, it is as if the universe, which has usually existed conceptually as a Fact (even if the Fact were Berkeley's God) but a Fact which it was the aim of all science and philosophy to reveal, becomes instead a changing reality whose laws are remade at each instant by everything living, but most particularly man, man raised to a neo-medieval summit where the truth is not what one has felt yesterday or what one expects to feel tomorrow but rather truth is no more nor less than what one feels at each instant in the perpetual climax of the present.

What is consequent therefore is the divorce of man from his values, the liberation of the self from the Super-Ego of society. The only Hip morality (but of course it is an ever-present morality) is to do what one feels whenever and wherever it is possible, and—this is how the war of the Hip and the Square begins—to be engaged in one primal battle: to open the limits of the possible for oneself, for oneself alone, because that is one's need. Yet in widening the arena of the possible, one widens it reciprocally for others as well, so that the nihilistic fulfillment of each man's desire contains its antithesis of human cooperation.

If the ethic reduces to Know Thyself and Be Thyself, what makes it radically different from Socratic moderation with its stern conservative respect for the experience of the past is that the Hip ethic is immoderation, childlike in its adoration of the present (and indeed to respect the past means that one must also respect such ugly consequences of the past as the collective murders of the State). It is this adoration of the present which contains the affirmation of Hip, because its ultimate logic surpasses even the unforgettable solution of the Marquis de Sade to sex, private property, and the family, that all men and women have absolute but temporary rights over the bodies of all other men and women—the nihilism of Hip proposes as its final tendency that every social restraint and category be removed, and the affirmation implicit in the proposal is that man would then prove to be more creative than murderous and so would not destroy himself. Which is exactly what separates Hip from the authoritarian philosophies which now appeal to the conservative and liberal temper—what haunts the middle of the twentieth century is that faith in man has been lost, and the appeal of authority has been that it would restrain us from ourselves. Hip, which would return us to ourselves, at no matter what price in individual violence, is the affirmation of the barbarian, for it requires a primitive passion about human nature to believe that individual acts of violence are always to be preferred to the collective violence of the State; it takes literal faith in the creative possibilities of the human being to envisage acts of violence as the catharsis which prepares growth.

Whether the hipster's desire for absolute sexual freedom contains any genuinely radical conception of a different world is of course another matter, and it is possible, since the hipster lives with his hatred, that many of them are the material for an elite of storm troopers ready to follow the first truly magnetic leader whose view of mass murder is phrased in a language which reaches their emotions. But given the desperation of his condition as a psychic outlaw, the hipster is equally a candidate for the most reactionary and most radical of movements, and so it is just as possible that many hipsters will come—if the crisis deepens—to a radical comprehension of the horror of society, for even as the radical has had his incommunicable dissent confirmed in his experience by precisely the frustration, the denied opportunities, and the bitter years which his ideas have cost him, so the sexual adventurer deflected from his goal by the implacable animosity of a society constructed to deny the sexual radical as well may yet come to an equally bitter comprehension of the slow relentless inhumanity of the conservative power which controls him from without and from within. And in being so controlled, denied, and starved into the attrition of conformity, indeed the hipster may come to see that his condition is no more than an exaggeration of the human condition, and

332 · <i>NORMAN MAILER</i>

if he would be free, then everyone must be free. Yes, this is possible too, for the heart of Hip is its emphasis upon courage at the moment of crisis, and it is pleasant to think that courage contains within itself (as the explanation of its existence) some glimpse of the necessity of life to become more than it has been.

It is obviously not very possible to speculate with sharp focus on the future of the hipster. Certain possibilities must be evident, however, and the most central is that the organic growth of Hip depends on whether the Negro emerges as a dominating force in American life. Since the Negro knows more about the ugliness and danger of life than the white, it is probable that if the Negro can win his equality, he will possess a potential superiority, a superiority so feared that the fear itself has become the underground drama of domestic politics. Like all conservative political fear it is the fear of unforeseeable consequences, for the Negro's equality would tear a profound shift into the psychology, the sexuality, and the moral imagination of every white alive.

With this possible emergence of the Negro, Hip may erupt as a psychically armed rebellion whose sexual impetus may rebound against the antisexual foundation of every organized power in America, and bring into the air such animosities, antipathies, and new conflicts of interest that the mean empty hypocrisies of mass conformity will no longer work. A time of violence, new hysteria, confusion and rebellion will then be likely to replace the time of conformity. At that time, if the liberal should prove realistic in his belief that there is peaceful room for every tendency in American life, then Hip would end by being absorbed as a colorful figure in the tapestry. But if this is not the reality, and the economic, the social, the psychological, and finally the moral crises accompanying the rise of the Negro should prove insupportable, then a time is coming when every political guidepost will be gone, and millions of liberals will be faced with political dilemmas they have so far succeeded in evading, and with a view of human nature they do not wish to accept. To take the desegregation of the schools in the South as an example, it is quite likely that the reactionary sees the reality more closely than the liberal when he argues that the deeper issue is not desegregation but miscegenation. (As a radical I am of course facing in the opposite direction from the White Citizen's

Councils—obviously I believe it is the absolute human right of the Negro to mate with the white, and matings there will undoubtedly be, for there will be Negro high school boys brave enough to chance their lives.) But for the average liberal whose mind has been dulled by the committee-ish cant of the professional liberal, miscegenation is not an issue because he has been told that the Negro does not desire it. So, when it comes, miscegenation will be a terror, comparable perhaps to the derangement of the American Communists when the icons to Stalin came tumbling down. The average American Communist held to the myth of Stalin for reasons which had little to do with the political evidence and everything to do with their psychic necessities. In this sense it is equally a psychic necessity for the liberal to believe that the Negro and even the reactionary Southern white are eventually and fundamentally people like himself, capable of becoming good liberals too if only they can be reached by good liberal reason. What the liberal cannot bear to admit is the hatred beneath the skin of a society so unjust that the amount of collective violence buried in the people is perhaps incapable of being contained, and therefore if one wants a better world one does well to hold one's breath, for a worse world is bound to come first, and the dilemma may well be this: given such hatred, it must either vent itself nihilistically or become turned into the cold murderous liquidations of the totalitarian state.

6

No matter what its horrors the twentieth century is a vastly exciting century for its tendency is to reduce all of life to its ultimate alternatives. One can well wonder if the last war of them all will be between the black and the whites, or between the women and the men, or between the beautiful and ugly, the pillagers and managers, or the rebels and the regulators. Which of course is carrying speculation beyond the point where speculation is still serious, and yet despair at the monotony and bleakness of the future have become so engrained in the radical temper that the radical is in danger of abdicating from all imagination. What a man feels is the impulse for his creative effort, and if an alien but nonetheless passionate instinct about the meaning of life has come so unexpectedly from a virtually illiterate people, come out of the most intense conditions of exploitation, cruelty, violence, frustration, and lust, and yet has succeeded as an instinct in keeping this tortured people alive, then it is perhaps possible that the Negro holds more of the tail of the expanding elephant of truth than the radical, and if this is so, the radical humanist could do worse than to brood upon the phenomenon. For if a revolutionary time should come again, there would be a crucial difference if someone had already delineated a neo-Marxian calculus aimed at comprehending every circuit and process of society from ukase to kiss as the communications of human energy—a calculus capable of translating the economic relations of man into his psychological relations and then back again, his productive relations thereby embracing his sexual relations as well, until the crises of capitalism in the twentieth century would yet be understood as the unconscious adaptations of a society to solve its economic imbalance at the expense of a new mass psychological imbalance. It is almost beyond the imagination to conceive of a work in which the drama of human energy is engaged, and a theory of its social currents and dissipations, its imprisonments, expressions, and tragic wastes is fitted into some gigantic synthesis of human action where the body of Marxist thought, and particularly the epic grandeur of *Das Kapital* (that first of the major *psychologies* to approach the mystery of social cruelty so simply and practically as to say that we are a collective body of humans whose life-energy is wasted, displaced, and procedurally stolen as it passes from one of us to another) —where particularly the epic grandeur of *Das Kapital* would find its place in an even more God-like view of human justice and injustice, in some more excruciating vision of those intimate and institutional processes which lead to our creations and disasters, our growth, our attrition, and our rebellion.

1957

EDWIN ARLINGTON ROBINSON

(1869–1935)

Descended on his mother's side from one of America's earliest poets, Anne Bradstreet, Robinson is remembered today as one of the greatest poets America has produced. He was born in Head Tide, Maine, but when he was a year old, his family moved to Gardiner, in the same state. To Robinson, the community in which he grew up was one of typical Yankee commercalism, with its eye on, and its values in, "the main chance," but hiding beneath its surfaces the silent and interior agonies that make hell "more than half of paradise." Gardiner became the "Tilbury Town" of some of Robinson's most memorable poems.

By the time Robinson was graduated from Gardiner High School in 1889, his father's income had all but disappeared. Despite incipient poverty and the town's purse-lipped disapproval of his "wastefulness," Robinson spent four years of what seemed like idleness trying to bring his long-standing and secret love—the writing of poetry—to fruition. He entered Harvard in 1891, but when his father died, Robinson had to leave Cambridge with only two years of higher education behind him. Unsuccessfully, he tried both to publish poems and to enter business. When his mother died in 1896, Robinson felt free to leave Maine and go to New York to be a poet.

New York paid no attention to his arrival. He had to underwrite his first volume of poems, *The Torrent and the Night Before* (1896) in a private printing. The book attracted no attention. In 1897 he published *Children of the Night* (which included most of poems of the previous volume), but again publication cost him money and brought him no success. *Cap-*

tain Craig, the first of his long poems, saw print in 1902. Yet by 1905, in order to keep his frail body and his imaginative soul together, Robinson had to work as a timekeeper, checking loads of stone in the New York City subway that was then being built. But that year, which seemed to be the nadir of his failure, was the beginning of his rise. Kermit Roosevelt had been given a copy of Robinson's poems and, impressed by them, recommended them to his father, the President. Theodore Roosevelt thought so highly of the poems that, after inquiring about the fate of the poet, he gave him a job in the New York Customs House, a sinecure which afforded Robinson time to write. Moreover, the President wrote a review of high praise for Robinson in *The Outlook,* and from that time on both publishers and public became interested.

In 1910 *The Town Down the River* (dedicated to Theodore Roosevelt) finally brought reputation to Robinson, but full recognition and distinction came to him in 1916 with *The Man Against the Sky.* As an established poet, Robinson maintained his residence in New York City, but spent his summers in the MacDowell colony, an artists' retreat in Peterboro, New Hampshire, where he did much of his writing. The first of his famous Arthurian poems, *Merlin,* appeared in 1917, followed by *Lancelot* (1920), and *Tristram* (1927), which won the Pulitzer Prize, as did his first *Collected Poems* in 1921. *Tristram* was by all odds his most popular and best-selling book, even becoming a large book club's monthly selection for its members.

Although the "new poetry" movement, a renaissance of American creativity beginning about 1912, was at its height during the early years of Robinson's success, he was never identified with any critical "school" or avant-garde group. Robinson's innovations were not in form——he utilized standard forms such as the sonnet and quatrain, and remained, as Robert Frost has said, "content with the old ways to be new." What really attracted readers, however, was Robinson's modern sensibility, equally apparent in poems about commercial New York and poems about medieval subjects. His bleak world is filled with a humanity whose objects and goals are uncertain, a world from which any easy teleological optimism has departed. Yet, although he was essentially naturalistic, he never partook of the strong determinism or the total pessimism that permeated the work of so many of his contemporary experimental and revolutionary literary colleagues. The blackness of his universe is punctuated by gleams of light that, however uncertain, illuminate the grim nobility of a race that incredibly refuses to cut its throat and die. Robinson's glimpses of universal human anguish that eventuates so often in defeat, suicide, and depersonalization—particularly in a blindly smug commercialist America—are touched with wonder at the stubbornly noble perpetuation of human life. "I've always told you it's a hell of a place," said Robinson, speaking of the universe. "That's why it must mean something."

In addition to the titles mentioned above, Robinson's books include *Avon's Harvest* (1921), *The Man Who Died Twice* (1924), *Modred* (1929), *The Prodigal Son* (1929), *Cavender's House* (1929), *Nicodemus* (1932), *Talifer* (1933), and *King Jasper* (1935). Some editions of Robinson's work are *Collected Poems* (1921); *The Collected Poems of Edwin Arlington Robinson*, 5 vols. (1927); *Collected Poems of Edwin Arlington Robinson* (1937); L. Thompson, ed., *Tilbury Town, Selected Poems of Edwin Arlington Robinson* (1953); and M. D. Zabel, ed., *Selected Poems of Edwin Arlington Robinson* (1965).
Studies of the man and his work are to be found in L. R. Morris, *The Poetry of Edwin Arlington Robinson* (1923); B. R. Redman, *Edwin Arlington Robinson* (1926); M. Van Doren, *Edwin Arlington Robinson* (1927); L. M. Beebe, *Aspects of the Poetry of Edwin Arlington Robinson* (1928); C. Cestre, *An Introduction to Edwin Arlington Robinson* (1930); W. Brown, *Next Door to a Poet* (1937); L. Lippincott, *A Bibliography of the Writings and Criticisms of Edwin Arlington Robinson* (1937); H. Hagedorn, *Edwin Arlington Robinson* (1938); E. Kaplan, *Philosophy in the Poetry of Edwin Arlington Robinson* (1940); R. Torrence, ed., *Selected Letters of Edwin Arlington Robinson* (1940); C. J. Weber, ed., *Letters of Edwin Arlington Robinson . . .* (1943); D. Sutcliffe, ed., *Untriangulated Stars: Letters of Edwin Arlington Robinson . . .* (1947); Y. Winters, *Edwin Arlington Robinson* (1947); E. Neff, *Edwin Arlington Robinson* (1948); E. Barnard, *Edwin Arlington Robinson* (1952); E. S. Fussell, *Edwin Arlington Robinson* (1954); C. T. Davis, ed., *Selected Early Poems and Letters* (1960); L. Coxe, *Edwin Arlington Robinson* (1962); W. R. Robinson, "Edwin Arlington Robinson," *Dissertation Abstracts*, XXIV (1963); L. Untermeyer, *Edwin Arlington Robinson* (1963); and C. P. Smith, *Where the Light Fails: A Portrait of Edwin Arlington Robinson* (1965).

Supremacy

There is a drear and lonely tract of hell
From all the common gloom removed afar:
A flat, sad land it is, where shadows are,

Whose lorn estate my verse may never tell.
I walked among them and I knew them well:
Men I had slandered on life's little star
For churls and sluggards; and I knew the scar
Upon their brows of woe ineffable.

But as I went majestic on my way,
Into the dark they vanished, one by one,   10
Till, with a shaft of God's eternal day,
The dream of all my glory was undone,—
And, with a fool's importunate dismay,
I heard the dead men singing in the sun.

1892

The House on the Hill

They are all gone away,
   The House is shut and still,
There is nothing more to say.

Through broken walls and gray
   The winds blow bleak and shrill:
They are all gone away.

Nor is there one to-day
   To speak them good or ill:
There is nothing more to say.

Why is it then we stray   10
   Around that sunken sill?
They are all gone away,

And our poor fancy-play
   For them is wasted skill:
There is nothing more to say.

There is ruin and decay
   In the House on the Hill:
They are all gone away,
There is nothing more to say.

1894

Credo

I cannot find my way: there is no star
In all the shrouded heavens anywhere;
And there is not a whisper in the air
Of any living voice but one so far
That I can hear it only as a bar
Of lost, imperial music, played when fair
And angel fingers wove, and unaware,
Dead leaves to garlands where no roses are.

No, there is not a glimmer, nor a call,
For one that welcomes, welcomes when he fears,   10
The black and awful chaos of the night;
For through it all—above, beyond it all—
I know the far-sent message of the years,
I feel the coming glory of the Light.

1896

George Crabbe

Give him the darkest inch your shelf allows,
Hide him in lonely garrets, if you will,—
But his hard, human pulse is throbbing still
With the sure strength that fearless truth endows.
In spite of all fine science disavows,
Of his plain excellence and stubborn skill
There yet remains what fashion cannot kill,
Though years have thinned the laurel from his brows.

Whether or not we read him, we can feel
From time to time the vigor of his name   10
Against us like a finger for the shame
And emptiness of what our souls reveal
In books that are as altars where we kneel
To consecrate the flicker, not the flame.

1896

John Evereldown

"Where are you going to-night, to-night,—
　　Where are you going, John Evereldown?
There's never the sign of a star in sight,
　　Nor a lamp that's nearer than Tilbury Town.
Why do you stare as a dead man might?
Where are you pointing away from the light?
And where are you going to-night, to-night,—
　　Where are you going, John Evereldown?"

"Right through the forest, where none can see,
　　There's where I'm going, to Tilbury Town.　　　16
The men are asleep,—or awake, may be,—
　　But the women are calling John Evereldown.
Ever and ever they call for me,
And while they call can a man be free?
So right through the forest, where none can see,
　　There's where I'm going, to Tilbury Town."

"But why are you going so late, so late,—
　　Why are you going, John Evereldown?
Though the road be smooth and the way be straight,
　　There are two long leagues to Tilbury Town.　　20
Come in by the fire, old man, and wait!
Why do you chatter out there by the gate?
And why are you going so late, so late,—
　　Why are you going, John Evereldown?"

"I follow the women wherever they call,—
　　That's why I'm going to Tilbury Town.
God knows if I pray to be done with it all,
　　But God is no friend to John Evereldown.
So the clouds may come and the rain may fall,
The shadows may creep and the dead men crawl,—　　30
But I follow the women wherever they call,
　　And that's why I'm going to Tilbury Town."

　　　　　　　　　　　　　　　　　　1896

Aaron Stark

Withal a meager man was Aaron Stark—
Cursed and unkempt, shrewd, shriveled, and morose.
A miser was he, with a miser's nose,
And eyes like little dollars in the dark.
His thin, pinched mouth was nothing but a mark;
And when he spoke there came like sullen blows
Through scattered fangs a few snarled words and close,
As if a cur were chary of its bark.

Glad for the murmur of his hard renown,
Year after year he shambled through the town—   10
A loveless exile moving with a staff;
And oftentimes there crept into his ears
A sound of alien pity, touched with tears—
And then (and only then) did Aaron laugh.

1896

Zola

Because he puts the compromising chart
Of hell before your eyes, you are afraid;
Because he counts the price that you have paid
For innocence, and counts it from the start,
You loathe him. But he sees the human heart
Of God meanwhile, and in His hand was weighed
Your squeamish and emasculate crusade
Against the grim dominion of his art.

Never until we conquer the uncouth
Connivings of our shamed indifference   10
(We call it Christian faith) are we to scan
The racked and shrieking hideousness of Truth
To find, in hate's polluted self-defence
Throbbing, the pulse, the divine heart of man.

1896

The Clerks

I did not think that I should find them there
When I came back again; but there they stood,
As in the days they dreamed of when young blood
Was in their cheeks and women called them fair.
Be sure, they met me with an ancient air,—
And yes, there was a shop-worn brotherhood
About them; but the men were just as good,
And just as human as they ever were.

And you that ache so much to be sublime,
And you that feed yourselves with your descent,   10
What comes of all your visions and your fears?
Poets and kings are but the clerks of Time,
Tiering the same dull webs of discontent,
Clipping the same sad alnage of the years.

1896

Dear Friends

Dear friends, reproach me not for what I do,
Nor counsel me, nor pity me; nor say
That I am wearing half my life away
For bubble-work that only fools pursue.
And if my bubbles be too small for you,
Blow bigger then your own: the games we play
To fill the frittered minutes of a day,
Good glasses are to read the spirit through.

And whoso reads may get him some shrewd skill;
And some unprofitable scorn resign,   10
To praise the very thing that he deplores;
So, friends (dear friends), remember, if you will,
The shame I win for singing is all mine,
The gold I miss for dreaming is all yours.

1896

The Dead Village

Here there is death. But even here, they say,—
Here where the dull sun shines this afternoon
As desolate as ever the dead moon
Did glimmer on dead Sardis,—men were gay;
And there were little children here to play,
With small soft hands that once did keep in tune
The strings that stretch from heaven, till too soon
The change came, and the music passed away.

Now there is nothing but the ghosts of things,—
No life, no love, no children, and no men;   10
And over the forgotten place there clings
The strange and unrememberable light
That is in dreams. The music failed, and then
God frowned, and shut the village from His sight.

1896

Luke Havergal

Go to the western gate, Luke Havergal,
There where the vines cling crimson on the wall,
And in the twilight wait for what will come.
The leaves will whisper there of her, and some,
Like flying words, will strike you as they fall;
But go, and if you listen she will call.
Go to the western gate, Luke Havergal—
Luke Havergal.

No, there is not a dawn in eastern skies
To rift the fiery night that's in your eyes;   10
But there, where western glooms are gathering,
The dark will end the dark, if anything:
God slays Himself with every leaf that flies,
And hell is more than half of paradise.
No, there is not a dawn in eastern skies—
In eastern skies.

Out of a grave I come to tell you this,
Out of a grave I come to quench the kiss
That flames upon your forehead with a glow
That blinds you to the way that you must go.   20
Yes, there is yet one way to where she is, ,
Bitter, but one that faith may never miss.
Out of a grave I come to tell you this—
To tell you this.

There is the western gate, Luke Havergal,
There are the crimson leaves upon the wall.
Go, for the winds are tearing them away,—
Nor think to riddle the dead words they say,
Nor any more to feel them as they fall;
But go, and if you trust her she will call.   30
There is the western gate, Luke Havergal—
Luke Havergal.

                    1896

Cliff Klingenhagen

Cliff Klingenhagen had me in to dine
With him one day; and after soup and meat,
And all the other things there were to eat,
Cliff took two glasses and filled one with wine
And one with wormwood. Then, without a sign,
For me to choose at all, he took the draught
Of bitterness himself, and lightly quaffed
It off, and said the other one was mine.

And when I asked him what the deuce he meant
By doing that, he only looked at me   10
And smiled, and said it was a way of his.
And though I know the fellow, I have spent
Long time a-wondering when I shall be
As happy as Cliff Klingenhagen is.

                    1897

Richard Cory

Whenever Richard Cory went down town,
We people on the pavement looked at him:
He was a gentleman from sole to crown,
Clean favored, and imperially slim.

And he was always quietly arrayed,
And he was always human when he talked;
But still he fluttered pulses when he said,
"Good-morning," and he glittered when he walked.

And he was rich—yes, richer than a king—
And admirably schooled in every grace: 10
In fine, we thought that he was everything
To make us wish that we were in his place.

So on we worked, and waited for the light,
And went without the meat, and cursed the bread;
And Richard Cory, one calm summer night,
Went home and put a bullet through his head.

                                                      1897

Reuben Bright

Because he was a butcher and thereby
Did earn an honest living (and did right),
I would not have you think that Reuben Bright
Was any more a brute than you or I;
For when they told him that his wife must die,
He stared at them, and shook with grief and fright,
And cried like a great baby half that night,
And made the women cry to see him cry.

And after she was dead, and he had paid
The singers and the sexton and the rest,   10
He packed a lot of things that she had made
Most mournfully away in an old chest
Of hers, and put some chopped-up cedar boughs
In with them, and tore down the slaughter-house.

                                                      1897

The Woman and the Wife

I. The Explanation

"You thought we knew," she said, "but we were wrong.
This we can say, the rest we do not say;
Nor do I let you throw yourself away
Because you love me. Let us both be strong,
And we shall find in sorrow, before long,
Only the price Love ruled that we should pay:
The dark is at the end of every day,
And silence is the end of every song.

"You ask me for one proof that I speak right,
But I can answer only what I know;   10
You look for just one lie to make black white,
But I can tell you only what is true—
God never made me for the wife of you.
This we can say,—believe me! . . . Tell me so!"

II. The Anniversary

"Give me the truth, whatever it may be.
You thought we knew, now tell me what you miss:
You are the one to tell me what it is—
You are a man, and you have married me.
What is it worth to-night that you can see
More marriage in the dream of one dead kiss   20
Than in a thousand years of life like this?
Passion has turned the lock, Pride keeps the key.

"Whatever I have said or left unsaid,
Whatever I have done or left undone,—
Tell me. Tell me the truth. . . . Are you afraid?
Do you think that Love was ever fed with lies
But hunger lived thereafter in his eyes?
Do you ask me to take moonlight for the sun?"

1902

Miniver Cheevy

Miniver Cheevy, child of scorn,
    Grew lean while he assailed the seasons;
He wept that he was ever born,
    And he had reasons.

Miniver loved the days of old
    When swords were bright and steeds were prancing;
The vision of a warrior bold
    Would set him dancing.

Miniver sighed for what was not,
    And dreamed, and rested from his labors;   10
He dreamed of Thebes and Camelot,
    And Priam's neighbors.

Miniver mourned the ripe renown
    That made so many a name so fragrant;
He mourned Romance, now on the town,
    And Art, a vagrant.

Miniver loved the Medici,
    Albeit he had never seen one;
He would have sinned incessantly
    Could he have been one.   20

Miniver cursed the commonplace
    And eyed a khaki suit with loathing;
He missed the mediaeval grace
    Of iron clothing.

Miniver scorned the gold he sought,
    But sore annoyed was he without it;
Miniver thought, and thought, and thought,
    And thought about it.

Miniver Cheevy, born too late,
    Scratched his head and kept on thinking;   30
Miniver coughed, and called it fate,
    And kept on drinking.

1907

Doctor of Billiards

Of all among the fallen from on high,
We count you last and leave you to regain
Your born dominion of a life made vain
By three spheres of insidious ivory.
You dwindle to the lesser tragedy—
Content, you say. We call, but you remain.
Nothing alive gone wrong could be so plain,
Or quite so blasted with absurdity.

You click away the kingdom that is yours,
And you click off your crown for cap and bells;   10
You smile, who are still master of the feast,
And for your smile we credit you the least;
But when your false, unhallowed laugh occurs,
We seem to think there may be something else.

1910

For a Dead Lady

No more with overflowing light
Shall fill the eyes that now are faded,
Nor shall another's fringe with night
Their woman-hidden world as they did.
No more shall quiver down the days
The flowing wonder of her ways,
Whereof no language may requite
The shifting and the many-shaded.

The grace, divine, definitive,
Clings only as a faint forestalling;   10
The laugh that love could not forgive
Is hushed, and answers to no calling;
The forehead and the little ears
Have gone where Saturn keeps the years;
The breast where roses could not live
Has done with rising and with falling.

The beauty, shattered by the laws
That have creation in their keeping,

No longer trembles at applause,
Or over children that are sleeping;   20
And we who delve in beauty's lore
Know all that we have known before
Of what inexorable cause
Makes Time so vicious in his reaping.

                                        1910

How Annandale Went Out

"They called it Annandale—and I was there
To flourish, to find words, and to attend:
Liar, physician, hypocrite, and friend,
I watched him; and the sight was not so fair
As one or two that I have seen elsewhere:
An apparatus not for me to mend—
A wreck, with hell between him and the end,
Remained of Annandale; and I was there.

"I knew the ruin as I knew the man;
So put the two together, if you can,   10
Remembering the worst you know of me.
Now view yourself as I was, on the spot—
With a slight kind of engine. Do you see?
Like this . . . You wouldn't hang me? I thought not."

                                        1910

Cassandra

I heard one who said: "Verily,
    What word have I for children here?
Your Dollar is your only Word,
    The wrath of it your only fear.

"You build it altars tall enough
    To make you see, but you are blind;
You cannot leave it long enough
    To look before you or behind.

"When Reason beckons you to pause,
    You laugh and say that you know best;   10

But what it is you know, you keep
    As dark as ingots in a chest.

"You laugh and answer, 'We are young;
    O leave us now, and let us grow.'—
Not asking how much more of this
    Will Time endure or Fate bestow.

"Because a few complacent years
    Have made your peril of your pride,
Think you that you are to go on
    Forever pampered and untried?   20

"What lost eclipse of history,
    What bivouac of the marching stars,
Has given the sign for you to see
    Millenniums and last great wars?

"What unrecorded overthrow
    Of all the world has ever known,
Or ever been, has made itself
    So plain to you, and you alone?

"Your Dollar, Dove and Eagle make
    A Trinity that even you   30
Rate higher than you rate yourselves;
    It pays, it flatters, and it's new.

"And though your very flesh and blood
    Be what your Eagle eats and drinks,
You'll praise him for the best of birds,
    Not knowing what the Eagle thinks.

"The power is yours, but not the sight;
    You see not upon what you tread;
You have the ages for your guide,
    But not the wisdom to be led.   40

"Think you to tread forever down
    The merciless old verities?

And are you never to have eyes
   To see the world for what it is?

"Are you to pay for what you have
   With all you are?"—No other word
We caught, but with a laughing crowd
   Moved on. None heeded, and few heard.

                                            1914

Eros Turannos

[*Love, the Tyrant*]

She fears him, and will always ask
   What fated her to choose him;
She meets in his engaging mask
   All reasons to refuse him;
But what she meets and what she fears
Are less than are the downward years,
Drawn slowly to the foamless weirs
   Of age, were she to lose him.

Between a blurred sagacity
   That once had power to sound him,
And Love, that will not let him be   10
   The Judas that she found him,
Her pride assuages her almost,
As if it were alone the cost.—
He sees that he will not be lost,
   And waits and looks around him.

A sense of ocean and old trees
   Envelops and allures him;
Tradition, touching all he sees,
   Beguiles and reassures him;   20
And all her doubts of what he says
Are dimmed with what she knows of days—
Till even prejudice delays
   And fades, and she secures him.

The falling leaf inaugurates
   The reign of her confusion;
The pounding wave reverberates
   The dirge of her illusion;
And home, where passion lived and died,
Becomes a place where she can hide,   30
While all the town and harbor side
   Vibrate with her seclusion.

We tell you, tapping on our brows,
   The story as it should be,—
As if the story of a house
   Were told, or ever could be;
We'll have no kindly veil between
Her visions and those we have seen,—
As if we guessed what hers have been,
   Or what they are or would be.   40

Meanwhile we do no harm; for they
   That with a god have striven,
Not hearing much of what we say,
   Take what the god has given;
Though like waves breaking it may be,
Or like a changed familiar tree,
Or like a stairway to the sea
   Where down the blind are driven.

                               1914

Flammonde

The man Flammonde, from God knows where,
With firm address and foreign air,
With news of nations in his talk
And something royal in his walk,
With glint of iron in his eyes,
But never doubt, nor yet surprise,
Appeared, and stayed, and held his head
As one by kings accredited.

Erect, with his alert repose
About him, and about his clothes,   10

He pictured all tradition hears
Of what we owe to fifty years.
His cleansing heritage of taste
Paraded neither want nor waste;
And what he needed for his fee
To live, he borrowed graciously.

He never told us what he was,
Or what mischance, or other cause,
Had banished him from better days
To play the Prince of Castaways.   20
Meanwhile he played surpassing well
A part, for most, unplayable;
In fine, one pauses, half afraid
To say for certain that he played.

For that, one may as well forego
Conviction as to yes or no;
Nor can I say just how intense
Would then have been the difference
To several, who, having striven
In vain to get what he was given,   30
Would see the stranger taken on
By friends not easy to be won.

Moreover, many a malcontent
He soothed and found munificent;
His courtesy beguiled and foiled
Suspicion that his years were soiled;
His mien distinguished any crowd,
His credit strengthened when he bowed;
And women, young and old, were fond
Of looking at the man Flammonde.   40

There was a woman in our town
On whom the fashion was to frown;
But while our talk renewed the tinge
Of a long-faded scarlet fringe,
The man Flammonde saw none of that,
And what he saw we wondered at—
That none of us, in her distress,
Could hide or find our littleness.

There was a boy that all agreed
Had shut within him the rare seed   50
Of learning. We could understand,
But none of us could lift a hand.
The man Flammonde appraised the youth,
And told a few of us the truth;
And thereby, for a little gold,
A flowered future was unrolled.

There were two citizens who fought
For years and years, and over nought;
They made life awkward for their friends,
And shortened their own dividends.   60
The man Flammonde said what was wrong
Should be made right; nor was it long
Before they were again in line,
And had each other in to dine.

And these I mention are but four
Of many out of many more.
So much for them. But what of him—
So firm in every look and limb?
What small satanic sort of kink
Was in his brain? What broken link   70
Withheld him from the destinies
That came so near to being his?

What was he, when we came to sift
His meaning, and to note the drift
Of incommunicable ways
That make us ponder while we praise?
Why was it that his charm revealed
Somehow the surface of a shield?
What was it that we never caught?
What was he, and what was he not?   80

How much it was of him we met
We cannot ever know; nor yet
Shall all he gave us quite atone
For what was his, and his alone;
Nor need we now, since he knew best,

Nourish an ethical unrest:
Rarely at once will nature give
The power to be Flammonde and live.

We cannot know how much we learn
From those who never will return,   90
Until a flash of unforeseen
Remembrance falls on what has been.
We've each a darkening hill to climb;
And this is why, from time to time
In Tilbury Town, we look beyond
Horizons for the man Flammonde.

                                                    1915

Bewick Finzer

Time was when his half million drew
    The breath of six per cent;
But soon the worm of what-was-not
    Fed hard on his content;
And something crumbled in his brain
    When his half million went.

Time passed, and filled along with his
    The place of many more;
Time came, and hardly one of us
    Had credence to restore,   10
From what appeared one day, the man
    Whom we had known before.

The broken voice, the withered neck,
    The coat worn out with care,
The cleanliness of indigence,
    The brilliance of despair,
The fond imponderable dreams
    Of affluence,—all were there.

Poor Finzer, with his dreams and schemes,
    Fares hard now in the race,   20
With heart and eye that have a task

When he looks in the face
Of one who might so easily
    Have been in Finzer's place.

He comes unfailing for the loan
    We give and then forget;
He comes, and probably for years
    Will he be coming yet,—
Familiar as an old mistake,
    And futile as regret.

30

1916

Veteran Sirens

[Ninon de l'Enclos: famous French courtesan]

The ghost of Ninon would be sorry now
To laugh at them, were she to see them here,
So brave and so alert for learning how
To fence with reason for another year.

Age offers a far comelier diadem
Than theirs; but anguish has no eye for grace,
When time's malicious mercy cautions them
To think a while of number and of space.

The burning hope, the worn expectancy,
The martyred humor, and the maimed allure,   10
Cry out for time to end his levity,
And age to soften its investiture;

But they, though others fade and are still fair,
Defy their fairness and are unsubdued;
Although they suffer, they may not forswear
The patient ardor of the unpursued.

Poor flesh, to fight the calendar so long;
Poor vanity, so quaint and yet so brave;
Poor folly, so deceived and yet so strong,
So far from Ninon and so near the grave.   20

1916

The Man Against the Sky

Between me and the sunset, like a dome
Against the glory of a world on fire,
Now burned a sudden hill,
Bleak, round, and high, by flame-lit height made higher,
With nothing on it for the flame to kill
Save one who moved and was alone up there
To loom before the chaos and the glare
As if he were the last god going home
Unto his last desire

Dark, marvelous, and inscrutable he moved on   10
Till down the fiery distance he was gone,
Like one of those eternal, remote things
That range across a man's imaginings
When a sure music fills him and he knows
What he may say thereafter to few men,—
The touch of ages having wrought
An echo and a glimpse of what he thought
A phantom or a legend until then;
For whether lighted over ways that save,
Or lured from all repose,   20
If he go on too far to find a grave,
Mostly alone he goes.

Even he, who stood where I had found him,
On high with fire all round him,
Who moved along the molten west,
And over the round hill's crest
That seemed half ready with him to go down,
Flame-bitten and flame-cleft,
As if there were to be no last thing left
Of a nameless unimaginable town,—   30
Even he who climbed and vanished may have taken
Down to the perils of a depth not known,
From death defended though by men forsaken,
The bread that every man must eat alone;
He may have walked while others hardly dared
Look on to see him stand where many fell;
And upward out of that, as out of hell,
He may have sung and striven

To mount where more of him shall yet be given,
Bereft of all retreat,   40
To sevenfold heat,—
As on a day when three in Dura shared
The furnace, and were spared
For glory by that king of Babylon
Who made himself so great that God, who heard,
Covered him with long feathers, like a bird.

Again, he may have gone down easily,
By comfortable altitudes, and found,
As always, underneath him solid ground
Whereon to be sufficient and to stand   50
Possessed already of the promised land,
Far stretched and fair to see:
A good sight, verily,
And one to make the eyes of her who bore him
Shine glad with hidden tears.
Why question of his ease of who before him,
In one place or another where they left
Their names as far behind them as their bones,
And yet by dint of slaughter, toil and theft,
And shrewdly sharpened stones,   60
Carved hard the way for his ascendency
Through deserts of lost years?
Why trouble him now who sees and hears
No more than what his innocence requires,
And therefore to no other height aspires
Than one at which he neither quails nor tires?
He may do more by seeing what he sees
Than others eager for iniquities;
He may, by seeing all things for the best,
Incite futurity to do the rest.   70

Or with an even likelihood,
He may have met with atrabilious eyes
The fires of time on equal terms and passed
Indifferently down, until at last
His only kind of grandeur would have been,
Apparently, in being seen.
He may have had for evil or for good
No argument; he may have had no care
For what without himself went anywhere

To failure or to glory, and least of all   80
For such a stale, flamboyant miracle;
He may have been the prophet of an art
Immovable to old idolatries;
He may have been a player without a part,
Annoyed that even the sun should have the skies
For such a flaming way to advertise;
He may have been a painter sick at heart,
With Nature's toiling for a new surpise;
He may have been a cynic, who now, for all
Of anything divine that his effete   90
Negation may have tasted,
Saw truth in his own image, rather small,
Forbore to fever the ephemeral,
Found any barren height a good retreat
From any swarming street,
And in the sun saw power superbly wasted;
And when the primitive old-fashioned stars
Came out again to shine on joys and wars
More primitive, and all arrayed for doom,
He may have proved a world a sorry thing   100
In his imagining,
And life a lighted highway to the tomb.

Or, mounting with infirm unsearching tread,
His hopes to chaos led,
He may have stumbled up there from the past,
And with an aching strangeness viewed the last
Abysmal conflagration of his dreams,—
A flame where nothing seems
To burn but flame itself, by nothing fed;
And while it all went out,   110
Not even the faint anodyne of doubt
May then have eased a painful going down
From pictured heights of power and lost renown,
Revealed at length to his outlived endeavor
Remote and unapproachable forever;
And at his heart there may have gnawed
Sick memories of a dead faith foiled and flawed
And long dishonored by the living death
Assigned alike by chance
To brutes and hierophants;   120
And anguish fallen on those he loved around him

May once have dealt the last blow to confound him,
And so have left him as death leaves a child,
Who sees it all too near;
And he who knows no young way to forget
May struggle to the tomb unreconciled.
Whatever suns may rise or set
There may be nothing kinder for him here
Than shafts and agonies;
And under these   130
He may cry out and stay on horribly;
Or, seeing in death too small a thing to fear,
He may go forward like a stoic Roman
Where pangs and terrors in his pathway lie,—
Or, seizing the swift logic of a woman,
Curse God and die.

Or maybe there, like many another one
Who might have stood aloft and looked ahead,
Black-drawn against wild red,
He may have built, unawed by fiery gules   140
That in him no commotion stirred,
A living reason out of molecules
Why molecules occurred,
And one for smiling when he might have sighed
Had he seen far enough,
And in the same inevitable stuff
Discovered an odd reason too for pride
In being what he must have been by laws
Infrangible and for no kind of cause.
Deterred by no confusion or surprise   150
He may have seen with his mechanic eyes
A world without a meaning, and had room,
Alone amid magnificence and doom,
To build himself an airy monument
That should, or fail him in his vague intent,
Outlast an accidental universe—
To call it nothing worse—
Or, by the burrowing guile
Of Time disintegrated and effaced,
Like once-remembered mighty trees go down   160
To ruin, of which by man may now be traced
No part sufficient even to be rotten,
And in the book of things that are forgotten

Is entered as a thing not quite worth while.
He may have been so great
That satraps would have shivered at his frown,
And all he prized alive may rule a state
No larger than a grave that holds a clown;
He may have been a master of his fate,
And of his atoms,—ready as another   170
In his emergence to exonerate
His father and his mother;
He may have been a captain of a host,
Self-eloquent and ripe for prodigies,
Doomed here to swell by dangerous degrees,
And then give up the ghost.
Nahum's great grasshoppers were such as these,
Sun-scattered and soon lost.

Whatever the dark road he may have taken,
This man who stood on high   180
And faced alone the sky,
Whatever drove or lured or guided him,—
A vision answering a faith unshaken,
An easy trust assumed by easy trials,
A sick negation born of weak denials,
A crazed abhorrence of an old condition,
A blind attendance on a brief ambition,—
Whatever stayed him or derided him,
His way was even as ours;
And we, with all our wounds and all our powers,   190
Must each await alone at his own height
Another darkness or another light;
And there, of our poor self dominion reft,
If inference and reason shun
Hell, Heaven, and Oblivion,
May thwarted will (perforce precarious,
But for our conservation better thus)
Have no misgiving left
Of doing yet what here we leave undone?
Or if unto the last of these we cleave,   200
Believing or protesting we believe
In such an idle and ephemeral
Florescence of the diabolical,—
If, robbed of two fond old enormities,
Our being had no onward auguries,

What then were this great love of ours to say
For launching other lives to voyage again
A little farther into time and pain,
A little faster in a futile chase
For a kingdom and a power and a Race   210
That would have still in sight
A manifest end of ashes and eternal night?
Is this the music of the toys we shake
So loud,—as if there might be no mistake
Somewhere in our indomitable will?
Are we no greater than the noise we make
Along one blind atomic pilgrimage
Whereon by crass chance billeted we go
Because our brains and bones and cartilage
Will have it so?   220
If this we say, then let us all be still
About our share in it, and live and die
More quietly thereby.

Where was he going, this man against the sky?
You know not, nor do I.
But this we know, if we know anything:
That we may laugh and fight and sing
And of our transience here make offering
To an orient Word that will not be erased,
Or, save in incommunicable gleams   230
Too permanent for dreams,
Be found or known.
No tonic and ambitious irritant
Of increase or of want
Has made an otherwise insensate waste
Of ages overthrown
A ruthless, veiled, implacable foretaste
Of other ages that are still to be
Depleted and rewarded variously
Because a few, by fate's economy,   240
Shall seem to move the world the way it goes;
No soft evangel of equality,
Safe-cradled in a communal repose
That huddles into death and may at last
Be covered well with equatorial snows—
And all for what, the devil only knows—
Will aggregate an inkling to confirm

The credit of a sage or of a worm,
Or tell us why one man in five
Should have a care to stay alive   250
While in his heart he feels no violence
Laid on his humor and intelligence
When infant Science makes a pleasant face
And waves again that hollow toy, the Race;
No planetary trap where souls are wrought
For nothing but the sake of being caught
And sent again to nothing will attune
Itself to any key of any reason
Why man should hunger through another season
To find out why 'twere better late than soon   260
To go away and let the sun and moon
And all the silly stars illuminate
A place for creeping things,
And those that root and trumpet and have wings,
And herd and ruminate,
Or dive and flash and poise in rivers and seas,
Or by their loyal tails in lofty trees
Hang screeching lewd victorious derision
Of man's immortal vision.

Shall we, because Eternity records   270
Too vast an answer for the time-born words
We spell, whereof so many are dead that once
In our capricious lexicons
Were so alive and final, hear no more
The Word itself, the living word
That none alive has ever heard
Or ever spelt,
And few have ever felt
Without the fears and old surrenderings
And terrors that began   280
When Death let fall a feather from his wings
And humbled the first man?
Because the weight of our humility,
Wherefrom we gain
A little wisdom and much pain,
Falls here too sore and there too tedious,
Are we in anguish or complacency,
Not looking far enough ahead
To see by what mad couriers we are led

Along the roads of the ridiculous,   290
To pity ourselves and laugh at faith
And while we curse life bear it?
And if we see the soul's dead end in death,
Are we to fear it?
What folly is here that has not yet a name
Unless we say outright that we are liars?
What have we seen beyond our sunset fires
That lights again the way by which we came?
Why pay we such a price, and one we give
So clamoringly, for each racked empty day   300
That leads one more last human hope away,
As quiet fiends would lead past our crazed eyes
Our children to an unseen sacrifice?
If after all that we have lived and thought,
All comes to Nought,—
If there be nothing after Now,
And we be nothing anyhow,
And we know that,—why live?
'Twere sure but weaklings, vain distress
To suffer dungeons where so many doors   310
Will open on the cold eternal shores
That look sheer down
To the dark tideless floods of Nothingness
Where all who know may drown.

                                                  1916

The Mill

The miller's wife had waited long,
    The tea was cold, the fire was dead;
And there might yet be nothing wrong
    In how he went and what he said:
"There are no millers any more,"
    Was all that she had heard him say;
And he had lingered at the door
    So long that it seemed yesterday.

Sick with a fear that had no form
    She knew that she was there at last;   10

And in the mill there was a warm
  And mealy fragrance of the past.
What else there was would only seem
  To say again what he had meant;
And what was hanging from a beam
  Would not have heeded where she went.

And if she thought it followed her,
  She may have reasoned in the dark
That one way of the few there were
  Would hide her and would leave no mark: 20
Black water, smooth above the weir
  Like starry velvet in the night,
Though ruffled once, would soon appear
  The same as ever to the sight.

                                        1919

Mr. Flood's Party

Old Eben Flood, climbing alone one night
Over the hill between the town below
And the forsaken upland hermitage
That held as much as he should ever know
On earth again of home, paused warily.
The road was his with not a native near;
And Eben, having leisure, said aloud;
For no man else in Tilbury Town to hear:

"Well, Mr. Flood, we have the harvest moon
Again, and we may not have many more;   10
The bird is on the wing, the poet says,
And you and I have said it here before.
Drink to the bird." He raised up to the light
The jug that he had gone so far to fill,
And answered huskily: "Well, Mr. Flood,
Since you propose it, I believe I will."

Alone, as if enduring to the end
A valiant armor of scarred hopes outworn,
He stood there in the middle of the road

Like Roland's ghost winding a silent horn.   20
Below him, in the town among the trees,
Where friends of other days had honored him,
A phantom salutation of the dead
Rang thinly till old Eben's eyes were dim.

Then, as a mother lays her sleeping child
Down tenderly, fearing it may awake,
He set the jug down slowly at his feet
With trembling care, knowing that most things break;
And only when assured that on firm earth
It stood, as the uncertain lives of men   30
Assuredly did not, he paced away,
And with his hand extended paused again:

"Well, Mr. Flood, we have not met like this
In a long time; and many a change has come
To both of us, I fear, since last it was
We had a drop together. Welcome home!"
Convivially returning with himself,
Again he raised the jug up to the light;
And with an acquiescent quaver said:
"Well, Mr. Flood, if you insist, I might.   40

"Only a very little, Mr. Flood—
For auld lang syne. No more, sir; that will do."
So, for the time, apparently it did,
And Eben evidently thought so too;
For soon amid the silver loneliness
Of night he lifted up his voice and sang,
Secure, with only two moons listening,
Until the whole harmonious landscape rang—

"For auld lang syne." The weary throat gave out,
The last word wavered; and the song being done,   50
He raised again the jug regretfully
And shook his head, and was again alone.
There was not much that was ahead of him,
And there was nothing in the town below—
Where strangers would have shut the many doors
That many friends had opened long ago.

1920

New England

Here where the wind is always north-north-east
And children learn to walk on frozen toes,
Wonder begets an envy of all those
Who boil elsewhere with such a lyric yeast
Of love that you will hear them at a feast
Where demons would appeal for some repose,
Still clamoring where the chalice overflows
And crying wildest who have drunk the least.

Passion is here a soilure of the wits,
We're told, and Love a cross for them to bear;   10
Joy shivers in the corner where she knits
And Conscience always has the rocking-chair,
Cheerful as when she tortured into fits
The first cat that was ever killed by Care.

1923

Karma

Christmas was in the air and all was well
With him, but for a few confusing flaws
In divers of God's images. Because
A friend of his would neither buy nor sell,
Was he to answer for the axe that fell?
He pondered; and the reason for it was,
Partly, a slowly freezing Santa Claus
Upon the corner, with his beard and bell.

Acknowledging an improvident surprise,
He magnified a fancy that he wished   10
The friend whom he had wrecked were here again.
Not sure of that, he found a compromise;
And from the fulness of his heart he fished
A dime for Jesus who had died for men.

1923

AMY LOWELL

(1874–1925)

A member of a venerable Massachusetts family that included
James Russell Lowell, an internationally famous astronomer,
and a Harvard President, Amy Lowell, with her cigar smoking
and her bellicose eccentricities, hardly fitted the general stereo-
type of the Boston Brahmin. Born in Brookline, she was educated in traditional patrician fashion by private tutors and travel
in Europe. She had no fixed ideas about a career, but in 1902
she began to devote herself rigorously to a study of the writing
of poetry, inspired—so the story goes—by a performance of
Eleanora Duse.

In 1910 the *Atlantic Monthly*, historically a Brahmin haven,
printed her first published poem, and two years later she published a conventional and undistinguished volume of verses, *A
Dome of Many-Coloured Glass*. Then in 1913, in England, she
met Ezra Pound and the group of poets—including Hilda Doolittle, Richard Aldington and John Gould Fletcher—who called
themselves "Imagists." (In 1914 Pound edited an anthology
of their poems called *Des Imagistes*.) The Imagists were in the
vanguard of the "new poetry" movement, rebelling against
the "pretty" language and moralizing attitudes characteristic
of much traditional poetry. Miss Lowell enthusiastically caught
the contagious excitement of the group—she tended toward
enthusiasm and largeness in every way—and immediately
wrested leadership from the hapless Pound.

For the next decade, she kept the "new poetry" in the public
eye. With her ample resources of cash and energy, she brought
out regular editions of *Some Imagist Poets*, traveled widely to
lecture, read to, and bully audiences, and generally crusaded
with great relish for her cause. In 1914 she published her sec-

ond volume of poems, *Sword Blades and Poppy Seed*, which gave clear indication of the new influences on her work. Her next volume of poetry, *Men, Women and Ghosts* (1916), was sandwiched between two critical studies of the influences upon, and directions of, the poetic renaissance: *Six French Poets* (1915) and *Tendencies in Modern American Poetry* (1917).

The first issue of *Some Imagist Poets* in 1915 announced a manifesto of imagism; its statements, hotly discussed at the time, have become a commonplace in modern poetry. The six principles enunciated insisted that poetry (1) should "use the language of common speech," employing "always the *exact* word"; (2) should create new rhythms for new moods, not "copy old rhythms, which merely echo old moods. . . . In poetry a new cadence means a new idea"; (3) should allow the poet "absolute freedom in the choice of subject"; (4) should "present an image . . . and not deal in vague generalities, however magnificent and sonorous"; (5) should be "hard and clear, never blurred or indefinite"; and (6) should have "concentration" as its "very essence."

Some of Miss Lowell's other books, in addition to the titles mentioned above, are *Can Grande's Castle* (1918); *Pictures of the Floating World* (1919); *A Critical Fable* (1922); *What's O'Clock* (1925); *John Keats* (1925); *The Madonna of Carthagena* (1927); and *Poetry and Poets: Essays* (1930). L. Untermeyer edited *The Complete Poetical Works of Amy Lowell* (1955).

Studies of Miss Lowell and her works are to be found in J. G. Fletcher, "Miss Lowell's Discovery," *Poetry*, VI (1915); W. Bryher, *Amy Lowell* (1918); C. Aiken, *Scepticisms* (1919); R. Hunt and R. Snow, *Amy Lowell* (1921); P. H. Boynton, *Some Contemporary Americans* (1924); J. Farrar, *The Literary Spotlight* (1924); H. Monroe, *Poets and Their Art* (1926); C. Wood, *Amy Lowell* (1926); E. S. Sergeant, *Fire Under the Andes* (1927); G. Hughes, *Imagism and the Imagists* (1931); J. L. Lewes, "Amy Lowell," *Dictionary of American Biography*, XV (1933–1934); S. F. Damon, *Amy Lowell* (1935), the standard biography; F. Greenslet, *The Lowells and Their Seven Worlds* (1946); G. Arms and J. M. Kuntz, *Poetry Explication* (1950); A. Tate, *Sixty American Poets* (1954); H. Gregory, *Amy Lowell: Portrait of the Poet in Her Time* (1958); and W. T. Scott, *Exiles and Fabrications* (1961).

Patterns

I walk down the garden-paths,
And all the daffodils

Are blowing, and the bright blue squills.
I walk down the patterned garden-paths
In my stiff, brocaded gown.
With my powdered hair and jewelled fan,
I too am a rare
Pattern. As I wander down
The garden-paths.

My dress is richly figured,   10
And the train
Makes a pink and silver stain
On the gravel, and the thrift
Of the borders.
Just a plate of current fashion,
Tripping by in high-heeled, ribboned shoes.
Not a softness anywhere about me,
Only whalebone and brocade.
And I sink on a seat in the shade
Of a lime tree. For my passion   20
Wars against the stiff brocade.
The daffodils and squills
Flutter in the breeze
As they please.
And I weep;
For the lime-tree is in blossom
And one small flower has dropped upon my bosom.

And the plashing of waterdrops
In the marble fountain
Comes down the garden-paths.   30
The dripping never stops.
Underneath my stiffened gown
Is the softness of a woman bathing in a marble basin,
A basin in the midst of hedges grown
So thick, she cannot see her lover hiding,
But she guesses he is near,
And the sliding of the water
Seems the stroking of a dear
Hand upon her.
What is Summer in a fine brocaded gown!   40
I should like to see it lying in a heap upon the ground.
All the pink and silver crumpled up on the ground.

I would be the pink and silver as I ran along the paths,
And he would stumble after,
Bewildered by my laughter.
I should see the sun flashing from his sword-hilt and the
    buckles on his shoes.
I would choose
To lead him in a maze along the patterned paths,
A bright and laughing maze for my heavy-booted lover.
Till he caught me in the shade,   50
And the buttons of his waistcoat bruised my body as
    he clasped me,
Aching, melting, unafraid.
With the shadows of the leaves and the sundrops,
And the plopping of the waterdrops,
All about us in the open afternoon—
I am very like to swoon
With the weight of this brocade,
For the sun sifts through the shade.

Underneath the fallen blossom
In my bosom,   60
Is a letter I have hid.
It was brought to me this morning by a rider from the
    Duke.
"Madam, we regret to inform you that Lord Hartwell
Died in action Thursday se'nnight."
As I read it in the white, morning sunlight,
The letters squirmed like snakes.
"Any answer, Madam?" said my footman.
"No," I told him.
"See that the messenger takes some refreshment.
No, no answer."   70
And I walked into the garden,
Up and down the patterned paths,
In my stiff, correct brocade.
The blue and yellow flowers stood up proudly in the sun,
Each one.
I stood upright too,
Held rigid to the pattern
By the stiffness of my gown.
Up and down I walked,
Up and down.   80

In a month he would have been my husband.
In a month, here, underneath this lime,
We would have broke the pattern;
He for me, and I for him,
He as Colonel, I as Lady,
On this shady seat.
He had a whim
That sunlight carried blessing.
And I answered. "It shall be as you have said."
Now he is dead.   90

In Summer and in Winter I shall walk
Up and down
The patterned garden-paths
In my stiff, brocaded gown.
The squills and daffodils
Will give place to pillared roses, and to asters, and to snow.
I shall go
Up and down,
In my gown.
Gorgeously arrayed,   100
Boned and stayed.
And the softness of my body will be guarded from embrace
By each button, hook, and lace.
For the man who should loose me is dead,
Fighting with the Duke in Flanders,
In a pattern called a war.
Christ! What are patterns for?

                                                   1915

Lilacs

Lilacs,
False blue,
White,
Purple,
Color of lilac,
Your great puffs of flowers
Are everywhere in this my New England.
Among your heart-shaped leaves
Orange orioles hop like music-box birds and sing

Their little weak soft songs;   10
In the crooks of your branches
The bright eyes of song sparrows sitting on spotted eggs
Peer restlessly through the light and shadow
Of all Springs.
Lilacs in dooryards
Holding quiet conversations with an early moon;
Lilacs watching a deserted house
Settling sideways into the grass of an old road;
Lilacs, wind-beaten, staggering under a lopsided shock of
    bloom
Above a cellar dug into a hill.   20
You are everywhere.
You were everywhere.
You tapped the window when the preacher preached his
    sermon,
And ran along the road beside the boy going to school.
You stood by pasture-bars to give the cows good milking,
You persuaded the housewife that her dish pan was of
    silver
And her husband an image of pure gold.
You flaunted the fragrance of your blossoms
Through the wide doors of Custom Houses—
You, and sandal-wood, and tea,   30
Charging the noses of quill-driving clerks
When a ship was in from China.
You called to them: "Goose-quill men, goose-quill men,
May is a month for flitting,"
Until they writhed on their high stools
And wrote poetry on their letter-sheets behind the propped-
    up ledgers.
Paradoxical New England clerks,
Writing inventories in ledgers, reading the "Song of Solo-
    mon" at night,
So many verses before bed-time,
Because it was the Bible.   40
The dead fed you
Amid the slant stones of graveyards.
Pale ghosts who planted you
Came in the night-time
And let their thin hair blow through your clustered stems.
You are of the green sea,
And of the stone hills which reach a long distance.

You are of elm-shaded streets with little shops where they
   sell kites and marbles,
You are of great parks where everyone walks and nobody
   is at home.
You cover the blind sides of greenhouses   50
And lean over the top to say a hurry-word through the
   glass
To your friends, the grapes, inside.

Lilacs,
False blue,
White,
Purple,
Color of lilac,
You have forgotten your Eastern origin,
The veiled women with eyes like panthers,
The swollen, aggressive turbans of jeweled Pashas.
Now you are a very decent flower,
A reticent flower,
A curiously clear-cut, candid flower,
Standing beside clean doorways,
Friendly to a house-cat and a pair of spectacles,
Making poetry out of a bit of moonlight
And a hundred or two sharp blossoms.
Maine knows you;
Has for years and years;
New Hampshire knows you,   70
And Massachusetts
And Vermont.
Cape Cod starts you along the beaches to Rhode Island;
Connecticut takes you from a river to the sea.
You are brighter than apples,
Sweeter than tulips,
You are the great flood of our souls
Bursting above the leaf-shapes of our hearts,
You are the smell of all Summers,
The love of wives and children,   80
The recollection of the gardens of little children,
You are State Houses and Charters
And the familiar treading of the foot to and fro on a road
   it knows.
May is lilac here in New England,
May is a thrush singing "Sun up!" on a tip-top ash-tree,

May is white clouds behind pine-trees
Puffed out and marching upon a blue sky.
May is a green as no other,
May is much sun through small leaves,
May is soft earth,   90
And apple-blossoms,
And windows open to a South wind.
May is a full light wind of lilac
From Canada to Narragansett Bay.

Lilacs,
False blue,
White,
Purple,
Color of lilac,
Heart-leaves of lilac all over New England,   100
Roots of lilac under all the soil of New England,
Lilac in me because I am New England,
Because my roots are in it,
Because my leaves are of it,
Because my flowers are for it,
Because it is my country
And I speak to it of itself
And sing of it with my own voice
Since certainly it is mine.

1920

EDNA ST. VINCENT MILLAY

(1892–1950)

Born in Rockland, Maine, Edna St. Vincent Millay became one of the New Englanders who took a stance against the Yankee rigidity and propriety which had helped to nourish the Victorians and against which the postwar young writers rebelled.

She had begun writing poems at an early age, and in 1912 she attracted wide attention in Mitchell Kennerley's *The Lyric Year* with her poem "Renascence." Appropriately enough, she began her career with a small furor. Kennerley did not award her any prize money from his annual *Zeitgeist* anthology, and controversy arose because many readers thought her poem should have received recognition. She entered Barnard College, transferred to Vassar where she came to like the stage, and in the year of her graduation—1917—published *Renascence*, her first volume of poetry. Upon graduating, she moved to Greenwich Village and immediately became a leader of female bohemianism *pour épater le bourgeois*. She supported herself by writing articles and short stories (using various pseudonyms) and associated herself with some productions of the Provincetown Players, of Eugene O'Neill fame, in their Macdougal Street Playhouse.

In 1920 she became a spiritual leader of the Jazz Age Lost Generation when she published *A Few Figs from Thistles*, a deliberately and impishly iconoclastic book of verse in which the "flaming youth" of the postwar era found suitable phrases and attitudes, as they were to do in Fitzgerald and Hemingway. In the following year she published *Second April*, but she did not reach the top of her spiritual bent or display the sensual delicacy of her lyricism until 1923, when she published *The Harp Weaver and Other Poems. The Harp Weaver* and her love sonnets constitute her best work. Interested in many genres, Miss Millay also wrote five plays, one of which, *The King's Henchman* (1926), was used as the libretto of an opera by Deems Taylor and performed at the Metropolitan Opera House in 1927.

In the 1930's and 1940's, Miss Millay's output not only became smaller but changed direction from the romantic and passionate lyricism of her earlier books to an increasing concern with the hard historical events of the world about her. *The Murder of Lidice* (1942) exemplifies the change.

Other books, by Miss Millay, in addition to those mentioned above, are *The Lamp and the Bell* (1921), *Distressing Dialogues* (1924), *The Buck in the Snow and Other Poems* (1928), *Fatal Interview* (1931), *Wine from These Grapes* (1934), *Conversation at Midnight* (1937), *Huntsman, What Quarry?* (1939), and *Make Bright the Arrows* (1940). Some Collections are *Three Plays* (1926); *Collected Sonnets of Edna St. Vincent Millay* (1941); *Collected Lyrics of Edna St. Vincent Millay* (1943); *Mine the Harvest*, edited by Norma Millay (1954); and the *Collected Poems of Edna St. Vincent Millay*, edited by Norma Millay (1956).

Studies of Miss Millay and her work are to be found in H. Monroe, *Poets and Their Art* (1926); A. Kreymborg, *Our Singing Strength* (1929); E. Atkins, *Edna St. Vincent Millay and Her Times* (1936); K. Yost, *A Bibliography of the Works of Edna St. Vincent Millay* (1937); F. B. Millett, *Contemporary American Authors* (1940); A. Tate, *Sixty American Poets, 1896–1944* (1945); V. Sheean, *The Indigo Bunting* (1951); A. R. Macdougall, ed., *The Letters of Edna St. Vincent Millay* (1952); E. Wilson, *The Shores of Light* (1952); A. Tate, *Sixty American Poets* (1954); T. Shafter, *Edna St. Vincent Millay* (1957); and M. Gurko, *Restless Spirit: The Life of Edna St. Vincent Millay* (1962).

Euclid Alone Has Looked on Beauty Bare

Euclid alone has looked on Beauty bare.
Let all who prate of Beauty hold their peace,
And lay them prone upon the earth and cease
To ponder on themselves, the while they stare
At nothing, intricately drawn nowhere
In shapes of shifting lineage; let geese
Gabble and hiss, but heroes seek release
From dusty bondage into luminous air.
O blinding hour, O holy, terrible day,
When first the shaft into his vision shone   10

Of light anatomized! Euclid alone
Has looked on Beauty bare. Fortunate they
Who, though once only and then but far away,
Have heard her massive sandal set on stone.

1920

I Know I Am But Summer to Your Heart

I know I am but summer to your heart,
And not the full four seasons of the year;
And you must welcome from another part
Such noble moods as are not mine, my dear.
No gracious weight of golden fruits to sell
Have I, nor any wise and wintry thing;
And I have loved you all too long and well
To carry still the high sweet breast of Spring.
Wherefore I say: O love, as summer goes,
I must be gone, steal forth with silent drums   10
That you may hail anew the bird and rose
When I come back to you, as summer comes.
Else will you seek, at some not distant time,
Even your summer in another clime.

1922

Justice Denied in Massachusetts

Let us abandon then our gardens and go home
And sit in the sitting-room.
Shall the larkspur blossom or the corn grow under this
    cloud?
Sour to the fruitful seed
Is the cold earth under this cloud,
Fostering quack and weed, we have marched upon but
    cannot conquer;
We have bent the blades of our hoes against the stalks of
    them.
Let us go home, and sit in the sitting-room.
Not in our day
Shall the cloud go over and the sun rise as before,   10
Beneficent upon us
Out of the glittering bay,

And the warm winds be blown inward from the sea
Moving the blades of corn
With a peaceful sound.
Forlorn, forlorn,
Stands the blue hay-rack by the empty mow.
And the petals drop to the ground,
Leaving the tree unfruited.
The sun that warmed our stooping backs and withered the
    weed uprooted—   20
We shall not feel it again.
We shall die in darkness, and be buried in the rain.

What from the splendid dead
We have inherited—
Furrows sweet to the grain, and the weed subdued—
See now the slug and the mildew plunder.
Evil does overwhelm
The larkspur and the corn;
We have seen them go under.

Let us sit here, sit still,   30
Here in the sitting-room until we die;
At the step of Death on the walk, rise and go;
Leaving to our children's children this beautiful doorway,
And this elm,
And a blighted earth to till
With a broken hoe.

                                    1927

Oh, Sleep Forever in the Latmian Cave

Oh, sleep forever in the Latmian cave,
Mortal Endymion, darling of the Moon!
Her silver garments by the senseless wave
Shouldered and dropped and on the shingle strewn,
Her fluttering hand against her forehead pressed,
Her scattered looks that trouble all the sky,
Her rapid footsteps running down the west—
Of all her altered state, oblivious lie!
Whom earthen you, by deathless lips adored,
Wild-eyed and stammering to the grasses thrust,   10

And deep into her crystal body poured
The hot and sorrowful sweetness of the dust:
  Whereof she wanders mad, being all unfit
  For mortal love, that might not die of it.

1931

VACHEL LINDSAY

(1879–1931)

Born of pioneer stock from Kentucky and Indiana in a Spring-field, Illinois, house where Abraham Lincoln had been enter-tained, and brought up in the evangelism and fundamentalism of the Campbellites, Vachel Lindsay had every reason to combine the zeal of piety with the folk materials and democratic politics of "the common man." The merger of Lindsay's ideals and mystiques is indicated by his poetic heroes, ranging from Gov-ernor Altgeld of Illinois, who pardoned three anarchists unjustly imprisoned during the Haymarket affair, to General William Booth, the founder of the Salvation Army.

His wide schoolboy reading combined with his father's evan-gelism—and his mother's desire that Vachel be a painter—to produce in him an early ambition to be an American folk artist. He attended Hiram College from 1897 to 1900, then went to the Chicago Art Institute for three years, and was enrolled in the New York School of Art in 1904–1905. New York, however, was not particularly interested in buying draw-ings by Vachel Lindsay, and in 1905 he began to give vent to his impulse for populist reform. His increasing interest in poetry was shared with lecturing for the Anti-Saloon League and the YMCA, where he also taught art.

In 1906 he began walking tours as a vagabond minstrel and reformer. In 1908 he toured the East and Midwest, and in 1912 the Midwest and the Southwest, chanting poems in re-turn for food and lodging and distributing his little pamphlet, *Rhymes to be Traded for Bread.* Reflections of his journeys are to be found in his *Adventures While Preaching the Gospel of Beauty* (1914) and *A Handy Guide for Beggars* (1916). His public chanting made him the most sensational of the "prairie poets," a term designating Lindsay, Edgar Lee Masters, and Carl Sandburg. There is no doubt that interest in Lindsay was nurtured by the attention paid to the "new poetry" movement, but Lindsay differed from the "new poets" in many ways.

First of all, he did not agree with the sentiment of Jolas' "Manifesto of the Word" that "The common reader be damned." In his rebellion against the commercialism of middle-class values, Lindsay, formed as he was in the fervor of Mid-western fundamentalist Protestantism and the progressive politics of Midwestern agrarian populism, conceived of art and poetry as messiahs that would release the true American energy and resurrect the common man into a New World of beauty. His trinity comprised Andy Jackson, Abe Lincoln, and Walt Whitman. Furthermore, although the "prairie poets" for a while broke away from traditional poetry, Lindsay did not follow the path of the free verse experimentalists.

Feeling that his vagabond's message of the "Gospel of Beauty" would make poetry a real idiom of the redeemed common man, he did not want his poetry to be part of the new and esoteric literary cults, read only by the ultra-sophisticated reader. Conceiving of his "national reciting tours" as "the higher vaudeville," he employed the thumping rhyme and beat of the hymn, jazz, circus music, spirituals, and the Salva-tion Army band—something, he felt, that would catch up and be recognized by everyone. The "Gospel of Beauty" that he preached involved a "new localism" in which people would be exalted and filled with pride by building bright and beautiful communities based on the folk myths and values of the new democracy. Although his poetry does not rate in the first rank and probably does not have enduring quality, there is no question that, in the listening, his dramatic chants had a sensa-tionally effective impact.

Discovered by Harriet Monroe's *Poetry* magazine, which began publication in 1912, Lindsay published "General William Booth Enters into Heaven" in an issue of 1913. So enthusiasti-cally was this new voice received, that *General William Booth Enters into Heaven and Other Poems* was published in the same year and his performances became the hit of the Chicago lit-erary salons. Although his 1913 volume of poetry did not re-ceive wide popular recognition, *The Congo and Other Poems* (1914) established for Lindsay a national reputation. *The Chinese Nightingale and Other Poems* (1917) was also well and widely received.

Lindsay, however, was unable to sustain the enthusiastic surge of his poetry. His pathetic, naive, and beautiful faith in a national rebirth of beauty and spirituality through folk poetry was negated in a history that discouraged him. Exhausted by his many recitation tours, financially impoverished and hardly able to support his wife and two children, and given to fits of depression (fed by a life-long guilt that he had not honored his parents' wish that he go into the ministry), he killed himself in 1931.

Some other of Lindsay's books, besides those mentioned above, are *The Art of the Moving Picture* (1915), revised and enlarged in 1922; *The Golden Whales of California and Other Rhymes in the American Language* (1920); *The Daniel Jazz and Other Poems* (1920); *The Golden Book of Springfield* (1920); *Going-to-the Sun* (1923); *Going-to-the Stars* (1926); *The Litany of Washington Street* (1929); and *Every Soul Is a Circus* (1929). There is no collected edition of Lindsay's complete works, but some of his poems are available in the *Collected Poems of Vachel Lindsay* (1925) and M. Harris, ed., *Selected Poems of Vachel Lindsay* (1963).

Studies of Lindsay and his work are to be found in C. Aiken, *Scepticisms* (1919); S. Graham, *Tramping with a Poet in the Rockies* (1922); C. Van Doren, *Many Minds* (1924); H. Monroe, *Poets and Their Art* (1926); T. K. Whipple, *Spokesmen* (1928); A. Kreymborg, *Our Singing Strength* (1929); A. E. Trombley, *Vachel Lindsay, Adventurer* (1929); H. Spencer, ed., *Selected Poems of Vachel Lindsay* (1931); E. L. Masters, *Vachel Lindsay; A Poet in America* (1935); H. H. Clark, ed., *Major American Poets* (1936); A. J. Armstrong, ed. *Letters of Nicholas Vachel Lindsay to A. Joseph Armstrong* (1940); F. B. Millett, *Contemporary American Authors* (1940); G. Arms and J. M. Kuntz, *Poetry Explication* (1950); M. Harris, *The City of Discontent* (1952); A. Tate, *Sixty American Poets, 1896–1944* (1954); E. Ruggles, *The West-Going Heart* (1959); M. Yatron, *America's Literary Revolt* (1959) and P. Viereck, "The Crack-Up of American Optimism," *Modern Age*, IV (1960).

General William Booth Enters into Heaven

(To be sung to the tune of "The Blood of the Lamb" with indicated instruments)

I

(*Bass drum beaten loudly.*)
Booth led boldly with his big bass drum—
(Are you washed in the blood of the Lamb?)
The Saints smiled gravely and they said: "He's come."
(Are you washed in the blood of the Lamb?)

Walking lepers followed, rank on rank,
Lurching bravos from the ditches dank,
Drabs from the alleyways and drug fiends pale—
Minds still passion-ridden, soul-powers frail:—
Vermin-eaten saints with moldy breath,
Unwashed legions with the ways of Death—   10
(Are you washed in the blood of the Lamb?)

(*Banjos.*)
Every slum had sent its half-a-score
The round world over. (Booth had groaned for more.)
Every banner that the wide world flies
Bloomed with glory and transcendent dyes.
Big-voiced lasses made their banjos bang,
Tranced, fanatical they shrieked and sang:—
"Are you washed in the blood of the Lamb?"
Hallelujah! It was queer to see
Bull-necked convicts with that land make free.   20
Loons with trumpets blowed a blare, blare, blare
On, on upward thro' the golden air!
(Are you washed in the blood of the Lamb?)

II

(*Bass drum slower and softer.*)
Booth died blind and still by faith he trod,
Eyes still dazzled by the ways of God.
Booth led boldly, and he looked the chief
Eagle countenance in sharp relief,
Beard a-flying, air of high command
Unabated in that holy land.

(*Sweet flute music.*)
Jesus came from out the court-house door,   30
Stretched his hands above the passing poor.
Booth saw not, but led his queer ones there
Round and round the mighty court-house square.
Then, in an instant all that blear review
Marched on spotless, clad in raiment new.
The lame were straightened, withered limbs uncurled
And blind eyes opened on a new, sweet world.

(*Bass drum louder.*)
Drabs and vixens in a flash made whole!

Gone was the weasel-head, the snout, the jowl!
Sages and sibyls now, and athletes clean,   40
Rulers of empires, and of forests green!

    (*Grand chorus of all instruments. Tambourines to the
       foreground.*)
The hosts were sandalled, and their wings were fire!
(Are you washed in the blood of the Lamb?)
But their noise played havoc with the angel-choir.
(Are you washed in the blood of the Lamb?)
Oh, shout Salvation! It was good to see
Kings and Princes by the Lamb set free.
The banjos rattled and the tambourines
Jing-jing-jingled in the hands of Queens.

    (*Reverently sung, no instruments.*)
And when Booth halted by the curb for prayer   50
He saw his Master thro' the flag-filled air.
Christ came gently with a robe and crown
For Booth the soldier, while the throng knelt down.
He saw King Jesus. They were face to face,
And he knelt a-weeping in that holy place.
Are you washed in the blood of the Lamb?

                      1913

Abraham Lincoln Walks at Midnight

    (*In Springfield, Illinois*)

It is portentous, and a thing of state
That here at midnight, in our little town
A mourning figure walks, and will not rest,
Near the old court-house pacing up and down,

Or by his homestead, or in shadowed yards
He lingers where his children used to play,
Or through the market, on the well-worn stones
He stalks until the dawn-stars burn away.

A bronzed, lank man! His suit of ancient black,
A famous high top-hat and plain worn shawl   10
Make him the quaint great figure that men love,
The prairie-lawyer, master of us all.

He cannot sleep upon his hillside now.
He is among us:—as in times before!
And we who toss and lie awake for long
Breathe deep, and start, to see him pass the door.

His head is bowed. He thinks on men and kings.
Yea, when the sick world cries, how can he sleep?
Too many peasants fight, they know not why,
Too many homesteads in black terror weep.   20

The sins of all the war-lords burn his heart.
He sees the dreadnaughts scouring every main.
He carries on his shawl-wrapped shoulders now
The bitterness, the folly and the pain.

He cannot rest until a spirit-dawn
Shall come;—the shining hope of Europe free:
The league of sober folk, the Workers' Earth,
Bringing long peace to Cornland, Alp and Sea.

It breaks his heart that kings must murder still,
That all his hours of travail here for men   30
Seem yet in vain. And who will bring white peace
That he may sleep upon his hill again?

                                              1914

The Santa-Fé Trail

(A Humoresque)

(*I asked the old negro: "What is that bird that sings so well?" He answered: "That is the Rachel-Jane." "Hasn't it another name—lark, or thrush, or the like?" "No. Jus' Rachel-Jane."*)

I. In Which a Racing Auto Comes from the East

This is the order of the music of the
morning:—

To be sung delicately, to an improvised tune.

First, from the far East comes but a
crooning.
The crooning turns to a sunrise singing.
Hark to the *calm*-horn, *balm*-horn, *psalm*-horn.
Hark to the *faint*-horn, *quaint*-horn, *saint*-horn. . . .

Hark to the *pace*-horn, *chase*-horn, *race*-horn.

To be sung or read with great speed.

And the holy veil of the dawn has gone.
Swiftly the brazen car comes on.
It burns in the East as the sunrise burns.
I see great flashes where the far trail turns.   10
Its eyes are lamps like the eyes of dragons.
It drinks gasoline from big red flagons.
Butting through the delicate mists of the morning,
It comes like lightning, goes past roaring.
It will hail all the windmills, taunting, ringing,
Dodge the cyclones,
Count the milestones,
On through the ranges the prairie-dog tills—
Scooting past the cattle on the thousand hills. . . .
Ho for the *tear*-horn, *scare*-horn, *dare*-horn,

To be read or 20 *sung in a rolling bass, with some deliberation.*

Ho for the *gay*-horn, *bark*-horn, *bay*-horn.

Ho for Kansas, land that restores us
When houses choke us, and great books bore us!
Sunrise Kansas, harvesters' Kansas,
A million men have found you before us.
A million men have found you before us.

II. In Which Many Autos Pass Westward

I want live things in their pride to remain.

In an even, deliberate, narrative manner.

I will not kill one grasshopper vain
Though he eats a hole in my shirt like a door.
I let him out, give him one chance more.   30
Perhaps, while he gnaws my hat in his whim,
Grasshopper lyrics occur to him.
I am a tramp by the long trail's border,
Given to squalor, rags and disorder.
I nap and amble and yawn and look,
Write fool-thoughts in my grubby book,
Recite to the children, explore at my ease,
Work when I work, beg when I please,
Give crank-drawings, that make folks stare
To the half-grown boys in the sunset glare,   40
And get me a place to sleep in the hay
At the end of a live-and-let-live day.
I find in the stubble of the new-cut weeds

A whisper and a feasting, all one needs:
The whisper of the strawberries, white and red
Here where the new-cut weeds lie dead.

But I would not walk all alone till I die
Without some life-drunk horns going by.
And up round this apple-earth they come
Blasting the whispers of the morning dumb:— 50
Cars in a plain realistic row.
And fair dreams fade
When the raw horns blow.

On each snapping pennant
A big black name:—
The careering city
Whence each car came.
They tour from Memphis, Atlanta, Savannah,
Tallahassee and Texarkana.
They tour from St. Louis, Columbus,   *Like a train- 60*
    Manistee,   *caller in a Union*
They tour from Peoria, Davenport, Kankakee.   *Depot.*
Cars from Concord, Niagara, Boston,
Cars from Topeka, Emporia, and Austin.
Cars from Chicago, Hannibal, Cairo.
Cars from Alton, Oswego, Toledo.
Cars from Buffalo, Kokomo, Delphi,
Cars from Lodi, Carmi, Loami.
Ho for Kansas, land that restores us
When houses choke us, and great books bore us!
While I watch the highroad   70
And look at the sky,
While I watch the clouds in amazing grandeur
Roll their legions without rain
Over the blistering Kansas plain—
While I sit by the milestone
And watch the sky,
The United States
Goes by.

Listen to the iron-horns, ripping, racking.   *To be given very*
                                               harshly, with a
Listen to the quack-horns, slack and   *snapping ex- 80*
    clacking.   *plosiveness.*

Way down the road, trilling like a toad,
Here comes the *dice*-horn, here comes the *vice*-horn,
Here comes the *snarl*-horn, *brawl*-horn, *lewd*-horn,
Followed by the *prude*-horn, bleak and squeaking:—
(Some of them from Kansas, some of them from Kansas.)
Here comes the *hod*-horn, *plod*-horn, *sod*-horn,
Nevermore-to-*roam*-horn, *loam*-horn, *home*-horn.
(Some of them from Kansas, some of them from Kansas.)

> Far away the Rachel-Jane *To be read or*
> *sung, well-nigh in*
> Not defeated by the horns *a whisper.* 90
> Sings amid a hedge of thorns:—
> "Love and life,
> Eternal youth—
> Sweet, sweet, sweet, sweet,
> Dew and glory,
> Love and truth,
> Sweet, sweet, sweet, sweet,"

WHILE SMOKE-BLACK FREIGHTS ON THE *Louder and*
louder, faster and
DOUBLE-TRACKED RAILROAD, *faster.*
DRIVEN AS THOUGH BY THE FOUL FIEND'S OX-GOAD,
SCREAMING TO THE WEST COAST, SCREAMING TO THE
EAST, 100
CARRY OFF A HARVEST, BRING BACK A FEAST,
AND HARVESTING MACHINERY AND HARNESS FOR THE BEAST,
THE HAND-CARS WHIZ, AND RATTLE ON THE RAILS,
THE SUNLIGHT FLASHES ON THE TIN DINNER-PAILS.

And then, in an instant, ye modern men, *In a rolling bass,*
with increasing de-
Behold the procession once again, *liberation.*
The United States goes by!
Listen to the iron-horns, ripping, racking, *With a snapping*
explosiveness.
Listen to the *wise*-horn, desperate-to-*ad-*
vise horn,
Listen to the *fast*-horn, *kill*-horn, *blast*-horn. . . . 110

> Far away the Rachel-Jane *To be sung or read*
> *well-nigh in a*
> Not defeated by the horns *whisper.*
> Sings amid a hedge of thorns:—
> "Love and life,
> Eternal youth,
> Sweet, sweet, sweet, sweet,
> Dew and glory,
> Love and truth.
> Sweet, sweet, sweet, sweet."

The mufflers open on a score of cars
With wonderful thunder,
CRACK, CRACK, CRACK,
CRACK-CRACK, CRACK-CRACK,
CRACK, CRACK, CRACK,
Listen to the gold-horn . . .
Old horn . . .
Cold horn . . .

To be bawled 120 in the beginning with a snapping explosiveness, ending in a languorous chant.

And all the tunes, till the night comes down
On hay-stack, and ant-hill, and wind-bitten town.
Then far in the west, as in the beginning,
Dim in the distance, sweet in retreating,
Hark to the faint-horn, quaint-horn, saint-
   horn,
Hark to the calm-horn, balm-horn, psalm-horn. . . .

To be sung 130 to exactly the same whispered tune as the first five lines.

They are hunting the goals that they
   understand:—
San Francisco and the brown sea-sand.

This section beginning sonorously, ending in a languorous whisper.

My goal is the mystery the beggars win.
I am caught in the web the night-winds spin.
The edge of the wheat-ridge speaks to me.
I talk with the leaves of the mulberry tree.
And now I hear, as I sit all alone   140
In the dusk, by another big Santa-Fé stone,
The souls of the tall corn gathering round
And the gay little souls of the grass in the ground.
Listen to the tale the cottonwood tells.
Listen to the windmills, singing o'er the wells.
Listen to the whistling flutes without price
Of myriad prophets out of paradise.
Harken to the wonder
That the night-air carries. . . .
Listen . . . to . . . the . . . whisper . . .   150
Of . . . the . . . prairie . . . fairies
   Singing o'er the fairy plain:—
   "Sweet, sweet, sweet, sweet.
   Love and glory,
   Stars and rain,
   Sweet, sweet, sweet, sweet. . . ."

To the same whispered tune as the Rachel-Jane song —but very slowly.

1914

CARL SANDBURG

(1878–1967)

The best-known of "the prairie poets," Carl Sandburg early became identified with folk idioms whose use was given a rationale by the farmer-labor progressivism of the heartland. Born in Galesburg, Illinois, the locale (Knox College) of the fourth in the Lincoln-Douglas debates of the famous series of 1858, Sandburg was the son of illiterate Swedish immigrants. His father, at the time of Sandburg's birth, was a railroad-gang blacksmith.

Sandburg's sympathies with labor, however, were not caused only by his origins. When he was thirteen years old, he began working on a milk route, which was the first of an amazing variety of jobs that took him through trucking, brickyard work, barbershop work, theater work, dishwashing, migratory field-labor, soldiering, editing, newspaper reporting, and the rich experiences of the life of a hobo. He was a housepainter in Galesburg when, in 1898, he enlisted in the army to go to Puerto Rico during the Spanish-American war. When he was mustered out, he worked his way through Lombard College in Galesburg, but left in 1902, a short time before he completed his final year. As a reporter, he wandered from place to place, becoming more and more confirmed in the folk orientation which had already created in him, even before he had reached his sixteenth birthday, the determination to be either a poet or a hobo. For a while he was an organizer for Wisconsin's Social-Democratic Party, and in 1910 he was secretary to the Socialist mayor of Milwaukee, Emil Seidel.

In 1904, encouraged by a former teacher at Lombard, Sandburg had privately printed a thirty-nine-page pamphlet of twenty-two poems called *In Reckless Ecstasy*. These poems indicated only slightly the direction that Sandburg's mature work would take. Ten years later, when he published "Chicago" and other pieces in *Poetry* magazine, he became a recognized part of the "new poetry" movement. In 1916, Sandburg's *Chicago Poems* excited much controversy over his use of folk idiom, a free form of verse, and "unpoetical," industrial subject matter. The controversy established his reputation. Like Whitman, whose tradition he follows, and like Lindsay, Sandburg was impelled by the desire to become the poetic voice of the myths and values and enduring toughness of the common, laboring man.

In some of his poems, such as "Fog" and "Nocturne in a Deserted Brickyard," Sandburg was influenced by the Imagists. It is such muscular, Whitmanesque poems as *Cornhuskers* (1918), however, for which Sandburg will be remembered. In them, the vocations and lives of the "common man" are related to a sweeping and affirmative vision of the panorama of America, the sense of which is communicated with romantic tenderness, optimism, and joy. In 1920 he published *Smoke and Steel*, followed by *Slabs of the Sunburned West* in 1922 and *Good Morning, America* in 1928. It was during the 1920's that Sandburg began his lecture tours, in which he read his poems, talked about folk tales, and sang folk songs to the accompaniment of his own guitar. The materials, as well as the spirit of these tours, appeared in *The American Songbag* (1927) and *The People, Yes* (1936).

In addition to his poems, Sandburg is widely known for his children's stories, the most famous of which are the *Rootabaga Stories* (1922), and most especially for his monumental biography of Lincoln: *The Prairie Years* (2 vols., 1926) and *The War Years* (4 vols., 1939).

Some other Sandburg books, besides those mentioned above, are *Potato Face* (1930), *Early Moon* (1930), *Home Front Memo* (1943), and *Remembrance Rock* (1948), his only novel. There is no collected edition of the works of Carl Sandburg. His poems may be found in *Complete Poems* (1950), and M. Van Doren, ed., *Harvest Poems, 1910–1960* (1960). *The Sandburg Range* (1957) offers representative selections from his entire work.

In addition to Sandburg's autobiographical *Always the Young Strangers* (1953), studies of the man and his work are to be found in C. Aiken, *Scepticisms* (1919); S. P. Sherman, *Americans* (1922); H. Hansen, *Midwest Portraits* (1923); P. Rosenfeld, *Port of New York* (1924); C. Van Doren, *Many Minds* (1924); B. Weirick, *From Whitman to Sandburg in American Poetry* (1924); T. K. Whipple, *Spokesmen* (1928); A. Kreymborg, *Our Singing Strength* (1929); M. Cowley, ed., *After the Genteel Tradition* (1937); B. Deutsch, "Poetry for the People," *English Journal*, XXVI (1937); V. Loggins, *I Hear America* (1937); K. Detzer, *Carl Sandburg* (1941); H. W. Wells, *The American Way of Poetry* (1943); H. Gregory and M. Zaturenska, *A History of American Poetry, 1900–1940* (1946); T. Shaw, *Carl Sandburg: A Bibliography* (1948); D. G. Hoffman, "Sandburg and 'The People': His Literary Populism Reappraised," *Antioch Review*, X (1950); W. C. Williams, "Carl Sandburg's Complete Poems," *Poetry*, LXXVIII (1951); A. Tate, *Sixty American Poets, 1896–1944* (1954); and G. Allen, "Carl Sandburg: Fire and Smoke," *South Atlantic Quarterly*, LIX (1960); R. Crowder, *Carl Sandburg* (1964); and H. Durnell, *The America of Carl Sandburg* (1965). Russell B. Nye's *Midwestern Progressive Politics* provides an excellent background for an understanding of some of the native motives and sympathies that impelled Sandburg, Masters, and Lindsay.

Nocturne in a Deserted Brickyard

Stuff of the moon
Runs on the lapping sand
Out to the longest shadows.
Under the curving willows,
And round the creep of the wave line,
Fluxions of yellow and dusk on the waters
Make a wide dreaming pansy of an old pond in the night.

w. 1910
p. 1916

Fog

The fog comes
on little cat feet.

It sits looking
over harbor and city
on silent haunches
and then moves on.

w. 1912
p. 1916

Chicago

Hog Butcher for the World,
Tool Maker, Stacker of Wheat,
Player with Railroads and the Nation's Freight Han-
    dler;
Stormy, husky, brawling,
City of the Big Shoulders:

They tell me you are wicked and I believe them, for I
    have seen your painted women under the gas lamps
    luring the farm boys.
And they tell me you are crooked and I answer: Yes, it is
    true I have seen the gunman kill and go free to kill
    again.
And they tell me you are brutal and my reply is: On the
    faces of women and children I have seen the marks of
    wanton hunger.
And having answered so I turn once more to those who
    sneer at this my city, and I give them back the sneer
    and say to them:
Come and show me another city with lifted head singing
    so proud to be alive and coarse and strong and cun-
    ning.   10
Flinging magnetic curses amid the toil of piling job on job,
    here is a tall bold slugger set vivid against the little soft
    cities;
Fierce as a dog with tongue lapping for action, cunning as
    a savage pitted against the wilderness,
        Bareheaded,
        Shoveling,
        Wrecking,
        Planning,
        Building, breaking, rebuilding,
Under the smoke, dust all over his mouth, laughing with
    white teeth,
Under the terrible burden of destiny laughing as a young
    man laughs,
Laughing even as an ignorant fighter laughs who has never
    lost a battle,   20

Bragging and laughing that under his wrist is the pulse, and
   under his ribs the heart of the people,
      Laughing!
Laughing the stormy, husky, brawling laughter of Youth,
   half-naked, sweating, proud to be Hog Butcher, Tool
   Maker, Stacker of Wheat, Player with Railroads and
   Freight Handler to the Nation.

                                                    1914

To a Contemporary Bunkshooter

You come along . . . tearing your shirt . . . yelling about
   Jesus.
   Where do you get that stuff?
   What do you know about Jesus?
Jesus had a way of talking soft and outside of a few bankers and higher-ups among the con men of Jerusalem
   everybody liked to have this Jesus around because he
   never made any fake passes and everything he said
   went and he helped the sick and gave the people hope.
You come along squirting words at us, shaking your fist
   and call us all dam fools so fierce the froth slobbers
   over your lips . . . always blabbing we're all going
   to hell straight off and you know all about it.

I've read Jesus' words. I know what he said. You don't
   throw any scare into me. I've got your number. I
   know how much you know about Jesus.
He never came near clean people or dirty people but they
   felt cleaner because he came along. It was your
   crowd of bankers and business men and lawyers hired
   the sluggers and murderers who put Jesus out of the
   running.
I say the same bunch backing you nailed the nails into
   the hands of this Jesus of Nazareth. He had lined
   up against him the same crooks and strong-arm men
   now lined up with you paying your way.

This Jesus was good to look at, smelled good, listened
   good. He threw out something fresh and beautiful
   from the skin of his body and the touch of his hands
   wherever he passed along.

You slimy bunkshooter, you put a smut on every human
blossom in reach of your rotten breath belching
about hell-fire and hiccupping about this Man who
lived a clean life in Galilee.   10
When are you going to quit making the carpenters build
emergency hospitals for women and girls driven crazy
with wrecked nerves from your gibberish about Jesus?
—I put it to you again: Where do you get that stuff?
What do you know about Jesus?

Go ahead and bust all the chairs you want to. Smash a
whole wagon-load of furniture at every performance.
Turn sixty somersaults and stand on your nutty
head. If it wasn't for the way you scare the women
and kids I'd feel sorry for you and pass the hat.
I like to watch a good four-flusher work, but not when he
starts people puking and calling for the doctors.
I like a man that's got nerve and can pull off a great
original performance, but you—you're only a bug-
house pedlar of second-hand gospel—you're only
shoving out a phoney imitation of the goods this Jesus
wanted free as air and sunlight.

You tell people living in shanties Jesus is going to fix it
up all right with them by giving them mansions in the
skies after they're dead and the worms have eaten 'em.
You tell $6 a week department store girls all they need
is Jesus; you take a steel trust wop, dead without
having lived, grey and shrunken at forty years of age,
and you tell him to look at Jesus on the cross and he'll
be all right.
You tell poor people they don't need any more money
on pay day and even if it's fierce to be out of a job,
Jesus'll fix that up all right, all right—all they gotta
do is take Jesus the way you say.
I'm telling you Jesus wouldn't stand for the stuff you're
handing out. Jesus played it different. The bankers
and lawyers of Jerusalem got their sluggers and murderers to go after Jesus just because Jesus wouldn't
play their game. He didn't sit in with the big thieves.

I don't want a lot of gab from a bunkshooter in my religion.

I won't take my religion from any man who never works
   except with his mouth and never cherishes any memory except the face of the woman on the American
   silver dollar.   20
I ask you to come through and show me where you're
   pouring out the blood of your life.
I've been to this suburb of Jerusalem they call Golgotha,
   where they nailed Him, and I know if the story is
   straight it was real blood ran from His hands and
   the nail-holes, and it was real blood spurted in red
   drops where the spear of the Roman soldier rammed
   in between the ribs of this Jesus of Nazareth.

                                                         1914

I Am the People, the Mob

I am the people—the mob—the crowd—the mass.
Do you know that all the great work of the world is done
   through me?
I am the workingman, the inventor, the maker of the
   world's food and clothes.
I am the audience that witnesses history. The Napoleons
   come from me and the Lincolns. They die. And then I
   send forth more Napoleons and Lincolns.
I am the seed ground. I am a prairie that will stand for
   much plowing. Terrible storms pass over me. I forget.
   The best of me is sucked out and wasted. I forget. Everything but Death comes to me and makes me work and
   give up what I have. And I forget.
Sometimes I growl, shake myself and spatter a few red
   drops for history to remember. Then—I forget.
When I, the People, learn to remember, when I, the People,
   use the lessons of yesterday and no longer forget who
   robbed me last year, who played me for a fool,—then
   there will be no speaker in all the world say the name:
   "The People," with any fleck of a sneer in his voice or
   any far-off smile of derision.
The mob—the crowd—the mass—will arrive then.

                                                      w. 1914
                                                      p. 1916

Grass

Pile the bodies high at Austerlitz and Waterloo.
Shovel them under and let me work—
      I am the grass; I cover all.

And pile them high at Gettysburg
And pile them high at Ypres and Verdun.
Shovel them under and let me work.
Two years, ten years, and passengers ask the conductor:
      What place is this?
      Where are we now?

      I am the grass.   10
      Let me work.

                1918

FROM

The People, Yes

[The People Will Live On]

    The people will live on.
The learning and blundering people will live on.
    They will be tricked and sold and again sold
And go back to the nourishing earth for rootholds,
    The people so peculiar in renewal and comeback,
    You can't laugh off their capacity to take it.
The mammoth rests between his cyclonic dramas.

The people so often sleepy, weary, enigmatic,
    is a vast huddle with many units saying:
    "I earn my living.   10
    I make enough to get by
    and it takes all my time.
    If I had more time
    I could do more for myself
    and maybe for others.
    I could read and study
    and talk things over

and find out about things.
It takes time.
I wish I had the time."   20

The people is a tragic and comic two-face:
hero and hoodlum: phantom and gorilla twisting to moan with a gargoyle mouth: "They
buy me and sell me . . . it's a game . . .
sometime I'll break loose. . . ."

Once having marched
Over the margins of animal necessity,
Over the grim line of sheer subsistence,
    Then man came
To the deeper rituals of his bones,
To the lights lighter than any bones,
To the time for thinking things over,
To the dance, the song, the story,
Or the hours given over to dreaming,
    Once having so marched.

Between the finite limitations of the five senses
and the endless yearnings of man for the beyond
the people hold to the humdrum bidding of work and food
while reaching out when it comes their way
for lights beyond the prison of the five senses,
for keepsakes lasting beyond any hunger or death.
    This reaching is alive.
The panderers and liars have violated and smutted it.
    Yet this reaching is alive yet
    for lights and keepsakes.

The people know the salt of the sea
and the strength of the winds
lashing the corners of the earth.
The people take the earth
as a tomb of rest and a cradle of hope.   50
Who else speaks for the Family of Man?
They are in tune and step
with constellations of universal law.

The people is a polychrome,
a spectrum and a prism

held in a moving monolith,
a console organ of changing themes,
a clavilux of color poems
wherein the sea offers fog
and the fog moves off in rain   60
and the labrador sunset shortens
to a nocturne of clear stars
serene over the shot spray
of northern lights.

The steel mill sky is alive.
The fire breaks white and zigzag
shot on a gun-metal gloaming.
Man is a long time coming.
Man will yet win.
Brother may yet line up with brother: 70

This old anvil laughs at many broken hammers.
    There are men who can't be bought.
    The fireborn are at home in fire.
    The stars make no noise.
    You can't hinder the wind from blowing.
    Time is a great teacher.
    Who can live without hope?
In the darkness with a great bundle of grief the people
    march.
In the night, and overhead a shovel of stars for keeps, the
    people march:
"Where to? what next?"

                                                         1936

ROBERT FROST
(1874–1963)

There is an amusing irony in the fact that Robert Frost, who was so strongly associated with the rhythms and circumstances of clear, cold, northern Yankee country, should have been named Robert Lee and should have been born in San Francisco because the southern sympathies of his father caused the family to move to California from New England, where the clan had lived for nine generations. When Robert was ten years old, his father died, and his mother moved the family back to New England, to his grandfather's home in Lawrence, Massachusetts. Later, Frost was introduced to New Hampshire when his mother moved there to teach school.

In 1892 Frost was graduated from the Lawrence High School, where he was co-valedictorian with Elinor White, whom he later married. He spent a few months at Dartmouth on his grandfather's money, but did not like the experience and left. He worked in mills, tramped around the country, wrote poems, and enrolled for two years in Harvard. Always poor—a cobbler, a teacher, a journalist, a farmer—Frost kept writing poems. But nobody bought them. Frost's case was like that of Robinson: too good for the easy nonsense of the newspaper "poet's corners," too far ahead of his times to attract publishers. In twenty years, until 1913, Frost earned an average of $10 a year selling poems. Nevertheless determined to write, and unwilling (as he said) to scandalize the family any longer with his poor poet-farmer existence, he sold the farm his grandfather had given him and took his wife and four children to England. England was a logical choice: the cost of living was low there and the "new poetry" movement had already begun in the work of some of the Georgian poets who became his friends.

While in England he published his first volume, *A Boy's Will*

(1913). English readers applauded Frost's work as Americans had been unwilling to do. In the next year he published what is perhaps his best single volume, the magnificent *North of Boston*. Again the English took delighted notice, acclaiming the way in which the simple, dramatic presentation of New England materials grew, with quiet lyricism, into complex and subtle meanings. Further, the English were the first to note the breathtaking control with which Frost managed to combine the necessities of a given form's rhythm with the natural patterns of truly common speech, bringing to perfection the intentions of such poets as Wordsworth and Robinson. In 1915 both books were republished in the United States, and Frost felt that now that his books had "gone home," he should, too. When he got off the boat, he was astonished by the eagerness with which American critics and publishers scurried to acclaim the works of Robert Frost. To paraphrase his own words, the land was his before he was the land's.

In the face of his enthusiastic reception, he moved to a farm in New Hampshire, and then, in 1919, to one in Vermont, where he settled. The honors accumulated as the now-familiar titles appeared: *Mountain Interval* in 1916, *New Hampshire* in 1923, *West Running Brook* in 1928, *A Further Range* in 1936. Mr. Frost received four Pulitzer prizes, and as early as the 1920's he began to receive honors, lectureships, fellowships, and poet-in-residenceships from many universities, colleges, and writers' conferences. Eagerly sought everywhere, he toured the entire country with his readings.

Although in his materials Frost was a regional poet, his poems are universal. He insisted that poems begin in delight and end in wisdom, that they present a classically clear dramatization which makes the reader recognize what he had forgotten he knew. The dramatic presentation is followed in the reader's mind by an "after image," the slow dawning of meditative content that is the final result of the misleadingly simple and rustic perception of the hard object. Like Robinson, Frost was a modern poet, whose sensibilities were suspended between belief and doubt. His attitudes toward nature, for instance, demonstrate in the earlier work a tough-minded trust in natural purpose; in some of the later poems, however, nature tends to be more antagonistic than beneficent. Held beautifully in this "modern" suspension, Frost's poems all insist that whatever man can know of the experience beyond easy belief must be discovered in an Emersonian way by the individual, whose inner identity is shaped in solitude by nature. And, in turn, nature's being and meanings are shaped by the musings and perceptions and sensibilities of the single inner man. Hating conformity and distrusting "collectivistic love," Frost yet managed to suggest that the individual's tough journey into nature and experience flowers most fully in a translation from the self to the other, from the private to the public, from the personal to the racial. It is no wonder that he has so often been spoken of in association with the tough New England Transcendentalists who preceded him.

Some other books by Frost include *A Way Out* (1929), *A Witness Tree* (1942), *A Masque of Reason* (1945), *Steeple Bush* (1947), and *A Masque of Mercy* (1947). Some editions of his poems are *Collected Poems* (1930, 1939); the *Complete Poems* (1949), the standard work to date; L. Untermeyer, ed., *The Road Not Taken* (1951); *In the Clearing* (1962); and R. Graves, ed., *Selected Poems of Robert Frost* (1963).

Studies of the man and his work are to be found in A. Lowell, *Tendencies in Modern American Poetry* (1917); C. Van Doren, *Many Minds* (1924); G. B. Munson, *Robert Frost* (1927); T. K. Whipple, *Spokesmen* (1928); S. Cox, *Robert Frost* (1929); G. R. Elliott, *The Cycle of Modern Poetry* (1929); C. Ford, *The Less Travelled Road* (1935); M. Van Doren, "The Permanence of Robert Frost," *American Scholar*, V (1936); W. B. S. Clymer and C. R. Green, *Robert Frost, A Bibliography* (1937); R. Thornton, ed., *Recognition of Robert Frost* (1937); R. P. Coffin, *New Poetry of New England* (1939); L. Thompson, *Fire and Ice* (1942); L. and E. Mertins, *The Intervals of Robert Frost* (1947); G. Arms and J. M. Kuntz, *Poetry Explication* (1950); H. H. Waggoner, *The Heel of Elohim* (1950); R. Jarrell, *Poetry and the Age* (1953); S. Cox, *Swinger of Birches* (1957); R. L. Cook, *The Dimensions of Robert Frost* (1958); J. Lynen, *The Pastoral Art of Robert Frost* (1960); G. Nitchie, *Human Values in the Poetry of Robert Frost* (1960); E. S. Sergeant, *Robert Frost* (1960); E. Isaacs, *An Introduction to Robert Frost* (1962); M. B. Anderson, *Robert Frost and John Bartlett* (1963); R. A. Brower, *The Poetry of Robert Frost* (1963); J. R. Doyle, Jr., *The Poetry of Robert Frost* (1963); R. Squires, *The Major Themes of Robert Frost* (1963); L. Untermeyer, ed., *The Letters of Robert Frost to Louis Untermeyer* (1963); E. C. Lathem and L. Thompson, eds., *Robert Frost, Farm-Poultryman* (1964); F. B. Adams, *To Russia with Frost* (1964); J. Gould, *Robert Frost* (1964); J. F. Lynen, *The Pastoral Art of Robert Frost* (1964); F. D. Reeve, *Robert Frost in Russia* (1964); L. Thompson, ed., *Selected Letters of Robert Frost* (1964); L. Untermeyer, *Robert Frost* (1964); D. Grant, *Robert Frost and His Reputation* (1965); L. Mertins, *Robert Frost* (1965); D. Smythe, *Robert Frost Speaks* (1965); P. Gerber, *Robert Frost* (1966); E. Lathem, ed., *Interviews with Robert Frost* (1966); and L. Thompson, *Robert Frost: The Early Years* (1966).

Mowing

There was never a sound beside the wood but one,
And that was my long scythe whispering to the ground.
What was it it whispered? I knew not well myself;
Perhaps it was something about the heat of the sun,
Something, perhaps, about the lack of sound—
And that was why it whispered and did not speak.
It was no dream of the gift of idle hours,
Or easy gold at the hand of fay or elf:
Anything more than the truth would have seemed too weak
To the earnest love that laid the swale in rows,   10
Not without feeble-pointed spikes of flowers
(Pale orchises), and scared a bright green snake.
The fact is the sweetest dream that labor knows.
My long scythe whispered and left the hay to make.

w. 1901
p. 1913

Reluctance

Out through the fields and the woods
    And over the walls I have wended;
I have climbed the hills of view
    And looked at the world, and descended;
I have come by the highway home,
    And lo, it is ended.

The leaves are all dead on the ground,
    Save those that the oak is keeping
To ravel them one by one
    And let them go scraping and creeping   10
Out over the crusted snow,
    When others are sleeping.

And the dead leaves lie huddled and still,
    No longer blown hither and thither;
The last lone aster is gone;
    The flowers of the witch-hazel wither;
The heart is still aching to seek,
    But the feet question 'Whither?'

Ah, when to the heart of man
    Was it ever less than a treason   20
To go with the drift of things,
    To yield with a grace to reason,
And bow and accept the end
    Of a love or a season?

w. 1901
p. 1913

The Death of the Hired Man

Mary sat musing on the lamp-flame at the table
Waiting for Warren. When she heard his step,
She ran on tip-toe down the darkened passage
To meet him in the doorway with the news
And put him on his guard. 'Silas is back.'
She pushed him outward with her through the door
And shut it after her. 'Be kind,' she said.
She took the market things from Warren's arms
And set them on the porch, then drew him down
To sit beside her on the wooden steps.   10

'When was I ever anything but kind to him?
But I'll not have the fellow back,' he said.
'I told him so last haying, didn't I?
If he left then, I said, that ended it.
What good is he? Who else will harbor him
At his age for the little he can do?
What help he is there's no depending on.
Off he goes always when I need him most.
He thinks he ought to earn a little pay,
Enough at least to buy tobacco with,   20
So he won't have to beg and be beholden.
"All right," I say, "I can't afford to pay
Any fixed wages, though I wish I could."
"Someone else can." "Then someone else will have to."
I shouldn't mind his bettering himself
If that was what it was. You can be certain,
When he begins like that, there's someone at him
Trying to coax him off with pocket-money,—

In haying time, when any help is scarce.
In winter he comes back to us. I'm done.'   30

'Sh! not so loud: he'll hear you,' Mary said.

'I want him to: he'll have to soon or late.'

'He's worn out. He's asleep beside the stove.
When I came up from Rowe's I found him here,
Huddled against the barn-door fast asleep,
A miserable sight, and frightening, too—
You needn't smile—I didn't recognize him—
I wasn't looking for him—and he's changed.
Wait till you see.'

                    'Where did you say he'd been?'

'He didn't say. I dragged him to the house,   40
And gave him tea and tried to make him smoke.
I tried to make him talk about his travels.
Nothing would do: he just kept nodding off.'

'What did he say? Did he say anything?'

'But little.'

                    'Anything? Mary, confess
He said he'd come to ditch the meadow for me.'

'Warren!'

                    'But did he? I just want to know.'

'Of course he did. What would you have him say?
Surely you wouldn't grudge the poor old man
Some humble way to save his self-repect.   50
He added, if you really care to know,
He meant to clear the upper pasture, too.
That sounds like something you have heard before?
Warren, I wish you could have heard the way
He jumbled everything. I stopped to look

Two or three times—he made me feel so queer—
To see if he was talking in his sleep.
He ran on Harold Wilson—you remember—
The boy you had in haying four years since.
He's finished school, and teaching in his college.   60
Silas declares you'll have to get him back.
He says they two will make a team for work:
Between them they will lay this farm as smooth!
The way he mixed that in with other things.
He thinks young Wilson a likely lad, though daft
On education—you know how they fought
All through July under the blazing sun,
Silas up on the cart to build the load,
Harold along beside to pitch it on.'

'Yes, I took care to keep well out of earshot.'   70

'Well, those days trouble Silas like a dream.
You wouldn't think they would. How some things linger!
Harold's young college boy's assurance piqued him.
After so many years he still keeps finding
Good arguments he sees he might have used.
I sympathize. I know just how it feels
To think of the right thing to say too late.
Harold's associated in his mind with Latin.
He asked me what I thought of Harold's saying
He studied Latin like the violin   80
Because he liked it—that an argument!
He said he couldn't make the boy believe
He could find water with a hazel prong—
Which showed how much good school had ever done him.
He wanted to go over that. But most of all
He thinks if he could have another chance
To teach him how to build a load of hay—'

'I know, that's Silas' one accomplishment.
He bundles every forkful in its place,
And tags and numbers it for future reference,   90
So he can find and easily dislodge it
In the unloading. Silas does that well.
He takes it out in bunches like big birds' nests.
You never see him standing on the hay

He's trying to lift, straining to lift himself.'

'He thinks if he could teach him that, he'd be
Some good perhaps to someone in the world.
He hates to see a boy the fool of books.
Poor Silas, so concerned for other folk,
And nothing to look backward to with pride,   100
And nothing to look forward to with hope,
So now and never any different.'
Part of a moon was falling down the west,
Dragging the whole sky with it to the hills.
Its light poured softly in her lap. She saw it
And spread her apron to it. She put out her hand
Among the harp-like morning-glory strings,
Taut with the dew from garden bed to eaves,
As if she played unheard some tenderness
That wrought on him beside her in the night.   110
'Warren,' she said, 'he has come home to die:
You needn't be afraid he'll leave you this time.'

'Home,' he mocked gently.

                          'Yes, what else but home?
It all depends on what you mean by home.
Of course he's nothing to us, any more
Than was the hound that came a stranger to us
Out of the woods, worn out upon the trail.'

'Home is the place where, when you have to go there,
They have to take you in.'

                          'I should have called it
Something you somehow haven't to deserve.'   120

Warren leaned out and took a step or two,
Picked up a little stick, and brought it back
And broke it in his hand and tossed it by.
'Silas has better claim on us you think
Than on his brother? Thirteen little miles
As the road winds would bring him to his door.
Silas has walked that far no doubt today.

Why didn't he go there? His brother's rich,
A somebody—director in the bank.'

'He never told us that.'

                    'We know it though.'   130

'I think his brother ought to help, of course.
I'll see to that if there is need. He ought of right
To take him in, and might be willing to—
He may be better than appearances.
But have some pity on Silas. Do you think
If he had any pride in claiming kin
Or anything he looked for from his brother,
He'd keep so still about him all this time?'

'I wonder what's between them.'

                       'I can tell you.
Silas is what he is—we wouldn't mind him—   140
But just the kind that kinsfolk can't abide.
He never did a thing so very bad.
He don't know why he isn't quite as good
As anybody. Worthless though he is,
He won't be made ashamed to please his brother.'

'*I* can't think Si ever hurt anyone.'

'No, but he hurt my heart the way he lay
And rolled his old head on that sharp-edged chair-back.
He wouldn't let me put him on the lounge.
You must go in and see what you can do.   150
I made the bed up for him there tonight.
You'll be surprised at him—how much he's broken.
His working days are done; I'm sure of it.'

'I'd not be in a hurry to say that.'

'I haven't been. Go, look, see for yourself.
But, Warren, please remember how it is:
He's come to help you ditch the meadow.

He has a plan. You mustn't laugh at him.
He may not speak of it, and then he may.
I'll sit and see if that small sailing cloud   **160**
Will hit or miss the moon.'

                                 It hit the moon.
Then there were three there, making a dim row,
The moon, the little silver cloud, and she.
Warren returned—too soon, it seemed to her,
Slipped to her side, caught up her hand and waited.

'Warren?' she questioned.

                               'Dead,' was all he answered.
                                         w. 1905
                                         p. 1914

Mending Wall

Something there is that doesn't love a wall,
That sends the frozen-ground-swell under it,
And spills the upper boulders in the sun;
And makes gaps even two can pass abreast.
The work of hunters is another thing:
I have come after them and made repair
Where they have left not one stone on a stone,
But they would have the rabbit out of hiding,
To please the yelping dogs. The gaps I mean,
No one has seen them made or heard them made,   **10**
But at spring mending-time we find them there.
I let my neighbor know beyond the hill;
And on a day we meet to walk the line
And set the wall between us once again.
We keep the wall between us as we go.
To each the boulders that have fallen to each.
And some are loaves and some so nearly balls
We have to use a spell to make them balance:
'Stay where you are until our backs are turned!'
We wear our fingers rough with handling them.
Oh, just another kind of outdoor game,
One on a side. It comes to little more:
There where it is we do not need the wall:

He is all pine and I am apple orchard.
My apple trees will never get across
And eat the cones under his pines, I tell him.
He only says, 'Good fences make good neighbors.'
Spring is the mischief in me, and I wonder
If I could put a notion in his head:
'*Why* do they make good neighbors? Isn't it   30
Where there are cows? But here there are no cows.
Before I built a wall I'd ask to know
What I was walling in or walling out,
And to whom I was like to give offense.
Something there is that doesn't love a wall,
That wants it down.' I could say 'Elves' to him,
But it's not elves exactly, and I'd rather
He said it for himself. I see him there
Bringing a stone grasped firmly by the top
In each hand, like an old-stone savage armed.   40
He moves in darkness as it seems to me,
Not of woods only and the shade of trees.
He will not go behind his father's saying,
And he likes having thought of it so well
He says again, 'Good fences make good neighbors.'

                                                      1914

After Apple-Picking

My long two-pointed ladder's sticking through a tree
Toward heaven still,
And there's a barrel that I didn't fill
Beside it, and there may be two or three
Apples I didn't pick upon some bough.
But I am done with apple-picking now.
Essence of winter sleep is on the night,
The scent of apples: I am drowsing off.
I cannot rub the strangeness from my sight
I got from looking through a pane of glass   10
I skimmed this morning from the drinking trough
And held against the world of hoary grass.
It melted, and I let it fall and break.
But I was well
Upon my way to sleep before it fell,
And I could tell

What form my dreaming was about to take.
Magnified apples appear and disappear,
Stem end and blossom end,
And every fleck of russet showing clear.   20
My instep arch not only keeps the ache,
It keeps the pressure of a ladder-round.
I feel the ladder sway as the boughs bend.
And I keep hearing from the cellar bin
The rumbling sound
Of load on load of apples coming in.
For I have had too much
Of apple-picking: I am overtired
Of the great harvest I myself desired.
There were ten thousand thousand fruit to touch,   30
Cherish in hand, lift down, and not let fall.
For all
That struck the earth,
No matter if not bruised or spiked with stubble,
Went surely to the cider-apple heap
As of no worth.
One can see what will trouble
This sleep of mine, whatever sleep it is.
Were he not gone,
The woodchuck could say whether it's like his   40
Long sleep, as I describe its coming on,
Or just some human sleep.

                                                1914

The Road Not Taken

Two roads diverged in a yellow wood,
And sorry I could not travel both
And be one traveler, long I stood
And looked down one as far as I could
To where it bent in the undergrowth;

Then took the other, as just as fair,
And having perhaps the better claim,
Because it was grassy and wanted wear;
Though as for that the passing there
Had worn them really about the same,   10

And both that morning equally lay
In leaves no step had trodden black.
Oh, I kept the first for another day!
Yet knowing how way leads on to way,
I doubted if I should ever come back.

I shall be telling this with a sigh
Somewhere ages and ages hence:
Two roads diverged in a wood, and I—
I took the one less traveled by,
And that has made all the difference.   20

w. 1915
p. 1916

Birches

When I see birches bend to left and right
Across the lines of straighter darker trees,
I like to think some boy's been swinging them.
But swinging doesn't bend them down to stay
As ice-storms do. Often you must have seen them
Loaded with ice a sunny winter morning
After a rain. They click upon themselves
As the breeze rises, and turn many-colored
As the stir cracks and crazes their enamel.
Soon the sun's warmth makes them shed crystal shells   10
Shattering and avalanching on the snow-crust—
Such heaps of broken glass to sweep away
You'd think the inner dome of heaven had fallen.
They are dragged to the withered bracken by the load,
And they seem not to break; though once they are bowed
So low for long, they never right themselves:
You may see their trunks arching in the woods
Years afterwards, trailing their leaves on the ground
Like girls on hands and knees that throw their hair
Before them over their heads to dry in the sun.   20
But I was going to say when Truth broke in
With all her matter-of-fact about the ice-storm
I should prefer to have some boy bend them
As he went out and in to fetch the cows—
Some boy too far from town to learn baseball,

Whose only play was what he found himself,
Summer or winter, and could play alone.
One by one he subdued his father's trees
By riding them down over and over again
Until he took the stiffness out of them,   30
And not one but hung limp, not one was left
For him to conquer. He learned all there was
To learn about not launching out too soon
And so not carrying the tree away
Clear to the ground. He always kept his poise
To the top branches, climbing carefully
With the same pains you use to fill a cup
Up to the brim, and even above the brim.
Then he flung outward, feet first, with a swish,
Kicking his way down through the air to the ground.   40
So was I once myself a swinger of birches.
And so I dream of going back to be.
It's when I'm weary of considerations,
And life is too much like a pathless wood
Where your face burns and tickles with the cobwebs
Broken across it, and one eye is weeping
From a twig's having lashed across it open.
I'd like to get away from earth awhile
And then come back to it and begin over.
May no fate willfully misunderstand me   50
And half grant what I wish and snatch me away
Not to return. Earth's the right place for love:
I don't know where it's likely to go better.
I'd like to go by climbing a birch tree,
And climb black branches up a snow-white trunk
Toward heaven, till the tree could bear no more,
But dipped its top and set me down again.
That would be good both going and coming back.
One could do worse than be a swinger of birches.

w. 1915
p. 1916

The Oven Bird

There is a singer everyone has heard,
Loud, a mid-summer and a mid-wood bird,

Who makes the solid tree trunks sound again.
He says that leaves are old and that for flowers
Mid-summer is to spring as one to ten.
He says the early petal-fall is past
When pear and cherry bloom went down in showers
On sunny days a moment overcast;
And comes that other fall we name the fall.
He says the highway dust is over all.   10
The bird would cease and be as other birds
 But that he knows in singing not to sing.
 The question that he frames in all but words
 Is what to make of a diminished thing.

1916

The Need of Being Versed in Country Things

The house had gone to bring again
To the midnight sky a sunset glow.
Now the chimney was all of the house that stood,
Like a pistil after the petals go.

The barn opposed across the way,
That would have joined the house in flame
Had it been the will of the wind, was left
To bear forsaken the place's name.

No more it opened with all one end
For teams that came by the stony road   10
To drum on the floor with scurrying hoofs
And brush the mow with the summer load.

The birds that came to it through the air
At broken windows flew out and in,
Their murmur more like the sigh we sigh
From too much dwelling on what has been.

Yet for them the lilac renewed its leaf,
And the aged elm, though touched with fire;
And the dry pump flung up an awkward arm;
And the fence post carried a strand of wire.   20

For them there was really nothing sad.
But though they rejoiced in the nest they kept,

One had to be versed in country things
Not to believe the phoebes wept.

w. 1920
p. 1923

Fire and Ice

Some say the world will end in fire,
Some say in ice.
From what I've tasted of desire
I hold with those who favor fire.
But if it had to perish twice,
I think I know enough of hate
To say that for destruction ice
Is also great
And would suffice.

w. 1920
p. 1923

Stopping by Woods on a Snowy Evening

Whose woods these are I think I know
His house is in the village though;
He will not see me stopping here
To watch his woods fill up with snow

My little horse must think it queer
To stop without a farmhouse near
Between the woods and frozen lake
The darkest evening of the year.

He gives his harness bells a shake
To ask if there is some mistake.   10
The only other sound's the sweep
Of easy wind and downy flake.

The woods are lovely, dark and deep.
But I have promises to keep,
And miles to go before I sleep,
And miles to go before I sleep.

1923

Once by the Pacific

The shattered water made a misty din.
Great waves looked over others coming in,
And thought of doing something to the shore
That water never did to land before.
The clouds were low and hairy in the skies,
Like locks blown forward in the gleam of eyes.
You could not tell, and yet it looked as if
The shore was lucky in being backed by cliff,
The cliff in being backed by continent;
It looked as if a night of dark intent   10
Was coming, and not only a night, an age.
Someone had better be prepared for rage.
There would be more than ocean-water broken
Before God's last *Put out the Light* was spoken.

w. 1926
p. 1928

Spring Pools

These pools that, though in forests, still reflect
The total sky almost without defect,
And like the flowers beside them, chill and shiver,
Will like the flowers beside them soon be gone,
And yet not out by any brook or river,
But up by roots to bring dark foliage on.

The trees that have it in their pent-up buds
To darken nature and be summer woods—
Let them think twice before they use their powers
To blot out and drink up and sweep away   10
These flowery waters and these watery flowers
From snow that melted only yesterday.

w. 1927
p. 1928

Tree at My Window

Tree at my window, window tree,
My sash is lowered when night comes on;
But let there never be curtain drawn
Between you and me.

Vague dream-head lifted out of the ground,
And thing next most diffuse to cloud,
Not all your light tongues talking aloud
Could be profound.

But, tree, I have seen you taken and tossed,
And if you have seen me when I slept,   10
You have seen me when I was taken and swept
And all but lost.

That day she put our heads together,
Fate had her imagination about her,
Your head so much concerned with outer,
Mine with inner, weather.

w. 1927
p. 1928

Two Tramps in Mud Time

Or, A Full-Time Interest

Out of the mud two strangers came
And caught me splitting wood in the yard.
And one of them put me off my aim
By hailing cheerily 'Hit them hard!'
I knew pretty well why he dropped behind
And let the other go on a way.
I knew pretty well what he had in mind:
He wanted to take my job for pay.

Good blocks of oak it was I split,
As large around as the chopping block;   10
And every piece I squarely hit
Fell splinterless as a cloven rock.

The blows that a life of self-control
Spares to strike for the common good
That day, giving a loose to my soul,
I spent on the unimportant wood.

The sun was warm but the wind was chill.
You know how it is with an April day
When the sun is out and the wind is still,
You're one month on in the middle of May.   20
But if you so much as dare to speak,
A cloud comes over the sunlit arch,
A wind comes off a frozen peak,
And you're two months back in the middle of March.

A bluebird comes tenderly up to alight
And turns to the wind to unruffle a plume
His song so pitched as not to excite
A single flower as yet to bloom.
It is snowing a flake: and he half knew
Winter was only playing possum.   30
Except in color he isn't blue,
But he wouldn't advise a thing to blossom.

The water for which we may have to look
In summertime with a witching-wand,
In every wheelrut's now a brook,
In every print of a hoof a pond.
Be glad of water, but don't forget
The lurking frost in the earth beneath
That will steal forth after the sun is set
And show on the water its crystal teeth.   40

The time when most I loved my task
These two must make me love it more
By coming with what they came to ask.
You'd think I never had felt before
The weight of an ax-head poised aloft,
The grip on earth of outspread feet,
The life of muscles rocking soft
And smooth and moist in vernal heat.

Out of the woods two hulking tramps
(From sleeping God knows where last night,   50

But not long since in the lumber camps).
They thought all chopping was theirs of right.
Men of the woods and lumberjacks,
They judged me by their appropriate tool.
Except as a fellow handled an ax,
They had no way of knowing a fool.

Nothing on either side was said.
They knew they had but to stay their stay
And all their logic would fill my head:
As that I had no right to play   60
With what was another man's work for gain.
My right might be love but theirs was need.
And where the two exist in twain
Theirs was the better right—agreed.

But yield who will to their separation,
My object in living is to unite
My avocation and my vocation
As my two eyes make one in sight.
Only where love and need are one,
And the work is play for mortal stakes,
Is the deed ever really done
For Heaven and the future's sakes.

                                                    1934

Neither Out Far Nor In Deep

The people along the sand
All turn and look one way.
They turn their back on the land.
They look at the sea all day.

As long as it takes to pass
A ship keeps raising its hull;
The wetter ground like glass
Reflects a standing gull.

The land may vary more;
But wherever the truth may be—   10
The water comes ashore,
And the people look at the sea.

They cannot look out far.
They cannot look in deep.
But when was that ever a bar
To any watch they keep?

1934

Desert Places

Snow falling and night falling fast, oh, fast
In a field I looked into going past,
And the ground almost covered smooth in snow,
But a few weeds and stubble showing last.

The woods around it have it—it is theirs.
All animals are smothered in their lairs.
I am too absent-spirited to count;
The loneliness includes me unawares.

And lonely as it is that loneliness
Will be more lonely ere it will be less—   10
A blanker whiteness of benighted snow
With no expression, nothing to express.

They cannot scare me with their empty spaces
Between stars—on stars where no human race is.
I have it in me so much nearer home
To scare myself with my own desert places.

1934

Departmental

Or, The End of My Ant Jerry

An ant on the tablecloth
Ran into a dormant moth
Of many times his size.
He showed not the least surprise.

His business wasn't with such.
He gave it scarcely a touch,
And was off on his duty run.
Yet if he encountered one
Of the hive's enquiry squad
Whose work is to find out God   10
And the nature of time and space,
He would put him onto the case.
Ants are a curious race;
One crossing with hurried tread
The body of one of their dead
Isn't given a moment's arrest—
Seems not even impressed.
But he no doubt reports to any
With whom he crosses antennae,
And they no doubt report   20
To the higher up at court.
Then word goes forth in Formic:
'Death's come to Jerry McCormic,
Our selfless forager Jerry.
Will the special Janizary
Whose office it is to bury
The dead of the commissary
Go bring him home to his people.
Lay him in state on a sepal.
Wrap him for shroud in a petal.   30
Embalm him with ichor of nettle.
This is the word of your queen.'
And presently on the scene
Appears a solemn mortician;
And taking formal position
With feelers calmly atwiddle,
Seizes the dead by the middle,
And heaving him high in air,
Carries him out of there.
No one stands round to stare.   40
It is nobody else's affair.

It couldn't be called ungentle.
But how thoroughly departmental.

w. 1935
p. 1936

Come In

As I came to the edge of the woods,
Thrush music—hark!
Now if it was dusk outside,
Inside it was dark.

Too dark in the woods for a bird
By sleight of wing
To better its perch for the night,
Though it still could sing.

The last of the light of the sun
That had died in the west   10
Still lived for one song more
In a thrush's breast.

Far in the pillared dark
Thrush music went—
Almost like a call to come in
To the dark and lament.

But no, I was out for Stars:
I would not come in.
I meant not even if asked,
And I hadn't been.   20

1941

The Gift Outright

The land was ours before we were the land's.
She was our land more than a hundred years
Before we were her people. She was ours
In Massachusetts, in Virginia,
But we were England's, still colonials,
Possessing what we still were unpossessed by,
Possessed by what we now no more possessed.
Something we were withholding made us weak
Until we found out that it was ourselves

We were withholding from our land of living, 10
And forthwith found salvation in surrender.
Such as we were we gave ourselves outright
(The deed of gift was many deeds of war)
To the land vaguely realizing westward,
But still unstoried, artless, unenhanced,
Such as she was, such as she would become.

1942

STEPHEN VINCENT BENÉT

(1898–1943)

It is not often that a military background results in a taste for serious literature, but such is the case in the family of Stephen Vincent Benét, whose father, grandfather, and great-grandfather were professional army officers. His father and grandfather so successfully encouraged the reading of poetry that Stephen, his brother, William Rose, and his sister, Laura, all turned into writers.

Benét was born in Bethlehem, Pennsylvania, and educated in San Francisco and Georgia, where his father was stationed. Despite the peripatetic life of army posts and military academies, Benét early turned to writing. While still a schoolboy, he published juvenile verses in *Saint Nicholas* and had a volume of dramatic monologues, *Five Men and Pompey*, in print when he entered Yale in 1915. While an undergraduate, he published a prize-winning poem, *The Drug Shop: or, Endymion in Edmonstoun* (1917), as a separate little book. In his senior year, he was editor of the *Yale Literary Magazine*, which was receiving contributions from classmates Philip Barry, Archibald Mac-Leish, and Thornton Wilder. He was graduated in 1919, after having worked in an Army decoding office with James Thurber. Two years later he earned his Master's degree, his thesis being a volume of poems, *Heavens and Earth*, published in 1920.

From Yale he went to the Sorbonne, where he met Rosemary Carr, a Paris correspondent for Chicago and London papers, and in 1921 he married her. By 1922, when the Benéts returned to the States, Stephen had published two novels, *The Beginning of Wisdom* (1921) and *Young People's Pride* (1922), and had settled down seriously to the business of being a professional author. A prolific writer, he turned out many short stories, poems, and articles.

Influenced by his father's library of American military history, he had developed early a sense of the growth of the Republic, a sense that was to be the central thread of his best work. Particularly intrigued by the Civil War, he used a Guggenheim award in 1926 to go to Paris in order to write an epic poem of that struggle. In 1928 the work was completed and published. It was *John Brown's Body*, which won immediate honors and wide popular success. The poem displayed Benét's enraptured and romantic feeling for the American panorama and the folk elements in its cultural history, as had the earlier *The Ballad of William Sycamore* (1923) and as *The Devil and Daniel Webster* (1936) was to do later.

For a long time Benét had been revolving in his mind an idea for an epic about American westering, taking the pioneers across the Atlantic and then across the continent. The poem was never finished, but part of it was published posthumously as *Western Star* in 1944. The interruption in his work was occasioned by the depression, fascism, and Nazism. Enamored of the myth of the American Dream, of the infinite possibilities of the Republic, he directed his writing powers against the disillusionment and rising totalitarianism of the depression years with an exalted dedication to the American democracy he loved. *Burning City* (1936) and *We Stand United, and Other Radio Scripts* (1945) are examples of this work. His feverish activity on behalf of the common man's collective stake in democracy and individual freedom undermined his frail health, and he died before he was forty-five years old.

Some other books by Benét are *King David* (1923), *Tiger Joy* (1925), *The Barefoot Saint* (1929), *A Book of Americans,* with his wife (1933), *Our Singing Strength* (1929); M. D. Zabel, "The American Grain," *Poetry,* XLVIII (1936); F. B. Millett, *Contemporary American Authors* (1940); W. R. Benét, "My Brother Steve . . . ," *Saturday Review of Literature,* XXVI (March 27, 1943)—this issue contains a symposium of ten articles on

Benét; W. R. Benét and J. Farrar, *Stephen Vincent Benét* (1943); C. La Farge, "The Narrative Poetry of Stephen Vincent Benét," *Saturday Review of Literature*, XXVII (August 5, 1944); G. Maddocks, "Stephen Vincent Benét: A Bibliography," *Bulletin of Bibliography*, XX (1951); F. H. Jackson, "Stephen Vincent Benét and History," *Historian* XVII (1954); A. Tate, *Sixty American Poets* (1954); C. Fenton, *Stephen Vincent Benét* (1958); C. Fenton, ed., *Selected Letters of Stephen Vincent Benét* (1960); P. Stroud, *Stephen Vincent Benét* (1962); G. Abbe, ed., *Stephen Vincent Benét on Writing* (1964).

American Names

I have fallen in love with American names,
The sharp names that never get fat,
The snakeskin-titles of mining-claims,
The plumed war-bonnet of Medicine Hat,
Tucson and Deadwood and Lost Mule Flat.

Seine and Piave are silver spoons,
But the spoonbowl-metal is thin and worn,
There are English counties like hunting-tunes
Played on the keys of the postboy's horn,
But I will remember where I was born.   10

I will remember Carquinez Straits,
Little French Lick and Lundy's Lane,
The Yankee ships and the Yankee dates
And the bullet-towns of Calamity Jane.
I will remember Skunktown Plain.

I will fall in love with a Salem tree
And a rawhide quirt from Santa Cruz,
I will get me a bottle of Boston sea
And a blue-gum nigger to sing me blues.
I am tired of loving a foreign muse.   20

Rue des Martyrs and Bleeding-Heart-Yard,
Senlis, Pisa, and Blindman's Oast,
It is a magic ghost you guard
But I am sick for a newer ghost,
Harrisburg, Spartanburg, Painted Post.

Henry and John were never so,
And Henry and John were always right?
Granted, but when it was time to go
And the tea and the laurels had stood all night,
Did they never watch for Nantucket Light?   30

I shall not rest quiet in Montparnasse.
I shall not lie easy at Winchelsea.
You may bury my body in Sussex grass,
You may bury my tongue at Champmédy.
I shall not be there. I shall rise and pass.
Bury my heart at Wounded Knee.

                                                        1927

FROM

John Brown's Body

Invocation

American muse, whose strong and diverse heart
So many men have tried to understand
But only made it smaller with their art,
Because you are as various as your land,

As mountainous-deep, as flowered with blue rivers,
Thirsty with deserts, buried under snows,
As native as the shape of Navajo quivers,
And native, too, as the sea-voyaged rose.

Swift runner, never captured or subdued,
Seven-branched elk beside the mountain stream,   10
That half a hundred hunters have pursued
But never matched their bullets with the dream,

Where the great huntsmen failed, I set my sorry
And mortal snare for your immortal quarry.

You are the buffalo ghost, the broncho-ghost
With dollar-silver in your saddle-horn,
The cowboys riding in from Painted Post,

The Indian arrow in the Indian corn,
And you are the clipped velvet of the lawns
Where Shropshire grows from Massachusetts' sods,   20
The grey Maine rocks—and the war-painted dawns
That break above the Garden of the Gods.

The prairie-schooners crawling toward the ore
And the cheap car, parked by the station-door.

Where the skyscrapers lift their foggy plumes
Of stranded smoke out of a stony mouth
You are that high stone and its arrogant fumes,
And you are ruined gardens in the South

And bleak New England farms, so winter-white
Even their roofs look lonely, and the deep   30
The middle grainland where the wind of night
Is like all blind earth sighing in her sleep.

A friend, an enemy, a sacred hag
With two tied oceans in her medicine-bag.

They tried to fit you with an English song
And clip your speech into the English tale.
But, even from the first, the words went wrong,
The catbird pecked away the nightingale.

The homesick men begot high-cheekboned things
Whose wit was whittled with a different sound   40
And Thames and all the rivers of the kings
Ran into Mississippi and were drowned.

They planted England with a stubborn trust.
But the cleft dust was never English dust.

Stepchild of every exile from content
And all the disavouched, hard-bitten pack
Shipped overseas to steal a continent
With neither shirts nor honor to their back.

Pimping grandee and rump-faced regicide,
Apple-cheeked younkers from a windmill-square,   50
Puritans stubborn as the nails of Pride,

Rakes from Versailles and thieves from County Clare,
The black-robed priests who broke their hearts in vain
To make you God and France or God and Spain.

These were your lovers in your buckskin-youth.
And each one married with a dream so proud
He never knew it could not be the truth
And that he coupled with a girl of cloud.

And now to see you is more difficult yet   60
Except as an immensity of wheel
Made up of wheels, oiled with inhuman sweat
And glittering with the heat of ladled steel.

All these you are, and each is partly you,
And none is false, and none is wholly true.

So how to see you as you really are,
So how to suck the pure, distillate, stored
Essence of essence from the hidden star
And make it pierce like a riposting sword.

For, as we hunt you down, you must escape
And we pursue a shadow of our own   70
That can be caught in a magician's cape
But has the flatness of a painted stone.

Never the running stag, the gull at wing,
The pure elixir, the American thing.

And yet, at moments when the mind was hot
With something fierier than joy or grief,
When each known spot was an eternal spot
And every leaf was an immortal leaf,

I think that I have seen you, not as one,
But clad in diverse semblances and powers,   80
Always the same, as light falls from the sun,
And always different, as the differing hours.

Yet, through each altered garment that you wore
The naked body, shaking the heart's core.

All day the snow fell on that Eastern town
With its soft, pelting, little, endless sigh
Of infinite flakes that brought the tall sky down
Till I could put my hands in the white sky

And taste cold scraps of heaven on my tongue
And walk in such a changed and luminous light   90
As gods inhabit when the gods are young.
All day it fell. And when the gathered night

Was a blue shadow cast by a pale glow
I saw you then, snow-image, bird of the snow.

And I have seen and heard you in the dry
Close-huddled furnace of the city street
When the parched moon was planted in the sky
And the limp air hung dead against the heat.

I saw you rise, red as that rusty plant,
Dizzied with lights, half-mad with senseless sound,   100
Enormous metal, shaking to the chant
Of a triphammer striking iron ground.

Enormous power, ugly to the fool,
And beautiful as a well-handled tool.

These, and the memory of that windy day
On the bare hills, beyond the last barbed wire,
When all the orange poppies bloomed one way
As if a breath would blow them into fire,

I keep forever, like the sea-lion's tusk
The broken sailor brings away to land,   110
But when he touches it, he smells the musk,
And the whole sea lies hollow in his hand.

So, from a hundred visions, I make one,
And out of darkness build my mocking sun.

And should that task seem fruitless in the eyes
Of those a different magic sets apart

To see through the ice-crystal of the wise
No nation but the nation that is Art,

Their words are just. But when the birchbark-call
Is shaken with the sound that hunters make   120
The moose comes plunging through the forest-wall
Although the rifle waits beside the lake.

Art has no nations—but the mortal sky
Lingers like gold in immortality.

This flesh was seeded from no foreign grain
But Pennsylvania and Kentucky wheat,
And it has soaked in California rain
And five years tempered in New England sleet

To strive at last, against an alien proof
And by the changes of an alien moon,   130
To build again that blue, American roof
Over a half-forgotten battle-tune

And call unsurely, from a haunted ground,
Armies of shadows and the shadow-sound.

In your Long House there is an attic-place
Full of dead epics and machines that rust,
And there, occasionally, with casual face,
You come awhile to stir the sleepy dust;

Neither in pride nor mercy, but in vast
Indifference at so many gifts unsought,   140
The yellowed satins, smelling of the past,
And all the loot the lucky pirates brought.

I only bring a cup of silver air,
Yet, in your casualness, receive it there.

Receive the dream too haughty for the breast,
Receive the words that should have walked as bold
As the storm walks along the mountaincrest
And are like beggars whining in the cold.

The maimed presumption, the unskilful skill,
The patchwork colors, fading from the first,   150

And all the fire that fretted at the will
With such a barren ecstasy of thirst.

Receive them all—and should you choose to touch them
With one slant ray of quick, American light,
Even the dust will have no power to smutch them,
Even the worst will glitter in the night.

If not—the dry bones littered by the way
May still point giants toward their golden prey.

1928

EZRA POUND

(1885–   )

Almost the direct antithesis of the Midwestern poets who were
first heralded in the pages of Harriet Monroe's Chicago magazine, *Poetry*, Ezra Pound loves neither America, democracy, nor
poetry of "the common man." Probably more influential than
any other modern American poet except Eliot (if Pound and
Eliot really can be called American poets any longer), Pound
often has been the center of hot literary, critical, and political
controversy.

He was born in Hailey, Idaho, but spent his formative years
in the East, where he attended the University of Pennsylvania
and Hamilton College. He taught Romance languages for two
years at the University of Pennsylvania, took his Master's degree there in 1906, and then went to Europe to do research
on Lope de Vega, the Spanish dramatist and poet. In 1907 he
was dismissed from an instructorship at Wabash College, Indiana, and feeling that the United States had little room for
an experimental poet and critic, he left for England in 1908. He
remained in London for the next ten years, turning out dramati-
cally new poetry, translations, and essays. One of the group
which included T. E. Hulme, Pound turned against romanticism;
in his classical insistence upon hard, precise poetry stripped of
sentimentality, he helped to found the "Imagists." In 1914
he edited *Des Imagistes* and a revolutionary little magazine appropriately named *Blast*.

As an innovator, Pound not only introduced readers to Japanese, Chinese, Italian, Latin, French and Provençal poetry
through his own translations—his recondite and esoteric learning is enormous—but, as the foreign correspondent of *Poetry*,
he also championed many new writers. Robert Frost, Hilda Doo-

little, T. S. Eliot, D. H. Lawrence, William Butler Yeats, James
Joyce, and the French symbolistes all owe something of their
impact on the American literary imagination in the early twentieth century to the catalytic action of Ezra Pound.

His own poetry, essentially, is composed of two enormous
undertakings—*Personae* and *Cantos*. *Personae* (as well as
Cantos) is a part of Pound's attempt to create a literary heritage
in which all the culture of the past becomes the common possession of writers of the present—a concept which has deeply influenced the criticism and poetry of T. S. Eliot. Thus, in Pound's
poetry, one is as apt to find a Chinese ideogram as to find the
most abstruse contemporary allusions. The first book of
Personae was published in 1909, expanded in 1913, and
brought out as *Personae: The Collected Poems* in 1926. The
1926 volume includes the 1909 volume of *Personae* as well as
Exultations (1909), *Ripostes* (1912), *Lustra* (1916), *Homage
to Sextus Propertius* which first appeared in *Quia Pauper Amavi*
(1919), and *Hugh Selwyn Mauberley* (1920).

The *Cantos* are still being written. They were to have stopped
after 100 cantos were completed, but Pound's design has
changed. Pound's ambitious plan in the *Cantos* is nothing less
than an epic commentary on human civilization in which social
and political ideas are defined by means of every imaginable
kind of allusion and, sometimes, even by private free association. The first three cantos appeared in *Poetry* magazine, in
the American edition of *Lustra* (1917), and in *Quia Pauper
Amavi*. They have since expanded in *A Draft of XVI Cantos*
(1925); *A Draft of Cantos XVII-XXVII* (1928); *A Draft of
XXX Cantos* (1930); *Eleven New Cantos: XXXI-XLI* (1934);
The Fifth Decad of Cantos (1937); *Cantos LII-LXXI* (1940);
The Pisan Cantos (1948); *Section: Rock Drill* (1956), which
increased the number of cantos to ninety-five; and *Throne*
(1960), which brings the number of cantos to 109. Based upon
Dante's organization of *The Divine Comedy*, the *Cantos* have
challenged readers to find the relationships that will form
meaningful divisions. There are almost as many readings and
evaluations of the *Cantos* as there are critics. In 1949, the
Pisan Cantos received the first annual Bollingen award for poetry. The selection of Pound by the committee, composed of
the Fellows in American Literature of the Library of Congress,
touched off a furious debate on the social responsibility of the
poet.

Controversy still rages about Pound—there are those who

defend to the death everything he writes, and there are those who condemn it all and are still incensed by the granting of the Bollingen award. His importance as an influence and innovator, however, is unassailable. He has affected poets as varied as Eliot, MacLeish, and Hart Crane; his translations (some of the most famous are *Cathay*, from the Chinese, 1915; *Noh*, from the Japanese, 1916; *Certain Noble Plays of Japan*, 1916; and *The Sonnets and Ballate of Guido Cavalcanti*, 1912) are splendid achievements; his various defenses of the experimental in art, literature, sculpture, and music have been ground-break·· ing efforts.

Pound's thought generally has been leavened with a mystique about usury, the state, and social credit that has led him to fascism and an insanely unquenchable anti-Semitism. Thus such sane and interesting prose works as *Pavannes and Divisions* (1918), *Instigations* (1920), *How to Read* (1931), and *Make It New* (1934) unfortunately must stand with such frenetic out-pourings as the *ABC of Economics* (1933) and *Jefferson and/or Mussolini* (1935). In 1924 Pound settled in Rapallo, Italy, and became an advocate of fascism under Mussolini. During World War II, he made regular anti-American broadcasts on Radio Rome's "American Hour." In 1945 he was captured, brought back to the United States after a thirty-four-year absence that had been broken only by one brief visit, and indicted for treason. He was found insane and committed to St. Elizabeth's hospital in Washington, where he remained until 1958, when the treason charges against him were dropped. Upon his release he returned to Italy, where the first thing he did was to make the fascist salute.

Some other of Pound's books are *A Lume Spento* (1908), H. Kenner, ed.; *Provença* (1910); *Canzoni* (1911); *Gaudier-Brzeska* (1910); *Indiscretions* (1923); *The ABC of Reading* (1934); *Culture* (1938); *Money Pamphlets by Pound* (1950–1952); *The Translations of Ezra Pound* (1953, 1963, 1964); and *Pavannes and Divagations* (1958).

Editions and studies of the man and his work are to be found in T. S. Eliot, *Ezra Pound: His Metric and Poetry* (1917); C. Aiken, *Scepticisms* (1919); T. S. Eliot, ed., *Selected Poems* (1928, 1959); G. Hughes, *Imagism and the Imagists* (1931); F. R. Leavis, *New Bearings in English Poetry* (1932); E. Sitwell, *Aspects of Modern Poetry* (1934); R. P. Blackmur, *The Double Agent* (1935); A. Amdur, *The Poetry of Ezra Pound* (1936); C. Norman, ed., *The Case of Ezra Pound* (1948); A. Tate, *On the Limits of Poetry* (1948); The editors of *Poetry*, eds., *The Case Against the Saturday Review of Literature* (1949); *Quarterly Review of Litertaure*, V (1949)——a special Pound Issue;

M. Schlauch, "The Anti-Humanism of Ezra Pound," *Science and Society*, XIII (1949); *Selected Poems* (1949, 1957); D. D. Paige, ed., *The Letters of Ezra Pound, 1907–1941* (1950); P. Russell, ed., *An Examination of Ezra Pound* (1950); H. Kenner, *The Poetry of Ezra Pound* (1951); B. Deutsch, *Poetry in Our Time* (1952); H. H. Watts, *Ezra Pound and "The Cantos"* (1952); J. H. Edwards, *A Preliminary Checklist of the Writings of Ezra Pound* (1953); R. Aldington, *Ezra Pound and T. S. Eliot* (1954); T. S. Eliot, ed., *The Literary Essays of Ezra Pound* (1954); L. Leary, ed., *Motive and Method in the Cantos of Ezra Pound: English Institute Essays* (1954); J. J. Espey, *Ezra Pound's Mauberley* (1955); M. Moore, *Predilections* (1955); J. Edwards and W. Vasse, Jr., *Annotated Index to the Cantos of Ezra Pound* (1957); C. Emery, *Ideas into Action: A Study of Pound's Cantos* (1959); W. V. O'Connor and E. Stone, eds., *A Casebook on Ezra Pound* (1959); C. Norman, *Ezra Pound* (1960); M. Rosenthal, *A Primer of Ezra Pound* (1960); G. Dekker, *The Cantos of Ezra Pound* (1963); L. S. Dembo, *The Confucian Odes of Ezra Pound* (1963); W. V. O'Connor, *Ezra Pound* (1963); W. Sutton, ed., *Ezra Pound: A Collection of Critical Essays* (1963); D. Davie, *Ezra Pound: Poet as Sculptor* (1964); G. Giovannini, *Ezra Pound and Dante* (1964); R. G. Howarth, *Two Modern Writers: Ezra Pound and Edith Sitwell* (1964); N. Stock, *Poet in Exile: Ezra Pound* (1964); J. P. Sullivan, *Ezra Pound and Sextus Propertius* (1964); special Pound issue of *Agenda*, IV (Oct.–Nov., 1965); P. Hutchins, *Ezra Pound's Kensington* (1965); N. Stock, ed., *Ezra Pound—Perspectives* (1966); and J. Cornell, *The Trial of Ezra Pound* (1966).

A Virginal

No, no! Go from me. I have left her lately.
I will not spoil my sheath with lesser brightness,
For my surrounding air has a new lightness;
Slight are her arms, yet they have bound me straitly
And left me cloaked as with a gauze of æther;
As with sweet leaves; as with a subtle clearness.
Oh, I have picked up magic in her nearness
To sheathe me half in half the things that sheathe her.

No, no! Go from me. I have still the flavor,
Soft as spring wind that's come from birchen bowers. 10
Green come the shoots, aye April in the branches,
As winter's wound with her sleight hand she staunches,
Hath of the trees a likeness of the savor:
As white their bark, so white this lady's hours.

1909

In a Station of the Metro

The apparition of these faces in the crowd;
Petals on a wet, black bough.

1912

The River-Merchant's Wife: A Letter*

While my hair was still cut straight across my forehead
I played about the front gate, pulling flowers.
You came by on bamboo stilts, playing horse,
You walked about my seat, playing with blue plums.
And we went on living in the village of Chokan:
Two small people, without dislike or suspicion.

At fourteen I married My Lord you.
I never laughed, being bashful.
Lowering my head, I looked at the wall.
Called to, a thousand times, I never looked back.

At fifteen I stopped scowling,
I desired my dust to be mingled with yours
Forever and forever and forever.
Why should I climb the look out?

At sixteen you departed,
You went into far Ku-to-yen, by the river of swirling
    eddies,
And you have been gone five months.
The monkeys make sorrowful noise overhead.
You dragged your feet when you went out.
By the gate now, the moss is grown, the different mosses, 20
Too deep to clear them away!

The leaves fall early this autumn, in wind.
The paired butterflies are already yellow with August
Over the grass in the West garden;
They hurt me. I grow older.

* The poem is a translation from Li Po (701–762), the great Chinese
poet [Ed.].

If you are coming down through the narrows of the river
    Kiang,
Please let me know beforehand,
And I will come out to meet you
    As far as Cho-fu-sa.

By Rihaku
1916

FROM

Hugh Selwyn Mauberley

Life and Contacts

Vocat Æstus in Umbram
[Summer summons us into the shade]
    —Nemesianus EC. IV.

E. P. Ode pour l'Election de Son Sepulchre

[Ode on the Choice of his Tomb]

For three years, out of key with his time,
He strove to resuscitate the dead art
Of poetry; to maintain "the sublime"
In the old sense. Wrong from the start—

No, hardly, but seeing he had been born
In a half-savage country, out of date;
Bent resolutely on wringing lilies from the acorn;
Capaneus; trout for factitious bait;

Ἴδμεν γάρ τοι πάνθ', ὅσ' ἐνὶ Τροίῃ
[Ἴδμεν . . . Τροίῃ: for we know all things that are in Troy]
Caught in the unstopped ear;   10
Giving the rocks small lee-way
The chopped seas held him, therefore, that year.

His true Penelope was Flaubert,
He fished by obstinate isles;
Observed the elegance of Circe's hair
Rather than the mottoes on sun-dials.

Unaffected by "the march of events,"
He passed from men's memory in *l'an trentiesme*
De son eage; the case presents
[*l'an . . . eage:* the thirtieth year of his life]
No adjunct to the Muses' diadem.   20

II

The age demanded an image
Of its accelerated grimace,
Something for the modern stage,
Not, at any rate, an Attic grace;

Not, not certainly, the obscure reveries
Of the inward gaze;
Better mendacities
Than the classics in paraphrase!

The "age demanded" chiefly a mould in plaster,
Made with no loss of time,   30
A prose kinema, not, not assuredly, alabaster
Or the "sculpture" of rhyme.

III

The tea-rose tea-gown, etc.
Supplants the mousseline of Cos,
The pianola "replaces"
Sappho's barbitos.

Christ follows Dionysus,
Phallic and ambrosial
Made way for macerations;
Caliban casts out Ariel   40

All things are a flowing,
Sage Heracleitus says;
But a tawdry cheapness
Shall outlast our days.

Even the Christian beauty
Defects—after Samothrace;
We see τὸ καλὸν [τὸ καλὸν: the beautiful]
Decreed in the market place.

Faun's flesh is not to us,
Nor the saint's vision.   50
We have the press for wafer;
Franchise for circumcision.

All men, in law, are equals.
Free of Pisistratus,
We choose a knave or an eunuch
To rule over us.

O bright Apollo,
τίν' ἄνδρα, τίν' ἥρωα, τίνα θεὸν
[τίν' . . . θεὸν: what man, what hero, what god]
What god, man, or hero
Shall I place a tin wreath upon!   60

IV

These fought in any case,
and some believing,
          pro domo, in any case . . .

Some quick to arm,
some for adventure,
some from fear of weakness,
some from fear of censure,
some for love of slaughter, in imagination,
learning later . . .
some in fear, learning love of slaughter;   70

Died some, pro patria,
          non "dulce" non "et decor" . . .
walked eye-deep in hell
believing in old men's lies, then unbelieving
came home, home to a lie,
home to many deceits,
home to old lies and new infamy;
usury age-old and age-thick
and liars in public places.

Daring as never before, wastage as never before.   80
Young blood and high blood,

fair cheeks, and fine bodies;
fortitude as never before

frankness as never before,
disillusions as never told in the old days,
hysterias, trench confessions,
laughter out of dead bellies.

V

There died a myriad,
And of the best, among them,
For an old bitch gone in the teeth,   90
For a botched civilization,

Charm, smiling at the good mouth,
Quick eyes gone under earth's lid,

For two gross of broken statues,
For a few thousand battered books.

Yeux Glauques [Glaucous Eyes]

Gladstone was still respected,
When John Ruskin produced
"King's Treasuries"; Swinburne
And Rossetti still abused.

Fœtid Buchanan lifted up his voice   100
When that faun's head of hers
Became a pastime for
Painters and adulterers.

The Burne-Jones cartons
Have preserved her eyes;
Still, at the Tate, they teach
Cophetua to rhapsodize;

Thin like brook-water,
With a vacant gaze.
The English Rubaiyat was still-born   110

In those days.
The thin, clear gaze, the same
Still darts out faunlike from the half-ruin'd face,
Questing and passive. . . .
"Ah, poor Jenny's case" . . .

Bewildered that a world
Shows no surprise
At her last maquero's
Adulteries.

Envoi (1919)

Go, dumb-born book, 120
Tell her that sang me once that song of Lawes:
Hadst thou but song
As thou hast subjects known,
Then were there cause in thee that should condone
Even my faults that heavy upon me lie,
And build her glories their longevity.

Tell her that sheds
Such treasure in the air,
Recking naught else but that her graces give
Life to the moment, 130
I would bid them live
As roses might, in magic amber laid,
Red overwrought with orange and all made
One substance and one colour
Braving time.

Tell her that goes
With song upon her lips
But sings not out the song, nor knows
The maker of it, some other mouth,
May be as fair as hers, 140
Might, in new ages, gain her worshippers,
When our two dusts with Waller's shall be laid,
Siftings on siftings in oblivion,
Till change hath broken down
All things save Beauty alone.

1920

T. S. ELIOT
(1888–1965)

Probably the most influential poet and critic on the American
literary scene in the first half of the twentieth century, T. S.
Eliot, like his mentor, Ezra Pound, early in life ceased to associate himself with America.

He was born in St. Louis to a New England family with pre-
Revolutionary roots, which had transplanted itself, through
Eliot's grandfather, to the Midwest. The grandfather, a minister,
established the first Unitarian Church in St. Louis and founded
Washington University. Eliot was educated at Harvard, where
he received his Bachelor's and Master's degrees, and where he
edited the *Harvard Advocate*. Influenced by Babbitt and San-
tayana, he continued his studies in philosophy at the Sorbonne
for a year, at Harvard for three more years, and at Oxford
during the year of 1914, when he was twenty-six years old
and when the war broke out. From then on, Eliot remained in
England.

He supported himself in London by schoolteaching and by
working in Lloyd's bank, meanwhile writing poems in which he
expressed his philosophic dismay at the disintegration of religious values in the Western, Protestant world. *Prufrock and
Other Observations* appeared in 1917, *Poems* in 1919, and
occasional pieces in *The Egoist*, which he edited from 1917 to
1919. In 1922 Eliot published *The Waste Land* and began
editing *The Criterion*, which became a respected and influential
magazine. Although Eliot's other works had attracted deep
attention, sometimes bewildered, sometimes enthusiastic, it was
The Waste Land that established him as a pace setter in modern literature. The multitudinous allusions in the poem showed
the influence of Pound's concept of the heritage of all human
past history as the materials of the modern poet; the associa-

tional method indicated Eliot's interest in the methods of juncture utilized by the "metaphysical" poets and the attendant possibility of creating meaning, through imagery, simultaneously rather than chronologically; and the content of the poem articulated the sense of despair that intellectuals felt in the postwar era. Perhaps more than any single poem in English, *The Waste Land* broke the hold of convention and ushered in modern poetry. An entire generation of poets was formed by it, including such well-known writers as Stephen Spender, W. H. Auden, C. Day Lewis, Archibald MacLeish, Conrad Aiken, Hart Crane, and the "Fugitives."

In 1925, Eliot left the employ of Lloyd's bank to become a member of the board of Faber and Faber, London publishers. Two years later he became a British subject and a communicant in the Church of England. A year later, in the preface to *For Lancelot Andrewes* (1928), Eliot enunciated his famous self-definition as a "classicist in literature, a royalist in politics, and an Anglo-Catholic in religion." Like Pound, he was at least partially led to this position by his disgust for the mass culture of American democracy; although the self-definition has been hotly debated, even by his admirers, there is no question that it reflected attitudes that began to appear in the subtle and magnificently controlled religious aspects of Eliot's poetry. His faith resulted in the affirmation of *Ash Wednesday* (1930), the play *Murder in the Cathedral* (1935), and the universally revered *Four Quartets* (1943); these poems counterpoint the sense of dismal spiritual decay in the modern world of the earlier *Prufrock* and *The Wasteland*. In 1948 Eliot received the Nobel Prize for literature and continued to write plays that were vehicles for his spiritual probings: *The Cocktail Party* (1950), *The Confidential Clerk* (1953), and *The Elder Statesman* (1958). Except for *Murder in the Cathedral*, the plays (which include *The Rock*, 1934, and *The Family Reunion*, 1939) have neither exerted the influence nor enjoyed the universal approval of the poetry.

Eliot's literary essays, which had made him the reigning critical influence of the 1920's and 1930's (and, perhaps, the 1940's), were first presented in *The Sacred Wood* (1920). In *Homage to John Dryden* (1924), Eliot revived the seventeenth century as a model for English poetry, and in such works as *Selected Essays* (1932, 1950), *The Use of Poetry and the Use of Criticism* (1933), *Shakespeare & the Stoicism of Seneca* (1927), *John Dryden the Poet, the Dramatist, the Critic* (1932),

446 · *T. S. ELIOT*

and *Essays, Ancient & Modern* (1936), he contributed greatly toward the freeing of the literary imagination in criticism from nineteenth-century romanticism and moralism. (He had, however, since recanted some of his judgments, particularly of such writers as Milton and Keats.) He insisted on depersonalization of the author in the work, on hard thought and clear, precise imagery which would become an "objective correlative" for the mood the poet wishes to evoke.

The radical classicism of his taste and the radical experimentalism of his poetry, which rearranged critical tastes and literary pantheons, are closely related to his social thought. Eliot refined Pound's concept of the relationship between history and literature to the assumption that the true heritage of Western literature is to be found in the Christian tradition, particularly the non-dissociated sensibilities of the presumably unific medieval Christianity that flowered for the last and most glorious moment in the poetry of the seventeenth century. Such works as *After Strange Gods* (1934) and *The Idea of a Christian Society* (1939), in their most important aspects, resulted in a revaluation of "tradition and the individual talent."

Some other of Eliot's works are *The Journey of the Magi* (1927), *Animula* (1929), *Dante* (1929), *Marina* (1930), *Sweeney Agonistes* (1932), *Elizabethan Essays* (1934), *The Music of Poetry* (1942), *The Classics and the Man of Letters* (1942), *On Poetry* (1947), *Milton* (1947), *Notes Toward the Definition of Culture* (1948), *From Poe to Valery* (1948), *The Aims of Poetic Drama* (1949), *Poetry and Drama* (1951), *The Three Voices of Poetry* (1953), *American Literature and the American Language* (1953), *Religious Drama: Mediaeval and Modern* (1954), *The Literature of Politics* (1955), *The Frontiers of Criticism* (1956), and *On Poetry and Poets* (1957). *The Collected Poems, 1909–1935* (1936) has been superseded by *The Complete Poems and Plays* (1952), containing all the central work to that date.

Studies of the man and his work are to be found in G. Williamson, *The Talent of T. S. Eliot* (1929); T. McGreevy, *Thomas Stearns Eliot* (1931); A. Oras, *The Critical Ideas of T. S. Eliot* (1932); H. R. Williamson, *The Poetry of T. S. Eliot* (1933); F. O. Matthiessen, *The Achievement of T. S. Eliot* (1935, 1958); A. C. Partridge, *T. S. Eliot* (1937); B. Rajan, ed., *T. S. Eliot: A Study of His Writings* (1947); C. Sansom, *The Poetry of T. S. Eliot* (1947); R. March and Tambimuttu, eds., *T. S. Eliot: A Symposium* (1948); L. Unger, ed., *T. S. Eliot: A Selected Critique* (1948); F. Wilson, *Six Essays on the Development of T. S. Eliot* (1948); V. Brombert, *The Criticism of T. S. Eliot* (1949); E. Drew, *T. S. Eliot: The Design of His Poetry*

(1949); H. L. Gardner, *The Art of T. S. Eliot* (1949); K. Smidt *Poetry and Belief in the Work of T. S. Eliot* (1949); L. Unger, *The Art of T. S. Eliot* (1949); A. Mordell, *T. S. Eliot's Deficiencies as a Social Critic* (1951); R. H. Robbins, *The T. S. Eliot Myth* (1951); D. Maxwell, *The Poetry of T. S. Eliot* (1952); D. C. Gallup, *T. S. Eliot: A Bibliography* (1953); G. Williamson, *A Reader's Guide to T. S. Eliot* (1953); R. Aldington, *Ezra Pound and T. S. Eliot* (1954); G. Smith, Jr., *T. S. Eliot's Poetry and Plays* (1956); H. Kenner, *Invisible Poet: T. S. Eliot* (1959); P. E. Jones, *The Plays of T. S. Eliot* (1960); G. Wright, *The Poet in the Poem: The Personae of Eliot, Yeats, and Pound* (1960); L. Freed, *T. S. Eliot: Aesthetics and History* (1962); N. Frye, *T. S. Eliot* (1963); A. G. George, *T. S. Eliot: His Mind and Art* (1963); C. H. Smith, *T. S. Eliot's Dramatic Theory and Practice* . . . (1963); E. Thompson, *T. S. Eliot: The Metaphysical Perspective* (1963); P. R. Headings, *T. S. Eliot* (1964); H. Howarth, *Notes on Some Figures Behind T. S. Eliot* (1965); G. Jones, *Approach to the Purpose: A Study of the Poetry of T. S. Eliot* (1965); H. Gardner, *T. S. Eliot and the English Poetic Tradition* (1965); F. Lu, *T. S. Eliot* (1966); and A. Tate, ed., Eliot issue of *Sewanee Review*, LXXIV, 1966.

The Love Song of J. Alfred Prufrock

S'io credesse che mia risposta fosse
A persona che mai tornasse al mondo,
Questa fiamma staria senza piu scosse.
Ma perciocche giammai di questo fondo
Non torno vivo alcun, s'i'odo il vero,
Senza tema d'infamia ti rispondo.

[If I believed that my answer were to a person who could
return to the world, this flame would quiver no more; but
since, if I hear truth, never from this depth did any man
return, I answer thee without fear of infamy (DANTE, *Inferno*, xxvii, 61–66.]

Let us go then, you and I,
When the evening is spread out against the sky
Like a patient etherised upon a table;
Let us go, through certain half-deserted streets,
The muttering retreats
Of restless nights in one-night cheap hotels
And sawdust restaurants with oyster-shells:
Streets that follow like a tedious argument
Of insidious intent
To lead you to an overwhelming question . . .   10
Oh, do not ask, "What is it?"
Let us go and make our visit.

In the room the women come and go
Talking of Michelangelo.

The yellow fog that rubs its back upon the window-
panes,
The yellow smoke that rubs its muzzle on the window-
panes
Licked its tongue into the corners of the evening,
Lingered upon the pools that stand in drains,
Let fall upon its back the soot that falls from chimneys,
Slipped by the terrace, made a sudden leap,   20
And seeing that it was a soft October night,
Curled once about the house, and fell asleep.

And indeed there will be time
For the yellow smoke that slides along the street,
Rubbing its back upon the window-panes;
There will be time, there will be time
To prepare a face to meet the faces that you meet;
There will be time to murder and create,
And time for all the works and days of hands
That lift and drop a question on your plate;   30
Time for you and time for me,
And time yet for a hundred indecisions,
And for a hundred visions and revisions,
Before the taking of a toast and tea.

In the room the women come and go
Talking of Michelangelo.

And indeed there will be time
To wonder, "Do I dare?" and, "Do I dare?"
Time to turn back and descend the stair,
With a bald spot in the middle of my hair—   40
(They will say: "How his hair is growing thin!")
My morning coat, my collar mounting firmly to the chin,
My necktie rich and modest, but asserted by a simple pin—
(They will say: "But how his arms and legs are thin!")
Do I dare
Disturb the universe?
In a minute there is time
For decisions and revisions which a minute will reverse.

For I have known them all already, known them all:—
Have known the evenings, mornings, afternoons,
I have measured out my life with coffee spoons;   50
I know the voices dying with a dying fall
Beneath the music from a farther room.
    So how should I presume?

And I have known the eyes already, known them all—
The eyes that fix you in a formulated phrase,
And when I am formulated, sprawling on a pin,
When I am pinned and wriggling on the wall,
Then how should I begin
To spit out all the butt-ends of my days and ways?
    And how should I presume?   60

And I have known the arms already, known them all—
Arms that are braceleted and white and bare
(But in the lamplight, downed with light brown hair!)
Is it perfume from a dress
That makes me so digress?
Arms that lie along a table, or wrap about a shawl.
    And should I then presume?
    And how should I begin?

           . . . ʹ .

Shall I say, I have gone at dusk through narrow streets   70
And watched the smoke that rises from the pipes
Of lonely men in shirt-sleeves, leaning out of win-
    dows? . . .

    I should have been a pair of ragged claws
Scuttling across the floors of silent seas.

           . . . . .

And the afternoon, the evening, sleeps so peacefully!
Smoothed by long fingers,
Asleep . . . tired . . . or it malingers,
Stretched on the floor, here beside you and me.
Should I, after tea and cakes and ices,
Have the strength to force the moment to its crisis?   80
But though I have wept and fasted, wept and prayed,

Though I have seen my head (grown slightly bald) brought
    in upon a platter,
I am no prophet—and here's no great matter;
I have seen the moment of my greatness flicker,
And I have seen the eternal Footman hold my coat, and
    snicker,
And in short, I was afraid.

    And would it have been worth it, after all,
After the cups, the marmalade, the tea,
Among the porcelain, among some talk of you and me,
Would it have been worth while,   90
To have bitten off the matter with a smile,
To have squeezed the universe into a ball
To roll it toward some overwhelming question,
To say: "I am Lazarus, come from the dead,
Come back to tell you all, I shall tell you all"—
If one, settling a pillow by her head,
    Should say: "That is not what I meant at all;
    That is not it, at all."

    And would it have been worth it, after all,
Would it have been worth while,   100
After the sunsets and the dooryards and the sprinkled
    streets,
After the novels, after the teacups, after the skirts that
    trail along the floor—
And this, and so much more?—
It is impossible to say just what I mean!
But as if a magic lantern threw the nerves in patterns on a
    screen:
Would it have been worth while
If one, settling a pillow or throwing off a shawl,
And turning toward the window, should say:
    "That is not it at all,
    That is not what I meant, at all."   110

      · · · · ·

No! I am not Prince Hamlet, nor was meant to be;
Am an attendant lord, one that will do
To swell a progress, start a scene or two,
Advise the prince; no doubt, an easy tool,
Deferential, glad to be of use,

Politic, cautious, and meticulous;
Full of high sentence, but a bit obtuse;
At times, indeed, almost ridiculous—
Almost, at times, the Fool.

I grow old . . . I grow old . . .   120
I shall wear the bottoms of my trousers rolled.

Shall I part my hair behind? Do I dare to eat a peach?
I shall wear white flannel trousers, and walk upon the
   beach.
I have heard the mermaids singing, each to each.

I do not think that they will sing to me.

I have seen them riding seaward on the waves
Combing the white hair of the waves blown back
When the wind blows the water white and black.

We have lingered in the chambers of the sea
By sea-girls wreathed with seaweed red and brown   130
Till human voices wake us, and we drown.

                                                      1915

Morning at the Window

They are rattling breakfast plates in basement kitchens,
And along the trampled edges of the street
I am aware of the damp souls of housemaids
Sprouting despondently at area gates.

The brown waves of fog toss up to me
Twisted faces from the bottom of the street,
And tear from a passer-by with muddy skirts
An aimless smile that hovers in the air
And vanishes along the level of the roofs.

                                                      1916

Sweeney Among the Nightingales

ὤμοι πέπληγμαι καιρίαν πληγὴν ἔσω.
[Alas, I am struck by a timely blow within]

Apeneck Sweeney spreads his knees
Letting his arms hang down to laugh,
The zebra stripes along his jaw
Swelling to maculate giraffe.

The circles of the stormy moon
Slide westward toward the River Plate,
Death and the Raven drift above
And Sweeney guards the hornèd gate.

Gloomy Orion and the Dog
Are veiled; and hushed the shrunken seas;   10
The person in the Spanish cape
Tries to sit on Sweeney's knees

Slips and pulls the table cloth
Overturns a coffee-cup,
Reorganized upon the floor
She yawns and draws a stocking up;

The silent man in mocha brown
Sprawls at the window-sill and gapes;
The waiter brings in oranges
Bananas figs and hothouse grapes;   20

The silent vertebrate in brown
Contracts and concentrates, withdraws;
Rachel *née* Rabinovitch
Tears at the grapes with murderous paws;

She and the lady in the cape
Are suspect, thought to be in league;
Therefore the man with heavy eyes
Declines the gambit, shows fatigue,

Leaves the room and reappears
Outside the window, leaning in,   30
Branches of wistaria
Circumscribe a golden grin;

The host with someone indistinct
Converses at the door apart,
The nightingales are singing near
The Convent of the Sacred Heart,

And sang within the bloody wood
When Agamemnon cried aloud,
And let their liquid siftings fall
To stain the stiff dishonoured shroud.   40

                                                   1918

Gerontion

Thou hast nor youth nor age
But as it were an after dinner sleep
Dreaming of both.

Here I am, an old man in a dry month,
Being read to by a boy, waiting for rain.
I was neither at the hot gates
Nor fought in the warm rain
Nor knee deep in the salt marsh, heaving a cutlass,
Bitten by flies, fought.
My house is a decayed house,
And the jew squats on the window sill, the owner,
Spawned in some estaminet of Antwerp,
Blistered in Brussels, patched and peeled in London.   10
The goat coughs at night in the field overhead;
Rocks, moss, stonecrop, iron, merds.   [merds: dung]
The woman keeps the kitchen, makes tea,
Sneezes at evening, poking the peevish gutter.
                        I an old man,
A dull head among windy spaces.

Signs are taken for wonders. "We would see a sign!"
The word within a word, unable to speak a word,
Swaddled with darkness. In the juvescence of the year
Came Christ the tiger

In depraved May, dogwood and chestnut, flowering
    judas,   20
To be eaten, to be divided, to be drunk
Among whispers; By Mr. Silvero
With caressing hands, at Limoges
Who walked all night in the next room;

By Hakagawa, bowing among the Titians;
By Madame de Tornquist, in the dark room
Shifting the candles; Fräulein von Kulp
Who turned in the hall, one hand on the door. Vacant
    shuttles
Weave the wind. I have no ghosts,
An old man in a draughty house   30
Under a windy knob.

After such knowledge, what forgiveness? Think now
History has many cunning passages, contrived corridors
And issues, deceives with whispering ambitions,
Guides us by vanities. Think now
She gives when our attenton is distracted
And what she gives, gives with such supple confusions
That the giving famishes the craving. Gives too late
What's not believed in, or if still believed,
In memory only, reconsidered passion. Gives too soon   40
Into weak hands, what's thought can be dispensed with
Till the refusal propagates a fear. Think
Neither fear nor courage saves us. Unnatural vices
Are fathered by our heroism. Virtues
Are forced upon us by our impudent crimes.
These tears are shaken from the wrath-bearing tree.

The tiger springs in the new year. Us he devours. Think
    at last
We have not reached conclusion, when I
Stiffen in a rented house. Think at last
I have not made this show purposelessly   50
And it is not by any concitation
Of the backward devils.
I would meet you upon this honestly.
I that was near your heart was removed therefrom
To lose beauty in terror, terror in inquisition.
I have lost my passion: why should I need to keep it

Since what is kept must be adulterated?
I have lost my sight, smell, hearing, taste and touch:
How should I use it for your closer contact?

These with a thousand small deliberations   60
Protract the profit of their chilled delirium,
Excite the membrane, when the sense has cooled,
With pungent sauces, multiply variety
In a wilderness of mirrors. What will the spider do,
Suspend its operations, will the weevil
Delay? De Bailhache, Fresca, Mrs. Cammel, whirled
Beyond the circuit of the shuddering Bear
In fractured atoms. Gull against the wind, in the windy
     straits
Of Belle Isle, or running on the Horn,
White feathers in the snow, the Gulf claims,   70
And an old man driven by the Trades
To a sleepy corner.
                    Tenants of the house,
Thoughts of a dry brain in a dry season.

                                        1920

The Waste Land *

*"Nam Sibyllam quidem Cumis ego ipse oculis meis vidi
in ampulla pendere, et cum illi pueri dicerent: Σίβυλλα τί
θέλεις; respondebat illa: ἀποθανεῖν θέλω."*

["For I once myself, with my own eyes, saw the Cumaean
Sibyl hanging caged in glass jar, and when boys said to
her: 'Sibyl, what do you wish?' she would answer: 'I wish
die.' "]

For Ezra Pound

il miglior fabbro.
[the better craftsman]

* "Not only the title, but the plan and a good deal of the incidental
symbolism of the poem were suggested by Miss Jessie L. Weston's book
on the Grail legend: *From Ritual to Romance* (Cambridge). Indeed, so
deeply am I indebted, Miss Weston's book will elucidate the difficulties
of the poem much better than my notes can do; and I recommend it
(apart from the great interest of the book itself) to any who think such
elucidation of the poem worth the trouble. To another work of anthropology I am indebted in general, one which has influenced our generation
profoundly; I mean *The Golden Bough*; I have used especially the two
volumes *Adonis, Attis, Osiris.* Anyone who is acquainted with these works
will immediately recognize in the poem certain references to vegetation
ceremonies." (Eliot)

I. The Burial of the Dead

April is the cruellest month, breeding
Lilacs out of the dead land, mixing
Memory and desire, stirring
Dull roots with spring rain.
Winter kept us warm, covering
Earth in forgetful snow, feeding
A little life with dried tubers.
Summer surprised us, coming over the Starnbergersee
With a shower of rain; we stopped in the colonnade,
And went on in sunlight, into the Hofgarten,   10
And drank coffee, and talked for an hour.
Bin gar keine Russin, stamm' aus Litauen, echt deutsch.
And when we were children, staying at the arch-duke's,
My cousin's, he took me out on a sled,
And I was frightened. He said, Marie,
Marie, hold on tight. And down we went.
In the mountains, there you feel free.
I read, much of the night, and go south in the winter.

      What are the roots that clutch, what branches grow
Out of this stony rubbish? Son of man,   20
You cannot say, or guess, for you know only
A heap of broken images, where the sun beats,
And the dead tree gives no shelter, the cricket no relief,
And the dry stone no sound of water. Only
There is shadow under this red rock
(Come in under the shadow of this red rock),
And I will show you something different from either
Your shadow at morning striding behind you
Or your shadow at evening rising to meet you;
I will show you fear in a handful of dust.   30

> *Frisch weht der Wind*
> *Der Heimat zu,*
> *Mein Irisch Kind,*
> *Wo weilest du?*

[Line 12. "I am no Russian, I come from Lithuania, true German."]
[20. "Cf. Ezekiel II, i." (Eliot)]
[23. "Cf. Ecclesiastes, XII, v." (Eliot)]
[31. "V. Tristan und Isolde, I, verses 5–8" (Eliot). "Fresh blows the wind toward home; my Irish child (i.e., sweetheart) where do you wait?"]

"You gave me hyacinths first a year ago;
"They called me the hyacinth girl."
—Yet when we came back, late, from the Hyacinth garden,
Your arms full, and your hair wet, I could not
Speak, and my eyes failed, I was neither
Living nor dead, and I knew nothing,   40
Looking into the heart of light, the silence.
Oed' und leer das Meer.

   Madame Sosostris, famous clairvoyante,
Had a bad cold, nevertheless
Is known to be the wisest woman in Europe,
With a wicked pack of cards. Here, said she,
Is your card, the drowned Phoenician Sailor,
(Those are pearls that were his eyes. Look!)
Here is Belladonna, the Lady of the Rocks,
The lady of situations.   50
Here is the man with three staves, and here the Wheel
And here is the one-eyed merchant, and this card,
Which is blank, is something he carries on his back,
Which I am forbidden to see. I do not find
The Hanged Man. Fear death by water.
I see crowds of people, walking round in a ring.
Thank you. If you see dear Mrs. Equitone,
Tell her I bring the horoscope myself:
One must be so careful these days.

   Unreal City,   60
Under the brown fog of a winter dawn,
A crowd flowed over London Bridge, so many,

[42. "Id. III, verse 24" (Eliot). "Desolate and empty [is] the sea."
This phrase is sung by a shepherd appointed by the dying Tristan to
watch for the approach of Isolde's ship.]
   [46. "I am not familiar with the exact constitution of the Tarot pack
of cards, from which I have obviously departed to suit my own convenience. The Hanged Man, a member of the traditional pack, fits my purpose in two ways: because he is associated in my mind with the Hanged
God of Frazer, and because I associate him with the hooded figure in
the passage of the disciples to Emmaus in Part V. The Phoenician
Sailor and the Merchant appear later; also the 'crowds of people,' and
Death by Water is executed in Part IV. The Man with Three Staves (an
authentic member of the Tarot pack) I associate, quite arbitrarily, with
the Fisher King himself" (Eliot).]
   [48. Cf. Ariel's song in *The Tempest* (I, 2, 398).]
   [60. "Cf. Baudelaire:
      'Fourmillante cité, cité pleine de rêves,
      'Où le spectre en plein jour raccroche le passant' " (Eliot).
"Swarming city, city filled with dreams, where the ghost in full daylight
accosts the passerby."]

I had not thought death had undone so many.
Sighs, short and infrequent, were exhaled,
And each man fixed his eyes before his feet.
Flowed up the hill and down King William Street,
To where Saint Mary Woolnoth kept the hours
With a dead sound on the final stroke of nine.
There I saw one I knew, and stopped him, crying: "Stetson!
"You who were with me in the ships at Mylae!   70
"That corpse you planted last year in your garden,
"Has it begun to sprout? Will it bloom this year?
"Or has the sudden frost disturbed its bed?
"Oh keep the Dog far hence, that's friend to men,
"Or with his nails he'll dig it up again!
"You! hypocrite lecteur!—mon semblable,—mon frère!"

II. A Game of Chess

The Chair she sat in, like a burnished throne,
Glowed on the marble, where the glass
Held up by standards wrought with fruited vines
From which a golden Cupidon peeped out   80
(Another hid his eyes behind his wing)
Doubled the flames of sevenbranched candelabra
Reflecting light upon the table as
The glitter of her jewels rose to meet it,

[63. "Cf. *Inferno*, III, 55–57:
'si lunga tratta
di gente, ch'io non avrei mai creduto
che morte tanta n'avesse disfatta' " (Eliot). "So long a train of people; I would never have believed that death had undone so many." The passage refers to those in the Vestibule of Hell—those who chose neither good nor evil, but lived only for themselves. They are separated from the positive sinners (Who had at least *done* something) lest the truly wicked be given an occasion for exaltation.]
[64. "Cf. *Inferno*, IV, 25–7:
'Quivi, secondo che per ascoltare,
'non avea pianto, ma' che di sospiri,
'che l'aura eterna facevan tremare.' " (Eliot). "Here there was no complaint to be heard, only sighs, which caused the eternal air to tremble." The passage refers to Limbo, where the virtuous who lived before Christ are consigned to a life without pain, but also without hope or salvation.]
[68. "A phenomenon which I have often noticed." (Eliot)]
[74. "Cf. the Dirge in Webster's *White Devil*" (Eliot). This dirge, sung by a crazed mother whose son is burying the brother he killed, is in V, IV, 97–98 of the play.]
[76. "V. Baudelaire. Preface to *Fleurs du Mal*" (Eliot). "Hypocritical reader!—my double,—my brother!"]
[77. "Cf. *Antony and Cleopatra*, II, ii, 1, 190" (Eliot).]

From satin cases poured in rich profusion;
In vials of ivory and coloured glass
Unstoppered, lurked her strange synthetic perfumes,
Unguent, powdered, or liquid—troubled, confused
And drowned the sense in odours; stirred by the air
That freshened from the window, these ascended   90
In fattening the prolonged candle-flames,
Flung their smoke into the laquearia,
Stirring the pattern on the coffered ceiling.
Huge sea-wood fed with copper
Burned green and orange, framed by the coloured stone,
In which sad light a carvèd dolphin swam.
Above the antique mantel was displayed
As though a window gave upon the sylvan scene
The change of Philomel, by the barbarous king
So rudely forced; yet there the nightingale   100
Filled all the desert with inviolable voice
And still she cried, and still the world pursues,
'Jug Jug' to dirty ears.
And other withered stumps of time
Were told upon the walls; staring forms
Leaned out, leaning, hushing the room enclosed.
Footsteps shuffled on the stair.
Under the firelight, under the brush, her hair
Spread out in fiery points
Glowed into words, then would be savagely still.   110

      "My nerves are bad to-night. Yes, bad. Stay with me.
"Speak to me. Why do you never speak. Speak.
      "What are you thinking of? What thinking? What?
"I never know what you are thinking. Think."

      I think we are in rats' alley
Where the dead men lost their bones.

[92. "Laquearia. V. *Aeneid*, I, 726:
      dependent lychni laquearibus aureis incensi, et noctem flammis
      funalia vincunt" (Eliot). "Blazing lamps hang from the golden
ceiling, and torches rout the night with flame." The context of the passage is the banquet Dido gives for Aeneas; when Aeneas leaves Carthage,
Dido commits suicide.]
      [98. "Sylvan scene. V. Milton, *Paradise Lost*, IV, 140" (Eliot). The
phrase occurs in Milton's description of Eden.]
      [99. "Cf. Ovid, *Metamorphoses*, VI Philomela" (Eliot). King Tereus,
after raping Philomela, cut out her tongue to silence her; subsequently she
turned into a nightingale.]
      [103. "Cf. Part III, l. 204" (Eliot).]
      [115. "Cf. Part III, l. 195" (Eliot).]

    "What is that noise?"

                  The wind under the door.

"What is that noise now? What is the wind doing?"

                  Nothing again nothing.   120

                       "Do

"You know nothing? Do you see nothing? Do you re-
    member

"Nothing?"

    I remember

Those are pearls that were his eyes.

"Are you alive, or not? Is there nothing in your head?"

                               But

O O O O that Shakespeherian Rag—

It's so elegant

So intelligent   130

"What shall I do now? What shall I do?"

"I shall rush out as I am, and walk the street

"With my hair down, so. What shall we do to-morrow?

"What shall we ever do?"

                  The hot water at ten.

And if it rains, a closed car at four.

And we shall play a game of chess,

Pressing lidless eyes and waiting for a knock upon the
    door.

    When Lil's husband got demobbed, I said—

I didn't mince my words, I said to her myself,   140

HURRY UP PLEASE ITS TIME

Now Albert's coming back, make yourself a bit smart.

He'll want to know what you done with that money he
    gave you

To get yourself some teeth. He did, I was there.

You have them all out, Lil, and get a nice set,

[118. "Cf. Webster: 'Is the wind in that door still?'" (Eliot). When the surgeon in John Webster's *The Devil's Law Case* (III, ii) finds the stabbed Duke still breathing, he exclaims, "Is the wind in that doore still?"]

[125. "Cf. Part I, ll. 37, 48" (Eliot).]

[138. "Cf. the game of chess in Middleton's *Women Beware Women*" (Eliot). In Act II, scene ii of Middleton's play, a mother-in-law is distracted by means of a game of chess while her daughter-in-law is being seduced in another room.]

[139. demobbed: demobilized]

[141. The bartender's call announcing closing time has here, and throughout the remainder of the scene, grim spiritual implications.]

He said, I swear, I can't bear to look at you.
And no more can't I, I said, and think of poor Albert,
He's been in the army four years, he wants a good time,
And if you don't give it him, there's others will, I said.
Oh is there, she said. Something o' that, I said.   150
Then I'll know who to thank, she said, and give me a
    straight look.
HURRY UP PLEASE ITS TIME
If you don't like it you can get on with it, I said.
Others can pick and choose if you can't.
But if Albert makes off, it won't be for lack of telling.
You ought to be ashamed, I said, to look so antique.
(And her only thirty-one.)
I can't help it, she said, pulling a long face,
It's them pills I took, to bring it off, she said.
(She's had five already, and nearly died of young George.)
                                                             160
The chemist said it would be all right, but I've never been
    the same.
You *are* a proper fool, I said.
Well, if Albert won't leave you alone, there it is, I said,
What you get married for if you don't want children?
HURRY UP PLEASE ITS TIME
Well, that Sunday Albert was home, they had a hot gam-
    mon,
And they asked me in to dinner, to get the beauty of it
    hot—
HURRY UP PLEASE ITS TIME
HURRY UP PLEASE ITS TIME
Goonight Bill. Goonight Lou. Goonight May. Goonight.
                                                             170
Ta ta. Goonight, Goonight.
Good night, ladies, good night, sweet ladies, good night,
    good night.

III. The Fire Sermon

The river's tent is broken: the last fingers of leaf
Clutch and sink into the wet bank. The wind

[172. Cf. *Hamlet,* IV, v, Ophelia's mad scene.]
[III. Eliot explains the title in his note to l. 308.]

Crosses the brown land, unheard. The nymphs are departed.
Sweet Thames, run softly, till I end my song.
The river bears no empty bottles, sandwich papers,
Silk handkerchiefs, cardboard boxes, cigarette ends
Or other testimony of summer nights. The nymphs are departed.
And their friends, the loitering heirs of city directors— 180
Departed, have left no addresses.
By the waters of Leman I sat down and wept . . .
Sweet Thames, run softly till I end my song,
Sweet Thames, run softly, for I speak not loud or long.
But at my back in a cold blast I hear
The rattle of the bones, and chuckle spread from ear to ear.
A rat crept softly through the vegetation
Dragging its slimy belly on the bank
While I was fishing in the dull canal
On a winter evening round behind the gashouse 190
Musing upon the king my brother's wreck
And on the king my father's death before him.
White bodies naked on the low damp ground
And bones cast in a little low dry garret,
Rattled by the rat's foot only, year to year.
But at my back from time to time I hear
The sound of horns and motors, which shall bring
Sweeney to Mrs. Porter in the spring.
O the moon shone bright on Mrs. Porter
And on her daughter 200
They wash their feet in soda water

[176. "V. Spenser, *Prothalamion*" (Eliot). The line is the refrain from Spenser's pastoral poem (1596).]
[182. Cf. Psalms 137:1. Lac Leman is the French name for Lake Geneva.]
[192. "Cf. *The Tempest*, I, ii" (Eliot).]
[196. "Cf. Marvell, *To His Coy Mistress*" (Eliot). The pertinent lines in Marvell's poem read, "But at my back I always hear/Time's wingèd chariot hurrying near."]
[197. "Cf. [John] Day, *Parliament of Bees* [c. 1641]:
" 'When of the sudden, listening, you shall hear,
" 'A noise of horns and hunting, which shall bring
" 'Actaeon to Diana in the spring,
" 'Where all shall see her naked skin . . .' " (Eliot).]
[198. Sweeney is the type of the modern sensual man in Eliot's poems. See, for example, "Sweeney Among the Nightingales."]
[199. "I do not know the origin of the ballad from which these lines are taken: it was reported to me from Sydney, Australia" (Eliot). Mrs. Porter is a brothel-keeper in the version of the ballad alluded to by Eliot.]

Et O ces voix d'enfants, chantant dans la coupole!

Twit twit twit
Jug jug jug jug jug jug
So rudely forc'd.
Tereu

Unreal City
Under the brown fog of a winter noon
Mr. Eugenides, the Smyrna merchant
Unshaven, with a pocket full of currants   210
C.i.f. London: documents at sight,
Asked me in demotic French
To luncheon at the Cannon Street Hotel
Followed by a weekend at the Metropole.

At the violet hour, when the eyes and back
Turn upward from the desk, when the human engine waits
Like a taxi throbbing waiting,
I Tiresias, though blind, throbbing between two lives,

[202. "V. Verlaine, *Parsifal*" (Eliot). "And O the voices of the children singing in the choir loft!" The Porters' foot-washing is ironically juxtaposed to the washing of Parsifal's feet in preparation for his seeing the Holy Grail, during which ceremony the children sing in the choir loft.]

[210. "The currants were quoted at a price 'carriage and insurance free to London'; and the Bill of Lading, etc., were to be handed to the buyer upon payment of the sight draft" (Eliot).]

[218. "Tiresias, although a mere spectator and not indeed a 'character,' is yet the most important personage in the poem, uniting all the rest. Just as the one-eyed merchant, seller of currants, melts into the Phoenician Sailor, and the latter is not wholly distinct from Ferdinand Prince of Naples, so all the women are one woman, and the two sexes meet in Tiresias. What Tiresias *sees*, in fact, is the substance of the poem. The whole passage from Ovid is of great anthropological interest:

. . . Cum Iunone iocos et maior vestra profecto est
Quam, quae contingit maribus', dixisse, 'voluptas.'
Illa negat; placuit quae sit sententia docti
Quaerere Tiresiae: venus huic erat utraque nota.
Nam duo magnorum viridi coeuntia silva
Corpora serpentum baculi violaverat ictu
Deque viro factus, mirabile, femina septem
Egerat autumnos; octavo rursus eosdem
Vidit et 'est vestrae si tanta potentia plagae,'
Dixit 'ut auctoris sortem in contraria mutet,
Nunc quoque vos feriam!' percussis anguibus isdem
Forma prior rediit genetivaque venit imago.
Arbiter hic igitur sumptus de lite iocosa
Dicta Iovis firmat; gravius Saturnia iusto
Nec pro materia fertur doluisse suique
Iudicis aeterna damnavit lumina nocte,
At pater omnipotens (neque enim licet inrita cuiquam
Facta dei fecisse deo) pro lumine adempto
Scire futura dedit poenamque levavit honore' " (Eliot), "Jupiter,
gay with nectar, put aside his weighty responsibilities and joked with

Old man with wrinkled female breasts, can see
At the violet hour, the evening hour that strives   220
Homeward, and brings the sailor home from sea,
The typist home at teatime, clears her breakfast, lights
Her stove, and lays out food in tins.
Out of the window perilously spread
Her drying combinations touched by the sun's last rays,
On the divan are piled (at night her bed)
Stockings, slippers, camisoles, and stays.
I Tiresias, old man with wrinkled dugs
Perceived the scene, and foretold the rest—
I too awaited the expected guest.   230
He, the young man carbuncular, arrives,
A small house agent's clerk, with one bold stare,
One of the low on whom assurance sits
As a silk hat on a Bradford millionaire.
The time is now propitious, as he guesses,
The meal is ended, she is bored and tired,
Endeavours to engage her in caresses
Which still are unreproved, if undesired.
Flushed and decided, he assaults at once;
Exploring hands encounter no defence;   240
His vanity requires no response,
And makes a welcome of indifference.
(And I Tiresias have foresuffered all
Enacted on this same divan or bed;
I who have sat by Thebes below the wall
And walked among the lowest of the dead.)
Bestows one final patronising kiss,
And gropes his way, finding the stairs unlit . . .

Juno in her idle moments, saying, 'Decidedly your sex has greater pleasure in love than we men.' She denied it. They thereupon agreed to ask the opinion of Tiresias, who had experienced the pleasures of both sexes. For he had, with a blow of his staff, once separated the bodies of two enormous serpents who were coupling in a green wood. Immediately (incredible as it may seem) he was transformed into a woman and remained in such form for seven autumns. In the eighth, he again saw the same serpents, and said: 'If the stroke I gave you is so powerful as to change the giver's sex, I shall now strike you again.' Having struck the snakes again, he returned to his former sex and shape. Chosen to be the umpire of this sportive argument, he confirmed the opinion of Jupiter; but the daughter of Saturn thereupon fell into such a fit of pique so out of proportion to its cause that she condemned the umpire to an eternity of darkness. But the omnipotent father (since no god may negate the acts of another god) gave him knowledge of the future as compensation for his blindness, thus lightening his suffering with this honor." *Metamorphoses,* III, 320–38.]

[221. "This may not appear as exact as Sappho's lines, but I had in mind the 'longshore' or 'dory' fisherman, who returns at nightfall" (Eliot).]

She turns and looks a moment in the glass,
Hardly aware of her departed lover;   250
Her brain allows one half-formed thought to pass:
"Well now that's done: and I'm glad it's over."
When lovely woman stoops to folly and
Paces about her room again, alone,
She smoothes her hair with automatic hand,
And puts a record on the gramophone.

"This music crept by me upon the waters"
And along the Strand, up Queen Victoria Street.
O City city, I can sometimes hear
Beside a public bar in Lower Thames Street,   260
The pleasant whining of a mandoline
And a clatter and a chatter from within
Where fishmen lounge at noon: where the walls
Of Magnus Martyr hold
Inexplicable splendour of Ionian white and gold.

      The river sweats
      Oil and tar
      The barges drift
      With the turning tide
      Red sails   270
      Wide
      To leeward, swing on the heavy spar.
      The barges wash
      Drifting logs
      Down Greenwich reach
      Past the Isle of Dogs.
            Weialala leia
            Wallala leialala

[253. "V. Goldsmith, the song in *The Vicar of Wakefield*" (Eliot).
The lines alluded to appear in Chapter XXIV of the novel (1776).
"When lovely woman stoops to folly,/And finds too late that men betray,/
What charm can soothe her melancholy?/What art can wash her guilt
away?/The only art her guilt to cover,/To hide her shame from every
eye,/To give repentance to her lover,/And wring his bosom—is to die."]
[257. "V. *The Tempest*, as above [ll. 48, 192]" (Eliot).]
[264. "The interior of St. Magnus Martyr is to my mind one of the
finest among Wren's interiors. See *The Proposed Demolition of Nineteen
City Churches* (P. S. King & Son, Ltd.)" (Eliot).]
[266. "The Song of the (three) Thames-daughters begins here. From
line 292 to 306 inclusive they speak in turn. V. *Götterdämmerung*, III, i:
the Rhinedaughters" (Eliot). In Wagner's opera the Rhinedaughters lament
the lost beauty of their river ever since the gold of the Nibelungs was
stolen from them.]

Elizabeth and Leicester
Beating oars   280
The stern was formed
A gilded shell
Red and gold
The brisk swell
Rippled both shores
Southwest wind
Carried down stream
The peal of bells
White towers
             Weialala leia   290
             Wallala leialala

"Trams and dusty trees.
Highbury bore me. Richmond and Kew
Undid me. By Richmond I raised my knees
Supine on the floor of a narrow canoe."

    "My feet are at Moorgate, and my heart
    Under my feet. After the event
    He wept. He promised 'a new start.'
    I made no comment. What should I resent?"

    "On Margate Sands.   300
    I can connect
    Nothing with nothing.
    The broken fingernails of dirty hands.
    My people humble people who expect
    Nothing."
               la la

[279. "V. Froude, *Elizabeth,* Vol. I, ch. iv, letter of De Quadra to Philip of Spain:

'In the afternoon we were in a barge, watching the games on the river. (The queen) was alone with Lord Robert and myself on the poop, when they began to talk nonsense, and went so far that Lord Robert at last said, as I was on the spot there was no reason why they should not be married if the queen pleased' " (Eliot).]
[293. "Cf. *Purgatorio,* V, 133:

    'Ricorditi di me, che son la Pia;
    'Siena mi fe', disfecemi Maremma' " (Eliot). "Remember me, who am La Pia; Sienna made me, Maremma unmade me." In Purgatory, Dante meets Pia de' Tolomei among those who died by violence before complete repentance. Pia was murdered by her husband in his castle in Maremma—in contrast to the Highbury girl's "undoing" in the pleasure resorts of Richmond and Kew.]

To Carthage then I came
Burning burning burning burning
O Lord Thou pluckest me out
O Lord Thou pluckest   310

burning

IV. Death by Water

Phlebas the Phoenician, a fortnight dead,
Forgot the cry of gulls, and the deep sea swell
And the profit and loss.
                    A current under sea
Picked his bones in whispers. As he rose and fell
He passed the stages of his age and youth
Entering the whirlpool.
                    Gentile or Jew
O you who turn the wheel and look to windward,   320
Consider Phlebas, who was once handsome and tall as you.

V. What the Thunder Said

After the torchlight red on sweaty faces
After the frosty silence in the gardens
After the agony in stony places
The shouting and the crying
Prison and palace and reverberation
Of thunder of spring over distant mountains
He who was living is now dead
We who were living are now dying
With a little patience   330

[307. "V. St. Augustine's *Confessions:* 'to Carthage then I came, where a cauldron of unholy loves sang all about mine ears' " (Eliot).]

[308. "The complete text of the Buddha's Fire Sermon (which corresponds in importance to the Sermon on the Mount) from which these words are taken, will be found translated in the late Henry Clarke Warren's *Buddhism in Translation* (Harvard Oriental Series). Mr. Warren was one of the great pioneers of Buddhist studies in the Occident" (Eliot).]

[309. "From St. Augustine's *Confessions* again. The collocation of these two representatives of eastern and western asceticism, as the culmination of this part of the poem, is not an accident" (Eliot).]

[V. What the Thunder Said. "In the first part of Part V three themes are employed: the journey to Emmaus [Luke 24], the approach to the Chapel Perilous (see Miss Weston's book) and the present decay of eastern Europe" (Eliot).]

Here is no water but only rock
Rock and no water and the sandy road
The road winding above among the mountains
Which are mountains of rock without water
If there were water we should stop and drink
Amongst the rock one cannot stop or think
Sweat is dry and feet are in the sand
If there were only water amongst the rock
Dead mountain mouth of carious teeth that cannot spit
Here one can neither stand nor lie nor sit   340
There is not even silence in the mountains
But dry sterile thunder without rain
There is not even solitude in the mountains
But red sullen faces sneer and snarl
From doors of mudcracked houses
                              If there were water

And no rock
If there were rock
And also water
And water   350
A spring
A pool among the rock
If there were the sound of water only
Not the cicada
And dry grass singing
But sound of water over a rock
Where the hermit-thrush sings in the pine trees
Drip drop drip drop drop drop drop
But there is no water

Who is the third who walks always beside you?   360
When I count, there are only you and I together
But when I look ahead up the white road
There is always another one walking beside you
Gliding wrapt in a brown mantle, hooded

[357. "This is *Turdus aonalaschkae pallasii*, the hermit-thrush which I have heard in Quebec County. Chapman says (*Handbook of Birds of Eastern North American*) 'it is most at home in secluded woodland and thickety retreats. . . . Its notes are not remarkable for variety or volume, but in purity and sweetness of tone and exquisite modulation they are unequalled.' Its 'water-dripping song' is justly celebrated" (Eliot).]
[360. "The following lines were stimulated by the account of one of the Antarctic expeditions (I forget which, but I think one of Shackleton's): it was related that the party of explorers, at the extremity of their strength, had the constant delusion that there was *one more member* than could actually be counted" (Eliot).]

I do not know whether a man or a woman
—But who is that on the other side of you?

What is that sound high in the air
Murmur of maternal lamentation
Who are those hooded hordes swarming
Over endless plains, stumbling in cracked earth   370
Ringed by the flat horizon only
What is the city over the mountains
Cracks and reforms and bursts in the violet air
Falling towers
Jerusalem Athens Alexandria
Vienna London
Unreal

A woman drew her long black hair out tight
And fiddled whisper music on those strings
And bats with baby faces in the violet light   380
Whistled, and beat their wings
And crawled head downward down a blackened wall
And upside down in air were towers
Tolling reminiscent bells, that kept the hours
And voices singing out of empty cisterns and exhausted
    wells.

In this decayed hole among the mountains
In the faint moonlight, the grass is singing
Over the tumbled graves, about the chapel
There is the empty chapel, only the wind's home.
It has no windows, and the door swings,   390
Dry bones can harm no one.
Only a cock stood on the rooftree
Co co rico co co rico

[367–77. "Cf. Hermann Hesse, *Blick ins Chaos* [1920]: 'Schon ist halb
Europa, schon ist zumindest der halbe Osten Europas auf dem Wege zum
Chaos, fährt betrunken im heiligen Wahn am Abgrund entlang und singt
dazu, singt betrunken und hymnisch wie Dmitri Karamasoff sang. Ueber
diese Lieder lacht der Bürger beleidigt, der Heilige und Seher hört sie
mit Tränen' " (Eliot). "Already half of Europe, or at least half of Eastern
Europe, is on the road to chaos, moving drunkenly along with a kind
of holy folly into the abyss and singing drunken hymns as Dmitri Karamazov (in Dostoevsky's *The Brothers Karamazov*) did. The burgher
laughs scornfully at these songs, while the saint and seer hear them with
tears."]
[388. The chapel is the Chapel Perilous (cf. *From Ritual to Romance*),
where the seeking knight endures supernatural ordeals in preparation
for seeing the Grail.]

In a flash of lightning. Then a damp gust
Bringing rain

Ganga was sunken, and the limp leaves
Waited for rain, while the black clouds
Gathered far distant, over Himavant.
The jungle crouched, humped in silence.
Then spoke the thunder   400
DA
Datta: what have we given?
My friend, blood shaking my heart
The awful daring of a moment's surrender
Which an age of prudence can never retract
By this, and this only, we have existed
Which is not to be found in our obituaries
Or in memories draped by the beneficent spider
Or under seals broken by the lean solicitor
In our empty rooms   410
DA
Dayadhvam: I have heard the key
Turn in the door once and turn once only
We think of the key, each in his prison
Thinking of the key, each confirms a prison
Only at nightfall, aethereal rumours
Revive for a moment a broken Coriolanus
DA
Damyata: The boat responded

[396. Ganga is the Ganges, a river sacred to Hindus.]
[398. Himavant is the Himalaya Mountains.]
[402. " 'Datta, dayadhvam, damyata' (Give, sympathize, control). The
fable of the meaning of the Thunder is found in the Brihadaranyaka—
Upanishad, 5, 1. A translation is found in Deussen's Sechzig Upanishads
des Veda, p. 489" (Eliot).]
[408. "Cf. Webster, The White Devil, V, vi:
                            '. . . they'll remarry
    Ere the worm pierce your winding-sheet, ere the spider
    Make a thin curtain for your epitaphs' " (Eliot).]
[412. "Cf. Inferno, XXXIII, 46:
    'ed io sentii chiavar l'uscio di sotto
    all'orribile torre' " (Eliot). "And I heard the door of the hor-
rible tower being locked up below." This was said to Dante by Count
Ugolino, who, being condemned to starve to death, ate the flesh of his
sons and grandsons after they had died of starvation in his cell.
    "Also F. H. Bradley, Appearance and Reality, p. 346. "My external sen-
sations are no less private to myself than are my thoughts or my feelings.
In either case my experience falls within my own circle, a circle closed on
the outside; and, with all its elements alike, every sphere is opaque to
the others which surround it. . . . In brief, regarded as an existence
which appears in a soul, the whole world for each is peculiar and private
to that soul' " (Eliot).]

Gaily, to the hand expert with sail and oar   420
The sea was calm, your heart would have responded
Gaily, when invited, beating obedient
To controlling hands

                     I sat upon the shore
Fishing, with the arid plain behind me
Shall I at least set my lands in order?
London Bridge is falling down falling down falling down
Poi s'ascose nel foco che gli affina
Quando fiam uti chelidon—O swallow swallow
Le Prince d'Aquitaine à la tour abolie   430
These fragments I have shored against my ruins
Why then Ile fit you. Hieronymo's mad againe.
Datta. Dayadhvam. Damyata.
        Shantih shantih shantih

                                 1922

[425. "V. Weston: *From Ritual to Romance;* chapter on the Fisher
King" (Eliot).]
    [428. "V. *Purgatorio,* XXVI, 148:

     ' "Ara vos prec, per aquella valor
     "que vos guida al som de l'escalina,
     "sovegna vos a temps de ma dolor."

        Poi s'ascose nel foco che gli affina" ' " (Eliot). " 'I now pray
you by that Power which guides you to the top of this stairway, remember my sufferings in due season.' He then hid himself in the fire which
refines them." This is said to Dante by the Provençal poet, Arnaut
Daniel, consigned to the seventh ledge of Purgatory, where the lusts of
the flesh are purified by fire.]
    [429. "V. *Pervigilium Veneris.* Cf. Philomela in Parts II and III"
(Eliot). "When shall I be like the swallow"; the *Pervigilium Veneris* is a
second-century Latin poetic celebration of the natural world on the festival
of Venus.]
    [430. "V. Gerard de Nerval, Sonnet *El Desdichado*" (Eliot). "The
Prince of Aquitaine at the ruined tower."]
    [432. "V. Kyd's *Spanish Tragedy* [1594]" (Eliot). The first sentence
occurs in IV, i, 67, and means "I'll accommodate you." (Hieronymo, at
the King's request, writes an entertainment for the court, by which
mechanism he kills his son's murderers.) The second sentence is the sub-
title of the play.]
    [434. "Shantih. Repeated as here, a formal ending to an Upanishad,
'The Peace which passeth understanding' is our equivalent to this word"
(Eliot). Cf. Philippians, 4:7.]

Animula

'Issues from the hand of God, the simple soul'
To a flat world of changing lights and noise,
To light, dark, dry or damp, chilly or warm;
Moving between the legs of tables and of chairs,
Rising or falling, grasping at kisses and toys,

Advancing boldly, sudden to take alarm,
Retreating to the corner of arm and knee,
Eager to be reassured, taking pleasure
In the fragrant brilliance of the Christmas tree,
Pleasure in the wind, the sunlight and the sea;   10
Studies the sunlit pattern on the floor
And running stags around a silver tray;
Confounds the actual and the fanciful,
Content with playing-cards and kings and queens,
What the fairies do and what the servants say.
The heavy burden of the growing soul
Perplexes and offends more, day by day;
Week by week, offends and perplexes more
With the imperatives of 'is and seems'
And may and may not, desire and control.   20
The pain of living and the drug of dreams
Curl up the small soul in the window seat
Behind the *Encyclopaedia Britannica*.
Issues from the hand of time the simple soul
Irresolute and selfish, misshapen, lame,
Unable to fare forward or retreat,
Fearing the warm reality, the offered good,
Denying the importunity of the blood,
Shadow of its own shadows, spectre in its own gloom,
Leaving disordered papers in a dusty room;   30
Living first in the silence after the viaticum.

    Pray for Guiterriez, avid of speed and power,
For Boudin, blown to pieces,
For this one who made a great fortune,
And that one who went his own way.
Pray for Floret, by the boarhound slain between the yew
      trees,
Pray for us now and at the hour of our birth.

                                        1929

FROM

Four Quartets

Burnt Norton

τοῦ λόγου δ'ἐόντος ξυνοῦ ζώουσιν οἱ πολλοὶ ὡς ἰδίαν ἔχοντες
φρόνησιν.
[Although reason is a common possession, most men go
on thinking that they have understanding peculiarly their
own.]

I. p. 77. Fr. 2.

ὁδὸς ἄνω κάτω μία καὶ ὡυτή.
[The voyage up and the voyage down are the same.]

I. p. 89. Fr. 60.

Diels: *Die Fragmente der Vorsokratiker* (Herakleitos).

I

Time present and time past
Are both perhaps present in time future,
And time future contained in time past.
If all time is eternally present
All time is unredeemable.
What might have been is an abstraction
Remaining a perpetual possibility
Only in a world of speculation.
What might have been and what has been
Point to one end, which is always present.   10
Footfalls echo in the memory
Down the passage which we did not take
Towards the door we never opened
Into the rose-garden. My words echo
Thus, in your mind.
                    But to what purpose
Disturbing the dust on a bowl of rose-leaves
I do not know.
              Other echoes
Inhabit the garden. Shall we follow?
Quick, said the bird, find them, find them,
Round the corner. Through the first gate,   20
Into our first world, shall we follow
The deception of the thrush? Into our first world.
There they were, dignified, invisible,

Moving without pressure, over the dead leaves,
In the autumn heat, through the vibrant air,
And the bird called, in response to
The unheard music hidden in the shrubbery,
And the unseen eyebeam crossed, for the roses
Had the look of flowers that are looked at.
There they were as our guests, accepted and accepting.   30
So we moved, and they, in a formal pattern,
Along the empty alley, into the box circle,
To look down into the drained pool.
Dry the pool, dry concrete, brown edged,
And the pool was filled with water out of sunlight,
And the lotos rose, quietly, quietly,
The surface glittered out of heart of light,
And they were behind us, reflected in the pool.
Then a cloud passed, and the pool was empty.
Go, said the bird, for the leaves were full of children,   40
Hidden excitedly, containing laughter.
Go, go, go, said the bird: human kind
Cannot bear very much reality.
Time past and time future
What might have been and what has been
Point to one end, which is always present.

II

Garlic and sapphires in the mud
Clot the bedded axle-tree.
The trilling wire in the blood
Sings below inveterate scars   50
And reconciles forgotten wars.
The dance along the artery
The circulation of the lymph
Are figured in the drift of stars
Ascend to summer in the tree
We move above the moving tree
In light upon the figured leaf
And hear upon the sodden floor
Below, the boarhound and the boar
Pursue their pattern as before   60
But reconciled among the stars.

      At the still point of the turning world. Neither flesh nor
      fleshless;

Neither from nor towards; at the still point, there the
    dance is,
But neither arrest nor movement. And do not call it fixity,
Where past and future are gathered. Neither movement
    from nor towards,
Neither ascent nor decline. Except for the point, the still
    point,
There would be no dance, and there is only the dance.
I can only say, *there* we have been: but I cannot say where.
And I cannot say, how long, for that is to place it in time.

    The inner freedom from the practical desire,   70
The release from action and suffering, release from the
    inner
And the outer compulsion, yet surrounded
By a grace of sense, a white light still and moving,
Erhebung without motion, concentration
Without elimination, both a new world
And the old made explicit, understood
In the completion of its partial ecstasy,
The resolution of its partial horror.
Yet the enchainment of past and future
Woven in the weakness of the changing body,   80
Protects mankind from heaven and damnation
Which flesh cannot endure.
                      Time past and time future
Allow but a little consciousness.
To be conscious is not to be in time
But only in time can the moment in the rose-garden,
The moment in the arbour where the rain beat,
The moment in the draughty church at smokefall
Be remembered; involved with past and future.
Only through time time is conquered.

III

Here is a place of disaffection   90
Time before and time after
In a dim light: neither daylight
Investing form with lucid stillness
Turning shadow into transient beauty
With slow rotation suggesting permanence
Nor darkness to purify the soul
Emptying the sensual with deprivation

Cleansing affection from the temporal.
Neither plenitude nor vacancy. Only a flicker
Over the strained time-ridden faces   100
Distracted from distraction by distraction
Filled with fancies and empty of meaning
Tumid apathy with no concentration
Men and bits of paper, whirled by the cold wind
That blows before and after time,
Wind in and out of unwholesome lungs
Time before and time after.
Eructation of unhealthy souls
Into the faded air, the torpid
Driven on the wind that sweeps the gloomy hills of Lon-
     don,   110
Hampstead and Clerkenwell, Campden and Putney,
Highgate, Primrose and Ludgate. Not here
Not here the darkness, in this twittering world.

     Descend lower, descend only
Into the world of perpetual solitude,
World not world, but that which is not world,
Internal darkness, deprivation
And destitution of all property,
Desiccation of the world of sense,
Evacuation of the world of fancy,   120
Inoperancy of the world of spirit;
This is the one way, and the other
Is the same, not in movement
But abstention from movement; while the world moves
In appetency, on its metalled ways
Of time past and time future.

                              IV
Time and the bell have buried the day,
The black cloud carries the sun away.
Will the sunflower turn to us, will the clematis
Stray down, bend to us; tendril and spray   130
Clutch and cling?
Chill
Fingers of yew be curled
Down on us? After the kingfisher's wing
Has answered light to light, and is silent, the light is still
At the still point of the turning world.

V

Words move, music moves
Only in time; but that which is only living
Can only die. Words, after speech, reach
Into the silence. Only by the form, the pattern,   140
Can words or music reach
The stillness, as a Chinese jar still
Moves perpetually in its stillness.
Not the stillness of the violin, while the note lasts,
Not that only, but the co-existence,
Or say that the end precedes the beginning,
And the end and the beginning were always there
Before the beginning and after the end.
And all is always now. Words strain,
Crack and sometimes break, under the burden,   150
Under the tension, slip, slide, perish,
Decay with imprecision, will not stay in place,
Will not stay still. Shrieking voices
Scolding, mocking, or merely chattering,
Always assail them. The Word in the desert
Is most attacked by voices of temptation,
The crying shadow in the funeral dance,
The loud lament of the disconsolate chimera.

    The detail of the pattern is movement,
As in the figure of the ten stairs.   160
Desire itself is movement
Not in itself desirable;
Love is itself unmoving,
Only the cause and end of movement,
Timeless, and undesiring
Except in the aspect of time
Caught in the form of limitation
Between un-being and being.
Sudden in a shaft of sunlight
Even while the dust moves   170
There rises the hidden laughter
Of children in the foliage
Quick now, here, now, always—
Ridiculous the waste sad time
Stretching before and after.   w. 1934
                                                   p. 1936

Tradition and the Individual Talent

I

In English writing we seldom speak of tradition, though we occasionally apply its name in deploring its absence. We cannot refer to 'the tradition' or to 'a tradition'; at most, we employ the adjective in saying that the poetry of So-and-son is 'traditional' or even 'too traditional.' Seldom, perhaps, does the word appear except in a phrase of censure. If otherwise, it is vaguely approbative, with the implication, as to the work approved, of some pleasing archæological reconstruction. You can hardly make the word agreeable to English ears without this comfortable reference to the reassuring science of archæology.

Certainly the word is not likely to appear in our appreciations of living or dead writers. Every nation, every race, has not only its own creative, but its own critical turn of mind; and is even more oblivious of the shortcomings and limitations of its critical habits than of those of its creative genius. We know, or think we know, from the enormous mass of critical writing that has appeared in the French language, the critical method or habit of the French; we only conclude (we are such unconscious people) that the French are 'more critical' than we, and sometimes even plume ourselves a little with the fact, as if the French were the less spontaneous. Perhaps they are; but we might remind ourselves that criticism is as inevitable as breathing, and that we should be none the worse for articulating what passes in our minds when we read a book and feel an emotion about it, for criticizing our own minds in their work of criticism. One of the facts that might come to light in this process is our tendency to insist, when we praise a poet, upon those aspects of his work in which he least resembles anyone else. In these aspects or parts of his work we pretend to find what is individual, what is the peculiar essence of the man. We dwell with satisfaction upon the poet's difference from his predecessors, especially his immediate predecessors; we endeavour to find something that can be isolated in order to be enjoyed. Whereas if we approach a poet without this prejudice we shall often find that not only the best, but the most individual parts of his work

may be those in which the dead poets, his ancestors, assert their immortality most vigorously. And I do not
mean the impressionable period of adolescence, but the
period of full maturity.

Yet if the only form of tradition, of handing down, consisted in following the ways of the immediate generation
before us in a blind or timid adherence to its suc-
cesses, 'tradition' should positively be discouraged. We have
seen many such simple currents soon lost in the sand; and
novelty is better than repetition. Tradition is a matter of
much wider significance. It cannot be inherited, and if you
want it you must obtain it by great labour. It involves, in
the first place, the historical sense, which we may call
nearly indispensable to anyone who would continue to be a
poet beyond his twenty-fifth year; and the historical sense
involves a perception, not only of the pastness of the past,
but of its presence; the historical sense compels a man to
write not merely with his own generation in his bones, but
with a feeling that the whole of the literature of Europe
from Homer and within it the whole of the literature of his
own country has a simultaneous existence and composes a
simultaneous order. This historical sense, which is a sense
of the timeless as well as of the temporal and of the timeless and of the temporal together, is what makes a writer
traditional. And it is at the same time what makes a writer
most acutely conscious of his place in time, of his own
contemporaneity.

No poet, no artist of any art, has his complete meaning
alone. His significance, his appreciation is the appreciation
of his relation to the dead poets and artists. You cannot
value him alone; you must set him, for contrast and comparison, among the dead. I mean this as a principle of
æsthetic, not merely historical, criticism. The necessity
that he shall conform, that he shall cohere, is not onesided;
what happens when a new work of art is created is something that happens simultaneously to all the works of art
which preceded it. The existing monuments form an ideal
order among themselves, which is modified by the introduction of the new (the really new) work of art among
them. The existing order is complete before the new work
arrives; for order to persist after the supervention of novelty, the *whole* existing order must be, if ever so slightly, altered; and so the relations, proportions, values of each

work of art toward the whole are readjusted; and this is conformity between the old and the new. Whoever has approved this idea of order, of the form of European, of English literature will not find it preposterous that the past should be altered by the present as much as the present is directed by the past. And the poet who is aware of this will be aware of great difficulties and responsibilities.

In a peculiar sense he will be aware also that he must inevitably be judged by the standards of the past. I say judged, not amputated, by them; not judged to be as good as, or worse or better than, the dead; and certainly not judged by the canons of dead critics. It is a judgment, a comparison, in which two things are measured by each other. To conform merely would be for the new work not really to conform at all; it would be not new, and would therefore not be a work of art. And we do not quite say that the new is more valuable because it fits in; but its fitting in is a test of its value—a test, it is true, which can only be slowly and cautiously applied, for we are none of us infallible judges of conformity. We say: it appears to conform, and is perhaps individual, or it appears individual, and may conform; but we are hardly likely to find that it is one and not the other.

To proceed to a more intelligible exposition of the relation of the poet to the past: he can neither take the past as a lump, an indiscriminate bolus, nor can he form himself wholly on one or two private admirations, nor can he form himself wholly upon one preferred period. The first course is inadmissible, the second is an important experience of youth, and the third is a pleasant and highly desirable supplement. The poet must be very conscious of the main current, which does not at all flow invariably through the most distinguished reputations. He must be quite aware of the obvious fact that art never improves, but that the material of art is never quite the same. He must be aware that the mind of Europe—the mind of his own country—a mind which he learns in time to be much more important than his own private mind—is a mind which changes, and that this change is a development which abandons nothing *en route,* which does not superannuate either Shakespeare, or Homer, or the rock drawing of the Magdalenian draughtsmen. That this development, refinement perhaps, complication certainly, is not, from the point of view of the artist, any improvement. Perhaps not even an improvement from the point of view of the psychologist or not to the extent which we imagine; perhaps only in the end based upon a complication in economics and machinery. But the difference between the present and the past is that the conscious present is an awareness of the past in a way and to an extent which the past's awareness of itself cannot show.

Someone said: 'The dead writers are remote from us because we *know* so much more than they did.' Precisely, and they are that which we know.

I am alive to a usual objection to what is clearly part of my programme for the *métier* [craft] of poetry. The objection is that the doctrine requires a ridiculous amount of erudition (pedantry), a claim which can be rejected by appeal to the lives of poets in any pantheon. It will even be affirmed that much learning deadens or perverts poetic sensibility. While, however, we persist in believing that a poet ought to know as much as will not encroach upon his necessary receptivity and necessary laziness, it is not desirable to confine knowledge to whatever can be put into a useful shape for examinations, drawing-rooms, or the still more pretentious modes of publicity. Some can absorb knowledge, the more tardy must sweat for it. Shakespeare acquired more essential history from Plutarch than most men could from the whole British Museum. What is to be insisted upon is that the poet must develop or procure the consciousness of the past and that he should continue to develop this consciousness throughout his career.

What happens is a continual surrender of himself as he is at the moment to something which is more valuable. The progress of an artist is a continual self-sacrifice, a continual extension of personality.

There remains to define this process of depersonalization and its relation to the sense of tradition. It is in this depersonalization that art may be said to approach the condition of science. I therefore invite you to consider, as a suggestive analogy, the action which takes place when a bit of finely filiated platinum is introduced into a chamber containing oxygen and sulphur dioxide.

II .

Honest criticism and sensitive appreciation is directed not upon the poet but upon the poetry. If we attend to the confused cries of the newspaper critics and the *susurrus* [murmuring] of popular repetition that follows, we shall hear the names of poets in great numbers; if we seek not Blue-book knowledge but the enjoyment of poetry, and ask for a poem, we shall seldom find it. I have tried to point out the importance of the relation of the poem to other poems by other authors, and suggested the conception of poetry as a living whole of all the poetry that has ever been written. The other aspect of this Impersonal theory of poetry is the relation of the poem to its author. And I hinted, by an analogy, that the mind of the mature poet differs from that of the immature one not precisely in any valuation of 'personality,' not being necessarily more interesting, or having 'more to say,' but rather by being a more finely perfected medium in which special, or very varied, feelings are at liberty to enter into new combinations.

The analogy was that of the catalyst. When the two gases previously mentioned are mixed in the presence of a filament of platinum, they form sulphurous acid. This combination takes place only if the platinum is present; nevertheless the newly formed acid contains no trace of platinum, and the platinum itself is apparently unaffected: has remained inert, neutral, and unchanged. The mind of the poet is the shred of platinum. It may partly or exclusively operate upon the experience of the man himself; but, the more perfect the artist, the more completely separate in him will be the man who suffers and the mind which creates; the more perfectly will the mind digest and transmute the passions which are its material.

The experience, you will notice, the elements which enter the presence of the transforming catalyst, are of two kinds: emotions and feelings. The effect of a work of art upon the person who enjoys it is an experience different in kind from any experience not of art. It may be formed out of one emotion, or may be a combination of several; and various feelings, inhering for the writer in particular words or phrases or images, may be added to compose the final result. Or great poetry may be made without the direct use of any emotion whatever: composed out of feelings solely. Canto XV of the *Inferno* (Brunetto Latini) is a working up of the emotion evident in the situation; but the effect, though single as that of any work of art, is obtained by considerable complexity of detail. The last quatrain gives an image, a feeling attaching to an image, which 'came,' which did not develop simply out of what precedes, but which was probably in suspension in the poet's mind until the proper combination arrived for it to add itself to. The poet's mind is in fact a receptacle for seizing and storing up numberless feelings, phrases, images, which remain there until all the particles which can unite to form a new compound are present together.

If you compare several representative passages of the greatest poetry you see how great is the variety of types of combination, and also how completely any semi-ethical criterion of 'sublimity' misses the mark. For it is not the 'greatness,' the intensity, of the emotions, the components, but the intensity of the artistic process, the pressure, so to speak, under which the fusion takes place, that counts. The episode of Paolo and Francesca employs a definite emotion, but the intensity of the poetry is something quite different from whatever intensity in the supposed experience it may give the impression of. It is no more intense, furthermore, than Canto XXVI, the voyage of Ulysses, which has not the direct dependence upon an emotion. Great variety is possible in the process of transmutation of emotion: the murder of Agamemnon, or the agony of Othello, gives an artistic effect apparently closer to a possible original than the scenes from Dante. In the *Agamemnon,* the artistic emotion approximates to the emotion of an actual spectator; in *Othello* to the emotion of the protagonist himself. But the difference between art and the event is always absolute; the combination which is the murder of Agamemnon is probably as complex as that which is the voyage of Ulysses. In either case there has been a fusion of elements. The ode of Keats contains a number of feelings which have nothing particular to do with the nightingale, but which the nightingale, partly perhaps because of its attractive name, and partly because of its reputation, served to bring together.

The point of view which I am struggling to attack is perhaps related to the metaphysical theory of the substantial unity of the soul: for my meaning is, that the poet has, not a 'personality' to express, but a particular medium, which is only a medium and not a personality, in which impressions and experiences combine in peculiar and unexpected ways. Impressions and experiences which are important for the man may take no place in the poetry, and those which become important in the poetry may play quite a negligible part in the man, the personality.

I will quote a passage which is unfamiliar enough to be regarded with fresh attention in the light—or darkness—of these observations:

> And now methinks I could e'en chide myself
> For doating on her beauty, though her death
> Shall be revenged after no common action.
> Does the silkworm expend her yellow labours
> For thee? For thee does she undo herself?
> Are lordships sold to maintain ladyships
> For the poor benefit of a bewildering minute?
> Why does yon fellow falsify highways,
> And put his life between the judge's lips,
> To refine such a thing—keeps horse and men
> To beat their valours for her? . . .

In this passage (as is evident if it is taken in its context) there is a combination of positive and negative emotions: an intensely strong attraction toward beauty and an equally intense fascination by the ugliness which is contrasted with it and which destroys it. This balance of contrasted emotion is in the dramatic situation to which the speech is pertinent, but that situation alone is inadequate to it. This is, so to speak, the structural emotion, provided by the drama. But the whole effect, the dominant tone, is due to the fact that a number of floating feelings, having an affinity to this emotion by no means superficially evident, have combined with it to give us a new art emotion.

It is not in his personal emotions, the emotions provoked by particular events in his life, that the poet is in any way remarkable or interesting. His particular emotions may be simple, or crude, or flat. The emotion in his poetry will be a very complex thing, but not with the complexity of the emotions of people who have very complex or unusual emotions in life. One error, in fact, of eccentricity in poetry is to seek for new human emotions to express; and in this search for novelty in the wrong place it discovers the perverse. The business of the poet is not to find new emotions, but to use the ordinary ones and, in working them up into poetry, to express feelings which are not in actual emotions at all. And emotions which he has never experienced will serve his turn as well as those familiar to him. Consequently, we must believe that 'emotion recollected in tranquillity' is an inexact formula. For it is neither emotion, nor recollection, nor, without distortion of meaning, tranquillity. It is a concentration, and a new thing resulting from the concentration, of a very great number of experiences which to the practical and active person would not seem to be experiences at all; it is a concentration which does not happen consciously or of deliberation. These experiences are not 'recollected,' and they finally unite in an atmosphere which is 'tranquil' only in that it is a passive attending upon the event. Of course this is not quite the whole story. There is a great deal, in the writing of poetry, which must be conscious and deliberate. In fact, the bad poet is usually unconscious where he ought to be conscious, and conscious where he ought to be unconscious. Both errors tend to make him 'personal.' Poetry is not a turning loose of emotion, but an escape from emotion; it is not the expression of personality, but an escape from personality. But, of course, only those who have personality and emotions know what it means to want to escape from these things.

III

ὁ δὲ νοῦς ἴσως θειότερόν τι καὶ ἀπαθές ἐστιν [*Possibly the mind is something divine and therefore independent*].

This essay proposes to halt at the frontier of metaphysics or mysticism, and confine itself to such practical conclusions as can be applied by the responsible person interested in poetry. To divert interest from the poet to the poetry is a laudable aim: for it would conduce to a juster estimation of actual poetry, good and bad. There are many people who appreciate the expression of sincere emotion in verse, and there is a smaller number of people who can appreciate technical excellence. But very few know when there is an expression of *significant* emotion, emotion which has its life in the poem and not in the history of the poet. The emotion of art is impersonal. And the poet cannot reach this impersonality without surrendering himself wholly to the work to be done. And he is not likely to know what is to be done unless he lives in what is not merely the present, but the present moment of the past, unless he is conscious, not of what is dead, but of what is already living.

1919

WALLACE STEVENS

(1879–1955)

Wallace Stevens was born in Reading, Pennsylvania, and followed his father's footsteps into the law. After graduation from Harvard, he attended the New York University Law School, and from 1904 to 1916 was a successful lawyer in New York. While he was practicing law, he wrote poems slowly and painstakingly, publishing only occasionally in avant-garde magazines, mostly in Harriet Monroe's *Poetry*. These fugitive pieces attracted to Stevens the attention of a small group of sophisticated readers who, impressed by the meticulousness of his experimentation, watched with interest his attempt to evolve a style that would be the perfect vehicle for his ideas.

In 1916 he moved to Hartford, Connecticut, where he entered the employ of an insurance firm. He continued to produce sparsely, but became known, among the cognoscenti, as "a man to watch." It was not until 1923 that he published his first volume of poems, *Harmonium*. At forty-four, he became known as one of the new "younger" poets. Eight years later Stevens issued an enlarged and revised edition of *Harmonium*. In 1934 he became vice president of the Hartford Accident and Indemnity Company, becoming a productive poet as he became a successful insurance executive—living proof that poetry and "real life" can mix, after all. In the following year he published *Ideas of Order*, followed by *Owl's Clover* in 1936 and *The Man with the Blue Guitar and Other Poems* in 1937. With these volumes Stevens became a leading American poet.

Stevens' poetry occasionally has been called "escapist." That is, it is "difficult" poetry, not given to ready paraphrase, following poetic rather than rational logic, and, like much contemporary poetry, not adapted to the easy understanding that the followers of Whitman wished to emotionalize and sanctify. But this man of business and worldy affairs was not concerned with poetry that escaped the problems of the world. Indeed, he tried to create a poetry of ideas that would illuminate reality rather than run from it. In *The Necessary Angel* (1951), he explained his vision of poetry. For him, poetry was the voice of the imagination; reality was not the object but the imaginative perception of the object in all its relations. The poem, as the voice of imaginative sight, illuminates "things" through subtly ordered and toned ideas so that the marriage of thing and idea, man and circumstance, is made visible. It is not escapism, therefore, but witty ideational abstraction precisely articulated in just the combination of words that show the very process of abstraction, that makes Stevens' poetry difficult. It is innovational poetry, at once Transcendental and classical.

In *Parts of a World* (1942), Stevens offered more poems that sought to use the microcosm as an exposition of the cosmos. Stevens' poetry is generally concerned with man's loss of a sense of the universe, corresponding to man's loss of God. Unlike Eliot, however, Stevens did not attempt to discover God in ritual or supernaturalism or institutionalized Christianity. In fact, in Stevens' poetry there is a naturalistic insistence on the actual world as the sole reality, on man as the creator of God. But in its attempt to create an abiding and unified sense of cosmic purpose through the order of ideas made possible by the poetic logic of the imagination, Stevens' poetry may be called religious. Following the publication of *Notes Toward a Supreme Fiction* (1942), *Esthetique du Mal* (1945), *Transport to Summer* (1947), *Three Academic Pieces* (1947), and *A Primitive like an Orb* (1948), Stevens won the second annual Bollingen Prize in 1949.

Stevens' other books include *The Auroras of Autumn* (1950) and S. F. Morse, ed., *Opus Posthumous* (1957). The standard work, *Collected Poems*, was issued in 1954. His daughter, Holly Stevens, published his *Letters* in 1966.

Studies of the man and his work are to be found in the Wallace Stevens issue of the *Harvard Advocate*, CXXVII (December, 1940); W. V. O'Connor, *The Shaping Spirit: A Study of Wallace Stevens* (1950); S. F. Morse, *Wallace Stevens* (1950); S. F. Morse, *Wallace Stevens: A Preliminary Checklist of His Published Writings, 1898–1954* (1954); *Perspective*, VII (Autumn 1954)—a Wallace Stevens issue; R. Pack, *Wallace Stevens* (1958); F. Kermode, *Wallace Stevens* (1961);

A. Brown and R. S. Haller, eds., *The Achievement of Wallace Stevens* (1962); M. Boroff, ed., *Wallace Stevens: A Collection of Critical Essays* (1963); D. Fuchs, *The Comic Spirit of Wallace Stevens* (1963); T. F. Walsh, *Concordance to the Poetry of Wallace Stevens* (1963); J. Enck, *Wallace Stevens: Images and Judgments* (1964); S. F. Morse, J. R. Bryer, and J. N. Riddel, eds., *Wallace Stevens Checklist and Bibliography of Stevens Criticism* (1964); H. W. Wells, *Introduction to Wallace Stevens* (1964); E. P. Nassar, *Wallace Stevens . . .* (1965); R. H. Pearce and J. H. Miller, eds., *The Act of the Mind: Essays on the Poetry of Wallace Stevens* (1965); J. N. Riddel, *The Clairvoyant Eye: The Poetry and Poetics of Wallace Stevens* (1965); F. Doggett, *Stevens' Poetry of Thought* (1966); and H. J. Stern, *Wallace Stevens* (1966).

The Worms at Heaven's Gate

Out of the tomb, we bring Badroulbadour,
Within our bellies, we her chariot.
Here is an eye. And here are, one by one,
The lashes of that eye and its white lid.
Here is the cheek on which that lid declined,
And, finger after finger, here, the hand,
The genius of that cheek. Here are the lips,
The bundle of the body and the feet.

Out of the tomb we bring Badroulbadour.

1916

A High-Toned Old Christian Woman

Poetry is the supreme fiction, madame.
Take the moral law and make a nave of it
And from the nave build haunted heaven. Thus,
The conscience is converted into palms,
Like windy citherns hankering for hymns.
We agree in principle. That's clear. But take
The opposing law and make a peristyle,
And from the peristyle project a masque
Beyond the planets. Thus, our bawdiness,
Unpurged by epitaph, indulged at last,   10
Is equally converted into palms,
Squiggling like saxophones. And palm for palm,

Madame, we are where we began. Allow,
Therefore, that in the planetary scene
Your disaffected flagellants, well-stuffed,
Smacking their muzzy bellies in parade,
Proud of such novelties of the sublime,
Such tink and tank and tunk-a-tunk-tunk,
May, merely may, madame, whip from themselves
A jovial hullabaloo among the spheres.   20
This will make widows wince. But fictive things
Wink as they will. Wink most when widows wince.

1922

The Emperor of Ice-Cream

Call the roller of big cigars,
The muscular one, and bid him whip
In kitchen cups concupiscent curds.
Let the wenches dawdle in such dress
As they are used to wear, and let the boys
Bring flowers in last month's newspapers.
Let be be finale of seem.
The only emperor is the emperor of ice-cream.

Take from the dresser of deal,
Lacking the three glass knobs, that sheet   10
On which she embroidered fantails once
And spread it so as to cover her face.
If her horny feet protrude, they come
To show how cold she is, and dumb.
Let the lamp affix its beam.
The only emperor is the emperor of ice-cream.

1922

Peter Quince at the Clavier

I

Just as my fingers on these keys
Make music, so the selfsame sounds
On my spirit make a music, too.

Music is feeling, then, not sound;
And thus it is that what I feel,
Here in this room, desiring you,

Thinking of your blue-shadowed silk,
Is music. It is like the strain
Waked in the elders by Susanna.

Of a green evening, clear and warm,   10
She bathed in her still garden, while
The red-eyed elders watching, felt

The basses of their beings throb
In witching chords, and their thin blood
Pulse pizzicati of Hosanna.

II

In the green water, clear and warm,
Susanna lay.
She searched
The touch of springs,
And found   20
Concealed imaginings.
She sighed,
For so much melody.

Upon the bank, she stood
In the cool
Of spent emotions.
She felt, among the leaves,
The dew
Of old devotions.

She walked upon the grass,   30
Still quavering.
The winds were like her maids,
On timid feet,
Fetching her woven scarves,
Yet wavering.

A breath upon her hand
Muted the night.

She turned—
A cymbal crashed,
And roaring horns.   40

III

Soon, with a noise like tambourines,
Came her attendant Byzantines.

They wondered why Susanna cried
Against the elders by her side;

And as they whispered, the refrain
Was like a willow swept by rain.

Anon, their lamps' uplifted flame
Revealed Susanna and her shame.

And then, the simpering Byzantines
Fled, with a noise like tambourines.   50

IV

Beauty is momentary in the mind—
The fitful tracing of a portal;
But in the flesh it is immortal.

The body dies; the body's beauty lives.
So evenings die, in their green going,
A wave, interminably flowing.
So gardens die, their meek breath scenting
The cowl of winter, done repenting.
So maidens die, to the auroral
Celebration of a maiden's choral.   60
Susanna's music touched the bawdy strings
Of those white elders; but, escaping,
Left only Death's ironic scraping.
Now, in its immortality, it plays
On the clear viol of her memory,
And makes a constant sacrament of praise.

                                        1915, 1923

Sunday Morning

I

Complacencies of the peignoir, and late
Coffee and oranges in a sunny chair,
And the green freedom of a cockatoo
Upon a rug mingle to dissipate
The holy hush of ancient sacrifice.
She dreams a little, and she feels the dark
Encroachment of that old catastrophe,
As a calm darkens among water-lights.
The pungent oranges and bright, green wings
Seem things in some procession of the dead,   10
Winding across wide water, without sound.
The day is like wide water, without sound,
Stilled for the passing of her dreaming feet
Over the seas, to silent Palestine,
Dominion of the blood and sepulchre.

II

Why should she give her bounty to the dead?
What is divinity if it can come
Only in silent shadows and in dreams?
Shall she not find in comforts of the sun,
In pungent fruit and bright, green wings, or else   20
In any balm or beauty of the earth,
Things to be cherished like the thought of heaven?
Divinity must live within herself:
Passions of rain, or moods in falling snow;
Grievings in loneliness, or unsubdued
Elations when the forest blooms; gusty
Emotions on wet roads on autumn nights;
All pleasures and all pains, remembering
The bough of summer and the winter branch.
These are the measures destined for her soul.   30

III

Jove in the clouds had his inhuman birth.
No mother suckled him, no sweet land gave
Large-mannered motions to his mythy mind
He moved among us, as a muttering king,
Magnificent, would move among his hinds,
Until our blood, commingling, virginal,

With heaven, brought such requital to desire
The very hinds discerned it, in a star.
Shall our blood fail? Or shall it come to be
The blood of paradise? And shall the earth   40
Seem all of paradise that we shall know?
The sky will be much friendlier then than now,
A part of labor and a part of pain,
And next in glory to enduring love,
Not this dividing and indifferent blue.

IV

She says, "I am content when wakened birds,
Before they fly, test the reality
Of misty fields, by their sweet questionings;
But when the birds are gone, and their warm fields
Return no more, where, then, is paradise?"   50
There is not any haunt of prophecy,
Nor any old chimera of the grave,
Neither the golden underground, nor isle
Melodious, where spirits gat them home,
Nor visionary south, nor cloudy palm
Remote on heaven's hill, that has endured
As April's green endures; or will endure
Like her remembrance of awakened birds,
Or her desire for June and evening, tipped
By the consummation of the swallow's wings.   60

V

She says, "But in contentment I still feel
The need of some imperishable bliss."
Death is the mother of beauty; hence from her,
Alone, shall come fulfilment to our dreams
And our desires. Although she strews the leaves
Of sure obliteration on our paths,
The path sick sorrow took, the many paths
Where triumph rang its brassy phrase, or love
Whispered a little out of tenderness,
She makes the willow shiver in the sun   70
For maidens who were wont to sit and gaze
Upon the grass, relinquished to their feet.
She causes boys to pile new plums and pears
On disregarded plate. The maidens taste
And stray impassioned in the littering leaves.

VI

Is there no change of death in paradise?
Does ripe fruit never fall? Or do the boughs
Hang always heavy in that perfect sky,
Unchanging, yet so like our perishing earth,
With rivers like our own that seek for seas   80
They never find, the same receding shores
That never touch with inarticulate pang?
Why set the pear upon those river-banks
Or spice the shores with odors of the plum?
Alas, that they should wear our colors there,
The silken weavings of our afternoons,
And pick the strings of our insipid lutes!
Death is the mother of beauty, mystical,
Within whose burning bosom we devise
Our earthly mothers waiting, sleeplessly.   90

VII

Supple and turbulent, a ring of men
Shall chant in orgy on a summer morn
Their boisterous devotion to the sun,
Not as a god, but as a god might be,
Naked among them, like a savage source.
Their chant shall be a chant of paradise,
Out of their blood, returning to the sky;
And in their chant shall enter, voice by voice,
The windy lake wherein their lord delights,
The trees, like serafin, and echoing hills,   100
That choir among themselves long afterward.
They shall know well the heavenly fellowship
Of men that perish and of summer morn.
And whence they came and whither they shall go
The dew upon their feet shall manifest.

VIII

She hears, upon that water without sound,
A voice that cries, "The tomb in Palestine
Is not the porch of spirits lingering.
It is the grave of Jesus, where he lay."
We live in an old chaos of the sun,   110
Or old dependency of day and night,
Or island solitude, unsponsored, free,

Of that wide water, inescapable.
Deer walk upon our mountains, and the quail
Whistle about us their spontaneous cries;
Sweet berries ripen in the wilderness;
And, in the isolation of the sky,
At evening, casual flocks of pigeons make
Ambiguous undulations as they sink,
Downward to darkness, on extended wings.   120

                                        1915, 1923

Anecdote of the Jar

I placed a jar in Tennessee,
And round it was, upon a hill.
It made the slovenly wilderness
Surround that hill.

The wilderness rose up to it,
And sprawled around, no longer wild.
The jar was round upon the ground
And tall and of a port in air.

It took dominion everywhere.
The jar was gray and bare.   10
It did not give of bird or bush,
Like nothing else in Tennessee.

                                        1919, 1923

Thirteen Ways of Looking at a Blackbird

I

Among twenty snowy mountains,
The only moving thing
Was the eye of the blackbird.

II

I was of three minds,
Like a tree
In which there are three blackbirds.

III

The blackbird whirled in the autumn winds.
It was a small part of the pantomime.

IV

A man and a woman
Are one.
A man and a woman and a blackbird
Are one.

10

V

I do not know which to prefer,
The beauty of inflections
Or the beauty of innuendoes,
The blackbird whistling
Or just after.

VI

Icicles filled the long window
With barbaric glass.
The shadow of the blackbird
Crossed it, to and fro.
The mood
Traced in the shadow
An indecipherable cause.

20

VII

O thin men of Haddam,
Why do you imagine golden birds?
Do you not see how the blackbird
Walks around the feet
Of the women about you?

VIII

I know noble accents
And lucid, inescapable rhythms;
But I know, too,
That the blackbird is involved
In what I know.

30

IX

When the blackbird flew out of sight,
It marked the edge
Of one of many circles.

X

At the sight of blackbirds
Flying in a green light,
Even the bawds of euphony
Would cry out sharply.

40

XI

He rode over Connecticut
In a glass coach.
Once, a fear pierced him,
In that he mistook
The shadow of his equipage
For blackbirds.

XII

The river is moving.
The blackbird must be flying.

XIII

It was evening all afternoon.
It was snowing
And it was going to snow.
The blackbird sat
In the cedar-limbs.

50

1923

A Postcard from the Volcano

Children picking up our bones
Will never know that these were once
As quick as foxes on the hill;

And that in autumn, when the grapes
Made sharp air sharper by their smell
These had a being, breathing frost;

And least will guess that with our bones
We left much more, left what still is
The look of things, left what we felt

At what we saw. The spring clouds blow   10
Above the shuttered mansion-house,
Beyond our gate and the windy sky

Cries out a literate despair.
We knew for long the mansion's look
And what we said of it became

A part of what it is . . . Children,
Still weaving budded aureoles,
Will speak our speech and never know,

Will say of the mansion that it seems
As if he that lived there left behind   20
A spirit storming in blank walls,

A dirty house in a gutted world,
A tatter of shadows peaked to white,
Smeared with the gold of the opulent sun.

1936

Of Modern Poetry

The poem of the mind in the act of finding
What will suffice. It has not always had
To find: the scene was set; it repeated what
Was in the script.
                    Then the theatre was changed
To something else. Its past was a souvenir.

It has to be living, to learn the speech of the place.
It has to face the men of the time and to meet
The women of the time. It has to think about war
And it has to find what will suffice. It has
To construct a new stage. It has to be on that stage   10
And, like an insatiable actor, slowly and
With meditation speak words that in the ear,
In the delicatest ear of the mind, repeat,
Exactly, that which it wants to hear, at the sound
Of which, an invisible audience listens,
Not to the play, but to itself, expressed
In an emotion as of two people, as of two
Emotions becoming one. The actor is
A metaphysician in the dark, twanging
An instrument, twanging a wiry string that gives   20
Sounds passing through sudden rightnesses, wholly
Containing the mind, below which it cannot descend,
Beyond which it has no will to rise.
                                     It must
Be the finding of a satisfaction, and may
Be of a man skating, a woman dancing, a woman
Combing. The poem of the act of the mind.

                                                        1940

A Rabbit as King of the Ghosts

The difficulty to think at the end of day,
When the shapeless shadow covers the sun
And nothing is left except light on your fur—

There was the cat slopping its milk all day,
Fat cat, red tongue, green mind, white milk
And August the most peaceful month.

To be, in the grass, in the peacefulest time,
Without that monument of cat,
The cat forgotten in the moon;

And to feel that the light is a rabbit-light,   10
In which everything is meant for you
And nothing need be explained;

Then there is nothing to think of. It comes of itself;
And east rushes west and west rushes down,
No matter. The grass is full

And full of yourself. The trees around are for you,
The whole of the wideness of night is for you,
A self that touches all edges,

You become a self that fills the four corners of night.
The red cat hides away in the fur-light   20
And there you are humped high, humped up,

You are humped higher and higher, black as stone—
You sit with your head like a carving in space
And the little green cat is a bug in the grass.

1942

The World as Meditation

[I have spent too much time practising my violin and travelling. But the essential exercise of a composer—meditation—nothing has ever kept me from that. . . . I live in a permanent dream that never ceases, night or day.]

J'ai passé trop de temps à travailler mon violon, à voyager. Mais l'exercice essentiel du compositeur—la méditation—rien ne l'a jamais suspendu en moi. . . . Je vis un rêve permanent, qui ne s'arrête ni nuit ni jour.

GEORGES ENESCO

Is it Ulysses that approaches from the east,
The interminable adventurer? The trees are mended.
That winter is washed away. Someone is moving

On the horizon and lifting himself up above it.
A form of fire approaches the cretonnes of Penelope,
Whose mere savage presence awakens the world in which
she dwells.

She has composed, so long, a self with which to welcome
him,
Companion to his self for her, which she imagined,
Two in a deep-founded sheltering, friend and dear friend.

The trees had been mended, as an essential exercise   10
In an inhuman meditation, larger than her own.
No winds like dogs watched over her at night.

She wanted nothing he could not bring her by coming alone.
She wanted no fetchings. His arms would be her necklace
And her belt, the final fortune of their desire.

But was it Ulysses? Or was it only the warmth of the sun
On her pillow? The thought kept beating in her like her
heart.
The two kept beating together. It was only day.

It was Ulysses and it was not. Yet they had met,
Friend and dear friend and a planet's encouragement.   20
The barbarous strength within her would never fail.

She would talk a little to herself as she combed her hair,
Repeating his name with its patient syllables,
Never forgetting him that kept coming constantly so near.
                                        1952

ROBINSON JEFFERS

(1887–1962)

Many poetic American sensibilities have been subjected to the spectacle of human evil, misery, and stupidity. Some, like Poe, react in horror; others, like Robinson, in agony. But no one has reacted with such nihilistic hatred as has Robinson Jeffers. Misanthropic seems too mild a word to characterize the mind behind the poems.

Jeffers was born in Pittsburgh, Pennsylvania, the son of a learned professor and theologian. Under the father's tutelage, Jeffers could read Greek when he was five years old and several modern languages at fifteen. By that time he was also well acquainted with the homelands of those languages, having traveled widely on the Continent and having been educated in Switzerland and Germany. When he returned to the United States, he enrolled in Occidental College, from which he was graduated at eighteen. He took several years of graduate courses in English and medicine at the University of Southern California, studied further in Zurich, and took courses in law, forestry, and zoology at the University of Washington. The diversity and extent of his education was symptomatic of uncertainty about his career, but by 1911 Jeffers was sure that what he really wanted to do was to write poetry.

In 1912 the legacy of a cousin afforded him a small independent income which allowed him to realize his ambition. In 1914 Jeffers and his bride, deterred from European travel by the war, went instead to Carmel, at the base of California's magnificent Monterey peninsula. Enchanted by the country, the great granite cliffs of Big Sur farther down the coast, the heavy surf, and the wind-tortured trees, Jeffers found the emotional home that suited his temperament and made Carmel his physical residence. He built a stone house himself, together with a tower called "Hawk's Tower," where he wrote his poetry in virtual isolation.

His first two volumes, *Flagons and Apples* (1912) and *Californians* (1916) neither attracted much attention nor gave much indication of what was to come. But in *Tamar and Other Poems* (1924), the long rolling lines, with rhythms like the Big Sur surf, the shocking subject matter, the bleak, black view of man, sensationally announced Jeffers' presence in American literature. His presence was established by the other volumes that appeared by the time the 1920's drew to a close: *Roan Stallion, Tamar, and Other Poems* (1925); *The Women at Point Sur* (1927); *Poems* (1928); *An Artist* (1928); *Cawdor* (1928); and *Dear Judas and Other Poems* (1929).

By the time the decade was over, there was no question about Jeffers' revulsion from human existence and his love for the awesome, great, stark forces of nature typified by the country in which he lived. His poems indicate a hard naturalism in which God is nothing other than physical existence itself, marred only by one scrofulous disease: people. The conditions of physical existence necessitate both pain and beauty. But people are too weak for pain, too insensitive for beauty; the few aspiring souls who attempt to embrace both are, like hurt hawks, doomed to extinction anyway. Time and the incredible, overwhelming physical processes of the cosmos go on, indifferent to the muck of that crawling insect, man. For Jeffers, the universe, epitomized by the Pacific Coast scenery of which he writes, will be clean, silent, and peacefully pure only when man and his blighting civilization are totally annihilated.

Reacting against what he found precious, abstruse, and fantastic in modern poetry, Jeffers utilized his free but beautifully controlled heavy rhythms to write narratives that tell of the incest, terror, horror, solipsism, and meaninglessness of human life and to prophesy its doom. Indeed, Jeffers felt his views were corroborated by World War I, the depression aftermath, World War II, and the atomic bomb; his certitude that human society will wipe itself out has grown. Writing about World War II, for example, he treated Nazism merely as one more instance of what has been and of the worst that is yet to come. Indifferent to whether England or Germany would emerge triumphant, he insisted that the spectacle would be worth watching only if it finally meant the end of man. "If civilization goes down," he said, "that would be an event to contemplate. But," he lamented, "it will not be in our time, alas, my dear, it will not be in our time."

Some of Jeffers' other works include *Apology for Bad Dreams* (1930), *Descent to the Dead* (1931), *Thurso's Landing* (1932), *Give Your Heart to the Hawks* (1933), *Solstice and Other Poems* (1935), *Beaks of Eagles* (1936), *Such Counsels You Gave to Me* (1937), *Two Consolations* (1940), *Be Angry at the Sun* (1941), *Medea* (1946), *The Double Axe and Other Poems* (1948), *Hungerfield and Other Poems* (1954), and *The Beginning and the End and Other Poems* (1963). *The Selected Poetry of Robinson Jeffers* was published in 1938. There is no collected edition of his works.

Studies of the man and his work are to be found in G. Sterling, *Robinson Jeffers* (1926); L. Adamic, *Robinson Jeffers* (1929); S. S. Alberts, *A Bibliography of the Works of Robinson Jeffers* (1933); B. Deutsch, *This Modern Poetry* (1935); M. B. Bennett, *Robinson Jeffers and the Sea* (1936); R. Gilbert, *Shine, Perishing Republic* (1936); W. Van Wyck, *Robinson Jeffers* (1938); E. Greenan, *Of Una Jeffers* (1939); D. Schwartz and F. Taylor, "The Enigma of Robinson Jeffers," *Poetry*, LV (1939); F. I. Carpenter, "The Values of Robinson Jeffers," *American Literature*, X (1940); L. C. Powell, *Robinson Jeffers: The Man and His Work* (1940); R. W. Short, "The Tower Beyond Tragedy," *Southern Review*, VII (1941); R. Gilbert, *Four Living Poets* (1944); G. Arms and J. M. Kuntz, *Poetry Explication* (1950); H. H. Waggoner, *The Heel of Elohim* (1950; A. Tate, *Sixty American Poets, 1896–1944* (1954); L. C. Powell, "The Double Marriage of Robinson Jeffers," *Southwest Review*, XLI (1956); R. Squires, *The Loyalties of Robinson Jeffers* (1956); M. C. Monjian, *Robinson Jeffers* (1958); and O. Seidlin, "The Oresteia Today: A Myth Dehumanized," *Thought*, XXXIV (1959); F. I. Carpenter, *Robinson Jeffers* (1962); and M. B. Bennett, *The Stone Mason of Tor House* (1966).

Shine, Perishing Republic

While this America settles in the mould of its vulgarity,
    heavily thickening to empire,
And protest, only a bubble in the molten mass, pops and
    sighs out, and the mass hardens,

I sadly smiling remember that the flower fades to make
    fruit, the fruit rots to make earth.
Out of the mother; and through the spring exultances, ripe-
    ness and decadence; and home to the mother.

You making haste haste on decay: not blameworthy; life is
    good, be it stubbornly long or suddenly

A mortal splendor: meteors are not needed less than mountains: shine, perishing republic.

But for my childen, I would have them keep their distance
from the thickening center; corruption
Never has been compulsory, when the cities lie at the
monster's feet there are left the mountains.

And boys, be in nothing so moderate as in love of man, a
clever servant, insufferable master.
There is the trap that catches noblest spirits, that caught—
they say—God, when he walked on earth.   10
                                                              1924

To the Stone-Cutters

Stone-cutters fighting time with marble, you foredefeated
Challengers of oblivion
Eat cynical earnings, knowing rock splits, records fall down,
The square-limbed Roman letters
Scale in the thaws, wear in the rain. The poet as well
Builds his monument mockingly;
For man will be blotted out, the blithe earth die, the brave
sun
Die blind, his heart blackening:
Yet stones have stood for a thousand years, and pained
thoughts found
The honey peace in old poems.   10
                                                              1924

Boats in a Fog

Sports and gallantries, the stage, the arts, the antics of
dancers,
The exuberant voices of music,
Have charm for children but lack nobility; it is bitter
earnestness
That makes beauty; the mind
Knows, grown adult.
                    A sudden fog-drift muffled the ocean,
A throbbing of engines moved in it,

At length, a stone's throw out, between the rocks and the
vapor,
One by one moved shadows
Out of the mystery, shadows, fishing-boats, trailing each
other,
Following the cliff for guidance,   10
Holding a difficult path between the peril of the sea-fog
And the foam on the shore granite.
One by one, trailing their leader, six crept by me,
Out of the vapor and into it,
The throb of their engines subdued by the fog, patient and
cautious,
Coasting all around the peninsula
Back to the buoys in Monterey harbor. A flight of pelicans
Is nothing lovelier to look at;
The flight of the planets is nothing nobler; all the arts
lose virtue
Against the essential reality   20
Of creatures going about their business among the equally
Earnest elements of nature.

                                                            1925

Roan Stallion

The dog barked; then the woman stood in the doorway,
        and hearing iron strike stone down the steep road
Covered her head with a black shawl and entered the light
        rain; she stood at the turn of the road.
A nobly formed woman; erect and strong as a new tower;
        the features stolid and dark
But sculptured into a strong grace; straight nose with a
        high bridge, firm and wide eyes, full chin,
Red lips; she was only a fourth part Indian; a Scottish
        sailor had planted her in young native earth,
Spanish and Indian, twenty-one years before. He had
        named her California when she was born;
That was her name; and had gone north.
                                She heard the hooves and
        wheels come nearer, up the steep road.
The buckskin mare, leaning against the breastpiece, plodded
        into sight round the wet bank.

The pale face of the driver followed; the burnt-out eyes;
    they had fortune in them. He sat twisted
On the seat of the old buggy, leading a second horse by a
    long halter, a roan, a big one,   10
That stepped daintily; by the swell of the neck, a stallion.
    "What have you got, Johnny?" "Maskerel's stallion.
Mine now. I won him last night, I had very good luck."
    He was quite drunk. "They bring their mares up here
    now.
I keep this fellow. I got money besides, but I'll not show
    you." "Did you buy something, Johnny,
For our Christine? Christmas comes in two days, Johnny."
    "By God, forgot," he answered laughing.
"Don't tell Christine it's Christmas; after while I get her
    something, maybe." But California:
"I shared your luck when you lost: you lost *me* once,
    Johnny, remember? Tom Dell had me two nights
Here in the house: other times we've gone hungry: now
    that you've won, Christine will have her Christmas.
We share your luck, Johnny. You give me money, I go
    down to Monterey to-morrow,
Buy presents for Christine, come back in the evening. Next
    day Christmas." "You have wet ride," he answered
Giggling. "Here money. Five dollar; ten; twelve dollar.
    You buy two bottles of rye whiskey for Johnny."   20
"All right. I go to-morrow."
                    He was an outcast Hollander; not old, but
    shriveled with bad living.
The child Christine inherited from his race blue eyes, from
    his life a wizened forehead; she watched
From the house-door her father lurch out of the buggy
    and lead with due respect the stallion
To the new corral, the strong one; leaving the wearily
    breathing buckskin mare to his wife to unharness.

Storm in the night; the rain on the thin shakes of the roof
    like the ocean on rock streamed battering; once
    thunder
Walked down the narrow canyon into Carmel valley and
    wore away westward; Christine was wakeful
With fears and wonders; her father lay too deep for storm
    to touch him.
                    Dawn comes late in the year's dark,

Later into the crack of a canyon under redwoods; and
    California slipped from bed
An hour before it; the buckskin would be tired; there was
    a little barley, and why should Johnny
Feed all the barley to his stallion? That is what he would
    do. She tiptoed out of the room.   30
Leaving her clothes, he'd waken if she waited to put them
    on, and passed from the door of the house
Into the dark of the rain; the big black drops were cold
    through the thin shift, but the wet earth
Pleasant under her naked feet. There was a pleasant smell
    in the stable; and moving softly,
Touching things gently with the supple bend of the un-
    clothed body, was pleasant. She found a box,
Filled it with sweet dry barley and took it down to the
    old corral. The little mare sighed deeply
At the rail in the wet darkness; and California returning
    between two redwoods up to the house
Heard the happy jaws grinding the grain. Johnny could
    mind the pigs and chickens. Christine called to her
When she entered the house, but slept again under her
    hand. She laid the wet night-dress on a chair-back
And stole into the bedroom to get her clothes. A plank
    creaked, and he wakened. She stood motionless
Hearing him stir in the bed. When he was quiet she
    stooped after her shoes, and he said softly,   40
"What are you doing? Come back to bed." "It's late, I'm
    going to Monterery, I must hitch up."
"You come to bed first. I been away three days. I give you
    money, I take back the money
And what you do in town then?" She sighed sharply and
    came to the bed.
                He reaching his hands from it
Felt the cool curve and firmness of her flank, and half
    rising caught her by the long wet hair.
She endured, and to hasten the act she feigned desire; she
    had not for long, except in dream, felt it.
Yesterday's drunkenness made him sluggish and exacting;
    she saw, turning her head sadly,
The windows were bright gray with dawn; he embraced
    her still, stopping to talk about the stallion.
At length she was permitted to put on her clothes. Clear
    daylight over the steep hills;

Gray-shining cloud over the tops of the redwoods; the
  winter stream sang loud; the wheels of the buggy
Slipped in deep slime, ground on washed stones at the
  road-edge. Down the hill the wrinkled river smothered
  the ford.   50
You must keep to the bed of stones: she knew the way by
  willow and alder: the buckskin halted midstream,
Shuddering, the water her own color washing up to the
  traces; but California, drawing up
Her feet out of the whirl onto the seat of the buggy swung
  the whip over the yellow water
And drove to the road.
                         All morning the clouds were racing
  northward like a river. At noon they thickened.
When California faced the southwind home from Mon-
  terey it was heavy with level rainfall.
She looked seaward from the foot of the valley; red rays
  cried sunset from a trumpet of streaming
Cloud over Lobos, the southwest occident of the solstice.
  Twilight came soon, but the tired mare
Feared the road more than the whip. Mile after mile of
  slow gray twilight.
          Then, quite suddenly, darkness.
"Christine will be asleep. It is Christmas Eve. The ford.
  That hour of daylight wasted this morning!"
She could see nothing; she let the reins lie on the dash-
  board and knew at length by the cramp of the wheels
                                                              60
And the pitch down, they had reached it. Noise of wheels
  on stones, plashing of hooves in water; a world
Of sounds; no sight; the gentle thunder of water; the
  mare snorting, dipping her head, one knew,
To look for footing, in the blackness, under the stream.
  The hushing and creaking of the sea-wind
In the passion of invisible willows.
                              The mare stood still; the woman
  shouted to her; spared whip,
For a false leap would lose the track of the ford. She
  stood. "The baby's things," thought California,
"Under the seat: the water will come over the floor"; and
  rising in the midst of the water
She tilted the seat; fetched up the doll, the painted wooden
  chickens, the woolly bear, the book

Of many pictures, the box of sweets: she brought them
    all from under the seat and stored them, trembling,
Under her clothes, about the breasts, under the arms; the
    corners of the cardboard boxes
Cut into the soft flesh; but with a piece of rope for a
    girdle and wound ₒabout the shoulders   70
All was made fast. The mare stood still as if asleep in the
    midst of the water. Then California
Reached out a hand over the stream and fingered her
    rump; the solid wet convexity of it
Shook like the beat of a great heart. "What are you wait-
    ing for?" But the feel of the animal surface
Had wakened a dream, obscured real danger with a dream
    of danger. "What for? for the water-stallion
To break out the stream, that is what the rumpstrains
    for, him to come up flinging foam sidewise,
Fore-hooves in air, crush me and the rig and curl over his
    woman." She flung out with the whip then;
The mare plunged forward. The buggy drifted sidelong:
    was she off ground? Swimming? No: by the splashes.
The driver, a mere prehensile instinct, clung to the side-
    irons of the seat and felt the force
But not the coldness of the water, curling over her knees,
    breaking up to the waist
Over her body. They'd turned. The mare had turned up
    stream and was wallowing back into shoal water.   80
Then California dropped her forehead to her knees, hav-
    ing seen nothing, feeling a danger,
And felt the brute weight of a branch of alder, the pendu-
    lous light leaves brush her bent neck
Like a child's fingers. The mare burst out of water and
    stopped on the slope to the ford. The woman climbed
    down
Between the wheels and went to her head. "Poor Dora,"
    she called her by her name, "there, Dora. Quietly,"
And led her around, there was room to turn on the mar-
    gin, the head to the gentle thunder of the water.
She crawled on hands and knees, felt for the ruts, and
    shifted the wheels into them. "You can see, Dora.
I can't. But this time you'll go through it." She climbed
    into the seat and shouted angrily. The mare
Stopped, her two forefeet in the water. She touched with
    the whip. The mare plodded ahead and halted.

Then California thought of prayer: "Dear little Jesus,
Dear baby Jesus born to-night, your head was shining 90
Like silver candles. I've got a baby too, only a girl. You
    had light wherever you walked.
Dear baby Jesus give me light." Light streamed: rose,
    gold, rich purple, hiding the ford like a curtain.
The gentle thunder of water was a noise of wing-feathers,
    the fans of paradise lifting softly.
The child afloat on radiance had a baby face, but the
    angels had birds' heads, hawks' heads,
Bending over the baby, weaving a web of wings about
    him. He held in the small fat hand
A little snake with golden eyes, and California could see
    clearly on the under radiance
The mare's pricked ears, a sharp black fork against the
    shining light-fall. But it dropped; the light of heaven
Frightened poor Dora. She backed; swung up the water,
And nearly oversetting the buggy turned and scrambled
    backward; the iron wheel-tires rang on boulders.
Then California weeping climbed between the wheels.
    Her wet clothes and the toys packed under   100
Dragged her down with their weight; she stripped off
    cloak and dress and laid the baby's things in the
    buggy;
Brought Johnny's whiskey out from under the seat;
    wrapped all in the dress, bottles and toys, and tied
    them
Into a bundle that would sling over her back. She un-
    harnessed the mare, hurting her fingers
Against the swollen straps and the wet buckles. She tied
    the pack over her shoulders, the cords
Crossing her breasts, and mounted. She drew up her shift
    about her waist and knotted it, naked thighs
Clutching the sides of the mare, bare flesh to the wet
    withers, and caught the mane with her right hand,
The looped-up bridle-reins in the other. "Dora, the baby
    gives you light." The blinding radiance
Hovered the ford. "Sweet baby Jesus give us light." Cata-
    racts of light and Latin singing
Fell through the willows; the mare snorted and reared:
    the roar and thunder of the invisible water;
The night shaking open like a flag, shot with the flashes;
    the baby face hovering; the water   110

Beating over her shoes and stockings up to the bare
    thighs; and over them, like a beast
Lapping her belly; the wriggle and pitch of the mare
    swimming; the drift, the sucking water; the blinding
Light above and behind with not a gleam before, in the
    throat of darkness; the shock of the forehooves
Striking bottom, the struggle and surging lift of the
    haunches. She felt the water streaming off her
From the shoulders down; heard the great strain and sob
    of the mare's breathing, heard the horseshoes grind
    on gravel.
When California came home the dog at the door snuffed
    at her without barking; Christine and Johnny
Both were asleep; she did not sleep for hours, but kindled
    fire and knelt patiently over it,
Shaping and drying the dear-bought gifts for Christmas
    morning.

    She hated (she thought) the proud-necked stallion.
He'd lean the big twin masses of his breast on the rail, his
    red-brown eyes flash the white crescents,   120
She admired him then, she hated him for his uselessness,
    serving nothing
But Johnny's vanity. Horses were too cheap to breed. She
    thought, if he could range in freedom,
Shaking the red-roan mane for a flag on the bare
    hills.
        A man brought up a mare in April;
Then California, though she wanted to watch, stayed
    with Christine indoors. When the child fretted
The mother told her once more about the miracle of the
    ford; her prayers to the little Jesus
The Christmas Eve when she was bringing the gifts
    home; the appearance, the lights, the Latin singing,
The thunder of wing-feathers and water, the shining
    child, the cataracts of splendor down the darkness.
"A little baby," Christine asked, "the God is a baby?"
    "The child of God. That was his birthday.
His mother was named Mary: we pray to her too: God
    came to her. He was not the child of a man
Like you or me. God was his father: she was the stallion's
    wife—what did I say—God's wife,"   130

She said with a cry, lifting Christine aside, pacing the
planks of the floor. "She is called more blessed
Than any woman. She was so good, she was more loved."
"Did God live near her house?" "He lives
Up high, over the stars; he ranges on the bare blue hill of
the sky." In her mind a picture
Flashed, of the red-roan mane shaken out for a flag on the
bare hills, and she said quickly, "He's more
Like a great man holding the sun in his hand." Her mind
giving her words the lie, "But no one
Knows, only the shining and the power. The power, the
terror, the burning fire covered her over . . ."
"Was she burnt up, mother?" "She was so good and
lovely, she was the mother of the little Jesus.
If you are good nothing will hurt you." "What did she
think?" "She loved, she was not afraid of the hooves—
Hands that had made the hills and sun and moon, and
the sea and the great redwoods, the terrible strength,
She gave herself without thinking." "You only saw the
baby, mother?" "Yes, and the angels about him,   140
The great wild shining over the black river." Three times
she had walked to the door, three times returned,
And now the hand that had thrice hung on the knob,
full of prevented action, twisted the cloth
Of the child's dress that she had been mending. "Oh, oh,
I've torn it." She struck at the child and then em-
braced her
Fiercely, the small blond sickly body.
                              Johnny came in, his face
reddened as if he had stood
Near fire, his eyes triumphing "Finished," he said, and
looked with malice at Christine. "I go
Down valley with Jim Carrier; owes me five dollar, fifteen
I charge him, he brought ten in his pocket.
Has grapes on the ranch, maybe I take a barrel red wine
instead of money. Be back to-morrow.
To-morrow night I tell you—Eh, Jim," he laughed over
his shoulder, "I say to-morrow evening
I show her how the red fellow act, the big fellow. When
I come home." She answered nothing, but stood
In front of the door, holding the little hand of her daugh-
ter, in the path of sun between the redwoods,   150

While Johnny tied the buckskin mare behind Carrier's
    buggy, and bringing saddle and bridle tossed them
Under the seat. Jim Carrier's mare, the bay, stood with
    drooped head and started slowly, the men
Laughing and shouting at her; their voices could be heard
    down the steep road, after the noise
Of the iron-hooped wheels died from the stone. Then one
    might hear the hush of the wind in the tall red-
    woods,
The tinkle of the April brook, deep in its hollow.

                               Humanity is the
    start of the race; I say
Humanity is the mold to break away from, the crust to
    break through, the coal to break into fire,
The atom to be split.
                     Tragedy that breaks man's face and a white
    fire flies out of it; vision that fools him
Out of his limits, desire that fools him out of his limits,
    unnatural crime, inhuman science,
Slit eyes in the mask; wild loves that leap over the walls
    of nature, the wild fence-vaulter science,
Useless intelligence of far stars, dim knowledge of the
    spinning demons that make an atom,   160
These break, these pierce, these deify, praising their God
    shrilly with fierce voices: not in man's shape
He approves the praise, he that walks lightning-naked on
    the Pacific, that laces the suns with planets,
The heart of the atom with electrons: what is humanity
    in this cosmos? For him, the last
Least taint of a trace in the dregs of the solution; for
    itself, the mould to break away from, the coal
To break into fire, the atom to be split.

                        After the child slept, after
    the leopard-footed evening
Had glided oceanward, California turned the lamp to its
    least flame and glided from the house.
She moved sighing, like a loose fire, backward and for-
    ward on the smooth ground by the door.
She heard the night-wind that draws down the valley like
    the draught in a flue under clear weather

Whisper and toss in the tall redwoods; she heard the
 tinkle of the April brook deep in its hollow. 170
Cooled by the night the odors that the horses had left
 behind were in her nostrils; the night
Whitened up the bare hill; a drift of coyotes by the river
 cried bitterly against moonrise;
Then California ran to the old corral, the empty one
 where they kept the buckskin mare,
And leaned, and bruised her breasts on the rail, feeling
 the sky whiten. When the moon stood over the hill
She stole to the house. The child breathed quietly. Her-
 self: to sleep? She had seen Christ in the night at
 Christmas.
The hills were shining open to the enormous night of the
 April moon: empty and empty,
The vast round backs of the bare hills? If one should ride
 up high might not the Father himself
Be seen brooding His night, cross-legged, chin in hand,
 squatting on the last dome? More likely
Leaping the hills, shaking the red-roan mane for a flag
 on the bare hills. She blew out the lamp.
Every fiber of flesh trembled with faintness when she
 came to the door; strength lacked, to wander 180
Afoot into the shining of the hill, high enough, high
 enough . . . the hateful face of a man had taken
The strength that might have served her, the corral was
 empty. The dog followed her, she caught him by the
 collar,
Dragged him in fierce silence back to the door of the
 house, latched him inside.
     It was like daylight
Out-doors and she hastened without faltering down the
 footpath, through the dark fringe of twisted oak-
 brush,
To the open place in a bay of the hill. The dark strength
 of the stallion had heard her coming; she heard him
Blow the shining air out of his nostrils, she saw him in
 the white lake of moonlight
Move like a lion along the timbers of the fence, shaking
 the nightfall
Of the great mane; his fragrance came to her; she leaned
 on the fence;

He drew away from it, the hooves making soft thunder
    in the trodden soil.
Wild love had trodden it, his wrestling with the stranger,
    the shame of the day   190
Had stamped it into mire and powder when the heavy
    fetlocks
Strained the soft flanks. "Oh, if I could bear you!
If I had the strength. O great God that came down to
    Mary, gently you came. But I will ride him
Up into the hill, if he throws me, if he tramples me, is it
    not my desire
To endure death?" She climbed the fence, pressing her
    body against the rail, shaking like fever,
And dropped inside to the soft ground. He neither threat-
    ened her with his teeth nor fled from her coming,
And lifting her hand gently to the upflung head she
    caught the strap of the headstall,
That hung under the quivering chin. She unlooped the
    halter from the high strength of the neck
And the arch the storm-cloud mane hung with live dark-
    ness. He stood; she crushed her breasts
On the hard shoulder, an arm over the withers, the other
    under the mass of his throat, and murmuring   200
Like a mountain dove, "If I could bear you." No way, no
    help, a gulf in nature. She murmured, "Come,
We will run on the hill. O beautiful, O beautiful," and
    led him
To the gate and flung the bars on the ground. He threw
    his head downward
To snuff at the bars; and while he stood, she catching
    mane and withers with all sudden contracture
And strength of her lithe body, leaped, clung hard, and
    was mounted. He had been ridden before; he did
    not
Fight the weight but ran like a stone falling;
Broke down the slope into the moon-glass of the stream,
    and flattened to his neck
She felt the branches of a buck-eye tree fly over her, saw
    the wall of the oak-scrub
End her world: but he turned there, the matted branches
Scraped her right knee, the great slant shoulders   210
Laboring the hill-slope, up, up, the clear hill. Desire had
    died in her

At the first rush, the falling like death, but now it revived,
She feeling between her thighs the labor of the great
    engine, the running muscles, the hard swiftness,
She riding the savage and exultant strength of the world.
    Having topped the thicket he turned eastward,
Running less wildly; and now at length he felt the halter
    when she drew on it; she guided him upward;
He stopped and grazed on the great arch and pride of the
    hill, the silent calvary. A dwarfish oakwood
Climbed the other slope out of the dark of the unknown
    canyon beyond; the last wind-beaten bush of it
Crawled up to the height, and California slipping from
    her mount tethered him to it. She stood then,
Shaking. Enormous films of moonlight
Trailed down from the height. Space, anxious whiteness,
    vastness. Distant beyond conception the shining   220
    ocean
Lay light like a haze along the ledge and doubtful world's
    end. Little vapors gleaming, and little
Darknesses on the far chart underfoot symbolized wood
    and valley; but the air was the element, the moon-
Saturate arcs and spires of the air.
                              Here is solitude, here on the
    calvary, nothing conscious
But the possible God and the cropped grass, no witness,
    no eye but that misformed one, the moon's past
    fullness.
Two figures on the shining hill, woman and stallion, she
    kneeling to him, brokenly adoring.
He cropping the grass, shifting his hooves, or lifting the
    long head to gaze over the world,
Tranquil and powerful. She prayed aloud, "O God, I
    am not good enough, O fear, O strength, I am
    draggled
Johnny and other men have had me, and O clean power!
    Here am I," she said, falling before him,
And crawled to his hooves. She lay a long while, as if
    asleep, in reach of the fore-hooves, weeping. He
    avoided
Her head and the prone body. He backed at first; but
    later plucked the grass that grew by her shoulder.   230
The small dark head under his nostrils: a small round
    stone, that smelt human, black hair growing from it:

The skull shut the light in it: it was not possible for any
  eyes
To know what throbbed and shone under the sutures of
  the skull, or a shell full of lightning
Had scared the roan strength, and he'd have broken
  tether, screaming, and run for the valley.
                                        The atom bounds-breaking,
Nucleus to sun, electrons to planets, with recognition
Not praying, self-equaling, the whole to the whole, the
  microcosm
Not entering nor accepting entrance, more equally, more
  utterly, more incredibly conjugate
With the other extreme and greatness; passionately per-
  ceptive of identity. . . .
                        The fire threw up figures
And symbols meanwhile, racial myths formed and dis-
  solved in it, the phantom rulers of humanity   240
That without being are yet more real than what they are
  born of, and without shape, shape that which makes
  them:
The nerves and the flesh go by shadowlike, the limbs and
  the lives shadowlike, these shadows remain, these
  shadows
To whom temples, to whom churches, to whom labors
  and wars, visions and dreams are dedicate:
Out of the fire in the small round stone that black moss
  covered, a crucified man writhed up in anguish;
A woman covered by a huge beast in whose mane the
  stars were netted, sun and moon were his eyeballs,
Smiled under the unendurable violation, her throat swollen with the storm and blood-flecks gleaming
On the stretched lips; a woman—no, a dark water, split
  by jets of lightning, and after a season
What floated up out of the furrowed water, a boat, a fish,
  a fire-globe?
                    It had wings, the creature,
And flew against the fountain of lightning, fell burnt out
  of the cloud back to the bottomless water . . .
Figures and symbols, castlings of the fire, played in her
  brain; but the white fire was the essence,   250
The burning in the small round shell of bone that black
  hair covered, that lay by the hooves on the hilltop.

She rose at length, she unknotted the halter; she walked
   and led the stallion; two figures, woman and stallion,
Came down the silent emptiness of the dome of the hill,
under the cataract of the moonlight.

The next night there was moon through cloud. Johnny
   had returned half drunk toward evening, and
   California
Who had known him for years with neither love nor
   loathing to-night hating him had let the child Christine
Play in the light of the lamp for hours after her bedtime;
   who fell asleep at length on the floor
Beside the dog; then Johnny: "Put her to bed." She
   gathered the child against her breasts, she laid her
In the next room, and covered her with a blanket. The
   window was white, the moon had risen. The mother
Lay down by the child, but after a moment Johnny stood
   in the doorway. "Come drink." He had brought
   home
Two jugs of wine slung from the saddle, part payment
   for the stallion's service; a pitcher of it   260
Was on the table, and California sadly came and emptied
   her glass. Whiskey, she thought,
Would have erased him till to-morrow; the thin red
   wine . . .
"We have a good evening," he laughed, pouring it.
"One glass yet then I show you what the red fellow did."
   She moving toward the house-door his eyes
Followed her, the glass filled and the red juice ran over
   the table. When it struck the floor-planks
He heard and looked. "Who stuck the pig?" he muttered
   stupidly, "here's blood, here's blood," and trailed his
   fingers
In the red lake under the lamplight. While he was looking
   down the door creaked, she had slipped out-doors.
And he, his mouth curving like a faun's imagined the
   chase under the solemn redwoods, the panting
And unresistant victim caught in a dark corner. He
   emptied the glass and went outdoors
Into the dappled lanes of moonlight. No sound but the
   April brook's. "Hey Bruno," he called, "find her.   270

Bruno, go find her." The dog after a little understood
    and quested, the man following.
When California crouching by an oak-bush above the
    house heard them come near she darted
To the open slope and ran down hill. The dog barked at
    her heels, pleased with the game, and Johnny
Followed in silence. She ran down to the new corral, she
    saw the stallion
Move like a lion along the timbers of the fence, the dark
    arched neck shaking the nightfall
Of the great mane; she threw herself prone and writhed
    under the bars, his hooves backing away from her
Made muffled thunder in the soft soil. She stood in the
    midst of the corral, panting, but Johnny
Paused at the fence. The dog ran under it, and seeing the
    stallion move, the woman standing quiet,
Danced after the beast, with white-toothed feints and
    dashes. When Johnny saw the formidable dark
    strength
Recoil from the dog, he climbed up over the fence.   280

The child Christine waked when her mother left her
And lay half dreaming, in the half-waking dream she
    saw the ocean come up out of the west
And cover the world, she looked up through clear water
    at the tops of the redwoods. She heard the door
    creak
And the house empty; her heart shook her body, sitting
    up on the bed, and she heard the dog
And crept toward light, where it gleamed under the
    crack of the door. She opened the door, the room
    was empty,
The table-top was a red lake under the lamplight. The
    color of it was terrible to her;
She had seen the red juice drip from a coyote's muzzle
    her father had shot one day in the hills
And carried him home over the saddle: she looked at the
    rifle on the wall-rack: it was not moved:
She ran to the door, the dog was barking and the moon
    was shining: she knew wine by the odor
But the color frightened her, the empty house frightened
    her, she followed down hill in the white lane of moon-
    light   290

The friendly noise of the dog. She saw in the big horse's
    corral, on the level shoulder of the hill,
Black on white, the dark strength of the beast, the dancing
    fury of the dog, and the two others.
One fled, one followed; the big one charged, rearing; one
    fell under his fore-hooves. She heard her mother
Scream: without thought she ran to the house, she dragged
    a chair past the red pool and climbed to the rifle,
Got it down from the wall and lugged it somehow through
    the door and down the hillside, under the hard weight
Sobbing. Her mother stood by the rails of the corral, she
    gave it to her. On the far side
The dog flashed at the plunging stallion; in the midst of
    the space the man, slow-moving, like a hurt worm
Crawling, dragged his body by inches toward the fence-
    line. Then California, resting the rifle
On the top rail, without doubting, without hesitance,
Aimed for the leaping body of the dog, and when it stood,
    fired. It snapped, rolled over, lay quiet.   300
"O mother, you've hit Bruno!" "I couldn't see the sights in
    the moonlight," she answered quietly. She stood
And watched, resting the rifle-butt on the ground. The
    stallion wheeled, freed from his torment, the man
Lurched up to his knees, wailing a thin and bitter bird's
    cry, and the roan thunder
Struck; hooves left nothing alive but teeth tore up the
    remnant. "O mother, shoot, shoot!" Yet California
Stood carefully watching, till the beast having fed all his
    fury stretched neck to utmost, head high,
And wrinkled back the upper lip from the teeth, yawning
    obscene disgust over—not a man—
A smear on the moon-lake earth: then California moved
    by some obscure human fidelity
Lifted the rifle. Each separate nerve-cell of her brain flam-
    ing the stars fell from their places
Crying in her mind: she fired three times before the
    haunches crumpled sidewise, the forelegs stiffening,
And the beautiful strength settled to earth: she turned
    then on her little daughter the mask of a woman   310
Who has killed God. The night-wind veering, the smell
    of the spilt wine drifted down hill from the house.
                                1925

Hurt Hawks

I

The broken pillar of the wing jags from the clotted shoulder,
The wing trails like a banner in defeat,
No more to use the sky forever but live with famine
And pain a few days: cat nor coyote
Will shorten the week of waiting for death, there is game
without talons.
He stands under the oak-bush and waits
The lame feet of salvation; at night he remembers freedom
And flies in a dream, the dawns ruin it.
He is strong and pain is worse to the strong, incapacity is
worse.
The curs of the day come and torment him   10
At distance, no one but death the redeemer will humble that
head,
The intrepid readiness, the terrible eyes.
The wild God of the world is sometimes merciful to those
That ask mercy, not often to the arrogant.
You do not know him, you communal people, or you have
forgotten him;
Intemperate and savage, the hawk remembers him;
Beautiful and wild, the hawks, and men that are dying,
remember him.

II

I'd sooner, except the penalties, kill a man than a hawk;
but the great redtail
Had nothing left but unable misery
From the bone too shattered for mending, the wing that
trailed under his talons when he moved.   20
We had fed him six weeks, I gave him freedom,
He wandered over the foreland hill and returned in the eve-
ning, asking for death,
Not like a beggar, still eyed with the old
Implacable arrogance. I gave him the lead gift in the twi-
light.
What fell was relaxed,

Owl-downy, soft feminine feathers; but what
Soared: the fierce rush: the night-herons by the flooded
    river cried fear at its rising
Before it was quite unsheathed from reality.

                          1928

JOHN CROWE RANSOM

(1888–)

John Crowe Ransom has been the leading spirit of the "New Criticism." Born the son of a minister in Pulaski, Tennessee, he graduated in 1909 from Vanderbilt University, in Nashville, the scene of one of his great areas of influence. From Vanderbilt he went as a Rhodes Scholar to Oxford, where he remained for three years; upon completion of his British education, he returned to Vanderbilt where he was a professor of English for twenty-three years, where he helped found *The Fugitive,* and where he became the mentor of poets and critics who included Cleanth Brooks, Allen Tate, and Robert Penn Warren.

In 1930 he published *God without Thunder* and contributed to *I'll Take My Stand,* both attacks on the contemporary adoration of science, which, Ransom felt, abstracted knowledge to the point where it robbed men of a full recognition of experience. It is small wonder that the Edgar Allen Poe who wrote "Sonnet —to Science" attracted Ransom's group and became the subject of a detailed investigation by one of Ransom's colleagues, Allen Tate. Ransom's reputation during the years at Vanderbilt was based upon his poetry as well as his social ideas; in 1919 he published his first book of verse, *Poems about God.* He has produced only a few slim volumes of poetry, the core of which has been collected in *Selected Poems* (1945). Ransom's poetry has been praised for qualities that stand high in the values of the "New Critics" and, indeed, in the values of many other critics since the revolution of the "new poetry" movement: wit, irony, classically precise diction, and an avoidance of all traces of sentimentality.

In 1937 he moved to Gambier, Ohio, to take a professorship at Kenyon College; there he founded the influential *Kenyon Review*. Since then, his reputation has rested more on his literary criticism than on his poetry. He has produced two important critical books, *The World's Body* (1938) and *The New Criticism* (1941).

Others of Ransom's works include *Chills and Fever* (1924); *Two Gentlemen in Bonds* (1926); and *Poems and Essays* (1955).

Studies of the man and his work are to be found in A. Tate, "Poetry and the Absolute," *Sewanee Review*, XXXV (1927); R. P. Warren, "John Crowe Ransom; A Study in Irony," *Virginia Quarterly Review*, XI (1935); D. Schwartz, "The Isolation of Modern Poetry," *Kenyon Review* (Spring, 1941); Y. Winters, *The Anatomy of Nonsense* (1943); A. Tate, ed., *A Southern Vanguard* (1947); R. W. Stallman, "John Crowe Ransom: A Bibliography," *Sewanee Review*, LVI (1948); *Sewanee Review*, LXV (Summer, 1948)—an issue of "Homage to John Ransom"; M. Blum, "The Fugitive Particular: John Crowe Ransom, Critic," *Western Review*, XIV (1950); G. Warrerman, "The Irony of John Crowe Ransom," *University of Kansas City Review*, XXIII (1956); J. L. Stewart, *John Crowe Ransom* (1962); and K. F. Knight, *The Poetry of John Crowe Ransom* (1964).

Piazza Piece

—I am a gentleman in a dustcoat trying
To make you hear. Your ears are soft and small
And listen to an old man not at all,
They want the young men's whispering and sighing.
But see the roses on your trellis dying
And hear the spectral singing of the moon;
For I must have my lovely lady soon,
I am a gentleman in a dustcoat trying.

—I am a lady young in beauty waiting
Until my truelove comes, and then we kiss.   10
But what grey man among the vines is this
Whose words are dry and faint as in a dream?
Back from my trellis, Sir, before I scream!
I am a lady young in beauty waiting.

1919, 1955

Bells for John Whiteside's Daughter

There was such speed in her little body,
And such lightness in her footfall,
It is no wonder that her brown study
Astonishes us all.

Her wars were bruited in our high window.
We looked among orchard trees and beyond
Where she took arms against her shadow,
Or harried unto the pond

The lazy geese, like a snow cloud
Dripping their snow on the green grass,   10
Tricking and stopping, sleepy and proud,
Who cried in goose, Alas,

For the tireless heart within the little
Lady with rod that made them rise
From their noon apple-dreams and scuttle
Goose-fashion under the skies!

But now go the bells, and we are ready,
In one house we are sternly stopped
To say we are vexed at her brown study,
Lying so primly propped.   20

1924, 1955

Antique Harvesters

(SCENE: *Of the Mississippi the bank sinister, and of the
Ohio the bank sinister.*)

Tawny are the leaves turned but they still hold,
And it is harvest; what shall this land produce?
A meager hill of kernels, a runnel of juice;
Declension looks from our land, it is old.
Therefore let us assemble, dry, grey, spare,
And mild as yellow air.

"I hear the croak of a raven's funeral wing."
The young men would be joying in the song

Of passionate birds; their memories are not long.
What is it thus rehearsed in sable? "Nothing."   10
Trust not but the old endure, and shall be older
Than the scornful beholder.

We pluck the spindling ears and gather the corn.
One spot has special yield? "On this spot stood
Heroes and drenched it with their only blood."
And talk meets talk, as echoes from the horn
Of the hunter—echoes are the old men's arts,
Ample are the chambers of their hearts.

Here come the hunters, keepers of a rite.
The horn, the hounds, the lank mares coarsing by   20
Under quaint archetypes of chivalry;
And the fox, lovely ritualist, in flight
Offering his unearthly ghost to quarry;
And the fields, themselves to harry.

Resume, harvesters. The treasure is full bronze
Which you will garner for the Lady, and the moon
Could tinge it no yellower than does this noon;
But grey will quench it shortly—the field, men, stones.
Pluck fast, dreamers; prove as you amble slowly
Not less than men, not wholly.   30

Bare the arm, dainty youths, bend the knees
Under bronze burdens. And by an autumn tone
As by a grey, as by a green, you will have known
Your famous Lady's image; for so have these;
And if one say that easily will your hands
More prosper in other lands,

Angry as wasp-music be your cry then:
"Forsake the Proud Lady, of the heart of fire,
The look of snow, to the praise of a dwindled choir,
Song of degenerate specters that were men?   40
The sons of the fathers shall keep her, worthy of
What these have done in love."

True, it is said of our Lady, she ageth.
But see, if you peep shrewdly, she hath not stooped;
Take no thought of her servitors that have drooped,

For we are nothing; and if one talk of death—
Why, the ribs of the earth subsist frail as a breath
If but God wearieth.

1924, 1955

The Equilibrists

Full of her long white arms and milky skin
He had a thousand times remembered sin.
Alone in the press of people traveled he,
Minding her jacinth, and myrrh, and ivory.

Mouth he remembered: the quaint orifice
From which came heat that flamed upon the kiss,
Till cold words came down spiral from the head.
Grey doves from the officious tower illsped.

Body: it was a white field ready for love,
On her body's field, with the gaunt tower above,   10
The lilies grew, beseeching him to take,
If he would pluck and wear them, bruise and break.

Eyes talking: Never mind the cruel words,
Embrace my flowers, but not embrace the swords.
But what they said, the doves came straightway flying
And unsaid: Honor, Honor, they came crying.

Importunate her doves. Too pure, too wise,
Clambering on his shoulder, saying, Arise,
Leave me now, and never let us meet,
Eternal distance now command thy feet.   20

Predicament indeed, which thus discovers
Honor among thieves, Honor between lovers.
O such a little word is Honor, they feel!
But the grey word is between them cold as steel.

At length I saw these lovers fully were come
Into their torture of equilibrium;
Dreadfully had forsworn each other, and yet
They were bound each to each, and they did not forget.

And rigid as two painful stars, and twirled
About the clustered night their prison world,   30
They burned with fierce love always to come near,
But Honor beat them back and kept them clear.

Ah, the strict lovers, they are ruined now!
I cried in anger. But with puddled brow
Devising for those gibbeted and brave
Came I descanting: Man, what would you have?

For spin your period out, and draw your breath,
A kinder saeculum begins with Death.   [saeculum: cycle]
Would you ascend to Heaven and bodiless dwell?
Or take your bodies honorless to Hell?   40

In Heaven you have heard no marriage is,
No white flesh tinder to your lecheries,
Your male and female tissue sweetly shaped
Sublimed away, and furious blood escaped.

Great lovers lie in Hell, the stubborn ones
Infatuate of the flesh upon the bones;
Stuprate, they rend each other when they kiss,
                              [stuprate: violated]
The pieces kiss again, no end to this.

But still I watch them spinning, orbited nice.
Their flames were not more radiant than their ice.   50
I dug in the quiet earth and wrought the tomb
And made these lines to memorize their doom:—

Epitaph

Equilibrists lie here; stranger, tread light;
Close, but untouching in each other's sight;
Mouldered the lips and ashy the tall skull,
Let them lie perilous and beautiful.

                                        1927, 1955

WILLIAM CARLOS WILLIAMS
(1883–1963)

A prolific writer, Williams was a novelist (*A Voyage to Pagany*, 1928; *White Mule*, Part I, 1937; Part II, 1940; *The Build-Up*, 1952), a playwright (*Many Loves*, 1958), a short-story writer (*The Knife of the Times*, 1932; *Life along the Passaic River*, 1938), and an essayist (*The Great American Novel*, 1923; *In the American Grain*, 1925; *Selected Essays of William Carlos Williams*, 1954). But he is best known as a poet, and the best-known of his poems is *Paterson*, of which the first four volumes were collected in 1951. Book V appeared in 1958, and the whole epic had been in continuous growth since 1946.

Born in Rutherford, New Jersey, Williams had a European preparatory education following his education in the New York public schools and prior to his enrollment at the University of Pennsylvania, where he earned his M.D. in 1906. An acquaintance of Pound at the University, Williams associated himself with the expatriate when he met him again in Europe, where Williams had gone to study pediatrics. Always interested in poetry, Williams' eagerness to write was intensified by discussions with the young experimentalists of the new poetry movement. He took his excitement back home with him to New Jersey, where, from 1910, he successfully practiced medicine until his retirement.

In a way Williams was the opposite of John Crowe Ransom in that for him science furnished a realistic perception that is an entree to poetry. His practice in the industrial New Jersey of Paterson and his view of the lives led there, set against the history of the city, led to his epic poems. The recipient of many awards for his writing, Williams continued to work out his iconoclastic and tough-minded poetry, in which the poet "by use of his imagination and the language he hears," tries to lift "the material conditions and appearances of his environment to the sphere of the intelligence, where they will have new currency." It is not what a poet says that counts for Williams, but "what he makes, with such intensity of perception that it lives with an intrinsic movement of its own to verify its authenticity."

Williams' other books include Go Go (1923), Adam & Eve & The City (1936), The Complete Collected Poems of William Carlos Williams: 1906–1938 (1938); The Broken Span (1941); Selected Poems (1949); Collected Later Poetry of William Carlos Williams (1950); Make Light of It (1950); Collected Earlier Poems of William Carlos Williams (1951); The Autobiography of William Carlos Williams (1951); The Desert Music and Other Poems (1954); Journey to Love (1955); and Pictures from Breughel (1962).

Studies of the man and his work, besides The Autobiography of William Carlos Williams (1951), are to be found in P. Rosenfeld, Port of New York (1924); K. Burke, "The Methods of William Carlos Williams," Dial, LXXXII (1927); R. Lechlitner, "The Poetry of William Carlos Williams," Poetry, LIV (1939); Briarcliff Quarterly, III (Oct., 1946)—a Williams issue; F. Morgan, "William Carlos Williams: Imagery, Rhythm, Form," Sewanee Review, LV (1947); V. Koch, William Carlos Williams (1950); J. Benett, "The Lyre and the Sledgehammer," Hudson Review, V (1952); R. Ellmann, "William Carlos Williams: The Doctor in Search of Himself," Kenyon Review, XIV (1952); Perspective, VI (Autumn–Winter, 1953)—a Williams issue; F. J. Hoffman, "Williams and His Muse," Poetry, LXXXIV (1954); Sister M. B. Quinn, "William Carlos Williams: A Testament of Perpetual Change," PMLA, LXX (1955); F. Thompson, "The Symbolic Structure of Paterson," Western Review, XIX (1955); J. C. Thirlwall, ed., The Selected Letters of William Carlos Williams (1957); E. Heal, ed., I Wanted to Write a Poem: The Autobiography of the Works of a Poet (1958); L. C. Martz, "The Unicorn in Paterson: William Carlos Williams," Thought, XXXV (1960); W. Sutton, "Dr. Williams' Paterson and the Quest for Form," Criticism, II (1960); J. M. Brinnin, William Carlos Williams (1963); L. W. Wagner, The Poems of William Carlos Williams: A Critical Study (1964); L. W. Wagner, "A Decade of Discovery, 1953–1963: Checklist of Criticism, William Carlos Williams' Poetry," Twentieth Century Criticism, X (1964); J. H. Miller, ed., William Carlos Williams (1966); and M. L. Rosenthal, ed., The William Carlos Williams Reader (1966).

Tract

I will teach you my townspeople
how to perform a funeral—
for you have it over a troop
of artists—
unless one should scour the world—
you have the ground sense necessary.

See! the hearse leads.
I begin with a design for a hearse.
For Christ's sake not black—
nor white either—and not polished!   10
Let it be weathered—like a farm wagon—
with gilt wheels (this could be
applied fresh at small expense)
or no wheels at all:
a rough dray to drag over the ground.

Knock the glass out!
My God—glass, my townspeople!
For what purpose? Is it for the dead
to look out or for us to see
how well he is housed or to see   20
the flowers or the lack of them—
or what?
To keep the rain and snow from him?
He will have a heavier rain soon:
pebbles and dirt and what not.
Let there be no glass—
and no upholstery! phew!
and no little brass rollers
and small easy wheels on the bottom—
my townspeople what are you thinking of!   30

A rough plain hearse then
with gilt wheels and no top at all.
On this the coffin lies
by its own weight.

                No wreaths please—
especially no hot-house flowers.
Some common memento is better,

something he prized and is known by:
his old clothes—a few books perhaps—
God knows what! You realize
how we are about these things,   40
my townspeople—
something will be found—anything—
even flowers if he had come to that.
So much for the hearse.

For heaven's sake though see to the driver!
Take off the silk hat! In fact
that's no place at all for him
up there unceremoniously
dragging our friend out to his own dignity!
Bring him down—bring him down!   50
Low and inconspicuous! I'd not have him ride
on the wagon at all—damn him—
the undertaker's understrapper!
Let him hold the reins
and walk at the side
and inconspicuously too!

Then briefly as to yourselves:
Walk behind—as they do in France,
seventh class, or if you ride
Hell take curtains! Go with some show   60
of inconvenience; sit openly—
to the weather as to grief.
Or do you think you can shut grief in?
What—from us? We who have perhaps
nothing to lose? Share with us
share with us—it will be money
in your pockets.

            Go now
I think you are ready.

                                    w. 1916
                                    p. 1920

Danse Russe

If I when my wife is sleeping
and the baby and Kathleen
are sleeping
and the sun is a flame-white disk
in silken mists
above shining trees—
if I in my north room
dance naked, grotesquely
before my mirror
waving my shirt round my head   10
and singing softly to myself:
"I am lonely, lonely,
I was born to be lonely,
I am best so!"
If I admire my arms, my face,
my shoulders, flanks, buttocks
against the yellow drawn shades—

Who shall say I am not
the happy genius of my household?

1917

Queen-Ann's-Lace

Her body is not so white as
anemone petals nor so smooth—nor
so remote a thing. It is a field
of the wild carrot taking
the field by force; the grass
does not raise above it.
Here is no question of whiteness,
white as can be, with a purple mole
at the center of each flower.
Each flower is a hand's span   10
of her whiteness. Wherever
his hand has lain there is
a tiny purple blemish. Each part
is a blossom under his touch

to which the fibers of her being
stem one by one, each to its end,
until the whole field is a
white desire, empty, a single stem,
a cluster, flower by flower,
a pious wish to whiteness gone over—   20
or nothing.

                                                    1921

By the Road to the Contagious Hospital

By the road to the contagious hospital
under the surge of the blue
mottled clouds driven from the
northeast—a cold wind. Beyond, the
waste of broad, muddy fields
brown with dried weeds, standing and fallen

patches of standing water
the scattering of tall trees

All along the road the reddish
purplish, forked, upstanding, twiggy   10
stuff of bushes and small trees
with dead, brown leaves under them
leafless vines—

Lifeless in appearance, sluggish
dazed spring approaches—

They enter the new world naked,
cold, uncertain of all
save that they enter. All about them
the cold, familiar wind—

Now the grass, tomorrow   20
the stiff curl of wildcarrot leaf

One by one objects are defined—
It quickens: clarity, outline of leaf

But now the stark dignity of
entrance—Still, the profound change
has come upon them: rooted they
grip down and begin to awaken

1923

Wheelbarrow

so much depends
upon

a red wheel
barrow

glazed with rain
water

beside the white
chickens

1923

The Yachts

Contend in a sea which the land partly encloses
shielding them from the too heavy blows
of an ungoverned ocean which when it chooses
tortures the biggest hulls, the best man knows
to pit against its beatings, and sinks them pitilessly.
Mothlike in mists, scintillant in the minute

brilliance of cloudless days, with broad bellying sails
they glide to the wind tossing green water
from their sharp prows while over them the crew crawls

ant-like, solicitously grooming them, releasing,   10
making fast as they turn, lean far over and having
caught the wind again, side by side, head for the mark.
In a well guarded arena of open water surrounded by
lesser and greater craft which, sycophant, lumbering

and flittering follow them they appear youthful, rare
as the light of a happy eye, live with the grace
of all that in the mind is feckless, free and
naturally to be desired. Now the sea which holds them

is moody, lapping their glossy sides, as if feeling
for some slightest flaw but fails completely.   20
Today no race. Then the wind comes again. The yachts

move, jockeying for a start, the signal is set and they
are off. Now the waves strike at them but they are too
well made, they slip through, though they take in canvas.

Arms with hands grasping seek to clutch at the prows.
Bodies thrown recklessly in the way are cut aside.
It is a sea of faces about them in agony, in despair

until the horror of the race dawns staggering the mind,
the whole sea becomes an entanglement of watery bodies
lost to the world, bearing what they cannot hold. Broken 30

beaten, desolate, reaching from the dead to be taken up
they cry out, failing, failing! their cries rising
in waves still as the skillful yachts pass over.

                                                            1935

Burning the Christmas Greens

Their time past, pulled down
cracked and flung to the fire
—go up in a roar

All recognition lost, burnt clean
clean in the flame, the green
dispersed, a living red,
flame red, red as blood wakes
on the ash—

and ebbs to a steady burning
the rekindled bed become   10
a landscape of flame

At the winter's midnight
we went to the trees, the coarse
holly, the balsam and
the hemlock for their green

At the thick of the dark
the moment of the cold's
deepest plunge we brought branches
cut from the green trees

to fill our need, and over
doorways, about paper Christmas
bells covered with tinfoil
and fastened by red ribbons

we stuck the green prongs,
in the windows hung
woven wreaths and above pictures
the living green. On the

mantle we built a green forest
and among those hemlock
sprays put a herd of small
white deer as if they

were walking there. All this!
and it seemed gentle and good
to us. Their time past,
relief! The room bare. We

stuffed the dead grate
with them upon the half burnt out
log's smoldering eye, opening
red and closing under them

and we stood there looking down.
Green is a solace
a promise of peace, a fort
against the cold (though we

did not say so) a challenge
above the snow's

hard shell. Green (we might
have said) that, where

small birds hide and dodge
and lift their plaintive
rallying cries, blocks for them   50
and knocks down

the unseeing bullets of
the storm. Green spruce boughs
pulled down by a weight of
snow—Transformed!

Violence leaped and appeared.
Recreant! roared to life
as the flame rose through and
our eyes recoiled from it.

In the jagged flames green   60
to red, instant and alive. Green!
those sure abutments . . . Gone!
lost to mind

and quick in the contracting
tunnel of the grate
appeared a world! Black
mountains, black and red—as

yet uncolored—and ash white,
an infant landscape of shimmering
ash and flame and we, in   70
that instant, lost,

breathless to be witnesses,
as if we stood
ourselves refreshed among
the shining fauna of that fire.

                                                    1944

E. E. CUMMINGS
(1894–1962)

The change from E. E. Cummings to "e. e. cummings" is an indication of the poet's attempt to concentrate all objects into hard, separate words liberated from the usual hierarchies demanded by normal usage. The consequent mechanics of Cummings' poetry made him one of the most controversial figures on the modern literary horizon, although recent studies and his continued output made him less the subject of bitter vilification or total adoration and more the subject of critical understanding.

Cummings was born in Cambridge, Massachusetts, the son of a Harvard English professor who accepted the pastorate of Boston's Old South Church in 1905 and remained in that post until 1926. Recognizing his father's former employer as a passably decent educational institution, Cummings attended Harvard and received his B.A. in 1915 and his M.A. a year later. In 1917, like many other young men who later became writers in the 1920's, Cummings volunteered for ambulance service in the war and served in France with the small but famous Norton Harjes Ambulance Corps. By a chilling error concerning censorship, he was indicted for treason and was imprisoned in a French detention camp for several months. When he was released, he joined the United States Army. Mustered out, he returned to Paris two years after the war was over in order to study painting.

All the while, however, he was writing and publishing occasional poems; his novel, *The Enormous Room*, Cummings' account of his detention camp experiences and one of the very best books to come out of World War I, appeared in 1922. In the following year he published *Tulips and Chimneys*, his first volume of verse. Henceforth he was a poet. From the very beginning of his career, Cummings' experiments with syntax and typography made him the center of raging debate; but, in reality, he was only one more member of the iconoclastic and radical literary generation which combined postwar disillusionment with the excitement of experimentation in the arts and sciences. His lower-case typography, for example, was a deliberate attempt to allow words to assume a symbolic presence which would generate meanings that had coherence in the associational workings of the mind rather than in the grammatical logic of conventional expectations. (Sigmund Freud, James Joyce, and Gertrude Stein were no small influences in the literature produced by Cummings' generation.) The titles of some of his works indicate how unusual the books looked to his contemporaries: & (1925); *Is 5* (1926); *Him* (1927); *CIOPW* (1931); *VV (Viva: Seventy New Poems)*, (1931); *Eimi* (1933); *No Thanks* (1935); *1/20 (One over Twenty): Poems* (1936); *1 x 1* (1944).

His subject matter and attitudes sometimes seem brutal and perhaps even shocking, particularly when he is excoriating business ethics, the middle class, commercialism, patriotism. However, some of his lyrics and love poems are among the most exquisite in the language, and it is probably as a lyricist, as well as an experimentalist, that Cummings will be remembered. In addition to several other awards and honors, Cummings won the Bollingen Prize in 1957.

Some other works by Cummings are *Anthropos: The Future of Art* (1945); *Santa Claus: A Morality* (1946); *i: six nonlectures* (1953); and G. J. Firmage, ed., *E. E. Cummings: A Miscellany* (1958, rev. 1965). Most of the earlier poems are collected in *Poems, 1923–1954* (1954); to which must be added the later works: *95 Poems* (1958); *100 Selected Poems* (1959); and *50 Poems* (1960).
Studies of the man and his work are to be found in P. Rosenfeld, *Men Seen* (1925); R. P. Blackmur, *The Double Agent* (1935); B. Deutsch, *This Modern Poetry* (1935); F. B. Millett, *Contemporary American Authors* (1940); J. Arthos, "The Poetry of E. E. Cummings," *American Literature*, XIV (1943); *The Harvard Wake*, No. 5 (Spring, 1946)—a Cummings issue; K. Shapiro, "Prosody as the Meaning," *Poetry*, LXXIII (1949); P. Lauter, *E. E. Cummings: Index to First Lines and Bibliography of Works by and about the Poet* (1955); R. Von Abele, " 'Only to Grow': Change in the Poetry of E. E. Cummings," *PMLA*, LXX (1955); N. Friedman, "Diction, Voice, and Tone: The Poetic Language of E. E. Cummings," *PMLA*, LXXII (1957); C. Norman, *The Magic-Maker: E. E. Cummings* (1958, rev. 1965); G. J. Firmage, *E. E. Cummings: A Bibliography* (1960,

rev. 1964); N. Friedman, *E. E. Cummings: The Art of His Poetry* (1960); S. V. Baum, ed., *EETI:eec* (1961); N. Friedman, *e. e. cummings: The Growth of a Writer* (1964); B. A. Marks, *E. E. Cummings* (1964); and R. E. Wegner, *The Poetry and Prose of E. E. Cummings* (1965).

[*in Just-spring*]

in Just-
spring   when the world is mud-
luscious the little
lame balloonman

whistles   far   and wee

and eddieandbill come
running from marbles and
piracies and it's
spring

when the world is puddle-wonderful

the queer
old balloonman whistles
far   and   wee
and bettyandisbel come dancing

from hop-scotch and jump-rope and

it's
spring
and
     the

          goat-footed   20

balloonMan   whistles
far
and
wee

                                                        1920

[*Thy fingers make early flowers*]

Thy fingers make early flowers of
all things.
thy hair mostly the hours love:
a smoothness which
sings, saying
(though love be a day)
do not fear, we will go amaying.

thy whitest feet crisply are straying.
Always
thy moist eyes are at kisses playing,   10
whose strangeness much
says; singing
(though love be a day)
for which girl art thou flowers bringing?

To be thy lips is a sweet thing
and small.
Death, Thee i call rich beyond wishing
if this thou catch,
else missing.
(though love be a day   20
and life be nothing, it shall not stop kissing).

1923

[*Buffalo Bill's defunct*]

Buffalo Bill's
defunct
      who used to
      ride a watersmooth-silver
            stallion
and break onetwothreefourfive pigeonsjustlikethat
              Jesus

he was a handsome man
           and what i want to know is
how do you like your blueeyed boy
Mister Death

1923

[O Thou to whom the musical white spring]

O Thou to whom the musical white spring

offers her lily inextinguishable,
taught by thy tremulous grace bravely to fling

Implacable death's mysteriously sable
robe from her redolent shoulders,
                    Thou from whose
feet reincarnate song suddenly leaping
flameflung, mounts, inimitably to lose
herself where the wet stars softly are keeping

their exquisite dreams—O Love! upon thy dim   10
shrine of intangible commemoration,
(from whose faint close as some grave languorous hymn

pledged to illimitable dissipation
unhurried clouds of incense fleetly roll)

i spill my bright incalculable soul.

                                        1924

["next to of course god]

"next to of course god america i
love you land of the pilgrims' and so forth oh
say can you see by the dawn's early my
country 'tis of centuries come and go
and are no more what of it we should worry
in every language even deafanddumb
thy sons acclaim your glorious name by gorry
by jingo by gee by gosh by gum
why talk of beauty what could be more beautiful than these heroic happy dead   10
who rushed like lions to the roaring slaughter
they did not stop to think they died instead
then shall the voice of liberty be mute?"

He spoke.   And drank rapidly a glass of water

                                        1926

[somewhere i have never travelled]

somewhere i have never travelled,gladly beyond
any experience,your eyes have their silence:
in your most frail gesture are things which enclose me,,
or which i cannot touch because they are too near

your slightest look easily will unclose me
though i have closed myself as fingers,
you open always petal by petal myself as Spring opens
(touching skilfully,mysteriously) her first rose

or if your wish be to close me,i and
my life will shut very beautifully,suddenly,   10
as when the heart of this flower imagines
the snow carefully everywhere descending;

nothing which we are to perceive in this world equals
the power of your intense fragility:whose texture
compels me with the colour of its countries,
rendering death and forever with each breathing

(i do not know what it is about you that closes
and opens;only something in me understands
the voice of your eyes is deeper than all roses)
nobody,not even the rain,has such small hands   20

               1931

[i sing of Olaf]

i sing of Olaf glad and big
whose warmest heart recoiled at war:
a conscientious object-or

his well-belovéd colonel(trig
westpointer most succinctly bred)
took erring Olaf soon in hand;
but—though an host of overjoyed
noncoms(first knocking on the head
him)do through icy waters roll
that helplessness which others stroke   10

with brushes recently employed
anent this muddy toiletbowl,
while kindred intellects evoke
allegiance per blunt instruments—
Olaf(being to all intents
a corpse and wanting any rag
upon what God unto him gave)
responds,without getting annoyed
"I will not kiss your f.ing flag"

straightway the silver bird looked grave   20
(departing hurriedly to shave)

but—though all kinds of officers
(a yearning nation's blueeyed pride)
their passive prey did kick and curse
until for wear their clarion
voices and boots were much the worse,
and egged the firstclassprivates on
his rectum wickedly to tease
by means of skilfully applied
bayonets roasted hot with heat—   30
Olaf(upon what were once knees)
does almost ceaselessly repeat
"there is some s. I will not eat"

our president,being of which
assertions duly notified
threw the yellowsonofabitch
into a dungeon,where he died

Christ(of His mercy infinite)
i pray to see;and Olaf,too

preponderatingly because   40
unless statistics lie he was
more brave than me:more blond than you.

                                        1931

[anyone lived in a pretty how town]

anyone lived in a pretty how town
(with up so floating many bells down)
spring summer autumn winter
he sang his didn't he danced his did.

Women and men(both little and small)
cared for anyone not at all
they sowed their isn't they reaped their same
sun moon stars rain

children guessed(but only a few
and down they forgot as up they grew
autumn winter spring summer)
that noone loved him more by more

when by now and tree by leaf
she laughed his joy she cried his grief
bird by snow and stir by still
anyone's any was all to her

someones married their everyones
laughed their cryings and did their dance
(sleep wake hope and then)they
said their nevers they slept their dream   20

stars rain sun moon
(and only the snow can begin to explain
how children are apt to forget to remember
with up so floating many bells down)

one day anyone died i guess
(and noone stooped to kiss his face)
busy folk buried them side by side
little by little and was by was

all by all and deep by deep
and more by more they dream their sleep   30
noone and anyone earth by april
wish by spirit and if by yes.

Women and men(both dong and ding)
summer autumn winter spring
reaped their sowing and went their came
sun moon stars rain

1940

HART CRANE

(1899–1932)

Hart Crane spent his brief life in an agony of suspense between angrily rejecting and struggling to accept the world
about him. He rejected college, business, commerce, and the
vulgarity of America. Yet, like F. Scott Fitzgerald, he saw in
America's vast meretricious beauty a power that he tried to
understand, accept, and express. He came as close as he
was ever to come in *The Bridge*, one of the most compelling
of all modern poems.

Born in Garretsville, Ohio, Crane grew up in Cleveland, coming to hate the Midwest and all it stood for in his mind: a
dollar-sign gilt, bars restrictive, and a Babbitt rampant. As a
youth he was deeply affected by the bad marriage of his
parents, whose eventual separation widened even further the
fissure between himself and his father. He repudiated his
father's candy business and gravitated to New York, drifting
through various jobs as a clerk, salesman, and mechanic, and
through various visits to the West Indies sugar plantation of
his mother's family. By 1922 he was settled in New York,
barely earning an irregular and unhappy living as an advertising writer. Yet all the while he continued to write poetry,
which he had begun to do at the age of thirteen. He immersed
himself in the avant-garde company of the people who were
associated with such little magazines as *The Seven Arts* and
The Little Review.

White Buildings (1926), the first of the two books he published, did little to win him general recognition, although it
was hailed by the cognoscenti. He attempted to write poetry
whose images and metaphors would make their own relation-

ships and meanings, and, like E. E. Cummings and Emily Dickinson, he used words in unaccustomed and startling ways; the general effect was one which tended to destroy the understanding that is communicated by the customary means of logical syntax, verbal definition, and grammar. To many readers, much of his poetry remains obscure.

Crane brooded about the kinds of images which would bear and bare his mystical sense of American energy and history, and express the central symbol of his mystique, The Brooklyn Bridge. From his mean room in Brooklyn Heights, Crane commanded a sweeping view of the bridge, and like Whitman, who had brooded over the same harbor before him, Crane determined to be the modern voice of that inarticulate yet fantastic complex that is America. In opposition to the repudiation of Eliot and his followers, Crane tried to express the vision that transcends the brutality, vulgarity, and commercialism of America and that makes it more than a convenient image of the modern-day wasteland of Western civilization. *The Bridge*, in brief, is an imaginative attempt to discover the unifying myth of our time and of America itself.

Although *The Bridge* won *Poetry* magazine's award for 1930, Crane felt no more "arrived," no more at home in the world, than he had before. He won a Guggenheim award in 1931 to go to Mexico in order to write an epic poem about that country. He failed to do so. Depressed by his failure, troubled by his homosexuality, anxious about the awaiting actuality of America, which he felt was so destructive of his re-creative mythic vision, unhappy about his family and life itself, he committed suicide by jumping from the stern of the ship that was returning him to New York from Mexico.

The *Collected Poems*, edited with an excellent introduction by Waldo Frank in 1933, includes the poems of *White Buildings*, *The Bridge*, and additional early and late fugitive pieces.

Studies of the man and his work are to be found in G. B. Munson, *Destinations* (1928); R. P. Blackmur, *The Double Agent* (1935); A. Tate, *Reactionary Essays on Poetry and Ideas* (1936); P. Horton, *Hart Crane* (1937, 1957); F. O. Matthiessen, "Hart Crane," *Dictionary of American Biography, Supplement One* (1944); Y. Winters, *In Defense of Reason* (1947); B. Weber, *Hart Crane* (1948); B. Ghiselin, "Bridge into the Sea," *Partisan Review*, XVI (1949); S. K. Coffman, Jr., "Symbolism in *The Bridge*," *PMLA*, LXVI (1951); B. Weber, ed., *The Letters of Hart Crane* (1953); F. J. Hoffman, *The Twenties* (1955); L. Dembo, "The Unfractioned Idiom of Hart Crane's *The Bridge*," *American Literature*, XXVII (1955); H. D. Rowe,

Hart Crane: A Bibliography (1955); J. Kloucek, "The Framework of Hart Crane's *The Bridge,*" *Midwest Review* (1960); S. Hazo, *Hart Crane: An Introduction and Interpretation* (1963); V. Quinn, *Hart Crane* (1963); and M. K. Spears, *Hart Crane* (1965).

Voyages: II

And yet this great wink of eternity,
Of rimless floods, unfettered leewardings,
Samite sheeted and processioned where
Her undinal vast belly moonward bends,
Laughing the wrapt inflections of our love;

Take this Sea, whose diapason knells
On scrolls of silver snowy sentences,
The sceptred terror of whose sessions rends
As her demeanors motion well or ill,
All but the pieties of lovers' hands.   10

And onward, as bells off San Salvador
Salute the crocus lustres of the stars,
In these poinsettia meadows of her tides,—
Adagios of islands, O my Prodigal,
Complete the dark confessions her veins spell.

Mark how her turning shoulders wind the hours,
And hasten while her penniless rich palms
Pass superscription of bent foam and wave,—
Hasten, while they are true,—sleep, death, desire,
Close round one instant in one floating flower.   20

Bind us in time, O seasons clear, and awe.
O minstrel galleons of Carib fire,
Bequeath us to no earthly shore until
Is answered in the vortex of our grave
The seal's wide spindrift gaze toward paradise.

                                        1926

The Bridge

Proem: To Brooklyn Bridge

How many dawns, chill from his rippling rest
The seagull's wings shall dip and pivot him,
Shedding white rings of tumult, building high
Over the chained bay waters Liberty—

Then, with inviolate curve, forsake our eyes
As apparitional as sails that cross
Some page of figures to be filed away;
—Till elevators drop us from our day . . .

I think of cinemas, panoramic sleights
With multitudes bent toward some flashing scene   10
Never disclosed, but hastened to again,
Foretold to other eyes on the same screen;—

And Thee, across the harbor, silver-paced
As though the sun took step of thee, yet left
Some motion ever unspent in thy stride,—
Implicitly thy freedom staying thee!

Out of some subway scuttle, cell or loft
A bedlamite speeds to thy parapets,
Tilting there momently, shrill shirt ballooning,
A jest falls from the speechless caravan.   20

Down Wall, from girder into street noon leaks,
A rip-tooth of the sky's acetylene;
All afternoon the cloud-flown derricks turn . . .
Thy cables breathe the North Atlantic still.

And obscure as that heaven of the Jews,
Thy guerdon . . . Accolade thou dost bestow
Of anonymity time cannot raise:
Vibrant reprieve and pardon thou dost show.

O harp and altar, of the fury fused,
(How could mere toil align thy choiring strings)   30
Terrific threshold of the prophet's pledge,
Prayer of pariah, and the lover's cry,—

Again the traffic lights that skim thy swift
Unfractioned idiom, immaculate sigh of stars,
Beading thy path—condense eternity:
And we have seen night lifted in thine arms.

Under thy shadow by the piers I waited;
Only in darkness is thy shadow clear.
The City's fiery parcels all undone,
Already snow submerges an iron year . . .   40

O Sleepless as the river under thee,
Vaulting the sea, the prairies' dreaming sod,
Unto us lowliest sometime sweep, descend
And of the curveship lend a myth to God.

Van Winkle

[*Streets spread past store and factory-sped by sunlight and
her smile . . .*]

Macadam, gun-grey as the tunny's belt,
Leaps from Far Rockaway to Golden Gate:
Listen! the miles a hurdy-gurdy grinds—
Down gold arpeggios mile on mile unwinds.

Times earlier, when you hurried off to school,
—It is the same hour though a later day—
You walked with Pizarro in a copybook,
And Cortez rode up, reining tautly in—
Firmly as coffee grips the taste,—and away!

There was Priscilla's cheek close in the wind,
And Captain Smith, all beard and certainty,
And Rip Van Winkle, bowing by the way,—
"Is this Sleepy Hollow, friend—?" And he—

[*Like Memory, she is time's truant, shall take you by the
hand . . .*]

And Rip forgot the office hours,
                              and he forgot the pay;
      Van Winkle sweeps a tenement
                   down town on Avenue A,—

The grind-organ says . . . Remember, remember
The cinder pile at the end of the backyard
Where we stoned the family of young
Garter snakes under . . . And the monoplanes
We launched—with paper wings and twisted
Rubber bands. . . . Recall—recall
                              the rapid tongues
That flittered from under the ash heap day
After day whenever your stick discovered
Some sunning inch of unsuspecting fibre—   70
It flashed back at your thrust, as clean as fire.

And Rip was slowly made aware
      that he, Van Winckle, was not here
      Nor there. He woke and swore he'd seen Broadway
      a Catskill daisy chain in May—

So memory, that strikes a rhyme out of a box,
Or splits a random smell of flowers through glass—
Is it the whip stripped from the lilac tree
One day in spring my father took to me,
Or is it the Sabbatical, unconscious smile   80
My mother almost brought me once from church
And once only, as I recall—?

It flickered through the snow screen, blindly
It forsook her at the doorway, it was gone
Before I had left the window. It
Did not return with the kiss in the hall.

Macadam, gun-grey as the tunny's belt,
Leaps from Far Rockaway to Golden Gate . . .
Keep hold of that nickel for car-change, Rip,—
Have you got your *"Times"*—?   90
And hurry along, Van Winkle—it's getting late!

The River

[. . . *and past the din and slogans of the year*—]

Stick your patent name on a signboard
brother—all over—going west—young man
Tintex—Japalac—Certain-teed Overalls ads
and lands sakes! under the new playbill ripped
in the guaranteed corner—see Bert Williams what?
Ministrels when you steal a chicken just
save me the wing, for if it isn't
Erie it ain't for miles around a
Mazda—the telegraphic night coming on Thomas   100

a Ediford—and whistling down the tracks
a headlight rushing with the sound—can you
imagine—while an EXPRESS makes time like
SCIENCE—COMMERCE and the HOLYGHOST
RADIO ROARS IN EVERY HOME WE HAVE THE NORTHPOLE
WALLSTREET AND VIRGINBIRTH WITHOUT STONES OR
WIRES OR EVEN RUNning brooks connecting ears
and no more sermons windows flashing roar
Breathtaking—as you like it . . . eh?

                         So the 20th Century—so
whizzed the Limited—roared by and left   110
three men, still hungry on the tracks, ploddingly
watching the tail lights wizen and converge, slipping gimleted and neatly out of sight.

                    *

[*to those whose addresses are never near*]

The last bear, shot drinking in the Dakotas,
Loped under wires that span the mountain stream.
Keen instruments, strung to a vast precision
Bind town to town and dream to ticking dream.
But some men take their liquor slow—and count
—Though they'll confess no rosary nor clue—
The river's minute by the far brook's year.   120
Under a world of whistles, wires and steam

Caboose-like they go ruminating through
Ohio, Indiana—blind baggage—
To Cheyenne tagging . . . Maybe Kalamazoo.

Time's renderings, time's blendings they construe
As final reckonings of fire and snow;
Strange bird-wit, like the elemental gist
Of unwalled winds they offer, singing low
My Old Kentucky Home and *Casey Jones,
Some Sunny Day*. I heard a road-gang chanting so.   130
And afterwards, who had a colt's eyes—one said,
"Jesus! Oh I remember watermelon days!" And sped
High in a cloud of merriment, recalled
"—And when my Aunt Sally Simpson smiled," he
      drawled—
"It was almost Louisiana, long ago."

"There's no place like Booneville though, Buddy,"
One said, excising a last burr from his vest,
"—For early trouting." Then peering in the can,
"—But I kept on the tracks." Possessed, resigned,
He trod the fire down pensively and grinned,   140
Spreading dry shingles of a beard. . . .

                                        Behind

My father's cannery works I used to see
Rail-squatters ranged in nomad raillery,
The ancient men—wifeless or runaway
Hobo-trekkers that forever search
An empire wilderness of freight and rails.
Each seemed a child, like me, on a loose perch,
Holding to childhood like some termless play.
John, Jake, or Charley, hopping the slow freight
—Memphis to Tallahassee—riding the rods,   150
Blind fists of nothing, humpty-dumpty clods.

   [*but who have touched her, knowing her without name*]

Yet they touch something like a key perhaps.
From pole to pole across the hills, the states
—They know a body under the wide rain;
Youngsters with eyes like fjords, old reprobates
With racetrack jargon,—dotting immensity

They lurk across her, knowing her yonder breast
Snow-silvered, sumac-stained or smoky blue,
Is past the valley-sleepers, south or west.
—As I have trod the rumorous midnights, too.   160

And past the circuit of the lamp's thin flame
(O Nights that brought me to her body bare!)
Have dreamed beyond the print that bound her name.
Trains sounding the long blizzards out—I heard
Wail into distances I knew were hers.
Papooses crying on the wind's long mane
Screamed redskin dynasties that fled the brain,
—Dead echoes! But I knew her body there,
Time like a serpent down her shoulder, dark,
And space, an eaglet's wing, laid on her hair.   170

                    [*nor the myths of her fathers* . . .]

Under the Ozarks, domed by Iron Mountain,
The old gods of the rain lie wrapped in pools
Where eyeless fish curvet a sunken fountain
And re-descend with corn from querulous crows.
Such pilferings make up their timeless eatage,
Propitiate them for their timber torn
By iron, iron—always the iron dealt cleavage!
They doze now, below axe and powder horn.

And Pullman breakfasters glide glistening steel
From tunnel into field—iron strides the dew—   180
Straddles the hill, a dance of wheel on wheel.
You have a half-hour's wait at Siskiyou,
Or stay the night and take the next train through.
Southward, near Cairo passing, you can see
The Ohio merging,—borne down Tennessee;
And if it's summer and the sun's in dusk
Maybe the breeze will lift the River's musk
—As though the waters breathed that you might know
Memphis Johnny, Steamboat Bill, Missouri Joe.
Oh, lean from the window, if the train slows down,   190
As though you touched hands with some ancient clown,
—A little while gaze absently below
And hum *Deep River* with them while they go.

Yes, turn again and sniff once more—look see,
O Sheriff, Brakeman and Authority—
Hitch up your pants and crunch another quid,
For you, too, feed the River timelessly.
And few evade full measure of their fate;
Always they smile out eerily what they seem.
I could believe he joked at heaven's gate—   200
Dan Midland—jolted from the cold brake-beam.

Down, down—born pioneers in time's despite,
Grimed tributaries to an ancient flow—
They win no frontier by their wayward plight,
But drift in stillness, as from Jordan's brow.

You will not hear it as the sea; even stone
Is not more hushed by gravity . . . But slow,
As loth to take more tribute—sliding prone
Like one whose eyes were buried long ago

The River, spreading, flows—and spends your dream.   210
What are you, lost within this tideless spell?
You are your father's father, and the stream—
A liquid theme that floating niggers swell.

Damp tonnage and alluvial march of days—
Nights turbid, vascular with silted shale
And roots surrendered down of moraine clays:
The Mississippi drinks the farthest dale.

O quarrying passion, undertowed sunlight!
The basalt surface drags a jungle grace
Ochreous and lynx-barred in lengthening might;   220
Patience! and you shall reach the biding place!

Over De Soto's bones the freighted floors
Throb past the City storied of three thrones.
Down two more turns the Mississippi pours
(Anon tall ironsides up from salt lagoons)

And flows within itself, heaps itself free.
All fades but one thin skyline 'round . . . Ahead
No embrace opens but the stinging sea;
The River lifts itself from its long bed,

Poised wholly on its dream, a mustard glow,   230
Tortured with history, its one will—flow!
—The Passion spreads in wide tongues, chocked and slow,
Meeting the Gulf, hosannas silently below.

III. Cutty Sark

> *O, the navies old and oaken,*
> *O, the Temeraire no more!*
>   —MELVILLE

I met a man in South Street, tall—
a nervous shark tooth swung on his chain.
His eyes pressed through green grass
—green glasses, or bar lights made them
so—
    shine—
        GREEN—   240
            eyes—
stepped out—forgot to look at you
or left you several blocks away—

in the nickel-in-the-slot piano jogged
"Stamboul Nights"—weaving somebody's nickel
    sang—

    O Stamboul Rose—dreams weave the rose!

    Murmurs of Leviathan he spoke,
    and rum was Plato in our heads . . .
"It's S.S. *Ala*—Antwerp,—now remember kid
to put me out at three she sails on time.   250
I'm not much good at time any more keep
weakeyed watches sometimes snooze—" his bony hands
got to beating time . . . "A whaler once—
I ought to keep time and get over it—I'm a
Democrat—I know what time it is—No
I don't want to know what time it is—that
damned white Arctic killed my time . . ."

    O Stamboul Rose—drums weave—

"I ran a donkey engine down there on the Canal
in Panama—got tired of that—   260
then Yucatan selling kitchenware—beads—
have you seen Popocatepetl—birdless mouth
with ashes sifting down—?

             and then the coast again . . ."

    Rose of Stamboul O coral Queen—
    teased remnants of the skeletons of cities—
    and galleries, galleries of watergutted lava
    snarling stone—green—drums—drown

Sing!
"—that spiracle!" he shot a finger out the door . . .
"O life's a geyser—beautiful—my lungs—   270
No—I can't live on land—!"

I saw the frontiers gleaming of his mind;
or are there frontiers—running sands sometimes
running sands—somewhere—sands running . . .
Or they may start some white machine that sings.
Then you may laugh and dance the axletree—
steel—silver—kick the traces—and know—

    ATLANTIS ROSE drums wreathe the rose,
    the star floats burning in a gulf of tears
    and sleep another thousand—

                  interminably   280
long since somebody's nickel—stopped—
playing—

A wind worried those wicker-neat lapels, the
swinging summer entrances to cooler hells . . .
Outside a wharf truck nearly ran him down
—he lunged up Bowery way while the dawn
was putting the Statue of Liberty out—that
torch of hers you know—

I started walking home across the Bridge . . .

                 *

Blithe Yankee vanities, turreted sprites, winged   290
                    British repartees, skil-
ful savage sea-girls

that bloomed in the spring—Heave, weave
those bright designs the trade winds drive . . .

   Sweet opium and tea, Yo-ho!
   Pennies for porpoises that bank the keel!
   Fins whip the breeze around Japan!

Bright skysails ticketing the line, wink round the Horn
to Frisco, Melbourne . . .
                              Pennants, parabolas—
clipper dreams indelible and ranging,
baronial white on lucky blue!   300

   Perrenial-*Cutty*-trophied-*Sark!*

Thermopylae, Black Prince, Flying Cloud through Sunda
—scarfed of foam, their bellies veered green esplanades,
locked in wind-humors, ran their eastings down;

   at Java Head freshened the nip
   (sweet opium and tea!)
   and turned and left us on the lee . . .

Buntlines tusseling (91 days, 20 hours and anchored!)
                              Rainbow, Leander
(last trip a tragedy)—where can you be
Nimbus? and you rivals two—   310

      a long tack keeping—

                              Taeping?
                              Ariel?

                              1930

MARIANNE MOORE

(1887–   )

Like Wallace Stevens, Marianne Moore mixed business and poetry. After she was graduated from Bryn Mawr in 1909, she enrolled for a year in courses in business administration in the Metzger Institute in Carlisle, Pennsylvania. For four years thereafter, she taught business in a Carlisle School, at the end of which time, in 1915, *Poetry* and *The Egoist* (soon to be edited by T. S. Eliot) first published some of her poems. From that time on, she abandoned the business of business for the business of professional writing.

Like T. S. Eliot, she was born in St. Louis, and, also like him, she turned toward England, where her first volume, *Poems* (1921), arranged by Hilda Doolittle and other of the Imagists, was published. Her first volume to be published in America, *Observations* (1924), won an award from the *Dial*, which she began to edit from the following year until 1929. When the *Dial* folded, to take its place among the other extinct and exciting experimental magazines of the postwar era, Miss Moore moved to Brooklyn, the residence with which she became identified, though she transferred to Manhattan in 1966.

Like Hart Crane, E. E. Cummings, and the entire generation of poets influenced by T. S. Eliot, she has written poems in which the condensed metaphor transcends conventional grammatical logic, drawing experience out of the chaotic welter of things seen and compacting it to order and meaning.

Like Marianne Moore and no one else, she presents the thing seen with a precise clarity of detail whose simplicity is expanded with the wit of the metaphysical poets, to whom she has often been compared. Wide general recognition came to her with the publication of *Selected Poems* in 1935, and her *Collected Poems* (1951) won her the National Book Award, the Bollingen Award, and the Pulitzer Prize. Her complete translation of La Fontaine's fables appeared in 1954 and *Complete Poems* in 1967.

Miss Moore's other books are *The Pangolin and Other Verse* (1936), *What Are Years* (1941), *Nevertheless* (1944), *A Face* (1949), *Predilections* (criticism, 1955), *Like a Bulwark* (1956), *O To Be a Dragon* (1959), *A Marianne Moore Reader* (1961), and *Tell Me, Tell Me* (1966).

Studies of Miss Moore and her work are to be found in L. Untermeyer, *American Poetry since 1900* (1923); P. Rosenfeld, *Men Seen* (1925); William Carlos Williams, "Marianne Moore," *Dial*, LXXVIII (1925); G. B. Munson, *Destinations* (1928); A. Kreymborg, *Our Singing Strength* (1929); R. P. Blackmur, *The Double Agent* (1935); T. S. Eliot, introduction to the *Selected Poems of Marianne Moore* (1935); M. D. Zabel, *Literary Opinion in America* (1937); K. Burke, "Motives and Motifs in the Poetry of Marianne Moore," *Accent*, II (1942); R. Jarrell, "Thoughts about Marianne Moore," *Partisan Review*, XIX (1952); W. D. Snodgrass, "Elegance in Marianne Moore," *Western Review*, XIX (1954); R. Beloof, "Prosody and Tone: The 'Mathematics' of Marianne Moore," *Kenyon Review*, XX (1958); M. Borroff, "Dramatic Structure in the Poetry of Marianne Moore," *Literary Review* (1958); E. P. Sheehy and A. Lohf, *The Achievement of Marianne Moore: A Bibliography, 1907–1957* (1958); B. F. Engel, *Marianne Moore* (1964); and J. Garrigue, *Marianne Moore* (1965).

Poetry*

I, too, dislike it: there are things that are important beyond
     all this fiddle.
  Reading it, however, with a perfect contempt for it, one
     discovers in
  it after all, a place for the genuine.
    Hands that can grasp, eyes
    that can dilate, hair that can rise
      if it must, these things are important not because a

high-sounding interpretation can be put upon them but
     because they are
  useful. When they become so derivative as to become
     unintelligible,
  the same thing may be said for all of us, that we
    do not admire what   10

* See Editor's note on page 566.

        we cannot understand: the bat
           holding on upside down or in quest of something to

eat, elephants pushing, a wild horse taking a roll, a tireless
        wolf under
        a tree, the immovable critic twitching his skin like a
           horse that feels a flea, the base-
        ball fan, the statistician—
           nor is it valid
               to discriminate against "business documents and

school-books"; all these phenomena are important. One
        must make a distinction
        however: when dragged into prominence by half poets,
           the result is not poetry,

nor till the poets among us can be "literalists of   20
        the imagination"—above
           insolence and triviality and can present

for inspection, imaginary gardens with real toads in them,
        shall we have
        it. In the meantime, if you demand on the one hand,
        the raw material of poetry in
           all its rawness and
           that which is on the other hand
               genuine, then you are interested in poetry.

                                   1921

The Fish

wade
through black jade.
    Of the crow-blue mussel-shells, one keeps
    adjusting the ash-heaps;
        opening and shutting itself like

an
injured fan.
    The barnacles which encrust the side
    of the wave, cannot hide
        there for the submerged shafts of the   10

sun,
split like spun
    glass, move themselves with spotlight swiftness
    into the crevices—
        in and out, illuminating

the
turquoise sea
    of bodies. The water drives a wedge
    of iron through the iron edge
        of the cliff; whereupon the stars,   20

pink
rice-grains, ink
    bespattered jelly-fish, crabs like green
    lilies, and submarine
        toadstools, slide each on the other.

All
external
    marks of abuse are present on this
    defiant edifice—
        all the physical features of   30

Ac-
cident—lack
    of cornice, dynamite grooves, burns, and
    hatchet strokes, these things stand
        out on it; the chasm-side is

dead.
Repeated
    evidence has proved that it can live
    on what cannot revive
        its youth. The sea grows old in it.   40
                                                              1921

A Grave

Man looking into the sea,
taking the view from those who have as much right to
    it as you have to it yourself,

it is human nature to stand in the middle of a thing,
but you cannot stand in the middle of this; the sea has
    nothing to give but a well excavated grave.
The firs stand in a procession, each with an emerald
    turkey-foot at the top,
reserved as their contours, saying nothing; repression, how-
    ever, is not the most obvious characteristic of the sea;
the sea is a collector, quick to return a rapacious look.
There are others besides you who have worn that look— 10
whose expression is no longer a protest; the fish no longer
    investigate them
for their bones have not lasted:
men lower nets, unconscious of the fact that they are
    desecrating a grave,
and row quickly away—the blades of the oars
moving together like the feet of water-spiders as if there
    were no such thing as death.
The wrinkles progress upon themselves in a phalanx—
    beautiful under networks of foam,
and fade breathlessly while the sea rustles in and out of
    the seaweed;
the birds swim through the air at top speed, emitting cat-
    calls as heretofore—
the tortoise-shell scourges about the feet of the cliffs, in
    motion beneath them;
and the ocean, under the pulsation of lighthouses and noise
    of bell-buoys,   20
advances as usual, looking as if it were not that ocean in
    which dropped things are bound to sink—
in which if they turn and twist, it is neither with volition
    nor consciousness.

                                           1924

Editors' note: In her *Complete Poems* (1967) Marianne Moore relegated
to an appendix the version of "Poetry" quoted on page 563, and substi-
tuted this much shorter version.

Poetry

    I, too, dislike it.
        Reading it, however, with a perfect contempt for it,
                                one discovers in
    it, after all, a place for the genuine.

ARCHIBALD MACLEISH

(1892–   )

In 1928, Archibald MacLeish published *The Hamlet of A. MacLeish*. In 1930 he published *New Found Land*. Between these books there solidified a growing change in MacLeish's perspectives that in some ways makes the two works seem ages rather than a mere two years apart. The first derivatively reflected the modish despair over the spiritual decay of Western civilization that permeated the thought and writing of the expatriates who adopted the attitudes of Pound and Eliot. The later work bursts with an affirmative sense of American idealism and folk destiny that is akin to the feeling for the Republic which one finds in the work of MacLeish's Yale classmate, Stephen Vincent Benét. Throughout the continuation of MacLeish's career, his work has generally reflected the second mood rather than the first.

Born in Glencoe, Illinois, MacLeish attended a Connecticut preparatory school and Yale University, from which he was graduated in 1915. While at Harvard Law School, where he studied for the bar after completing his undergraduate work, he published two volumes of verse, *Songs for a Summer Day* (1915) and *Tower of Ivory* (1917). When the United States entered World War I, he enlisted as a private and emerged from the army as an artillery captain. Following the war, he practiced law unhappily in Boston from 1919 to 1923, when, surrendering to the more puissant sirens of poetry, he moved with his wife and children to Paris. In Europe he came to know Pound and Eliot, learning his craft under their influence. The books he published there, *The Happy Marriage and Other*

Poems (1924), *The Pot of Earth* (1925), *Nobodaddy* (1926), *Streets in the Moon* (which, in 1926, first won him wide acceptance), reflected the impact that anthropology and myth (via Frazer), Pound, Eliot, and the French symbolistes had on the "lost generation" expatriates.

But on his return to the United States in 1928, MacLeish increasingly was captured by an enlarging social consciousness that became aware of the ironic discrepancies between the American dream and various aspects of the American actuality. He began to feel that many concerns of the expatriate artists, of all genres, had little responsible relationship to life. The change was embodied in *New Found Land* and, especially, *Conquistador* (1932), which he wrote out of an extended visit to Mexico. The combined sense of American affirmation and radical social consciousness became particularly pronounced a year later in *Frescoes for Mr. Rockefeller's City*, which satirizes the attitudes and practices of American big business. Mac-Leish's antipathy to American commercialism grew out of the materials he assembled and researched while he was an editor of *Fortune* magazine.

In 1939 President Roosevelt appointed him Librarian of Congress, a post he kept until 1944, when he became an Assistant Secretary of State for a year. During the 1930's and 1940's, again like Benét, MacLeish became acutely disturbed by the rise of totalitarianism evidenced by the waxing of fascist power; he tried to combat it and the depression "blues" by communicating a rallying sense of hope and purpose to the American people. His verse drama *Panic* (1935) and his verse plays for radio, *The Fall of the City* (1937) and *Air Raid* (1938), together with the commentary of *Land of the Free* (1938), the poetry of *Public Speech* (1936), and *America Was Promises* (1940), the declaration of *The Irresponsibles* (1940), and the exhortation of *The American Cause* (1941), *A Time to Speak* (1941), and *A Time to Act* (1942) were announcements of his sense of immediacy and of the social uses of literature during a time when he felt democracy was imperiled.

MacLeish headed the American delegation to UNESCO in 1946. In 1949 he became a professor of English at Harvard, retiring in 1967. His *J.B.: A Play in Verse* (1958), based on the story of Job, was produced on Broadway in 1959 and won a Pulitzer Prize, as did his *Collected Poems, 1917–1952* (1953). His latest work, *Poetry and Experience* (1961), is a critical study.

Some other of MacLeish's works are *Einstein* (1929), *American Story* (1944), *Actfive* (1948), and *Songs for Eve* (1955).

Studies of the man and his work are to be found in A. Kreymborg, *Our Singing Strength* (1929); M. U. Schappes, "The Directions of Archibald MacLeish," *Symposium*, III (1932); B. Deutsch, *This Modern Poetry* (1935); A. Mizener, "The Poetry of Archibald MacLeish," *Sewanee Review*, XLIV (1938); C. Brooks, *Modern Poetry and the Tradition* (1939); E. Honig, "History, Document, and Archibald MacLeish," *Sewanee Review*, XLVIII (1940); O. Cargill, *Intellectual America* (1941); E. M. Sickels, "Archibald MacLeish and American Democracy," *American Literature*, XV (1943); R. Whittemore, "MacLeish and the Democratic Pastoral," *Sewanee Review*, LXI (1953); A. Tate, *Sixty American Poets, 1896–1944* (1954); R. Eberhart, "Outer and Inner Verse Drama," *Virginia Quarterly Review*, XXXIV (1958); W. V. Bush, ed., *The Dialogues of Archibald MacLeish and Mark Van Doren* (1964); and S. L. Falk, *Archibald MacLeish* (1965).

You, Andrew Marvell

And here face down beneath the sun
And here upon earth's noonward height
To feel the always coming on
The always rising of the night:

To feel creep up the curving east
The earthy chill of dusk and slow
Upon those under lands the vast
And ever climbing shadow grow

And strange at Ecbatan the trees
Take leaf by leaf the evening strange   10
The flooding dark about their knees
The mountains over Persia change

And now at Kermanshah the gate
Dark empty and the withered grass
And through the twilight now the late
Few travelers in the westward pass

And Baghdad darken and the bridge
Across the silent river gone
And through Arabia the edge
Of evening widen and steal on   20

And deepen on Palmyra's street
The wheel rut in the ruined stone
And Lebanon fade out and Crete
High through the clouds and overblown

And over Sicily the air
Still flashing with the landward gulls
And loom and slowly disappear
The sails above the shadowy hulls

And Spain go under and the shore
Of Africa the gilded sand   30
And evening vanish and no more
The low pale light across that land:

Nor now the long light on the sea

And here face downward in the sun
To feel how swift how secretly
The shadow of the night comes on . . .

                     1926

American Letter

FOR GERALD MURPHY

The wind is east but the hot weather continues,
Blue and no clouds, the sound of the leaves thin,
Dry like the rustling of paper, scored across
With the slate-shrill screech of the locusts.
                             The tossing of
Pines is the low sound. In the wind's running
The wild carrots smell of the burning sun.
Why should I think of the dolphins at Capo di Mele?
Why should I see in my mind the taut sail
And the hill over St.-Tropez and your hand on the tiller?
Why should my heart be troubled with palms still?   10
I am neither a sold boy nor a Chinese official
Sent to sicken in Pa for some Lo-Yang dish.
This is my own land, my sky, my mountain:
This—not the humming pines and the surf and the sound
At the Ferme Blanche, nor Port Cros in the dusk and the
    harbor

Floating the motionless ship and the sea-drowned star.
I am neither Po Chü-i nor another after
Far from home, in a strange land, daft
For the talk of his own sort and the taste of his lettuces.
This land is my native land. And yet   20
I am sick for home for the red roofs and the olives,
And the foreign words and the smell of the sea fall.
How can a wise man have two countries?
How can a man have the earth and the wind and want
A land far off, alien, smelling of palm-trees
And the yellow gorse at noon in the long calms?

It is a strange thing—to be an American.
Neither an old house it is with the air
Tasting of hung herbs and the sun returning
Year after year to the same door and the churn   30
Making the same sound in the cool of the kitchen
Mother to son's wife, and the place to sit
Marked in the dusk by the worn stone at the wellhead—
That—nor the eyes like each other's eyes and the skull
Shaped to the same fault and the hands' sameness.
Neither a place it is nor a blood name.
America is West and the wind blowing.
America is a great word and the snow,
A way, a white bird, the rain falling,
A shining thing in the mind and the gulls' call.   40
America is neither a land nor a people,
A word's shape it is, a wind's sweep—
America is alone: many together,
Many of one mouth, of one breath,
Dressed as one—and none brothers among them:
Only the taught speech and the aped tongue.
America is alone and the gulls calling.
It is a strange thing to be an American.
It is strange to live on the high world in the stare
Of the naked sun and the stars as our bones live.   50
Men in the old lands housed by their rivers.
They built their towns in the vales in the earth's shelter.
We first inhabit the world. We dwell
On the half earth, on the open curve of a continent.
Sea is divided from sea by the day-fall. The dawn
Rides the low east with us many hours;
First are the capes, then are the shorelands, now

The blue Appalachians faint at the day rise;
The willows shudder with light on the long Ohio:
The Lakes scatter the low sun: the prairies   60
Slide out of the dark: in the eddy of clean air
The smoke goes up from the high plains of Wyoming:
The steep Sierras rise: the struck foam
Flames at the wind's heel on the far Pacific
Already the noon leans to the eastern cliff:
The elms darken the door and the dust-heavy lilacs.

It is strange to sleep in the bare stars and to die
On an open land where few bury before us:
(From the new earth the dead return no more.)
It is strange to be born of no race and no people.   70
In the old lands they are many together. They keep
The wise past and the words spoken in common.
They remember the dead with their hands, their mouths
    dumb.
They answer each other with two words in their meeting.
They live together in small things. They eat
The same dish, their drink is the same and their proverbs.
Their youth is like. They are like in their ways of love.
They are many men. There are always others beside them.
Here it is one man and another and wide
On the darkening hills the faint smoke of the houses.   80
Here it is one man and the wind in the boughs.

Therefore our hearts are sick for the south water.
The smell of the gorse comes back to our night thought.
We are sick at heart for the red roofs and the olives;
We are sick at heart for the voice and the foot fall . . .
Therefore we will not go though the sea call us.

This, this is our land, this is our people,
This that is neither a land nor a race. We must reap
The wind here in the grass for our soul's harvest:
Here we must eat our salt or our bones starve.   90
Here we must live or live only as shadows.
This is our race, we that have none, that have had
Neither the old walls nor the voices around us,
This is our land, this is our ancient ground—
The raw earth, the mixed bloods and the strangers,
The different eyes, the wind, and the heart's change.

These we will not leave though the old call us.
This is our country-earth, our blood, our kind.
Here we will live our years till the earth blind us—

The wind blows from the east. The leaves fall.   100
Far off in the pines a jay rises.
The wind smells of haze and the wild ripe apples.

I think of the masts at Cette and the sweet rain.

                                        1927

Speech to Those Who Say Comrade

The brotherhood is not by the blood certainly,
But neither are men brothers by speech—by saying so:
Men are brothers by life lived and are hurt for it.

Hunger and hurt are the great begetters of brotherhood:
Humiliation has gotten much love:
Danger I say is the nobler father and mother.

Those are as brothers whose bodies have shared fear
Or shared harm or shared hurt or indignity.
Why are the old soldiers brothers and nearest?

For this: with their minds they go over the sea a little 10
And find themselves in their youth again as they were in
Soissons and Meaux and at Ypres and those cities:

A French loaf and the girls with their eyelids painted
Bring back to aging and lonely men
Their twentieth year and the metal odor of danger.

It is this in life which of all things is tenderest—
To remember together with unknown men the days
Common also to them and perils ended:

It is this which makes of many a generation—
A wave of men who having the same years   20
Have in common the same dead and the changes.

The solitary and unshared experience

Dies of itself like the violations of love
Or lives on as the dead live eerily:

The unshared and single man must cover his
Loneliness as a girl her shame for the way of
Life is neither by one man nor by suffering.

Who are the born brothers in truth? The puddlers
Scorched by the same flame in the same foundries,
Those who have spit on the same boards with the blood
    in it,   30

Ridden the same rivers with green logs,
Fought the police in the parks of the same cities,
Grinned for the same blows, the same flogging,

Veterans out of the same ships, factories,
Expeditions for fame: the founders of continents:
Those that hid in Geneva a time back,

Those that have hidden and hunted and all such—
Fought together, labored together: they carry the
Common look like a card and they pass touching.

Brotherhood! No word said can make you brothers!   40
Brotherhood only the brave earn and by danger or
Harm or by bearing hurt and by no other.

Brotherhood here in the strange world is the rich and
Rarest giving of life and the most valued,
Not to be had for a word or a week's wishing.

                                              1936

ALLEN TATE

(1899–   )

Allen Tate was born in Clark County, Kentucky, and attended Vanderbilt University in Nashville, Tennessee. By the time he was graduated in 1922, he had impressed Donald Davidson and John Crowe Ransom, his teachers, as well as classmates including Robert Penn Warren, as a young man who would make his mark in the world of letters. He left the South after graduation and, in the immemorial fashion of millions, went to New York to see where that mark was to be made. He free-lanced as he could, wrote poetry, and kept constant contact with the remarkable Vanderbilt group.

In 1924 he married novelist Caroline Gordon and four years later published his first volume, *Mr. Pope and Other Poems*. These poems, together with two biographies, *Stonewall Jackson* (1928) and *Jefferson Davis* (1929), and the volume that first won him general recognition as a poet, *Poems, 1928–1931* (1932), indicated the literary and social attitudes that were represented in *I'll Take My Stand* (1930), to which he contributed. Tate's belief in the values of tradition, social order, the heritage of the ante-bellum South, and religion, as well as his beliefs about poetry—classical hardness and precision together with an intellectual toughness that will allow a fit and highly educated audience to give a poem all that it demands—were articulated in one of his important books, *Reactionary Essays on Poetry and Ideas* (1936).

For several years Tate taught in the English departments of various southern colleges as well as at Princeton, and from 1942 to 1944 he occupied the chair of poetry in the Library of Congress. From 1944 to 1946 he was editor of the *Sew-*

575

anee Review, and he joined the English department of the University of Minnesota in 1951. Since then he has published *The Forlorn Demon* (1953), *The Man of Letters in the Modern World* (1955), and *Collected Essays* (1959); his *Sixty American Poets, 1896–1944* (1945, with bibliography by Francis Cheney) was revised in 1954.

Some other of Tate's books include *Selected Poems* (1937); *The Fathers* (1938); *Reason in Madness* (1941); *The Winter Sea* (1944); *Poems, 1922–1947* (1948); and *Two Conceits for the Eye to Sing, If Possible* (1950).

Statements about Mr. Tate, his work, and his school are to be found in C. Glicksberg, "Allen Tate and Mother Earth," *Sewanee Review*, XLV (1937); D. Schwartz, "The Poetry of Allen Tate," *Southern Review*, V (1940); A. Mizener, " 'The Fathers' and Realistic Fiction," *Accent*, VII (1947); A. Tate, ed., *A Southern Vanguard* (1947); R. C. Beatty, "Allen Tate as Man of Letters," *South Atlantic Quarterly*, XLVII (1948); C. Amyx, "The Aesthetics of Allen Tate," *Western Review*, XIII (1949); V. Koch, "The Poetry of Allen Tate," *Kenyon Review*, XI (1949); M. K. Spears, "The Criticism of Allen Tate," *Sewanee Review*, LXVII (1949); R. G. Davis, "The New Criticism and the Democratic Tradition," *American Scholar*, XVIV (1949–1950); L. D. Rubin, Jr., "The Serpent in the Mulberry Bush," *Hopkins Review*, VI (1953); A. Tate, *Sixty American Poets* (1954); W. B. Arnold, *The Social Ideas of Allen Tate* (1955); E. Vivas, *Creation and Discovery* (1955); R. Foster, "Narcissus as Pilgrim: Allen Tate," *Accent*, XVII (1957); J. Bradbury, *The Fugitives: A Critical Account* (1958); L. Cowan, *The Fugitive Group* (1959); R. R. Purdy, ed., *Fugitive's Reunion* (1959); *Sewanee Review*, LXVII (Autumn, 1959)—a Tate issue; R. K. Meiners, *The Last Alternatives: A Study of the Works of Allen Tate* (1963); and G. Hemphill, *Allen Tate* (1964).

Death of Little Boys

When little boys grown patient at last, weary,
Surrender their eyes immeasurably to the night,
The event will rage terrific as the sea;
Their bodies fill a crumbling room with light.

Then you will touch at the bedside, torn in two
Gold curls now deftly intricate with gray
As the windowpane extends a fear to you
From one peeled aster drenched with the wind all day

And over his chest the covers in the ultimate dream
Will mount to the teeth, ascend the eyes, press back   10

The locks—while round his sturdy belly gleam
Suspended breaths, white spars above the wreck:

Till all the guests come in to look, turn down
Their palms, and delirium assails the cliff
Of Norway where you ponder, and your little town
Reels like a sailor drunk in a rotten skiff.

The bleak sunshine shrieks its chipped music then
Out to the milkweed amid the fields of wheat.
There is a calm for you where men and women
Unroll the chill precision of moving feet.   20

                                                  1928

Ode to the Confederate Dead

Row after row with strict impunity
The headstones yield their names to the element,
The wind whirrs without recollection;
In the riven troughs the splayed leaves
Pile up, of nature the casual sacrament
To the seasonal eternity of death;
Then driven by the fierce scrutiny
Of heaven to their election in the vast breath,
They sough the rumor of mortality.

Autumn is desolation in the plot   10
Of a thousand acres where these memories grow
From the inexhaustible bodies that are not
Dead, but feed the grass row after rich row.
Think of the autumns that have come and gone!—
Ambitious November with the humors of the year,
With particular zeal for every slab,
Staining the uncomfortable angels that rot
On the slabs, a wing chipped here, an arm there:
The brute curiosity of an angel's stare
Turns you, like them, to stone,   20
Transforms the heaving air
Till plunged to a heavier world below
You shift your sea-space blindly
Heaving, turning like the blind crab.

Dazed by the wind, only the wind
The leaves flying, plunge

You know who have waited by the wall
The twilight certainty of an animal,
Those midnight restitutions of the blood
You know—the immitigable pines, the smoky frieze   30
Of the sky, the sudden call: you know the rage,
The cold pool left by the mounting flood,
Of muted Zeno and Parmenides.
You who have waited for the angry resolution
Of those desires that should be yours tomorrow,
You know the unimportant shrift of death
And praise the vision
And praise the arrogant circumstance
Of those who fall
Rank upon rank, hurried beyond decision—   40
Here by the sagging gate, stopped by the wall.

    Seeing, seeing only the leaves
    Flying, plunge and expire

Turn your eyes to the immoderate past,
Turn to the inscrutable infantry rising
Demons out of the earth—they will not last.
Stonewall, Stonewall, and the sunken fields of hemp,
Shiloh, Antietam, Malvern Hill, Bull Run.
Lost in the orient of the thick and fast
You will curse the setting sun.   50

    Cursing only the leaves crying
    Like an old man in a storm

You hear the shout, the crazy hemlocks point
With troubled fingers to the silence which
Smothers you, a mummy, in time.

                    The hound bitch
Toothless and dying, in a musty cellar
Hears the wind only.

                Now that the salt of their blood
Stiffens the saltier oblivion of the sea,

Seals the malignant purity of the flood,
What shall we who count our days and bow   60
Our heads with a commemorial woe
In the ribboned coats of grim felicity,
What shall we say of the bones, unclean,
Whose verdurous anonymity will grow?
The ragged arms, the ragged heads and eyes
Lost in these acres of the insane green?
The gray lean spiders come, they come and go;
In a tangle of willows without light
The singular screech-owl's tight
Invisible lyric seeds the mind   70
With the furious murmur of their chivalry.

    We shall say only the leaves
    Flying, plunge and expire

We shall say only the leaves whispering
In the improbable mist of nightfall
That flies on multiple wing:
Night is the beginning and the end
And in between the ends of distraction
Waits mute speculation, the patient curse
That stones the eyes, or like the jaguar leaps   80
For his own image in a jungle pool, his victim.

What shall we say who have knowledge
Carried to the heart? Shall we take the act
To the grave? Shall we, more hopeful, set up the grave
In the house? The ravenous grave?

                       Leave now

The shut gate and the decomposing wall:
The gentle serpent, green in the mulberry bush,
Riots with his tongue through the hush—
Sentinel of the grave who counts us all!

                              1928, 1948

ROBERT PENN WARREN
(1905–   )

A Kentuckian like Allen Tate, Robert Penn Warren, the best-known and most versatile of the "Fugitives," was born in the town of Guthrie. He was associated with *The Fugitive* during his stay at Vanderbilt, from which he was graduated in 1925. Two years later he earned the M.A. degree at the University of California, went on to Yale, and then, as a Rhodes Scholar, to Oxford, where he was awarded the B. Litt. in 1930. The year prior to his Oxford degree he had published his first book, *John Brown: The Making of a Martyr*. In 1934, after various teaching jobs in the South, he joined the English department of Louisiana State University; a year later the publication of *Thirty-Six Poems* won him recognition as a distinguished poet.

At Louisiana State University he was once more associated with Cleanth Brooks, with whom he had been a student at Vanderbilt and a Rhodes Scholar at Oxford. Together, in 1935, they founded and edited the influential *Southern Review*, which lasted until 1942, and in 1938 they edited *Understanding Poetry*, a "New Critical" textbook which, in its insistence upon close and formal analysis of poetic structures and techniques, revolutionized the teaching of literature in American colleges and universities. Warren inaugurated his career as a major novelist in 1939 with the publication of *Night Riders*. Since then he has written five other novels: *At Heaven's Gate* (1943); the widely known *All The King's Men* (1946); *World Enough and Time* (1950); *Band of Angels* (1955); and *The Cave* (1959).

Despite his activity as a novelist, Warren did not abandon

his function as teacher, critic, and poet. In 1942 he joined the English department of the University of Minnesota, and two years later he published *Selected Poems, 1923–1943*. This was followed by *The Rime of the Ancient Mariner* (1946), a critical study of Coleridge's symbolism. His production of poetry continued with *Brother to Dragons* (1953), *Promises* (1957), and *You, Emperors, and Others* (1960). Looking for new literary fields to conquer, Warren engaged the short story in *Blackberry Winter* (1946) and *The Circus in the Attic* (1947). He left Minnesota for Yale in 1951; retired five years later in order to devote his full time to writing, and has since resumed his association with Yale. In 1967 he won the Bollingen Award for poetry.

Some of his other works are *Eleven Poems on the Same Theme* (1942), and *Segregation, The Inner Conflict in the South* (1956), and *Selected Essays* (1958).

Studies of the man, his work, and his school are to be found in I. Hendry, "The Regional Novel: The Example of Robert Penn Warren," *Sewanee Review*, LIII (1945); N. R. Girault, "The Narrator's Mind as Symbol: An Analysis of *All the Kings' Men*," *Accent*, VII (1947); R. B. Heilman, "Melpomene as Wallflower; or The Reading of Tragedy," *Sewanee Review*, LV (1947); R. W. Stallman, "Robert Penn Warren: A Checklist of His Critical Writings," *University of Kansas City Review*, XIV (1947); E. Bentley, "The Meaning of Robert Penn Warren's Novels," *Kenyon Review*, X (1948); R. G. Davis, "The New Criticism and the Democratic Tradition," *American Scholar*, XVIV (1949–1950); *Folio*, XV (May, 1950), a Warren issue; J. Frank, "Romanticism and Reality in Robert Penn Warren," *Hudson Review*, IV (1951); C. Glicksberg, *American Literary Criticism, 1900–1950* (1951); W. V. O'Connor, *An Age of Criticism, 1900–1950* (1952); C. R. Anderson, "Violence and Order in the Novels of Robert Penn Warren," *Southern Renascence*, L. Rubin, Jr. and R. D. Jacobs, eds. (1953); A. Tate, *Sixty American Poets* (1954); F. McDowell, "Psychology and Theme in *Brother to Dragons*," *PMLA*, LXX (1955); W. M. Frohock, *The Novel of Violence in America* (1957); F. Sochatoff, ed., *All the King's Men: A Symposium* (1957); J. Bradbury, *The Fugitives: A Critical Account* (1958); L. Cowan, *The Fugitive Group* (1959); R. R. Purdy, ed., *Fugitive's Reunion* (1959); J. Stewart, "Robert Penn Warren and the Knot of History," *ELH*, XXVI (1959); L. Casper, *Robert Penn Warren* (1960); J. E. Hardy, "Robert Penn Warren's Double Hero," *Virginia Quarterly Review*, XXXVI (1960); *Modern Fiction Studies*, VI (Spring, 1960)—a Warren issue; *South Atlantic Quarterly*, LXII (1963) —a Warren issue; P. West, *Robert Penn Warren* (1964); C. H. Bohner, *Robert Penn Warren* (1965); J. L. Longley, ed., *Robert Penn Warren* (1965); and V. H. Strandberg, *A Colder Fire: The Poetry of Robert Penn Warren* (1965).

The Last Metaphor

The wind had blown the leaves away and left
The lonely hills and on the hills the trees;
One fellow came out with his mortal miseries
And said to himself: "I go where brown leaves drift

"On streams that reflect but cold the evening,
Where trees are bare, the rock is gray and bare,
And scent of the year's declension haunts the air,
Where only the wind and no tardy bird may sing."

He passed by a water, profound and cold,
Whereon remotely gleamed the violent west.   10
Stark rose a wood about a rocky crest;
Only the wind sang there, as he foretold.

So he took counsel of the heart alone
To be instructed of this desolation,
And when the tongue of the wind had found cessation
After such fashion he lifted up his own.

"The wind has blown the withered leaves away
And left the hills and on the hills the trees.
These thoughts are leaves which are as memories,
Mementoes of the phantom spring's decay.   20

"That bitterly cling if there rise no wind to blow.
I am as the tree and with it wave like season."
Again he heard the wind's deep diapason
And spoke again but not in music now.

"Assuredly the planet's tilt will bring
The accurate convulsion of the year—
The budding leaf, the green, and then the sere.
After winter burst the fetid spring,

"After April and the troubled sod
Fell summer on us with its deathly sheaf,   30
Autumnal ashes then and the brittle leaf
Whereunder fructified the crackling pod.

"Now flat and black the trees stand on the sky
Unreminiscent of the year's frail verdure.
Purged of the green that kept so fatal tenure
They are made strong; no leaf clings mortally."

And hence he made one invocation more,
Hoping for some winds beyond some last horizon
To shake the tree and so fulfill its season:
Before he went a final metaphor, 40

Not passionate this, he gave to the chill air,
Thinking that when the leaves no more abide
The stiff trees rear not up in strength and pride
But lift unto the gradual dark in prayer.

1931

Bearded Oaks

The oaks, how subtle and marine,
Bearded, and all the layered light
Above them swims; and thus the scene,
Recessed, awaits the positive night.

So, waiting, we in the grass now lie
Beneath the languorous tread of light:
The grasses, kelp-like, satisfy
The nameless motions of the air.

Upon the floor of light, and time,
Unmurmuring, of polyp made, 10
We rest; we are, as light withdraws,
Twin atolls on a shelf of shade.

Ages to our construction went,
Dim architecture, hour by hour:
And violence, forgot now, lent
The present stillness all its power.

The storm of noon above us rolled,
Of light the fury, furious gold,
The long drag troubling us, the depth:
Dark is unrocking, unrippling, still. 20

Passion and slaughter, ruth, decay
Descend, minutely whispering down,
Silted down swaying streams, to lay
Foundation for our voicelessness.

All our debate is voiceless here,
As all our age, the rage of stone;
If hope is hopeless, then fearless fear,
And history is thus undone.

Our feet once wrought the hollow street   30
With echo when the lamps were dead
At windows, once our headlight glare
Disturbed the doe that, leaping, fled.

I do not love you less that now
The caged heart makes iron stroke,
Or less that all that light once gave
The graduate dark should now revoke.

We live in time so little time
And we learn all so painfully,
That we may spare this hour's term
To practice for eternity.   40

                                                  1937

Revelation

Because he had spoken harshly to his mother,
The day became astonishingly bright,
The enormity of distance crept to him like a dog now,
And earth's own luminescence seemed to repel the night.

Roof was rent like loud paper tearing to admit
Sun-sulphurous splendor where had been before
But the submarine glimmer by kindly countenances lit,
As slow, phosphorescent dignities light the ocean floor.

By walls, by walks, chrysanthemum and aster,
All hairy, fat-petalled species, lean, confer,   10
And his ears, and heart, should burn at that insidious
    whisper

Which concerns him so; he knows; but he cannot make
out the words.

The peacock screamed, and his feathered fury made
Legend shake, all day, while the sky ran pale as milk;
That night, all night, the buck rabbit stamped in the
moonlight glade,
And the owl's brain glowed like a coal in the grove's
combustible dark.

When Sulla smote and Rome was rent, Augustine
Recalled how Nature, shuddering, tore her gown,
And kind changed kind, and the blunt herbivorous tooth
dripped blood;
At Duncan's death, at Dunsinane, chimneys blew down. 20

But, oh! his mother was kinder than ever Rome,
Dearer than Duncan—no wonder, then, Nature's frame
Thrilled in voluptuous hemispheres far off from his home;
But not in terror: only as the bride, as the bride.

In separateness only does love learn definition,
Though Brahma smiles beneath the dappled shade,
Though tears, that night, wet the pillow where the boy's
head was laid
Dreamless of splendid antipodal agitation;

And though across what tide and tooth Time is,
He was to lean back toward that recalcitrant face, 30
He would think, than Sulla more fortunate, how once he
had learned
Something important above love, and about love's grace.

1942

TWELVE CONTEMPORARY
POETS

Kenneth Fearing (1902–1961) was born in Chicago and, after graduating from the University of Wisconsin, held jobs as a millhand, salesman, reporter, and free-lance writer. *Angel Arms* (1929), *Poems* (1935), *Dead Reckoning* (1938), *Afternoon of a Pawnbroker* (1943), and *Stranger at Coney Island* (1949) are bitter and ironic verse satires of the spiritually dislocated and emotionally maladjusted life of the American middle class. *Collected Poems* appeared in 1940 and *New and Selected Poems* in 1956. His novels include *The Hospital* (1939), *Clark Gifford's Body* (1942), and *The Big Clock* (1946).

Some statements about his work are to be found in K. Burke, *Philosophy of Literary Form* (1941); M. Rosenthal, "The Meaning of Kenneth Fearing's Poetry," *Poetry*, LXIV (1944); H. Gregory and M. Zaturenska, *A History of American Poetry, 1900–1940* (1946); and J. P. Bishop, *Collected Essays of John Peale Bishop* (1948).

Richard Eberhart (1904–   ) was born in Austin, Minnesota, received his B.A. from Dartmouth in 1926, and four years later published his first book, *A Bravery of Earth*. He received his Master's degree from Cambridge University in 1933 and returned to the United States to teach at the St. Mark's School in Massachusetts from 1933 to 1942. During that time he published *Reading the Spirit* (1937) and *Song and Idea* (1942). He was in the Navy until 1946, meanwhile publishing *Poems, New and Selected* (1944). From 1947 to 1952 he was in a manufacturing business in Boston, during which time he published *Burr Oaks* (1947), *Brotherhood of Men* (1949), *An Herb Basket* (1950), *Selected Poems* (1951), and *The Visionary Farms* (1952). In 1952 he returned to teaching in the English departments of various colleges and universities and joined the staff at Dartmouth in 1956. He became Consultant in Poetry at the Library of Congress in *1953* (1953), *Great Praises* (1957), *Collected Poems, 1930–1960* (1960), *Collected Verse Plays* (1962), and *The Quarry* (1964).

Some statements about Eberhart's work are to be found in J. M. Brinnin, "Stigmata of Rapture," *Poetry*, LXI (1942); D. Daiches, "Towards the Proper Spirit," *Poetry*, LXVI (1945); R. Denney, "Idiomatic Kingdom," *Poetry*, LXXXV (1954); S. Rodman, "The Poetry of Richard Eberhart," *Perspectives USA*, No. 10 (1955); P. L. Thorslev, Jr., "The Poetry of Richard Eberhart," *Poets in Progress* (1962); D. Hoffman, "Hunting a Master Image: The Poetry of Richard Eberhart," *The Hollins Critics*, I (1964); and R. J. Mills, Jr., *Richard Eberhart* (1966).

Theodore Roethke (1908–1963) was born in Saginaw, Michigan, received his B.A. in 1929 and his M.A. in 1936 from the University of Michigan, and went on to teach in several colleges and universities. In 1941 he published *Open House*, followed, seven years later, by *The Lost Son and Other Poems*. *Praise to the End!* appeared in 1951 and the 1954 Pulitzer Prize-winner, *The Waking, Poems 1933–1953*, appeared in 1953. Roethke also won the Bollingen Award in 1958, following the publications of *Words for the Wind* in that year. *I Am! Says the Lamb* was published in 1961, *Sequence, Sometimes Metaphysical, Poems* in 1963, and *The Far Field* in 1964. In 1965 R. J. Mills, Jr., edited *On the Poet and His Craft*, a collection of Roethke's critical essays. From 1947 until his death Roethke was a member of the department of English at the University of Washington.

Some statements about his work are to be found in L. Foster, Jr., "Lyric Realist," *Poetry*, LVIII (1941); K. Burke, "The Vegetal Radicalism of Theodore Roethke," *Sewanee Review*, LVIII (1950); B. Deutsch, *Poetry in Our Time* (1952); C. Arnett, "Minimal to Maximal: Theodore Roethke's Dialectic," *College English*, XVIII (1957); R. J. Mills, Jr., *Theodore Roethke* (1963); A. Stein, ed., *Theodore Roethke: Essays on the Poetry* (1965); and W. J. Martz, ed., *The Achievement of Theodore Roethke* (1966).

Elizabeth Bishop (1911–   ) was born in Worcester, Massachusetts, and received her A.B. from Vassar in 1934. She consolidated her reputation during the next decade, publishing a book of poems, *North and South*, in 1946, winning a Guggenheim award in 1947, and becoming Consultant in Poetry to the Library of Congress, 1949–50. A member of the National Institute of Arts and Letters, she was awarded an Institute grant in literature in 1951. She received the Pulitzer Prize for *Poems: North and South/Cold Spring* in 1955. After many changes of residence—from the Northeast to Key West to Mexico in the 1940's—she settled in Brazil in 1962.

Some recent statements about her work and the milieu of contemporary poetry are J. A. Emig, "The Poem as Puzzle," *English Journal*, LII (1963); *Proceedings of the National Poetry Festival, 1962*, published by the Library of Congress in 1964; R. J. Mills, Jr., *Contemporary American Poetry* (1965); and A. Stevenson, *Elizabeth Bishop* (1966).

Delmore Schwartz (1913–1966) was born in Brooklyn, received his B.A. in 1935 from New York University, and continued his studies at Columbia, the University of Wisconsin, and Harvard. In 1938 he published *In Dreams Begin Responsibilities*. Two years later, he went to Harvard, where he taught until 1947, meanwhile publishing *Shenandoah* (1941) and *Genesis* (1943). He acted in editorial and review capacities for the *Partisan Review* and *The New Republic*. In 1948 *The World Is a Wedding* appeared, followed two years later by *Vaudeville for a Princess* and by *Summer Knowledge* in 1959, in which year he won the Bollingen Award. He published *Successful Love and Other Stories* in 1961. Among Schwartz's accomplishments is a translation (1939) of Rimbaud's *A Season in Hell*.

Some statements about his work are to be found in H. Politzer (M. Greenberg, tr.), "The Two Worlds of Delmore Schwartz," *Commentary*, X (1950); C. Aiken, *A Reviewer's ABC* (1958), ed. by R. Blanshard; and J. L. Halio, "Delmore Schwartz's Felt Abstractions," *Southern Review*, I (1965).

Karl Shapiro (1913–   ) was born in Baltimore and educated at the University of Virginia and Johns Hopkins. He has taught at Hopkins and has been editor of *Poetry*, but he published his first volume in very nonacademic surroundings. He was with the army in the South Pacific when *Person, Place and Thing* appeared in 1942, and *Essay on Rime* (1945), like the Pulitzer prizewinning *V-Letter and Other Poems* (1944), was composed while Shapiro was on overseas duty. A former Consultant in Poetry at the Library of Congress, Shapiro has also published *Trial of a Poet* (1947), *Poems 1940–1953* (1953), *Poems of a Jew* (1958), and *White-Haired Lover* (1968). He has taught English at the University of Nebraska, and was editor of *Prairie Schooner* from 1959–1963. He now teaches English at the University of Illinois at Chicago Circle.

Some statements about his work are to be found in M. Cowley, "Lively and Deadly Wit," *Poetry*, LXI (1943); D. Schwartz, "Karl Shapiro's Poetics," *Nation*, CLXI (1945); R. Richman, "Alchemy or Poetry; Discussion of Karl Shapiro's *Essay on Rime*," *Sewanee Review*, LIV (1946); F. O. Matthiessen, *The Responsibilities of the Critic* (1952); W. C. Williams, *Selected Essays* (1954); C. Aiken, *A Reviewer's ABC* (1958), ed. by R. Blanshard; J. G. Southworth, "The Poetry of Karl Shapiro," *English Journal*, LI (1962); and R. Slotkin, "The Contextual Symbol," *American Quarterly*, XXVIII (1966).

Randall Jarrell (1914–1965) was born in Nashville, Tennessee, and received both his B.A. and M.A. in his hometown from Vanderbilt University, where he studied with John Crowe Ransom and Robert Penn Warren. Like most of his contemporaries, he too served in World War II (Air Corps) and taught in various college and university English departments throughout the country. He published *Blood for a Stranger* (fiction, 1942); *Little Friend, Little Friend* (1945); *Losses* (1948); *Poetry and the Age* (essays, 1953); *Pictures from an Institution* (1954); *Selected Poems* (1955); *The Woman at the Washington Zoo* (1960), which won the National Book Award; *A Sad Heart at the Supermarket* (essays, 1962); *The Bat-Poet* (1964), *The Gingerbread Rabbit* (1964), and *The Animal Family* (1965), all children's books; and *The Lost World* (1965).

Some statements about Jarrell's work are to be found in P. Tyler, "The Dramatic Lyricism of Randall Jarrell," *Poetry*, LXXIX (1952); Sister M. B. Quinn, *The Metamorphic Tradition in Modern Poetry* (1955); C. M. Adams, *Randall Jarrell: A Bibliography* (1958); *Analects*, I (1961)—a Jarrell issue; and R. W. Flint, "On Randall Jarrell," *Commentary*, XLI (1966).

Robert Lowell (1917–   ), the great-grandnephew of James Russell Lowell, was born in Boston and educated in St. Mark's School (where Richard Eberhart has taught), Harvard, and Kenyon College, from which he received his B.A. in 1940. During World War II he spent some time in jail as a conscientious objector. He too has taught in the English departments of several colleges and universities and has been Consultant in Poetry at the Library of Congress. He has published *Land of Unlikeness* (1944), *Lord Weary's Castle* (1946), for which he was awarded the Pulitzer Prize in 1947, *Poems 1938–1949* (1950), *Life Studies* (1959), *Imitations* (1961), *Phaedra* (1961), *For the Union Dead* (1964), *The Old Glory* (1965), and *Near the Ocean* (1967).

Some statements about his work are to be found in A. Warren, "Double Discipline," *Poetry*, LXX (1947); L. Frankenberg, *Pleasure Dome* (1949); W. C. Jumper, " 'Whom Seek Ye?' A Note on Robert Lowell's Poetry," *Hudson Review*, IX (1956); R. Jarrell, *Poetry and the Age* (1953); Marius Bewley, *The Complex Fate* (1954); M. L. Rosenthal, *The Modern Poets* (1960); H. B. Staples, *Robert Lowell* (1962); J. Mazzaro, *The Poetic Themes of Robert Lowell* (1965); and W. Martz, ed., *The Achievement of Robert Lowell* (1966).

Richard Wilbur (1921–   ) was born in New York, received his B.A. from Amherst in 1942, and then went into the army for his World War II service. His M.A. came from Harvard in 1947; he taught at Wellesley, and then returned to teach at Harvard until 1954. In 1955 he joined the Department of English at Wesleyan University in Connecticut. A winner of the Prix de Rome of the American Academy of Arts and Letters in 1954, Wilbur has published *The Beautiful Changes and Other Poems* (1947), *Ceremony and Other Poems* (1950), *A Bestiary* (1955), *Things of This World* (1956), for which he was awarded the Pulitzer Prize in 1957, *Poems, 1943–1956* (1957), *Advice to a Prophet* (1961), and *The Poems of Richard Wilbur* (1963). Also among his accomplishments are a translation (1955) of Molière's *Le Misanthrope* and a collaboration on the lyrics for the Lillian Hellman-Leonard Bernstein musical dramatization of *Candide* (1956).

Some statements about his work are to be found in F. C. Golffing, "A Remarkable New Talent," *Poetry*, LXXI (1948); R. Jarrell, *Poetry and the Age* (1953); F. W. Warlow, "Richard Wilbur," *Bucknell Review*, VII (1958); J. G. Southworth, "The Poetry of Richard Wilbur," *College English*, XXII (1960); and F. E. Faverty, "Well-Open Eyes; or, The Poetry of Richard Wilbur," *Poets in Progress* (1962).

Born in Newark, New Jersey, in 1926, Allen Ginsberg first gained national attention—suddenly and spectacularly—as the author of *Howl and Other Poems* in 1956. Critics responded with cries of "treason!" "filth!" or "bravo!" as they hailed him as the new dean of the "beat" poets. His personal career has been romantic and erratic. During his school years and after earning his bachelor's degree from Columbia in 1949, he worked as a dishwasher, on cargo ships, as a night porter, as a spot welder, and, for those he began to gather around him, as a guru. He has published *Kaddish, Poems 1958–1960* (1961), *Empty Mirror* (1962), and *Reality Sandwishes* (1963). He has read his poetry and lectured in many universities and in many nations. For a while he resided in India, living the life of a holy man and studying Indian poetry and philosophy. With his shoulder-length hair, his full, shaggy beard, and his full, shaggy reputation, he is a familiar figure in the community of twentieth-century dissent. He consciously and deliberately has chosen Whitman as his American ancestor, for in Whitman he finds the sense of vocation he admires: that of the seer and the prophet of transcendental, antiestablishmentarian love and vision.

Recent evaluations of the man and his poetry include A. Grossman, "Allen Ginsberg: The Jew as American Poet," *Judaism*, XI (1962); L. A. Haselmayer, "Beat Prophet and Beat Wit," *Iowa English Yearbook*, 6 (1962); and B. Hunsberger, "Kit Smart's 'Howl,' " *Wisconsin Studies in Contemporary Literature*, VI (1965). J. W. Erlich edited *Howl of the Censor* in 1961, a transcript of the trial which found *Howl* not to be obscene.

The tragically short life of Sylvia Plath (1932–1963) nevertheless allowed her enough time to produce three books and two children, and to establish a reputation as a writer whose poems have had particular impact upon readers at midcentury. Her poems are signs of the passionate rebelliousness that characterizes a radical re-examination of Western values since the beginning of the cold war. She was born in Boston, Massachusetts, and was educated at the Wellesley High School and at Smith College. For a while, at Boston University, she was a student of Robert Lowell, who wrote about her warmly and sorrowfully when she died. Miss Plath won a Fulbright Scholarship to Cambridge University, where she met the English poet Ted Hughes, whom she married in 1956. Her books are *The Colossus* (1960), a book of poems; *The Bell Jar*, a novel written under the pseudonym of "Victoria Lucas," and *Ariel*, which was published posthumously in 1965.

A recent comment on her work is to be found in A. R. Jones, "Necessity and Freedom: The Poetry of Robert Lowell, Sylvia Plath, and Anne Sexton," *Critical Quarterly*, VII (1965).

The selection of contemporary poets for an anthology of American literature is complicated by an embarrassment of riches. Without question, the United States is experiencing a literary renaissance, spearheaded by poetry. There are more good, skilled—even brilliant—poets on the scene at the present moment than ever before in the history of the nation. There are not only older contemporaries like Conrad Aiken and Mark Van Doren and Louise Bogan and John Peale Bishop, and middle-aged contemporaries like Muriel Rukeyser and Howard Nemerov and John Ciardi and John Malcolm Brinnin and Jean Garrigue, but also an enormous number of people of various ages who have reputations that are relatively newly established: W. D. Snodgrass, Robert Pack, Isabella Gardner, W. S. Merwin, James Wright, Donald Hall, Denise Levertov, Anne Sexton, Lawrence Ferlinghetti, Philip Booth, James Dickey are just a very few of the many who immediately come to mind. With room for only one more poem, the editors decided not to choose it from among the established poets. Any single choice would be insufficient. Therefore, the editors have deliberately chosen a poet whose reputation is about to become established, a representative of the many unknown young people who are just publishing books of poetry, and whose poems published so far promise much. In selecting James Scully, the editors have tried to present a sample of the best poetry of the most immediate moment, in order to indicate that in the few years between the revisions of any anthology nowadays, new stars rise and America offers a glimpse of continually expanding literary galaxies.

The youngest writer in this book, James Scully was born in New Haven, Connecticut, in 1937. The recipient of a National Defense Fellowship, he completed his Ph.D. at the University of Connecticut, where he now teaches poetry after having taught at Rutgers in 1963–64. He spent the year of 1962–63 in Rome, writing poetry as a Fellow of the Ingram Merrill Foundation. His first book of poetry is *The Marches* (1967), which won the Lamont Poetry Prize as the year's best first book of poems.

KENNETH FEARING

Dirge

1-2-3 was the number he played but today the number
      came 3-2-1;
   bought his Carbide at 30 and it went to 29; had the
      favorite at Bowie but the track was slow—

O, executive type, would you like to drive a floating
      power, knee-action, silk upholstered six? Wed a Holly-
      wood star? Shoot the course in 58? Draw to the ace,
      king, jack?
   O, fellow with a will who won't take no, watch out for
      three cigarettes on the same, single match; O, demo-
      cratic voter born in August under Mars, beware of
      liquidated rails—

Denouement to denouement, he took a personal pride in
      the certain, certain way he lived his own, private life,
   But nevertheless, they shut off his gas; nevertheless, the
      bank foreclosed; nevertheless, the landlord called;
      nevertheless, the radio broke,

And twelve o'clock arrived just once too often,
   just the same he wore one grey tweed suit, bought one
      straw hat, drank one straight Scotch, walked one
      short step, took one long look, drew one deep breath,
   just one too many,

And wow he died as wow he lived,   10
   going whop to the office and blooie home to sleep and
      biff got married and bam had children and oof got
      fired,
   zowie did he live and zowie did he die,

With who the hell are you at the corner of his casket,
      and where the hell we going on the right-hand silver
      knob, and who the hell cares walking second from

the end with an American Beauty wreath from why
the hell not,

Very much missed by the circulation staff of the New
York Evening Post; deeply, deeply mourned by the
B.M.T.,

Wham, Mr. Roosevelt; pow, Sears Roebuck; awk, big
dipper; bop, summer rain;
bong, Mr., bong, Mr., bong, Mr., bong.

1935

RICHARD EBERHART

The Groundhog

In June, amid the golden fields,
I saw a groundhog lying dead.
Dead lay he; my senses shook,
And mind outshot our naked frailty.
There lowly in the vigorous summer
His form began its senseless change,
And made my senses waver dim
Seeing nature ferocious in him.
Inspecting close his maggots' might
And seething cauldron of his being,   10
Half with loathing, half with a strange love,
I poked him with an angry stick.
The fever arose, became a flame
And Vigour circumscribed the skies,
Immense energy in the sun,
And through my frame a sunless trembling.
My stick had done nor good nor harm.
Then stood I silent in the day
Watching the object, as before;
And kept my reverence for knowledge   20
Trying for control, to be still,
To quell the passion of the blood;
Until I had bent down on my knees
Praying for joy in the sight of decay.
And so I left: and I returned

In Autumn strict of eye, to see
The sap gone out of the groundhog,
But the bony sodden hulk remained.
But the year had lost its meaning,
And in intellectual chains   30
I lost both love and loathing,
Mured up in the' wall of wisdom.
Another summer took the fields again
Massive and burning, full of life,
But when I chanced upon the spot
There was only a little hair left,
And bones bleaching in the sunlight
Beautiful as architecture;
I watched them like a geometer,
And cut a walking stick from a birch.   40
It has been three years, now.
There is no sign of the groundhog.
I stood there in the whirling summer,
My hand capped a withered heart,
And thought of China and of Greece,
Of Alexander in his tent;
Of Montaigne in his tower,
Of Saint Theresa in her wild lament.

1936

The Fury of Aerial Bombardment

You would think the fury of aerial bombardment
Would rouse God to relent; the infinite spaces
Are still silent. He looks on shock-pried faces.
History, even, does not know what is meant.

You would feel that after so many centuries
God would give man to repent; yet he can kill
As Cain could, but with multitudinous will,
No farther advanced than in his ancient furies.

Was man made stupid to see his own stupidity?
Is God by definition indifferent, beyond us all?   10
Is the eternal truth man's fighting soul
Wherein the Beast ravens in its own avidity?

Of Van Wettering I speak, and Averill,
Names on a list, whose faces I do not recall
But they are gone to early death, who late in school
Distinguished the belt feed lever from the belt holding
   pawl.

1947

THEODORE ROETHKE

Dolor

I have known the inexorable sadness of pencils,
Neat in their boxes, dolor of pad and paper-weight,
All the misery of manila folders and mucilage,
Desolation in immaculate public places,
Lonely reception room, lavatory, switchboard,
The unalterable pathos of basin and pitcher,
Ritual of multigraph, paper-clip, comma,
Endless duplication of lives and objects.
And I have seen dust from the walls of institutions,
Finer than flour, alive, more dangerous than silica,   10
Sift, almost invisible, through long afternoons of tedium,
Dropping a fine film on nails and delicate eyebrows,
Glazing the pale hair, the duplicate gray standard faces.

1943

The Waking

I wake to sleep, and take my waking slow.
I feel my fate in what I cannot fear.
I learn by going where I have to go.

We think by feeling. What is there to know?
I hear my being dance from ear to ear.
I wake to sleep, and take my waking slow.

Of those so close beside me, which are you?
God bless the Ground! I shall walk softly there,
And learn by going where I have to go.

Light takes the Tree; but who can tell us how? 10
The lowly worm climbs up a winding stair;
I wake to sleep, and take my waking slow.

Great Nature has another thing to do
To you and me; so take the lively air,
And, lovely, learn by going where to go.

This shaking keeps me steady. I should know.
What falls away is always. And is near.
I wake to sleep, and take my waking slow.
I learn by going where I have to go.

1953

ELIZABETH BISHOP

The Man-Moth *

* Newspaper misprint for "mammoth."

Here, above,
cracks in the buildings are filled with battered moonlight.
The whole shadow of Man is only as big as his hat.
It lies at his feet like a circle for a doll to stand on,
and he makes an inverted pin, the point magnetized to the moon.
He does not see the moon; he observes only her vast properties,
feeling the queer light on his hands, neither warm nor cold,
of a temperature impossible to record in thermometers.

But when the Man-Moth
pays his rare, although occasional, visits to the surface, 10
the moon looks rather different to him. He emerges
from an opening under the edge of one of the sidewalks
and nervously begins to scale the faces of the buildings.
He thinks the moon is a small hole at the top of the sky,
proving the sky quite useless for protection.
He trembles, but must investigate as high as he can climb.

Up the façades,
his shadow dragging like a photographer's cloth behind
him,
he climbs fearfully, thinking that this time he will manage
to push his small head through that round clean opening   20
and be forced through, as from a tube, in black scrolls on
the light.
(Man, standing below him, has no such illusions.)
But what the Man-Moth fears most he must do, although
he fails, of course, and falls back scared but quite unhurt.

Then he returns
to the pale subways of cement he calls his home. He flits,
he flutters, and cannot get aboard the silent trains
fast enough to suit him. The doors close swiftly.
The Man-Moth always seats himself facing the wrong way
and the train starts at once at its full, terrible speed,   30
without a shift in gears or a gradation of any sort.
He cannot tell the rate at which he travels backwards.

Each night he must
be carried through artificial tunnels and dream recurrent
dreams.
Just as the ties recur beneath his train, these underlie
his rushing brain. He does not dare look out the window,
for the third rail, the unbroken draught of poison,
runs there beside him. He regards it as a disease
he has inherited the susceptibility to. He has to keep
his hands in his pockets, as others must wear mufflers.   40

If you catch him,
hold up a flashlight to his eye. It's all dark pupil,
an entire night itself, whose haired horizon tightens
as he stares back, and closes up the eye. Then from the
lids
one tear, his only possession, like the bee's sting, slips.
Slyly he palms it, and if you're not paying attention
he'll swallow it. However, if you watch, he'll hand it over,
cool as from underground springs and pure enough to
drink.

1955

DELMORE SCHWARTZ

Starlight Like Intuition Pierced the Twelve

The starlight's intuitions pierced the twelve,
The brittle night sky sparkled like a tune
Tinkled and tapped out on the xylophone.
Empty and vain, a glittering dune, the moon
Arose too big, and, in the mood which ruled,
Seemed like a useless beauty in a pit;
And then one said, after he carefully spat:
"No matter what we do, he looks at it!

"I cannot see a child or find a girl
Beyond his smile which glows like that spring moon."   10
"—Nothing no more the same," the second said,
"Though all may be forgiven, never quite healed
The wound I bear as witness, standing by;
No ceremony surely appropriate,
Nor secret love, escape or sleep because
No matter what I do, he looks at it——"

"Now," said the third, "no thing will be the same:
I am as one who never shuts his eyes,
The sea and sky no more are marvellous,
And I no longer understand surprise!"   20
"Now," said the fourth, "nothing will be enough
—I heard his voice accomplishing all wit:
No word can be unsaid, no deed withdrawn
—No matter what is said, he measures it!"

"Vision, imagination, hope or dream,
Believed, denied, the scene we wished to see?
It does not matter in the least: for what
Is altered, if it is not true? That we
Saw goodness, as it is—*this* is the awe
And the abyss which we will not forget,   30
His story now the sky which holds all thought:
No matter what I think, think of it!"

"And I will never be what once I was,"
Said one for long as narrow as a knife,
"And we will never be what once we were;
We have died once; this is a second life."
"My mind is spilled in moral chaos," one
Righteous as Job exclaimed, "now infinite
Suspicion of my heart stems what I will
—No matter what I choose, he stares at it!"   40

"I am as one native in summer places
—Ten weeks' excitement paid for by the rich;
Debauched by that and then all winter bored,"
The sixth declared. "His peak left us a ditch!"
"He came to make this life more difficult,"
The seventh said, "No one will ever fit
His measure's heights, all is inadequate:
No matter what I do, what good is it?"

"He gave forgiveness to us: what a gift!"
The eighth chimed in. "But now we know how much   50
Must be forgiven. But if forgiven, what?
The crime which was will be; and the least touch
Revives the memory: what is forgiveness worth?"
The ninth spoke thus: "Who now will ever sit
At ease in Zion at the Easter feast?
No matter what the place, he touches it!"

"And I will always stammer, since he spoke,"
One, who had been most eloquent, said, stammering.
"I looked too long at the sun; like too much light,
So too much goodness is a boomerang,"   60
Laughed the eleventh of the troop. "I must
Try what he tried: I saw the infinite
Who walked the lake and raised the hopeless dead:
No matter what the feat, he first accomplished it!"

So spoke the twelfth; and then the twelve in chorus:
"Unspeakable unnatural goodness is
Risen and shines, and never will ignore us;
He glows forever in all consciousness;
Forgiveness, love, and hope possess the pit,

And bring our endless guilt, like shadow's bars: 70
No matter what we do, he stares at it!

What pity then deny? what debt defer?
We know he looks at us like all the stars,
And we shall never be as once we were,
This life will never be what once it was!"

1950, 1959

The True-Blue American

Jeremiah Dickson was a true-blue American,
For he was a little boy who understood America, for he
    felt that he must
Think about *everything;* because that's *all* there is to
    think about,
Knowing immediately the intimacy of truth and comedy,
Knowing intuitively how a sense of humor was a necessity
For one and for all who live in America. Thus, natively,
    and
Naturally when on an April Sunday in an ice cream
    parlor Jeremiah
Was requested to choose between a chocolate sundae
    and a banana split
He answered unhesitatingly, having no need to think of it
Being a true-blue American, determined to continue as
    he began: 10
Rejecting the either-or of Kierkegaard, and many another
    European;
Refusing to accept alternatives, refusing to believe the
    choice of between;
Rejecting selection; denying dilemma; electing absolute
    affirmation: knowing
    in his breast

    The infinite and the gold
    Of the endless frontier, the deathless West.

"Both: I will have them both!" declared this true-blue
    American

In Cambridge, Massachusetts, on an April Sunday, in-
    structed
  By the great department stores, by the Five-and-Ten,
Taught by Christmas, by the circus, by the vulgarity and
    grandeur of   20
  Niagara Falls and the Grand Canyon,
Tutored by the grandeur, vulgarity, and infinite appetite
    gratified and
  Shining in the darkness, of the light
On Saturdays at the double bills of the moon pictures,
The consummation of the advertisements of the imagina-
    tion of the light
Which is as it was—the infinite belief in infinite hope—of
    Columbus,
  Barnum, Edison, and Jeremiah Dickson.

                                                          1959

KARL SHAPIRO

Troop Train

It stops the town we come through. Workers raise
Their oily arms in good salute and grin.
Kids scream as at a circus. Business men
Glance hopefully and go their measured way.
And women standing at their dumbstruck door
More slowly wave and seem to warn us back,
As if a tear blinding the course of war
Might once dissolve our iron in their sweet wish.

Fruit of the world, O clustered on ourselves
We hang as from a cornucopia   10
In total friendliness, with faces bunched
To spray the streets with catcalls and with leers.
A bottle smashes on the moving ties
And eyes fixed on a lady smiling pink
Stretch like a rubber-band and snap and sting
The mouth that wants the drink-of-water kiss.

And on through crummy continents and days,
Deliberate, grimy, slightly drunk we crawl,
The good-bad boys of circumstance and chance,
Whose bucket-helmets bang the empty wall   20
Where twist the murdered bodies of our packs
Next to the guns that only seem themselves.
And distance like a strap adjusted shrinks,
Tightens across the shoulder and holds firm.

Here is a deck of cards; out of this hand
Dealer, deal me my luck, a pair of bulls,
The right draw to a flush, the one-eyed jack.
Diamonds and hearts are red but spades are black,
And spades are spades and clubs are clovers—black.
But deal me winners, souvenirs of peace.   30
This stands to reason and arithmetic,
Luck also travels and not all come back.

Trains lead to ships and ships to death or trains,
And trains to death or trucks, and trucks to death,
Or trucks lead to the march, the march to death,
Or that survival which is all our hope;
And death leads back to trucks and trains and ships,
But life leads to the march, O flag! at last
The place of life found after trains and death
—Nightfall of nations brilliant after war.   40
                                                   1943

The Conscientious Objector

The gates clanged and they walked you into jail
More tense than felons but relieved to find
The hostile world shut out, the flags that dripped
From every mother's windowpane, obscene
The bloodlust sweating from the public heart,
The dog authority slavering at your throat.
A sense of quiet, of pulling down the blind
Possessed you. Punishment you felt was clean.

The decks, the catwalks, and the narrow light
Composed a ship. This was a mutinous crew   10

Troubling the captains for plain decencies,
A *Mayflower* brim with pilgrims headed out
To establish new theocracies to west,
A Noah's ark coasting the topmost seas
Ten miles above the sodomites and fish.
These inmates loved the only living doves.

Like all men hunted from the world you made
A good community, voyaging the storm
To no safe Plymouth or green Ararat;
Trouble or calm, the men with Bibles prayed,   20
The gaunt politicals construed our hate.
The opposite of all armies, you were best
Opposing uniformity and yourselves;
Prison and personality were your fate.

You suffered not so physically but knew
Maltreatment, hunger, ennui of the mind.
Well might the soldier kissing the hot beach
Erupting in his face damn all your kind.
Yet you who saved neither yourselves nor us
Are equally with those who shed the blood   30
The heroes of our cause. Your conscience is
What we come back to in the armistice.

                                                1947

RANDALL JARRELL

Losses

It was not dying: everybody died.
It was not dying: we had died before
In the routine crashes—and our fields
Called up the papers, wrote home to our folks,
And the rates rose, all because of us.
We died on the wrong page of the almanac,
Scattered on mountains fifty miles away;
Diving on haystacks, fighting with a friend,
We blazed up on the lines we never saw.

We died like aunts or pets or foreigners.   10
(When we left high school nothing else had died
For us to figure we had died like.)

In our new planes, with our new crews, we bombed
The ranges by the desert or the shore,
Fired at towed targets, waited for our scores—
And turned into replacements and woke up
One morning, over England, operational.
It wasn't different: but if we died
It was not an accident but a mistake
(But an easy one for anyone to make).   20
We read our mail and counted up our missions—
In bombers named for girls, we burned
The cities we had learned about in school—
Till our lives wore out; our bodies lay among
The people we had killed and never seen.
When we lasted long enough they gave us medals;
When we died they said, "Our casualties were low."

They said, "Here are the maps"; we burned the cities.

It was not dying—no, not ever dying;
But the night I died I dreamed that I was dead,   30
And the cities said to me: "Why are you dying?
We are satisfied, if you are; but why did I die?"

                                                       1944

Nestus Gurley

Sometimes waking, sometimes sleeping,
Late in the afternoon, or early
In the morning, I hear on the lawn,
On the walk, on the lawn, the soft quick step,
The sound half song, half breath: a note or two
That with a note or two would be a tune.
It is Nestus Gurley.

It is an old
Catch or snatch or tune
In the Dorian mode: the mode of the horses   10
That stand all night in the fields asleep

Or awake, the mode of the cold
Hunter, Orion, wheeling upside-down,
All space and stars, in cater-cornered Heaven.
When, somewhere under the east,
The great march begins, with birds and silence;
When, in the day's first triumph, dawn
Rides over the houses, Nestus Gurley
Delivers to me my lot.

As the sun sets, I hear my daughter say: 20
"He has four routes and makes a hundred dollars."
Sometimes he comes with dogs, sometimes with children,
Sometimes with dogs and children.
He collects, today.
I hear my daughter say:
"Today Nestus has got on his derby."
And he says, after a little: "It's two-eighty."
"How could it be two-eighty?"
"Because this month there're five Sundays: it's two-eighty."

He collects, delivers. Before the first, least star   30
Is lost in the paling east; at evening
While the soft, side-lit, gold-leafed day
Lingers to see the stars, the boy Nestus
Delivers to me the Morning Star, the Evening Star
—Ah no, only the Morning *News,* the Evening *Record*

Of what I have done and what I have not done
Set down and held against me in the Book
Of Death, on paper yellowing
Already, with one morning's sun, one evening's sun.

Sometimes I only dream him. He brings then   40
News of a different morning, a judgment not of men.
The bombers have turned back over the Pole,
Having met a star. . . . I look at that new year
And, waking, think of our Moravian Star
Not lit yet, and the pure beeswax candle
With its red flame-proofed paper pompom
Not lit yet, and the sweetened
Bun we brought home from the love-feast, still not eaten,
And the song the children sang: *O Morning Star—*

And at this hour, to the dew-hushed drums   50
Of the morning, Nestus Gurley

Marches to me over the lawn; and the cat Elfie,
Furred like a musk-ox, coon-tailed, gold-leaf-eyed,
Looks at the paper boy without alarm
But yawns, and stretches, and walks placidly
Across the lawn to his ladder, climbs it, and begins to purr.
I let him in,
Go out and pick up from the grass the paper hat
Nestus has folded: this tricorne fir for a Napoleon
Of our days and institutions, weaving   60
Baskets, being bathed, receiving
Electric shocks, Rauwolfia. . . . I put it on
—Ah no, only unfold it.
There is dawn inside; and I say to no one
About—
          it is a note or two
That with a note or two would—
                              say to no one
About nothing: "He delivers dawn."

When I lie coldly   70
—Lie, that is, neither with coldness nor with warmth—
In the darkness that is not lit by anything,
In the grave that is not lit by anything
Except our hope: the hope
That is not proofed against anything, but pure
And shining as the first, least star
That is lost in the east on the morning of Judgment—
May I say, recognizing the step
Or tune or breath. . . .
                        recognizing the breath,   80
May I say, "It is Nestus Gurley."

                                              1960

ROBERT LOWELL

Mr. Edwards and the Spider

I saw the spiders marching through the air,
Swimming from tree to tree that mildewed day
   In latter August when the hay
    Came creaking to the barn. But where
      The wind is westerly,
Where gnarled November makes the spiders fly
Into the apparitions of the sky,
They purpose nothing but their ease and die
Urgently beating east to sunrise and the sea;

    What are we in the hands of the great God?   10
    It was in vain you set up thorn and briar
       In battle array against the fire
        And treason crackling in your blood;
          For the wild thorns grow tame
    And will do nothing to oppose the flame;
    Your lacerations tell the losing game
    You play against a sickness past your cure.
How will the hands be strong? How will the heart endure?

    A very little thing, a little worm,
    Or hourglass-blazoned spider, it is said,   20
       Can kill a tiger. Will the dead
       Hold up his mirror and affirm
         To the four winds the smell
    And flash of his authority? It's well
    If God who holds you to the pit of hell,
    Much as one holds a spider, will destroy,
Baffle and dissipate your soul. As a small boy

    On Windsor Marsh, I saw the spider die
    When thrown into the bowels of fierce fire:
       There's no long struggle, no desire   30
       To get up on its feet and fly—
         It stretches out its feet

And dies. This is the sinner's last retreat;
Yes, and no strength exerted on the heat
Then sinews the abolished will, when sick
And full of burning, it will whistle on a brick.

But who can plumb the sinking of that soul?
Josiah Hawley, picture yourself cast
   Into a brick-kiln where the blast
    Fans your quick vitals to a coal—   40
     If measured by a glass,
  How long would it seem burning! Let there pass
A minute, ten, ten trillion; but the blaze
Is infinite, eternal: this is death,
To die and know it. This is the Black Widow, death.

                                      1944

After the Surprising Conversions

September twenty-second, Sir: today
I answer. In the latter part of May,
Hard on our Lord's Ascension, it began
To be more sensible. A gentleman
Of more than common understanding, strict
In morals, pious in behavior, kicked
Against our goad. A man of some renown,
An useful, honored person in the town,
He came of melancholy parents; prone
To secret spells, for years they kept alone—   10
His uncle, I believe, was killed of it:
Good people, but of too much or little wit.
I preached one Sabbath on a text from Kings;
He showed concernment for his soul. Some things
In his experience were hopeful. He
Would sit and watch the wind knocking a tree
And praise this countryside our Lord has made.
Once when a poor man's heifer died, he laid
A shilling on the doorsill; though a thirst
For loving shook him like a snake, he durst   20
Not entertain much hope of his estate
In heaven. Once we saw him sitting late
Behind his attic window by a light
That guttered on his Bible; through that night
He meditated terror, and he seemed

Beyond advice or reason, for he dreamed
That he was called to trumpet Judgment Day
To Concord. In the latter part of May
He cut his throat. And though the coroner
Judged him delirious, soon a noisome stir   30
Palsied our village. At Jehovah's nod
Satan seemed more let loose amongst us: God
Abandoned us to Satan, and he pressed
Us hard, until we thought we could not rest
Till we had done with life. Content was gone.
All the good work was quashed. We were undone.
The breath of God had carried out a planned
And sensible withdrawal from this land;
The multitude, once unconcerned with doubt,
Once neither callous, curious nor devout,   40
Jumped at broad noon, as though some peddler groaned
At it in its familiar twang: "My friend,
Cut your own throat. Cut your own throat. Now! Now!"
September twenty-second, Sir, the bough
Cracks with the unpicked apples, and at dawn
The small-mouth bass breaks water, gorged with spawn.
                                                                    1950

Skunk Hour

(For Elizabeth Bishop)

Nautilus Island's hermit
heiress still lives through winter in her Spartan cottage;
her sheep still graze above the sea.
Her son's a bishop. Her farmer
is first selectman in our village;
she's in her dotage.

Thirsting for
the hierarchic privacy
of Queen Victoria's century,
she buys up all   10
the eyesores facing her shore,
and lets them fall.

The season's ill—
we've lost our summer millionaire,

who seemed to leap from an L. L. Bean
catalogue. His nine-knot yawl
was auctioned off to lobstermen.
A red fox stain covers Blue Hill.

And now our fairy
decorator brightens his shop for fall;⁣ 20
his fishnet's filled with orange cork,
orange, his cobbler's bench and awl;
there is no money in his work,
he'd rather marry.

One dark night,
my Tudor Ford climbed the hill's skull;
I watched for love-cars. Lights turned down,
they lay together, hull to hull,
where the graveyard shelves on the town. . . .
My mind's not right.⁣ 30

A car radio bleats,
"Love, O careless Love. . . ." I hear
my ill-spirit sob in each blood cell,
as if my hand were at its throat. . . .
I myself am hell;
nobody's here—

only skunks, that search
in the moonlight for a bite to eat.
They march on their soles up Main Street:
white stripes, moonstruck eyes' red fire⁣ 40
under the chalk-dry and spar spire
of the Trinitarian Church.

I stand on top
of our back steps and breathe the rich air—
a mother skunk with her column of kittens swills the garbage pail.
She jabs her wedge-head in a cup
of sour cream, drops her ostrich tail,
and will not scare.

1958

RICHARD WILBUR

Juggler

A ball will bounce, but less and less. It's not
A light-hearted thing, resents its own resilience.
Falling is what it loves, and the earth falls
So in our hearts from brilliance,
Settles and is forgot.
It takes a sky-blue juggler with five red balls

To shake our gravity up. Whee, in the air
The balls roll round, wheel on his wheeling hands,
Learning the ways of lightness, alter to spheres
Grazing his finger ends,   10
Cling to their courses there,
Swinging a small heaven about his ears.

But a heaven is easier made of nothing at all
Than the earth regained, and still and sole within
The spin of worlds, with a gesture sure and noble
He reels that heaven in,
Landing it ball by ball,
And trades it all for a broom, a plate, a table.

Oh, on his toe the table is turning, the broom's
Balancing up on his nose, and the plate whirls   20
On the tip of the broom! Damn, what a show, we cry:
The boys stamp, and the girls
Shriek, and the drum booms
And all comes down, and he bows and says good-bye.

If the juggler is tired now, if the broom stands
In the dust again, if the table starts to drop
Through the daily dark again, and though the plate
Lies flat on the table top,
For him we batter our hands
Who has won for once over the world's weight.   30

1949

Advice to a Prophet

When you come, as you soon must, to the streets of our
    city,
Mad-eyed from stating the obvious,
Not proclaiming our fall but begging us
In God's name to have self-pity,

Spare us all words of the weapons, their force and range,
The long numbers that rocket the mind;
Our slow, unreckoning hearts will be left behind,
Unable to fear what is too strange.

Nor shall you scare us with talk of the death of the race.
How shall we dream of this place without us?—   **10**
The sun mere fire, the leaves untroubled about us,
A stone look on the stone's face?

Speak of the world's own change. Though we cannot con-
    ceive
Of an undreamt thing, we know to our cost
How the dreamt cloud crumbles, the vines are blackened by
    frost,
How the view alters. We could believe,

If you told us so, that the white-tailed deer will slip
Into perfect shade, grown perfectly shy,
The lark avoid the reaches of our eye,
The jack-pine lose its knuckled grip   **20**

On the cold ledge, and every torrent burn
As Xanthus once, its gliding trout
Stunned in a twinkling. What should we be without
The dolphin's arc, the dove's return,

These things in which we have seen ourselves and spoken?
Ask us, prophet, how we shall call
Our natures forth when that live tongue is all
Dispelled, that glass obscured or broken

In which we have said the rose of our love and the clean
Horse of our courage, in which beheld   **30**

The singing locust of the soul unshelled,
And all we mean or wish to mean.

Ask us, ask us whether with the worldless rose
Our hearts shall fail us; come demanding
Whether there shall be lofty or long standing
When the bronze annals of the oak-tree close.

1961

ALLEN GINSBERG

A Supermarket in California

What thoughts I have of you tonight, Walt Whitman, for
I walked down the sidestreets under the trees with a headache self-conscious looking at the full moon.

In my hungry fatigue, and shopping for images, I went
into the neon fruit supermarket, dreaming of your enu-
merations!

What peaches and what penumbras! Whole families
shopping at night! Aisles full of husbands! Wives in the
avocados, babies in the tomatoes!—and you, Garcia Lorca,
what were you doing down by the watermelons?   10

I saw you, Walt Whitman, childless, lonely old grubber,
poking among the meats in the refrigerator and eyeing the
grocery boys.

I heard you asking questions of each: Who killed the
pork chops? What price bananas? Are you my Angel?

I wandered in and out of the brilliant stacks of cans following you, and followed in my imagination by the store
detective.

We strode down the open corridors together in our solitary fancy tasting artichokes, possessing every frozen delicacy, and never passing the cashier.   21

Where are we going, Walt Whitman? The doors close in
an hour. Which way does your beard point tonight?

(I touch your book and dream of our odyssey in the supermarket and feel absurd.)

Will we walk all night through solitary streets? The trees

add shade to shade, lights out in the houses, we'll both be
lonely.   28
  Will we stroll dreaming of the lost America of love past
blue automobiles in driveways, home to our silent cottage?

  Ah, dear father, graybeard, lonely old courage-teacher,
what America did you have when Charon quit poling his
ferry and you got out on a smoking bank and stood watching the boat disappear on the black waters of Lethe?

                                                             1956

SYLVIA PLATH

Daddy

You do not do, you do not do
Any more, black shoe
In which I have lived like a foot
For thirty years, poor and white,
Barely daring to breathe or Achoo.

Daddy, I have had to kill you.
You died before I had time—
Marble-heavy, a bag full of God,
Ghastly statue with one grey toe
Big as a Frisco seal   10

And a head in the freakish Atlantic
Where it pours bean green over blue
In the waters of beautiful Nauset.
I used to pray to recover you.
Ach, du.

In the German tongue, in the Polish town
Scraped flat by the roller
Of wars, wars, wars.
But the name of the town is common.
My Polack friend   20

Says there are a dozen or two.
So I never could tell where you
Put your foot, your root,
I never could talk to you.
The tongue stuck in my jaw.

It stuck in a barb wire snare.
Ich, ich, ich, ich,
I could hardly speak.
I thought every German was you.
And the language obscene   30

An engine, an engine
Chuffing me off like a Jew.
A Jew to Dachau, Auschwitz, Belsen.
I began to talk like a Jew.
I think I may well be a Jew.

The snows of the Tyrol, the clear beer of Vienna
Are not very pure or true.
With my gypsy ancestress and my weird luck
And my Taroc pack and my Taroc pack
I may be a bit of a Jew.   40

I have always been scared of *you,*
With your Luftwaffe, your gobbledygoo.
And your neat moustache
And your Aryan eye, bright blue.
Panzer-man, panzer-man, O You—

Not God but a swastika
So black no sky could squeak through.
Every woman adores a Fascist,
The boot in the face, the brute
Brute heart of a brute like you.   50

You stand at the blackboard, daddy,
In the picture I have of you,
A cleft in your chin instead of your foot
But no less a devil for that, no not
Any less the black man who

Bit my pretty red heart in two.
I was ten when they buried you.
At twenty I tried to die
And get back, back, back to you.
I thought even the bones would do.   60

But they pulled me out of the sack,
And they stuck me together with glue.
And then I knew what to do.
I made a model of you,
A man in black with a Meinkampf look

And a love of the rack and the screw.
And I said I do, I do.
So daddy, I'm finally through.
The black telephone's off at the root,
The voices just can't worm through.   70

If I've killed one man, I've killed two—
The vampire who said he was you
And drank my blood for a year,
Seven years, if you want to know.
Daddy, you can lie back now.

There's a stake in your fat black heart
And the villagers never liked you.
They are dancing and stamping on you.
They always *knew* it was you.
Daddy, daddy, you bastard, I'm through.   80

1962

JAMES SCULLY

Crew Practice

(Lake Bled, in Jugoslavia)
FOR MY SON, JOHN

I'd wave the gnats away and try
to tell you, *no one is more dear,*
unable to tell, or think why

and justify our life besides,
hardly in touch. As like that shell's,
fanning water, our shadow glides

down to the dark bottom, beneath
consideration nearly . . . Past
the feudal castle, with each breath

striding much like a galley or   10
a leggy water bug, men drop
airs, ages lost in the Great War,

the Austro-Hungarian Empire
and pine island astern—where still
an alpine church upholds its spire

but holds it, also, upside-down
in the water mirror, as though
gravity dragged images down

and drained them off. So many lives.
Caretakers raking the far shore   20
burn off a winter of wet leaves,

the column of smoke leans. Swallows
blow over all day, worrying
sunset—like quick following harrows

until the sky yields. In widening rings
they orbit, then come back as bats
stroking raggedly on damp wings

(as will the dark, frantic for more,
beat circles over the lamplit
footpath, still darker than before)　　　　　　30

equipment in perfect order.
Whenever overtaken, I
duck, nor trust anyone's radar,

not even theirs. Then, when I look
at what comes true, or listen, hard
by the flat tension of a lake

while gooseflesh rises, recalling
how the coxswain's regular bark
marked time, forced rising and falling,

or out of habit dream on Proust,　　　　　　40
how little we know or love, those
we know the best and love the most,

then, man to man, this heartless view
tempts me almost to tell a lie,
and wish you better than I do.

　　　　　　　　　　　　　　1965

INDEX OF AUTHORS, TITLES, AND FIRST
LINES OF POEMS

My long two-pointed ladder's sticking through a tree, 411

CONTENTS OF OTHER VOLUMES
IN THIS SERIES

Colonial and Federal · To 1800

The American Romantics · 1800–1860

☆ ☆ ☆

Nation and Region · 1860–1900

DATE DUE

JUN 10 '03		